LITTLEBROOK

by

Geoffrey H Hutson

LITTLEBROOK

by

Geoffrey H Hutson

ISBN: 978-0-9560578-1-5

Published by Geoffrey H Hutson in conjunction with Writersworld Ltd

Copy edited by Sue Croft

Printed and bound by www.printondemand-worldwide.com

www.writersworld.co.uk

WRITERSWORLD
2 Bear Close
Woodstock
Oxfordshire
OX20 1JX
England

DEDICATION

This book is dedicated to

Ken, Pete and Stella

and to the memory of our dear parents Bill and Kate

and to my wife Betty and our son John

It is also dedicated to the very many friends I had
during my boyhood years,
growing up in the village of
Littlebourne in Kent

ACKNOWLEDGEMENTS

I wish to acknowledge the debt I owe to Graham Cook who, by his searching overview of the world of publishing, saw the need for a new and very much more viable system of publishing based upon the simple principle of Print-on-Demand. His company, Writersworld Ltd, runs smoothly and efficiently.

Following this I have to record my sincere thanks to Writersworld's talented and conscientious copy editor, Sue Croft, and to Charles Leveroni, the cover designer, for his work in creating Littlebrook's excellent cover, so evocative of the period.

Finally I would like to record my special appreciation to my friend Liz Webster who is the only person to have read the entire manuscript of LITTLEBROOK before it was sent off to Writersworld Ltd.

PREFACE

Geoffrey Hutson was born and grew up in the village of Littlebourne near Canterbury in Kent. During the 1930s he went to St George's Primary School in Canterbury and Simon Langton Grammar School for Boys.

A Chartered Physicist and Chartered Engineer, he is now retired after a lifetime in the teaching profession, preceded by five years during World War II in the R.E.M.E. having been trained at the Royal Military College of Science as an expert in electronics. His teaching career spanned Matriculation to Degree level, the latter in Atomic Physics and Electronics.

He has written academic textbooks for Arnolds of London and the McGraw-Hill Publishing Company. Notably his McGraw-Hill textbook 'COLOUR TELEVISION THEORY: PAL-System Principles & Receiver Circuitry' became a standard textbook for the subject. Over 30,000 English language copies were sold together with Portuguese and Spanish translations used in Europe, Brazil and Latin America respectively.

With Writersworld Ltd in October 2008 he published his latest academic book, 'THE BIG BANG: Shameful Pseudo Science', which is gaining acclaim and may well become a defining work in this field where frustrated physicists, blunting their noses against Infinity, seek an easy way out.

'LITTLEBROOK' is Geoffrey's first work of fiction and was researched and written over a period of years. Littlebrook is a fictitious Kentish village situated between the city of Canterbury and the English Channel coast. It should be noted that, with the exception of one character close to his heart, the characters portrayed and the incidents described are entirely imaginary.

However, as is to be expected, there are echoes of Littlebourne . . . in Littlebrook.

CONTENTS

INTRODUCTION

The book is a truly fascinating glimpse of life in the English countryside, deep in the rural heart of the County of Kent, in the 1920s.

Whimsical, intriguing, starkly realistic, often bizarre, humorous, quirky and incongruous, in places sad, tragic and at times eerie and macabre, the people the reader will meet move against a background now gone forever, yet tantalisingly seeming to be still there, within reach— recreated in these richly entertaining pages.

Journey in your imagination through a dreamlike world of hop gardens and oast houses, windmills and wheelwrights, orchards and woodlands, gamekeepers and dogs, rabbit-potters and ferreters, traction engines and threshing machines, malt-houses and brewers, saddlers and blacksmiths, carriers and horses, steam-ploughing and buried treasure, fairgrounds and fortune-tellers, miniature railways and a wall-of-death, gallopers and dodgem cars, bell-towers and bell ringers, mediaeval coastal castles and sea-defences.

Visit a flea-circus with an eccentric Dean of the Church of England; see the horizon broaden from Kent to California, from the white cliffs of Dover to San Francisco by courtesy of the Royal Navy; meet the film men from Los Angeles on location in Kent.

Hear of all these people and events, and much more, as seen through the eyes of the many remarkable characters you will get to know.

For those who seek a brief escape from the modern world, read this nostalgic work of fiction . . . that could so easily be fact. The social and technological background against which the stories are structured is accurately portrayed, and makes a fascinating contribution towards the social history of the times.

PROLOGUE

If fleeting memories and a fictional spell,
Create reminders of people who once did dwell;
If scenes and buildings here described,
Evoke pictures of places that now have died;
Then maybe existing in Time's domain,
Real life was there and forever will remain.

If people are found whose memory rings true,
It could be they were known not only by you;
If some are unpleasant and thought not nice,
Then leave them alone and think not twice;
For a figment of imagination all may be,
With both wheat and chaff just invented by me.

If in the still air of the misty marshes,
Fancies flit like a will o' the wisp that passes;
Then perhaps in travelling through life's brief span,
Like Omar Khayyám's so eager young man;
'I came out of the same door as in I went',
In the beautiful Garden of England that is Kent.

G. H. Hutson
The Somerset Levels: 2009

Chapter 1

AN UNWELCOME MESSAGE FOR THE MILLER'S MATE

triggers awesome events in the lives of four people

In the gathering dusk of the chill November evening, Ockham Mill stood out starkly against the clear, twilight sky. The steady breeze that had served the windmill so well during the day was showing signs of slackening as night fell, and an overnight frost was expected. Already a thin mist lay low on the flat fields around the area, lapping the rounded base of the flat-topped hill which the mill crowned so attractively. Viewed from a distance, so well did the windmill complement the smooth, symmetrical shape of the knoll that it seemed almost as though that prominent geographical feature had been designed especially to provide an ideal place to plant the fine-looking, picturesque old building.

Inside the mill the day's work was coming to an end. With a sigh of relief Ted Knowles—right-hand man to the irascible owner of the mill—disengaged the drive mechanism from the runner stone of the pair of millstones which had been in use that afternoon, and humped to one side the last sack of flour of the day's production quota. It had been a hard, ten-hour day and he was tired, very tired. As was usual on Fridays, Ted had worked the mill on his own since midday. His boss, the Miller, known as Dusty to the locals, took Friday afternoon off each week.

The Miller did not much like being called 'Dusty', for he was a pompous, self-important fellow who was not at all happy to be addressed by such a common nickname. He found it demeaning and out-of-line with the image he had of himself.

Aware of this sensitivity on the part of the arrogant Miller, some men delighted in loudly using the name on social occasions to needle him and stir him up a bit. Perversely, his obvious discomfiture and disgruntled reaction pleased them. There was for him no easy, face-saving way out of this niggling little private vicious circle, so in theory he had to grin and bear it. In practice, although he suffered it in silence, he did precious little grinning as he did so. On the contrary he often produced a glowering scowl—a most agreeable bonus for his friendly, smiling, innocent-looking tormentors.

Even this visual reaction had to be guarded against if he could manage to control himself, for there had been an occasion when it had led to an expression of feigned concern for his welfare, the comment itself being the vehicle for yet another calculated use of his so-welcome and pride-pricking nickname.

"You're not looking too well, Dusty," someone had said. "Shall I fetch you a glass of water?"

This apparently kind enquiry had focused sympathetic attention on him, which had done nothing to lessen his irritation and acute embarrassment. And addressed to a man whose addiction to Scotch whisky was legendary, even the reference to water had carried an intended innuendo which neither he, nor several others present, missed.

There had been nothing so far about this particular day which made it different from any other Friday. As yet there was nothing to indicate that the day was to prove a marked turning point in the mill's long history—the start, indeed of a series of fateful events for those whose lives were closely bound up with it. For this seemingly normal Friday had a lethal sting in its tail.

Wearily, Ted made his way up the four flights of well-worn wooden steps, from the ground floor to the top of the five-storey, brick-built, tower-type windmill. When he started up the fourth flight, just above his head was the 'cap'—the top section of the mill—containing the heavy wooden windshaft and its associated massive machinery. This main driving shaft was mounted horizontally, diametrically across the circular tower. The four large windsails were connected to one end of the windshaft, which was pivoted on two bearings, one at its neck, the other at the far end.

The whole cap section of the mill was mobile. It could be turned through a complete circle to bring the windsails into the wind, whatever the wind's direction. It was

1

mounted on a toothed runner-rail that was fixed to the rim of the wall at the top of the fourth floor.

Fixed concentrically on the windshaft was the huge, strongly-built, wooden brake wheel, so called because one of its two important functions was to enable the windsails to be stopped by the application of a brake to its wide rim. Its second job was to act as the main driving wheel for the large, vertical, wooden driving shaft.

This two-section driving shaft looked what it was—part of a tree-trunk. It passed right down through the mill to the ground floor where its steel-capped end was pivoted in an iron bearing set in concrete. Its second main pivot was halfway up, on the floor of the third storey. This floor was of very heavy construction since it had to carry the weight of the grain stores. These consisted of two large bins filled through the trapdoors set in the floor of the fourth storey immediately above them.

The massive vertical shaft was constructed of two pieces joined at the centre by an iron section which formed the pivot that passed through a steel bearing set in the extremely strong, third-storey floor.

Mounted on the top of the vertical driving shaft was a sturdy, horizontal, wooden cog wheel called the 'wallower'. This heavy-duty cog wheel bore iron teeth on its rim, which meshed with matching iron teeth built out on the inward-facing surface of the brake wheel's wooden rim.

For a man like Ted, who liked mechanical things, this huge, impressive machinery never ceased to please him. Visitors were always astounded at the sheer size of it all. They tended to stand and gaze at it with awe, especially if they were lucky enough to see it working. But the Miller did not encourage visitors when the mill was working for it was a very busy, confined place and positively dangerous to the unwary.

Ted paused part-way up the fourth flight of wooden stairs, with his head and shoulders poking through the square hatchway that led into the cap. From this vantage point, just above floor-level, he glanced around, as was his habit, to check that all was well before he shut down the machinery.

Above his head the large brake wheel rotated ponderously, in time with the fifty-foot diameter windsails which were turning slowly in the moderate breeze, completing about five turns in one minute. The 'wallower' had fewer teeth around its rim than the brake wheel had on its surface, so the vertical driving shaft went between three and four times faster than the windsails, completing some fifteen to twenty revolutions per minute.

Below Ted were various mechanisms which were driven by other cog wheels mounted on the vertical driving shaft that formed their axle.

One of these, a large spur wheel situated below the ceiling of the ground floor below, drove, via speed-increasing gear wheels, the top or 'runner' stones, of the two pairs of millstones positioned directly above it on the floor of the second storey. One set of millstones ground wheat grain to make flour. The other, having coarser surfaces, ground barley grain into barley meal.

The 48" diameter stones, when running at 150 revolutions per minute, needed an input power of about 5hp and could turn out 180lb of fine flour per hour from 5 bushels of wheat. At the same speed and power-input the meal stones turned out 300lb of meal from 5 bushels of barley, but could handle 10 bushels per hour to yield 600lb when set up to produce coarsely-ground meal for cattle-feeding purposes. A smaller mill, situated a few miles away, developed rather less than half this power and used stones of only 30" diameter, running at 250 revolutions per minute and handling about one-half of these quantities. These figures were normal for moderate winds.

The second, smaller cog wheel was also on the ground floor, where it drove the

2

mill's hoist system for lifting sacks of grain from the ground floor to the third floor, through square hatches in the floors. Having reached this fourth storey the sacks of grain were emptied as required, down chutes under the trap-doors into the storage bins on the floor below.

Both these two cog wheels were now disengaged from the mechanisms they drove, because the mill had stopped work for the day and was being shut down for the night. Even with the workloads entirely disconnected in this way, the windsails had to develop a great deal of power just to turn the shafts. The free-running load was very considerable indeed, because of the sheer weight of the shafts and wheels and the friction in their bearings.

A high proportion of the available driving force from the windsails was used merely to turn the 'engine' before it did any productive work at all. But nobody was the least bit concerned about this low efficiency. Captured energy from the winds was free. It was there in abundance for the taking. The massively-built mill machinery went on using it year after year, repaying over and over again the high initial cost of constructing the mill.

The mill made its own characteristic sounds as it worked away, driven by the force of the wind sighing and whistling through its sails. Inside there was always a continuous background noise, a deep rumbling, creaking sound of moving machinery, augmented by the higher-pitched, unmistakeable sound of the millstones when they were grinding grain and, less often, by the sound of the pulley wheels and sack-lifting gear as, from time to time, it was operated. The whole structure vibrated and, to those who worked inside one, a mill seemed to have a life of its own.

Ted was so used to working in this environment that he was not bothered by the noise nor even, so it seemed, was consciously aware of it—unless, that is, it suddenly changed in some abnormal way. This he would notice immediately and quickly investigate, because it could well signify trouble which had to be minimised by, if necessary, the rapid shutting down of the workings, so as to obviate damage. A breakdown was very inconvenient because of the tight schedule they worked to, and could be costly both in terms of lost production and of repair work by the millwrights.

Standing where he was, on the final flight of steps, Ted was in the best position to make an overall examination of the parts of the turning mechanism on which it was necessary to keep a close watch. He both looked and listened while making this brief check. Satisfying himself that all was well, he mounted the few final steps and walked across the floor of the cap to the point where the mill's brake chain hung down from its pulley wheel which was fixed high up in the roof's timbers.

Reaching up he grasped the chain in both hands and began to pull it downwards. Above his head the chain passed over its 1' diameter wheel and down to the end of the very strong, wooden lever arm, known in the mill as the brake 'staff'. The staff was pivoted at its far end and as Ted pulled it upwards by means of the chain, a short linking chain attached to the staff near the pivot exerted a powerful pull on the massive braking system, to begin the process of bringing the mill's machinery to a halt. The long length of the staff provided the leverage needed to enable one man to work the huge brake.

The brake itself consisted of a series of curved sections of stout wood which extended over two-thirds of the way around the huge brake wheel. These linked, iron-backed, curved brake sections were pulled to bring them into contact with the rim of the brake wheel, producing a friction which gradually increased as the chain was pulled downwards. Today the wind was moderate and the task not too difficult. In a strong wind, however, the braking friction needed to bring the massive windsails to a halt was formidable indeed: in a gale it was awesome. Each mill had its history of tales to tell of frightening experiences during a sudden onslaught of gale-force winds.

As the brake wheel slowed down, Ted watched for a white mark painted on its side to approach top-dead-centre and increased his pull to stop the wheel near enough at this point.

When aligned in this position the windsails outside formed a St Andrew's cross, or letter X, against the background of the tall mill tower. The Miller insisted on this being done whenever the mill was still. He had an obsession about it and was adamant that it should always be done. It was generally agreed that a mill looked best with the sails set like this. Some Millers only did this for a Sunday rest-day and on public holidays. Others never bothered at all at any time. But Ted's employer had his mill set like this each evening and whenever it was at rest. Once, Ted had been careless in his braking and the next day the Miller had been quick to take him to task about it. His remark was terse and to the point.

"Ted," he said, as he walked into the mill, "you didn't leave the mill set tidy last night. It's a bad advert! A sloppy mill grinds poor flour! See to it tonight. I don't ever want to see that again!"

A taciturn and disgruntled sort of man, he was difficult to please at the best of times, so Ted, with few exceptions, avoided trouble by keeping to the rules.

Having stopped the wheel turning, Ted leant over the wooden safety guard-rail to hook the chain over its locking spike, keeping it securely in its tightened state. At times of high winds, or when anybody was working up in the cap near the mechanism, it was customary to further tighten up and lock the brake as a safety measure. To do this it was necessary to stand on steps to lean further in over the guard-rail and knock a prepared oak wedge under the brake staff near its pivot. This ensured that the wheel could not inadvertently start turning. The machinery was very dangerous and over the years there had been nasty accidents in the mill. There was not much room to move and it was all too easy to get caught up in the huge cog wheels.

Satisfying himself that the brake chain was secure, Ted let go of it and momentarily grabbed the guard-rail with his left hand as he stepped backwards. As he did so he noticed that the rail had some 'give' in it. Grasping it with both hands he shook it to check it and found that it had partially given way in the joint at one end. He made a mental note that this essential safety rail must be examined closely, and repaired, when the millwright made his next visit. This was due in five weeks' time, the week after Christmas, when he had some maintenance work to carry out on the windsails.

Extinguishing the top-floor oil lamp Ted made his way down the steps, carrying the mill's lantern. On the way down he put out the lamps, one after another, as he passed the vantage points where they hung. This was an established routine on late-autumn and winter evenings, a routine reversed when they were lit up in the darkness of the early morning hour at which work started each day.

In winter Ted started the day by lighting up the mill from the bottom upwards, and then set the sails in motion, repeating the sequence in reverse order at night. His progress in the morning could be marked by an observer by the lighting-up of the small windows set in the inward-sloping, high round wall of the tower mill. There were two such windows, diametrically opposite one another, on each of the four working floors of the mill.

Similarly, at night, his progress downwards could be marked by the corresponding going-out of these lights as he made his way downwards. It was not unusual for a late customer on his way up the lane to the mill, situated at the top of the hill which formed its prominent, high, windy location, to see the lights start to go out and to hurry himself to get there before it was too late. After the long working day such 'fag-end' visitors were

4

not the most popular customers at the mill, although they could not be turned away.

Finally, on this bleak November evening, Ted turned out the ground floor lights, went out—locking the main door of the mill behind him—and made his way round to the tool store behind the main buildings where he kept his bicycle under cover every day when at work in the mill.

He did not know, as he trudged along the path and opened the door, that his mundane, well-ordered life was about to change dramatically and would never be the same again.

In the light of his lantern he spotted immediately a white envelope clipped into an upright position on the handlebar of his bike. It was held there securely by the spring-loaded, roller-lever brake spindle, neatly fastened under one of the stop-lugs on the rolling rod.

Printed in bold capital letters on the envelope were the words,

TO TED KNOWLES

PRIVATE AND CONFIDENSHULL

Ted stood quite still for some moments, his gaze riveted upon the envelope. He was acutely aware that something very strange was afoot and he had a sinking feeling in the pit of his stomach. Something was wrong; of that he already felt quite sure. Instinctively he knew that the envelope signalled serious trouble. Its very manner of coming must mean that it was nasty.

His eye was arrested momentarily by the misspelling of the last word. It rang a bell in his head. He had seen the word spelt in that curious way somewhere before, but he couldn't remember where. His brow furrowed as he tried hard to recall where it had been, but he failed, and the unanswered question sank into his subconscious mind to bug him, on and off, for a long time to come.

At length, hanging the lantern on a nail stuck in an overhead rafter, he closed the door to shut out the outside world and took hold of the envelope, pulling on the brake-lever to release it from the grasp of the brake's return spring.

Methodically he took out his penknife and neatly split the flap open. Inside was a single sheet of paper folded in two places. Opening it out he held it under the light of the lantern to read it.

At first he didn't quite take it in. On a more careful study of the words his heart sank. The message it carried was all too stark and clear. It was written in the form of a simple poem, crude and childish maybe, but carrying in its lines a chillingly cruel cutting edge that seemed to slice into his very guts, so sharp was its emotional impact. The words were:

FRIDAY IS THE MILLER'S DAY

Whilst you are working in his mill, Ted,
The Miller is working on your Mildred.
Whilst you grind his corn for our bread,
The Miller grinds your wife in his bed.

With an ashen face he sat down on a wooden box and buried his face in his hands. As the full implication of the message sank in, his shoulders shook as he sobbed for a while, uncontrollably. There was no question of his not believing the truth of the brutal revelation, for with a sudden blinding light many slightly out-of-kilter happenings and curiously inexplicable incidents, focused into an all-too meaningful pattern.

There was no need for him to indulge in a Sherlock Holmes style of systematic dovetailing together of a series of small clues to build into a final, inescapable proof of guilt. Beyond any doubt whatsoever he knew that the two people having the greatest influence on his life—his wife and his employer—were deceiving him. He felt physically sick.

The one he had loved dearly since he was a lad of seventeen, and she the same age. The other, twenty years his senior, he had learnt to tolerate but never to like, since he had entered his employ thirteen years ago. By necessity he had worked with him daily, and over the years had developed a resistance to his not very likeable personality traits and general unpleasantness. He had grown a thick skin; he had had to do so.

The Miller was not a nice man. It is doubtful whether any single living person, not even his own wife, could dispute that. He was by nature both selfish and spiteful, a greedy grabber whose own self-interest came first at all times, irrespective of repercussions on other people, no matter what their circumstance.

By a curious quirk of character he attended Church each Sunday, for both morning and evening services, and seldom missed. Inevitably the contradiction between his seeming dedication to the Christian philosophy, demonstrated on Sundays, and the way he went about his weekday life with no apparent reference to the tenets of this faith whatsoever, caused him to be labelled a downright hypocrite.

There were those who said he was such a bloody rogue that he went to Church on Sunday to balance the books. It was as though any amount of skulduggery during weekdays could be prevented from affecting his destiny on Judgement Day by the simple pay-as-you-go routine of attending Church on Sunday to seek absolution, to 'free him up' so that he could behave as a miserable, dishonest bastard all the week!

Certainly no stranger, observing his dignified and solemn demeanour as he performed his duties as a sidesman in Church on Sundays, would ever suspect that next morning he would make Shakespeare's Shylock look like a soft touch.

This was the background against which Ted's personal drama was set.

From a feeling of great despair and sorrow he soon became consumed by a bitter, burning anger. Never impulsive in anything he did, Ted's natural reaction was to think, think and think again, before he responded in any way to the impact of the life-shattering message spelt out on the paper in his hand.

So he started by getting his priorities straight. First of all he decided that nobody in the world would ever hear, from him, a single word about the letter. Certainly no one would henceforth see the letter itself because he resolved to destroy it in the privacy of his own garden when he got home.

As for the writer of the poison-pen letter, whoever that was would never have the satisfaction of knowing that he had even read it. He was shut in the store shed, completely out of sight, and even if the writer were lurking nearby with a malicious desire to see how he reacted to the message, for all that person would ever know he might have chucked it away without even reading it.

Nor would he mention its content to his wife or the Miller, not at least until he had thought the matter through: and probably never. That was not to say he would not act upon the substance of its content; that was a different matter altogether.

Perhaps it was Ted's addiction to the game of poker that led him to decide instinctively to play his cards close to his chest and show no outward sign of his emotions. It was reaction which was to serve him well. In effect he retired within himself, determined to think the matter through entirely on his own, act on his own, and at no stage involve any other living person at all. That way, his instinct told him, he would remain in charge of his own destiny, retaining, for a while at least, an advantage over the two people who, with himself, completed the eternal triangle now revealed.

So it was that in the evening of what had started off as an innocent, routine day of his commonplace life, Ted was now caught up in a real-life drama. When looked at from a future date it was to appear more like a Victorian melodrama than events in the lives of ordinary people living in the quiet, peaceful tranquillity of the English countryside.

Ted's return from the mill never ran to a precise timetable. Each day had its unpredictable variations and he went home when the work was finished, not when the mill's large wall-clock told him to. As a result he was able to conceal from the outside world that this day was in any way different from other days. By the time he reached home he was calm, collected and in control of himself.

As always, his wife had a hot meal ready for him. It was her habit to stand his plate on a slowly-steaming saucepan of water to keep the meal hot. Sometimes it stood there for quite a long time, particularly on a Friday, as was the case on this fateful night.

Always a quiet, thoughtful man, if his wife noticed anything at all it was simply that he was preoccupied, presumably as so often before, due to some problems and difficulties he had experienced during his day at the mill. Seldom, if ever, did he volunteer any information about such matters and nor did she ever press him. Truth to tell she didn't want to know anyway. And on the following morning normality was the order of the day.

The apparent outward mildness of Ted became his strength. This, combined with his strong, natural inner determination and lone-wolf disposition, enabled him to act upon the information he had received in a completely unobtrusive manner.

Though bitter indeed about his wife's infidelity, he had no doubt that it was the Miller who was largely to blame for it. Two years earlier Ted and his wife had suffered a traumatic tragedy which had deeply affected their previously uneventful and relatively very happy married life. It had marked them both indelibly: scarred their very souls.

Their little nine-year old daughter, an only child and the centre of their lives, had died of scarlet fever. Always a delicate child, little Jenny did not stand a chance as she was not strong enough to withstand this serious illness. When scarlet fever was diagnosed she had been removed immediately to the nearest fever isolation hospital. This very small establishment, virtually a one-ward hospital, was located, as were similar ones elsewhere, well out in the country away from centres of population.

The very words, isolation hospital, struck a chord of fear in the hearts of adults and children alike. The name had a deadly serious ring, as did the two diseases diphtheria and scarlet fever, chiefly associated with it. Once inside there, a patient could not be visited. At best they could only be viewed through a window. The comforting presence to children of their mother and father was denied them, not needlessly by hard-hearted officialdom but by what was deemed to be a necessity, to prevent the spread of these highly infectious and dangerous diseases.

Ted and Mildred both felt, like others in similar circumstances, that the compulsory removal of their daughter from home had itself caused such an emotional disturbance to her that this, despite the well-intentioned reasons for it, had contributed to her going under.

Their hearts had sunk when the local Doctor, assisted by the District Nurse, had taken a swab of Jenny's throat. Her very sore throat, an angry-looking rash and other symptoms, already indicated a high probability that her illness was scarlet fever. When this had been confirmed she had to be told she must go to hospital for a few weeks to make her better. She pleaded with them not to make her go, but they had to steel themselves to face the inevitable. Neither of them would ever forget her agonised sobbing as she was carried out of the house to the waiting ambulance. Her tortured and terrified cries of "Mummy, I don't want to go," were the last words they ever heard from her. Within three days Jenny was dead.

Both Ted and his wife were devastated by their loss. Each reacted in their own way, impelled by their very different temperaments. Ted, whose work kept him fully occupied for up to ten hours a day, got through the ordeal better than his wife. It was early spring at the time and when not at work at the mill he slogged away on his allotment, coming home tired out each day so that he slept through sheer exhaustion.

Mildred, however, was of a different type. She mooned around the home all day, or wandered the woodland paths, lost in a sad world of melancholy. When Ted was home with her she hardly appeared to notice his presence. Often, when he spoke to her, she seemingly did not hear him, being lost in a reverie in a world of her own from which he felt excluded. Ted watched helplessly as she moped about the home and garden. She performed her household duties like an automaton, doing those routine things she had done for years, in a curiously detached way. It was as though she were sleep-walking.

At night while Ted slept she lay awake—sometimes for hours on end. And soon after Jenny died she moved into her little daughter's bedroom. Ted felt guilty because he could sleep while she could not. Perhaps without justification he came to think that Mildred thought he grieved less for Jenny than she did—even, in some tortuous way, that she blamed him for her death.

Be that as it may, their normal life as man and wife ceased when their only child died. They became two people living under the same roof yet sharing no communication of spirit or common purpose. Mildred went her own way and Ted did not question what she did or how she passed her days. He just hoped that time would eventually soften their grief and heal their wounded souls, as so many well-meaning friends assured them it would. Perhaps then they would be able to resume a semblance of their previous life, though he knew it could never be the same again.

As days had given way to weeks and weeks to months, this travesty of their previous life continued and became the norm. Compelled by the necessity to work, in order to live, Ted kept on ploughing his lonely furrow. Meanwhile Mildred lived out her days in her own solitary, sad, shadowy domain, virtually isolated from the outside world. Or so Ted had thought. But not any more. Not after he had read that terrible, vicious little message.

Two years had wrought their silent changes in Mildred's life unbeknown to Ted, blinkered as he was on the treadmill of his routine existence. Suddenly, on this fateful Friday, he had been catapulted out of his state of limbo to be confronted with a starkly different personal world.

He felt that Mildred's morbid state of mind had contributed to her out-of-character liaison with the Miller. How and when it had started he did not know. What he did know for sure was that the obnoxious Miller, now perceived by him to be even more vile and despicable than he had thought before, had fastened on Mildred in her condition of vulnerable misery, like a vulture descending upon its weakened prey.

The more Ted dwelt upon it, the greater grew his silent hatred of his employer. Gradually the wheels of dramatic fate began to turn like the windsails of the mill in a strengthening wind. But the implacable force driving the engines of destiny came not from without but from the gathering storm within himself. The throbbing of the machinery in the mill during the days seemed to give a dreadful momentum to the black thoughts of his troubled mind. Soon the ferment in his head began to focus into a sharpening picture of the pathway ahead that he must tread. At length he knew what he had to do to burst his way out of the consuming nightmare that was burning up his fevered mind.

Strangely, once having decided what to do, his mind quietened. All his mental energy was now directed at working out how to do what he had to do. Stripped of uncertainty he became a deadly and dangerous man, fired by an emotion as old as mankind itself.

Soon, cautiously but inexorably, he began to act; there would be no stopping him now. The goddess Nemesis had whispered her age-old message in Ted's ear. The Miller's fate was sealed. Only the date of his doomsday remained to be determined.

The mill's geographical position was well chosen and very fortunate. At its hilltop position the prevailing winds blew directly across very flat land from the open sea beyond the horizon. As the crow flies, the coastline of this peninsula of South-east England was some twenty miles away, depending upon the direction, and inshore winds from the North-east round to the South-west were little impaired by the high ground. Only from the North-west and West was the mill in the lea of a land mass, and even then any significant high ground was distant from it.

Although there were frustrating days of little wind, on average, over a one-year span, the mill did well and enjoyed a higher proportion of windy productive days than many mills further inland.

When the mill was becalmed Ted usually had plenty of work to do in and around the establishment keeping the mill clean and in good working order. During days when there was little to do he worked in the Miller's large garden. His boss watched him closely and made sure he had more than enough to do. This he did by always instructing Ted what next he must do when he'd finished the job he was then doing. Potential respite periods were in this way not present in the Miller's work schedule for his right-hand man. He built them out of the system, an attention to detail typical of his niggardly nature.

Occasionally, when there had been a prolonged period of calm air and a backlog of 'grinding' work had built up, if the wind got up in the night Ted would be winkled out to start the mill running during the hours of darkness. By shiftwork and bringing in an old retired hand, the mill would be kept running day and night until it had caught up with itself.

During normal periods of more or less continuous production the mill worked for six days each week, with Sunday a day of rest. At such times Ted and the Miller ran it together as a two-man operation for most of the time, each of them having one half day off during the week. On Wednesdays Ted finished work at 1 o'clock and on Fridays the Miller went off at lunchtime, but in his case seldom stayed later than midday.

Because these two afternoons involved a one-man operation of the mill, it almost always meant the one left on his own had to work an extra hour or so before the assigned workload was completed. So on Wednesday afternoon the Miller was extra late home and similarly on Friday evening Ted was late. To a later generation this would have made something of a nonsense of Ted's so-called 5½ day week since he paid back part of his half day off by working unpaid overtime on Fridays. However, a good many people worked a 6 day week anyway, so Ted did not complain; the arrangement was not unreasonable by the prevailing standards and he enjoyed his midweek break on Wednesdays.

On the Friday of the week following the Friday evening when he had received his bolt-from-the-blue message, Ted resolved to do a little discreet checking up. He made his plans carefully.

The mill, built on the knoll, was at the highest point in an area of hedged fields, all in use as pasture land for sheep and cattle. An unmade road ran down from it to join a narrow lane which curved round the foot of the knoll. It was the perfect location for a windmill, making it the dominating feature of the landscape for miles around.

About half a mile down the lane was the Miller's spacious, pleasant bungalow home. It was set in extensive, well-cultivated gardens having lawns, flower beds, areas of attractive shrubs, a greenhouse, a sizeable vegetable plot and a small orchard. The garden was further enhanced by small, winding stream of sparklingly clear water that had been diverted to encompass a fishpond. The continuous gentle flow of water kept the pond-water permanently crystal clear so that a variety of goldfishes and other species could always be seen in and around the carefully-selected water plants growing in the pond. The Miller's wife had an artistic eye and the garden was well-planned. All in all the local people regarded the Miller's home as a very nice set-up. It was quite an estate in its own right and bore eloquent testimony to his prowess as a money-grubber, for it was by local standards a luxury home, a 'dream of a place', far beyond the reach of most people in the neighbourhood.

Looking down from the top floor of the mill, the Miller's bungalow could be clearly seen. The lane swept in an arc round the foot of the knoll, passing by the gravel driveway which formed the entrance to his estate. It was the back of the bungalow which could be seen from the mill, with the lane passing to the far side of his front garden. A wide, paved terrace ran along the back of the bungalow with five broad, stone steps leading down from the terrace to a lawned area. On either side of the steps, stretching from one end of the terrace to the other, ran a bank formed into an attractive, cared-for rockery.

Ted's very much more modest home lay in the opposite direction of the lane. His cottage, one of a group of four, was some two miles away on the fringe of the parish of Littlebrook. He had a good-sized garden supplemented by an allotment not far up the road. It had been a happy enough haven, up until the loss of his little girl. The fact that by comparison to his own the Miller's home was almost palatial in its size and aspect, had never been a source of concern to Ted. This was the way things were. It was the Miller's good fortune that he had inherited the well-established mill from his father.

Now, though, Ted's mood was different, very different. Anger, hatred and deep resentment fuelled his emotions. Not content with the wealth he already possessed, his rich, greedy, grasping employer had now stolen his wife.

One of Ted's most prized possessions was a pair of ex-Army World War1 binoculars. They were stamped with a broad arrow signifying their War Department origin and also by the date, 1916. Similarly marked was their strong, leather carrying case, complete with a lanyard. When he cycled off to work that Friday morning Ted had the binoculars slung over his shoulders. On arrival at the mill he concealed them in the store shed where they remained until the Miller went home soon after midday for his accustomed Friday afternoon off.

As soon as his boss was safely off the premises Ted collected his binoculars and took them to the top floor of the mill. Standing a little back from the window on the side of the tower overlooking the Miller's house, he spent some checking out what he could see of the estate. He knew the layout of the property very well because of his frequent visits when he made up his hours working in the gardens.

Carefully he scanned along the back of the bungalow and found that he could see to ground level right across the building. Near the left-hand corner under a glazed porchway was the back door leading into the kitchen. To the right of the door was the long kitchen window. Next to this was the dining room window and further along still were French doors giving direct access to the garden from the Miller's main spacious lounge. Built out from the right-hand corner of the building was the large bay window of the Miller's main bedroom, giving a pleasant aspect across the garden. All the remaining windows and the front-door were out of sight.

Having satisfied himself that he could see a good part of the bungalow Ted left his binoculars on the deep ledge beneath the narrow window set in the three-foot thick wall of the mill.

He then went to collect his lunch box from the carrier of his bicycle and made himself comfortable in his usual corner of the store shed to enjoy his snack of sandwiches and cake.

Conscious, however, of the necessity to make up time to give himself some leeway later on, he cut short his normal lunch break and got busy making inroads on the workload that had to be cleared that day.

Just before 2o'clock he disengaged the grinding wheels and went up to the top of the mill to his observation point. As expected, within a few minutes he saw the Miller and his wife Rebecca come out of the back door, lock it after them and walk round the corner of the bungalow out of his field of vision. He knew that they were on their way to the detached garage built on that side of the dwelling.

Not long afterwards he saw the Miller's tan-coloured car chug into view. It was a 1922 Morris Bullnose two-seater saloon which he had bought second-hand the previous year from a local farmer. Ted noticed that the boot lid was up and he could see a large, wickerwork basket standing on the dicky seat, clear evidence that the Miller's wife was on her way to her weekly Women's Institute meeting held in the Littlebrook village hall every Friday afternoon. He knew that the basket would contain home-made cakes baked by Rebecca, together with sundry items from their garden, all destined for the weekly WI bring-and-buy sale.

One of the things that had immediately clicked in Ted's mind when he read the poisonous little note about the Miller's weekly assignation with Mildred was that, regular as clockwork, Rebecca was taken by her husband every Friday to her afternoon meeting. He always returned to collect her at half-past nine in the evening when the weekly whist-drive run by the WI ended.

Rebecca was Treasurer of the Littlebrook branch of the WI and a pillar of the local organisation. The wicker basket, along with the various items provided by her, usually contained bags of flour packed and supplied to the WI at a small discount by the Miller himself. He never failed to seek some business advantage from any activities that he or his wife got involved with.

Ted now knew that this weekly sale of flour was not his employer's only vested interest in Rebecca's WI commitment. He had been quick to work out that this regular Friday arrangement left the Miller safely at home on his own between 3 o'clock and 9 o'clock in the evening with his own wife conveniently busily occupied with her own affairs about three miles away and unable to come home until he fetched her.

At the same time Ted himself had perforce to work late at the mill, leaving Mildred to her own devices: all in all a very nice combination of circumstances, just right, Ted had concluded, for a conniving, scheming bastard like the Miller!

Having seen the car disappear down the lane, Ted returned to his work, resolving to go back up to his observation point at intervals during the afternoon to see what he could discover.

Allowing half an hour or so for the Miller's round trip, when next Ted looked out he saw straightaway that the back door of the bungalow was open, indicating that his boss had already arrived back. Shortly afterwards he saw the Miller himself walk in from the garden and close the door behind him.

When he made his next scrutiny at about 3 o'clock there was no sign of life. Presumably the Miller was inside the bungalow but whether he had company, or was alone, it was not possible to tell. Maybe, Ted thought, Mildred might already be in there with him. He began to wonder whether he was ever likely to learn anything significant from his remote position. This he had half expected and in any event he knew that ultimately—if not today then on some future Friday afternoon—he would almost certainly have to make some personal foray into the Miller's home grounds to seek absolute verification of the truth of the accusation in the letter. To Ted, justice demanded no less.

On his next visit to the mill top, at about a quarter to four, his heart gave a leap as soon as he raised his glasses to his eyes. Round the back of the bungalow, propped up against the wall by the kitchen door, was a lady's bicycle. It was a tall, black, looped-framed machine, with straight handlebars onto which a wicker basket was strapped. Low on the front forks was a red-painted, carbide gas-lamp, and fixed on the back carrier was an open-topped, wooden box. Unmistakeably it was Mildred's bike. It most certainly had not been there just over half an hour ago, so during the interval it was evident that his wife had arrived. No doubt, over perhaps a long period of similar visits, Mildred's arrival was timed to perfection. With a sickening feeling Ted knew that his strong conviction that the letter was true would be proved before the day was out.

Scanning along the windows he looked for signs of life. It was getting a little dusky since the evenings were drawing in at this time of the year. The windows appeared as areas of blackness and he could see nothing at all inside the bungalow. As he watched, however, a light came on in the room where the French windows were and he quickly switched his attention to that room.

Peering intently he could see signs of movement in the room. At one stage the portly form of the Miller passed by the window. Shortly afterwards a female figure passed by, taking off a top coat as she did so. He saw the coat, then a hat, tossed onto a chair. Then the figure walked towards the window and stopped still.

Focusing his glasses Ted saw that it was indeed Mildred standing there. With a start he saw that she appeared to be staring directly at him. He ducked back instinctively but realised that although she was undoubtedly looking at the mill there was no possibility whatsoever that, with the naked eye, she could have seen him standing there looking at her through his binoculars.

As yet there were no lights on in the mill, which gave him added reassurance that he was well and truly out of sight. Quickly he went down the four flights of stairs to the ground floor and lit the lamps. Following normal routine he climbed up again, lighting the lamps from floor to floor. On his way up, as he passed the windows, he was careful not to look towards the bungalow.

On reaching the top floor, though, just before lighting the lamps, he stood in the twilight, well back from the window, and took up his binoculars again to look at the lighted window of the Miller's plush lounge. As he watched, first one then the other of the two figures moved into his line of vision to stop, facing one another, immediately opposite the French doors.

Each held a glinting brandy glass. In his other hand the Miller clutched a bottle of familiar appearance. It was clearly a whisky bottle—'Johnnie Walker', the Miller's favourite brand, as Ted could plainly see by the shape of the bottle which was of square section rather than the more normal rounded shapes of other brands. Pouring a quantity first into Mildred's glass, then his own, he stood the bottle on a side-table and raised his glass to clink it against Mildred's. They each took a drink then turned and moved away from the window.

As they did so, Ted noticed the Miller place his arm around Mildred's shoulders and steer her across the room to the end where he knew there to be a large inglenook fireplace which formed the centre of attraction in the well-furnished lounge—presumably, Ted rightly guessed, to establish her on the comfortable settee facing the fire. A moment later the Miller reappeared at the window and pulled the heavy velvet curtains across the French doors to blot out the view. All very cosy, Ted thought, very cosy indeed.

There was nothing more Ted could do from his present remote position so he turned from the window and lit the top-floor lamps. Collecting his binoculars he then moved swiftly down to the ground floor.

His next move he had more or less worked out during the afternoon while spying out the land. He knew that the next hour or so would be crucial and for this period he intended to devote his time wholly to his detective work. Meanwhile, with the grinding-stones out of action but the windsails still steadily rotating as they had been all afternoon, it would appear to the outside world that he was fully occupied with his milling duties. The machinery would continue to rumble away without harm, leaving him free to pursue his private, unhappy business.

Moving out of the mill he paused for a few moments to satisfy himself that nobody was in sight. Locking the mill door he hurried round to the back of the buildings and clambered through the thick hedgerow into the field that adjoined the mill. His route down to the bungalow was well mapped out in his mind. Ducking his head below the level of the hedges he hurried from one field to another, avoiding open ground but otherwise following a more or less direct line from the mill to the Miller's home, cutting off the corner of the meandering lane which led to the front of the bungalow.

Within ten minutes he had reached the field immediately to the rear of the Miller's back garden. From now on he knew he had to take great care not to be seen, either from inside the bungalow or by anybody who happened to pass along the lane itself. This presented little difficulty. There was plenty of cover and he was all too familiar with the lie of the land.

Slipping through a gap in the hedge he moved quickly from cover to cover and in a matter of a few moments was safely positioned, well out of sight, in the shrubbery, with only the rear lawn separating him from the back of the bungalow.

The light in the lounge was still on, so Ted flitted silently across the lawn to the bungalow and edged his way along the wall to the French doors. Peering through a small slit between the curtains which covered the doors he saw straightaway there was nobody in the room, but he spotted Mildred's coat and hat slung on an armchair.

Looking to the right he noticed a dim light behind the curtains across the corner bay-window of the Miller's main bedroom. Moving silently along the wall he reached the corner but found that the curtains completely covered the large curved windows, preventing him from seeing anything at all of the inside of the room. Passing round the corner of the bungalow he came next to a small window, built out to form a small bay allowing the side garden to be seen from the bedroom, to complement the view from the main window. Carefully Ted approached the window and spotted a gap at the edge of the curtain. With extreme caution he crept to the window and looked into the room.

What he saw shocked him. Though he was in truth expecting something of the kind, nonetheless the reality made his heart miss a beat. Stretched out on her back on the Miller's large double bed was his wife Mildred, stark naked and looking expectantly towards the door. Further along the outside wall Ted could see that the bathroom light was on and almost immediately there came the sound of water gushing down the outside drain through a pipe which obviously came from the bath itself.

Ted kept his eyes glued to the window. A few minutes later the bathroom door opened and the Miller entered the room wearing a colourful dressing gown tied with a dark blue sash. He was leering at Mildred and not taking his eyes off her as he crossed the room.

It was obvious he could hardly wait to get at Mildred. Tossing his towel onto a chair he stripped off his gown with great urgency and threw it also on the chair.

Ted thought he looked repulsive and revolting, absolutely revolting. From his slobbering mouth down over his ape-like chest, covered as it was with a mass of black hair, to his ugly pot-belly below which there was ample evidence what act he was now rampantly ready to perform, and with the flabby body supported on surprisingly skinny white spindly legs, the man looked positively obscene.

How his wife could possibly feel anything but revulsion for this foul creature Ted could not begin to understand. To him the Miller looked to be just about the last man a woman would be expected to welcome into bed with her. Yet welcome him Mildred certainly did. She was ready and waiting, not with the appearance of resigned, abject submission, but with obvious, eager anticipation. She reached up and positively dragged him down on top of her.

What followed was to remain a nightmarish picture in Ted's memory for the rest of his life. Sickened and disgusted by what he saw he at length turned away from the dreadful scene to make his way back to the mill. But he was sufficiently in control of his emotions to go back the way he had come, with the same caution, so that nobody would see his movements. Later on, any such witness of his visit might be dangerous. This much Ted remembered with prudent forethought.

In the event he was successful in this intention. No one saw him either come or go, nor did anybody ever know that Ted had witnessed the ravishing of his wife by his employer.

Back at the mill he took up his duties where he had left off and continued normally until the day's work was done.

It was further testimony to his self-control that by the time he arrived home his behaviour was indistinguishable from any other day. He was of course late home, as was usual on Friday evenings. Mildred was there awaiting his arrival with a hot meal all ready for him. Evidently plenty of experience had given her complete confidence in returning home from her intimate sexual romp with the Miller to face her husband with brazen effrontery. Ted could only stand by and observe—almost with disbelief—this hitherto unsuspected perfidy on the part of his wife.

As he sat silently munching his meal he determined that he would do his best to ensure that today's visit would be the last time Mildred would enjoy the lascivious attentions of the detestable Miller. If his plans worked out as well as he hoped they would, then before next Friday dawned the Miller would have ground his last corn and bedded his last woman.

Later that evening as he rested in his armchair by the warm glow of the coal fire burning in the high grate of the black enamelled stove of their kitchen range, Ted went over again in his mind every detail of what it was he intended to do. By the time he went to bed he was quite satisfied in his mind that his scheme was foolproof.

Only one thing could extend the Miller's life from next week to the week after. By an ironical twist of fate only the failure of the prevailing wind to continue to blow could give him a short reprieve. If the mill were in the doldrums by the middle of next week—a situation that would make the Miller curse at length because they were so busy—then he would live to curse another day. Otherwise his doom was assuredly sealed. A cruel paradox for a man whose worldly wealth depended upon the wind.

Having come to this grim conclusion, Ted fell asleep as soon as he lay down his head and slept like a log. It was the kind of sleep poets like to call 'the untroubled sleep of a simple labouring man'. In reality it was the sleep of exhaustion. Ted had lived through a long and punishing day, physically, mentally and emotionally; so he flaked out.

By contrast, in the next room his wife was in bed but not asleep. She lay awake staring at the ceiling in the light of her small bedside oil-lamp. Presently she would read for a while. For the moment she was savouring in her mind's eye the events in the bungalow that afternoon. The Miller had become an addiction. She enjoyed his ardent attentions and loved the luxury of his home. How she wished she could live there all the time.

For quite some time Mildred lay day-dreaming of how life might then be. It was as though the dreadful void left by the loss of her little daughter had been filled by the excitement of her assignations with the Miller, and the dream world she created around him. These thoughts filled her mind and she no longer agonised by the hour over the cruel fate which had plucked little Jenny from the land of the living. At length, with a deep sigh, she picked up her book and read for a while until she too felt drowsy and could sleep.

If this unhappily estranged married couple dreamt at all, it is highly probable that the same person featured in both their dreams. He was the common factor in their otherwise separate emotional worlds. But whereas to Mildred he would appear as the acme of her deepest romantic yearnings, to Ted he would be the epitome of a selfish, despicable villain, a human louse whose proper destiny ought to be to have his bloated body crushed to pulp.

Their diametrically opposite viewpoints created these very different but in both cases grossly distorted images of a man who, to a detached, neutral observer, would have appeared neither as good nor as bad as they individually pictured him to be.

Unluckily for the Miller, however, his fate would not be determined by a neutral adjudicator. Life seldom works out like that. Only the few get their strictly just deserts based upon coolly balanced judgments. And he was not to be one of them.

15

Chapter 2

DRAMA IN THE WINDMILL
restless windsails signal a disaster within

During the next few days there was nothing to give the slightest indication that dramatic events were in the offing. A close observer, though, had there been one familiar with the normal routines in the mill, might have noticed that Ted spent more time than usual busy up in the cap. The Miller didn't notice because Ted made those extra visits to the cap when his boss was well out of the way. However, despite this precaution, Ted made sure he carried out some routine maintenance on each occasion. An unexpected interruption, well signalled as it would be by the clumping of boots up the wooden steps, would have afforded him ample time to switch from his abnormal clandestine activities to his legitimate work. He made sure that there was plenty of clear evidence around to show the nature of such work. Ted was nothing if not careful; there was little or no chance of his being found out. In the event he was never interrupted so these precautions proved unnecessary. So far, so good—for Ted, that is, but not, alas, for the Miller.

On Wednesday morning of the next week, Ted, first at the mill as was normal, opened up the establishment and made his way up to the cap to set the windsails turning. Before releasing the brake he made one or two final preparations, taking only a few minutes to complete these well-planned finishing touches to his master plan. He then unhooked the taut brake chain from its fastening and slackened it off, allowing the huge windsails to start turning the machinery ready for the day's work. Then, pausing to peer down below to make sure the Miller was not yet around, he shifted the short, strongly-built portable steps permanently kept in the cap to a position under the brake chain's pulley wheel. Quickly he climbed the steps and spent just a few seconds only making a final adjustment to the chain, Satisfied that all was well he replaced the steps and made his way to the bottom of the mill.

When the Miller arrived Ted had already engaged the drive to the grinding-stones to begin production. Last thing the previous evening they had used the sack-hoisting machinery to lift a load of corn to the fourth storey of the mill, stacking the sacks methodically, ready to be dealt with the following day, and then finally emptying several of the sacks down the chute to fill the grain bin on the floor below.

Meanwhile the flour bin on the ground floor was completely empty and all was thus made ready to start grinding the next customer's corn as soon as the mill started working in the morning. One of the ways the Miller maintained his high standards and preserved his reputation was to ensure that his flour and barley-meal bins were completely emptied every night. All production for each day was bagged up before the mill was closed down. Cleanliness was vital, the more so because try as they might, they could not eliminate mice and rats from the premises. Both grain waiting to be milled and flour or barley-meal already ground, had to be securely bagged up, with the exception of the grain in the third-storey storage bins which were well closed and secure against any foraging rats or mice.

As the Miller grunted his greeting of 'Good morning, Ted' to his well-trained and conscientious right-hand man, he noted with satisfaction that flour was already beginning to run out of the spout into the flour bin. He went up to the first floor to check that all was well with the grinding-stones and that their grain-feeding assembly was working normally.

Everything was fine. The simple gravity-feed system was working smoothly and efficiently. Now that production had started the grain which they had left ready in the storage-bin on the floor above him was moving steadily down the feed-pipe to the grain hopper located immediately above the grinding stones.

A rotating 'damsel wheel' vibrated the grain-shaker which caused a continuous fine feed of grain to fall through the central eye-hole of the top runner stone. Once inside, caught between the two stones, the movement of the runner stone combined with the shaped and grooved surfaces of this pair of stone wheels, caused the grain to move outwards towards the periphery of the stones, being crushed and finely ground into powder as it traversed to the edge of the lower stationary stone. By the time it reached the outlet pipe from the lower stone, the farmer's corn had been converted into finely ground flour.

As he always did, the Miller went to the ground floor and tested the flour by taking some in his right hand and rubbing his thumb on it. Long experience made this an effective way of assessing that the grinding-stones were properly set and still functioning efficiently. Periodically they had to be taken out and re-set by a stone-dresser, a job which was always done for the Miller by a visiting expert who serviced many mills in the county. The flour in the bin was warm because of the friction-grinding process and this factor was subconsciously also checked by the Miller as he 'felt' the flour. He would have found difficulty in defining what exactly the qualities were that he automatically noted as he 'felt' the quality of his flour, but he certainly knew when it was right and when it was becoming below par.

Work proceeded steadily throughout the morning and bags of flour gradually accumulated to mark the progress of their labours. When the output reached a certain level Ted went up to the fourth storey to undo some more sacks of grain and shoot the contents into the storage bin below. Production was in this way continuous. There was little verbal communication between the two men during the morning. Long practice of working together made them work as a two-man team, following established routines with little need to exchange words.

Against the back ground of the rumbling and clatter of the machinery, the swish, swish, swish of the huge windsails outside and the vibrating of the whole fabric of the entire mill, each man was lost in his own thoughts. They carried out their complementary actions quite automatically, like component parts of the whole mill-machine. Once in production the mill and the men became a combined unit which ran with well-ordered efficiency. Sacks of grain went in at the top and bags of flour piled up at the bottom. It was a well-organised factory, powered by the seldom-failing wind that blew across the fields where the corn was grown.

By the end of the morning an impressive output had been achieved. At 1 o'clock Ted, now covered, as was the Miller himself, with a fine, grey-white powdery dust, was ready to be away for his lunch and his half-day off.

It was never made easy for Ted to make his departure on a Wednesday afternoon. Far from smilingly wishing him a pleasant afternoon, the Miller, by his sulky expression and grunted comments always contrived to make Ted feel uneasy—almost guilty—when he went off for his well-earned few hours of freedom. The Miller's unconcealed displeasure and reluctance to let him go off, tugged at Ted like a restraining cord from which he had to break away by conscious effort in order to leave the mill.

This day was no different. The Miller's departing words to Ted were, "Well, I suppose you'd better be off then and leave me to finish this lot on my own."

They were the last words the Miller was ever to speak to Ted. As he cycled from the back of the mill past the mill door on his way home he caught a glimpse of his employer's disgruntled-looking face watching him go off down the path. The almost scowling face was his last visual image of the man, matching in mood the tone of the last words he had heard from him. The possibility that he would almost certainly never see the Miller alive again did not trouble Ted in the least.

Thinking back afterwards he did in fact conclude that he had never left the mill in a happier state of mind. He felt as though he were cycling off from a stiflingly oppressive life into the fresh air of an unknown future. Quite simply he was excited, perhaps even elated, and full of vague expectations and hopes of a happier life ahead of him.

Following his normal habits Ted went off home, had his lunch and spent the afternoon in his garden. He was at pains to ensure that there would be nothing unusual in his pattern of behaviour during this particular Wednesday afternoon and evening.

When the light began to fade he made his way indoors, washed and changed, had his tea, rested up and read his newspaper for a while. Then, at opening time, he took himself off to his local pub for his usual long Wednesday evening of relaxation. He always enjoyed these extra hours of freedom on Wednesdays.

After a glass or two of beer his regular card-school companions had arrived. Wednesday was early-closing day for local shops and a small group of men, like Ted, enjoyed this bit of mid-week extra relaxation. He and his small group of cronies spent the evening either playing cards or, if not, darts or dominoes or shove-ha'penny, whatever took their fancy. No matter what the game was there was always a small element of gambling in it, to add to the spice of the evening. Stakes were modest indeed but they added to the fun.

Shortly after 8 o'clock that evening their play was suddenly interrupted. The street door opened abruptly and Brendan Evans, the local village Policeman entered the pub with obvious urgency. Looking round he spotted Ted and called to him across the bar without preamble.

"Ted, you're wanted straight away up at the mill," he said in a tone of voice which in itself was enough to indicate that something serious was afoot. "There's been a bad accident. My Sergeant has asked me to fetch you as fast as I can."

Scrambling to his feet Ted lost no time in hurrying across the room to follow the Policeman outside. Waiting there with its engine running was a Talbot delivery van, a vehicle Ted instantly recognised. It belonged to Ralph Comber, the baker at Ockhambury, a village about two miles from Littlebrook. Ted knew that Molly Comber was a close friend of the Miller's wife and quite often spent Wednesday afternoons at the bungalow. As at Littlebrook, Wednesday was early-closing day at Ockhambury and the baker would run his wife over to see her friend, returning to pick her up during the evening.

Ralph Comber was at the wheel of the Talbot and as soon as Constable Evans and Ted had jumped aboard he drove off toward the mill with as much speed as he could. It seemed that the Miller had failed to arrive home at his usual time and, although his wife was not worried at first because he was quite often late on Wednesdays, she at length became more and more anxious. When Ralph Comber arrived to pick up his wife he had volunteered to run up the lane to the mill in his van to see if all was well.

When he arrived he sensed that something was wrong. Lights were still burning in the mill, but inside all was quiet. The windsails were not turning and all the machinery was still. Of the Miller there was no sign. Ralph entered the mill and called out to the Miller several times, but there was no reply. He climbed the steps to the next floor to check around the place but the scurrying of a rat on the floor above him told him only too well that the mill was unattended. Nonetheless he decided to check the floors above in case the Miller had been taken ill, and he climbed the flights of steps one after the other, calling out as he went.

At length he reached the cap. Aghast, what he saw there was a sight more shocking and horrible than anything he had witnessed in his life before, and one that was to remain etched in his memory to the end of his days.

The mutilated body of the Miller was hanging head downwards, terribly crushed in the gearing above Ralph's head, and an awful pool of blood lay on the floor beneath the mangled body.

Ralph had rushed down the steps and out of the mill to carry his terrible news to the Miller's wife. From the bungalow the Littlebrook village Policeman was contacted by telephone. He in turn summoned the local Doctor, the District Nurse and lastly his own area Police Sergeant whose presence was mandatory on matters as serious as this.

Nothing of course could be done for the Miller by the Doctor. He had been dead long before Ralph had reached the mill and left to tell Rebecca what had happened. Ralph had advised Rebecca to stay with Molly at her bungalow and he himself returned to be at the mill when help arrived.

They couldn't even extricate the Miller's body from the machinery. The expert knowledge of Ted was required to organise that and the Police Sergeant had asked Ralph to fetch him as quickly as possible, with Brendan Evans travelling with Ralph to tell Ted what the situation was that would confront him at the mill.

As the van travelled along the lane round the foot of the knoll, Ted looked up at the dark outline of the mill silhouetted against the clear, moonlit night sky. The windsails signalled a grim message to him, one unnoticed by the others. Almost, but not quite, the sails made a vertical St George's cross against the sky. They had certainly not been brought to a standstill by the practised use of the brake, to rest in their well-known St Andrew's position. It was clear to him they had stopped in an arbitrary position, not a controlled one. That told him much, already.

When the Talbot chugged its way up the steep hill with the baker nervously grinding his gears as he changed down to its lowest gear for the hard climb, a small knot of people could be seen gathered outside the mill door awaiting their arrival.

As they got out Ted glanced up at the sails and saw that they were not in fact perfectly still. The wind up there, though not strong, was still exerting a powerful twist to the sails. As the wind gusted, the sails took up a bit to turn nearer to the vertical then, after the gust, they settled back a little way. He watched for a moment as this spasmodic to and fro movement of the sails followed the whims of the gusty wind. His expert familiarity with the workings of the huge machine provided him with an accurate picture in his mind's eye of what was going on high in the cap, long before he climbed the steps.

As he walked towards the mill door the Doctor reached out his hand and clutched Ted's arm,

"Prepare yourself for a shock, Ted," he said in a concerned voice. "What you are going to see is an awful sight, but we must all do our best to cope with it tonight. The task will tax your strength, I'm afraid, but we need your help up there to get him out."

"Yes," said Ted with his face set grimly, "the Police have told me what to expect."

Standing to one side the group waited for Ted to lead the way into the mill. He was followed by the Sergeant and the Doctor. Outside the local Policeman took charge and shut the mill's main gate to prevent any more sightseers—some were already heading up the lane from the pub—from entering the precincts. Ralph was meanwhile despatched back to the Miller's bungalow with the District Nurse. The Doctor, as ever, had his priorities right. The Miller was beyond help but his wife would need all the support they could give her.

When Ted had climbed the last flight of steps up into the cap it was all he could do to prevent himself from being physically sick. It was a truly awful spectacle. For several minutes the party of three just stood in silence and gazed at the gruesome scene. The Miller's torn and twisted body, together with a splintered section of the guard-rail, was trapped between the brake wheel and the wallower cog wheel it drove. Congealed blood was everywhere and the Doctor commented quietly that a main artery had been severed, causing this massive loss of blood.

"The poor fellow," he went on, must have died almost instantaneously. One arm has been pulled out of its socket and his head is virtually severed. He could not possibly have known much about it. If he had to die it's a mercy he did not suffer a lingering death in dreadful pain alone in this place. What we must do now is get his body out of there and off to the mortuary."

"Before we do that," the Police Sergeant intervened, "we'd better first try to make out exactly what happened. There will have to be an inquest, naturally. How did he come to fall in there like that, do you think, Ted?"

Ted had been studying the machinery with close attention.

"It's all too plain what went wrong," he said gravely. "Look up there!" Ted pointed to the brake chain jammed hard between the side of the large pulley wheel and its U-shaped guide bracket.

"What's happened, then?" asked the Sergeant.

"Well," responded Ted, "to bring the windsails to a halt we have to pull on that chain to operate the brake. The chain must have jumped off the pulley wheel. It looks to me as though the guide-bracket that keeps it over the wheel has worked loose and the chain's gone down the side of it. The Miller must have jerked it a bit sideways instead of keeping it square-on to the pulley wheel when he pulled it."

"What did he do then, do you think?" asked the Sergeant. "Did he get up there to try to free the chain?"

"No," said Ted with a grim face. "He would know that was impossible. The weight of the brake-staff keeps it too tight. One man couldn't shift it—not easily, anyway. But he wouldn't even try. When the brake chain gives trouble we climb up there and bang that large wooden wedge under the far end of the brake-staff to lift it upwards to apply the brake. That stops the sails turning and at the same time slackens the far end of the chain. Then we can knock the chain back up onto the pulley wheel."

"Bit dangerous that, isn't it?" commented the Doctor.

"Not really, for us," answered Ted. "We know the dangers and watch what we are doing. The guard-rail holds you back from the brake wheel. You just have to be careful not to let your coat, or a scarf, say, be caught up by the cogs and dragged into the gear wheels there."

Ted paused a moment or two, studying the awful scene thoughtfully.

"You can see what happened, though," he continued. "He climbed up to reach the brake lever, leaning across the guard-rail. Under his heavy weight the guard-rail has splintered at the far end and broken off. He must have pitched head downwards over the wallower wheel there. His arm must have got caught in the cogs between the brake wheel and the wallower so that he was pulled straight into the machinery and torn apart."

"Yes," said the Sergeant, "that's plain enough. Not much doubt about that, is there? At least we can see exactly what happened. That's always a help to everybody in a fatal accident like this. If we can do so, we have to explain to the Coroner how an accident came to happen. Sometimes nobody can tell and we never do find out. At least in a case like this the Coroner is able to warn others in similar situations of the possible dangers."

"Well then," intervened the Doctor grimly, "now we know how he got in there what we've got to do is to get him out again, as cleanly as we can."

It was all too obvious that this in itself was going to be no easy task. Somehow, what was left of the Miller had to be extricated from the meshed cog teeth gripping him. The whole system was jammed up. It was a seemingly hopeless mess.

The Police Sergeant turned to Ted.

"What do you suggest, Ted?" he asked. "How can we possibly release him from those wheels?"

As they watched, the windsails, straining as they were to turn under the force of the wind, kept turning the brake wheel slightly, running part way up the next tooth on the cogs to squash the terrible mess of clothing, wood, flesh and bones. The gory mash formed a wodge that blocked the rotation of the wheel. As the wind gusts fell off, the wheel appeared to back off slightly as though working against a spring. Ted knew that this very small movement of the brake wheel which they could see in front of them corresponded to a very noticeable movement of the tips of the windsails as seen outside. There was a tremendous leverage involved. That is how the system worked.

Ted also knew, but didn't say, that if the wind picked up, the brake wheel would overcome the resistance of the mess blocking it and that the Miller's body would then be cut into two pieces by the immense force. The iron teeth on both the brake wheel and the wallower-wheel meshing with it, would simply cut through the pitiful mess now jamming them. He knew full well what they had to do.

"Wait here a little while," he said to his two companions. "I'll go down and luff the cap round a quarter-turn to get the sails out of the wind. Then we shall be able to lever the brake wheel backwards to release the body."

So saying, Ted hurried down the steps and out of the door to the concrete apron surrounding the base of the tower. Directly opposite to the windsails the cap overhead stuck out in a structure carrying the fan-tail. This section of the cap was there to give a measure of automatic alignment of the windsails into the wind. A propeller wheel, having its axis at right-angles to the windsails' axle, turned an arrangement of cogs and a worm-gear to force the entire cap of the mill to turn on its mounting. In a strong wind the turning force was enough to align the cap correctly, bringing the windsails squarely on into the wind.

In a moderate wind, however, it would barely do so and the cap would stop short of optimum alignment. In a light wind it failed to work adequately at all. To overcome this difficulty the mill was fitted with the traditional hand-operated chain system which had been all that was available prior to the development of the fan-tail automatic alignment device. A long, endless chain hung down from the projecting fan-tail housing high above.

It was part of their routine each day to check the alignment of the windsails from time to time. The fan-tail carried a weather-cock mounted well up above the housing where they could see it without difficulty when standing on the apron below. All they had to do was pull on the chain, hand over hand, to rotate the mill cap above them until the windsails lined up facing the direction from which the wind was coming. As the cap above them turned, they walked round the concrete apron underneath, pulling the chain until the correct alignment was achieved. With the wind full on the face of the huge windsails they rotated with awesome force, even in a moderate breeze.

As Ted appeared from the door Brendan Evans quickly joined him.

"What's to do, Ted?" the Policeman asked, anxious to know what was happening.

"I'm going to luff the cap round a bit to turn the sails out of the wind," Ted explained. "We have to get the wind off the sails to stop the brake wheel trying to turn. Until we do that there's no chance of us backing it off to get his body out. The force is too great. He's trapped solidly in the gearing. If the wind gets up he will get chopped in half completely."

Brendan Evans winced at this gruesome prospect while Ted walked round the side of the mill, grabbed the hanging chain and began to pull it down, hand-over-hand, in a well-practised way. High above their heads, as he pulled the chain, it moved over a cog wheel and the huge cap slowly turned out of the wind.

Ted mentally noticed that the Policeman, used no doubt to dealing with life's ever-

22

present quota of tragedies, was sufficiently detached to be able to interest himself in how the mechanism of the alignment system above them worked. The thought struck him that it was all part of the same process by which people get hardened to things by constant exposure to them—just like he'd got used to working day after day with the miserable bastard whose bloated body was now jamming up the works, squashed up in the gearing high in the mill above their heads.

For all his experience of life in the raw, Brendan Evans would have been extremely startled had he been able to read these markedly unsympathetic thoughts in the mind of the Miller's right-hand man, working with such quiet efficiency beside him.

Having luffed the windsails round out of the wind, Ted hurried back into the mill and ran up the steps to the top. There was a spring in his step for he suddenly realised that he was now very much the man in charge of the mill!

On arrival back at the top he briskly took charge of events and got busy straight away with the unpleasant task of getting the Miller's body out of the gear wheels.

He'd picked up some empty grain sacks from the floor below. He placed four of these over the pool of blood beneath the Miller's body and passed another to the Police Sergeant.

"If you put this round his body and hang on to him, I'll lever the brake wheel backwards to free him," Ted said, with the assurance of a man who knew exactly what had to be done.

When the Sergeant was ready Ted picked up a large, heavy length of timber and inserted it through the brake wheel just behind one of the massive pieces of timber that formed the box-like framework structure of the centre of the wheel. With the end of his lever wedged at a suitable anchoring point behind the wheel, Ted heaved with all his strength and succeeded in inching the wheel back a notch or two. The Doctor saw what he was about and added his strength to Ted's on his improvised lever system. After several successive heaves they finally managed to back off the huge wheel sufficiently to allow the Sergeant to pull what was left of the Miller free, and allow his body to slump on the rough sacking spread below him on the floor.

An ambulance from the Canterbury City Hospital had by this time reached the mill, and soon afterwards the ambulance crew carried the Miller away from his mill, his departure for the last time, to deposit him in the mortuary.

In due course a verdict of Accidental Death was recorded by the Coroner at an inquest and the Miller was laid to rest in the Littlebrook churchyard, alongside his father.

Meanwhile it fell to Ted to clean up the awful mess at the mill with the help of Toby Twist, a retired mill-hand now called back to work full-time at the mill until a replacement could be found. Toby had spent most of his working life at the mill and they were lucky to have him on call.

Ted and his elderly mate did not talk much while they were engaged in their stomach-churning task of removing the last traces of the Miller from the massive machinery that had destroyed him. The great teeth on the cog wheels carried stark evidence of the way the trapped body had been dragged in, to be horrifyingly crushed and torn apart. It was not a pleasant job. They both had to fight back almost overwhelming feelings of nausea.

"Cor, strewth, Ted," muttered Toby as they paused to rest a moment, his face ashen with the horror of it all. "Reminds me of Harry Rayner's meat-mincing machine in that den of his behind the slaughterhouse. Makes you realise we are all made of meat, just like the stuff he cuts up on his butcher's slab. Never quite thought of it like that before, had you?"

Ted's face went greener than ever as he struggled not to heave his guts up. He made no reply; he couldn't. His condition was not helped by Toby's further observations.

"Only hope my missus doesn't shove a dollop of sausage meat in the frying pan along with the egg and bacon when I get home tonight," he said. "She's fond of doing that when I'm late home and she has a fry-up for my supper. Don't suppose I shall ever be able to look at mince-meat or sausages again as long as I live without remembering the mashed-up Miller's meat in these wheels."

"Ease up, Toby," grunted Ted. "It's bad enough having to face this job, without hearing your bloody awful comments."

"Sorry, Ted," responded Toby. "Never seen anything like this before. A bit more than I can take, this is. I'm not thinking what I'm saying. Sorry, mate!"

With that they carried on their gruesome task in silence, each doing his best not to think about what it was they were clearing up.

It was not until they came to the floor that Ted's strong constitution finally gave way.

"Cor, bloody 'ell, Ted! Look down there," Toby said, pointing to a place beneath the windshaft where lay the remains of a dinner-plate sized puddle of congealed blood. It showed signs of being scuffed and smudged all over and from it, extending in a trail to a point under the woodwork by the steps, was the unmistakeable signs of rats having gone to and fro across the floor. Somehow that made it worse than ever. Beyond doubt the rats, a constant menace in the mill, had homed in on this unexpected supply of unique nourishment and trafficked across the floor before Ralph Comber's arrival had scared them away. The presence of rats' droppings here and there in the revolting mess showed they had been around quite some time before getting scared off.

"Just fancy that," commented Ted in a hushed tone. "Rats gorging themselves on the Miller's blood. What a way to end his days at the mill! Hated those rats, he did. Never could get rid of them for long, hard as he used to try. They were too cunning for him. There are too many places around this old place where they can hide away. Good job he didn't know there'd come a day when they stuffed their stinking guts with his blood!"

That was too much for Ted. With a hand held tightly over his mouth he hurried down the steps out into the fresh air and was violently sick by the hedge. It was quite a while before he was able to rejoin Toby and finish their unenviable task of cleaning up the top floor. At length it was done and with great relief they went below to occupy themselves with more congenial duties.

Gradually the fuss subsided and the pressing need for production to be maintained impelled all concerned to concentrate upon their work and try to put the tragedy behind them.

Unable to secure the immediate services of the millwright, who worked to a tight schedule and was too heavily engaged to come in straightaway, a local builder was called in to carry out the repairs necessary to restore safety in the cap. A carpenter rebuilt the guard-rail arrangement, to protect those working there from being caught up, as was the Miller, in the dangerous machinery which turned with such awesome momentum.

With the help of the blacksmith, an improved system of guide-hoops and U-brackets was fitted to prevent the brake chain from jumping off its pulley wheel and slipping down the side of the wheel, as it had done before. This simple defect was judged to have been the primary cause of the Miller's fatal accident.

At length everything was back to normal in the cap. But it was not a place anyone liked to go more often than was necessary, especially after dark in the flickering light of the oil-lamps. Ted felt particularly ill-at-ease up there, a feeling that was to stay with him for a long time to come.

Chapter 3

AN EYE FOR AN EYE

a doom-laden voice from the past
is remembered

Ted noticed, and was not alone in doing so, that Mildred appeared much more upset even than the Miller's wife herself by the death of his detested boss. This may have puzzled others but it certainly didn't surprise him.

To preserve what he hoped was the delusion that he knew nothing of Mildred's secret association with the odious man, he felt it necessary to comment upon her seemingly unnatural and excessive grief.

"I can't understand why you're so upset about him," Ted said one day when he found her, for the umpteenth time, sobbing in her bedroom. "It's not as though he was a nice bloke," he went on, with a hard edge to his voice. "He was a miserable, selfish, greedy, fat-gutted old bastard. Nobody liked him, so far as I know. I certainly didn't. Good riddance to the old devil, I say! He never did me any favours, that's for sure!"

"I just can't get over the dreadful way he died," sobbed Mildred. "Getting caught up and torn to pieces in that horrid great wheel was a terrible way to die! I keep thinking about it. I can't get it out of my mind."

"Well, you'll just have to try," remarked Ted without any trace of sympathy. "We still rely on the mill for our living. And so does his wife, Rebecca. You had better start feeling sorry for her for a change!"

This last jibe hit Mildred where it hurt most, and it started her wondering if Ted knew anything. Afterwards she made a determined effort to stop feeling sorry for herself. That was what she had been doing and she realised that it was having the effect of drawing attention to herself. That was something she certainly did not want. There was no future in it, least of all to bring her sympathy from other people. She was on her own, and now she knew it, only too well.

With the death of the Miller, Ted became of vital importance to the continued survival of the mill as a going concern, and in turn to the prosperity of Rebecca, the Miller's widow. She had to rely upon him to run things for her. At the mill he became the boss and worked very hard to make a success of it. Life for him was now entirely different now that he was no longer at the beck and call of another man, especially one as unpleasant as his late employer.

Not only did Ted look after the practical running of the windmill but he also assumed increasing responsibility for the administration of the place. It soon became evident to Rebecca that her future depended very much upon him. Fortunately she liked him and they got on well together. Ted spent more and more time at the bungalow working with her on matters connected with the business.

After several months had elapsed she decided to make Ted a partner in the business and discussed the proposition with her solicitor. On satisfying himself that she was quite sure she and Ted could work well together and that Ted was an honest, reliable man in whom they could have complete confidence, her solicitor drew up an agreement meeting her wishes. He accepted the validity of her argument; the proposed arrangement appeared a wise move for her to make because it secured Ted's permanent presence at the mill and gave him the best possible incentive to make a success of it.

When the proposition was put to Ted he not unnaturally jumped at it. It was a wonderful opportunity and presented him with the prospect of long-term security, together with the opportunity to enhance his standard of living by using his initiative in developing the business.

So Ted and Rebecca became partners in a joint concern. Previously Rebecca had played no part in the business at all. Her husband had never any inclination to give her a say in its running and kept her out of it. This approach was typical of him; he had to be the undisputed boss. He ran the mill and she ran the home. And that was that.

Now, given the opportunity, Rebecca enjoyed the responsibility and in truth her life was happier than it had been for a long time. She and Ted made a good team. They spent an increasing amount of time together and became very close friends.

It was clearly necessary for Ted to have a right-hand man at the mill to understudy him and run the mill for brief periods on his own when the need arose. He determined to choose his man carefully. It happened that there was young man in his early twenties upon whom Ted had his eye. He was well-known to Ted and exactly the right type. Since leaving school he had been earning his living working in a flour mill and knew the essentials of the trade well.

He was not, however, employed in another windmill but in a water mill situated not many miles away, using the reliable flow of the modest little river that passed along the valley through Littlebrook, having its origin in springs not many miles from the village. The river formed an attractive feature of the area and gathered strength from small streams as it followed the contours of the land and wound its way through the countryside towards the Channel coast.

It mattered little that the motive power of the mill in which he worked was water, not wind. Ted knew it would only be a matter of time before he became equally well-versed in the technicalities of a mill powered by wind, if only he could be persuaded to make the change.

Ted decided to see him and broach the matter. In his existing job Neville Page was the junior member in a team of four men employed at the water mill and could expect no promotion there in the near future. In Ted's present circumstances he was very conscious of the fact that the acquisition of the right kind of assistant was extremely important to him and could greatly influence the way things went in the next few years. So Ted offered Neville a substantially better job with, so far as they could then tell, good prospects of a permanent and safe future. Neville grabbed the chance and the deal was sealed, much to the satisfaction of both Ted and Rebecca.

Two weeks later Neville started work at the windmill. He quickly settled into the routine and the place ran with smooth efficiency. With some relief, Ted's temporary helper Toby Twist, fetched reluctantly out of his retirement in the emergency situation, returned to his more leisurely life. At the age of 72 the heavy work at the mill was really too much for him and his health would have suffered if he had attempted to put the clock back and carry so hard a full-time job for much longer. He went back to his garden and resumed his status as temporary relief-worker, on call at the mill when needed. Occasional extra income was welcome and the arrangement suited him very well.

Within one year of the Miller's untimely death the mill was running more successfully than it had ever done. Everybody was happy. Except, that is, for Mildred. She wasn't at all happy. She was the loser. Once again she took to wandering the woodland paths, lost in her own private world of frustrated dreams and melancholy thoughts.

Mildred was uncomfortably aware that she was the one who had made the break in her marriage. She had moved into her own bedroom and there she had remained. By her own choice she had virtually pushed Ted out of her life. Now she began to wonder. She watched him grow into a happier and more confident man. He had a certain air of self-assurance which she had never seen in him before: a successful business man with his own financial stake in the thriving mill.

Ted was working very hard, perhaps harder than he had ever done, but with the very great difference that now he was working for himself. The harder he worked, the more money he made. Somehow, though, however hard he worked, it did not seem to tire him as much as had his life under the domination of his difficult, demanding, deceitful, duplicitous and altogether thoroughly despicable—and now thankfully forever departed—employer. This man had oppressed and mentally wearied him, making hard work harder. Now the clouds had lifted and his spirits were lifted with them. In this free atmosphere he seemed to have boundless energy.

Life had changed very much. Capriciously, now that Mildred had wilfully, totally alienated Ted, she found herself wanting him back again. She began to brood on this and for the first time started to regret the actions she had taken and the shameful way she had deceived him.

And then—out of the blue one day— she was jolted out of her grey, self-centred world. In the wicker basket of her bike, when she dropped some shopping into it, she found a poisonous little note. Somebody, somewhere, had also been watching Ted, watching him with envy as he prospered and grew visibly happier by the day. And envy sometimes fosters spite. It certainly did so in this case.

In a venomous few words the writer let it be known that Ted and Rebecca were no longer just business partners. The message was crude and graphic, leaving nothing to the imagination.

The note was in a rather grubby envelope. On it, pencil-written in large letters, were the words,

TO MILDRED KNOWLES
PRIVATE AND CONFIDENSHULL

Had Ted caught a glimpse of the words on the envelope his memory would have received an immediate jolt. But he never did see it. As for Mildred, she did not even notice the curiously misspelt word.

The style of the message itself, childlike in its simple rhyming lines, but adult in its discernment and manner of expression, would also have registered with Ted. He would have been convinced that this, taken with the strangely spelt word on the envelope, showed beyond any shadow of doubt that the letter came from the same odious person as did his own similar one. It was the second vicious little poison-pen letter that the writer had fired like a lethal poison dart into his private world.

The words to Mildred, which Ted was never to see, were,

When the Miller was living you were his slave,
But now he is mouldering in his grave,
And you are mourning that he lost his life,
Your husband Ted is shagging his wife.

It was now Mildred's turn to be consumed by hatred and she reacted in a manner not unlike that in which her husband—unbeknown to her— had done under similar circumstances not so very long before. She destroyed the letter, determined no one else should ever see it, and set about proving whether or not what it said was true.

It did not take her long to establish the stark accuracy of the message. She watched Ted's movements carefully and, by a bizarre twist of fate, a virtual re-run of an earlier scene took place at the Miller's bungalow.

This time, though, it was Mildred who watched through the window. Inside, on the same bed, in surroundings she knew so well, she saw Ted and Rebecca acting out the same scene that their respective spouses had performed before.

Sick at heart, Mildred realised she was on the receiving end of her just deserts. Fate had dished out its classical judgement. She remembered a simple saying often repeated by her old grandfather when she was a little girl. In her mind she could hear his deep 'Old Father Time' voice droning out in his rich, broad Kentish accent the doom-laden words,

**'An eye for an eye,
A tooth for a tooth'**

Her Grandad, of whom she had been very fond, seemed to have a store of ancient sayings, time-honoured maxims and proverbs, which he had a habit of trotting out to fit events of day-to-day life in the countryside, especially those involving local personalities who, for good reasons or bad, happened to be well known.

How well, Mildred thought, this particular one seemed to fit her own present predicament. The words kept repeating over and over in her head as she stared through the window. As she watched, mesmerised by what she saw, she found herself adding words of her own as the remorseless logic of the message narrowed down to focus on what was happening there in front of her eyes.

**'An eye for an eye,
A double-cross for a double-cross,
A deceit for a deceit,
A bit on the side for a bit on the side,
An ADULTERY for an ADULTERY'**

The word *ADULTERY* surfaced from the depths of Mildred's memory, hitherto locked there in a vaguely remembered litany learnt as a young lass and now intoned in priestly fashion in her mind as one of the Bible's '*Thou shalt nots*'. It was a word never once used, either in thought or conversation, all her life; it was one that she had first come across in Confirmation classes.

During her liaison with the Miller she had certainly never come near remembering the word in association with her delightful activities with him on the bed she was now looking at.

But now, on the receiving end of betrayal, as the victim, her mind was stimulated by a deep anger which set it buzzing more feverishly by far than had the depth of any feelings of guilt she had experienced previously about allowing herself to be bedded by the Miller.

Out shot the formal, forbidding, frighteningly legalistic word *ADULTERY!* Nothing less! Plain, shameless *ADULTERY.* One of the Ten Commandments was being broken!

Brazenly-Busted on the Bouncing Bed by the Miller's Widow and her Husband Ted!

At the impact of the word Mildred instantly experienced sharply painful emotions. She was affronted, wounded, aggrieved, and felt terribly wronged. But only for the briefest of moments. Only for a moment was she able to indulge herself in the luxury of feeling the intense outrage and overwhelming self-pity of being the betrayed person; the injured party; the victim of *ADULTERY.*

For hard on the heels of this hurt to herself, new-born in her mind and fast beginning to be nurtured by gnawing at her guts, came once again the memory of her Grandfather's voice, growling out his much-used message.

'An eye for an eye!' intoned the voice from the past, with emphasis on the principle of repayment and rightful revenge.

The inference sank in, as suddenly as the self-pity had started to suppurate.

The *'eye'* that she was witnessing being dished out to her was the revenge *'eye'* of her Grandad's equation. *She* had provided the first *'eye'*, the big one. It had simply bounced back like a ball off a wall. *Hers* was the first *ADULTERY.* What she was seeing being enacted with such enthusiasm and obvious unadulterated pleasure on the bed, was the payoff for it; pure unadulterated adultery!

There was no escape from the realisation that she had forfeited her right to feel affronted and sorely wronged by the two people entangled on the bed. At length she could watch their antics no longer. They sickened her and she began to feel overcome by nausea.

Silently she went off home, her mind in a torment. It was a long time later that day before her mind quietened and her thoughts became more controlled.

It was not in the nature of things, though, that she accepted for very long the clinical balance of the scales of natural justice. By devious and twisted thinking, perhaps a natural process because her mind was likely to be more slanted towards excusing her own conduct than that of the other two, she finally came to feel more sinned against than guilty of sin herself. *Her* infidelity seemed more excusable to her than did Ted's!

However illogical her conclusion may have been, once arrived at it fuelled an increasing anger and bitter resentment against Ted and Rebecca. Conversely she became less remorseful about her liaison with the Miller. After all, he was dead and buried. But the other two were alive—very much alive and fully operational, as witness their uninhibited, vigorous, eager, rhythmic performance, seen through the garden window.

Her anger, though, became more and more focused upon Rebecca. Perversely Ted gradually became more and more desirable to her once again. Somehow it was as though the account between her and Ted had been squared. But the Miller being now out of the framework left Rebecca as the odd one out.

Mildred became burnt up with jealousy of Rebecca, jealous of her association with Ted, jealous of her life of luxury in the sumptuous comfort of her lovely bungalow and garden, and jealous too of her obvious happiness and contentment with the new circumstances of her life.

So she started her own solitary planning, as determined as Ted had been to act on her own, taking nobody into her confidence. She was equally as remorseless, equally as thorough, equally as implacable and, in the end, equally as successful.

Six weeks later Rebecca was dead.

A writer of a novel, however far-fetched, would not have dared dream up and describe such a clean-cut, surgical removal from the land of the living, of two people, by the cold-blooded planning of amateur assassins bent upon their work of merciless destruction in this mirror-image-balanced equation of cause and effect. Yet so it was. Once again, in a true life situation, fact proved stranger than fiction.

As in the case of her husband's death before her, the Coroner's verdict at Rebecca's inquest was Accidental Death. Nobody, as far as is known, ever suspected anything else. Or if they did, they didn't voice it.

People were used to fate dishing out unpredictable blows. Among the creatures of the countryside life and death existed side by side. Sometimes, in the same way, human beings ended their lives abruptly, even on a day when everything seemed set fair—but from natural causes, accidents, and sometimes even, occasionally, from suicides—but not murder. Murder was something that happened elsewhere! So suspicions were seldom aroused in connection with sudden deaths, however unexpected and dramatic.

There was certainly no recent or known local precedent for the successive accidental deaths of a husband and wife, especially at so short an interval between one tragedy and the other. But even this unique circumstance did not stimulate suspicion, for

30

local people were philosophical. The 'Old Man with his Scythe' went about his appointed task as 'The Grim Reaper' in a strange and relentless way. Nobody, it was said, ever knew who would be cut down next; his process of selection was inscrutable. The Miller certainly had no warning and neither did Rebecca.

There was much discussion among locals on the twin tragedies that had removed this couple from their midst. Some drew a little comfort from the fact that Rebecca's manner of dying was not so horrific as her husband's dreadful end.

Rebecca was ordained by fate to leave the scene in a rather more gentle way. Not that she was any less dead at the end of it!

It was her habit, after the loss of her husband, to cycle each week to her regular WI meeting. She could not drive their Bullnose Morris car and it had remained immobile in their garage since its owner had departed. As yet it had not even occurred to Rebecca that she might perhaps be able to learn to drive it herself. Driving motor cars was very much a man's world, and deeply implanted in her subconscious mind was the certainty of the scornful reaction her husband would have had to any suggestion that she might be able to drive the car herself. He would have scoffed at the very idea and she would have been laughed out of court! So she had not even considered the possibility.

Many people concluded later on that this was a very great pity because, had she have been able to use her car, she would most probably be still alive. Mildred, hearing this comment, privately disagreed with the conclusion. She alone knew that all that would have changed would have been the manner of Mildred's death: and it would likely have been a much less easy way to die.

So Rebecca had travelled about locally on her bike—to go to the village for shopping, to visit friends and, tragically as it turned out, to get to her WI functions. She did not much like cycling in the dark, but had no choice if she wanted to continue her usual evenings out. Ted had fixed up a carbide gas lamp on her bike, like the one he had fitted to Mildred's bike. The dim yellow light from this was just about sufficient to light her way, and also to let anybody else know that she was there.

On the way home from WI meetings she took shortcuts along footpaths. This was normal practice for cyclists in the district. One of these took her across a narrow bridge made of wooden planks, which crossed the river by the water mill where her employee Neville Page had done his miller's training. Along each side of the bridge was a waist-high wooden rail giving, it was felt, perfectly adequate safety for walkers.

It was here that Rebecca's life came to an end. In the dark, on a cold, blustery winter's night, she had apparently skidded on the wet, slippery surface and come off her bike. The Police concluded that she had pitched over the rail. Below her, very deep and ice-cold was the mill pool. Some ten feet deep, the pool was always treated with respect. Its mere appearance was malevolent, especially in the gloom of a cold winter evening.

Local boys knew only too well that it was highly dangerous to attempt to bathe in this dark, deep, treacherous pool. The rush of water from the millrace caused a swirling, churning whirlpool, difficult enough to get out of by a strong swimmer even in the heat of summer. It was deadly dangerous in the ice-cold of winter.

Rebecca, suddenly plunging headfirst into this maelstrom, fully dressed in her heavy winter clothing, stood no chance. She was not the first to die in this fateful place, nor was she to be the last. And the reputation of the place was such that heads nodded in ready acceptance of her accidental death. It is doubtful if anyone ever gave a second's thought to the possibility that there had been foul play.

There was in fact very nearly a double tragedy there that night. A later cyclist, travelling the same route, ran into Rebecca's bike and came off, fortunately saving himself from also pitching over the rail by grasping it and stopping his fall.

31

Happily for Mildred this second near-tragedy gave even greater credence to the verdict of Accidental Death on Rebecca.

Just before the footpath reached the river and the entry point to the wooden bridge, there was a fairly sharp turn. On each side of the path was a high privet hedge. The result of this turn in the pathway was that a cyclist's front wheel was on the turn coming into the open past the end of the hedge and had to be straightened to enter the bridge square-on. The man who ran into Rebecca's bike was moving too fast to stop. He hit the bike a split-second before he saw it, and off he came.

In a matter of moments he could see there had been a serious accident. Rebecca's bike lay across the path with its front wheel partially under the lower rail. The contents of the wicker basket fixed to her handlebars were scattered on the planks up to the edge of the bridge and further items were subsequently fished out of the river. Nursing a painful, badly-sprained wrist, the man hurried to the nearest house for assistance. In the light of a hurricane lamp a lady's body could be seen floating face-down on the water, turning in a widening circle like a floating log eddying towards the reeds along the bank, as driftwood frequently did at that point.

By the time the police had retrieved her body and the doctor made his examination, it was estimated that she had probably been in the river for over half an hour before being found. It was obviously just another accident—nobody's fault, just sheer bad luck!

Ted was mortified by the news. He had become very attached to Rebecca and her sudden death shocked him deeply. It was a situation he was totally unprepared for. Life had been going so well and the possibility that it could be so cruelly changed overnight was something he had not even remotely considered. They had seemed to be set fair for years to come, working happily together as partners and intimate friends.

His first priority had to be the practical one of ensuring that the mill continued to function normally so that business was not interrupted. This he did quite automatically. There was no problem about that.

What very quickly started to exercise his mind, though, causing him increasing anxiety, was the legal position. He owned a half share in the mill, a partnership in a thriving concern. But what, he wondered, was his position now? It was a question which he needed to have answered without delay, so he fixed an appointment to see the solicitor who had organised things for them.

Ted knew that as part of the partnership agreement the solicitor had advised Rebecca to have a clause written in which ensured the return of the business to her sole ownership in the event of Ted's death. This was fair because Ted was not buying his way into the business but having it given to him in return for the security to Rebecca of his continuing to manage and run the mill indefinitely. It was a fair deal for Ted because it increased his income substantially and gave him security for life.

In the event of the reverse circumstance of Rebecca predeceasing him, Ted had the assurance that his half-share in the mill would be preserved for the rest of his life.

Beyond that, though, he knew nothing. Presumably he would finish up with a new, as yet unknown partner. That could make a lot of difference to his life. In his anxiety he thought out a variety of repercussions, many of which would present him with difficulties and problems. For a start he had no money behind him. Doubtless his new partner would have. So, Ted reasoned, as likely as not he would finish up very much the junior partner.

Unknown to him, however, Rebecca had everything well organised. In due course, when the legal wheels had turned and probate granted, the solicitor, who had been nominated by Rebecca as sole executor of her estate, was able to put Ted's mind at rest.

But he made such a self-important meal of it that he prolonged Ted's unease quite unnecessarily.

There were two very important things that profoundly affected Ted's future. They had been organised by the solicitor on Rebecca's instructions in two steps, the first just a few weeks after the partnership had been set up, and the second some months later.

As these legal steps had been taken one at a time the solicitor told Ted about them one at a time. Tediously, in their chronological order, dealing with dates and data in his dry, legalistic manner, the pompous old man droned on ponderously to the bemused, rather overawed working man trying to take in the import of what was being said. The wording of the documents the solicitor read from was laboured and in parts virtually incomprehensible. Cynics were known to say that by the use of this complicated language solicitors made themselves seem to be a good deal cleverer than they actually were! Judging by the way he clearly savoured his reading, it was a fair comment about this particular member of the profession, if not for all of them.

Suddenly, though, when the solicitor at last summarised what it all meant, Ted's spirits lifted immensely. He could hardly believe what he had heard and had to get the salient points confirmed by seeking Yes or No answers to some simple questions—all of which reinforced the private and jaundiced view of the self-opinionated old solicitor that the scruffy fellow sitting in front of him was not worthy of the very great good fortune that had come his way.

In essence Rebecca's wishes were simple and unequivocal. Her first modification to her own original wishes concerning the disposal of her estate in the event of her predeceasing Ted, involved the ownership of the mill. After having thought about it for some time she felt she would like Ted to have the same security as she had. She instructed the solicitor to make an alteration in her Will directing that Ted should become the sole owner of the mill, inheriting, in effect, her half of the partnership.

On the solicitor's firm advice she did not tell Ted of this provision since it did not affect the existing agreement at all. It was part of the wily old boy's policy to impress upon his clients the wisdom of keeping their own council. He was particularly insistent that there was no reason whatsoever for Rebecca to divulge details of this arrangement to Ted. So Rebecca had taken his advice and said nothing, though she herself could see no reason why she should not pass on to Ted this comforting reassurance of his security should she die before him.

The solicitor forebore to tell her that it had been known for people who stood to gain from the death of another to contrive their departure earlier than normal natural circumstances would otherwise have ordained!

At a later date, when Rebecca had become more than just a little fond of Ted, she returned to the solicitor once again. She had thought long and hard about her Will in general. She and the Miller had no children and no close family ties at all. Their close family connections were distant ones. The people numbered among these were not in any way close friends or treasured family connections. There had been no help, not even a show of sympathy from any of them when her husband the Miller had died so tragically—a reflection perhaps of his almost universal unpopularity. Why, she figured, should any of them stand to benefit in any way from her estate should she die? The mere thought of it disturbed her.

But Ted—now he was a different matter altogether! Of all the people in the world he was the one Rebecca cared for most. Far and away the most. So she instructed the solicitor to destroy her previous Will and prepare a new one leaving everything she possessed in the world to Ted. Not that at the time she was in a morbid state of mind—in fact quite the opposite. Inwardly she felt sure that she would almost certainly outlive

Ted. But if fate decreed otherwise, then her mind was made up about what it was she wanted done on her behalf; she knew her mind and had absolutely no qualms about it.

Once again her trusted legal adviser enjoined her to keep her own counsel about these new provisions, which he duly wrote into her new Will as directed. He took the opportunity, as discreetly as he could, to find out from her if she had taken his advice and not told Ted or anyone else about her previous arrangements concerning the mill itself. He was quite satisfied after his talk with her that she had indeed treated the whole matter of her Will with complete secrecy.

As it turned out, it proved a good thing he had made these enquiries because, when Rebecca died so tragically, he had no reason to be suspicious about it.

When in due course he came to the moment when he told Ted about the contents of Rebecca's Will, Ted's unfeigned surprise was too obviously genuine for there to be any possibility that he'd had prior knowledge of his good fortune. Had he known, he would probably have found it hard, if not impossible, to manifest such signs of natural pleasure on hearing it, and certainly would not have made several tedious requests for confirmation of its terms.

Not for the first time in his long career of administering clients' estates, the solicitor found himself inwardly jealous of the recipient of such good fortune. Secretly, he also harboured the conviction that he personally, as the Miller's family solicitor of many years standing, more than deserved at least a rewarding slice of it. Sometimes people felt kindly disposed towards him and bequests came his way. But not from the Miller's widow! Rebecca had not any such feelings of long-term obligation towards him. She had quite properly regarded him as her paid servant, no more, no less!

So when it came to the end of the day, his function under Rebecca's instructions was the transfer her entire worldly estate; the mill; the bungalow with its furnishings, fittings and contents; the smart Morris Bullnose car; absolutely everything, to the fellow sitting in front of him—a working man who possessed nothing: nothing except the ability to work a windmill. A dusty, mucky, manual job. He did not like it one little bit.

The solicitor, when he finally, formally shook Ted's hand to wish him 'Good day', could not restrain himself from saying, without a smile or any sign of pleasure on his countenance,

"You are a very fortunate man, Mr Knowles. A very fortunate man indeed. I hope you prove worthy of the extreme generosity bestowed upon you by the wife of your former employer."

This lofty, supercilious remark, delivered by the pompous old solicitor as he looked down his nose at the man listening to him with obvious respect, was not recognised by Ted for the outrageously patronising comment it was. On the contrary, acting like the grateful recipient of charity dispensed by one of his betters, Ted replied earnestly, manifesting a sincere eagerness to impress.

"I'll do my best, I promise you, Sir," he said. "I'll try not to let you down. I'll work very hard, you can be sure of that. Thank you, Sir. Thank you for all you've done. You have been very kind." Fumbling with his cap, Ted awkwardly bid the solicitor goodbye and deferentially left the room.

The ego of the man he left behind was inflated even more by this display of diffidence and subservience. Standing with his back to his comfortable open fire, hand resting on his portly belly with his thumbs hooked in his waistcoat pockets, the puffed-up pompous ass positively preened himself. Though considered utterly insufferable by most of his peers he was totally unaware of the antipathy engendered by his manner, safely cocooned as he was in the comfortable conviction of his profound professional importance.

Ted departed from the solicitor's fusty premises with his head in the clouds. He still found it hard to take in what had happened and it took some time for all the full implications of his new circumstances to sink in. Far from his future being beset with potential problems and difficulties, the sky had suddenly cleared completely.

In effect he reasoned that, for the first time in his life he was truly master of his own destiny: a financially secure man with a well-established business of his own and a dream home to go with it. His sadness at the death of Rebecca was soon submerged by the excitement of contemplating the new life ahead of him.

Quickly, his head buzzing with ideas, he hurried home to tell Mildred the unbelievable news. It was an outcome far beyond her expectations and she too soon became totally preoccupied with plans for the future.

Almost without noticing it, Ted and Mildred became so infused with enthusiasm for the future that they found themselves in communion with each other once again. For the first time since the loss of their little daughter they began to think and act like a married couple, instead of two separate individuals living under the same roof but sharing no awareness of a common bond or mutual destiny.

Without putting it into words, Ted and Mildred had both decided to put the past behind them and start a new life together. Neither of them wanted to ask questions of the other because neither wanted to answer those questions that would be bound to follow their own. This unspoken resolution was to take them over the hump and lead to a resumption of their proper relationship as man and wife.

Fortuitously, but quite incredibly, their separate, secret, guilty consciences, arising so astonishingly from almost precisely equal past infidelities followed by dreadful acts of vengeance, silenced them both. So, buried of necessity, Ted and Mildred's traumatic past history did not raise its head to create a barrier between them.

Events from then on moved quickly.

Neville, Ted's by now well-established and much valued right-hand man, was soon to be married. Ted's cottage provided Neville and his wife with an immediately available home. It was not a usual circumstance for a young married couple to solve their housing problem with so little trouble. Quite naturally they were thrilled by their good fortune and their families were equally delighted to see them so quickly settled in a home of their own.

Meanwhile Ted and Mildred moved into the comparative luxury of the Miller's bungalow. It was still of course known to everyone as 'the Miller's bungalow', but that was all right by Ted because he himself was now 'the Miller'!

Life for the two of them became truly idyllic. Some of their friends remarked that they must have achieved happiness beyond their wildest dreams. This remark registered in Mildred's mind and she pondered it. She remembered very well what her so recently cherished 'wildest dream' had been, and realised that she had virtually achieved it—except that the man with her in the luxury bungalow was Ted and not the Miller.

But in the event that was a bonus, not a shortfall. For she soon became convinced that the 'new' Miller was a much better man with whom to share the rest of her life than the 'old' Miller would have been. Her new Ted was a far better companion than the Miller could ever have become. In her heart of hearts she was sure of that.

So Mildred figured out that she had indeed achieved happiness beyond her wildest dreams. And Ted was the 'beyond' bit! It was a strange twist of fate, something she could never have come near to imagining.

The supreme irony of this circumstance did not escape her. It brought to her mind another of her Grandfather's favourite sayings. In her head his voice resentfully and ruefully intoned the words, **'The Devil looks after his own!'** Like everything else about the Devil her Grandfather hadn't liked this habit of his at all. It rankled in the old man's mind. Under its pernicious, protective umbrella of inverted justice, nasty people profited from their nastiness, often, so it seemed, in direct proportion to the evilness of their way of life. This upside-down working of the Devil's idea of fair play had annoyed him and bugged him to the end of his days.

And in the memory of his granddaughter Mildred, he went on complaining about this system of sinners' rewards long after he'd left the scene. Fond though she had been of him, and happy though her memories of him were, Mildred sometimes wished he would shut-up making disturbing comments in her mind about matters that made her squirm with uneasy feelings of guilt and insecurity.

Alas, there was no escape, for he frequently appeared with startling clarity in her troubled dreams to voice his oft-repeated messages when she was a helpless captive in a confused, half-real, half-imagined world of frightening unfolding events from which she so often woke sorely disturbed in her mind . . . with a racing heart . . . sweating on the edge of some impending disaster . . . to lie awake with an ill-defined feeling of dread.

Mildred got so she feared these dreams, yet try as she might before falling asleep at night, she could not pre-condition her thoughts so that these unnerving experiences did not ensnare her over and over again. In truth the feared fear fed upon itself and she created the web which enmeshed and punished her; she was the victim of her own stark, deeply-etched memories of scenes known largely only to her, where she had been either a principal player or a silent solitary witness.

In effect she could not escape from herself and to this extent her otherwise seemingly perfect happiness was marred, flawed by the gnawing persistence of a troubled conscience. Though she could brush aside its unwelcome intrusion during her busy days, she was a hapless prey to its nagging attacks during the nights.

When she was asleep her subconscious mind made what it would of the vivid pictures and detailed information buried in her memory and she suffered as a fearful, locked-in, helpless puppet in the scenes generated by her highly active and inventive imagination. On occasions little Jenny, her lost daughter, featured in her tortured dreams, almost always pleading for help in a desperate situation—reaching out to her but agonisingly beyond her frantic grasp.

Sometimes, on the threshold of waking in the dead of night, she sensed a huge blackness that held within it a deep torment and a dreadful threat, so inescapable and all-enveloping that she suspected there to be a malevolent evil agency outside of herself, deliberately inflicting suffering upon her and seeking her destruction.

But whether initiated by her own feverish imagination, or fed by some external, primeval, remorseless, eternal evil force that was attracted to and fastened upon her vulnerable, beckoningly receptive fearful mind, mattered little. Her dreams were dominated for the rest of her life by a deep-rooted fear: a foreboding of an ultimate dreadful fate. And there was nothing she could do about it. Nothing at all.

Given the facts, there are those God-fearing souls with a strong belief in the workings of Holy Retribution who would have said that therein lay her punishment—albeit only the earthly part of it—with plenty more to come in the next world.

Fortunately perhaps for her, Mildred's personal philosophy did not embrace this awesome higher level of faith, so she was at least spared the travail of this long-term unhappy perspective.

But for all that, she suffered enough.

Chapter 4

THE NEW MIILLER AND HIS WIFE

learn to live each with their own
dreadful unshared secrets.

Both Ted and Mildred individually, in the midst of their mutual happiness, were in fact never free for long from their separate but equally graphic memories of past events. It was to be a long time before they felt secure, and they were never to be entirely free of the past. Every now and then each of them would be beset by periods of anxiety and worrying thoughts.

Sometimes, in the quiet of the evenings as he sat with a book in his comfortable, inherited armchair by the glowing log fire, Ted would gaze at Mildred, happily engrossed in her needlework, and turn things over in his mind. He knew that never in a million years would she ever suspect him of deliberately plotting the death of the Miller. There was nothing in his past behaviour to suggest to her, or to anyone else for that matter, that he might be capable of so dreadful an act. He wondered just what she would do if in some unpredictable way she ever found out the truth.

If something had triggered both their memories during the day, maybe perhaps simultaneously—Mildred would glance up from her work to see her husband contentedly relaxing by the fire, and also remember the past. Ted, she knew very well, would never ever suspect that she could have been in any way responsible for, or even remotely implicated in, the tragic death of the Miller's wife, much less that she had actually lain in wait that night for Rebecca and had stepped out from behind the hedge to push her in the back and give her a sideways heave so that she pitched over the safety rail into the icy waters below. She wondered just what he would do if in some unpredictable way he ever found out the truth.

And so they both carried on wondering. But fortunately for them they never did find out. Each in their separate way was equally successful in giving no cause for suspicion to anybody—except perhaps for the one solitary person about whom both were secretly anxious.

Only the writer of the poison-pen letters could possibly have dreamt up something as outrageous as what actually happened, and the writer, though indeed darkly suspicious, was caught on the horns of a dilemma.

If foul play were suspected in connection with the deaths of the Miller, then of his wife, it would almost certainly be discovered that the vindictive writer of the vicious notes had been responsible for initiating the events which followed. And writers of poison-pen letters were universally despised by everyone.

There was a further reason why the writer was in a cleft stick. There had been other similar poison-pen letters from the same source, distributed about the district every now and then over a long period of time, but never traced home. In the pubs there was sometimes murder in the air as infuriated men made plain what the fate of the writer would be if ever found.

Lack of discovery on past occasions had led to an arrogant, if in reality foolish over-confidence. When the writer started to think more deeply about it there seemed a strong possibility that previously nobody had looked very hard for the culprit because no serious repercussions had resulted from the letters. Nothing more, as far as could be judged, than a few blazing family rows and the sowing of suspicions where perhaps none had existed before.

But the present situation was altogether more serious. Two deaths—if indeed they had resulted from the two successive letters—that was a different matter! Very different! If murder was suspected and Ted and Mildred became implicated, then the hunt for the source of the stream of letters would surely begin in earnest. It would become a no-holds-barred affair.

For the first time, the malicious wielder of the vicious pen got scared and decided not to voice suspicions lest a series of searching investigations began. An avalanche could easily be started that would almost certainly engulf the person who incited the awful, implacable anger that led to the murders—if murders there had been.

As a result of these considerations, stemming from strong motives of self-preservation, both the recipients of the letters and the evil-minded sender of them, all kept quiet. The twin, sad, sudden and untimely departures from the land of the living of the Miller and his wife, went into history as Accidental Deaths.

As a bonus to local people, the specialist in the discovery of illicit affairs who had so delighted in stirring up trouble by dropping poisonous pen notes around, at selected, sensitive spots, revealing sordid details of these secret relationships, prudently decided to send no more of them. This did not stop the writer from enjoying the nefarious pleasure of observing these liaisons, but the iniquitous publicity machine was shut down.

So the windsails went on turning, the corn was ground and life for Ted and Mildred continued to prosper.

With the added responsibility and satisfaction of being a mill-owner Ted developed an increasing interest in the structure and history of windmills in general. Now that they had their own car they were able to get out and about much more than they had been able to before. So they set about visiting as many windmills as they could, within reasonable distance from home.

Chugging along in the Bullnose Morris Cowley car with a picnic hamper on the dicky seat behind them, and armed with a camera, they had a very pleasant time hunting down mills over a wide area. Many were situated not far from the coast, where favourable locations had been chosen as giving a good proportion of windy days. Those inland were similarly situated in well-chosen spots, on high ground and usually in open country. These locations made for enjoyable days out.

Although many of the mills they went to were still working and flourishing, Ted discovered that some of them had fallen into disuse and sadly were being allowed to decay. To him a mill was a faithful servant and deserved a better fate.

Many men who spent their lives working in windmills shared Ted's feeling that a mill had a character and spirit all of its own; that it was almost like a living being. Mills had their moods. Dormant and silent on a calm, airless day, they came to vibrant life when the wind blew. Like living creatures they responded to the elements and reacted to changes, sometimes in unpredictable ways. Ted thought it a very great pity that they became uneconomic to run and that they were allowed to rot away instead of being preserved as buildings, even if only for use as storage space. He was pleased to find, here and there, a small number which enterprising people had converted into comfortable homes. They made unusual and fascinating places in which to live.

After a time Ted became quite an authority on windmills. He built up an interesting collection of lantern slides and was much in demand to give talks to small groups of enthusiastic people.

In his travels he had found examples of mills of all the three categories into which they fell. There were several tower mills like his own—the strongest and most durable type of mill—in a good healthy state and going as well as ever. Also still in use were many of the picturesque smock-mills. These, of wooden construction, clad in overlapping planks or weatherboards, needed regular maintenance but lasted for generations if they were properly cared for. Of the third type, the post-mills, there were not many still working. As a rule they were very old structures and Master Millers of years gone by had either replaced them with the stronger, more efficient smock-mills or tower mills, or abandoned the trade altogether.

To complete his collection Ted was at pains to take photographs of what remained of these abandoned windmills and to find out all he could about their history.

Ted's enthusiasm did not stop when he was on holiday. In his slide collection he had some fine pictures of a mill he had visited in Suffolk. He and Mildred had been staying with relatives in Ipswich, a place they liked to visit because it allowed them to spend many happy days at Felixstowe by the sea.

Some miles away from where they stayed was a fine tower mill at Pakenham. it was truly a most striking sight. The eighty-foot high tower was painted jet black with its dome-shaped cap and its windsails in a contrasting bright white. Ted had been told that it took forty gallons of tar to decorate the high black tower, and some fifteen gallons of white paint to cover the cap and the four, fully-shuttered sails.

These facts, which Ted always trotted out to impress his audiences, gave some idea of the unusually large size of the attractive mill.

When pressed to say which of the many mills he had visited he liked the most, Ted singled out this one at Pakenham in Suffolk as a fine example of a tower mill.

As for smock-mills, he particularly liked the very nicely designed one situated at Sandwich in Kent. Painted all white, with its fine-looking fantail to turn the cap and its fully-shuttered, neatly-constructed windsails, this well-cared-for mill presented a picturesque building that was much admired.

Another similar one at Cranbrook in Kent also interested Ted because of its waist-high metal walkway staging, build out well above ground level in a neat, wrap-around balcony. Access to the balcony was through a door set high up in the side of the mill, three floors down from the top of the 75 foot high, octagonal building, at the junction of the tarred brickwork base and the white-painted woodwork of the rest of the structure above.

Hanging from the elegant, six-bladed fantail and its gearing was a weight-bearing rod for shutter control, and also a luffing chain. A mill-worker could walk round the balcony to get directly beneath the fantail whatever position the rotating cap was in, to get at these controls.

The balcony also gave ready access to the sails, should men have to climb them for repair purposes. There was a neat, four-rail safety fence running round the balcony. This, together with the supporting struts beneath the balcony's platform, gave the mill added attraction, in Ted's opinion, for the standard of craftsmanship in this octagonal building was very pleasing to the eye. There was something just right about it and Ted never passed through the district without calling to have another look at it.

A very impressive mill he had heard about but not yet visited was at Coleby Heath in Lincolnshire. Ted's cousin from Suffolk reckoned that this was a seven-storey tower mill worked by three pairs of sails. This six-sailed mill was bigger than any Ted had so far seen. One day he hoped to get a lantern-slide of it to include in his collection.

Ted and Neville worked hard to improve the Littlebrook windmill and to make it safer in all weathers. They were prompted to do this by a near-disaster that befell them on a stormy March night when the mill nearly got out of control. A sudden increase in wind strength, which quickly built up to gale force, caught them off-guard. The sails started to race at a frightening speed and the whole structure of the mill vibrated ominously.

Rushing up to the cap they had tried to apply the brake but the result was terrifying. The intense friction made the brake wheel rim and the brake blocks so hot that the cap was filled with a choking smoke and they had difficulty in breathing. Only by frantic trips up and down the steps, bringing water to throw over the brake wheel were they able to prevent a disastrous fire. Also, using a time-honoured practice, they put both sets of grinding wheels into action. This applied a braking load on the system to help check the speed. Fortunately both the barley and wheat bins were well-filled with grain at the time. They were lucky that it was a squall of short duration, rather than a sustained gale, that they experienced. At length, when the wind began to abate, they were able to tighten the grip of the brake and bring the machinery to a halt. But it was a near thing.

This incident, which could have destroyed Ted's happy security, caused him to think deeply about improvements in the mill to obviate the possibility of future troubles. He took expert advice on the matter and set in motion a plan of several successive steps to make the whole mill both more efficient and more safely controlled.

One major improvement was a complete replacement of the sails. In the original ones, spring-loaded shutters mounted in frames set in the sails were progressively shut to catch the wind by adding weights on a steel rod hanging down the side of the mill. This load turned the shutters against the force of a spring system. With no weights the shutters presented a minimum surface area to the wind, so the system was as nearly as possible, failsafe. However, the shutter control was not very convenient, needing constant adjustment, and also was not completely reliable and safe.

New 'patent' type sails were fitted with a much better shutter control system. They were automatically self-adjusting under normal weather conditions. In addition, they could be controlled by a manually operated gear-wheel which turned steel rods built into each sail along their spines.

The row of shutters in the sails presented their full face to the wind in mild weathers, but turned progressively to become more and more 'edge-on' to the wind as it increased.

If gale-force winds threatened, the shutters could be turned manually through ninety degrees so that they were completely edge-on. It was then only the framework of the sails that caught the wind.

Ted and Neville found, to their amazement, that with the shutters in this position there was still sufficient turning force during a gale-force wind to make it necessary to have the brakes fully engaged to stop the windsails from rotating.

They discovered this when they went to shut down the mill one evening. It happened that a squall was blowing up just at this crucial time. Though it was still their usual practice to stop the windsails by the use of the brakes, Ted decided on this occasion, because of the urgent need to hold down the speed, to turn the shutters fully out of the wind immediately, before they generated heat by applying the brake. It came as a surprise to them that the sails kept turning even with the shutters fully opened, and the mill did not come to a final standstill until the brake was applied.

After that Ted made it a rule that when they went home at night, if there was any likelihood of the wind getting up during the night, the shutters were fully opened and left in their edge-on position.

However, this was done after the brake had been applied so that Ted could first ensure that the mill was shut down with the windsails set to form a St Andrew's cross, in the traditional way.

In a wind that was not strong the sails would stop when the shutters were fully opened, and Ted found by experience that the drill had to be such that the alignment of the sails was first established by using the normal brake, after which the shutters could then be opened. Otherwise they would finish up with the windsails set in an arbitrary position.

Neville found his boss curiously pernickety on this point and was careful when he shut the mill down on his own to leave the sails set properly.

Dislike the Miller though he had, Ted had nonetheless inherited from him this obsession with leaving the mill 'set pretty'. Though reluctant to admit it, he had also inherited from his cantankerous and unpleasant employer a great deal of know-how on high-quality milling techniques and general mill management. This expertise had come down through the generations in the Miller's family. Neville in his turn got the benefit of this, but from a boss with a more agreeable manner than had been Ted's surly guide and mentor.

With the braking system also improved in design and other fire precautions introduced, Ted was able to face the future with less anxiety than he had suffered immediately after their nightmarish experience.

In his studies of old mills and mill ruins Ted learnt of many occasions when mills had ended their working lives by storm disasters of the kind that had so nearly afflicted his mill.

He heard of one smock-mill in particular which had 'run away' in a gale, becoming completely out of control. Choking smoke from the wooden brake-rim and the fully-applied brake blocks that had failed to stop the windsails turning had driven the men out of the cap. Down below, the furiously grinding stones ejected a stream of flour until the grain in the bin above ran out altogether. The millstones ran together without the lubrication of the flour and showers of sparks ignited nearby powder-dry woodwork. Fire had already started up in the cap and the mill was full of choking smoke. The whole structure was vibrating frighteningly and the noise was awful. In desperation the men had to run for their lives and get out of the mill, leaving it to its fate. The huge sails continued to rotate against the background of the burning mill. Then they themselves caught fire and the flaming woodwork rotated like a giant Catherine wheel. It was a truly awe-inspiring sight. The final spectacle of the burning mill made a dramatic picture which stayed in the memories of those who witnessed it for the rest of their lives.

Being not without imagination, Ted could see in his mind's eye his own mill, set proudly on the knoll, flaming away against the night sky while they all watched helplessly from the safety of the ground at the foot of the mill. As a result of these dreadful images of potential disaster he had resolved in his mind to do all he could, cost what it may, to render his mill safe from such a fate.

An old miller, who had worked in a post-type mill which had canvas sails, told Ted how his own mill had come near to destruction one night when he was a young man newly started at work in the mill. It frightened the life out of him, so he said.

Apparently their efforts to stop the mill in a gale-force wind, using the crude brake, caused the brake wheel to catch fire. In the choking white smoke the mill owner, a 'tough little bloke' according to the old man, had taken a swift decision. He let the brake off completely, put the fire out by chucking buckets of water over the burning brake wheel and ordered his two assistants to 'abandon ship'. With the brake off, the windsails turned at a frightening rate and by the time they got below the whole place was rocking with vibration. The noise in there was terrible.

Everybody thought the mill's last day had come. Like many before them they could do nothing but stand back and watch as it 'ran away' and destroyed itself. But, unexpectedly, it was saved by its own unsophisticated construction. The canvas on the sails was the first thing to go. First one sheet then another was torn off in the wind leaving just a skeleton framework for the wind to vent its spite upon. The mill's machinery stopped working and the awful vibration was reduced to just structural movement in the gale. Thus the mill survived to grind flour another day!

This story impressed Ted very much. Previously he had regarded the old post-mills, particularly those with canvas sails, as crude windmills of historic interest only. Their structure was simple but logical. The core of the mill was its post—essentially a carefully-selected tree trunk of sufficient rigid strength to do the job. The whole mill—its windsails; its machinery; its internal work-space; all of it was in effect pivoted around this post. A long pole extending at a angle downwards to just above ground level, enabled men to turn the whole mill into the wind by simply walking round the circular path pushing on the pole, using it as a lever and rotating the entire mill on its central supporting post.

In truth the mills, crude as they were, had their advantages. Ted learnt that some of them had been known to outperform their bigger, haughty brothers under certain weather conditions. With their lightweight sail frames but big areas of canvas, they were sometimes seen still slogging away producing flour with little more than a breeze to disturb the air. Like sailing ships utilising every breath of wind, there was something to be said for their canvas sails.

The old man told Ted of this with a great deal of pride. He said that there had been a large, posh smock-mill near enough to the little post-mill he worked in for both teams to be able to watch progress in their neighbour's mill. Often, he said, the sails of the smock-mill came to a standstill and production stopped, while their little mill kept going.

He reckoned that one day, when still a boy not long on the staff of the mill, his boss sent him over to the smock-mill when it had stopped and their post-mill was still going, to ask the Master Miller if they could grind some corn for him in the 'little old mill up the road'. He got a very dusty answer as did many apprentices in all trades, sent with great glee by their seniors who, with serious faces, dispatched them on all sorts of preposterous and sometimes hilarious errands. It was an occupational risk for wide-eyed boys at the start of their careers. The keener they were, and the more anxious to please, the more likely they were to be on the receiving end of these practical jokes, often ruefully recalled for years to come.

When the old man told Ted this story, remembered throughout the man's life, it created a very graphic image in Ted's mind, for he pictured his own late, but not lamented boss as the Master Miller of the smock-mill, greeting the small boy at the door of his stationary, moribund mill, and seeing over his shoulder the little poor relation of a thing—the ancient post-mill—still working away with its crude canvas sails rotating merrily in the very soft breeze. The mocking message from his small-time rival would have wound up the Miller to explosion point. He would not have been amused; there would have been no laughter at the door of the smock-mill. But Ted had smiled to himself at the delight there would have been amongst the Miller's staff behind him if they heard the boy deliver his message!

This amusing little story became part of Ted's mill lecture repertoire and always, when he told it, it was his own late boss whose picture he described as the infuriated Master Miller of the dormant smock-mill.

Just three years after he became sole owner of the mill Mildred presented Ted with a son and heir. The boy was a great joy to them both and gave their new life together even greater meaning. Little Ken Knowles was to grow up in a wonderful setting. Ted was proud of him, very proud indeed.

As he watched his small son in the garden of their lovely home during Ken's first summer, Ted thought how different his own start in life had been from that of his previous employer who had been the 'son of a Master Miller'. With immense satisfaction Ted saw his son as the potential inheritor of the windmill, a Master Miller's son with an assured prosperous future. One day Ken Knowles would be the Miller following in the footsteps of his widely respected father, Ted. Sometimes it seemed too good to be true.

Both Ted and Mildred in their different ways, but under the influence of similar inner compulsions, tried hard to concentrate on enjoying the present, and to look forward to the future and forget the past. Both succeeded in the first two of these three aims—

but not the third. Neither of them got anywhere near to achieving the last.

Some memories are too vivid, too deeply etched in the memory to be blotted out. Two such were those of the Miller's mangled body caught in the massive gear wheels high up in the cap of his mill, and of his wife's bedraggled body floating in the ice-cold water of the deep, malevolent-looking millpond behind the water mill.

By any count these must be rated as sobering nightmarish pictures to be harboured deeply and ineradicably in the memories of two outwardly normal people enjoying a prosperous life in the quiet beauty of the Kentish countryside. As dreadful memories they would have been disturbing enough under normal circumstances. They were made much worse for Ted and Mildred because each of them knew—and thought they alone knew—that while one of the two deaths was purely accidental the other was nothing less than coldly premeditated murder.

Small wonder that their dreams were often more grotesque and frightening than many created in the pages of horror stories. Neither of them knew what dreadful images and feelings of guilt plagued the mind of the other. But nobody ever knows what improbable pictures of past events lie buried in the memory of a neighbour's mind.

Some people, however, might have an inkling, or even, if gifted with acute perspicacity, make a good guess. Still others, troubled by vague suspicions, might try to probe the past by endeavouring to contact the dead in order to seek the truth straight from the spirit's mouth!

One such person was 'Old Motty' who claimed to be able to communicate with the dead. In his capacity of caretaker and gardener extraordinary in the village churchyard at Littlebrook, it fell to him to tend the graves of the Miller and Rebecca, buried side by side in the Miller's family plot. An observer might have noticed that Motty tended Rebecca's grave with more care than that of her husband. This disparity arose because, in common with a lot of people, Motty hadn't liked the Miller one little bit but, on the contrary, had always been extremely fond of Rebecca. In his simple book of judgement she was a nice lady and he a nasty man.

Both Ted and Mildred were secretly given to wondering just how much Old Motty knew. Like a lot of other local people they were never quite sure whether Motty really could communicate with the dead or was just a little 'screwy'—or maybe more than just a little. The disturbing thing was he spoke with such complete conviction and treated those disinclined to believe him with unconcealed contempt, as though their unwillingness to believe him merely stamped them as plain idiots unable to recognise what he saw as obvious fact. The disconcerting thing was that Motty was plainly a very shrewd old man. His deep-set eyes were bright and his gaze unnervingly penetrating.

To Ted and Mildred, to each without the other knowing, the mere thought of Motty was truly unnerving; they would have been very disturbed indeed had they been able to read his mind. Shrewd old boy that he was, it did not escape his notice that both of them were ill at ease when he met them. They didn't look him squarely in the eyes.

This set him wondering and pondering more than ever about the tragic circumstances of the Miller and his wife becoming residents in his territory as a result of untimely deaths. It didn't seem quite right.

The more he thought about it the more his imagination was triggered and the voices in his head spoke loudly to him as he mulled over the nature of the way these two people had met their ends. Pottering about in the quiet peace of the country churchyard he had plenty of time to think, and the names of the silent sleepers around him stimulated his subconscious mind. Not for the first time Motty did not like what the voices said to him. But on this issue he kept his own counsel for he was on dangerous ground.

He had learnt that some thoughts are best left unspoken; some matters are best left to be dealt with on Judgement Day.

The Vicar had long ago drummed that into him. He had become alarmed at the way Motty passed on the supposed opinions and comments of dead parishioners on matters of past and present concern. While sometimes outrageous, all too often these were disconcertingly plausible and left some people squirming with embarrassment at Motty's apparently 'authentic' disclosures.

So the Vicar had tried to shut Motty up where potential trouble could follow the topic of his 'ear-to-the-ground' type of information.

"At all costs, Mr Marsh," the Vicar had urged Motty, "don't pass on accusations, especially serious ones. Only trouble can come of that! Leave the Lord to deal with all such things in His own good way and in His own good time. You tend the graves and He will tend the souls."

As a result, Ted's and Mildred's separate secrets remained secure from revelation, even from this dangerous, if unlikely, source. And so their lives continued in a state of uneasy bliss.

To the outside world all appeared to be well at the windmill. Standing proudly and prominently on its private grassy hill with its impressive sails turning in the wind and its massive machinery rumbling away within, there were few people who passed by who were not captivated by it. A working windmill, in good order, well maintained and cared-for, made an attractive spectacle. Ted's mill was much admired; enthusiasts commented how it looked truly magnificent. A steady flow of corn went into it and a correspondingly satisfying stream of sacks of flour came out of it. Never in its life had it worked so well and so efficiently. Friends, neighbours, local people generally—all agreed that Ted Knowles had turned out to be a fine Master Miller.

"If the old Miller had to die," it was often said, "then he could not have wished his precious mill to land up in better hands." A somewhat ironical statement under the circumstances!

Yet the peace which reigned in the windmill was a troubled one. From time to time highly sensitive people visiting the mill were aware of an unease pervading the atmosphere of the place. Something somewhere was not quite right. This was especially so in the duskiness of a still evening when the machinery was not working and all was quiet except for the creaking of timbers and the soft sighing of a light breeze through the sails.

It may have been that the local people, knowing of the awful death of the previous Miller, were influenced by thinking about this dreadful tragedy as they stood in the rather awe-inspiring interior of the mill, dominated as it was by the massive, dangerous-looking machinery that filled so much of the space.

Or, it may have emanated from Ted himself, because often it was noticed that at times he did not seem to be quite 'with' those who were talking to him. He seemed preoccupied with his own thoughts, as though he were miles away. His thoughts of course were locked right there, inside the mill!

But then neither of these two possible causes of feelings of disquiet could explain why it was that now and again total strangers had this experience when Ted was not even present, and they knew nothing of the tragedy.

Perhaps the creaking timbers and soft, sighing, whistling sounds of air moving through the sails and in and about the lofty building, evoked a feeling that stifled voices were trying to tell of scenes and deeds of yesteryear, for violent emotions are said by some to create a lasting imprint on places where they are experienced, leaving a lingering trapped energy there which those who are super-sensitive are aware of.

Though sceptics would be scornful of such suggestions and dismiss them as fanciful moonshine there are certainly places here and there which—as did the old windmill—convey an indefinable something that defies rational argument and convincing explanation.

However hard-bitten the sceptics, it would have been difficult indeed for them to stand in Ted's mill beside those receptive to its powerful atmosphere and convince them that what they were sensing as an energy and force external to themselves was in fact generated by their own imagination.

Difficult is the wrong word—it would have been impossible, for the chill they felt penetrated to the very marrow of their bones. It was that unique other-world cold, the colder than cold spine-tingling chill of the supernatural.

Not everybody is sensitive to this unearthly cold, but those that are know full well it is there. So do some animals and they are not given to the duplicity of mental inventions, nor are they capable of displaying pretended fear. They are simply visibly and unaccountably scared of something unseen but of which they are acutely aware. Their instinct is to run and put space between themselves and this primeval presence of a permeating force they detect but cannot see or hear. Or can they?

Certainly Ted's dog would not go into the cap with him. Visiting the mill one wintry night to check something that was worrying him—nothing abnormal, purely a mechanical problem—he took his dog to keep him company. It would not go into the cap. It stood at the threshold at the top of the steps, whimpered and ran down to the floor below, looking up at Ted in a state of obvious abject fear. The experience did nothing to help Ted's confidence in going to the mill alone at night.

Neither would the windmill's resident cat, introduced by Neville to keep down the mice, following a method used in the watermill he had worked in, go into the cap. Neville tried to put it up there to hunt for prey, having found mouse droppings about the place. But it would not stay there. The hair stood up on its neck and it was plainly terrified. When he put it down it scurried down the steps and disappeared for several hours.

"Funny thing, that!" Neville said when he told Ted about it. "Scared stiff it was. Something about the place it didn't like, I suppose."

"No accounting for animals!" commented Ted gruffly. "Scared of shadows, some of them are. Perhaps the wind noises or the machinery frightened it. Maybe it will go up there and do its stuff when the place is quiet."

But the cat never did venture up there. The issue was shrugged off as just one of those things nobody understands.

Neville too dismissed the triviality from his mind. But Ted didn't. It added to his unease, an unease that was something he had to live with, an unease that never left him to the end of his days.

Chapter 5

"OLD MOTTY"
caretaker extraordinary of the churchyard

Precisely at eight o'clock in the morning, on days when he chose to do so, Motty Marsh would set out from his woodland cottage on his lengthy walk to the churchyard. His progress was painfully slow, for the years were beginning to tell on him though he hated to admit it. He was said to be much nearer ninety than eighty years old, but nobody really knew his age, and if he knew it himself, when asked he chose to be very vague about it. Clearly, it was a matter upon which he had no wish to dwell.

His aim when he made this particular journey was to reach his destination by nine o'clock, and he used his performance over this regularly repeated trip to monitor the state of his health. This was why he was so rigorously self-disciplined in keeping to his chosen departure time, every day he went there.

The Church clock would be striking nine just after—or to his chagrin sometimes just before—he reached his favourite seat along the hedge just inside the churchyard. If it were just after, Motty was pleased with himself and felt years younger all day. If it were just before, he didn't much like it, especially if he heard it strike when he was still a fair distance away. When this happened, he often invented good reasons for his poor performance such as a headwind—trouble with his guts—his dog Pug taking off into the wood after a rabbit—or people along his way stopping him to talk.

Having invented his reason, very soon afterwards he fully believed its truth himself. This was Motty's unconsciously developed way of blocking from his mind any disturbing, nagging thoughts that might suggest he was 'failing', for his carefully-timed walk had become a self-imposed measure of his physical ability. It was a challenge, and each day that he achieved his target was proof to him of his immediate prospects of safe survival. He preferred to remain a 'grave-tender' rather than a 'grave-dweller', a distinction which he was well qualified to make!

Well-known and recognised by all and sundry for miles around, there were few people who would pass him by without calling out a greeting as he made his way slowly along the roads.

Seen from the front, as an approaching figure, the dominant feature of Motty was a long, spade-shaped beard surmounted by a wide bushy crop of side-whiskers. His beard, side-whiskers, matching moustache and the frizzy fringe of hair that framed his long-serving grubby old cap, were uniformly greyish-white. One not too well-mannered beer-swiller, looking out of the window of Motty's local pub one Sunday morning, watching him coming slowly along the pathway on his way for his daily pint, commented, to the great amusement of the assembly, that "Old Motty coming towards you, creeping along with his beard nearly touching the ground, looks like some moth-eaten, mangy old sheep looking for grass to eat!"

Far from being offended by this somewhat ungentlemanly remark, duly reported to him when he entered, Motty enjoyed the joke and joined in the laughter. He liked a bit of good-natured banter and was more than capable of giving as good as he got. One of his great loves in life was a good hearty laugh and this, with his wicked sense of humour coupled with a penetrating shrewdness that caught people unawares, endeared him to those who knew him.

Not that Motty was always laughing. He could get very annoyed and ratty at times, usually though, to be fair to him, not without good reason. At one such time somebody was once heard to say, "Old Motty's getting hopping mad, but he can't hop, so he's getting a bloody sight madder every minute. Better give the old sod a pint before he does himself an injury!"

Seen from sideways-on, Motty presented a decidedly bent figure. With a pronounced forward stoop, he moved along as though he were intently searching the ground for any treasure it might yield. Following a lifetime of stooping work in the fields, in all weathers, gradually over the years he found it increasingly difficult to straighten up and his back had got markedly humped. With the onset of pain in his joints he had reached a stage some years ago when he found it impossible to stand up straight without suffering a great deal of discomfort. So he gave up trying.

These days he moved around and went about his daily business permanently looking at the ground when moving. To look up and see ahead, he would first stop, then slowly, and evidently so it seemed, painfully, bend his head backwards—with his eyeballs turned well up to minimise the amount of head-bending necessary—in order to see what he wanted to see, or to look at a person greeting him.

There was a time when a small group of young boys who habitually played in the woods near his home, took to having fun and games with him, leaving phoney articles for him to find on the pathway, or playing tricks that similarly relied for their success upon his close scrutiny of the ground as he passed along.

In this latter category there was a penny that he bent to pick up which leapt sideways just as he reached to clutch it and disappeared like a flash over the bank—too fast for him to see where it went! But the next one that he spotted some days later, when an attempt was made to repeat the success, was swiftly trapped under his walking stick. He could move his stick a lot faster than he could stoop!

With a grin of triumph and much satisfaction he bent down, pulled off the black thread that was stuck to its underside, and pocketed it. Four pairs of eyes watched him with dismay from the dense undergrowth, but utter silence prevailed. The score was now one to one.

A week later a third one appeared. This he again deftly trapped by a swift movement of his stick, only to find there was not thread attached to it but that it was securely stuck down with glue on to the flat surface of a large buried flintstone. Not to be defeated he worked away at it with his stout, multi-purpose pocketknife and pocketed that one as well. The silent watchers lost their investment once again. They had not expected him to persevere with such dogged determination.

The little game continued, with much inventiveness, on and off for some weeks, but with Motty becoming increasingly difficult to deceive. It culminated in an incident which finally caused the boys to give up. Motty was trapped by them when they cunningly operated several hundred yards from their normal area by the woodland path, where—well beyond the 'zone of suspicion'—they caught him unawares.

Motty found, no doubt to his great delight, what appeared to be a brand-new, full one-ounce packet of his favourite shag pipe tobacco lying on the pavement, apparently having been dropped by a fellow smoker. It was a well-known brand, cheap in price, and packed in a distinctive cylindrical roll rather than in the more usual square or rectangular packets.

This valuable find he pocketed with much satisfaction. What a gift from the Gods it was! When he arrived home, he unwrapped the paper packet to put the tobacco into his pouch and found it to be stuffed with a raw material he know only too well, both by sight and by smell: horse shit! Ruefully he grinned in silent amusement at this ingenious and successful deception, but promptly planned counter-measures.

The following Saturday morning when the boys, as was their regular habit, went to their supposedly secret camp concealed under dense undergrowth in a gulley near the road along the edge of the wood, they had a surprise waiting for them. They took their normal precautions in their approach to it, in order to preserve its security by never being seen near its location, copying the way they much admired of the wily skylark that deliberately lands away from its nest built on the ground, then scurries under the cover of tall grasses to get to it. They prided themselves on their proven successful security measures, knowing that other boys would long since have wrecked the place had they discovered it.

Their camp was a snug place, rain-proof except in very heavy downpours, built with much care from a framework of strong sticks covered with sacking and sundry pieces of old, rusty, corrugated iron sheets, the whole den being well camouflaged by branches and vegetation.

Inside it, to their dismay and horror, they found, in a very smelly heap on the floor, a goodly pile of the same raw material they had so kindly supplied for Motty's pleasure. By it was a small supply of old tobacco wrappers, ostensibly it seemed for their convenience in their clandestine manufacturing of bogus tobacco products. Stuck in the top of the heap, flying like a flag on a stick, was the unmistakeable, nice, new-looking wrapper that Motty had emptied in the privacy of his cottage with such abruptly blunted delight, as a thoroughly well-hooked sucker! He had now returned it, together with its contents, plus a generous quantity of the same, as interest on their investment!

They got the message and left Motty alone afterwards, lest his retaliatory action should become more severe, for the crafty old boy had demonstrated that their cover was blown. Not only that, they guessed correctly that he also knew their identities.

So the little contest ended, not without having provided some quiet pleasure for Motty, who truth to tell—old though he was—knew how boys ticked and enjoyed watching their antics. For their part the boys knew the old man's eyes could twinkle with fun, and for all his strange, ancient appearance he was known to be a good sport. They guessed that if they now left him alone, the account was square so their camp would remain secret and inviolate. Time proved them right!

When in motion, Motty was always supported by his strong, knotted old walking stick, cut and fashioned many years before by his own father when he had needed support himself. The handle of the stick was grasped tightly by Motty's gnarled right hand. Meanwhile, perhaps to counterbalance his body—looking as he did for all the world as though he were sure to tip over on his face, so great was his forward slant—he always had his left arm stuck up behind his back, with the elbow bent and the hand cupped as though to catch a cricket ball coming at him from behind.

Seen from the rear, as he made his way along, the chief point of note was Motty's coarsely-woven jacket with its hanging pockets that were always apparently loaded with heavy objects. The combination of these side-weights, his arched back and his stooping shoulders, had long since well and truly permanently deformed the jacket so that it had a distinctly 'inverted-U' shape. It was many years since the bottom edge of the jacket had been parallel to the ground.

Encompassed by this archway formed by his jacket, Motty's backside was neatly provided with a frame to look out of in much the same way as a doleful, worn-faced old monk gazes forlornly out of the stone arched window of an ancient monastery. In the seat of his baggy trousers was a large patch made of a different material from that of the trousers, a patch stitched on and re-stitched with heavy thread many times over the years by Motty's wife before she had 'been taken'. The trousers were made of heavy-duty corduroy, a traditionally hard-wearing material much favoured for its durability and warmth.

Just below the knees, Motty's trouser legs were tied around with string, a practice yielding many advantages to those accustomed to being out in the fields in all weathers, in a wide variety of ground conditions. Everything from the cold wind, dust, debris, earwigs, or any other creepy-crawlies, was discouraged from annoying the wearer by this not very elegant but commonplace and every effective countryman's device.

Despite his infirmities Motty regularly made his journey to the churchyard to pursue his self-imposed routine, unless compelled by bad weather, or a bout of sickness, to stay not very contentedly at home. He was employed, for a small wage, to keep the churchyard tidy. This he did conscientiously and in the main very satisfactorily, albeit very slowly. He was free to come and go as he liked. Usually he was to be found there three or four times a week.

Previous to his taking up these duties, before he retired from his normal job, for just on 56 years Motty had had no choice about going to work each day. For day after day, week after week, month after month, year in and year out—with the exception of a few days' holiday each year and odd times when he was too ill to go—Motty had got up early each morning and gone out in all weathers to earn his living as a farm labourer.

Of all things in his long life, nothing had given him so much pleasure as the privilege he now so thoroughly enjoyed of being able to decide each morning whether or not he would 'go to work'. There was no luxury greater than this control over his own life each day. If he awoke to find it raining and blowing he would stay where he was. If the sun were shining and the weather set fine, then out he would go, either to his part-time job or to work in his own garden, or just to wander slowly along the woodland paths with Pug, his tough little terrier dog.

To many people a churchyard hardly seems like a place to be happy in. Motty though, was quite contented there. It was quiet, peaceful, and he was his own boss. Nobody argued with him. The whole lot resting in there depended upon him and there was no messing about. For once in his life he was truly the 'Guv'nor'.

Once someone said, "Old Motty spends his days down there getting used to the place so's he'll feel at home when he goes there to stay full-time. He's getting to know the drill so he can come the old soldier when he joins up!"

Motty's regular visits to the churchyard, methodically working over its area during the spring, summer and autumn months, gave him a pretty good idea who was there. He also noted new arrivals. Some he welcomed as old friends. Others, whom he didn't like, were left in no doubt that he would rather they settled in somebody else's patch. Quite often newcomers were people younger than himself, sometimes very much younger. Occasionally, less often these days, the new residents were older than he was.

Motty didn't mind the younger ones; he didn't seek any priority to move in first, and didn't want any special treatment to allow him to jump the queue just because he was 'on the staff'. He figured that as the Boss up above 'took 'em in' at a steady rate on a more or less regular basis, each new arrival helped to keep him out of the current quota.

Increasingly though, over the years, the older he got, the more uneasy he became when someone older than himself came in. He didn't like it at all. It made him feel uncomfortable and he wished they'd had the decency to stay out a bit longer. As each one changed their status from somebody he would meet occasionally to have a yarn with, to a permanent resident in his domain who stuck around him for good reminding him he was on borrowed time, Motty was conscious of being a member of a diminishing community of his contemporaries in the village and the surrounding area. It made him feel more and more conspicuous, as though he stood out too invitingly as a ripe recruit, ready and waiting to be plucked out of the land of the living to join the army of the departed. Perhaps his desire not to be noticed was another contributory cause of his head to sink down between his shoulders.

Strangely, however, though he would have been happier if these older contemporaries of his had stayed in the land of the living, once they were duly buried and had been there a little while Motty became more reconciled to their presence. In a paradoxical way they added to the band of old friends around him, and after a bit he resumed contact with them, and included them in his 'conversations'!

It was well known that as he moved around his territory Motty sometimes talked to those lying near where he happened to be working. Their replies, naturally enough, being private, were not heard by anybody listening. The other side of each conversation Motty supplied—being 'heard' as he would assert—in his own mind, sometimes causing him to smile or even laugh aloud, but sometimes annoying him and making him ratty!

There were a good many of Motty's acquaintances among the inhabitants of the churchyard. Some were family, some old friends of whom he was very fond, but others he hadn't liked when they were alive and wished they would go away and get buried somewhere else now they were dead.

Since he was on his own in this quiet corner of the village, it seemed natural to Motty to have a word or two with those he knew, as he moved around. From time to time, people passing nearby, walking quietly on the grassy paths, would hear Motty's voice and pause awhile behind the hedge to listen. Some of Motty's comments were innocuous enough, but some became causes of much glee to be related with relish and passed from one person to another until they became legendary. These latter were more often than not associated with those he did not much care for.

Typical of these comments were Motty's kindly greeting when he came upon the rather sadly, but deliberately neglected, home of a particularly argumentative old skinflint who had been a pain-in-the-neck to all and sundry until he moved in about thirty years earlier, at a time when Motty was still in his youth in his late fifties, long before he started his work in the churchyard.

Moving towards a compost heap in the corner by the hedge, it appeared that Motty's memory was stirred when his eyes lit upon the moss-covered tombstone to spot the name.

Pausing a moment to prod the grave with his walking stick, his beard not much more than two feet above the ground, Motty growled, none too pleasantly,

"Ah! You're still there then, Bert Tomkin, eh? Huh! Huh! I remember you well enough, that I do. Miserable old bugger you were when you were alive, weren't you? Ain't got much to say for yourself now, though, 'ave you, you old sod! Shut *you* up shoving you out of the way in the corner, didn't they? 'Bloody good riddance' everybody said when you kicked the bucket. No tears shed for you, there weren't. Not enough to wet the arse of a gnat!"

With that, Motty had reportedly proceeded on his way, no doubt inwardly satisfied at having given the miserable occupant a piece of his mind to shut him up for a bit.

By chance one day, the Editor of one of the main County newspapers, published on Friday each week, happened to be in Motty's local pub when this oft-repeated story was being told. This pub, bearing the name of the famous East Kent County Regiment, 'The Buffs', was situated on the fringe of the village at the top of a fairly steep hill, adjacent to a large piece of woodland that extended over an area of several square miles.

Motty's cottage was upwards of half a mile beyond the pub, about 500 yards off the road, down a cart-track which ran along the edge of the dense wood. On the other side of the cart-track was an apple orchard with its disciplined rows of trees extending as far as the eye could see. Between the trees was grass, kept under control by periodic mowing, to give an attractive vista of wide green pathways over which the trees formed archways.

Looking down one such row, the impression was that of looking down a green tunnel. With sunlight causing dappled shadows and the tunnel appearing to the eye to narrow down in the distance to a small arch of blue sky at its far end, it would be difficult to imagine a more enchanting scene, or a more peaceful place to live. Occasionally the observer would see rabbits far down these long green tunnels, playing on the grass.

It was like looking through the wrong end of a telescope at a tiny fairyland world, distant yet, strangely, appearing tantalisingly just within reach. There was a beckoning compulsion to walk quietly down the tunnel to try to enter this wonderland miniature world. On a very still summer day there was a dreamlike quality to the place.

The Editor knew the area well and visited it from time to time when his business brought him from the County town of Maidstone to this delightful part of Kent. The ideally-placed pub, just off the road, was a nice stopping-off point.

As he sat enjoying his glass of Kentish beer in this farmland area with its rich mixture of woodlands, orchards, hop gardens, oast houses, water meadows and arable lands, where shepherds with their clever, well-trained dogs looked after scattered flocks of sheep, stockmen worked with their rich brown Jersey cows or black and white Friesians, and waggoners with their sturdy horses plodded their way around the roads and fields, he often felt there could be no place on earth more peaceful and restful than this. In the pub, seated on his own in a quiet corner, it was his habit to listen with great interest and no small amusement to the conversation of the locals as they drank their much-loved beer.

Sometimes he got ideas for stories as a result of listening to their good-natured conversation, interspersed as it was with guffaws of laughter and markedly country-flavoured repartee which was often more than a little bawdy in detail. This was just such a day for him.

The story about Motty in the churchyard addressing the departed Bert Tomkin, had much amused him, and the delightful picture it evoked in his mind's eye stimulated his experienced journalistic interest. Here could be the germ of a good country story. Of course he knew that stories such as the one he had just heard were often much exaggerated, and sometimes purely apocryphal. However, before he returned to this office, he thought he would take himself to the church to have a look around.

It was a nice day and as luck would have it, there was the bent figure of Motty, pottering about among the gravestones. His mere appearance was enough to persuade the Editor that—even without hearing Motty actually talking to his friends—there was material here for a story, with a photograph or two, of a very real old rural 'Man of Kent', at work in an interesting setting.

On arrival back at his office he briefed a reporter and sent him to do a feature about Motty in his churchyard. He was not to be disappointed. The story turned in by Mike, the young reporter given the assignment, was to be a real gem.

Mike's first move was to visit Littlebrook, make a few discreet enquiries about Motty's movements, and reconnoitre the churchyard. He was lucky in the plans he made as things do not always turn out right on expeditions of this type, but on this occasion they did. Subsequent events flowed along in a natural sequence, to present Mike with a wonderful little experience he was to remember for a long time.

During a pleasant half hour or so in Motty's pub, chatting with 'Old Mac' the publican and some 'locals', he was able by carefully steering the conversation in a not conspicuously inquisitive way, to gain the information he wanted about Motty's habitual movements. He also gathered some useful anecdotes about Motty, as well as a fairly accurate picture of his character and habits.

At the churchyard he had a good look round and selected a number of potential vantage points where he could conceal himself near to the main areas of the ground where Motty might conceivably be working. Then he worked out ways in which he could move from point to point without being seen.

Once having got his ground plan worked out, Mike went back to Maidstone determined to journey down to the village on the next fine day in time to get into position well before the zero hour of 9 am, the time when his researches had revealed that Motty started his working sessions at the churchyard. Sunday was never a day when Motty was at his work place, for obvious reasons, therefore Mike reasoned that Motty was likely to make a habit of going there for the first visit of a 'working week', on the first fine day of a week.

As luck would have it they were enjoying a fine spell of weather, and things augured well for the coming Monday.

The day dawned calm and clear, so Mike set off on his motorbike to chug along through the lovely Kentish countryside in the crisp morning air—a good start for what proved to be a good day for Mike.

On arrival Mike concealed his bike in a pre-determined place and took up a position under the straggling branches of an elder bush, a few yards along a bordering hedgerow near three wooden seats placed there for the convenience of visitors. His discreet investigations had established that Motty's days began at this point, where he rested a while after his long walk from home.

About fifteen minutes after he had settled into his vantage post, almost as if working to a predetermined script, the regular tap tap tap of a stick and the sound of shuffling feet warned him that Motty was on his way. By the church clock it was just after five minutes to nine when Motty opened the lych-gate and entered the precincts, followed eagerly by his lively little dog, 'Pug'. A good start to the day for Motty, as well as for Mike.

When the clock struck nine, Motty had already lowered himself thankfully on to one of the seats to get his breath back and survey the scene before starting his morning's work. Much to his satisfaction the day had begun with a win over the chiming clock. Leaning back against the rail of the seat, he looked up at the clock on the church tower, smiled to himself, and nodded his head slowly up and down. His first words of the day were apparently directed at the clock in person. When it had tolled out its booming nine strokes Mike heard Motty mutter, with evident mocking pride, "Beat you today, mate, didn't I? Beat you by a bloody mile!" Mike made his first entry in his notebook!

For a while Motty rested quietly on the seat with Pug lying at his feet. As he sat there he gazed around deciding where his attention was most needed. His practised eye summed up the existing condition of his estate, and he could see where he had stopped work on his last visit the previous week.

Mike, who also had been looking around, noticed an area of recently cut grass, adjacent to ground that was somewhat overgrown with grass and weeds. He thought Motty might well start his day's operations there. If he did Mike was well placed to watch proceedings and overhear any 'conversation'. As he sat there, though, Mike began to feel a trifle uneasy. What he was planning to do was nothing short of eavesdropping on an old man's private conversations with his friends and acquaintances.

Intending, as he certainly did, to introduce himself to Motty later on, and to get chatting with him to seek his permission to be 'written about', he made up his mind there and then that his article would be so written that Motty would enjoy its content rather than take exception to it. Motty was clearly well-liked locally. Mike determined that his piece in the County paper would further endear Motty to his friends, and enhance—not detract from—his reputation. Having in this way satisfied his conscience Mike settled down to his observations, feeling easier in his mind.

At length Motty got up and headed towards the church. Pug ran on ahead to get to a standpipe tap, put there for visitors so they could collect water for filling vases, and watering growing plants on the graves. A bucket, always full to overflowing from the dripping tap, was Pug's destination. He needed a drink.

Reaching the church, Motty disappeared round the back to reappear a few minutes later carrying the tools he wanted to meet his immediate needs. From his previous visit Mike knew that Motty's tools, and bits and pieces, were stored in the boiler house which was locked overnight by the Verger, and unlocked each morning. Finding the door open, Mike had peeped inside when he was wandering around the premises.

Apart from being a useful place to keep his equipment, the boiler house also served Motty as a place where he could shelter from the rain, if caught in a shower. In the winter, when the boiler was kept alight all the time, Motty could go in there for a 'warm-up' on the occasional visits he made to the churchyard at that period of the year, to check up that all was well.

Beside this room, which was built out from the wall of the church to accommodate the boiler, was a second wooden door which was never locked. This gave access to a small cubby-hole used as a storage place for members of the public who could leave pots, vases, jugs and small tools there. Motty tucked away some of his private things in this place.

Returning from the boiler room Motty dumped his tools at the edge of the recently cut area, where he had evidently decided to start operations. He did not resume his work straightaway though. Glancing down at the grave he said, "Shan't be long, Sam. Don't jump up! I'm just going to set my snares and traps. Be back soon, old mate—then I'll get you ship-shape again in no time!"

The words were as naturally spoken as though Sam were seated at the grave. Strangely, Mike didn't find this circumstance eerie. It was evident that in Motty's mind Sam was indeed there in person!

Motty now disappeared behind the church again, this time re-appearing carrying three galvanised-wire, cage-type traps tied together by a piece of string, and an old leather satchel. Pug was now in close attendance, in a state of some obvious excitement.

To the far side of the churchyard stood a very long, old barn, just behind the straggly hedgerow which marked the boundary of the church grounds on that side. Between the hedge and the barn were piles of rotting wood planks, and other unwanted, discarded articles and debris, dumped there over the years, together with old rusting sheets of corrugated iron, these partially covering the piles of wood. On his reconnaissance Mike had wandered into the farmyard and looked into the old barn. Inside were the sundry collection of farm implements, carts, harnesses, piles of hay and other paraphernalia so often found in old barns. Intrigued by its intricate wooden roof structure, he learnt later that a tithe barn had stood there in the 14th century and he determined to make it the subject of a future dedicated article.

Not far away, on the other side of the yard, were five very large 'dung-heaps'. These long mounds, each about six feet high, formed an invaluable, slowly-maturing reservoir of rotting manure. A sixth heap was being developed. There was an influx of farmyard manure from livestock continuously throughout the year. The heaps stood on a large area of concrete, roofed over to prevent rain water from leeching out 'goodness' from the material, but open on all sides to allow ready access for the air that is essential to the process of decay.

Depending upon the direction of the wind, residents of dwellings in the surrounding district would often have the air reaching them flavoured with an odour as unmistakably rural as the salt-laden air blowing in across seaweed-covered beaches is redolent of the sea.

Motty, in his working lifetime on a farm, had helped in the process of gradually building up, then taking down and distributing, dung-heaps such as these, over and over again. He liked the smell! So, for that matter, did Pug!

The dung-heaps were not really objectionable in their present more-or-less dormant state. At the traditional 'dung-spreading' time, however, anybody in the immediate vicinity and in the village generally, would receive on the breeze an all-pervading stench to remind them that this material was being shifted around the fields to play its time-honoured part in the farming year.

It was in the direction of this untidy boundary that Motty now headed. On a sharp, gruff command of "Find 'em, Pug! Seek 'em out, Boy! Seek 'em out!" the little terrier, with a bark of enthusiasm, set off with a dash, ahead of Motty, to the ragged hedgerow. On reaching it he began a feverish hunt in and out of the vegetation, around the bushes and straggly hedging, along the side of the barn, around and in and out of the piles of wood, his nose working overtime as he eagerly sought to sniff out his prey.

Mike guessed correctly that Motty and Pug were after rats, and he took out his binoculars to keep the pair under close observation. The environment along that side of the churchyard was ready-made for rat infestation, and Mike assumed that Motty had taken it upon himself to keep down these unwanted neighbours which no doubt at times invaded the church premises as they foraged around.

In a very short time Pug stopped his wanderings and exhibited a high degree of excitement as he concentrated his attention, with a great deal of intensive sniffing, at one point along the side of the barn.

Motty, long experienced in this routine, caught up with Pug to see what was causing his high level of enthusiasm. As so often before, Pug had found a recently used track leading to a hole at the base of the barn, and Pug's nose, snuffling and snorting eagerly, was pushed into this hole as far as it would go, his short tail wagging furiously.

Moving Pug away, Motty positioned one of his wire-cage traps under the tangle of nettles and brambles, so that its entrance faced the hole that formed the rat's front door. From a bag in his capacious pocket he had already taken out some of his prepared bait and put it into position inside the trap. Once inside, a rat would trigger the spring-loaded trap which then shut with a bang, leaving the captured rat to eat the bait at its leisure, its prospects thereafter being none too bright!

Meanwhile Pug had moved elsewhere to continue his eager hunting. No sooner had Motty settled his first trap to his satisfaction than Pug again indicated that he was onto another strong clue that rats had been present recently. This time the rats' pathway led to a scratched-out hole under the edge of a plank at the bottom of a heap of old wood pieces, covered over with a rusty sheet of corrugated iron. In such dry parts, under piles of rubbish, rats habitually moved in to set up home. Again Motty placed a trap facing the hole, in a strategic position.

It did not take long before the Pug and Motty partnership had located a hopeful place for the third trap, which was quickly in position. Having made his preparations to reduce the rat population, Motty then disappeared around the back of the church.

Mike had made some notes and taken a few photographs to record this part of the day's proceedings.

Not knowing how long Motty would be gone, Mike decided to stay where he was. After waiting for ten minutes he was beginning to think of nipping round to see what was happening, when Motty and Pug reappeared. It was not until later in the day that he discovered that during this period Motty had set a number of wire snares, just outside obviously 'active' rabbit holes, located in a grassy, bush-topped bank which ran along the side of the field bordering the grounds of the church.

Just beyond this rabbit-populated bank were several hedge-enclosed fields used for sheep, and also, in the case of one field, as a pasture for horses from a neighbouring farm. With a crystal-clear chalk-stream running through the fields, the whole area was covered with lush green grass. All in all it was a most pleasant place for rabbits to settle in, much to the convenience of Motty who, as a by-product of his 'official' duties, could supplement his diet with a rabbit pie when he wanted one, or sell the rabbits if he didn't want to eat them, in order to earn a little more cash.

Returning now to where he had left his tools, Motty had a word with his unseen friend before beginning his labours.

"Now then, old Sam, let's get you looking a bit tidier," he said. He took up his shears and began clipping the grass, continuing to talk to Sam as he did so.

"Fair number of rats under the old barn again, Sam. Must be a fair old crowd of them over there now. Not too worried about that, though, are we, old mate?" Here Motty began to chuckle away, apparently sharing a joke with Sam. "Worth a pint or two to me, they will be! I'll remember to drink your health when I cash in on them, that I will!"

Mike could not see the connection between rats and pints, but he was to learn later. His Editor, a much older man with more experience of the ways of the countryside, would not have needed the connection explained to him.

Busily, though not without many grunts and groans because bending and twisting about pained his troublesome joints, Motty finished clipping Sam's grassy surround and turned his attention to getting rid of some weeds. He pulled some up by the roots and then, with his sharpened hoe, undercut some dandelion and dock roots. These green plants he left on the surface to dry out and be raked up later with the cut grass.

With a parting comment to Sam of, "That's fixed you up again for a bit, Sam," he moved to Sam's neighbour and did the same for him.

Moving from grave to grave, with an occasional passing comment here and there, all of which Mike carefully recorded in his notebook, Motty slowly pursued his peaceful duties.

The nature of these sundry brief comments, which Mike was later to read over again as he prepared his article, clearly reflected Motty's attitude towards the inhabitants he addressed. Some he had obviously known well and others not. Some he had evidently liked, and others most certainly not!

One of those he spoke to and clearly remembered with affection, was a lady named Liz.

"How are you then, Liz?" he enquired, grinning mischievously. "Behaving yourself I 'ope, old girl, are you? Don't suppose you can get up to your old tricks these days though, can you, Liz? I 'spect the Guv'nor keeps his eye on you, eh! Not much chance for a randy old girl like you to get 'erself tumbled in the grass in 'ere without being spotted, is there? Wrong place to sin about in, this place is. Not in the front garden of the Lord's House! Poor old Liz, must be 'ard on you, old mate. Hee hee hee!"

Then, one place away from Liz, pausing to read the name on the tombstone, Motty said,

"Good morning, Albert 'odges. Didn't know you, mate. Nor did Liz, far as I know. Bet you've got to know 'er since you moved in 'ere alongside 'er though, ain't you, Albert?"

Motty chuckled gleefully to himself, evidently dwelling upon the implications of this meaningful remark, and then continued his comments to the silent stranger, Albert.

"Cor lummy duck, mate, you dropped in lucky being planted next to our old Liz, you did! Many's the feller in 'ere wot would swop places with you, old mate, any day of the week—that I do know. An' buy you a pint on the deal too. Bit of all right, our Liz is. It was your lucky day, Albert, when you died and got put down right by Liz. Most blokes would 'ave kicked the bucket before their time to get a billet like that. Good luck to you, old mate. Good luck! You enjoy yourself. If you ain't got stuck into our old Liz already, you wait until dark an' jump out of your 'ole an' get in alongside of 'er—she'll see you're all right! Don't be scared, mate! She won't 'urt you! She'll gobble you up, but she'll 'ave a job to kill you, won't she, Albert! You're safe enough, dead like you are!"

His continued happy chuckling showed Mike that these comments gave Motty cause for much inward satisfaction and merriment as he thought about his departed friend Liz, and presumably pictured the reception the unknown Albert might get when he paid her a visit. Mike could only speculate about the personality of 'Old Liz', and her relationship with Motty and his cronies in years gone by!

Meanwhile Motty moved on to an impressive grave which looked very new and expensive. On its imposing tombstone its owner's name was inscribed in ornate lettering, followed by a short eulogy marking the occupant out as somebody a bit special, if the words were to be believed. Motty's demeanour changed noticeably from one of cheerful familiarity, to one of deference and marked respect.

To Mike's eyes, this grave, with its obviously costly surround, its marble chips, and its various carved ornaments that complemented its large headstone, looked ostentatious and rather overdone. However, he watched Motty's reaction with interest.

"Nice morning, Mr Grant, Sir," Motty said, raising his knobbly old hand and touching his very grubby cap. "Pleased to see you looking so well settled-in, Sir, that I am. Right good job old Stony Charlie made of your 'eadstone too, Sir. The 'ole job's very smart, that it is, if you don't mind me saying so, Sir. Real 'alf-tidy job it is. Grave to be proud of you've got 'ere, Sir, if I may say so."

Motty then walked round looking intently at the grave from all angles. It was one of very recent origin and Motty looked it over with the eye of an expert. Examining a vase of flowers with evident pleasure and admiration, Motty then said approvingly,

"Lovely carnations your Missus 'as put 'ere, Sir. Best I've seen for many a year they are. I'll change their water for you, Sir, to keep 'em nice and fresh. Real specials they are. Need extra special care too, flowers like that do."

With that, as good as his word, Motty set off for the tap, returning a few minutes later with a watering can. He took out the flowers with great care, as though under observation by a critical watcher, threw the water out of the vase and re-filled it from the can. Then, again with marked care, he re-arranged the flowers to establish an attractive display.

"There you are, Mr Grant, Sir," he said. "That will do 'em a power of good, that will. Beauties they are! Real beauties! Everybody in 'ere will enjoy looking at those."

Putting the vase back in its place on the grave Motty prepared to move on, and touched his cap respectfully.

"Goodbye then, Sir," he said. "I'll be back to see you in a few days to make sure everything's all right. I 'ope you keep well. Try to keep your spirits up, as they say. You'll soon settle in, like the others round you 'ave. It's a good place to be, in 'ere is, if you've got to be buried. Bone yards don't come no better, that they don't. With that encouraging remark he then made his way on to his next task.

Mike found on later enquiry that the man, Roderick Grant, whose name he had noted from the inscription, had been a highly respected and much liked figure in the neighbourhood for a great many years. His extensive estate and rambling mansion of a house gave him an exalted status in Motty's eyes. Not that his worldly goods alone would have been reason for Motty's assessment. His reputation and accolade were gained by behaviour and deeds, not by money—although his open-handed generosity with the latter did in fact fund some of his good deeds.

In marked contrast was Motty's manner to the occupant of a much less conspicuous grave further down the line.

"Huh! You're still 'ere then, Sid, you swindling old sod!" Motty grunted, surveying the grave with obvious distaste. "You can bloody well wait till next time, you can, afore I tidy you up! Never should 'ave been put 'ere in the first place at all, you shouldn't 'ave been. It ain't right to put a nasty old bastard like you in 'ere, 'longside nice people. It ain't right at all. The dung-'eap would 'ave been a better place to stick you in. Reckon the rats would 'ave liked the taste of a stinkin' old sod like you!"

Muttering to himself, Motty moved on, leaving—as he said he would—the territory around Sid untouched.

Mike made a mental note to enquire about the lifestyle of the departed Sid. A man who could evoke such a hostile reaction from an apparently generally good-natured old chap like Motty must have a history worth looking into. He was fast beginning to feel that there was plenty of material here for another potentially amusing article in the future.

The quiet tempo of events was suddenly interrupted. Pug, who had been spending his time happily pursuing his own interests, sniffing around the area with unceasing inquisitiveness and tireless energy, suddenly gave a sharp bark and raced away in the direction of the barn. His sharp ears had picked up the distant metallic clang which he knew from much previous experience came from the abrupt shutting of the spring-loaded flap in one of the rat-traps.

Motty dropped what he was doing, grabbed his stick, and began making his way after Pug, who, with excited barking, had reached the trap positioned at the base of the side of the barn.

Mike took up his binoculars to watch what was happening. He saw Motty bend down and move away from the barn, carrying the trap. As he turned, Mike could clearly see a rat moving frantically about inside the wire cage.

What he saw next he didn't much like. Having moved into open ground, far enough from the hedgerow to ensure the rat wouldn't get away, Motty simply opened the trap door and shook the rat out. It scurried away, hotly pursued by Pug. In a blur of activity, he saw Pug catch the rat by the scruff of the neck, shake it vigorously, and trot back to Motty, where, on a sharp word of command from his master, he dropped the now lifeless rat at Motty's feet.

In what was clearly a routine operation, Motty took out his sharp pocket knife, cut the tail off the rat, pulled a clump of grass out of the hedgerow, dropped the rat into the hole, replaced the grass, and made his way back to the barn. On the way Mike saw him shove the rat's tail into his top pocket and pause to pat his excited little dog, while repeating several times, "Good dog! Good dog! Good dog!"

So pleased was Pug with this successful job and with his master's congratulations, that he wagged his tail so furiously it seemed to Mike as though his whole body was wagged along with the tail.

In a few minutes Motty had re-baited the trap and placed it back in its previous position, hoping no doubt that another member of the rat community would choose to come out into the sunshine by the same route. He was not to be disappointed. By the time he left that day, that particular trap had caught three rats, part of a very satisfying rat-day for Motty, because one of the other two traps also proved successful. It, though, yielded an unexpected and very welcome bonus for Motty, in a little drama played out in front of the watching Mike, who really was seeing a side of country life that he had not known about before.

After dealing with the first rat, hardly had Motty resumed his work with his shears at the grave he had left, when Pug called him away from his work and the whole procedure was repeated again. This time it was the trap by the rotting pile of wood that Pug raced to. This rat was dealt with as expeditiously as the previous one, but here the similarity ended.

When Motty, having harvested its tail and buried the rat, returned to the pile of wood with the trap to re-position it, he found Pug already there with his nose stuck under the edge of a plank, at the exit hole where—following Pug's original instruction—he had placed the trap. Pug's whole manner evinced great excitement. Motty knew that just under the plank must be another rat, actually there now and almost within reach. Pug's eager snuffling, snorting, and vigorous wagging of his tail told his Master in plain language that live quarry was at hand!

Using a piece of wood as a lever, Motty lifted the plank about a foot off the ground and wedged it there. Pug was under it in a flash, snuffling about in a state of high excitement and clearly on to something of great interest. Shoving his nose in further he pulled out a tangled ball of debris. It was made of torn-up pieces of paper, odd bits of fur, feathers, and pieces of string, dry grass, and leaves. This Motty had immediately recognised as a rat's nest. And Pug's reaction told him, beyond any doubt, that the nest was 'live'.

Pushing Pug to one side, Motty bent down to poke about in the little heap of debris carefully. One by one he picked out six tiny baby rats that looked to Mike, through his binoculars, like small pieces of red meat.

These tiny creatures Motty then proceeded to tie, along with a stone, in a piece of old rag taken from the dump. With no hesitation, obviously carrying out 'normal procedure', Motty made his way over to the watering can and dumped his little parcel of infant rats into the water. Later on these were retrieved, well and truly drowned, wrapped in a piece of paper and shoved into Motty's top pocket to join the rats' tails already there—one of which was their Mum's!

After this entertaining diversionary exercise, Motty returned to his methodical work of tidying up between the graves.

Very shortly afterwards Mike heard approaching footsteps in the lane. The walker turned in through the lych-gate to crunch along the gravel path towards the church door.

Motty's cheerful greeting of "Mornin', Vicar", identified the visitor, who, calling out "Good morning, Mr. Marsh," walked over to have a word with his valued helper. Out of respect for Motty's 'official position' the Vicar always addressed him as 'Mr. Marsh'. In this he was an exception, for everybody else, young and old alike, called him Motty.

Mike, always the opportunist, thought this to be an excellent chance to establish his visit on an acceptable basis. Making his way quietly and unobtrusively back along the hedgerow, he stepped through a gap into the lane and then strode purposefully along to turn in through the lych-gate and make his way towards the church.

The Vicar, spotting him, walked over the grass to meet his visitor.

"Reverend Yelman?" queried Mike, as the Vicar approached him.

"Yes, that's me," replied the Vicar genially. "Can I help you?" He noted Mike's binoculars and camera and took him to be a holidaymaker or hiker calling in to see the church.

Mike identified himself and explained that he was assigned by his paper to do a feature on the village, and to interview some of the local personalities. The Vicar welcomed him, assured him of any assistance he could give him in the project, and escorted him on a tour of the church. During this time Mike obtained some useful background information to add authenticity to his so far somewhat covert operation.

In due course he turned the conversation to the subject of Motty. The Vicar's smiling reaction was immediate. Motty obviously gave great amusement to many people, and the Vicar willingly entertained Mike with stories of his eccentric but much-liked part-time 'caretaker' of the church grounds. In the course of this little talk he mentioned Motty's additional contribution to the welfare of the establishment, of waging a constant war against the rats, with the expert assistance of his little dog Pug.

This was fortuitous, because Mike was intrigued by Motty's curious behaviour in cutting off the rat's tails and carefully storing them away in his pocket. The Vicar came to the point without any prompting from Mike, who had been wondering how he could raise the subject without revealing that he'd had Motty under observation for some while.

He learnt that Motty was a keen member of the "Rat and Sparrow Club", the first of its kind that Mike had come across. The club had the specific purpose of keeping down the numbers of these two particularly troublesome pests, both of which were a very real nuisance and a cause of much concern in the locality.

Rats thrived because of the concentration of livestock in the area. Pigs, chickens, ducks, horses, sheep, goats, cows and home-bred 'tame' rabbits, created an environment where liberal supplies of food, and attractive dwelling places, made just the right conditions in which rats could live and multiply in rich comfort.

To a lesser extent sparrows also were a pest. They too had everything they needed for comfort, and were present in swarms. These, apart from their other not very popular activities, raided corn crops and damaged other produce, plants and fruit bushes, as well as competing with chickens for their supplied food.

The Rat & Sparrow Club was financed in small part by its members' fees, but in its essential activity it was supported by farmers and landowners, who saw this outlay on their part as a useful service to their business interests. The members profited from being in this club on a 'reward-for-success' basis.

Each week 'active' members of the club went to a 'head and tail count' meeting. Each in turn went up to the appointed secretary/treasurer. Here they undid their small parcels and counted out the sparrow heads and rats' tails, which they had brought along as evidence of their success.

Sparrow heads, cut off or sometimes just pulled off the dead sparrows, were counted, and then the rats' tails together with baby rats if any, were checked in. Tiny baby rats, not possessing tails of meaningful size, were brought along 'whole'. They quite logically each counted as equal to an adult rat's tail, since the destruction of the baby rats represented an equal reduction in the rat population on a one-to-one basis.

A rat's tail earned the member one penny, and a sparrow's head a halfpenny. This, to keen members, added up to a useful extra income, and often, in nice weather, the hobby was much enjoyed by those taking part in organised hunting forays. The dog population, in particular, enjoyed the rat-catching outings.

Later, in conversation over a pint with 'old Mac', the landlord at "The Buffs", Mike was to learn that some members, at certain times of the year, went out with large nets and lamps at night, to catch sparrows in quantity. The large nets, often having a rectangular rather than a circular frame, were pushed against ivy-covered walls where sparrows regularly roosted. Enough noise and disturbance encouraged the sparrows to attempt to make a getaway, only to be trapped in the net. With a swift downward sweep the net was placed flat on the ground, with the sparrows trapped under it to be gathered up under the light of a lantern by the hunters, providing a harvest of heads for eventual conversion into beer money!

Mike also learned that the club treasurer had to be careful to 'bag up', and dispose of, the heads and tails as they were 'paid for' at the weekly count. Rats' tails in particular could find their way round again next week if they were not taken out of circulation.

Old Mac also said that one enterprising man had made quite a profit from breeding tame rats and 'flogging' their tiny red offspring, which of course were indistinguishable from 'wild rats'. People apparently became suspicious at the unusual success of this unscrupulous member in locating rats' nets. Normally it was a bonus enjoyed only infrequently, for a member to unearth a nest.

So his little game was stopped. It made it bad, said Mac, for the others because, from what he'd heard, there always seemed to be a degree of suspicion directed at members handing in baby rats!

However, at the church, in advance of receiving this additional information about the activities of the Rat & Sparrow club, Mike did not divulge to the Vicar that he had already witnessed Motty earlier on at work at his rat catching. He did not want to reveal that he had, in effect, been spying on Motty going about his business, but resolved to sound Motty out himself later on, so that this aspect could be incorporated naturally into the article he would subsequently be writing. He was used to eliciting information he already had, from the people it concerned, to avoid the inference when it was published that it had been obtained by prying. But he had to do plenty of prying nonetheless. There were of course occasions when the paper did not mind this being obvious, if the matters were ones of public interest and those being criticised did not deserve any soft-footed protection. If they were outraged by exposure, and indignant at invasion of their privacy, then so what!

Motty, though, was different. Mike, already a bit uneasy about his clandestine role in studying him, had taken a liking to the strange old boy. Clearly the eccentric, curious-looking old fellow was vulnerable, an easy target for having fun poked at him. Mike's resolve to create a piece of interesting copy that would leave his readers with a likeable impression of 'Old Motty', was strengthened by his close observation of him, and by the Vicar's obvious affection for him.

At length, after an interesting and enjoyable conversation, the Vicar took Mike along to where Motty was working and introduced him. He explained the purpose of Motty's visit and Motty agreed to be 'interviewed' by Mike about the life in the village in general and about the churchyard in particular. The Vicar then took his leave, saying 'goodbye' to them both and going off to pursue his parochial duties.

Motty and Mike retired to one of the seats along the hedge, and there they sat for a good half-hour or so during which time Mike gleaned a wealth of information about village life, and Motty's experiences. He also broached the question of control of vermin around the precincts of the church, and very soon Motty was describing with some enthusiasm how he and his dog Pug successfully kept down the population of rats. Proudly he fished out of his pocket the rats' tails he had gathered that day, and then showed Mike the small collection of tiny baby rats he had wrapped up safely in a small packet ready for submission to his Club's tallyman later in the week. This gruesome collection of evidence was not a sight that gave Mike much pleasure, and he was glad when Motty stuffed the lot back into his top pocket store!

Before he left, Mike decided to test, as discreetly as he could, the possible truth or otherwise of the story his editor had heard in the pub, which had excited his interest in Motty Marsh in the first place.

"I suppose, Mr. Marsh," Mike said respectfully, "you know pretty well where everybody is buried in this churchyard?"

"Reckon I do. Yeah, reckon I do an' all," responded Motty, not without some pride in his superior knowledge in this respect.

"So I suppose, Mr. Marsh, that now and again you have visitors coming to ask you for help, wondering if they happen to know where they can find a particular grave?"

continued Mike cautiously, working his way gingerly towards his intended question.

"Oh aye! Oh aye! Many's the time I show's 'em where to go," Motty replied. "It 'appens a lot, that do. Vicar always sends people to ask me if they needs 'elp. Many's the time I'm the only one wot knows! Many's the time! Oh, aye!"

Now was the time for Mike to dip his toes in the water.

"Do you happen to know where a man named Bert Tomkin is buried, Mr. Marsh? I understand he died about thirty years ago."

If Mike had entertained any doubts about whether or not Motty would even know the name, they were instantly dispelled. Motty's reaction was electric. It was as though Mike had stuck a pin in him! He was immediately highly alert.

"Bert Tomkin, d'yer say? Bert Tomkin?" he asked sharply.

"Yes, that's the name. A man I know is interested in his family history and asked me to enquire where his grave is, while I was visiting Littlebrook church."

This was the best Mike could think of on the spur of the moment. He was startled at Motty's intense reaction.

"You ain't a relation o' Bert Tomkin, then?" Motty asked fiercely.

"No," replied Mike. "No, I know nothing of him at all."

"Think yourself bloody lucky, then," said Motty. "An' I wish I 'ad never known anything about 'im too. Biggest bloody twister I ever met, 'e was!"

"You don't seem to have liked him much," Mike commented wryly.

"Like 'im? Like 'im? Course I didn't bloody well like 'im! No more didn't nobody else wot knowed 'im like 'im, s'far as I know."

Motty paused for breath, obviously very het-up at the mere thought of Bert Tomkin. Then he continued in like vein.

"Right old twister 'e was! He said explosively. "Crafty as a mean old rat and slimy as a bloody slug, 'e was! Never ought to 'ave been put in 'ere at all, 'e shouldn't. If I 'ad my way I'd dig the bugger up and chuck 'im out. That's what I'd do. Chuck 'im out. Not even good enough for the dung 'eap 'e ain't. Spoil good shit 'e would in there. Like 'im, eh? Like 'im? 'Oo the 'ell would like an old sod same as 'im? Huh! Huh! Huh!"

Mike began to fear that Motty might have a heart attack or burst a blood vessel or something if he didn't stop him, so he interrupted him before his blood pressure rose even higher.

"Sorry I mentioned him, Mr. Marsh. Of course I had no idea his name would upset you like this or I wouldn't have asked about him."

"It ain't your fault, young man," Motty said. "You weren't to know. But I tell yer this. I'm staying 'ere. If you want to see 'is grave you go by yerself. Over in the corner there, that's where 'e is. See that bloody mess in the corner? That's 'im. An' you're welcome."

In the direction indicated Mike could see a plot where grass and weeds stood high above the surrounding, well-tended grass. Leaving Motty watching him balefully from the seat, Mike got up and walked over to look, identifying his quarry by name from the inscription on the moss-covered headstone. It was evident that nobody had made any attempt at tidying this particular grave and its surround for a long time. It was, Mike thought, sadly neglected. Having thought that, he quickly made a mental correction and took out the word 'sadly' because it would clearly have offended Motty! Perish the thought! It was tantamount to having sympathy with Motty's enemy!

On closer inspection, walking round the plot, he saw clear evidence of Motty's aversion to it. The grass between this grave and others bordering it was clearly divided exactly in half. The outer half was closely cut all round, but the inner half had high-standing grass and weeds looking so straight along the edges that he suspected Motty

63

pegged a line down during his periodic visits to make sure he did nothing whatsoever to improve the appearance of his unwelcome tenant's territory!

All in all Mike felt that the story his editor had heard was almost certainly founded on fact: very bizarre facts maybe, but facts nonetheless. He could well imagine Motty addressing Bert Tomkin in the terms attributed to him.

When he retraced his footsteps back from this excursion to rejoin the strongly-prejudiced caretaker, Motty made his last comment on the matter.

"I knows it's a disgrace over there," he said, "but when I first came 'ere I said to the Vicar I'd 'elp 'im 'ere with pleasure. But, I says to 'im, I'll never, never, never, touch that old bugger's grave over there. I told 'im straight I wouldn't do it. I wouldn't never bloody well touch it! Either somebody else does it, I says, or the miserable old sod can get out and do it 'imself 'cos I never would. And I never 'as! And I never will!"

Then, with some acknowledgment of fair treatment by his employer he added, "And Vicar's never asked me. Give 'im that. I 'ave to say, 'e's never asked me from that day to this. We don't speak about it. If I 'ad my way I'd build a fence round the miserable sod, that I would!"

"I can understand him not pressing you to do something you don't want to do," said Mike. "Reverend Yelman seems a very nice man to me and he told me how much he appreciates all you do for him here."

"Did 'e say that, eh?" said Motty, visibly pleased at this favourable comment. "Said that, did 'e? That was a nice thing to say, that was." Then, thoughtfully, he added, "Vicar's a good bloke, that's what 'e is, a good bloke!"

Mike, relieved at having reduced Motty's state of dangerous over-excitement, thought now was a good time to be off. He took two more photographs of Motty with his dog Pug, thanked Motty for his kind help, promised him that he would send copies of the photographs to him in a few days' time, said goodbye and left to return to Maidstone.

On the way out of the village Mike stopped at "The Buffs" for another chat with Old Mac and to drink a refreshing glass of Kentish beer. It was then that he gained his further insight into the workings of the Rat & Sparrow Club.

But when Old Mac told him about the enterprising member of the Club who had been caught breeding baby rats for illicit profit, Mike rather put his foot in it.

"It wasn't Old Motty who looks after the churchyard who worked that fast one, by any chance, was it?" Mike enquired.

Old Mac did not think this a clever question at all.

"It certainly was *not* Motty," he said emphatically. "A crafty, scheming old so-and-so he may be. But Old Motty is at heart an honest man. He'd be very upset if he knew you'd even asked the question. Plays the ball straight down the middle, our Motty does. Detests swindlers, he does, in whatever shape they come."

Mike apologised for the obviously unfair thought and told Old Mac how Motty had just been showing him a family of baby mice he'd caught that very day. When the landlord had mentioned baby rats, of course it had rung an immediate bell.

"Well, I can tell you something you can take for certain," Old Mac concluded. "When Motty hands those in to the Club's treasurer there won't be anybody there who queries where they came from. Old Motty would blow his top clean off if they did!"

Back at the church, when his visitor had gone, Motty took a drink of water from the tap and then sat in the sun to munch a hefty thick bread and cheese sandwich taken from his old leather satchel. Pug received a juicy bone from the same source. This he crunched away at, lying contentedly on the grass at Motty's feet.

Not long afterwards, Motty gathered up his tools, collected his three rat traps, and made preparations to go home. He had done enough for that day.

His last job before departing was to go to the rabbit-infested bank in the field behind the church, to see if he had been lucky and to collect his snares.

Pug, as soon as his master started to head for the bank, darted ahead excitedly to make his accustomed search of the area. Before Motty was anywhere near, several barks from Pug told him that either there was a rabbit in one of the snares or Pug had seen one run off. When he arrived he found Pug snuffling at, but not molesting, a rabbit caught fast in a snare. Pug had been trained not to touch a trapped rabbit, but if one ran off he would give chase, and more often than not catch it.

Quite often, a rabbit coming out of a hole would be killed by the slip-knot wire snare as it tightened around its neck. This one was not killed. It was securely held, but undamaged and alive.

It was a good thing Mike had not accompanied Motty because what happened next he would not have liked. He was rather squeamish and unaccustomed to country life. Many people in the country killed, cooked and ate at least some of their meat. But the majority of people in towns *bought*, cooked and ate theirs. Somebody else, somewhere else, did the killing. Some people didn't like the idea of animals being killed at all, but as long as they did not see it done most did not spend much time thinking about, or agonising about, this unavoidable step in the business of living and eating. They just enjoyed the eating.

Motty did not even think about such paradoxes. Crouching down he disentangled the rabbit from the snare, held it up clear of the ground by its back legs using his left hand, and chopped it hard behind the ears with the edge of his right hand. The rabbit was killed instantly.

Motty looked forward happily to a rabbit pie in a day or two's time. As part of an established routine since Motty lost his wife, a kindly neighbour helped him out by doing some cooking for him. She would take the rabbit, cook an appetising pie, have half of it herself and pass the other half to Motty. He supplied the meat; she did the cooking; and both profited by the co-operation. Motty really looked forward to, and thoroughly enjoyed, these lovely rabbit pies, with their crusty pastry, tasty meat, and rich gravy. What he didn't eat hot, he ate with equal relish later, cold, perhaps as part of his lunch when at work in the churchyard.

Taking up his satchel, to which he tied the rabbit, Motty retrieved his remaining snares, took up his stick, and, accompanied by the ever-enthusiastic Pug, began to tap tap tap his way back home. He had enjoyed his day. So had Pug!

At Maidstone, two days later, the Editor sat in his office, read Mike's article, and looked at the photographs.

It was a good story. Mike had done a good job, no question about that. Apart from striking out the words 'bugger' and 'sod', to insert instead the words 'blighter' and 'devil' in deference to the not inconsiderable number of people who would take exception to the appearance of these words in print, he left the article alone. Otherwise, those remarks of Motty's selected by Mike for inclusion in his piece, were left in verbatim. The end product had the ring of authenticity without being too offensive, and he felt sure the majority of the newspaper's regular readers throughout the county of Kent would enjoy reading it.

For a while, after going over this piece again, the Editor sat alone in his office, pondering the curious bizarre habits of this weathered old man pottering in a village churchyard, talking now and again to his various departed acquaintances.

In a way, or so it seemed to him, it was not all that inconsistent with the behaviour of many people for whom life hereafter was part of their deeply-believed philosophy and faith.

If, he mused, people lived on in some way in another world, where were they? To many people a graveside was a focal point, a point of contact where, usually quietly and silently, they communed with their departed loved ones.

Motty did the same. But he talked aloud. And in talking, his words and his feelings were not unlike those he would have spoken and felt if the people were still 'alive' in some way and had miraculously made their presence felt.

Except that is, the Editor thought as he smiled to himself, in the case of Bert Tomkin. One sight of him and doubtless Motty would be gone. There was clearly nothing much left to be said to the unlamented Mr.Tomkin, and no doubt Motty would avoid him like the plague, beating a hasty retreat with his little dog Pug hard on his heels.

Bert Tomkin, by all the evidence positively disliked when alive, was clearly destined to remain a parish pariah in his corner plot—at least while 'Old Motty' was alive.

But the Editor was grateful to the departed Bert, for his presence had provided the initial link which had given rise to what proved to be an article that subsequently created widespread amusement among the paper's readers.

As for Mike, the episode was in due course to have a very profound effect—in a way nobody could possibly have foreseen—upon the development of his career and the future of his entire life.

Chapter 6

BILL THE SADDLER
true friend not only to horses

There was no noise except the second-by-second 'tock' 'tock' 'tock' of the large shop-clock on the wall, the hissing of the gas mantle and the sundry clicks, clinks, tings, bumps, grunts and movements generated by Bill as he sat on his sturdy old stool stitching farm harness.

With deft, swift, perfectly aimed stabs, the awl in Bill's right hand pierced holes on a pre-marked grooved line along the edge of the side of the heavy leather strap, each stab being followed in a flash by two needles passing through the hole in opposite directions dragging a 'double-ended' length of waxed thread which he pulled tightly to make a 'dead-in-line', double-sided stitch along the leather.

The stitches were of perfectly uniform size, for the position of each awl hole had been previously marked by a stitch pricker tool that Bill had moved along the line made by his grooving gauge. For tough, hardened leather such as he was working on he used a pricking iron, a form of punch bearing a row of evenly spaced teeth. This was placed along the line of the groove and clouted with a mallet to cut a line of 'starter holes' for the sharp awl to pass into. For softer leather and lighter work, he used a toothed pricker wheel, a faster, easier method of running a line of pricked holes along the grooved stitching line. The heavier-duty pricking iron had to be progressively moved along in a 'move-clout-move-clout' routine, to run the length of the line: a more than somewhat tedious process. Using the wheel Bill simply pressed it into the groove, then ran it along in a swift easy action.

As Bill worked on, at a steady relentless pace, this procedure left behind a very precise, thoroughly professional and pleasing-looking line of stitching, binding together the heavy pieces of old, well-worn and none-too-supple leather. It was hard work, a fact evidenced by the strength of Bill's hands, wrists and arms, which were called upon to keep up this and similar routines for hour after hour.

Bill knew what he was about and was extremely good at his job. Trained initially for five years as an apprentice under a hard, unforgiving taskmaster, Bill subsequently had had many years' experience handling light and heavy harness of all descriptions. He did not spare himself, and everything he turned out had the unmistakeable mark about it of the true craftsman.

A rattle of the brass door latch, a loud, sharp, metallic 'ding' from the spring-loaded doorbell and an inrush of cold air from the street outside, announced the arrival of a customer.

It was a blustery, rainy, and dismal evening outside, but inside the shop there was a welcoming warmth from Bill's black, cylindrical Valor oil-stove, which, together with the soft yellowy light from the gas mantle created a 'cosy haven' feel to the shop and made it a nice place to come into from the dark, wintry village street outside.

The limited extent of the gaslight left dark corners and shadowy areas in the shop. This, with the warm glow of the burning wick shining through the mica window of the stove, and the flickering circles of light thrown on the ceiling through the vent holes in its round top, added to the comfortable, friendly, semi-domestic atmosphere.

With scarcely a glance up from his work, Bill identified his visitor, who, with a grunted, "Evening, Bill", settled himself with grateful comfort to lean in the corner between the edge of Bill's bench and the shop window behind him.

Beyond the words, "Rough old night, Tom", from Bill, no further communication took place between the two for several minutes. During this time Tom stoked his rough wooden briar pipe with tobacco from a battered, shallow, screw-topped tin, and carefully lit it to begin a steady, satisfying series of puffs as he watched, with close interest, Bill's work progressing.

Tom, a farm labourer who worked with horses, knew about harness and noted that Bill was working on a girth-strap. On closer inspection he saw that the girth-strap was part of a pile of harness lying on the floor against the wall under the clock, just a few feet away from Bill's side where he could get at it piece by piece as he worked methodically through it. By a coincidence he recognised it as a set of harness which had been dumped on the floor when he was last in the shop on a Saturday morning three weeks ago. It was brought in by an old waggoner from Mansted's Farm.

Tom remembered that Bill had been none too pleased at the condition of the harness. On seeing it an angry frown had disturbed the normally happy appearance of Bill's face as he picked up pieces of it and examined it closely. He clearly didn't like what he saw.

"This lot has been let go far too long!" he had commented gruffly. "Far too long. It's not good enough, this! It just won't do!"

"I know that, Bill," the old man had said, uncomfortably. "But you know what the Guv'nor's like. He won't have anything mended until it's falling apart. In fact he won't spend a penny on anything until he has to!"

The reason for Bill's sharp reaction was plain to see. It was the total wearing-away of part of the neck padding of the collar. On one side, at shoulder level, the coarse, off-white, blue-striped collar cloth had a large hole in it, and all that was left of the flock stuffing underneath it were hard, matted, dirty, flat pieces looking more like tree-bark than anything else. The threadbare, badly-worn cloth was in a very sorry state indeed, and all resilience had long since gone from the stuffing it covered.

All knew, without Bill saying it, that this must have left a raw place on the horse's neck, causing it pain as it pulled its heavy loads, especially as it turned at the end of a furrow when dragging a plough through heavy soil. The collar wore most at the points where the force on the horse's back was greatest, the very places where the animal needed the protection of the padded collar most of all.

Bill, who loved horses, never failed to speak up for them and Tom was not alone in being grateful to Bill for this, for he spoke with the authority of an expert, without fear or favour. The sum total of suffering of these faithful, powerful friends, who worked so hard in the countryside in all weathers, was mitigated by the undisguised anger of Bill when he saw evidence of neglect on the part of those working them.

It could be, and often was—as in the present case—due to a marked reluctance on the part of the farmers who owned the horses, to part with any money until they absolutely had to, an added source of annoyance to Bill since they would invariably be among those who kept him waiting months, sometimes even over a full year, between receiving his 'quarterly' accounts and paying them.

Some admired Bill for the unhesitating way in which he 'dressed down' those responsible for failing to ensure the proper care of horses, irrespective of their status. Others, more timid or perhaps more cynical, were surprised that he would risk the loss of a customer for the sake of a horse.

If he were conscious of these reactions to his behaviour, Bill never showed it. For him his response to cruelty to horses was automatic—as would have been that of his saddler father, of his blacksmith grandfather, and of the long line of village blacksmiths from whom Bill was descended. His love of horses and his uncompromising response to ill-treatment of them was built into his genes. He was not even aware that this gave him a natural aura of authority amongst countrymen, for few would wish to face up to, even less contradict or otherwise knowingly provoke him on this matter.

As a result, though it did not appear in any account book, a blasting from Bill yielded a profit of less pain to a good many horses living scattered around the countryside over an area of many square miles.

In his own good time, Tom, who meanwhile had been dwelling upon and pondering these matters having had his thoughts triggered off by the sight of the sadly-worn collar on the floor, started the business of the evening that had brought him to the shop at 7pm on this dismal day.

"Got trouble, Bill," he said, pausing to puff away at his pipe, awaiting—not in a calculated way, but because it was natural—the question which must come.

"What's up, Tom?" asked Bill between grunts as he heaved the stiff, wide strap further along through the jaws of the wooden saddler's knee-clamp, which was held in a vertical position by his knees, its end standing firmly on the floor.

"Down on my luck, I'm afraid!" answered Tom. "Lost my job, Bill. The farm's sold up and it seems the bloke coming in don't need me."

"Sorry to hear that, Tom old son," said Bill, glancing up now from his work to look Tom anxiously in the face, his kind heart stirred by Tom's obvious distress.

"What are you going to do, Tom?" he asked, his genuine concern sounding in the tone of his voice.

"Dunno yet, Bill. Been looking around and asking if anybody knows where there's a job going. Not much hope—so far as I can see—this time of year."

"No, Tom," agreed Bill sadly. "Bad time to get chucked out. Bad time of year to lose your job, and no mistake!"

There followed a pause during which Bill, bent over his work, continued stitching away mechanically, while pondering Tom's problem and quietly making up his mind to ask around his contacts in the following days to see if he could discover an opening for him.

Meanwhile Tom had been gathering his thoughts and framing his words, to approach the specific purpose of his visit. At length he proceeded.

"Got to raise some money somehow, Bill, till I get fixed up with something—if you see what I mean, like," he said, a little hesitatingly.

"Yes, Tom. I can quite see that. Things must be difficult for you. I can quite see that," said Bill sympathetically. Those who knew Bill well knew that when he used the words 'I can quite see that', he really *was* listening to them. Sometimes, when busy at his work, he was deeply preoccupied and did not always hear what was said to him, and people had to repeat themselves. Bill was aware of this failing, and the use of these words was his way of letting them know he'd heard what they said. During any prolonged serious discussion the phrase was used unwittingly by Bill, many times over.

Tom picked his way forward gingerly towards his rather delicate business.

"Got to sell a few things to tide me over, Bill. That's all I can do," he said, sounding as helpless as he felt. Then he took the plunge, and dived straight in to ask his leading question.

"I wondered if you'd buy my new bike back off me, Bill?" he said, looking anxiously at Bill's face.

Tom's 'new' bike was 'new' in the sense that he had bought it new off Bill some ten months earlier, to replace his 'old' bike—this of unknown age—but certainly over fifteen years old. He'd had it over ten years, purchased second-hand from Bill when it was at least five years old.

Tom was one of Bill's regulars. His new bike, a Hercules, had cost him £3.19s.6d and nobody needed reminding of the price because it had remained unchanged for two or three years.

"Yes, Tom old lad, of course I will," Bill replied with no hesitation at all. "I'll give you three pounds for it. How will that suit you?"

"Cor, Bill!" Tom exclaimed, with obvious relief. "That would help a lot, that would. That would give me a bit of time. Thanks, Bill, thanks. That will really help us along."

"Right-ho, Tom! Right-ho! You bring it along in the morning and I'll square up with you," said Bill, to seal the deal.

Silence descended on the shop again for a while, and Bill, watched intently by Tom, continued his unremitting work.

Tom meanwhile was thinking. Thinking about bikes and prices and values. He wondered if Bill, known to be a bit absent-minded and forgetful about business matters generally, had forgotten that he'd had his new bike getting on a year. People did not always take advantage of Bill when his forgetfulness stood to their advantage. Some did, but most didn't, because Bill was a good-hearted bloke and deserved fairness from his friends.

At length Tom spoke up again.

"That's a good bit more than I thought, Bill," he said, frowning and looking a bit worried. "A good bit more than I thought. The bike's nigh-on a year old you know, Bill. Mind you I've looked after it well, as you know—it looks pretty new still, but of course it has been used for nearly a year. No getting round that."

This put everything fair and square and eased Tom's mind. "You sure you won't lose on the deal, Bill?" he added, figuring that a profit added to £3 would put the price Bill had to sell it for, up so near to the price of new one, nobody would buy it.

"No, Tom—no—I won't lose out on that, don't you worry. That's fair, Tom. You've looked after the bike—I know that—and what's more I know you won't like parting with it either," Bill assured him smilingly.

And so the bargain was sealed.

There followed a period of silence while Bill worked away with long-practised attention to the detail of what he was doing while turning over Tom's problem in his mind. He knew how hard it must have been for Tom to bring himself to face parting with his new bike, so long saved for, and so carefully looked after since—with great satisfaction and much pleasure—he'd wheeled it out of the shop when he'd collected it, almost a year ago.

At length, Tom moved to go.

"Goodnight then, Bill," he said, at the door. "See you tomorrow then. And thank's again, Bill."

"Cheerio, Tom," Bill replied cheerfully. "Don't worry, old lad, something will turn up. I'm quite sure of that. These things work out all right in the end. Life's full of ups and downs!"

Tom went off out into the street, and Bill worked on in the shop. No other customer came in that evening. Nor did Bill expect one. It was a 'rough old night'.

At eight o'clock, his normal closing time, Bill dropped his tools, left everything exactly where it was; locked the shop-door; pulled down the gas lamp chain to put the light out and went upstairs to wash and shave. Half-an-hour later Bill was with his cronies in his favourite pub, the 'King George' just down the road, having his customary glass of pale ale. It was a daily routine and he never missed his end-of-the-day tonic of a few glasses of his much loved 'IPA', a sparkling, bottled pale ale. He seldom worked less than an eleven or twelve hour day and needed his two or three hours' relaxation each evening away from the worries of his business.

Tom's bike duly arrived at the shop the next morning and Tom received his £3. Bill knew this sum was exactly twice Tom's normal weekly wage. With care this would keep Tom and his family for perhaps three weeks. Tom set off to walk the five miles back to his isolated cottage to plan in his mind as he trudged along what steps to take next to cope with his serious personal and financial problems resulting from the loss of his job.

Later that day, carefully oiled to prevent it rusting, the bike was hung up by Bill at the back of his large bike shed, tucked away safely where it wouldn't be knocked.

Just over seven months later, Bill, still at his bench but now working with the shop door open enjoying the cool evening air after a hot summer's day, was humming, somewhat tonelessly, quietly to himself when Tom walked in. The broad grin on his face was enough to tell Bill that Tom was back on his feet.

"Want to buy a bike, Bill!" announced Tom, without preamble.

"Got yourself fixed up all right again then, Tom?" Bill asked, smilingly.

"Yes, Bill. Fine! Couldn't be better! I had to job around doing odds and sods for a few months, but now I've got a permanent job again. I've got a job on the same farm as Joan's brother Arthur." Joan was Tom's wife and they had three children. "The Gov'nor's one of the best," added Tom, "and one way and another things are pretty good. Pretty good, Bill, and that's a fact."

"Glad to hear that, Tom. Best news of the day that is. It must have been a worrying time for you. That's grand! Good-oh! Well done, Tom old lad, well done!" said Bill with real pleasure.

"I need a bike badly though, Bill," Tom continued. "It's a good two miles to the farm." Here he paused a bit, his brow puckered while he collected his thoughts. At length he went on. "Can't go to a new one though, Bill. That will have to wait a bit. Have you got a good second-hand one to keep me going, Bill?"

"Yes, Tom" answered Bill, barely able to suppress his excitement at the joyful moment that was soon to come.

"I've got just the bike for you, as it happens, Tom. Just the very bike. A better than usual second-hand one that hasn't been knocked about. I reckon it will suit you down to a T. Come and have a look to see if you like it. It's out in the bike shed.

Bill put down his ultra-sharp, harness-maker's leather cutting knife carefully, out of harm's way where his children wouldn't get at it, at the back of his cluttered bench. A vital and much prized tool, this knife had an ebony handle and a half-moon shaped blade made of the very best brightly-shining Sheffield steel.

He then led Tom out of the shop door and down the short driveway, or 'alley' as Bill called it, and through the wide shed doorway which stood open, resting on the side fence which separated Bill Gunstone's property from that of Harry Rayner the Butcher, whose shop was next door.

Inside the large shed Tom followed Bill as he picked his way through the obstacle course which the way through proved to be. Most of the content was bikes. Almost all of them were old ones; ladies' with their looped frames, some fitted with wickerwork baskets on their handlebars; men's, which—though many were battered— were mostly sturdy-framed machines with straight or turned-up handlebars and roller-lever brakes; but here and there were 'racers' with dropped handlebars and cable brakes; and, in lesser number, several children's bikes including one or two tiny 'fairy-cycles'.

Separated from the remainder, stacked with more care against the side of the shed, was Bill's modest stock of new ones. These were mainly still in their protective packaging. Put on by the manufacturers this consisted chiefly of a heavy, brown water-proofed paper, wrapped like bandages around all parts of the frame and mudguards.

Also in the shed were a small number of pushchairs and prams. Usually these needed wheel attention. Some were buckled and needed new spokes and 'tru-ing'; others were to be provided with new, solid rubber tyres which Bill could fit with practised ease, making them up as he went along from continuous coils of the tyring which he stocked in various sizes. This rather stiff, hard-wearing rubber tyring had a strong, coiled steel spring along its core. There was a 'trick' in fitting it and those not in the know literally got in a 'twist' trying to master the art of cutting and fixing it.

On the floor, here and there in piles and smaller heaps, was harness, kept in 'farm lots' so Bill could know where he was. Some of the heavy harness was old, stiff, and seemingly dauntingly difficult to handle and restore to a useable condition. Riding harness, by comparison, was soft, pliable, easy to handle, and a relative pleasure for Bill to work on.

Apart from this stuff, and in a different category altogether in Bill's mind, were a few motorbikes. Bill was very interested in motorbikes and had ridden them and repaired them for years. There were not many bikes on the roads with which he was not familiar and knowledgeable. As he walked on he reached out his hand as he passed one—a Norton, with its long, narrow, rectangular-sectioned tank—and pushed hard down on the brass plunger of the tank-mounted oil pump. He didn't like pump-handles left stuck up like this. In the rain, Bill said, water could run down the brass pump rod and maybe get in the oil. Near the racy-looking Norton was a Douglas machine with its engine partly dismantled. Bill was in the process of decarbonising this engine, a job he intended to finish on Sunday when he could work at it without being interrupted. He was doing the bike up to sell it to a customer who was anxious to get it on the road.

At the back of the shed was Bill's pride and joy, his Harley Davidson motorbike and sidecar. This was a monster of a machine. A twin-cylindered engine, powerful and reliable powered this 'outfit'. On it, and in it, with its large, boat-like, khaki-coloured sidecar, Bill chugged along carrying his wife Kate and their four children—three boys and a girl—to the seaside at Broadstairs to see his retired saddler Dad, at regular intervals.

On such journeys Bill wore the peaked cap back to front and protected his eyes with glass goggles held on by an elasticated strap around his head. Wearing the cap back-to-front was not done for affectation, but for 'streamlining' purposes. Worn the right way round, wind under the peak would quickly lift the cap off once Bill picked up speed. On arrival, the goggles were pushed up to be parked on the cap over his forehead. A man dressed like this, with his heavy-duty, rainproof motoring coat on, looked a bit like an intrepid World War aviator, and was unmistakeably a motorcyclist, one of the privileged minority, for most people rode pushbikes—not motorbikes! Bill was conscious of this somewhat dashing and glamorous image and did not hurry to take off this distinctive gear when he got off his bike.

Bill walked round the Harley Davidson to the far end of the shed. On the wall, just where he had left it, with a fine coating of dust sticking to the film of oil he'd rubbed over it for protection against rust—but otherwise immaculate—was Tom's 'new' bike.

Tom, who necessarily had to keep his eyes down as he picked his way after Bill through the packed shed, came to a stop alongside Bill, as Bill pointed up just above eye-level to the wall ahead.

"How about this one, Tom? Will that suit you?" Bill said, with a mischievous grin.

Tom looked up, and his eyes filled with tears.

"Bill", he half whispered, in a hoarse voice, choking back his tears. "Bill, that's my bike you've got up there!"

"That's right, Tom", said Bill. "It may have two wheels instead of four legs but I reckon that when a steed has found a good home, then that's where it ought to stay. So I've kept it for you!"

"How much do you want for it, Bill?" asked Tom, almost in a whisper.

"That will cost you three pounds, Tom," answered Bill. "A fair price that, for a bike as good as that one!"

Tom could not speak—he had a financial problem, which, under the circumstances, he didn't know how to put to Bill. But he need not have worried!

"And look, Tom," said Bill, who had worked out details of this little deal a long time ago, "I know that three pounds in one go would make you short after being out of work. So you give me one pound cash on the nail, and the other two quid you can pay me off at two bob a week. Shove the money away each week and bring it to me each time you get up to ten bob. That will give you twenty weeks to pay it off."

"I'll bring it along each Saturday evening, Bill," said Tom earnestly, conscious of the fact that Bill had guessed his cash problem and saved him the embarrassment of having to ask for 'easy terms'.

"No, you won't," said Bill. "No, you won't! I don't want you pumping your way right over here every week just to pay me two bob. Not likely! I can't have that! No, Tom. You store it away at home. And that will save me having to tot it up. I'd rather leave that to you to do."

"There's no profit for you in this deal, Bill," said Tom, with a worried look on his face.

"Of course there is, Tom," commented Bill emphatically. "Who sold you the bike in the first place?"

Bill lifted the bike carefully down from the wall and flicked the dust off it with a piece of rag.

"There you are then, Tom," he said, his face radiant with happiness. "She's all yours again, old lad! And none the worse for having had a rest in the stable for a bit!"

Tom put his arm around Bill's shoulder. "Thanks, Bill," he said chokingly. "You're a right good friend. I'll never forget this day. Never!"

He took a small leather purse from the inside pocket of his jacket and gently shot the contents—three gold half-sovereigns—on to the palm of his hand. Putting one back into the purse, he handed the other two to Bill.

"Here's the one pound deposit then, Bill," he said. "I wish I could pay you the three pounds cash. But one pound is just right for me now. Leaves me a bit to see me through till next pay day. It's nice to feel I'm getting out of the wood again. I didn't expect to be back on my new bike again though, that's for sure. Joan's going to be very surprised to see me ride home on that! I can't wait to see her face when she sees it!"

Picking up the bike, he carried it carefully back through the shed until he'd cleared all the obstacles and then wheeled it down the yard and out on to the pathway. Turning, he grabbed Bill's hand and shook it vigorously.

"Thanks again, Bill," he said, with deep sincerity, he eyes still brimming with tears. "Thanks. You're a real friend. Like I said, I'll not forget this day. Never. An' I'll be along with the money regular. I won't let you down, Bill, that I won't."

"I know that, Tom old lad," responded Bill smilingly. "I don't have any worries on that score. Wish I could say that for everybody, though!"

This warm compliment pleased Tom and it did his morale a lot of good to know that he had earned the trust of a man like Bill.

His immediate problem now solved, and in a way he could not have imagined, Tom prepared to go home to break the good news to his wife. He cocked his leg over the bar, sat on the saddle and turned to say goodbye to the man who had helped him over a difficult patch.

"Well I'll be off then, Bill," he said. "Cheerio—and thanks again. I'll see you again in five weeks' time." With that he cycled off down the road.

Bill watched him go, then returned to his work happily. Though he would never have expressed, nor had even thought about it that way, the profit Tom was so concerned about was the joy in Bill's heart as he savoured this long-planned little deal.

He had helped a genuine man over the hump and had thoroughly enjoyed doing so.

In the years ahead, dressed in his habitual manner in a brown garage coat with a broad, heavy, dark brown strap round his waist, and always with a wide, leather wrist-strap strengthening his left arm, Bill was to smile to himself as, now and again, his wandering thoughts threw up the memory of Tom and his 'new' bike.

As he worked away, so often as a solitary figure busily engaged at his bench, a picture of Tom's face when he had looked up and seen his precious bike hanging on the shed wall in front of him came clearly into Bill's mind. He smiled as he had before, with deep contentment and real pleasure at something that had worked out well. For that's the way Bill was.

Sometimes well-meaning friends and relatives criticised Bill for being far too free-and-easy over such business matters, and too generous by half ever to make his fortune. Sentiment and profitable business did not always go together, it was said—maybe a truism in the harsh world of practical reality.

Bill's response was always the same. He turned a deaf ear to these comments and never ever argued the point about such issues at all.

But those who knew him well could tell he'd heard what had been said, for he had a curious reaction to personal criticism or comments of a kind which he neither accepted as valid, nor wished to discuss. Perhaps it could be called his zero option because it put a stop to the immediate issue and didn't involve him in needlessly stressful debate.

He began to hum quietly to himself, softly but audibly. It was a strange, random, toneless hum—not a tuneful, melodious one. He was certainly not tone deaf but his 'don't want to know' hum was curiously discordant and random. It appeared to be an automatic reaction, almost a reflex action like a muscular twitch or blink. Perhaps it was provoked by a disturbance of his normal, smooth-flowing, contented, good-tempered thought patterns, as though the unwelcome comment had struck a discordant note in his mind and upset his equilibrium.

No doubt early in his married life his wife Kate must have been frustrated, if not infuriated, by Bill's unwillingness to get involved in what he saw as unnecessary controversy. But, his equal in kindliness and equanimity, she learnt to live with it. Some things no one can change, however hard they try, and Bill's anti-hassle hum was one of them! It was his built-in protection against disagreements, especially if they were potentially acrimonious. At such a time the humming went on for some few minutes and Bill's brow was furrowed by a deep frown. But he would not, and did not, argue!

Bill's natural philosophy was purely pragmatic. Having decided what he considered to be the right thing to do in any given circumstance, he just went ahead and did it. No amount of cajoling and badgering moved him one iota from his predetermined path. He simply ignored such unsolicited advice. Those who tendered it were given space and allowed to voice their opinions. If this gave them some sort of satisfaction, then so be it! But Bill ploughed his own furrow, whether right or wrong, advisable or not, in the eyes of others.

And it must be said that however illogical and unbusinesslike some of his actions were, they gave him many staunch friends and loyal customers who went out of their way to deal with him rather than with others to whom they could equally well have turned, sometimes with a faster result—but never a fairer one.

Men like Tom did not forget. To them, as to his happy family, Bill was tops.

Chapter 7

HARRY THE BUTCHER

founder-member of
'The Rabbit Shooters Club'

There were five men in the exclusive little group at Littlebrook that styled itself 'The Rabbit Shooters Club'. It was founded by Harry Rayner, the local butcher, as a means of getting out to do a bit of shooting now and again with some friends.

Apart from Cecil Elton, the gamekeeper over whose territory they worked, the members, like Harry, were local self-employed tradesmen who treated themselves to one day off each month 'to go shooting'. Cecil went with them because he thoroughly enjoyed their company, but would have been the last to praise their prowess as 'shots'.

The title of the Club, with its implicit declared purpose of their expeditions, gave a rather misleading impression of what they actually did on these special days out. It has to be said at the outset that the number of rabbits living in the vicinity was not much reduced by their activities.

To Cecil some might think these days must have been something of a busman's holiday, but he didn't regard it this way at all. It could hardly have been less like one of the many days he spent each year as the mastermind and central figure on one of the official 'shoots' conducted by his employers over sections of the many square miles of woodland he controlled.

Cecil was responsible for the rearing and care of partridges and pheasants as well as the efficient management of the extensive estate. It was his responsibility to ensure an adequate population of game birds and to look after the organisation of the shoots, while at the same time overseeing the commercial exploitation of the raw materials produced by the woodland itself. Whole areas were coppiced, being cropped in a methodical cyclic routine, area by area, from one year to another. A limited number of trees were felled, very selectively, when needed locally.

His days out with his four friends allowed him to enjoy the company of men he liked, in the countryside that he loved, with his special knowledge of the territory and the habits of wildlife, making his presence invaluable and his guidance openly appreciated. *That* was Cecil's pleasure, not of course the shooting which he did every day of his life. These 'Club Days' were markedly different from his normal working days.

By the nature of his calling, Cecil spent most of his time on his own, ranging out and about over his extensive territory with only his well-trained dogs as company. He had four dogs, each selected for its special talents. There were always two of these with him—sometimes three—but one was always left on duty at home. More often than not this was his powerful, formidable Alsatian, 'Bob', a superbly trained guard dog. No intruder would hang about long with Bob around. He had freedom to range all over Cecil's well-fenced large garden and knew full well what was expected of him. When Cecil was out on an anti-poacher mission, at any time of the day or night, Bob was always with him. Two of the other three dogs always accompanied Cecil when he joined his four friends on 'Club Days'.

Cecil was absorbingly interested in his job and thought himself a lucky man to hold it. He was a privileged witness of a continuous cycle of events influenced by the changing seasons each year. To a man as fascinated by the world he lived in as he was, and as chock-a-block full of information about it, there was added fulfilment in exciting the interest of others.

When out with his friends he enjoyed pointing out things going on around them about which they were previously often completely unaware. To survive in these woodlands living creatures had to be secretive in their habits and were by nature so furtive that they were alert to uninitiated human beings passing by, long before people spotted them. Wise to their ways Cecil knew where they were, and what they were about. Every now and again he would hold up a cautionary hand and keep the group of men still, to observe something of interest that they would most certainly have missed.

Given the chance to be with him on occasions in the woodlands, children found the experience fascinating for there was so much to see when told where to look, and how to go about it without scaring everything away before they got near.

Though he always carried a gun, Cecil seldom used it when out with his four friends. His shots were usually confined to the killing of any pests they came upon as they moved around. He left the rabbits for the others to have a pot at. He kept his ears and eyes open as they wandered the fields and woodlands together and was of course the natural leader of the group. They were very lucky to have him with them. For his part though, he felt equally lucky to have the opportunity to enjoy their company, for his was something of a solitary life normally, and they all got on very well together.

To all of them, these days were much looked forward to and very much enjoyed. If the weather on the appointed day turned out to be unfavourable, they all had the flexibility in their various working commitments to be able to postpone their outing until another better day a little later on. This way they were always out on their walks on fair or reasonable days. Their memories of past occasions were by this means always memories of happy, successful days, never of miserable, rainy, disappointing ones. Harry Rayner was the link man who fixed the dates.

Starting as the sun came up, they trudged the fields and woodlands over a wide area, following routes always determined by Cecil and which, though very varied, always brought them to his gamekeeper's cottage by about 11 am.

This isolated cottage was a delightful place to come upon, set as it was on the fringe of extensive woodlands, with rolling Kentish orchards to the other side of it. Cecil had a very large garden full of interest both in terms of the things he grew, and the animals he kept there. There was not much he and his family needed to stock their larder that he did not produce himself.

Cecil's attractive wife Enid, with her shock of beautiful, wavy fair hair and blue, mischievous eyes, was a great favourite with them all. With her they enjoyed a hot drink—usually cocoa—and cake, often hot and freshly-baked. This pleasant break from their exertions would usually last for about half-an-hour, after which out they went to continue their business of the day.

Like the first session, this second stage followed a route planned by Cecil. Because it was a day of relaxation, the pace was never hurried, and they made their way along in a casual manner. There was no sense of urgency and little evidence of any dedicated determination to hunt down their prey. Every now and again there would be an opportunity to take a pot-shot at a rabbit. Fortunately for the rabbits, they missed more often than they bagged one.

Sometimes the rabbits were 'put up' by the two dogs working under Cecil's directions. He, and they for that matter, knew where the rabbits were likely to be. The dogs were very well-disciplined. If they turned out a rabbit, perhaps from its 'squat' in a clump of long grass, or out of the undergrowth, they froze on a sharp command from Cecil. They did not give chase, otherwise their lives would have been at risk. Sooner or later one of them would have got shot. Cecil knew this only too well for his companions blasting off at the moving targets were none too accurate. They were very much inexperienced amateurs by his standards. So were the dogs aware of the danger, for they were wise to the ways of men with guns, and watchful of them.

By these leisurely proceedings only a few rabbits were shot during the outings. An expert in efficiency would certainly have dismissed the exercise as not a cost-effective way of keeping down rabbits or, indeed, of obtaining meat to eat. Nobody was the least bit worried on that score, however. The days were thoroughly enjoyed, and, since that was their primary objective, they had to be rated as successful.

Every now and again during their walk, Cecil pulled out from a pocket of his warm tweed waistcoat a large, much treasured 'railway-type' pocket watch that was securely fastened on a strong brass chain. He would look at the bright, white-enamelled face with its bold Roman numerals, to keep a check on the time. Without the others realising it, he would modify his intended route as they made their way along, to ensure that they arrived at their destination at about the same time each trip. Always, somewhat miraculously it must have seemed to the others, at about 1.45 pm they arrived at "The Buffs", their regular place of refreshment. They filed thankfully through the pub door to be greeted by 'Old Mac' the landlord. The pub was appropriately named—perhaps that is why he had been attracted to it in the first place—because Old Mac was an ex-regular soldier who had served in the Buffs, the famous East Kent Regiment with its long illustrious history that had its Regimental Headquarters at Canterbury. The landlord was very proud of his Regiment and of his military background, a fact reflected in his soldierly stance maintained throughout his life, and not least by the many anecdotes about his life in the Army which frequently laced his conversation—particularly stories about the Boer War.

Once comfortably settled in the pub, they each enjoyed their own favourite brew, more often than not either beer or bitter pulled from the barrels in the cellar below by Old Mac, using his polished, mahogany-handled beer pumps. Always, in the case of Harry, the choice was a bottle of Mackenson's Milk Stout. Old Mac, by long-established practice, served them with thick meat or cheese sandwiches especially prepared for them, and they tucked into these with relish, hungry after their morning's wanderings out in the brisk fresh air.

At 2.30pm, the official closing-time of the pub after which serving drinks was against the law until the evening opening-time came round, the five adjourned with Old Mac to a small room approached from behind the main bar, called the 'side room'. Here they yarned and drank with great contentment, enjoying a feeling of safe, comfortable isolation from the outside world.

At about 2.45pm, more often than the workings of pure chance would have ordained, the village policeman, Brendan Evans, arrived at the pub to make sure no 'law-breaking' out-of-hours selling of drinks to customers was taking place. This he checked by ostentatiously peering through the windows of "The Buff's" two bars—the Public Bar and the Saloon Bar—both of which looked out upon the asphalt parking area at the front. He would find, to his apparent official satisfaction, that the two bars were closed and no unlawful drinking was taking place.

Wandering round the side of the pub to visit the outside 'Gents', he would hear the sound of happy voices coming from the 'side room' that had access to the yard by a side door at the top of a few steps. Thus he would 'discover', also to his personal satisfaction, that a 'private party' of the landlord's personal guests were being entertained by him in his 'private' room.

By long-established custom he would tap the door discreetly, tapping out—not it seemed without a suggestion of ironic humour—the well-known Morse Code SOS warning signal. The response to this urgent message was immediate. The door opened and he was invited in to join those in legal danger; after which the party continued happily as before.

To preserve the amiable village bobby from being compromised by witnessing a flagrant breach of the law without exercising his authority to stop it, it was contrived that he did not see the passing of money in payment for drinks. Old Mac looked after the 'accounts' in a discreet way. But to give Brendan Evans his due, he did not impose upon the generosity of this convivial company, because, by devious means, he never failed to buy his round. This piece of jiggery-pokery was also organised by Old Mac in a clandestine way, so that Brendan was never placed in the invidious position of being seen to break the law himself. The landlord was too old a soldier to expose himself to unnecessary risks. He reasoned that to prosecute him the local bobby would necessarily have to prosecute himself at the same time. A small risk in Old Mac's book! The open invitation to Brendan Evans, in effect, made him fireproof!

Old Mac had fought through the Boer War and suffered a great deal of hardship in the process. His life had been at high risk on many occasions, too many times quite unnecessarily due to the ineptitude of those controlling his destiny. Now that he was his own man he did not shove his head over the top recklessly. He and the local bobby got on well together. They both had strong survival instincts and were both at heart kindly, good-natured men. And Old Mac, who during his life had seen more than his share of deprivation in his travels, was thoughtful and generous. Perhaps because of his memories of hunger in Africa when on long treks in enemy territory, no impoverished tramp out on the open road ever passed his pub without receiving a hunk of bread and cheese to help him on his way.

During these regular get-togethers in his convenient private 'side room' that was ostensibly not a bar but nonetheless snugly adjacent to all the facilities and goodies available in the two 'official' bars, if Old Mac, his friends, or the village policeman worried about the law governing the use of Licensed Premises, they certainly didn't show it by talking in whispers or behaving in a conspiratorial way. On the contrary, their happy voices and frequent bursts of laughter were heard issuing loudly from the premises, sometimes well on towards the evening opening-time.

They also regularly played cards, gambling with modest stakes. As added entertainment, Old Mac's talented resident daughter, Rose, sometimes joined by her sister Kate—wife of Bill Gunston the Saddler—both of whom were very good pianists, set them all singing with popular songs, usually of recent World War or the earlier Boer War origins.

All in all the Rabbit Shooters Club' members enjoyed this part of their day of leisure as much, if not more, than the shooting that was their declared purpose. No wonder their families found them so enthusiastic about their small exclusive 'Club'!

There were, of course, several other groups in the village following their own particular sporting interests. Some also sought out rabbits! Prominent amongst the latter, and by far the most effective if the number of rabbits destroyed were the yardstick, was the Littlebrook Ferret Club. Their systematic approach to winkling out rabbits put the operation on a highly efficient and businesslike basis.

The twin objectives of this Club, and others like it, were to reduce the highly damaging activities of the large rabbit population on the one hand, while at the same time providing a welcome inexpensive addition to the supply of meat for local consumption.

If the rabbits could have voted on the matter they would have preferred there to be twenty Rabbit Shooters Clubs—accepting the one they knew as the norm of a Club's standard of performance—to the single Ferret Club. Against this ruthless group they stood no chance at all. Against the pot-shotting activities of the meandering five friends in the Rabbit Shooters Club their chances of survival were so high that they saw little risk in the Club's activities.

However, for the rabbits of the district, when the Ferret Club arrived at the site of a thriving colony, it was a case of 'get out and run' straightaway, or face almost certain disaster if they stayed, or went further underground. In a grassy bank, amidst bushes and shrubs, very soon after the Ferret Club reached the site, all holes, except odd ones not spotted which happened to be hidden beneath bushes or undergrowth, were effectively sealed by pegged-down nets which would trap any escaping rabbit with no possibility of its breaking out into open ground.

Shortly after the netting operation was completed, down into the burrows would be popped hungry, marauding ferrets. The biological design of these vicious hunters was exactly suited to moving fast and frighteningly along the underground tunnels towards the rabbits, whose natures made them feel safe below ground in their excavated homes. Against these sharp-teethed, slender-bodied invaders they had no defence whatsoever except to run, and run fast. Straight up and out into the open air they headed where their superior speed would ensure their safety. But they didn't make it! They were caught up in their headlong rush by the mesh of the strong nets.

Any lucky rabbit that did happen to make its exit out of one of the un-netted holes would bolt for it. More often than not they were caught by one of the sharp-eyed, ever-vigilant terrier dogs which always accompanied the Club members.

And that was that! The odds were totally against the rabbits. It was not a case of the occasional rabbit now and again ending its career, as was the result of the desultory efforts of the carefree wandering men with their guns, but a whole community would be cleaned out in one fierce assault. The combination of the cunning of men and the deadly efficiency of the long-bodied, underground predators was too much for them.

Backing up this man and ferret team were the terrier dogs, which eagerly hunted around to sniff out the rabbits to let their masters know which burrows were occupied in the first place, and then stayed, bright-eyed and watchful, to run them down should they be successful in breaking out into the open. A rabbit's chances of survival in a localised community were slim indeed!

The only inconvenience ever suffered by the members of the Ferret Club was the odd occasion when one of their prized ferrets moved so fast it managed to catch, and sink its teeth into, one of the residents below ground. Then, when it failed to re-appear back at ground level—as a well-behaved ferret was expected to do—it had to be either 'dug out' or patiently waited for until it had finished its meal—and maybe had an after-dinner nap as well.

There was one small victory, if such it was, that the rabbit population achieved. For on rare occasions, where there were extensive, deep burrows, the men up above went home without one of their prized ferrets; which then subsequently supported itself as a solitary, free-ranging rabbit hunter—itself also hunted, as is the way of life in the wild.

In sharp contrast to the devastatingly efficient Ferret Club, the Rabbit Shooters Club was much more of a social enterprise than a single-minded, purposeful one. The outings of the five friends were really dedicated to the pursuit of pleasure. The potting of a few rabbits was almost a by-product of their day's relaxation from their normal, hard-working daily routines.

Harry Rayner, the village butcher, whose inspiration it was to start the small Club in the first place, was something of a central figure in the group. Cecil provided the expertise; Harry provided the essential ingredient of amusement, and on occasions uproarious hilarity, that made the days so memorable and enjoyable. Sometimes the hilarity was deliberately engendered by Harry himself. Often though, it came as a result of his natural demeanour and behaviour, being intrinsically comical.

An idea of this likelihood of his being a source of fun was given by Fred, the blacksmith, when asked by a stranger how he could identify Harry from those Harry was with in the local pub, to which the enquirer had been directed to winkle Harry out.

The stranger was seeking to meet the butcher about a confidential business matter of some urgency, and Harry, playing truant from his shop, was down at his favourite pub at a time when he would normally be expected to be at work.

Fred's off-the-cuff reply was graphic.

"You can't miss him," Fred had said reassuringly. "He has a bald head, a Friar-tuck fringe, an 'Old Bill' moustache like a worn-out yard broom, a pot-gutted belly like as though he's up-the-spout, a large, very wide arse and short legs. Nothing but a stomach with arms and legs really, you could say, seen from a distance! But he's a bloody good butcher though. I have to give him that. A good butcher but a piss-poor shot with his twelve-bore gun! So keep out of his way if he's carrying his gun! Shelter behind his big arse! It's the only place you'll be safe!"

This succinct, though unflattering picture of Harry, as described by one of his four fellow members of the exclusive Rabbit Shooters Club, was accurate, if more than a little crude, in its terms!

His appearance, or 'turnout', when on their days out, caused much amusement, not only among his four Club friends, but also among those locals who knew him. So far as 'togging out' was concerned, Harry was by far the most impressively equipped of the group. He had always fancied himself as a 'Country Gentleman', so did his best to look like one when he was off 'going shooting', like a man of leisure. With an expensive Harris Tweed jacket, stylish plus-fours, excellent quality brown walking boots, thick woollen socks, Scottish-style deerstalker hat with a little set of jay's feathers stuck behind its ribbon, and a fine double-barrelled shotgun resting, pointing downwards, professionally over his arm, he certainly looked the part. In fact he out-Gentlemanned some local 'genuine' Gentlemen, in the conventions of appearance if nothing else!

The fact that he seldom if ever hit anything, and 'couldn't shoot for nuts', provided an endless source of fun to the others who enjoyed many a laugh recounting Harry's exploits. He himself gave no sign of being upset by this good-natured leg-pulling and banter. At heart an optimist, Harry fully expected to get so good in the end that he would gain universal recognition as one of the best shots in the whole area. After all, he reasoned to himself privately, though the others didn't know it he had only comparatively recently even fired a twelve-bore for the first time, never mind hit anything with it. He would get better, of that he was sure!

Meanwhile he was content to join in with the fun and repartee, while privately getting much pleasure from contemplating the time, which, with his Toad of Toad Hall-like confidence, he was certain would come, when they would all stand to one side in awe as they watched him win acclaim and widespread respect as one of the best shots in the county of Kent.

His projection into the future took him further. When musing in his armchair before a large log fire, well-primed with the Scotch whisky he liked so much, which gave him such a warm feeling of well-being and did wonders for his confidence, he even got so far as imagining himself extending his activities into the field of rifle shooting, to take part, possibly even to win, the national rifle-shooting contests at Wisley. Why not! Somebody had to win. Why not Harry Rayner, the County of Kent's crackshot from the village of Littlebrook! Whatever else Harry could or could not do, he could certainly dream better than most.

Harry had a flourishing business and employed three men and one woman full-time. In addition there were two part-time delivery boys who took out meat orders on Saturdays in the large cane baskets which rested in strong frames attached to the handlebars and front-forks of their heavy-duty trade-bikes. This staff, a large one by village standards because Harry's business took in several surrounding villages and hamlets, supported and assisted him in the busy life of butchering.

More accurately, those who knew the family well would say that Harry, plus three men, one woman and two boys, were employed and directed by Ada, Harry's very capable wife. This formidable lady had the business acumen and dedicated, tireless energy necessary to hold the whole show together. Harry might have thought he was the boss and ran the business, but a few hours on the premises would be enough to identify who really held the reins. It was most certainly Ada who was at the heart of things, though Harry—as his friend Fred had testified to the stranger enquiring about him—was indeed a skilled, practical butcher. But he lacked Ada's drive and acute business sense and, whether he realised it or not, the marked success of the firm was largely dependent upon her. This didn't matter; Harry, Ada and their children, a son and two daughters, were a happy family and lived well. Harry and Ada made a good team, even if Harry's performance had to be stimulated by regular sharp prods from his watchful wife.

Looking out over her ample bosom from her position by the till in the enclosed glass-fronted pay-box when they were busy in the shop, customers would sometimes be a trifle embarrassed by a sharply-worded, dagger-like instruction from her to Harry to attend to their needs. His attention wandered, and he was apt to gossip to a crony who happened to come in, or start messing about cutting up meat, leaving customers rather too long to cool their heels waiting for his attention. But they felt for the genial, portly Harry and winced when his stern-looking wife called him to his task so abruptly on their behalf. He tended to jerk at the jolt of her verbal missile and hurry guiltily to the counter, like an inattentive schoolboy caught out by an autocratic schoolmistress. It made them feel uneasy, but, as compensation, ladies were often extra nice to Harry, extending to him an unspoken message of sympathy for his hen-pecked predicament. So Harry did all right, basked in the warmth of their affectionate understanding and suffered his apparent travail with the stoicism of a saint!

Purpose-built on the premises, as a detached brick building, was a slaughter house. Apart from Harry's home-reared pigs, kept at the bottom of his garden in on-site pigsties, pigs and other animals were bought in as needed. Harry and his assistants did all the slaughtering themselves. The slaughter house contained all the facilities needed to meet this function. Usually one day per week, regularly, was devoted to the business of slaughtering. It was hard, punishing work, nauseating to people with queasy stomachs who could not watch—much less take part in—this unavoidable but disturbing part of the business of providing meat to eat.

A pig on its way up the yard towards the slaughter house would always squeal and scream in an appalling way. They always did this, even if they were 'first in' and the smell of fresh blood was not yet in the air. It was commonly thought that pigs had a sixth-sense, and somehow knew what lay ahead. This view gained credence because they could normally be moved peacefully from place to place without squealing. On the face of it there was nothing about the last journey of the innocent, 'fortunate' pig that was first-in-line, to distinguish it from a normal trip. Whether they had a sixth-sense or not, the fact remained that the imminence of a slaughtering session at Harry's premises was heralded by an ear-splitting, unmistakeable and awful sound.

Thereafter, as each pig went to its doom, its path could be traced by a listener as it was part-driven, part-dragged from its sty to the slaughter house. Its terrified squealing within the building would suddenly, abruptly, cease. Immediately after the cessation of this frightful noise, a sharp report indicated that the humane-killer had put an end to the pig's existence.

Many children, who grew up within earshot of these dreadful squeals of sheer terror, never got the sound out of their ears. For them, a mention of squeals or screams of terror in a book, or perhaps in a newspaper story of a tragedy, evoked an automatic recall of this awful, terrifying, squealing sound of a doomed pig.

Perhaps because of the fact that the animals were frantic and couldn't easily be held still, the procedure in Harry's slaughter house was rather unexpected, and a little bizarre—or so rumour had it. For the pig, on arrival, was said to be hit with an 'almighty wallop' slap in the side of its belly, using a long-handled mallet having a heavy wooden ball as its head. This instrument resembled an ancient knob-kerrie bludgeon used years ago by warring tribes in parts of Africa. Hit with this, the pig reportedly fell, stunned and utterly winded, to lie on its side. A gun, called a 'humane-killer', was then held at its forehead. When 'fired', a steel spike was driven deeply into the head to kill the pig instantaneously.

Immediately afterwards, hung head-downwards, supported by its hooked back legs on a chain which passed over pulley wheels fitted overhead, the pig's throat was cut so that its blood poured out before the cleaning up of the carcass began.

Before the compulsory introduction of humane-killers, the procedure was said to have been the same, but the cutting of the throat was the death-dealing part of the procedure. The humane-killer brought instant death, instead of a slow bleeding to death. Some people thought the term 'slaughtered by use of a humane killer' was hardly an accurate description of a slaughtering process rumoured to have as its first step the landing of a massive blow to the stomach using a primitive bludgeon.

But that's the way it was done in Harry's place—or so local legend had it. The story was perhaps embellished and exaggerated by those who delighted in describing this colourful, if grim, picture of a pig's unhappy end in this den of death for animals destined for the delight of diners at their dinner-tables. For there were cronies of his who had an ulterior motive in saying that a pig was made utterly and completely immobile before Harry shot it. It fuelled a bit of fun when discussing his shooting ability!

The blood from the pig ran sideways across the gently sloping concrete floor, to a gulley running along the base of the wall of the slaughter house, to pass out through a hole that led to an external gulley, which took it away to be lost down a drain. If needed for any purpose, the blood could of course be intercepted and not allowed to run to waste. As an act that betokened the good neighbour that Harry was, during the tomato growing season he kept buckets of blood for his next-door neighbour, Bill the Saddler, to feed his tomatoes on. Bill swore by this tonic and attributed the annual success of his crop to his good fortune in having a liberal supply of this rich food for his plants so conveniently on tap.

After 'blooding', the pig was hauled up and swung round to be lowered into a large, wide-topped tub which was filled with scalding hot water boiled in a purpose-built copper in the corner of the building.

The fire under the copper was lit first thing in the morning by Harry, as his first job on slaughtering days. Thereafter it was kept burning all day. More often than not, various pieces of waste matter from animal carcasses would find its way on to the fire. This provided an unmistakeable smell on slaughtering days, to go with the unmistakeable squeals of terror. A nice package!

The smell of burning flesh and bones again created a lifelong capacity in those who lived nearby, to identify from their memory the same smell whenever it reached them, wherever they happened to be. It was not a pleasant thought when the memory was triggered by this macabre odour wafting on the breeze near a crematorium.

Small wonder that with these twin manifestations of the gruesome work going on there, people living near Harry's premises did not look forward to his regular slaughtering days.

When lowered into the boiling water, the coarse hair on the pig's body was rapidly completely shaved off using very sharp knives. Very shortly afterward, following a vigorous scrubbing, the pig was hauled clear of the tub. With its two hind legs pulled apart on the supporting chains, the carcass was neatly cut, and chopped down the middle as far as the neck, the unwanted guts having first been tumbled out into a bucket. It now had its head removed by deft surgery!

At this stage the pig had been transformed into two hygienically and scrupulously cleaned halves, plus a head which would be made into brawn. Ada herself made the brawn, which enjoyed widespread acclaim. It was her speciality.

Not long afterwards, what just a little earlier in the day had been a contented but mucky pig snuffling around in a smelly pigsty, became jointed sections of pork. These, further divided and jointed, looking very good with pink-white smooth skin, appeared on the butcher's slab, ultimately to finish as highly appetising joints of Harry's prime pork on somebody's dinner table.

Once cooked and on the table, the joint's so recent, earlier existence as part of a living animal, was not a matter of concern to those eating the pork. Non-meat eaters, on the other hand, could never come to terms with this aspect of the majority of the population's behaviour. But such vegetarians were dismissed somewhat contemptuously and disparagingly by Harry, as 'carrot nibblers'. Too many of those and he would have been out of a job!

Not only that, he was a great meat-eater himself, and tucked into with relish the products of his own labours. He thought those not eating it were depriving themselves of one of the good things of life.

Harry had no mean appetite. Apart from his much-savoured meat he was a consumer of plenty of other rich foods, with a well-developed and indulged taste for a variety of well-known brands of Scotch whisky. His impressive stomach and heavy stature bore witness to his love of the good life!

But his gradually increasing size, his flushed features and his heavy breathing, so noticeable when he exerted himself at all, were regarded with some concern by his family doctor who had a few quiet words with him on the desirability of moderation in all things.

Harry could appreciate the wisdom of this advice, but deferred acting upon it until tomorrow, today being too soon to start such an unwelcome process of abstemious damage limitation! And each succeeding tomorrow in turn became today, and today always remained too soon! So, slowly and insidiously he grew fatter, he flushed more, and he puffed more. And the heart attack that was to kill him moved remorselessly nearer, knocking out more and more tomorrows that with his great zest for life he might otherwise have enjoyed.

Meanwhile he met his doctor's occasional anxious reminders by pointing to examples of thin, sparely-built, mutual acquaintances, who, despite their desirable slimness—or 'narrow-guttedness' as Harry called it—had been knocked out by sudden death, while some other happy fatties like him lived on! It was not the first time that the doctor had met this justification of their lifestyle by grossly overweight patients, but he forbore to debate the point, knowing that Harry's happy disposition was a factor in his favour in the subtle determination of a person's state of health and ultimate destiny. And he didn't want to help wear away Harry's phlegmatic nag-proof protective armour which allowed him to work so well with his capable but assertive wife. The description 'Family Doctor' was a very apt one. Harry's medical man had a pretty shrewd idea of the life he led, and did not want to disturb his contented state of mind, for on balance he saw him as a very happy fellow, even if he were slowly eating and drinking himself to death!

Harry was widely respected as being a first-class butcher, a real example of a master tradesman. It was perhaps inevitable that his expert performance with a humane-killer gun in his slaughter house should be contrasted with his abysmal performance with his double-barrelled shotgun.

Fred the blacksmith, who among the five members of Harry's shooting club could always be relied upon to come up with pertinent comments (though some thought them at times too cruelly sarcastic for comfort) pointed out this contrasting performance in his own inimitable way.

"Harry Rayner," said Fred, "has trouble shooting rabbits. Yet he can hit a pig in the brain first shot, every time! He's never been known to miss! And what's more, he can do this with a 'single shot' gun, never mind his cartridge-loaded, double-barrelled gun which shoots out a shower of leadshot. But the pig does have to be poleaxed first, so that it lies still! Then Harry, who has a very steady hand, can hold the barrel of his gun with its nozzle resting on the pig's forehead, take careful aim, and fire. One shot. One pig. Bloody good he is! Bloody good! A born crack-shot! It's a privilege to know him. Some people go through life without ever meeting a marksman like him!"

This acidic comment was made in Harry's presence and made him squirm a bit, though he took it in good part and joined in the laughter. But despite his good humour and eternal optimism, when Harry was out shooting with his friends and missed a 'sitting shot', he did get more than a little despondent. This feeling was not alleviated by the barrage of good-humoured banter he underwent, especially if the others had held off and 'given' the shot to him. Missing a rabbit on the run was excusable; they all did that frequently. But a 'sitter', come upon by the luck of the game, ought never to be missed if the range were short. Or so his friends thought, and pointedly said with great emphasis, each time it happened.

Harry, who was not a chump (far from it), eventually got around to suspecting that sometimes the others gave him the shot in the hope that he would miss the target to provide them with some merriment at his expense. He was right!

This particular trick led to a bit of fun on one memorable and afterwards much-related occasion.

The idea was Cecil's, skilled as he was in the setting up of decoys in the course of his work. The four of them got together to organize a special day for Harry.

On the appointed day they met and set off as usual, Harry blissfully unaware of what was in store. Nothing that happened during the first hour or so was at all unusual. Events unfolded in the quite unpredictable way they always did. Or seemingly so.

For some unaccountable reason though, by the natural workings of chance apparently, nobody appeared to be able to shoot straight. One after the other, even the best of them, missed rabbits that normally would not have escaped.

Harry was secretly not at all displeased to hear his friends tormenting one another for their abysmal performance.

Even Cecil seemed a trifle irritated by the frustration of guiding them to good targets, only to see them missed.

"You're all bloody useless this morning!" he commented as yet another rabbit escaped to run off unscathed into cover.

Harry began to hope that he would, for once, be the successful one. He determined to make a special effort to hit any target he was first at.

"Maybe," the optimistic Harry secretly thought, "today the tide will turn and these cocky blighters will begin to learn what a mistake they have all made in writing me off as a dead loss, or worse-than-useless"—two assessments often made of his marksmanship! His spirits began to rise, as the others showed signs of increasing despondency.

When the time was approaching 10.30am they were heading towards Cecil's cottage for their accustomed cocoa and cake. The cart-track they were walking along, called the 'middle path' by local people, passed right across the main wood they were in. It ran from a road which bordered the wood on one side, to the far side where it met at a T-junction another similar cart-track running along that side of the wood.

Turning right up this track would take them directly to Cecil's cottage, situated about a quarter-of-a-mile up the track. The trees in the part of the wood they were in were comparatively thinly scattered, with grass, bushes, and groundcover plants between them. On the far side of the track was an orchard, with its characteristic lush green grass between the fruit trees.

Both the cart-track they were on, and the one it met, had hard stony surfaces, built up over generations of use by farm carts and other country traffic cutting through the wood from the main road. Cart ruts, which always appeared in wet wintry weather, were regularly filled with stones and rubble when they became a nuisance. As a result of this constant necessary maintenance over the years, a tolerably good surface was preserved.

Along the sides of the tracks were grassy edges where dandelions and other plants grew. Rabbits often came out of their hidden burrows to move into these open spaces where food was abundant. They were often to be seen in the distance by people moving along the tracks. This area was always a likely happy hunting ground for the shooting club members, so they moved along the track with vigilance.

Unseen by the group as they moved towards the distant T-junction at 10.30am precisely, Cecil's wife Enid left their cottage and walked along the track to take up a pre-arranged position behind some bushes along the orchard-side of the track. She was about ten yards from the T-junction. Picking up a short stick, to the middle of which was tied a piece of strong twine, she settled down to wait expectantly. The twine lay on the ground, running along the edge of the orchard, past the end of the centre path where her husband and his friends would emerge. It had been carefully routed by Cecil so that it would not get caught up or snagged, when pulled.

Following their usual practice, as the shooting party approached the junction of the tracks, they walked slowly and very cautiously. Sometimes, just around the bend, would be rabbits feeding along the verges in the quiet morning air. The sun was warm and the atmosphere peaceful. Conditions were propitious.

Cecil, as was the custom, walked carefully ahead, to peer around the corner to look in each direction for any signs of rabbits being about. Reaching the end, he held up his hand, motioning the others to stop. They could tell that Cecil had seen something of interest.

It 'happened' that Harry was nearest to Cecil at this moment. Cecil stepped backwards with great care and pointed to direct attention to the left, jabbing his forefinger towards the far side of the track.

"A sitter!" he whispered. "A real beauty! You'd better take it, Harry. The others are piss-poor this morning!"

His selection by the expert to take the shot raised Harry's morale even further. He crept forward, his gun cocked and ready. As he peered around the corner, where Cecil had pointed, he spotted at once a fine-looking specimen of 'rabbithood'. It was sitting in a bolt upright stance, typical of a rabbit in a state of watchful alertness, checking the area ahead before it moved. Its ears were pricked up and its head turned away so that it was looking up the track to the left. At the moment its eyes were turned away from Harry's position.

It was a wonderful 'sitting-shot'. A real gift. There was not a moment to lose, because watchful rabbits 'keep their eyes around them'. Harry knew only too well that any second the rabbit's head would turn and he would be spotted.

Carefully he raised his gun to his shoulder, steadied himself, took aim, and fired.

Simultaneously with the gun going off with the loud bang that shotguns make, the rabbit appeared to jump about one foot in the air and them fell on its side to lie still. Dead in its tracks!

"Well done, Harry," said Cecil. "Good shot! First bag of the day. Good for you, Harry boy. Well done! I'm glad somebody can still shoot! I was beginning to think we were going to go home with nothing in the bag!"

With these words of praise from their guide and mentor ringing in his ears Harry strode over the path towards his kill to collect it. As he went, he heard, with some inward satisfaction and glee, the disgruntled voice of Fred mutter to the others, "Huh! Huh! Bit of bloody luck that was! The gun must have gone off before Harry took aim. That's the only way he'd ever hit anything!"

"No wonder he's needled," thought Harry, as he crossed the path. "He's missed both his shots this morning. It'll do him good to stew for a change!"

With a feeling of great triumph, Harry bent down and picked up the rabbit. Alas, his triumph was short-lived. Abruptly his elation gave way to awful chagrin. For, round the neck of the rabbit, neatly tied on with a piece of black ribbon, was a black-bordered cardboard label. On it, printed in bold letters, were the words:

To
HARRY RAYNER
With the compliments of
The ESTATE MANAGEMENT

As Harry read the label and glanced over the path towards his comrades, the look on his face, and the appearance of him standing there with his trophy, set them all roaring with laughter.

The crowning insult to Harry's pride was his discovery that, because it was thought he would be bound to miss the rabbit anyway, to leave it sitting there after his gun had gone off and so spoil the fun by giving the game away, Cecil had enlisted the help of Enid. The rabbit had been skilfully propped up by Cecil using a clever arrangement of sticks and a heavy brick.

When she heard the gun go off, Enid, following her instructions, gave a sharp jerk to the twine. A key piece of wood, supporting Cecil's contrivance, dropped the brick on a pivoted stick, the other end of which shot the rabbit upwards like somebody on the end of a see-saw. To the watchers, the effect was very realistic. The rabbit behaved as shot rabbits often do; a sudden jump into the air then down they go, to lie still on the ground.

With characteristic attention to detail, Cecil had used stiff wire to hold the rabbit's ears pointing sharply upwards as listening rabbits' ears always do. A decoy had to look as though it were alive and Cecil was very experienced in setting up bird and animal decoys. The chosen rabbit was a fine specimen and completely undamaged so far as could be seen, for it had been trapped by Cecil—not shot and disfigured. And to add to Harry's discomfiture and the delight of his companions, a close examination failed to reveal any signs of damage by lead shot after he had shot it with such a display of professional competence and stridden over so importantly to retrieve it. Harry, who liked plenty of salt scattered over his food, found this gleeful scrutiny of the victim as painful as having some of the same rubbed into a wound. It was not pleasant. He cringed and he squirmed and without a doubt he looked decidedly unhappy! 'Caught by the short and curlies', as Cecil so succinctly put it!

There was a great deal of hilarity as the five friends and Enid retired in high spirits to the keeper's cottage for their accustomed morning break of cake and cocoa.

Harry's moment of triumph was to become a legend. The very next day, Bill the saddler, who had heard the delightful tale in the King George pub the previous evening, called to Harry over the fence between their premises, to start the day with a friendly greeting.

"Good morning, Harry. Shot any rabbits lately?" queried Bill, beaming from ear to ear with mischievous pleasure.

Harry grunted his response, grinning sheepishly.

"Good morning, Bill," he called, and left it as that. He did not particularly want to talk about rabbits so early in the morning!

Bill had a strong sense of humour and much enjoyed comedy situations. Harry also enjoyed a good joke, but not this one because he was very much on the receiving end of it! But he had to admit to himself that it had been a wonderfully executed little set-up into which he had blundered like a blind man. Somewhat ruefully he figured that Bill was just the first of many who would be expressing an interest in his shooting that day. He was right!

Not only that day, though, for it didn't stop there! The story became as much a part of his life as an arm or a leg. He was never allowed to forget it!

At length he got around to enjoying telling the story himself. The great amusement and loud laughter which the story always caused, coloured now by an honest admission of how completely he had been taken in, and what his private thoughts had been as the drama developed, put him centre stage. Though it did nothing to enhance his reputation as a marksman, at least it made him feel like a successful comedian. He liked that for he enjoyed raising a laugh. It was a bonus, a little reward for his discomfiture and suffering at the time!

Harry, alas, neither made it to Wisley to compete with a rifle, nor even for that matter got good enough with his double-barrelled 12-bore shotgun to hit anything much smaller than a barn door from more than twenty feet away. For he died suddenly one day, much before his time, seemingly snatched from life in his prime without having displayed any marked symptoms of serious illness.

But at least he died on a full stomach, sitting dozing in his large, comfortable armchair before a roaring log fire one Sunday afternoon on a bright, frosty, February day, having enjoyed a substantial meal of roast beef and Yorkshire pudding, with roast potatoes, parsnips and brussels sprouts, all served with rich gravy and followed by generous helpings of golden syrup treacle pudding—the whole then pickled with several generous glasses of whisky. All in all his favourite fare!

When found by his wife he was, so it seemed, sleeping peacefully, and so far as could be judged he simply went out in his slumbers.

At his feet, curled up on the carpet, lay his old, much loved, large, brown, shaggy, long-curly-coated dog Chop, of unknown breed but of well-known stirling qualities, and maybe Harry's truest friend.

Chop was also very still, for like his master he too was stone dead, an awe-inspiring circumstance which rocked everybody and made them silent and thoughtful. The vet said that Chop must have died of shock because he would have been immediately aware of the drastically changed 'presence' of his master, by whose side he lived for as many hours in each day as he was permitted to be there.

Somehow it comforted everybody to know that wherever Harry now was, his devoted companion was there by his side.

The Doctor took no pleasure from the sad confirmation of the accuracy of his worried warnings, but was comforted by the thought that Harry lived and died a fun-loving and happy man. And as is so often the case, people found many good things to say about Harry after his death. And in the main, they were genuinely felt and not hypocritical.

But none could find it possible to say of him that he had been a good shot, or even a promising one. A *keen* shot was the best that could be said of him. Even in a eulogy there are limits to the extent by which reasonable credulity may fairly be stretched. This was particularly true in connection with this facet of Harry's prowess because, long after his departure, his name was seldom mentioned in conversation without the story of the rabbit being recalled, and this rather destroyed for all time his hoped-for assessed ability as a marksman.

Still, he was a good butcher, and a nice bloke.

Chapter 8

HOP PICKING TIME
hard work but not all work

The hop gardens of Kent, growing as they did a high proportion of England's total crop of hops, were famous far beyond the boundaries of the county. Their high quality hops were much sought after by brewers of beer. Hops give beer its much-liked, thirst-quenching, bitter flavour and help it to 'keep'. There were many who said that Kentish hops were the finest in the world, a claim which brewers were happy to repeat in advertising their beers, for it gave them a special edge.

Early in its annual development a hop garden was characterised by lines of poles about fifteen to eighteen feet high, with an interlacing network of strong horizontal wires with tight, vertical and upward-slanting stringing. Brown coconut-fibre string, called coir, was used. Where possible the lines of poles were erected in an east-west direction so that the hop plants faced south to give them maximum exposure to sunlight. The object of the stringing was to provide a framework up which the twisting hop plants could grow. Like vines, hop plants can only thrive if they are given a supporting structure.

The long, twining stems were called hop bines, or sometimes hop binds, by the people who cultivated and picked them. A 'bine' or 'bind' is a clinging vine. The word 'bind' aptly describes the clinging habit of the flexible hop stems which travel upwards by twisting around the string in the same way that the ubiquitous bindweed—plague of so many gardeners—grows up every available support.

Hop garden poles of chestnut or larch wood were cut and prepared locally. Dipped in a preservative the poles lasted several years, as did the wire, but the stringing was replaced entirely every year.

Stringing the hop garden was one of the many skills that farm workers of the area needed to have. For the highest strings men worked on stilts. To an observer seeing them for the first time, there was something whimsical about the sight of men striding about on their long extended legs. It seemed unreal. Travellers on the railway lines through Kent would often catch a glimpse of these strange figures moving about among their army of ranks of tall, erect hop poles. On a misty day there was a dreamlike quality to this fleeting scene.

Ben Skinner, a well-known figure in the Littlebrook hop gardens, was a past master of this art. He was so expert at walking on stilts that people often told him he ought to be in a circus! The nearest he came to this was when he was doing his well-known 'stilt dance', with his assistant and close friend Bert Shrubsole.

Both were over six feet tall, but whereas Ben was a hefty, burly man, Bert was thin as a bean pole. On stilts they looked like two giants from another world. In their role as entertainers they were known as the 'Whoppers', and billed as 'Bert and Bessy Whoppers, the Long-legged Hoppers'.

To the music of an accordion, this dance was their contribution to the annual celebration bonfire party held on the evening of the last Saturday of the hop picking period. Ben became Bessy, the wife of the partnership, dressed in an elaborate, highly decorated dress, with all her womanly proportions greatly exaggerated to match her very long legs. Bert was Bessy's ultra-skinny partner. With equal inventiveness he appeared as a very lanky, pathetic, and vulnerable figure, very much at the mercy of his overpowering wife. Their routine, well worked out and practised beforehand, caused a riot of laughter with a barrage of shouted comments, some of them highly suggestive and bawdy. Theirs was the most eagerly awaited act of the evening.

As the hop plants grew, the stringing gradually disappeared beneath the attractive healthy green leaves of the climbing bines which twisted their way up and along the strings. At the top of the strings the bines dropped and tended to become a rather tangled bundle of growth called a 'head'. Eventually the whole area was a forest of green. On a sunny day, walking down the alleys formed by the lines of hop poles, with the lush green growth often partially closing the gap overhead, was a pleasing sensation. On a very hot day the dappled shade made the hop garden a cool place to be in. With the strong, unmistakeable aromatic smell of hops, the whole atmosphere was very pleasant and peaceful. Nothing else was quite like it. Being there was an enchanting experience and one enjoyed over and over again each succeeding year by the many people who were captivated by hop gardens, for they had a magic about them that registered deeply in the memory and beckoned back those spellbound by them.

The description 'garden' is an apt one. A hop garden is in a way a special form of flower garden, for the cone-like hops form on the flower heads of the female hop plants. When ripe, the hops are multi-scaled cones from two to four inches long. The yellowy-green scales, or bracts, are really the fruits of the plants. When ready for harvesting the masses of yellow-green hops hanging among the rich green leaves make the plantation an attractive and unique form of garden.

In the weeks before hop picking time there was an air of expectation around Littlebrook and villages like it that were close to extensive hop gardens. The rich green growth of the hop vines, creating its dense foliage of attractive leaves and developing hops, contrasted sharply with the skeletal, intricate array of poles and brown stringing seen earlier. The change from its bare 'all-string-and-poles' appearance, to the rich vegetation and mature hops, took place as the summer days passed by.

From time to time villagers from Littlebrook and the surrounding area would walk the gardens to monitor progress and assess the crop. Some enthusiasts made the journey each weekend. Under very favourable conditions hop plant stems grow fast, as much as several inches in a few days, so between one visit and another a marked change was often seen.

Not only the farm workers who attended them, but knowledgeable and experienced local hop pickers watched the development closely. There was a vested interest in a good crop of hops—for the farmer who owned them; the workers who tended them; the brewers who needed them; but perhaps most of all for those who would pick them. The rewards of hop picking constituted a welcome extra income for the families who took part. And there was the hop picking occasion itself. If the weather were good there was a real holiday atmosphere during the three to four weeks of the hop picking period. It was a communal effort and an enjoyable time.

An influx of pickers was needed to complement the local people in order to cope with this burst of activity. The hops, once ready for picking, had to 'come off' quickly to preserve their quality, and a much larger workforce than could be provided by the local population was needed to achieve this.

The temporary, incoming labour-force of pickers had to be provided with accommodation near their place of work, to allow them to stay away from home for the three or four weeks of the hop picking period. This accommodation was rudimentary indeed, and would have won no accolades if assessed as 'holiday homes'. Few complained about that, though. Hop picking was treated very much as a mixture of a working and camping holiday in the country. Nobody expected much comfort when 'out camping', and they certainly didn't get it when they went hop picking.

Near each hop garden a grassy area was set off permanently for what was really a campsite. On each such plot a collection of 'hopper huts' was built, arranged in rows of adjoining compartments, each giving sleeping accommodation for two or three adults, or sometimes adults and children. They were very small places to live in, with no 'home comforts'.

Usually the huts were made of wood, with corrugated-iron roofs. Less often they were made entirely of corrugated-iron, or sometimes the walls were of brick. Each compartment had a door, often of the 'stable' type with upper and lower parts which were hinged separately, and a small window. The only furniture provided was a slatted platform to serve as a bed at night and a seat by day. A liberal supply of straw was at hand to be stuffed into palliasses, or sometimes into ordinary sacks, to act as simple mattresses.

A water tap was installed on site, and a row of earth latrines prepared. An essential feature was a communal area where campfires could be lit for cooking, or for evening get-togethers. Many a happy sing-song took place around these brightly burning fires during the evenings. In the shortening days of this time of year, part of each evening period was dark. This added to the camping feel of the place, especially if the weather were fine.

Many people brought their own oil-burning primus-stoves for cooking, and oil lamps for lighting their huts. The farmer would usually provide a few oil lanterns, or hurricane lamps, to light the latrine area by night. Candles were also widely used, and much in demand from the local shops during this period of the year.

These hopper huts were kept in good order by most farmers—though not by all—because they played an essential part in the farming year. Cleaned out and repaired during the year, they were 'made ready' in the weeks just before the picking season. A good supply of firewood was stacked on the site.

The shops and pubs in Kentish villages were stocked up and ready for the annual boost in the local population. Years of experience enabled those who had to make these preparations to know what supplies had to be laid on. It was estimated that upwards of fifty thousand extra people moved into the Kentish countryside during hop picking time.

In some districts where there were several hop gardens within a small area, the influx of people was very marked. And at weekends more 'strangers' than ever were around because it was customary for special excursions to be run, bringing relatives and friends to visit the hop pickers at their camp sites. A normally quiet and peaceful locality became transformed at weekends by this increase in population.

On the Saturday before the first Monday of hop picking, the visitors moved in. By all available means of transport hop pickers converged on the hop gardens of Kent.

In the Littlebrook area where there were three hop gardens within a radius of two miles, they came mainly from the East End of London, but also from the coastal areas, in particular from Dover and Deal. By tradition the same families tended to come each year. Children grew up with the annual hop picking holiday as part of their regular yearly routine.

Londoners usually came in special hop picking trains, called 'Hopping Specials'. On arrival in Kent they were picked up from the nearest railway station, which was some two miles from their destination, and taken direct to the hopper huts by farm transport.

Some parties travelled in seaside-type charabancs. An enterprising taxicab firm from Dover cashed in on this by using the two, open-topped charabancs which they ran for holiday excursions in the summer months. One of these, a bone-shaking 1918 GMC twenty-seater stalwart old vehicle, was a well-recognised regular visitor to Littlebrook each year. The other—a comparatively modern, fifteen-seater Chevrolet—had joined in when the tax firm had invested in their second motorbus.

On sunny dry days, these chugging charabancs, with their canvas hoods folded back, packed with happy people with their luggage, pots, pans, folding stools, small portable furniture, plus anything else they needed for their stay, were greeted by waves and smiles by locals who saw them passing by. The arriving visitors, often singing, noisy and excited, were in a boisterous mood as they approached their destination. Some local residents, who liked their normally quiet life, regarded the coming of the many visitors with some trepidation and were glad when they went away again. But they were in the minority, for many enjoyed the period each year, especially if they went hop picking themselves.

All in all the spirit of the arriving hop pickers was a light-hearted, happy one, and this was infectious. If the weather were good, the atmosphere was very much that of a holiday. To many the short period living in the countryside of Kent was the highlight of their year, looked forward to with great anticipation and talked about years later with nostalgia.

At the Littlebrook hopper huts it was always Ben Skinner and his right-hand man Bert Shrubsole who opened up the huts early on the Saturday morning, so that all was prepared for the people known to be coming that day. Ben was bailiff at Mansted's Farm, and very much the central figure controlling events during hop picking time.

The main party from London arrived in a group from the special train. Many of these were 'regulars' who spotted Ben and Bert straight away, and warm greetings were exchanged. Ben's first job was to allocate the accommodation and see to the issue of the essentials needed for the stay.

This first Saturday was a settling-in day. It was very important to make sure that all necessary domestic arrangements were sorted out because once picking started on Monday morning, nobody wanted to be delayed or deflected from the job in hand.

Always, there were enough 'old-stagers' around the hopper huts to help those there for the first time to get properly organised. Seen on a bleak rainy day in the winter, the hopper huts and the site looked a miserable place. On a sunny day during the season though, once occupied by the cheerful crowd of hop pickers, the atmosphere was transformed. It seemed an altogether different place.

There were usually a few among the newcomers who looked around disconsolately, wondering what they had let themselves in for and ready to go home again before they had even started! The regulars soon spotted them and reassured them. They would be quite all right, they were told, once they had settled in and got used to things. Usually this proved to be true, because it was the people rather than the place that mattered. And the people were a good-natured lot and it was easier to be happy among them, than miserable.

Now and again though, some people didn't wait to see, especially if it happened to be rainy and dismal when they arrived. They just took fright and cleared off home again. This did not happen often and they were soon replaced. There were not many ways of earning extra money, and few as pleasant as sitting out in a hop garden, busy picking and chatting with friends. When the weather cleared, new recruits were soon available to fill the gaps.

By the evening of the first Saturday, what with the journey down, and the busy time moving into the campsite, people were ready for a break. Many went off for a few hours to enjoy themselves.

Social activities of various kinds were laid on throughout the hop picking period, sometimes on weekday evenings, but in particular on Saturday afternoons and evenings. These functions attracted locals and visitors alike.

There were always more women and girls than men amongst the visitors because, in general, they were more likely to be available when needed for these weeks of part-time work on farms during the year.

Not surprisingly therefore, hop picking was a popular time of year for local young, and not-so-young men. In the pubs during the evenings, old acquaintances would meet up again, and liaisons of previous years happily resumed.

Some faces were eagerly sought out on this first Saturday evening to make sure expected friends had duly arrived for the new season. Two of these seekers were Percy Pringle, a local cobbler of amorous disposition, and his close friend Taffy Thomas, a self-employed woodcutter who shared the same interests. These dubious characters were known among their contemporaries as Pokum Percy and Randy Taffy, somewhat colourful descriptive names not without a logical basis for their adoption. Both spent their days largely on their own, Percy in his lock-up workshop on the outskirts of the village, and Taffy in woodland clearings, cutting and shaping coppiced wood for fencing and other farm purposes.

Taffy was very quick and adept at manufacturing the end-products, such as hurdles and wattles, from his cleverly sliced lengths of selected local woods. He cut the raw material, processed it, and then produced fully made end-products, all in his woodland workplace. It was creative, satisfying work which he enjoyed, particularly in warm fine weather. In effect his was a one-man factory with an assured market for the output.

Both men were to some extent 'loners'. Unlike Taffy though, Percy was married. Most people thought that the reason why Taffy was unmarried was because no woman in her senses would want to marry him anyway, assuming they had the chance to observe his behaviour and habits over a period of time. Not that he had ever shown any desire to give up his free-ranging status.

Percy on the other hand had been married a long time and had a family to support. But he had his life so organised that he could still spend a good part of his time to all intents and purposes as a single man. He was by profession a cobbler, but by inclination an ardent 'womaniser'.

Because of the limited amount of boot and shoe repairing work to be found in any one village, Percy had two workshops separated by some six miles. Between these he divided his working time, but his family home was in an isolated hamlet 'out in the sticks'. It was this isolated location of his home which had led Percy, once fully trained in cobbling skills, to fix himself up with a lock-up workshop in the nearest sizeable village.

After a few years, because he had been picking up a lot of extra work from there, he equipped and opened a second such workshop at Littlebrook. In time this became the more prosperous of the two, benefiting from the death of an elderly, well-established cobbler whose business closed down.

To give him his due, he worked hard and built up a good business between the two locations. One way and another he lived pretty well—and indulged himself pretty well too, in what he described as the 'delights of life'. Others, with no concession to delicacy, described these delights as 'boozing' and 'whoring'. It was fair comment!

By habit, he often slept for two or three nights in each of his workshops every week. This gave him long, efficient working days from Monday to Friday, during which he started early and finished late. But at 1 pm on Saturdays he went off home for the weekend, leaving all thoughts of cobbling behind him. Except that is, during hop picking time.

This special period called for 'special arrangements'. Then, as he earnestly explained to his wife, the heavy extra workload from the hop pickers at his Littlebrook shop 'tied him down' so that he needed to work Saturdays and Sundays as well! So, by force of circumstances, he had to stay in his workshop over Saturday and Sunday nights, to cope with this abnormal pressure of work. This freed Percy, along with his mate Taffy, to enjoy for three or four blissful weekends, a life of self-indulgence and seasonal pleasure.

In discussing their behaviour with a mutual acquaintance, Reverend Yelman, the Vicar—who knew more than most local people gave him credit for about what went on in the district over which he felt his position gave him an unwritten moral responsibility—described their life-style as one of 'reckless abandon' that was truly deplorable. It was his hope, when he voiced this strong comment, that it would promptly be passed back to the feckless pair by the holier-than-thou parishioner he was talking to, and cause them to veer back towards the straight and narrow.

By such devious means, coupled with strongly-loaded sermons which dwelt at length on the awful consequences of sin and debauchery, he did his best to counter the influx of so many temptations into his parish at this time of the year. Perhaps some were influenced by his efforts. But not so Percy and Taffy! They pursued their carnal intentions with single-minded determination!

When told of the Vicar's comments, issued in such stern terms from the pulpit, and warned with feigned concern by his friends of the dreadful consequences that would follow his escapades if he didn't mend his sinful ways, Taffy's reply was characteristically crude and uncompromising.

"If the Lord didn't want me to dip my wick," he said, "he wouldn't have given me one!"

It was not a response the Vicar would have cared to hear, being not the stuff of an Oxford Union debate, a forum where he had won his spurs with brief acclaim from his peers many years before, speaking on the very same subject! He had made an earnest, spirited defence of the Church's official stance on casual, illicit relationships of the kind in which Percy and Taffy were indulging. His audience was decidedly unsympathetic at the time. It was a sticky wicket. But his adversaries on that occasion at least opposed his unpopular position with argument rather more logical and amenable to reasoned debate than was Taffy's!

From uncomfortable previous experiences, the Vicar knew he could not handle an eyeball to eyeball confrontation with the recalcitrant Taffy. The man's ignorance was too much like impenetrable armour off which his verbal bullets bounced back and ricocheted harmlessly away, having no impact beyond stimulating the most disturbing reaction of further earthy, unrepeatable comments from Taffy, as the unrepentant fellow sought to justify the lecherous activities that he had no intention of forgoing to satisfy the Vicar's bleak philosophy of self-denial.

To Taffy it was pure kill-joy stuff. And he wanted nothing to do with it. He let it be known that he reckoned when he died it would be time enough for him to start going without his pleasures, and pointed out that he would be dead a long long time to make up for his comparatively few sinful years knocking off any woman who came near him!

That was the extent of his logic and as profound as he could get after giving the matter his serious consideration. It made the Vicar's ministry heavy-going! Small wonder he gave up trying, except, as on this occasion, by proxy!

Nothing much went on in the village without the locals knowing about it, especially if it involved a bit of scandal. So the actions of these two well-known womanisers were watched with interest. Not that Taffy made any secret of his activities. Far from it. Although Percy, understandably, was not all that keen on having his extra-marital affairs too widely broadcast, Taffy—on the contrary—liked to boast to all and sundry of his successes. This was especially true when he was well tanked-up with beer.

When a little tipsy, to the delight of all within hearing, Taffy not only gave vivid descriptions of his past escapades, but invented lurid, titillating details as he went along—no doubt voicing as accomplished deeds, excesses he'd dreamt up in the course of his private contemplation of his consuming obsession with women.

As a result of this well-known fact, in the pub where he was a regular he would be well-primed with beer by the assembled company in order to get him going.

Entertainment often has to be paid for, and it was worth investing a little money to encourage Taffy to talk. Since he liked his beer almost (but not quite) as much as he liked his women, Taffy did well out of this.

This ability of Taffy's to cash in on his carefree life, led a rather jealous crony of his to make a rueful comment.

"The crafty old blighter," he said, speaking of Taffy to his friends, "bashes away at a bit of spare until he's nearly creased, works up one hell of a thirst, then goes down to the pub and gets free beer all night on the strength of it!"

In effect, this is exactly what Taffy did do!

At the Ship Inn, on the evening of Saturday—the hop pickers' arrival day—the place was always packed. Regular customers got in position early in the Public and Saloon Bars, because by tradition they knew the night would be a lively and enjoyable one.

Soon after opening time visitors began to swell the normal modest numbers. Some were hailed as old friends, others were making their first tentative visit to a country pub, not knowing quite what to expect.

Percy and Taffy, spruced-up and expectant, awaited the arrival of their special friends, Glad and Clara from Camden Town. By 8 pm they were already in a happy state, fortified by a double whisky each and a couple of pints of beer.

Glad and Clara, now on their third trip to Littlebrook for hop picking, had arrived down from London that morning on the 'Hopper Special' train from London Bridge Station. They were all set to enjoy another paid 'holiday' in the country. Their date at the Ship that evening had been fixed up on the last night of their stay during the previous year, the assignment being for the evening of their day of arrival—the actual calendar date of the Saturday was not known until the farmer fixed it nearer the time.

There was no correspondence between the four of them during the intervening period so there was just that element of uncertainty on both sides about whether or not the meeting would materialise. Percy and Taffy watched the door anxiously as the visitors trickled in.

At 8.30pm their patience was rewarded and their anxiety dispelled. In walked the two ladies from Camden Town, to be greeted with great enthusiasm and excited relief by Percy and Taffy. Within a few minutes the four were happily settled at a corner table picking up where they had left off last year.

Thinking about where they had 'left off' the previous year had kept Percy and Taffy in a state of randy anticipation for several weeks past. Their expectations grew as the hops grew. Gleefully they had made their plans. 'Back at the ranch' in Percy's workshop-cum-residence wooden hut, provisions had been laid-in and domestic arrangements made.

Pride of place amongst the necessities of life, apart from the two camp beds, was a box of booze. In with several bottles of light-ale and brown-ale was tucked a bottle of whisky and a bottle of gin. Percy and Taffy liked whisky. Glad and Clara preferred gin. Taffy, when he'd collected the bottle of gin, had winked evilly at the publican Bill Martin behind the bar (who knew the score only too well) and commented with a wide grin, "This will oil their works up, Bill!"

As for the carefully prepared beds, which had an important part to play in the scheme of things, although strictly speaking only 'singles', they had proved to be quite capable of taking two people at a squeeze, and the kind intending hosts were not averse to having to put up with a bit of a squeeze!

Along with other local pubs, the Ship Inn was granted an extension of opening hours for this special hop picking first night, and the packed bars became progressively noisier as the evening went on. Oblivious of the rumpus going on around them the four reunited friends spent a very happy time together, drinking, talking, and making plans for the coming days when they would meet up.

By the time Bill, the landlord, made his time-honoured call for "Last drinks, Gentlemen, *IF* you please," the four of them were well and truly muzzy and merry.

To a chorus of laughter and shouted advice from all sides, Taffy unsteadily led Clara to the door, followed by Percy—trying hard to look dignified and sober—arm-in-arm with Glad.

When they got outside into the open air they were all hard put to it to stand steadily on their feet. It was about a quarter of a mile to Percy's cosy hut. That was just about as far as any of them could possibly have walked, but they set off in high spirits with much laughing and singing on the way.

A small group of village lads watched their progress up the road with close interest. Taffy's voice, always loud—possibly because his hearing was none too good—could be heard making it plain to Clara that she and Glad had no need to worry about having to walk all the way to the hopper huts that night. Percy, he assured her, would be quite willing to put them all up for the night!

Hearing this kind, thoughtful invitation by Taffy to his lady friend, caused an outburst of laughter from the lads.

"Dirty old devil!" sniggered Dicky Todd with mock indignation, addressing his laughing mates. "He's got it all worked out nicely, hasn't he? Cor! What a bloody hypocrite. By the time old Percy and Taffy have finished with them tonight they will be too shagged-out to go home to the hopper huts, even if they want to. It wouldn't surprise me if they will be so weak by tomorrow morning that old Taffy will have to push them up to the hop garden in his wheelbarrow. Cruelty to women, that's what it is. Next thing to cruelty to animals, that is. We ought to send for the R.S.P.C.W."

"What's that?" asked his younger brother Tim, who had been listening to Dicky with a worried look on his face.

"What's what?" responded Dicky, knowing full-well what his brother was querying, and wishing to make the most of his inspired invention.

"What's the R.S.P.C.W?" elaborated Tim.

"That's the Royal Society for the Prevention of Cruelty to Women. I should have thought you'd have known that!" replied Dicky, with apparent impatience, much to the amusement of the others.

"Well, I didn't", confessed Tim. "I've heard of the R.S.P.C.A., to help animals. But I didn't know there was one for women too."

"Of course there is," snapped Dicky. "Women cop a lot of cruelty, same as animals do. That's because men are stronger than women and some men knock women about!"

Tim now looked even more worried. He didn't like the sound of things at all. The two ladies had looked nice old things to him and he didn't like the idea of them walking into danger.

"Shouldn't we call out and tell them not to go into that hut, then?" he asked his older brother anxiously.

"No, you daft twit!" snorted Dicky. "Do you think they don't know what they are in-for inside that hut? They know what's coming to them all right, don't you worry. What's more they're looking forward to it! I heard old Taffy saying one day that women like it as much as men do. Huh! Don't you worry about them! I reckon they can't get inside old Percy's knocking-shop fast enough. It wouldn't surprise me to see them carry old Taffy out themselves in the morning, never mind the other way round. I bet it will do more harm to him than it will to them. Just look at the poor old sod! He looks half dead to me already. The strain could easily kill him tonight, I'm telling you—you wait and see!"

Tim was reassured by this superior wisdom from his big brother and stopped worrying. He began to perceive what it was all about. As the youngest member of the group he did not always grasp the implication of what his better-informed mates were on about, but was learning fast. What's more, he found the subjects they talked about with such glee, intensely interesting. Much more so than the sort of things his patient teacher at the village school was trying so hard to fire him off about.

Meanwhile Dicky's mind had been working on a bit, dwelling upon Taffy's possible imminent fate with a morbid fascination.

"I'm not joking about Taffy, you know", he said. "I heard our Dad say that Taffy would never make old bones. He said to Uncle Reg that the way old Taffy lives, drinking as much as he does, and knocking off one woman after another as fast as he can get his trousers down, he would most likely drop dead one of these days!"

"Could be tonight, the way he looks," observed Dicky's bosom pal, 'Sherbert' Dipstick. "He looks on his last legs now, to me!"

"I'll tell you what, if he does kick the bucket nobody will put a tombstone on his grave, that's for sure," remarked Dicky emphatically. "Dad said that so far as anybody knows old Taffy doesn't have any family or relatives at all, says he's a proper loner."

Dicky had no sooner made this observation than his face lit with sudden inspiration.

"I've got a good idea," he said, with much enthusiasm. "Let's get a notice ready to put on his grave when he dies. We can paint some words about him on a wooden board, nail it on one of those nice shaved poles he makes up in the woods, and ask old Motty to stick it at the end of his grave when they have made a mound of dirt, like they do for most people. At least he will have something there, and not just be left looking like half a row of spuds!"

His mates had a good laugh at this. But Dicky's brow was puckered. He was thinking about a suitable epitaph for Taffy's special replacement for a headstone.

"You can laugh," he said. "But I'm serious. I'll have a board ready by the time old Taffy drops dead. You wait and see!"

"What will you put on it, Dicky?" asked Tim.

"Don't know yet," answered Dicky. "I will have to compose him a little poem. It will come to me, in time. I'll have to think about it."

By the time the lads reached Percy's hut, the four had just succeeded in stumbling inside, with shrieks of laughter from the women intermingled with the sound of Taffy's loud, fruity, Welsh voice singing one of his well-known 'Sailors-Songs.'

Taffy had a repertoire of these songs remembered from his high life in the Royal Navy before and during the Great War. They were all carefully written out from memory on sheets of paper stowed in an old attaché case which stood against the wall behind his fireside chair in his bachelor cottage home.

Inside the case, along with his songs, were sundry papers bearing drawings, dirty stories and lewd pictures, collected over many years, much of it in foreign ports and distant parts of the world. Anything new that came his way, he duly added to this treasure chest of titillating material.

Occasionally Taffy would entertain his friends by delving into his store case to bring out juicy bits to show them, accompanied by bawdy comments and raucous laughter.

The battered case was locked by a small key that hung on his watch chain. On the lid, roughly painted in black letters were the words:

TAFFY THOMAS R.N.
PRIVATE AND CONFIDENSHULL

Taffy's songs, all pretty raw, didn't stop at describing the antics of British sailors and women in foreign ports, although this formed the subject of most of them. Usually they were sung to the tunes of well-known sea-shanties, with built-in strong chorus lines where all could join in.

The one the lads heard parts of, amidst peals of laughter from Glad and Clara, was different and a bit special. It seemed to involve, from the tantalising bits they managed to hear, not a fat woman and a British sailor, but a fat woman and a donkey! Agog with interest the lads were very disappointed when the door slammed shut to interrupt what seemed to be a story full of interest. They determined to ask old Taffy to tell them what happened when they next met him.

Shut outside they would have dearly loved to be a fly on the wall to watch proceedings inside the hut during the rest of the night. But Percy and Taffy, having previously suffered painfully from the taunting of local lads who had succeeded—or so they claimed—in peeping in the window during their hop picking razzles, had taken care to make their den of iniquity sight-proof if not sound-proof. So the door was securely bolted behind them when they went in. It wasn't very pleasant for Percy and Taffy to have their amorous performances described publicly in their own presence by people who claimed to have had ringside seats. This had happened one Sunday afternoon the previous year, and they still squirmed at the thought of it.

They had been sitting peacefully on the grass by the scoring hut at the recreation ground watching a village cricket match, when their peace was suddenly shattered by the arrival of three more spectators. One of them, as they flopped down on the grass, called out in a loud voice, for all in the vicinity to hear, a rather personal remark.

"Not surprised you need to lie out on the grass, you two fornicating old buggers!" announced the newcomer by way of introduction, a remark which alerted the attention of all those within earshot. "You must be right clapped-out, you must, after what we saw you up to last night in that cosy little knocking-shop of yours. And it wasn't boots and shoes you were knocking either!"

Then had followed a blow-by-blow account of Percy's and Taffy's actions with their two women in the cobblers hut the night before. For a time the undivided attention of those around them had switched from the cricket match to these firsthand accounts of such juicy events. With howls of laughter and many not very kind remarks from the crowd, poor Taffy and Percy had to listen to this free entertainment at their expense and suffer it with as good a grace as they could. It was not a nice time for them. Not a nice time at all.

Denials or protest were useless, for they simply added to the glee of their tormentors and the amusement of the audience, so they quickly shut up and suffered in silence. In any event, the unhappy pair were not even in a position to know that much of it was in fact invented as they went along by the inspired witnesses. A lot of it sounded all too much like the truth, bearing in mind that the truth itself was just a booze-fuddled vague memory in their day-after-the-night-before heads anyway. They hadn't forgotten though, what they had hoped would happen when they had laid their plans, and subsequently—each in his own unique, lewd and lusty thoughts—fantasised about, as they privately contemplated the pleasures to come as the day approached. Confused, unhappy, and helpless, they had no option but to sit it out until their tormentors had tired of their sport and turned their attention to the cricket!

So, with this miserable and embarrassing experience behind them, they had 'put the shutters up' as best they could, well in advance this year, to ensure their privacy.

As the lads, somewhat reluctantly, made their way up the road, the fading sounds of bumps, thumps and shrieks of laughter, along with snatches of Taffy's raucous voice emanating from the hut, gave plenty of food for thought to stimulate their imaginations.

With much gleeful laughter among themselves, there was no limit to the crudity of their highly inventive imaginings. They vied with one another to create lurid suggestions about what might be going on inside the den. Anything, from Percy's respected expertise as a cobbler, his mass of implements and tools, together with Taffy's known vast experience of foreign parts, was fair game to be somehow or other embodied in their mutually re-enforcing mental pictures of what might be happening back there in the hut in the dark of the night!

In between making his own contributions to the lurid suggestions, Dicky's mind had been busy with the problem of a fitting inscription for Taffy's future final resting place. It needed careful thought and a lot of going-over before he got it sorted out.

As they moved further away, feeling sorry they'd had to abandon the tantalising cobbler's hut for the night, Tim suddenly remembered the matter of Taffy's grave. He was quite sure Taffy was on his last legs and would soon be planted in the churchyard, to be cared for by Old Motty, like the rest of them dug in round there.

"Have you thought what to put on Taffy's grave yet, Dicky?" he asked his brother eagerly.

The question gave Dicky just the lead-in he wanted, to allow him to announce the product of his superior intellect. With great glee he answered Tim's enquiry.

"Oh yes," he replied, with a struggle to appear nonchalant. "Yes, I've made up something which ought to do the job, I reckon. Of course it wasn't easy! Things have got to be 'proper' and a bit sort of 'Holy like' to go in a place like that. It's not the stuff I usually write about in my poems."

"What is it, then?" asked Tim, who much admired his big brother's poetic genius.

"How about this?" said Dicky, barely able to suppress his own bottled-up laughter long enough to get the words out. "This is what I think we ought to put on the notice—

'Here lies Taffy
Dirty old shit,
Shagged himself to death,
Stupid bloody twit!'

—perhaps we can run a collection," he spluttered, delighted at the way the words came out, "and get it carved on a proper stone instead of on a notice board. What do you blokes think about that?"

There was a chorus of laughter from his friends in appreciation of this new display of poetic ability by Dicky. He was good at coming up with these little gems. And the more they laughed at them the better he got at dreaming them up. Secretly he spent a lot of time at home 'composing', as he liked to describe it. Sometimes he made a point of not hearing what people said when they spoke to him, but gazed into the far distance seemingly oblivious of their presence. His small brother Tim politely excused this apparent rudeness for him by explaining that Dicky was busy at his 'composing' and didn't hear anything when he was in the middle of it. Hidden away among Dicky's personal treasures was a rather scruffy, old school exercise book in which he carefully wrote out his masterpieces. It was not a book his parents or any other adults ever saw. His prepared epitaph for Taffy was similarly recorded, in due course, along with the others. It was shorter than most of his efforts. But he was quite proud of it.

After this further lift of their spirits, although still feeling a bit disappointed and frustrated at their inability to witness events inside the hut, the small group of lads went off home happily enough, leaving Percy and Taffy to get on with it tucked away in their safe haven.

Inside the hut Percy and Taffy did their best to bring the proceedings to a happy fruition, seriously impaired though they both were from the effects of over-priming their engines with too much alcohol.

On Sunday morning all was quiet in the village. As the church's peel of six bells rang out, pulled in well-rehearsed sequences by the local team of enthusiastic bell-ringers, people in the hopper huts got up leisurely and began their first day in the country. During the day they sorted out how to organise their feeding and living arrangements for the days ahead. It was a day of relaxation and a time to fix up all the little jobs around the place to ensure that life in the hopper hut community would be as comfortable as possible. For work was due to start in earnest next morning, and there would be little time to fuss about from then on.

Early on Monday morning people from the hopper huts, and from the village, began to trek along the paths to the hop gardens.

Ben Skinner and Bert Shrubsole, with their team of men from the farm, were at the hop garden at first light to get everything ready for the start. On this first picking day Ben and Bert organised the entire workforce, both locals and visitors, into suitable groups. Each small group was allocated a numbered row—or 'alley'—and installed themselves ready for action.

Something to sit on, like a camp stool or folding chair, was an essential, together with the bushel baskets provided for them to pick into. With shopping bags or wicker baskets containing food and drink for the day, people quickly settled into a routine.

A few of Ben's staff of farm workers were permanently around. Moving from alley to alley they cut down the hop bines a few at a time. Experience pickers worked their way along and through these cut-down trailing plants with practised speed. A steady rain of hops poured into the bushel baskets all day long. For convenience some preferred to pick into a bowl, a bucket, or a box placed on the ground between their knees, pausing every now and again to tip the contents into the bushel baskets.

When full, the bushel baskets were carried to, and emptied into, the large five-bushel 'Tally' baskets placed at the end of each row.

Care had to be taken not to crush-up fresh hops. Crushing spoilt their quality, so they were tipped lightly and carefully into the Tally baskets. Several times during the filling of the large baskets the hops were 'loosened-up' by spreading the fingers under them and lifting them upwards. Some people described this as 'fluffing them up'.

By the experts, this process was called 'hovering-up' the hops. To a newcomer it looked as though the pickers were trying to fill the basket with a minimum number of hops. It happened that this process suited both sides. The grower wanted this done to preserve the quality of the hops, and the hop pickers gladly went along with it. They took great pains to 'fluff' the hops and make their hard-won gatherings fill as many Tally baskets as possible each day.

New pickers felt a bit guilty doing this at first. It seemed too much like trying to make a little go a long way, until they became convinced that it was what the 'Boss' wanted them to do. They soon found out though, that even with the hops hovered-up in this way, it was hard enough to make any really significant sum of money in a week's continuous picking, anyway.

In some hop gardens Tally baskets were used which had inside them several loops of string, tied to the rim. These strings were pulled upwards to hover-up the hops; a method which safeguarded quality rather better than thrusting hands down into the pile.

It was not long before a marked disparity became evident between the rate at which various groups picked the hops. Some were really good at it, going at the job with a feverish intent as though their very lives depended upon it. Others treated the task in a more relaxed, less determined way, enjoying the social occasion and the chance to be in the countryside for a while, as much as an opportunity to clock-up a bit of extra cash.

Ben, who in the hop garden was known as the 'Tallyman', together with his right-hand man Bert, moved regularly to and fro along the edge of the rows. They were accompanied by a waggoner with his horse and cart.

The Tally baskets were emptied into sacks and loaded on to the cart. Each basket was recorded in Ben's 'Tally Book' against the name of the senior picker in charge in each alley. Ben and Bert were vigilant to see that the hops were 'clean' of leaves and stalks. Newcomers soon got to know that a good deal of care was needed in picking the hops. Otherwise, if they stripped-off leaves along with hops, the basket was rejected. It then had to be tipped out and carefully gone through by the pickers to take out the unwanted debris. This cost time and money, so it seldom happened twice to any one group. As with so many things, it was a question of learning the hard way.

It was left to the members of each group to keep a record of their own particular contribution in bushels to the daily total for their group. Eventually, on pay-days, they would receive their due proportion from the senior picker of their group. This person was paid by the Bailiff the total earned by their small team, and had the job of dividing it out.

In the case of local families it was often an annual ritual for various relatives and friends to join in when they could, perhaps for a few days, or part-days, during the hop picking period. Sometimes they came for personal profit and had their own efforts recorded, and at length rewarded. On occasions though, they simply donated their extra 'pick' to the family effort. Such visitors were welcome. It got a bit tedious filling a bushel basket, emptying it and starting all over again. To see a basket start to fill more quickly was very satisfying, as they chatted and worked together.

Among these temporary visitors was Percy. His mate Taffy was 'stuck up in the wood', to use his own lament, too far away from the hop garden to be able to nip in there during the day. He had to content himself with meeting Glad and Clara in the evenings and just dreaming of them during the day. In any event, at this time of the year he was extremely busy and could not afford to take time off from his work.

Percy, though, was conveniently placed not too far from the hop garden. So he made a point of roaming into the hive of activity now and again during the weekdays, to swap cobbling for hop picking for a spell. This gave him more time with the ladies from Camden Town. It was a pleasant change from his normally solitary life, to enjoy their company for a while.

Ben and Bert, working as they did, to and fro along the main cart-track which bordered the hop garden, were in a good position to spot the comings and goings of visitors. Seeing Percy sneaking along looking down the rows to find his lady friends, they took a delight in calling out a greeting and asking him pointed questions about his love life. Their loud and not very subtle enquiries caused much amusement to locals who heard them. Ben, grinning from ear to ear, asked Percy if he would confine his activities to picking hops while he was there and not interrupt the pickers who had more important things to do than talking to him about nightlife in 'Cobbler's Corner'.

Children, depending upon their age and inclinations, helped now and again for part of the day, but many soon tired of the tedious, concentrated business of picking, and in between whiles went off to play in the delightful surroundings. Most were allowed to enjoy their holiday and were not expected to work all day long with the 'grown-ups'.

Enterprising 'Ice Cream' men, 'Refreshment' stallholders, and sundry pedlars descended on the hop gardens to take advantage of the presence of so many people. They did well, for on many days it was hot and dusty work. And, to many, it was after all, a 'holiday' they were having.

With methodical, clockwork-like precision, once in motion the work in the hop gardens continued running smoothly through the successive days. The fragrant smell of hops pervaded the air of the whole district and made a powerful impact on anybody coming to the gardens for the first time. Only heavy rain could seriously interrupt proceedings.

As the days went by, viewed from the top of Littlebrook Hill, the local hop garden looked as though a plague of locusts was eating away the green stuff, working steadily along, remorselessly, from one end towards the other, destroying the crop completely.

Once having finished their 'alley', each group of pickers was moved along to the next available row. In this way the hops were harvested systematically from one end of the hop garden towards the other, leaving behind a bare, bedraggled scene. The hop-poles once more stood out starkly, as they had done before the hops were planted.

Meanwhile, other parallel activities picked up steam. At the heart of the whole business of harvesting the hops lay the Oast House.

It was to this ancient building that the cartloads of sacks of hops were delivered. At one end of the production line Ben and Bert checked off, and loaded, the sackfulls into the cart. At the other end a small team of men received the crop into the Oast House. The function of this purpose-built Oast House was to dry the hops and bag them up, ready for the brewers.

In turn, once the Oast House had produced a sufficient output, brewers' vehicles arrived to transport the long hop sacks into which the dried hops had been compressed, to the breweries where they were stored in the dry until needed.

At night all was quiet in the hop gardens and nothing stirred except the wild creatures that came out to live their nocturnal lifestyles while humans were out of the way. In the debris on the ground some found exotic food of a kind not usually sniffed-out on the farmland during the rest of the year. So hop picking was a good time of the year for them a well.

At the Oast House though, things were different. Work did not stop in there just because it was dark outside. Once started, the Oast House kept on working night and day until all the harvested hops had been dried.

And the Oast House, which had an atmosphere all its own, had a particular attraction at night, when the outside world was fast asleep. It was a fascinating place to visit, especially at night, and each year there was never a shortage of people wanting to have a look inside to see what went on in there.

Once having been in there, in the dead of night, the experience was not easily forgotten. It was a little eerie, and quite unique, a shadowy, dreamlike world, unlike anything most people had previously experienced.

There was about it a quality that seemed sure to suggest it must be haunted.

And indeed it was, by reputation, just such a place. It attracted ghosts, or so it seemed from the many stories of ghosts associated with it, in much the same way as a flame attracts moths. As a result it was studiously avoided by some sensitive souls who knew its reported history—especially after dark. Wild horses couldn't have driven them in there then! Some places are best left alone, particularly near midnight and in the still, small hours of the morning.

There are those who deem it wise not to meddle with things that are not understood, and to keep well away from old buildings and sites or ruins of buildings where strange happenings are too widely reported to be ignored.

In contrast there are those who like to flirt with danger and seek the excitement of strange experiences. To such people, places like the Oast House hold a beguiling fascination that beckons them in to sample for themselves whatever it is that has given the place it reputation. Sometimes people get more than they bargain for, and live to regret getting involved.

There was to be an occasion this year, long talked about locally in later years, when a small group of visitors to the Littlebrook Oast House were to have a very frightening experience, news of which was to travel far and wide to become an intriguing legend of stark occult manifestations—as magnetically fascinating to some as they were off-puttingly frightening to others.

Little could those involved have even remotely imagined that their scary, psychic experience would eventually attract the interest of people far away on the Pacific Coast of America, and would bring over an investigative team avid for unusual stories from the 'Old World' and who would subsequently recreate the story as part of a cinema feature film.

Chapter 9

TRAGEDY IN THE OAST HOUSE
day of destiny for the dryer

The red-brick Littlebrook Oast House was picturesque and much admired. There was, however, a story and a name associated with it that was as much a part of its history as its attractive architecture.

The story was of an event which had taken place many years before, on the Friday of the first week of hop picking. The year was 1876, and the name was Timothy Twylock, the dryer-in-charge of the Oast at that time.

Tim had been a dryer for over thirty years and had a first-class reputation as a highly experienced and competent man. The brewers had complete confidence in him and accepted the finished hops without question so long as they knew he had supervised the entire operation.

By long-established practice Tim stayed at the Oast day and night throughout the four weeks or so of the annual period during September and early October when the Oast was operational. He programmed his rest periods so that he, and only he, decided when each load in the kiln should first be turned, then later taken out to be spread on the extensive floor of the cooling room. There was a snug little niche built into the wall near the kiln fire where he took his few hours of sleep, on a simple bunk bed. If he left the premises at all, it was only for short periods during in-between times when nothing was going on which required his expert attention. He took his duties very seriously and was jealous of his reputation.

Soon after first light on the morning of the fateful day, with the Oast House going full blast and moving into its fifth day of operation for the new season, the busy routine of work was interrupted when a crow flew into the cowl on the Oast top and somehow got itself trapped inside.

Just how this happened nobody quite knew. It seemed that there was a gusty wind blowing on the day and it is thought probable that the cowl had moved suddenly, just as the crow was flying in to settle, as crows frequently did, on the wind vane arm. A bird sitting there on a rainy day, perched on the long arm just inside the cowl, was sheltered from the wind and rain. It was a good place for an intelligent crow to retire to, in between its forays in the fields and farmyards around the neighbourhood.

The trapped and injured crow, according to the story, made an awful noise cawing and fluttering up there in the cowl. Although, because the cowl was so high above the ground, it probably would not have been heard from outside, it most certainly was heard by the men spreading hops on the slatted drying surface above the fire in the kiln.

Access to the kiln was from the upper storey of the two-storey building. The men loading the hops in a thick, even layer above the fire were some twenty feet above ground level, standing inside the round tower, immediately under the conical roof of the Oast House kiln.

Looking up they could see the crow flapping about because the cowl was open to the sky on the weather vane side.

To attempt to get up to the cowl from the inside, supposing ladders were brought in, would have been difficult and hazardous in the extreme, since the furnace was burning and the Oast fully operational.

Access from the outside, however, was far simpler and ladders were quickly brought from the farm to get up to the crow. It wasn't a question of wanting to rescue it. Apart from the appalling racket it was making, it was certain to foul up the hops below and spread feathers in its frantic struggles to break free. Not only that, it might conceivably jam up the cowl and stop it turning freely in the wind. That would cause real trouble in the kiln below. Should the wind blow on the open side of the cowl, strong down-draughts would prevent the proper working of the drying system. So there was no help for it, the crow just had to come down so as not to interfere with the work.

One long ladder was put up to rest on the gutter of the main building of the Oast. This was a large, long, two-storey, brick-built, barn-like structure, with a normal ridge-tiled roof at one end of which was the tall round kiln with its high, slated roof surmounted by the cowl.

The rotating cowl was itself a sizeable structure, being over fourteen feet tall. Built on a round pivoted base, it was made of overlapping planks of wood slanting upwards to a small, flat-topped head. But for its truncated top, it looked rather like an enormous witch's hat, except that it was painted white instead of the traditional black of a pantomime witch's hat.

The long, broad-bladed weather-vane stuck out of the open side of the cowl so that it caught the wind, to turn the cowl. This ensured that the wind blew on the closed side of the cowl and strong down-draughts were thus prevented. In effect the cowl was a rotating chimney set upon the high conical roof of a round tower above the furnace.

The whole purpose of this spectacular structure was to provide a continuous, strong, upward-draught of air. This made the charcoal furnace burn brightly and strongly, providing a powerful upward stream of hot air to dry the hops spread on the drying bed of the kiln.

A second ladder was placed up the tiles from the gutter to the ridge of the main roof. Finally a third, long, extending ladder was stood on the ridge to lie on the tiles of the very steeply sloping, conical roof of the kiln.

Lashing these ladders, though a great nuisance because life was hectic enough without unwelcome diversions like this, did not take long. The drill was well enough known since from time to time the ladders were put up for maintenance work which had to be carried out on the buildings and the cowl.

Timothy Twylock, the man in charge of the Oast, took it upon himself to go up and 'fetch the crow out of it'. Fortunately the weather vane was pointing more or less along the ridge of the roof so that, above Timothy's head, the open side of the tall cowl yawned like a large open door above his head, as he climbed the third ladder towards it.

He was seen by the men below to climb off the top of the ladder and clamber inside the cowl. Standing with his toes on the circular woodwork of the bottom of the cowl, he grabbed the crow with both hands, wrung its neck and started to dislodge the trapped legs.

Accidents always seem, after the event, to have happened in an instant of time, leaving only a blurred memory of the sequence of events. Apparently a strong gust of wind caught the weather vane and swung the cowl round sharply through an angle of 45 degrees or so, as strong gusts of wind in squally weather were prone to do, without warning.

Timothy Twylock was caught off-balance, lost his footing, cried out in alarm, and reached out to cling to the strong arm of the weather vane. Two of his mates, standing below on the edge of the drying bed in the kiln, saw him hang there for a few seconds, with one hand clutching the weather vane arm and the other hand clutching the structure to the side of the cowl. Then, as inevitably it was bound to do, the wind shifted the cowl back towards its prevailing wind direction, wrenching Timothy's hands apart.

With a loud yell of "Look out there below!" directed apparently at his mates in the kiln, he lost hold and plummeted downwards, to crash with a splintering of woodwork right through the centre of the slatted laths of the drying bed, to fall headlong, amidst a shower of hops, into the white-hot furnace below.

Mercifully, so it was deduced because there were no screams of agony, his head must have struck the brick walls of the furnace so that he was at least knocked out, or killed outright, a fraction of a second before the flames and the fire consumed him.

The fire brigade was called immediately and to them fell the unpleasant task, after dousing the furnace, of removing what remained of poor Timothy Twylock.

Shocked and devastated with horror and grief, his comrades at the Oast had to clear the kiln completely. Urgently, the local builder moved in that same day and renewed the shattered drying-bed some sixteen feet above the top of the furnace.

Within twenty-four hours the furnace was re-lit, and the work of the Oast House resumed, as it had to do. Already a backlog of hops awaiting drying had built up. Picking of the ripened hops could not be held up, or soon part of the valuable crop would be lost.

There was about the place an unnatural silence among the team of men as they went about their work. Awed by the sudden death of Timothy Twylock, for so long the moving spirit of the Oast each year, the men went about their work like automatons, carrying out automatically the various jobs that had to be done with nothing more than an occasional muttered comment from one to another. The cheerful chatter, laughter, and repartee that normally brought life into the otherwise rather gloomy place, was entirely absent.

For many hours afterwards the awful stench of burnt flesh hung in the air. It was the same smell as that which emanated from the local village butcher's slaughter house once each week when, on slaughtering day, the area was pervaded by the smell from the boiler-fire chimney, as unwanted bits and pieces of bones, flesh, and hair, were chucked onto the fire. It was sickening to realise that the nauseating stench had come from the burning of their foreman and close friend, now gone forever from the Oast House which he had run for so long, with so much pride and dedication.

Just a few hours ago he had been working happily alongside them. Now he was gone.

Unlike normal times, there was little laughter at all at the Oast that year. Quietly and methodically the hops were processed. Out of respect for Timothy, every care was taken to ensure that the established high standards were maintained.

At length, just over four weeks later, the season came to an end and Timothy Twylock passed into history. But he was not forgotten. As year followed year, each newcomer to the team learnt about the dreadful accident. So his spirit lived on down the years, in the minds of the men working the Oast House.

And, as was predictable, his presence was felt in the dark of the night when men's thoughts turned to ghosts. This they frequently did, for in the dead of the night an Oast House could be a creepy, eerie place, evocative of thoughts of the supernatural.

It was in the nature of things in an Oast House that the pace of work was 'lumpy'. There were periods of intense activity, interspersed with slacker periods when some — and at times all—of the small workforce could rest up a bit: a time to sit down, have a welcome drink of beer or cider, and a chat. It was hot and dusty work in an Oast House, especially in and around the kiln, and frequent drinks were needed. Barrels of beer and cider were provided by the brewery to look after this need, a traditional 'perk' of the job, and one much appreciated by the men.

The beer drinkers took a proprietary interest in this strong beer, made in a brewery not many miles away from the Oast House. It was, after all, their own hops of previous years which gave the beer its bitter, thirst-quenching qualities. In this respect the hops travelled 'full circle'. This was a matter which gave some very real satisfaction to the thirsty drinkers as the cool, refreshing liquid ran down their parched throats.

These periods of relaxation occurred more during the night than the day. It was when sitting around the open stoking-hole of the kiln fire, deep in the night-hours, when, from time to time, discussion turned to ghostly topics. In the flickering firelight, with pools of darkness and semi-darkness around, it was easy to become convinced that another hidden spiritual world existed unseen there in the Oast with them. Yet, conversely, far from unseen themselves, they felt uncomfortably sure that their ghostly visitors were by no means unaware of the living men there with them in the night. Re-told legends became more real by the minute under these conditions where the backdrop, and atmosphere, was better than any stage-set could ever contrive to be.

During the day, the 'feel' of the place was very different. In any event, there was more to do during daylight hours. Some activities took place only during the day, so that—in between tending to the processes of drying the hops—these other matters occupied the time.

Then, more often than not, a swig from a tankard of beer, without an accompanying period of relaxation sitting down for a bit to have a yarn, was all there was time for. The ghostly apparitions of the murky, dim world of the night were driven away by the bright light of the day. And, if there were any ghost-originated, off-stage noises such as sounds which sent a shiver down their spines when they were alone in the night, these went unheard amidst the noise and bustle of the busy work-a-day life surrounding them.

The main additional duties of the day were connected with the arrival of fresh hops from the hop garden and the preparation of the finished, processed hops for departure.

Hops arrived at intervals throughout the day. They reached the Oast House in large sacks called hop 'pokes'. These were hauled up from the wagon below by a pulley and chain arrangement and stacked on the upper floor, adjacent to the kiln drying-bed where the hops were destined to go.

On some days, at much less frequent intervals, the brewer's transport came to the Oast House to fetch the finished products. The dried hops were carried in long sacks called 'hop pockets'. So 'pokes' went into, and 'pockets' came out of, the Oast House.

Hop pokes were made of a coarse, sacking-type material. In many areas they were brightly coloured, for identification purposes, to show their place of origin. This was necessary, particularly in some parts of Kent where a large Oast House complex containing several kilns all grouped together, belonging to a number of different farmers, serviced hop gardens from a wide area.

Each poke carried ten bushels, the equivalent of two full Tally baskets at the hop garden. But since the hops were lightly packed, following the 'hovering up' process at the hop garden, and not pressed in tightly, hop pokes were not heavy. They could be handled with ease. A farm wagon could carry an impressive-looking load of these large sacks, the limiting factor in determining the maximum load being one of space rather than weight.

Great care was taken, however, in the handling and stacking of the hop pokes, to prevent any crushing of the valuable crop. Everybody along the line was drilled in the need not to 'squash up' the hops.

A full hop poke had a great deal of 'seat-appeal'. It looked comfortable and felt nice and soft. So now and again some unsuspecting visitors plonked down on one to rest their weary feet awhile. Once spotted, though, they soon got up again—and did so much faster than they sat down. They were left in no doubt that a hop poke was not for sitting on!

This information invariably came to them in plain English, from a member of the Oast House staff. Normally polite and good-natured, they were inclined to get very annoyed if somebody wantonly damaged the precious hops. Occasionally their concern for the welfare of the hops and their irate reaction to somebody maltreating them, rebounded. A somewhat pompous, portly little man, who happened to have influential connections with the brewers, complained to the management. He didn't like the way he had been 'spoken to'. When he had sat down on a hop poke he was told to get off it in a manner to which he strongly objected. The graphic instruction was unequivocal. Bellowed across the floor from the far side of the Oast in a stentorian voice, the words were,

"Get your fat arse off that hop poke, you bloody idiot!"

The Oast worker was subsequently quietly complimented by his employer for his concern over the hops, but told to be more respectful to visitors in the future.

Fresh hops emptied out of the arriving pokes were spread out to a depth of up to two feet on the drying bed above the furnace in the kiln. Lightweight broad shovels called scuppets were employed in the Oast for moving hops around. They had a wooden frame which supported a working 'blade' made of canvas or hessian. This lightweight design ensured that the hops were not damaged when shovelled about. A scuppet acted as a scoop rather than a shovel.

Once on the drying bed the hops were 'hovered up', often by the use of a four-tined wooden fork. The tines were flat and blunt-ended. Using this gently and carefully, the hops were eased up to give a very loose layer. The object was to achieve maximum space between the hops for circulation of the rising hot air from the fire below, to give efficient drying of the load.

After several hours during which they were inspected at intervals by the dryer, he would at length declare them ready for turning. The drying bed itself, sometimes known as the 'staddle', was made of stout wooden slats or laths, spaced about half-an-inch apart. This platform was covered by an 'oast mat'. These special horse-hair mats were designed to allow hot air to pass through them freely. The unusual material was chosen because it was not damaged by heat, nor did it give off fumes to pollute the hops.

Once methodically turned using the scuppets and hovered up again by the flat-bladed forks, the hops needed about two further hours of drying time. When the dryer finally declared them ready, rakes were used to move the dried hops off the mat, to be taken out and onto the wooden cooling floor. A new load of hops was then spread on the drying bed. This process went on night and day throughout the four weeks or so of the hop picking period.

Most of the wooden floor area of the upper storey of the Oast was given over to the cooling operation. Loads from the kiln were shifted on to the floor in a systematic fashion so that each load had its correct total treatment. Experience over the long history of hop processing had shown that this cooling stage was important to the final quality of the finished product.

No stage in the sequence of treatments was arbitrary and just left to chance. The dryer saw to that. If good at his job, he was adept at judging the quality of the hops by feel, smell and general appearance. This is why the post of dryer was such an important one, and good experienced dryers were much valued by growers and brewers alike.

In his time Timothy Twylock had been outstandingly good, and, because of the way legendary figures gain rather than lose in prestige as the years pass, his standards came to be regarded as the epitome of the dryer's art.

On arrival from the hop garden freshly picked hops had a moisture content of between 65% and 85% by weight. On coming off the drying bed of the kiln, the moisture content was down to between 5% and 15%, but this level was not uniform throughout the mass of hops. Part of the hours hops spent spread out on the cooling floor was to allow their moisture content to equalize at a level of approximately 10%, which was judged to be about the optimum level for storage and handling purposes. Too high a moisture content and they would rot; too low and they would be too brittle so that they would be in danger of breaking down into fragments and dust when handled.

When fit to leave the cooling floor the hops were now safe from danger due to crushing, which previously would have led to decaying and spoiling. On the contrary the next stage was one which involved deliberately pressing and crushing the hops into storage sacks. These large cylindrical 'hop pockets' were from six to eight feet long and about two feet in diameter.

The requirement for proper care of the hops after drying was exactly opposite to that for the freshly picked hops. Crushing the fresh hops spoiled their quality, but conversely the preservation of the dried hops depended upon their being tightly compressed into a closely compacted mass. This prevented the intake of water vapour from the air. Dampness would have led to bacteriological decay and destructive rotting. A sniff of mildew from a hop pocket would indicate that its contents were useless to the brewer, and the lot would have to be dumped.

A press was needed to force the dried hops into this necessary compacted mass. The compression was achieved by a special machine called a hop press. An empty hop pocket was suspended in the machine with its mouth stretched open. The open neck of the hop pocket was conveniently arranged to be at floor level on the upper cooling floor of the Oast, and its body hung down from the ceiling of the ground floor, supported in a U-shaped sling.

Hops from the cooling floor were scooped into the open neck of the pocket using scuppets. At intervals, filling was interrupted while the press was used to force the hops hard down into the long pocket. Turning the handle of the large driving wheel of the press drove a flat metal disc, mounted on a rod, down into the pocket. The disc acted like a piston just fitting the cylindrical-shaped pocket.

Periodically, as filling progressed, the press was used. At length the strong pockets were tightly filled with closely compacted hops. When full of this solid mass of hops, the pocket's neck was sewn up, leaving two ears of the close woven sacking material to function as carrying-handles when the hop pockets were moved around.

A full hop pocket weighed between one and two hundredweights. An eight-foot-long, two-foot diameter sack, of this weight, was not easy to handle. When possible the full hop pockets were moved about on long trolleys. They were lifted by an overhead winch when it was necessary to move them off ground level and up on to the back of the brewer's transport vehicle.

The latter was sometimes a lorry, and sometimes a brewer's dray, pulled by the well-known brewer's Shire horses.

Brewer's draymen took a great pride in their horses and wagons. The sturdy Shire horses, with their distinctive, long-haired manes and fetlocks, were always well groomed. Their harnesses were well greased on the underside to keep the leather supple, then treated with saddle soap on the outside to keep the surface in prime condition and to impart a sheen to it. Regularly inspected, the harness was kept in immaculate repair by local skilled men like Bill the saddler, working under contract to the brewers.

To add to their impressive appearance, polished brasses and, often, coloured ribbons decorated the harness. Sometimes small, jingling bells hanging from the harness gave an added attraction, and warned of their coming.

Normally the draymen were employed delivering barrels of beer to the pubs and returning to the brewery with the empties. Fetching hops from the Oast House was a welcome change of routine for them.

Fully loaded with their normal deliveries of barrels of beer and crates of bottled beer, a brewer's dray was a very heavy load indeed. A pair of horses harnessed side by side was usually used. Of all working horses these magnificent brewer's Shires were often said to be among the best-treated horses of all. The whole outfit was a travelling advertisement for the brewers and most people would always pause in their activities to watch them go by.

It would have done a brewer's sales of beer no good at all if these much-loved, powerful but gentle horses were ever seen to be badly treated in any way. And on a hot day, the mere sight of the stacked barrels of beer was enough to stimulate an urgent thirst and often inspired people to pop into their local pub for a 'quick one'.

Very different, but of much interest—especially to small boys—were the chuffing Foden steam lorries sometimes used by brewers for beer deliveries. These had a very fast acceleration and ran smoothly. They did, however, puff out steam and smoke which made horse-pulled drays or petrol-driven lorries preferable for the collection of hop-pockets from Oast Houses. Any unwanted exposure to steam-borne smells could soon be picked up and absorbed by the dry hops and finish up tainting the taste of the beer, so care was needed to get the valuable, carefully-processed hops safely to the brewer's premises.

At the time when Ben Skinner was Tallyman in the hop garden, his opposite number in the Oast House was Arthur Marchant.

Arthur followed in the tradition of Timothy Twylock as dryer-in-charge. In a way it could fairly be said that his skills were directly attributable to the legendary master because they were handed down from one generation to the next. For his part, Timothy Twylock's expertise had been founded on the great deal of know-how passed on to him from earlier generations.

Somehow, to Arthur, it always seemed as though all things stemmed from Timothy Twylock. This was because history in the Oast seemed to start from the dreadful, abrupt end of the Master Dryer's life. Nobody ever referred back in time beyond this day. The men who manned the Oast immediately after his death went out of their way to do things as they knew he would have insisted they were done, had he still have been there. This started a tendency to refer to him in times of difficulty and ask the question "What would Timothy Twylock have done, to cope with this?"

Those who subsequently joined the team in later years were soon aware of this. In a curious but understandable way, Timothy Twylock became the original source of all hop-drying and Oast House management wisdom so far as future generations were concerned, at least in this particular Oast. The combination of his high reputation when alive, and the manner of his sudden death, resulted in him leaving his inimitable stamp upon the Oast for as long as it remained standing.

After the always very busy daylight hours, it was customary, in the more leisurely late evening hours, to welcome small parties of visitors to join the Oast House team around the fire. Such visitors were often relatives bringing along friends who particularly wanted to have a look and see what went on in an Oast House. Quite often they were attracted in the first place by stories they had heard of the cosy, yet a bit creepy feel of the Oast in the dead of night.

Usually, before it got too dark, they would have a look over the premises and were told of the various operations involved in the drying and packing of hops. Then they would settle down to sit on sundry boxes, baskets and benches around the stoking-hole of the brightly-glowing kiln fire, to enjoy the traditional refreshments.

Always available were baked potatoes, 'done to a turn' by cooking them in the hot ashes beneath the kiln fire. These were eaten with plenty of fresh farm butter and salt.

As for drink, there was beer or cider drawn from the inviting barrels propped up on their trestles.

No baked potato ever tasted better, nor glass of beer or cider more refreshing, than those consumed in the cosy-feeling, conspiratorial-like environment of the Oast at night. The so-much enjoyed refreshments and the inevitable swapping of yarns that followed, was what was remembered most in later years.

Arthur and his small team of men always looked forward to these social evenings, which brought a little light relief to their successive days and nights of work at the Oast. Sometimes they felt a bit like monks, cloistered in their rather cavernous and eerie buildings. Nights could seem very long, and to have visitors around, often until well after midnight, shortened the spell in a pleasant way. And now and again these get-togethers gave rise to extra-special occasions long talked about in later years.

Before the current hop picking season had started, Percy the cobbler and his mate Taffy the woodcutter, had asked permission to be allowed to bring along their hop picking lady friends, Glad and Clara from Camden Town, to see the Oast one evening.

Arthur readily agreed to this. He could see some fun arising from the visit. From time to time in the interim period he turned over in his mind, with increasing anticipatory glee, tentative plans to make the projected visit a really entertaining and memorable one.

In due course a date was made for the first Friday evening of the hop picking season. By coincidence, this was fifty years ago to the very day since Timothy Twylock had plunged to his untimely death at the Oast. The realisation that this macabre anniversary was coming up had planted the germ of an idea in Arthur's mind. It was a readymade opportunity for Arthur and his cronies to line up something a bit special for the amorous cobbler and his party.

A great deal of careful planning went into the preparation for this important evening visit. The occasion warranted something out of the ordinary, if only to honour the memory of the Oast's most famous dryer.

In the event they did their respected predecessor proud. So well did the evening go that they created another legend, a fitting sequel to the fifty-year-old legend of Timothy Twylock, Master-Dryer of the Littlebrook Oast House.

Chapter 10

AN EVENING VISIT TO THE HAUNTED OAST HOUSE

Motty unwittingly sets the scene

As arranged, Percy, Taffy, Glad and Clara duly arrived at the Oast House on Friday evening of the first week of hop picking. They reached there shortly before 10pm as instructed by Arthur. At this time Arthur and his team were scheduled to take a break and would be able to enjoy the company of the visitors. Little did Percy and his friends know that the occasion was to be one they would remember for the rest of their lives.

Arthur welcomed his visitors warmly and proceeded to show them over the Oast. As was logical they started where the hops came into the Oast House and saw the latest batch of full hop pokes that had arrived that afternoon, stacked by the upper-floor doorway. When this 'door in the wall' was opened to show them, they stood on the ledge to look down on the yard below where the farm carts from the hop garden pulled up. Above their heads, under the ridged, porch-like roof which projected out above the door, was the large pulley wheel with its hook-ended chain that was used both to haul up the pokes off the carts, and also to load the much heavier hop pockets from the ground floor up on to the brewery vehicles.

As always with visitors, the kiln with its glowing furnace was the main attraction. This was, after all, where the main action took place. It was the heart of the Oast House.

Arthur shepherded the group up the short flight of broad wooden steps which led into the kiln from the upper-floor area. On arrival inside the round walls of the kiln tower they stood for a while in silence, looking around the unfamiliar place with much interest.

Standing on the walkway that extended round the tower by the brick wall, they saw the deep layer of lightly-packed hops that was spread all over the 'oast mat'. The mat covered the closely-slatted drying-bed and the heated hops gave off a very strong, fresh, fragrant smell which they sniffed appreciatively. This pleasant smell permeated the entire Oast House and was immediately noticed by people visiting the Oast when they first stepped inside the building. It was a more concentrated version of the smell of the hop garden itself.

Standing there in the kiln, beneath the cowl high above their heads at the apex of the inward-sloping conical walls, with the heat from the glowing furnace under the drying-bed causing an up-draught of hot air through the hops, was a unique experience. It was thought-provoking. Enveloped as they were in the stifling, humid, atmosphere, suspended, so it seemed, between the dimly seen cowl above and the strongly burning fire below, made it a rather claustrophobic place in which to be. It was a strange, somewhat unreal world. Visitors, conscious of the furnace below, found themselves wondering how strong the slatted floor beneath the oast-mat was, and stepped backwards involuntarily to get close to the wall.

It was at this point in the tour that Arthur re-told the story of the tragic death of Timothy Twylock. In this unusual and impressive environment he did not need to be an accomplished raconteur to generate an intense interest. Told as it had actually happened fifty years ago, with no embellishments, the picture it evoked was awesome enough.

In their mind's eye, each of those with him could see a man hurtling down from the cowl high above, past where they now stood, to smash straight through the two-foot thick carpet of hops, carrying the slatted floor with him, to end his days consumed in the furnace below.

This dreadful vision planted the first uncomfortable awareness of the presence in the old building of an aura of bygone tragedy and drama. It set the scene for what was to follow and put the minds of the visitors into a highly receptive state. Thinking about it afterwards, Arthur—who was much more of an enlightened gardener than a perceptive psychologist—thought it had been a bit like raking up rich, highly fertile soil into a fine tilth to make it just right to sow seeds in. At the time he observed the thoughtful silence of his visitors as they stood looking around them thinking of the tragic death of the unfortunate man, and knew his planned evening had got off to the good start he wanted.

Moving back down the steps the group walked between the long, parallel beds of already-dried hops spread out on the cooling-room floor. These separated beds corresponded to successive batches of hops that had been processed in the kiln and now lay waiting until they were judged ready by Arthur to be loaded, via the hop press, into hop pockets.

Following a long-established practice, each person was given a small bag of dried hops as a memento of their visit to the Oast. Some people liked to keep these small bags of hops under their pillows at night, because not only did they like the smell of hops, but—as a bonus—this fragrance was said to be sleep-inducing. Years later they still retained their inimitable smell, much to the delight of people who came across these small bags of hops when rummaging about, turning out long-forgotten bits and pieces from drawers, cupboards, and sundry boxes of treasures stored away in the home.

After looking at the hops being scooped into a hop pocket, which was fitted—neck held widely opened—in the press, and watching the press at work for a while, the group moved to the ground floor beneath them where the partially-filled hop pocket hung suspended in its sling. It was a convenient way of packing the hops and moving them to the ground-floor, in one operation.

Standing upright, closely packed against one another, were full hop pockets awaiting collection by the brewer. They looked like tall, ram-rod stiff soldiers on parade, standing shoulder to shoulder in ranks. Thumping one with his large fist, Taffy—who fancied himself as a boxer—commented to Arthur,

"One of these, hung from the ceiling, would a make a bloody good punch bag."

Taffy was right. The closely-compacted mass of hops in the long, two-foot diameter tube, was resilient and would have stood a great deal of thumping. Arthur however, didn't like the idea at all!

"If you don't mind, Taffy," he said unsmilingly, "I'd rather you didn't thump those bags around like that. Those hops are worth money. There are plenty of things you can stuff into punch bags to bash about with those great fists of yours. It wouldn't make much sense to use valuable dried hops for a daft purpose like that!"

"Sorry, Arthur," muttered Taffy, suitably abashed. "I ought to have known better. I've often thought when I've seen them around that they looked as though they would make good punch bags. Seeing them close up like this, I just clouted one without thinking."

"It's all right, Taffy," said Arthur, with a wan smile. "It's just that we take so much trouble preparing the hops from the time they come in here to the time they go out, it goes against the grain to let anybody bash the pockets about. We like to see them go out of the Oast looking perfect."

Following this gentle reprimand, and having now finished their tour of the premises, the group made their way into the area in front of the kiln fire and settled themselves comfortably on the assortment of improvised seats put there for them.

Not long afterwards they were all thoroughly enjoying baked potatoes, along with either a glass of beer, or of cider, according to their choice.

There was a general sense of well-being among the group with Arthur and his mates swapping yarns with Percy, Taffy, Glad and Clara.

Without much prompting from Arthur, in the flickering light from the fire, against the dimly lit background of the space around them, the talk soon turned to the reputation of the Oast House as being haunted.

"Do you honestly believe," asked Clara, "that this Oast House really is haunted?"

"I know damn well it is!" responded Tubby Brightside, a veteran member of the Oast's staff, vehemently. "If you spent night after night in here, like we do, you would soon know that it's haunted too! There's no doubt about that!"

"You would an' all!" broke in Tubby's close friend and fellow veteran Oast-hand, Mike Buss. "I'll tell you what, I don't know many blokes who would volunteer to stay in this place on his own all night long! Especially in winter time. It's bad enough in here at hop picking time with the fire going strong and other blokes in here with you, and work going on all round you. Even then I don't mind admitting I'm sometimes scared stiff when the ghosts that live in here, or come visiting, are up and about. There's plenty goes on in this place that only spooks could make happen—strange, unnatural things."

"There is that!" confirmed Arthur, emphatically. "The place is haunted right enough, that's for sure. Dogs will soon tell you so, if you don't believe me! You try and bring a dog in here—especially at night time. I've never known a dog yet that would come in here without being dragged in—whining and slinking—with its tail tucked right back up between its legs. Dogs know, dogs do. They've got a sixth-sense. Instinct tells them when spirits are about. Dogs can smell better than we can. Nobody argues about that. And they can sense unnatural things better than we can, too. Fair gives you the willies it does, having a dog howl its head off in here at night. Scares us all worse than ever that does, I can tell you. Isn't that right, Tubby?"

"Too true it is," responded Tubby. "I've seen blokes having to drag dogs in here by their leads, many a time. Scared stiff they are, no matter how big and fierce they may be. Howl and carry-on something awful in here, they do. Makes it worse for us, that does, to see a great strong dog quivering with fright and covering its arse-hole up with its tail so spooks can't sniff around at it. That's a dog's way of trying to hide up. Sure sign of fear that is when a dog shuts its arse-hole down to a stranger. Just the opposite to raising its tail when it welcomes a friendly visitor to have a sniff. There's nothing a dog's master can do to stop it being scared, either. Even somebody like Cecil, the gamekeeper, for all his control over his dogs! Even he can't do a thing with them when in here, try as he might! And if that doesn't prove there are ghosts in here, then I don't know what does!"

"And cats too," contributed Will Tweddle, who at twenty-four years of age was the youngest member of Arthur's team. "You never see a cat in here. Never! Even if mice were queuing-up waiting to be eaten, a cat wouldn't come in here. Not even if it was starving, it wouldn't!"

This remark caused a laugh from the group, which interrupted Will's remarks. He wasn't joking though, or so it seemed, because he frowned and rounded on them straightaway.

"Ah! You might laugh!" he said earnestly. "So did Old Motty laugh when we told him about the cats. Motty said he knew the place was haunted right enough. But he reckoned his black cat Bob wouldn't be afraid. Motty says cats can put up with ghosts much better than dogs can. That's why witches use cats, especially black ones, for their spooky work, so he says. So he said we could borrow his cat Bob for a night or two to catch some mice for us. We were having a lot of trouble with them.

Well, he carried his cat down here one night, about two years ago it would be now. He brought it in here about nine o'clock that night to leave it with us, like he said he would. He carried it in here and when he put it down on the floor its hair all stood up on end, like the bristles on a dandy-brush. Scared out of its life, the old tom cat was. Terrible to see it was! Pitiful, I thought! Then, quick as a flash it bolted out of the door, and cleared off like a mad thing. Nowhere to be seen afterwards, it wasn't. And when old Motty got home, about two hours later, there was his cat, hiding in his toolshed, still shivering and scared out of its wits. Like Arthur said, some animals have got a sixth-sense. That cat knew all right!"

"Is he pulling our legs, Arthur?" said Percy.

"No, he's certainly not having you on," replied Arthur with conviction. "Old Motty quite thought his cat could put up with the ghosts in here. He said afterwards that the spirits in here must be mighty powerful ones to frighten his moggy like that. He says it was probably because Timothy Twylock would never allow cats in the Oast House. They say he reckoned there was nothing worse than cat's piss to destroy the goodness of hops. So Motty says it must have been Timothy Twylock's spirit in here that was so angry when the cat was brought in that the cat felt his presence real powerful-like. Makes sense, when you come to think about it. But Motty said it was the first time he'd known his old tom cat scared by ghosts, though he'd seen a good many of them in his time."

"Yes, if ever a place was haunted, this place is," commented Tubby. "There's no doubt about that. But if you don't believe us you can ask Old Motty himself. He's coming down presently, isn't he, Arthur?"

"He's supposed to be," answered Arthur. "He should be here soon, if he's coming at all. I reckon it's nigh on time for the pubs to chuck out now. He said he was going to the King George tonight, so he hasn't got far to walk. That's if he managed to get there in the first place. You can never be sure with him. Depends on how his back is. He's been having a bit of trouble lately. But apart from that, the old boy keeps pretty fit, considering his age. He must be knocking on a bit now."

"How old is he, Arthur?" asked Will.

"Nobody seems to know," replied Arthur. "He says he doesn't remember! He doesn't want to, if you ask me! Pretty well ninety, some say."

Pulling his much prized old timepiece out of the front pocket of his corded trousers by the long brass chain that secured it, Arthur checked the time.

"Yes," he said. "It's turned eleven o'clock. You'll probably hear the old blighter tap-tapping his way along here any moment now. I expect he'll make it. He doesn't miss the chance of a glass or two of free beer if he can help it! He likes his beer. Says the doctor told him it's what keeps him fit!"

"Knows a thing or two about ghosts and spirits, and things like that, Old Motty does, don't he, Arthur?" commented Tubby getting back to the subject.

"Yeah," replied Arthur, nodding his head thoughtfully. "They reckon he knows more than anybody in these parts for miles around, about things like that. More than Parson Yelman even. Old Motty knows more than the Parson does about spirits, so it's said. And they're not joking either. All the time he's spent in the churchyard, on his own, with only the dead to keep him company, has given him a bit of a sixth sense, the same as dogs and cats have. And he reckons some spirits talk to him, too. Talk straight into his mind when they speak. No sound at all, so he says. Yet he says he can still recognise the sound of somebody's voice. It all goes straight into his mind. Weird, isn't it!"

Arthur paused for a few moments to let this curious information sink in. Then he went on, much to the interest of those around him.

"Old Motty has many a talk with one or another of them, so he told me, according to who happens to be around the place when he's working there. They've kind of learnt to let him know what they want to say by whispering at him—right up inside his head—so he reckons. Gives you the creeps, just thinking about it, doesn't it! But he's so used to it, he thinks nothing of it. Nothing at all. Some people don't believe him, I know. But I wouldn't be too sure, I wouldn't. I've known too many times when he's been proved right, in the queer things he says. He's got special powers, there seems no doubt about that. Lots of people believe that, especially those who've known him a long time. They've learnt not to laugh-off what he says."

"Talk of the Devil! Here he comes now!" interrupted Taffy, who was nearest the door.

Conversation stopped, and all heads turned towards the door. From outside came the sound of Motty's voice, talking to his little dog Pug. They could hear the dog making a queer, whining, whimpering noise, not at all like the usual eager yapping normally associated with the perky little dog. Pug was one of those dogs that seemed to enjoy every minute of the day when they were out and about with their owners. But Pug clearly was not at all happy at the moment.

"All right! All right, dang you!" came Motty's voice. "I ain't a-goin' to make you go inside 'ere again. That I ain't. I knows you don't trust the spooks in 'ere. Not that they would 'urt you. I'll tie you up to this 'ere post 'ere. You can stay outside while I goes in for a bit. You'll be safe enough out 'ere, old mate. And 'ere's a couple of your fav'rite dog biscuit bones for you to crunch at. Brought them with me special I did 'cos I know you'd not like it at this place. That'll keep you 'appy for a bit. And sharpen-up your teeth for tomorrer's rattin' as well!"

Moments later the door opened and Old Motty, bent over at his usual forward-slanting angle, supported by his stout stick, came shuffling into the Oast.

Pausing in his stride he lifted his head up to gaze all around at the assembly.

"Evenin' all!" he said, cheerfully. "Cor lummy duck. You look as though you're doing all right. If ever a place looked cosy like, this old place does in 'ere! Right cosy you all looks to me!"

"Glad you could come, Motty," said Arthur. "Come and sit down over here and make yourself comfortable."

Thankfully Motty lowered himself down to sit on the upturned box prepared for him by Arthur, and was soon enjoying a long contented swig at the pint of beer passed to him. In no time at all the glass was empty.

"Cor! That goes down well, that does! Lovely," sighed Motty, thrusting this glass towards Arthur. "Beer don't come no better than that. Fill 'er up again, mate, will yer please. I've got a right sharp thirst tonight. An' that's a bit of good stuff they've dished you up with there, Arthur, that it is! Bit of the best that is!"

Motty was only too well aware that, by courtesy of the brewers, a plentiful supply of free beer was available at the Oast House each year during hop picking time. He had never been known to miss a visit to the Oast during this time of plenty, every year. And he usually contrived to show up at least once a week while the Oast was operational. But he was always a welcome visitor because he never failed to entertain the team working there.

Once he was settled down, furnished with another full glass, the conversation resumed where it had left off when he arrived.

"Been talking about the ghosts in the Oast here, Motty," said Arthur, to get matters rolling again. "These ladies here were asking if the place really is haunted."

"Not 'arf it ain't," spoke up Motty emphatically, his tone leaving no room for doubt. "Not 'arf! Ask my dog Pug out there if you don't believe me. He knows right enough. Dogs knows, dogs does. Poor little bugger's scared stiff just to be near the door, let alone be inside 'ere along with us. Shit 'imself 'e would if I made 'im come in 'ere!"

"They've been saying dogs can sense these things," said Glad, impressed by the conviction in the old man's voice. "We thought we heard your dog whimpering out there, as though something was upsetting it."

"They're quite right," confirmed Motty. "No doubt about it at all. Dogs can tell if spirits are about. They knows when ghosts are near them. But they can't see them, leastways we don't think they can, no more'n we can most times. That's what puts the shits up them. They knows they be there, but they can't see them."

"Do you think they can smell them?" asked Glad.

"No, I don't think so," replied Motty, a bit doubtfully. "Leastways they don't go sniffing around for them. Once spirits are about dogs don't do anything 'cept look scared stiff. Course the stink might be so powerful like, that they don't need to sniff. But I don't think they smell 'em out. I think they just knows they're there!"

Motty paused, and then it seemed his memory had been jogged about something, because he changed tack a bit.

"Reminds me of something," he said, looking across at Arthur. "Old Mac up at "The Buffs" was telling me only the other day about an 'aunted beer cellar under a pub at Sheerness on the Isle of Sheppey."

"Was that the "Ancient Britain" where he used to be before he came to Littlebrook?" interrupted Mike.

"No. It wasn't 'is pub," said Motty. "It was one not far from 'is, though. More an 'otel than a pub it was, I think. Leastways it was called an 'otel. The Regal 'otel I think Mac said, so far as I remember."

"More like the "Royal Hotel", I should think," interjected Tubby. "I've heard of one of that name somewhere up Sheppey way."

"Could 'ave been. I can't be sure," said Motty. "Anyway, Mac says the landlord there 'ad a big powerful dog—a Labrador, so Mac said. And there was no way 'is dog could be got down into the cellar. A funny, very low-ceilinged place it was, so Mac says, where they kept their beer and wine and things. Only about six feet of 'eadroom there was down there, and it was supposed to 'ave been connected to a smugglers' tunnel that led right down to the sea. The landlord showed Old Mac 'ow 'is dog carried on when he tried to get 'im to go down there. Pulled 'im down the wooden steps, 'e did, and the poor bleedin' dog nearly died of fright. All 'is 'air stood up on end along 'is neck and back. Old Mac felt sorry for the dog. Seemed cruel to Mac, it did, making the dog go through that just to prove the place was 'aunted."

"Could people feel anything?" asked Glad, clearly very intrigued by Motty's story.

"Mac says so," answered Motty. "Said it felt kind of creepy and wrong somehow down there, not warm, safe, and friendly, like 'is cellar is. Seems a sailor in the bar one night said it was all bullshit about the 'aunted cellar, so 'is mates bet 'im 'e wouldn't go down there on 'is own and stay there five minutes with the door shut on 'im. When they let 'im out 'is face was white as a sheet and 'is 'air was all a-standing on end, same as the landlord's dog used to be. Course 'is mates laughed their 'eads off at the sight of 'im. Told 'im 'e looked like a bloody whitewashed 'edge'og, they did. Scared the landlord proper! The Navy bloke looked so bad the landlord thought 'e was going to pass out on 'im. Snuff it like, there and then, from 'eart attack. Never allowed anybody else to try that lark again, 'e didn't. Too dangerous. Could 'ave 'ad somebody die of fright down there!"

"I must ask him about that," commented Arthur, interested in the story, which was quite new to him. "I'd like to hear more about that."

"Yeah, you do that," urged Motty. "Mac knows a lot about that 'aunted beer cellar. Plenty of proofs there were from local people about the ghosts in that cellar, accordin' to Mac. Seems a Sheerness paper once tried to get some photographs down there. But the spooks wouldn't 'ave none of that. They wouldn't allow the flashlight things they use to go off proper. Time after time they tried. And time after time they were like damp squibs on a firework night. In the end they gave up. The landlord said that the most scary place was one end where the cellar went off into a long room like the start of a blocked-off tunnel. As black as the ace of spades it was down there. And very cold! Uncommon cold! Sort of chilled your bones it did, so 'e said. Seems the ghosts didn't want that part lit up by a bright light, so some'ow or other the bloke with the camera couldn't get things to work proper. The spooks used their powers to bugger it all up for 'im. Gives you the creeps, don't it, to think o' that!

"An' I tell yer somethin' else," Motty went on, his keen old eyes moving from one to the other of them as they all sat gazing at him. "Some days the ghost played merry 'ell down there in the cellar. Banged about 'e did, an' tipped things over. An' the beer didn't pull up proper. The Landlord said 'e knew the ghost was upset about somethin', though course 'e didn't know what it were. So 'e used to stand a pint of beer in a glass on a barrel down there, afore 'e went to bed. That used to calm 'im down and the fuss stopped".

"Did the ghost drink the beer, then?" grinned Mike.

"In a manner of speakin', 'e did," answered Motty. "The glass was always empty in the morning, the landlord told Mac. But the beer was in a puddle on the floor and the glass moved to another place. Seems the ghost tipped the beer down 'is neck like, but o'course there bein' nothin' to 'im the beer ran straight through an' landed on the floor. But it must 'ave pleased the ghost 'cos 'e stopped sodding about an' things settled down again!"

There was a burst of laughter at this little story, and meanwhile Motty had a good swig of his beer. Then he got back to the business of the Oast House.

"But this old Oast we're in," he said, looking at the visitors, "this 'ere old Oast is the most 'aunted place for many a mile around, this is. Always 'as been 'aunted so far as I knows. My old Grandfather used to talk about it. 'E worked in 'ere 'e did. An' that's a-goin' back a piece, that is, ain't it?"

"Yeah! That certainly is getting back a bit, that is, Motty," observed Taffy with a smirk. "Ancient history that would be. Bloody ancient if it was in your Grandad's time!"

Motty glowered at him. He was never too happy about Taffy, who often made fun of him if he were allowed to get away with it. Once again Taffy had got his little needling dig in.

"Not so ainshun' that I didn't know 'im though, Taffy," Motty countered, with no time lost in thinking. "One thing's for sure, that's more'n you can say! You wouldn't be able to remember *your* Grandfather, not with what little brains you've got, pickled in whisky like they are. Nobody ever did know where the 'ell you came from anyway, not so far as I know. Born up in a tree, I shouldn't wonder. And chucked down like a rotten apple as soon as your mother saw you. Brought up as a baby by a bare-arsed baboon, I 'spect you were—judging by the smell of you!"

The laugh which followed restored Motty's equilibrium, at the expense of Taffy, who looked a little uncomfortable. It wasn't the first time he had got back more than he gave from Motty, old though the bent and bushy-bearded old graveyard goof was!

Motty, after a final glare at Taffy, continued his comments about the Oast House.

"People say," he went on, "that the 'auntin' in 'ere got a might of a lot worse after Timothy Twylock got killed in 'ere. I knows that's true, too. An it's wot you would expect, too. Just wot you would expect!"

"Why's that, Mr. Marsh?" intervened Clara, looking intensely interested. "Why would you expect it?"

"Cos 'e was 'appy in 'ere. 'E liked it 'ere, that's why," answered Motty. "Now 'e can't keep away from 'ere, yer see. Can't keep away 'e can't now 'e's dead. And of course, 'e brings 'is ghost mates along 'ere with 'im sometimes. Gets proper crowded with ghosts in 'ere then it does. Sort of meeting place for spirits this Oast is. Encourages 'em all in, 'e does, 'specially at 'op picking time. Proud of the Oast 'e was. Always showed people round this time of year 'e did. Now 'e shows spirits round. Just because they be dead don't mean they're not interested. Course they are. Same as you are."

"I see," said Clara. "I can understand that. This is where he would wish to be. I can see that."

"Yes," continued Motty. "Tim likes to see the 'ops drying each year. I knows that. Cos that was 'is life after all, weren't it? Checks up all the time, so they say. And puts things right sometimes, so I understand from spirits wot knows 'im well. When things goes wrong 'e gets thoughts into the 'eads of the blokes wot work in 'ere so's they knows wot's wot an' does wot 'e wants 'em to, to put things right. Course they don't know 'e does it. Gets all cocky like, they does. Thinks they're doing it all themselves, they does. Timothy Twylock don't mind that, though, 'e don't mind it one little bit. Just so long as the 'ops are looked after. That's all 'e cares about. Natchrull that is, when you thinks about it. Cos 'ops and 'op dryin' was 'is life!"

The apparent doubt cast upon their own abilities to manage in the Oast without help from a ghost did not pass unnoticed by the experts present. But it passed without comment.

Arthur, who was, after all, the dryer-in-charge, and the one most implicated by this angle, was not in the least bit concerned about any loss of face he might have suffered as a result of it. Far from it. He could hardly contain his excitement because Motty, quite by chance and good fortune, was inadvertently playing right into their hands. He was creating exactly the right atmosphere. Setting the scene very nicely for the evening's entertainment they had planned. Things couldn't be going better!

"You actually worked with Timothy Twylock, didn't you, Motty?" prompted Arthur, apparently with genuine, innocent interest.

"That I did!" said Motty. "And there ain't many blokes left as can say that either," he added with evident pride. "I was a bin-man in the 'op garden at the time 'e was killed. Out in the 'op garden at the very time, I was. Knowed 'im well, I did. And proud I am to say so too! Right proud, that I am. Best dryer in the 'ole o' Kent, so they used to say, Timothy Twylock was. Best of the lot, so 'twas said. An' there ain't been another one like 'im since, nor ever will be, most people say. Not never, ever, so 'tis said."

"Do you know how many years ago it was when he was killed, Motty?" asked Arthur, now bang on track and steering things along with consummate care.

"Not 'zactly," replied Motty. "Seems a long long time ago, that's all I knows. 'Arf a lifetime or more ago, I'd say!"

"Well, I'll tell you," said Arthur. "I worked it out a few weeks ago looking at the old Oast House Ledgers. Fifty year ago, Motty! That's when it was! Fifty years ago to this very night! The first hop picking Friday in the year 1876 was the day. And what's more, Timothy Twylock was 50 years old almost to the day. He got killed just two days after his 50th birthday. So if he were alive today, he would be almost 100 years old."

Motty looked very thoughtful. The information made quite a profound impact upon him.

"Cor lummy duck!" he said, with some feeling. "Fifty years ago this very day, was it? An' he'd be one hundred year old if he still lived. That makes today more'n a bit special, don't it? This 'ere day today's 'is 50th die-day as you might say, an' near enough 'is 100th birthday. Then I wouldn't mind bettin' 'is ghost is in this 'ere Oast House at this very minute. Sure to be! Ain't no doubt about that! No doubt at all! Tim wouldn't miss this day, stands to reason, don't it? No matter wot else 'e 'as on this week, 'e wouldn't miss bein' 'ere today, now would 'e? 'E's in 'ere somewhere this very minute, Bound to be! Stands to reason! 'Spect 'e's up there above us a-lookin' at the 'ops dryin' on the Oast mat. That's where 'e'll be. Just up there above our 'eads as we sit 'ere a-talkin' right now!"

There followed a short silence while the group around Motty dwelt upon the implications of what he had said. One or two of them looked around uneasily, shivering slightly despite the heat from the fire as they stared into shadowy spaces beyond the moving edges of the flickering light.

Glad and Clara had been listening to the conversation with close interest. The strange old man who spoke with such apparent conviction, had gripped their attention.

"Mr Marsh," ventured Glad, with some timidity, "how do you know that Timothy Twylock's spirit comes in here? An' how do you know he puts thoughts into people's heads?"

"Cos 'e told me so 'imself. That's 'ow," answered Motty; which seemed to him to be reason enough for anybody.

Glad looked puzzled, but Tubby came to her rescue.

"I expect you talk to him round in the churchyard, don't you, Motty?" he said, by way of clarification.

"That I do, every now and again," replied Motty. When 'e's there, that is."

Percy burst into laughter at this, and saw an opportunity to be funny, at Motty's expense.

"As he's buried there, he's always there, isn't he Motty? I can't see how he can wander far away from there! A bit kind of 'shut in' isn't he? Stuck there like!"

These comments raised a laugh from the company, but Motty bridled at this assertion and came straight back to put Percy in his place.

"You may know all about mend'ng boots and bloody shoes, Percy, but you know bugger-all about dead people an' spirits, that's for sure you don't. When you puts a dead man's body in 'is grave, that don't box 'is spirit up, down there along with 'is bones!" Surprised you should be so daft as to think so, Percy! I 'spect you think that the soul wot a spirit's made of is somethin' you could nail on the bottom of a bloody boot! Well, you can't! No more can you shut it in a box and keep it there forever, or until the wood rots to let it out. Thought as 'ow you'd know better than that!"

He paused a moment showing every sign of being genuinely shocked by Percy's abysmal lack of basic knowledge. His manner was like that of a schoolmaster who has discovered a gaping hole in a pupil's grasp of fundamentals. Then he summed up his feelings in no uncertain manner.

"Right bloody ignorant you must be, Percy, about things like that! Huh! Huh! Best not to open your great gob if all you can say are bloody stupid things like that!"

Motty glowered at Percy angrily. Beneath his bushy white eyebrows his deep-set eyes—turned-up to offset the characteristic, marked stoop of his bent form—appeared to challenge Percy not to make any further comments. Then he took a long swig at his beer, thrust the empty glass at Arthur, and expounded further on the difficult concept of human souls.

"Souls are funny things, souls are," he stated thoughtfully. "Nobody knows where a soul's stored in a man's body. Not even the best sawbones in the biggest London 'ospital could get one out of a man to look at. 'E wouldn't be able to find it, no matter where 'e carved around inside 'im. It would see 'im coming and get out of the bloody way. Fast! Go some place else it would where 'e couldn't get at it. Like be'ind an eyeball. The only way a sawbones would get it out would be to kill the man. An' then—even if 'e did that—'e still wouldn't be able to catch it. It would just slip through 'is fingers like a puff of wind and be off straight away to the spirit world.

"Yer see, a soul stays somewhere in a bloke's body whilst 'e's alive and never leaves its 'ome for a minute. It might dodge around a lot inside 'im—any place between 'is brain an' 'is balls, as yer might say—but never come out of 'im while 'e's breathin'. Never! But when 'e's dead it's as free as a fart. Once it gets changed from a soul to a spirit—an' that's wot 'appens when a man dies—then it can go wherever it likes. And it don't 'ang about gettin' anywhere either. In fact it takes no time at all to go where it wants, no matter 'ow far it is—that's the funny part about the way a spirit moves about."

Motty paused a moment, looking round his intently listening audience, conscious it seemed of how difficult it must be for ordinary people to understand such matters. Then he sought to explain in a bit more detail, this amazing mobility of free spirits. His audience lacked the long years of experience he had behind him, of being close to the subject, and the advantage of spending many many hours in the graveyard in the company of the dead. He could appreciate their difficulty only too well.

He remembered that he himself had puzzled a great deal during his early years in the churchyard, about where spirits were and how they managed to move around. And dwelling upon these things again now, stimulated by the interest of his companions, he remembered how the answer had come to him many years ago.

One sunny afternoon, on a day when the air was still, and all was quiet and peaceful in the churchyard, he was pondering these weighty matters while tending the grass around the grave of a close friend who had not long been a resident there, having moved in rather prematurely following a heart attack. His departed friend, himself a deep thinker, had quite fortuitously, in the course of conversation, answered many of the questions that had been bugging Motty for a long while. He passed on the gist of this talk now.

"My old mate Sam Larkin 'splained it to me a long time ago," he said. "Never forgotten it, I ain't. Must be nigh on twenty years now since they put dear old Sam down. Soon after 'e moved in round there I says to 'im one day, I says, 'Well, 'ow do you like it 'ere, Sam? Settled in, 'ave yer?' Took a minute or two 'fore 'e answered that, 'e did. Just as though 'e was a-thinkin' like, thinkin' a bit deep about it. Thought 'e'd buggered off at first, I did. Then Sam says somethin' I've always remembered. Cos it 'splained a lot that was a-puzzlin' me.

"'Motty,' 'e says to me, 'there ain't no such thing as 'ere or there to us dead-uns. Yer see,' 'e says, 'to us, 'ere is there, an' there is 'ere, so to speak. An 'ere is everywhere. And there is everywhere, too. Cos yer see, Motty,' Sam says, 'to us spirits, '*ere's* where we 'appens to be a-thinkin' about at the time. 'Ere is there, or anywhere, to us. Cos us spirits goes in a flash to where we thinks about. No body. No baggage. Not nothin' we spirits ain't got to lug around with us. Spirits is like thoughts. They don't need no transport.

"'Bit like live-uns' dreams. That's the best way I can 'splain it to yer, Motty,' 'e says. 'A live-un kind of pops all over the place in 'is dreams but don't take no time to get there, do 'e? One minute 'e can be eatin' winkles at Whitstable, next minute 'e can be on the pier at Margate—or round by the cathedral at Canterbury—then 'e can be back 'ome again in Littlebrook, diggin' 'is garden, say. But it don't take 'im no time at all to shift about, 'e just dreams 'e's anywhere an' 'e's there—in 'is dreams, like. No messin' about at all, travellin' between places.

"'But us spirits, we don't just dream it,' Sam says to me, 'we akchully does it. We goes where we thinks, an no messin' about at all.'

"That's 'ow Sam 'splained it to me," Motty concluded, with the air of a man who has dealt with something thoroughly, leaving no room for doubt.

"Can't quite see what he meant by that, Motty," said Taffy, his brow somewhat furrowed, reflecting his puzzlement.

Motty looked at Taffy a bit suspiciously to make sure that Taffy, like his mate Percy, wasn't making fun of him. The genuinely puzzled look on Taffy's face reassured him that Taffy was being serious for once.

"Takes gettin' used to, I know that, Taffy," conceded Motty." "I 'ad to think about it a lot afore I could see 'zactly wot Sam meant. You take Timothy Twylock. Now 'e likes this 'ere Oast 'ouse a lot, 'e does. Cos 'e was 'appy in 'ere afore 'e died. So 'e thinks about this place a lot an' that puts 'is spirit in 'ere. Like I just said, I shouldn't be surprised if 'e ain't in 'ere along with us now. At this very minute like!"

Some of the company looked markedly uncomfortable at this suggestion, and glanced around apprehensively.

Motty warmed to his subject, his mind alert and busy, for he could see that he was very much the centre of attention. Everybody was listening to him with obvious interest.

"Some queer things 'appen in the spirit world sometimes," he said.

"What do you mean?" asked Will, with rapt attention.

"Well, you take the blokes wot got killed in the War," explained Motty. "Them wot's got their names on the War Memorial stone, just up the road there. Old Sam's got to know a lot of them. Course 'e was dead a long time afore they were. And they ain't buried round at the churchyard, where Sam is, neither. They's buried out in France, they is, most of them. Makes no difference though, that don't. And age makes no difference to spirits. Sam says they all seems the same age in a queer manner of speaking like. They's wot age they think they be at the time when they speak to other spirits. Same as they's always at the place they 'appen to be thinkin' about at the time. So Sam says that age makes no difference. No more don't places make no difference either. Takes a bit of gettin' used to, that does!"

Turning to Taffy, who still looked very puzzled, he added a thoughtful, though rather loaded, comment.

"Not s'prised you finds it 'ard to understand, Taffy," he said meaningfully. "It's 'ard enough for me to think into, myself. Must be nigh-on bloody impossible for you, I 'spect!"

Motty paused again to further lubricate his throat with another long swig of beer and took the opportunity to thrust his glass at Arthur for another refill. Taking up where he had left off, he then went on with his observations.

"Sam says some of them killed in France hangs around this 'ere village a lot at times. Cos it was their 'ome after all. Natchrull they comes 'ere, ain't it?" he said, looking round for agreement.

"One of them—Alf Burns by name—told Sam that 'e sometimes sits on the steps of the War Memorial to read 'is name over. Likes to do that, 'e does. Makes 'im feel 'e ain't forgotten, it does, so 'e says. Then next minute off 'e goes over to France to sit on 'is 'eadstone in the War Cemetree."

For a few moments Motty was silent. His brow was furrowed even more deeply than normal, as though he were deep in thought about something. Nobody spoke, but all eyes were on him, waiting for him to continue his weird stories.

"I'll tell you somethin' queer that stuck in my mind," he said, having collected his thoughts. "Sam says, Alf told 'im what Sam called a funny little story about that-there Cemetree. Alf said that 'e and 'is mate Jack Twist was blowed-up together. Same time, same place, side by side they was. Some'ow though, seems their bodies got mixed up. Seems Jack got put down the 'ole marked Alf Burns, an' Alf got put in the next 'ole where the stone 'ad Jack Twist writ on it. Of course, when people went to visit their graves after

127

the War they goes and stands by the wrong stones. So they mourned an' grief'd away at the wrong grave, you see."

Clara looked at Motty, with tears in her eyes, obviously very moved by this strange little story.

"How very sad," she said. "Wouldn't you think they would be more careful?"

"Oh, it's all right," reassured Motty. "It got sorted out. Alf and Jack talked it over after the first relations came out there. An' they thought it was very sad, just the same like you does. So they decided to swap bones. Jack gave 'is bones to Alf. And Alf gave 'is bones to Jack. A fair swap it was, an' they shook 'ands on it. Seems they figured this put it all right. Cos yer see their spirits go to the grave with their own name on it, an' in the grave are bones wot belong to them, cos they've been given the bones to keep for good. Don't matter that they didn't grow the bones themselves. That don't matter at all, the way they sees it. So when a relation comes to the Cemetree, say to visit Alf, an' goes an' stands by the stone with Alf's name on it, everything's been sorted out proper, yer see. Alf's spirit belongs there and the bones wot are in the ground belongs to Alf. So that's all right, ain't it? They stan's an' mourns an' griefs in the right place. There ain't nothin' said 'bout it any more. Very good idea that was. Took a lot of thinkin' out, that did. Bloody clever I reckon that was."

Motty paused a few moments and looked hard at Percy, whose derisory laugh about what Motty had said had sparked off this long and learned talk about the mobility of spirits.

"And Percy," he said, speaking slowly and deliberately, "if you think about that when you gets back to that bloody cobbler's 'ut of your'n, p'raps you'll get to know a bit more about spirits an' won't be so quick to make jokes about things wot you don't understand. Best keep your mouth shut, my Dad used to say, 'bout things you knows nothin' about. Good advice for you too, that is, Percy. P'raps you'll remember that. Pity your old Dad didn't tell you things like that. Then your mouth wouldn't 'ave growed so big with talkin' so much bloody nonsense!" Motty's stern, censorious tone brooked no response and Percy kept quiet.

Motty's talk, though, had riveted the attention of everybody. It all seemed to make some sort of sense, and they began to look at Motty with something akin to respect, if not awe.

Tubby took up the conversation.

"Motty, tell me something," he said. "When you talk to a bloke round in the churchyard, from what you say he might not always be at home, as you might say—if you can call his grave his home."

"Quite right," responded Motty.

"So they don't always answer you, then, Motty?" Tubby went on.

"No, they sometimes don't answer," said Motty. "That's quite true. So then I knows they be busy someplace else, wherever they 'appens to be thinkin' about at the time. So I shuts up, and says no more for a bit."

Here Motty paused thoughtfully.

"Funny thing about that, though," he continued. "Like I said, they gets from place to place as fast as they thinks about it. And it seems they get to be kind of tuned-in to some extra-special livin' folk. It's a bit like 'ow a fiddle gets tuned-up to a pee-anner, I suppose. So's it can play with it proper like. They 'ave to be tuned-in to one another, don't they?

"But spirits don't get tuned-in to h'ordinry people. They can't, yer see. Never gets to speak to suchlike people at all, they don't. What's more, they don't try. Cos spirits knows who's special and who ain't. An' special ones don't grow on trees. Ain't many of them, there ain't. Ow many do you sittin' in 'ere know, for a start?"

Motty gazed around from one to another of his captive audience, but there was not response to his question.

"It 'appens I be one of them," he continued. "A gift, that's what it is. A gift! P'raps on account of my Grandfather bein' an extra special good fiddle player wot 'ad got musical ear'oles. Now me, I can't play a fiddle. My Dad could play a bit, though no ways so good as 'is Dad could. But the gift's come out in me as one wot can get tuned-in to spirits. Gifts gets to be 'anded down sometimes, don't they?"

Once again Motty took time out to have another swig at his beer and to collect his thoughts. He had the close attention of everybody, and nobody broke the spell by saying anything while he was having his drink. At length, duly refreshed, he picked up his line of thought again.

"So," he went on, "when they gets to know a live-un, very close like, an' gets used to talkin' to 'im straight into 'is 'ead like they do, a queer thing 'appens. When the live-un wot's partic'lar close to them starts to talk to them, then, bein' tuned-in like, they very soon senses that. An' when they senses it, they comes back quick as a flash to get back to where they knows the special one wot's a-talkin' to them is. Course, if it's me, they knows I'll be by their grave in the churchyard. So they scuttles back there like bloody lightnin'. Sometimes I don't even know they were not at 'ome, as yer might say, when I started to talk to them. P'raps they misses a few words. But I don't notice it. Cos they might just say 'Wot was that you said to me, Motty? I didn't quite catch that.' So I says it again and p'raps never knows they've only just come back an' wasn't there when I first spoke."

"They don't always come back when you talk to them though, I suppose, do they, Motty?" asked Will.

"Oh no. Course they don't", answered Motty. "Depends where they are, an' 'ow busy they are at the time. Course, if they're not doin' anythin' much and p'raps just day-dreamin' their time away, then like as not they'll 'ear me straight away and get back from wherever they are. Sometimes, though, they don't show up for weeks and weeks. A few I know ain't been around for more'n a year. Old sailors are like that, cos they've been all over the world in the Navy. So they 'as many a place they can think themselves away to. 'Spect some goes off back to Orstralia or New Zealand, cos they all likes it out there. That I do know."

"Could you talk to one now, Motty?" asked Percy, thinking he might put Old Motty on the spot by calling his bluff.

"Course I can't, you bloody twit!" responded Motty, with marked impatience. 'Ow the 'ell do yer think they'd find me? Might be anywhere, might'nt I? D'yer think they're bloody magicians or somethin'? I 'as to be at the normal meetin' place. The churchyard is the only place where I can speak to the spirits wot I knows personally. Cos that's where they're tuned-up to me at. You think of all the millions of people in the world. D'yer 'spect a spirit to go 'untin' about from one man to another looking for me?"

"I think I can understand that, Mr Marsh," said Clara helpfully. "That seems to make sense to me. It's like every other time people meet up. There has to be an agreed meeting place."

"That's quite right, that is," confirmed Motty. "Spirits only ever speaks to me when I'm in the churchyard. It's sort of the h'orfishull meetin' place. Even my old Dad, even 'e don't speak to me any place else but in the churchyard. 'E wouldn't think o' trying to speak to me at 'ome. Respects my private'sy more'n that, 'e does. An' I knows 'e wouldn't 'ave wanted 'is old Dad—that'd be my Grandfather—a-pokin' about the place when 'e died an' got to be a ghost. S'matter of fact, come to think on it, I can't remember my Dad speakin' to 'is Dad's spirit at all. Don't suppose my Dad 'ad the gift same as I 'ave or 'e would 'ave told me. An' 'e never did. Never even mentioned it, s'far as I can remember."

The conversation was interrupted by Will, who had pulled out his watch to look at the time.

"Excuse me, Arthur," he said, rather apologetically. "Do you mind if I pop home for a while to settle my old folks for the night. You know my Dad is none too well and I promised my Mum I'd look in before twelve o'clock to see they were all right until morning. I don't suppose I'll be gone for long."

"That's all right, Will," agreed Arthur. "You go off and see to them. You needn't hurry back. So long as you're here by half-past one when we change over the load up there. There's nothing much to do before then."

"Thanks, Arthur," said Will, and went off out into the night.

The door banged shut behind him. Those left inside heard him have a word with Pug before he made his way up the road. Pug whimpered a great deal when Will had gone off, leaving him alone out there once again. The little dog was clearly not all that happy tied up outside there in the dark. There was a mournful quality to the low noises he was making, which added to the unease of the visitors sitting in the dimly-lit interior of the eerie Oast House.

For a while there was silence by the fire and those present turned over in their minds the curious things Old Motty had said. Arthur filled the glasses of those who wanted topping up, starting with Motty whose empty glass held out yet again had reminded him of his duties as the host.

The air of well-being fostered by the warmth of the glowing fire, the congenial company and the plentiful supply of free beer, was tempered only by a feeling of vague disquiet—almost of foreboding—engendered by Motty's references to ghostly beings. His apparent near-conviction that unseen presences were there with them in the Oast, created a feeling that the longer they stayed the more likelihood there was that something supernatural might happen. It was a creepy sensation.

An air of expectancy pervaded the place as Percy and his friends sipped their drinks—lost for the moment in their own disturbed thoughts.

Arthur was well pleased. The scene was set. So far so good!

130

Chapter 11

GHOSTS IN THE OAST
a frightening experience for the visitors

Following the departure of Will, the subsequent pause for replenishment of glasses and a short period of quiet, Arthur re-opened the discussion.

Up until then he had listened to the conversation with great interest. Secretly he was delighted at the way the talk had flowed along, with no further impetus from him beyond his opening remark to Motty. Unwittingly Motty had made a better contribution to the evening's entertainment than he could ever have been 'scripted' to do. Now was the time, Arthur thought, to venture into the discussion himself and put forward a few ideas of his own.

"So far as I can understand," he said, looking round to capture the attention of the contemplative group sitting quietly sipping their drinks by the warm fire, "it seems that ghosts are not 'solid' like. What I mean is, they can't be touched, or felt, or knocked into, or pushed about, however hard you try. And seeing as how they have no weight—or substance like—they can't shift anything themselves by pushing at it, the same as we do. They haven't even got the strength of a little puff of wind."

"That's what I have always understood," intervened Glad. "They can even pass right though solid walls and through shut doors, so I've been told."

"'Course they can," interrupted Motty emphatically. "They just thinks their way through, if they wants to go in or out. Same as I said just now. They goes where they thinks—an' no messing'!"

"I see what you mean," said Glad. "Yes, it all makes sense when you stop to think about it. Ghosts are bound to go where they want with no trouble at all, aren't they? If they don't have a body to worry about, they don't have to bother about things being in their way, do they? What's more, I can see now that what you said before must be true. If there's no body to transport, then there can't be any travelling time getting them anywhere, can there? You know, Mr. Marsh, you have explained a lot of things I didn't understand, tonight."

Motty looked very gratified by this remark and was quick to repay the compliment with one of his own.

"I thought when I first see'd you, when I came in 'ere, that like as not you were a good thinker," he commented. "Not many people pick things up as quick as that. Shouldn't be s'prised if you ain't one of us special ones wot spirits can tune-in to, I shouldn't be s'prised at all."

Glad made no reply to this. She looked a bit uncomfortable, as though the idea of communicating with spirits did not much appeal to her.

Arthur was pleased with this little interchange of ideas between Glad and Motty. The conversation was now rolling along again nicely. He picked up his theme and continued on his pre-determined course, which was developing smoothly and naturally.

"My Uncle Felix," he said, "who is a pretty level-headed bloke himself, knows a lady who is a Spiritualist. An educated lady she is too, who knows a thing or two by all accounts. My Uncle says she's very serious-minded and knows what she's talking about.

"This lady says that though spirits can't shift things by their own strength the way we do, they can call upon living people and certain animals too, to do things for them. And not only that, she says they can call up forces of nature that we know nothing about, nor will ever know about, so it seems, until we are dead ourselves. For instance, they can make things go upwards instead of falling to the ground. And do lots of things like that, which are unnatural to us."

At this point Clara interrupted Arthur, but—as it turned out—helped rather than hindered him in his careful build-up of atmosphere.

"There are some special spirits, or demons, Arthur," she said, "that are extra powerful ones. There was a story about them in our local paper a few weeks ago. Some people had been messing about with something called an 'Ouija-board' to contact ghosts, and apparently they let loose this angry spirit amongst them. It was called a 'Poltergeist', so the experts said. It chucked things about all over the place and raised merry hell in the house. Frightened the life out of everybody, it did. Once they'd let it loose there was nothing they could do to make it go away. Everything and something was flying about the room as if there were a hurricane, yet there was no wind at all. In the end a Priest had to be called upon to get it out of the house. He came in and spoke some ancient words from the Bible to send it packing!"

"Oh yes," intervened Arthur, only too eager to exploit this bonus of added confirmation of his argument, "ordinary spirits can get the help of those Poltergeists if there's something they want done that they can't manage themselves. But I believe even spirits are a bit careful of involving them. They can soon get out of control, so I've heard, and go mad, causing real havoc. Proper demons they are, some of them! I expect it's a bit like calling in a murderer to kill a fly on the wall. Far too powerful for most jobs Poltergeists are, so I understand."

Arthur paused a moment, looking thoughtful and serious, weighing his words carefully.

"This Spiritualist lady," he went on, frowning slightly as if a bit worried, "said that it's dangerous for people to fool around with the world of spirits. She said it's possible to unleash dark and evil forces and people shouldn't meddle with things they don't understand or they will find themselves being used, and influenced by the spirits, in ways they would never even dream about!"

"That's just what it said in the story in our paper," Clara said. "The Priest they called in warned people not to play around with these things because they could put themselves in great danger. The Devil himself can soon move in on these meetings and nobody knows where such things can finish up. Once he gets a foot in the door, he doesn't go away again in a hurry!

It seems that another party of people took to sitting around a table with their fingers lightly resting on the top of it. And then they all willed the table to rise up off the floor and float. According to the story even a heavy table will sometimes lift up off the floor and float around the room, knocking over people and furniture as it goes.

This Priest begged people not to experiment with any of that kind of carry-on. Let's hope he scared people off! We don't want Poltergeists and mischief-making spirits mucking about in Camden Town. We've got enough trouble up there as it is, without inviting any more in!"

"I'll say we have," agreed Glad. "We can do without evil spirits and demons and things around there. To blazes with them! They can go to hell!"

"Huh! Huh! No need to tell them to go to 'ell, 'ell is just where evil spirits comes from in the first place!" interjected Motty, who showed by that remark how closely he had been following the discussion. "You won't upset them by telling them to go to 'ell, cos 'ell is 'ome to them! And they will go 'ome anyway when they gets 'ungry!"

"Seems too spooky for me, all that does," said Taffy. "Fair gives me the creeps just hearing about stuff like that. Folks must be plain daft to sod about with evil spirits like that. Bloody stupid if you ask me!"

Taffy wasn't at all keen on getting involved with ghosts. He spent too much time in the woods on his own to want to attract the attention of ghosts. By nature he was secretly more than a little scared of such things. And he had a fertile imagination. When it started to get dark while he was working in the woods, his imagination often got the better of him. This was especially true on a still, misty evening. There was something particularly scary about such days. They appeared the most spooky of all. Shapes seemed to loom up out of the shifting mist, and his mind started to play tricks with him. Scuffles, rustles, creaks and little sounds made by animals and birds carried far, and seemed to surround him, as he stood listening in the stillness of the dusk. On days like that he beat it for home just as soon as he could, and left his work for the next day when the daylight dispelled his fears.

Arthur began to get a bit uneasy by the turn of the discussion. He could see his guests being frightened off too early in the proceedings, so he tried to bring the conversation back under control.

"There's a lot of difference between conducting those so-called séances, and things like that, than just talking about such matters," he said reassuringly. "Of course it's asking for trouble to start calling up Poltergeists and rogue, destructive spirits like that. It's as daft as inviting the biggest thieving thug you can find to a Christmas Party, then filling his belly with beer, and expecting him to add to the fun and games of the evening. Oh no, that sort of thing is not for me. I'd never get mixed up in any hocus pocus like messing about with Ouija-boards, or séances, or dangerous things like that. No fear I wouldn't!"

"Quite right too!" said Percy. "No more would I, Arthur. Like you say, that's just asking for trouble, and people deserve what comes to them when they start messing about with things like that."

"They certainly do," Arthur said. "All the same, there are things you can do which aren't dangerous at all. Especially when it involves the ghosts of your own family and friends. There's no way they are going to do nasty things to you, or deliberately scare you, is there?"

"No, that's true, Arthur," said Tubby. "Of course they wouldn't. Stands to reason, that does. And come to think of it, I reckon it would upset them—especially if they couldn't find a way to tell you not to be scared. They have enough to put up with, with being dead—without living people they're fond of making them more miserable by getting frightened of them. It's unkind to friendly ghosts to get scared of them."

Arthur inwardly thanked Tubby for his help in getting matters into perspective and reducing the tension a little bit. It enabled him to get back on track.

"That Spiritualist lady I was telling you about," he went on, "told my Uncle that spirits can, if they like, let you know they're nearby by affecting one of your five senses—seeing, hearing, smelling, touching, or tasting. Not only that, some animals have that sixth-sense we've been talking about, and spirits can get hold of that as well."

"Well, I'm damned!" interrupted Taffy. "Now I can see what is meant by saying dogs and cats have a sixth sense. Can't say I've ever added up our senses like that, Arthur. Yeah. Now I see what it means. Seeing, hearing, smelling, touching and tasting—that does add up to five. And dogs and cats have those five, same as we do. Then they've got another one we don't have. And that makes six. The sixth sense. Now I see what people are getting at! Thanks for explaining that, Arthur."

Motty had been listening to this laborious process of Taffy's reasoning with growing impatience, and glowered at him.

"Huh! Glad there's *somethin'* you can understand, Taffy," he muttered. "Not much gets through that thick 'ead of yours, so far as I can see. S'prised you can even count up to six, now I come to think on it!"

A general chuckle greeted Motty's intervention. Taffy glared at him, but made no comment.

"Anyway," pursued Arthur, "the lady says that there's several things they can do if they're so minded. She says they can make lights or shadows that affect our eyes. They may not be normal lights or shadows, but we can see them. Then they can make noises happen. Queer, unnatural noises perhaps they may be, but we hear them all right—according to her. And they can create strange smells that get up our noses and work our sense of smell. Very peculiar smells some of them can be, too. Like no ordinary smells we know about. Unworldly smells, so she says—that's how she puts it.

Then they can affect us like as though we were being touched. And they can set us shivering because we suddenly feel cold. Sometimes in a warm house one room will suddenly feel awful cold. An eerie, dead-world cold it is too, according to her. Like no cold we usually feel. She says the spirits suck all the heat energy out of the room and somehow absorb it.

Not only that, they can leave horrible tastes in our mouths, like as though we've tasted extra nasty medicines. But she says these tastes are unlike anything we taste normally. You can't put a name to them. That's because they're spirit made, and not natural. She says the nearest thing to them is what some people call the taste of fear."

Arthur paused a moment while he checked over in his mind that he had covered the five senses. Satisfied that he had done so, he went on to deal with the sixth.

"As well as all those things, spirits can give out some kind of radiation—some energy we don't understand—that some animals like dogs and cats can pick up on, like we were talking about. That's what makes a dog or cat's hair stand on end, or a dog cringe and whimper and tuck its tail up between its legs. That's their sixth sense working, and the spirits go for it. That's the sense we don't have. At least not as strong as they have. This lady says that the sixth sense may be tied up to the sense that guides a homing-pigeon back to its loft. Not exactly the same thing, so she says, but something a few living creatures can do that we humans can't do."

"Pug 'as a sixth sense and no mistake," joined in Motty. "That's why 'e won't come in 'ere if 'e can 'elp it, for a start. An' I'll tell you somethin' else. There's a big ol' tomb round at the churchyard. Very ainshunt ol' tomb it is, with a slab that comes off the side an' steps leading down to a small vault place. This 'ere slab on the side got shifted one night and was left propped up lookin' like it might fall over an' 'urt somebody. We don't know who did it, but Parson Yelman 'e goes off an' gets Stony Charlie in to fix it up.

Pug was with me, watchin'. Soon as Charlie shifted the slab away from the tomb to see wot was wot down there, Pug started to go in there. But he just took one sniff at the stone steps leading down, looked in there, an' then 'e gives out an almighty loud 'owl, and ran like 'ell straight inside the church. Terrible chronic noise it were 'e made. Never 'eard the like, I ain't. When we gets in the church to get 'im out we finds 'im in the Parson's pulpit, tucked up under the shelf where the Parson keeps 'is big ol' church Bible. Pug knowed there was ghosts about, an' what's more 'e knew the safest place to go to! Not just inside the church, but up under the Bible. Just think on that! Parson 'e was right struck by that. Real 'mazed 'e were. Went white 'e did, a-thinkin' about it.

Made me proud of Pug, that did, to think 'e were that clever. Wot's that if it ain't a sixth sense a-workin' inside Pug's 'ead? Makes yer think, that do!"

There were expressions of astonishment from those gathered by the fire at Motty's impressive evidence of the existence of Pug's sixth sense.

Mike had something to contribute to the interesting discussion.

"It isn't only pigeons that can find their way home," he stated. "Dogs, cats and sometimes I think even horses, can find their way home. Especially cats, though. I know that is true because I can tell you of a case of it. Amazing thing it was too.

A mate of mine took his Mum's cat by train up to Tunbridge Wells, to his Aunt's house. It seems his Aunt was lonely and very miserable after her husband—that's my mate's Mum's brother Seb—kicked the bucket. So my mate's Mum gave her sister their cat, to keep 'er company. Well, my mate took the cat there in a basket, and left is there in Tunbridge Wells. That's over fifty miles away, that is, from where my mate's Mum lives near Margate.

Next week my mate's Mum had a letter from her sister to say that the cat had cleared off. She thought it must have gone for a walk, and got lost somewhere. Of course it didn't know its way around, and they reckoned it must have mooched off up the road like cats do, and couldn't find its way back. They gave it up for lost, and bought the old lady a kitten.

Then you'll never guess what happened. Nearly two years later the cat turned up back at my mate's house. Thin and hungry it was. But it came in the door from the garden, purring away as happy as you like to have got back home again. And there it stays to this very day. Nobody can figure out how it found its way back all that distance from Tunbridge Wells. But find its way it did, that's for sure. What's more, it went up there by rail, shut in a basket, and must have come back down by road, or across country. It seems like a miracle, doesn't it?"

"Don't know about a miracle! Sounds like a helluva tall story to me!" commented Percy scornfully.

"No, Percy!" insisted Mike vehemently. "You're quite wrong there. It certainly is *not* a tall story. That story is as true as I sit here in this Oast now. You can ask my mate Bruce Marshall himself if you don't believe me. It must have been that sixth sense Arthur's been talking about, working its wonders again as I see it. That cat came home over fifty miles on its own. Nobody carried it home. It walked on its own four legs, and spent almost two years getting there. Bloody marvellous, I think it was."

It was obvious Mike was quite sure of his facts, and those present could only marvel at this astounding feat.

The atmosphere in the Oast was now somewhat less strained and anxious and everyone was wide awake and full of interest. Arthur thought that now was the time to get things really moving.

"Here. I've got a good idea," he said, as if by sudden inspiration. "We know there are often ghosts around in this Oast House. Suppose we could find a way to ask them to give us a sign to prove they're in here with us. These must be friendly spirits, else why would they choose to hang about in here?"

"That's right, Arthur," spoke up Mike in support. "Any ghosts in here must be of a friendly turn of mind. Must be, mustn't they? They're almost certain to be spirits of people who worked in here. It sounds like a good idea to me, Arthur. Be interesting, that would, to see if we could get in touch with them. But how shall we go about it, Arthur?"

Arthur's brow puckered up noticeably, as though he were giving serious thought to the problem. The visitors sat silently watching him, not too sure that they altogether liked the sound of it.

"Well, let's see," went on Arthur hesitatingly, still contriving to manifest signs of intense mental concentration about a difficult matter. "Let's try and work something out. We'll all have to work together, I'm sure of that, to pull this off. It will need a bit of team-work I think. We shall have to combine our will-powers to build up enough strength of thought-energy to get through to them, I expect. I don't suppose for one minute any single one of us could get through on our own.

As I understand it, several people have to work together as a group to contact ghosts. It's a bit like needing a team of horses to pull a plough through heavy soil. One can't manage it on its own. It's not quite the same thing, I know, because there you are talking about physical pulling power. What we are after is mind-power. We've got to build it up to break through a kind of barrier, if you see what I mean."

"I think that's true," volunteered Clara. "That ties in with what we read in that article about the Ouija board party in Camden Town. They all sat round a table to call up the spirits."

"We don't want to get mixed up in a carry-on like that in here, though," Glad commented. "No bounds to what trouble that could cause us!"

"No, of course we don't," said Arthur. "We won't be asking the spirits to do anything likely to cause any sort of bother. All we'll do is just ask for a sign to prove to us that they are in here. That's all."

"What do you suggest then, Arthur?" asked Tubby, apparently keen to get on with things.

"Well, first of all, let's draw our seats round in a circle so that we can work together. Then we'll join hands and concentrate hard. When we are all ready we will sit quietly for a bit, to gather our strength. Then we will call out to the spirits and we'll all think as hard as we can, to will them to get through to us."

Motty had been listening to this with growing alarm. He didn't like the sound of it at all, and his manner showed it.

"Count me out, Arthur," he said abruptly. "I'm not a-goin' to muck about like that. Not bloody likely I'm not! You know what, if you're not careful . . ." Motty got no further with his intended warnings because they were all startled by an unexpected interruption from outside the door. Motty's dog, Pug, suddenly and unaccountably, had set up a long wailing howl, followed by another, and yet another.

Motty grabbed his stick and heaved himself to his feet. "What did I say!" he said in a very agitated voice. "Pug's got wind of the ghosts already. Somethin's up! That ain't no normal 'owl that ain't. 'E's sensed trouble, Pug 'as! 'E ain't 'owled like that since my ol' tom cat took ill an' died. I'm off, I am. Not staying in 'ere, I'm not. And," he said, turning to the four visitors, "if you've any sense you'll all bugger off out of 'ere pretty smartly too. No good will come of this. Those that plays at dangerous games gets 'urt. I'm off!"

"Here! Wait a minute, Motty. You're not really going home, are you? Don't go yet," pleaded Arthur, with evident anxiety in his voice. Without Motty, one of the key elements to create the right atmosphere for his carefully planned evening's entertainment would be gone.

"Too bloody true I'm a-goin'," replied Motty, in a tone leaving no room for doubt. "Not stoppin' in 'ere I'm not. You don't know wot your layin' up for yerselfs, you don't. Very powerful and uncommon crafty some spirits are. And if you upsets the like of them, they get 'ell of a lot more spiteful than any livin' man or woman wot you've knowed could ever be. They don't like being mucked about and made fools of, they don't. You know the words wot the Vicar says when 'e buries people. 'May they Rest in Peace', that's wot the Vicar says. T'ain't for nothin' them-there-words 'as come down to us from ainshunt times. Muckin' spirits about and a-stirrin' them up with meetin's and pokin' around at 'em with squeegee boards an' things, likely as not makes them 'oppin' bloody mad, so they gets right bloody nasty. An' soon as trouble starts, in'll come all the bloody demon spirits for miles around. They 'omes in on trouble—just wot they like, it is. No, Arthur! Sod that! I'm off, like I said!"

With that Motty stumped his way to the door. On reaching it, he turned to have a last word with the group left sitting around the fire.

"Mind what I say, now," he said. "There are things best not messed about with. Goodnight all—an' I 'ope I don't wake up in the mornin' to 'ear that 'alf of you are dead an' the rest carted off to the loony-bin!"

On that hopeful note, he opened the door, and went out. Meanwhile Pug had kept up his mournful, long-drawn-out wailing howls, which only ceased when his master appeared outside and untied him.

"Come on then, little mate," they heard Motty say. "We're a-goin' off home. Don't you worry, Pug—them in there can do wot they likes—but you an' me will get the 'ell out of it, just as fast as I can walk."

Silence descended on the group while the sound of Motty's progress up the road died away. Though they would be loath to admit it, each one of them harboured a nasty suspicion that there might be some truth in what Motty had said. The howling of the dog was inexplicable. Perhaps something in Motty's own highly disturbed state had communicated itself to the little dog, and triggered it off into an agitated, fearful state itself. Maybe it was just another example of the sixth sense working, with the dog picking up the unease of its master. Whatever the explanation, it had howled. Howled and howled, over and over again, in a most unnatural way. What's more, it had started only when the talk had turned to contacting the spirit world inside the Oast. It was disturbing and gave them all food for thought.

Glad and Clara looked positively worried. So, for that matter did Percy and Taffy.

"What a frighteningly eerie noise that dog made," said Clara with a shudder. "Gives you the creeps, doesn't it?"

"It does indeed," responded Glad. "An unworldly sound I think it was. Unworldly that's what it was. There's no other word for it."

The atmosphere was now noticeably uneasy. Arthur sensed that his guests would very soon be of a mind to abandon their proposed experiment if he didn't get a grip on the situation pretty quickly.

"Come on, then, let's get started," he said, in as normal a voice as he could muster. "Don't take any notice of Old Motty. He's well-known in these parts as one who spends his days thinking about spirits and talking to the dead. He's kind of preparing himself to join the happy throng, so people say. You mustn't let an old man like that interfere with what you do. He's a bit cranky, he is. Nobody believes what he says."

Percy and Taffy were not so sure about that. They had known Motty for a long time. Over the years, like a lot of other people, if they were really honest, they would have to admit that they were not at all sure Motty was as crazy as some folks made him out to be. Old as he was, his remarks were too often indicative of a shrewd mind buried behind his sunken but sharply penetrating eyes, for people to write him off as just daft. Strange he might be, but daft—no! Not by any means. Sometimes what he said was very far from being daft!

Neither of them, however, wished to appear scared in the eyes of their lady friends from London, so they kept quiet. And so the opportunity for them to opt out of the intended experiment in communication with the other world was lost.

"What do you want us to do, Arthur?" asked Percy in a flat tone of voice that was markedly lacking in enthusiasm and rather had about it a quality of resigned acquiescence.

Arthur got off the up-ended bushel basket he was sitting on and moved it to a point where it could form part of a circle of seats in the space in front of the fire.

"Draw your seats round," he instructed, describing an imaginary circle with his hands. "Space yourselves out so that we can all join hands to make an unbroken magic circle."

Somewhat reluctantly Percy, Taffy, Glad and Clara moved their seats until they, along with Mike, Tubby and Arthur, were sitting in a circle.

Arthur, watched by the others, took out his pocket watch, unfastened its chain from his trouser top and placed it on a box he had put in front of him. It was evident he had got something figured out that was going to need timing.

"To focus our will-power," he said, "we'd better concentrate on a particular time.

It's not far off midnight now, and from what I've always heard, twelve o'clock at night is a very special time for ghosts. There's something about the turn of a day which is like a door opening to them, making it easy for them to move from their world into ours. If you think about it, people often speak about haunting taking place at midnight."

"That's true," said Clara. "Somehow midnight always seems an especially frightening time. Perhaps that's why it's called the 'witching hour'!"

"What we'll do, then," continued Arthur, "is join hands just before midnight. We can hear the church clock striking clearly from in here, if we are all quiet. So I suggest that just before midnight, we call upon the ghosts to make a sign to us to show us they're here, inside the Oast House. Then we'll make our strongest possible will-power effort as the church clock strikes twelve, building up to a peak on the last stroke of the bell. We've got to 'will' them to give us a sign—urging them, just as hard as we can, in our minds."

"Wouldn't it be better to speak to just one particular ghost, rather than the lot of them?" suggested Tubby. "That way we would sort of focus our power on one spirit instead of spreading it all around the place."

"Yes, Tubby, maybe you're right," agreed Arthur. "Yes, that's a very good idea. If we all concentrate on the same one, then we ought to stand a better chance of breaking through the barrier and making contact. The obvious choice is Timothy Twylock himself. Like Motty said, tonight is an extra special occasion for him, so if any ghost is going to be in the building at midnight, then like as not it's going to be him."

"What shall we say if we all call out to him?" asked Mike. "It would be better if we all said the same thing at the same time or there will be just a babble of voices and nobody, not even a ghost, would be able to tell what we were on about."

"Good thinking, Mike," commented Arthur, inwardly delighted at the natural way the programme was now rolling. "Well now, let's think of something simple and straightforward that we can say together. Let me think now."

For some moments Arthur thought deeply about the problem, or gave every appearance of doing so, while the others sat looking at him, waiting for him to come up with a suggestion.

In the absence of conversation they all became acutely aware of the strange, isolated, out-of-this-world feel about the Oast House in the quiet of the night. The place became more and more eerie-feeling by the minute. Somewhere outside, to add even more to the dead-of-night atmosphere, came the distant hoot of an owl, a ghostly enough sound at the best of times. Under the present highly-charged circumstances it was enough to send an involuntary shiver down the spines of more than one of them, particularly Taffy, who associated the woeful sound with the unease of the gathering darkness in the woodlands he lived in so much. Arthur did not miss it himself, and with quiet satisfaction registered the bird's distant, mournful call as a welcome contribution from the wild. An unscripted sound effect provided with perfect timing!

At length Arthur's face lit up a bit and he spoke up with some satisfaction to tell them his suggested solution to the problem of what to say.

"How about this?" he asked. "Suppose we call out these two verses—

Timothy Twylock, is your ghost
Here with us inside this Oast?

On the twelfth stroke of midnight,
By the church bell,
Make us some signs, so we can tell!"

139

Turning to Clara, Arthur asked, "How about that? Do you think that ought to do the trick, Clara?"

Clara was a little startled at being singled out and deferred to, apparently as though Arthur considered her to be the most knowledgeable member of the group on the question of making contact with spirits. She presumed this must be due to her account of the newspaper article she had talked about. Not wishing to appear indecisive, she answered, with very little hesitation.

"Yes, Arthur," she replied. "I think that is very good. It's like you said it should be. It's simple and straightforward."

"Good," responded Arthur, with obvious satisfaction. "Then let's just practise saying it over quietly together, a few times. We must make sure we keep together, and get the words right. The message must be sharp and powerful, with no blurred edges. If we don't do that there's no chance of us getting through to him. They say it takes a mighty lot of concentration to break through the barrier to the spirit world."

Led by Arthur the group then went over the two verses—somewhat sheepishly and hesitatingly at first—but nevertheless working in unison and treating the matter seriously. Guided by their mentor they soon became word perfect and developed the lines into a rhythmic chant.

At length Arthur expressed himself satisfied and called a halt. "That's fine," he said, beaming with pleasure. "Couldn't be better. That should do the trick. That should get through to him if anything will."

Feeling very much in charge of the proceedings, he looked at his watch to check the time.

"Right," he said, in his best businesslike and authoritative voice. "Let's get down to it, then. It's nigh on twelve o'clock already, so we don't have much time. Let's join hands and start to concentrate. I'll watch the time and give you a count of three just before midnight. Then we must call out our message together, loudly and clearly. After that it's very important that we hold hands tightly and concentrate our minds as hard as we possibly can, to will the ghost to come through to us.

Remember now, it's got to be a combined effort of will-power. We must will him as hard as we can and carry on right up until we hear the clock striking midnight. Then we must sit very very still, as quietly as we can, counting the bell until it reaches twelve. That is the critical time. Either he will make his presence felt to us in whatever way he thinks fit, or the time will pass and nothing will happen. Is everybody clear?"

Arthur looked from one to the other round the circle to make sure everyone had got the message. Each in turn nodded confirmation that they were ready.

"Right, then," said Arthur, in a determined, positive manner. "Join hands and be ready for the count of three."

"Just a minute, Arthur," broke in Tubby. "How exactly do we 'will him' to come through to us? What thoughts do we drum up in our minds, like?"

"That's a good point you've raised there, Tubby," replied Arthur. "Come to think of it, we ought all to be going over the same words in our minds to make the thought-power as strong as possible. We must keep it simple, though. Sharp and simple. Let's think now. What can we say?"

He glanced anxiously at his watch, conscious that they had very few minutes to go and, frowning slightly, pondered for a few moments about what words to suggest. Then his frown lifted as the answer came to him, and he looked up at them to tell them what he had in mind. Another inspiration!

"I know," he said, "how about this? Suppose we keep on going over and over these words in our minds:

'Come on through, Timothy Twylock, come on through.'
'Come on through, Timothy Twylock, come on through.'

That's a simple enough message. If we all think that, as strongly as we can make it feel, perhaps that might stand a good chance of breaking through to him. I reckon if we all plead to him like, as hard as we possibly can, using the same thoughts, that ought to concentrate all our will-powers together in one almighty-strong, thought-power, cannon ball sort of thing and penetrate the shield between our two worlds. Got that, Tubby? Just grit your teeth, and go over those words with all your might!"

"Yes, Arthur," answered Tubby. "I've got the idea. I know what to do now. I'm right with you. Go ahead when you like, mate."

"Good," said Arthur. "Let's get organised. Join hands all round then. And be ready. It's about three minutes to twelve. And remember—keep very quiet so that we can all concentrate on what we're doing. We've got to get the 'feel' in the Oast House just right to contact the spirit world. Nobody knows how thoughts travel, but we've got to try to fill this Oast with thought-waves from our minds that are driven by will-power. So concentrate and think as hard as you can."

So saying, Arthur took up the hands of those on either side of him and the others followed suit, joining hands to complete the magic circle. Then—in what seemed a strangely eerie, hushed atmosphere—they sat and waited for the remaining minutes to tick away. All eyes were on Arthur as he gazed down at his pocket watch.

In the unusual silence within the old building, the ticking of this large old timepiece was clearly audible. As the seconds ticked away, the tension steadily grew. A palpable air of intense expectation that something unworldly was about to happen, pervaded the place. The four guests, clutching hands tightly, felt sure they were on the very edge of a supernatural experience, and their hearts quickened.

At length Arthur's body tensed.

"Get ready!" he hissed. "It's almost time. All together now. On the count of three. ONE . . . TWO . . . THREE . . . **NOW!**"

Seven voices rang out strongly and clearly, breaking the silence in the dimly-lit old Oast House:

> **"Timothy Twylock, is your ghost**
> **Here with us inside this Oast?**
> **On the twelfth stroke of midnight,**
> **By the church bell,**
> **Make us some signs, so we can tell!"**

When the chanting came to an end, Arthur gripped the hands of his partners more tightly than ever, and the heightened tension from him passed around the circle.

In the absolute silence all now concentrated hard, in the way they had been instructed. Their eyes were on Arthur, as he repeatedly silently mouthed the words:

> *'Come on through, Timothy Twylock, come on through.'*
> *'Come on through, Timothy Twylock, come on through.'*

Over and over again their mouths unconsciously followed his, as they dutifully played their part, contributing as strongly as they could.

Shortly after they had settled into this final stage of extreme concentration, the distant sound of the church bell began to toll the midnight hour.

Each one counted the strokes off in their mind. A slight forward nod of each head indicated how intently the bells' tolling was being counted. In a barely audible whisper

Arthur mouthed the numbers to make sure everybody knew the score, raising the level of his whispered count as the end approached.

"... seven ... eight ... nine ... ten ... ELEVEN ... TWELVE," he counted.

Hardly had the sound of the bell died away after the stroke of twelve when there rang though the Oast a heart-stopping sound which gripped the attention of the listeners. Seemingly from a point high above their heads, from the very top of the Oast where the cowl lay motionless in the still air of the quiet night, came an unearthly cry of anguish and warning.

"H e l p . . . H e l p . . . H e l p . . !" cried the fear-laden voice in long, drawn-out words which somehow carried in their tone a sound of hopeless despair.

"H e l p . . . H e l p . . . I can't hang on . . . I can't hang on . . . my fingers are slipping . . . H . e . . l . . . p . . . I'm going to fall . . . LOOK OUT . . . LOOK OUT DOWN THERE! . . . LOOK . . O . . . . U . . T!"

There followed a brief moment of utter silence, then came a dreadful wailing cry— a sound they were to remember for years to come:

"I'm going to die . . . Oh God, I'm going to D . . . I . . . . E . ."

The last, long drawn-out word 'DIE' seemed to hang in the air high up in the cowl, then—with awful speed—the sound appeared to travel downwards to become a bellow just above their heads.

Abruptly, with a splintering crash of woodwork, the sound of the approaching voice ceased.

Immediately following the sound of shattering woodwork there came a muffled whooshing sound from inside the fire, accompanied by a blinding flash of light which persisted for perhaps three or more seconds. It seemed like a prolonged flash of lightning, causing the area where the group sat to be brilliantly illuminated.

In the unnatural light their faces looked very white, with eyes wide open and mouths agape with surprise. A strong smell of sulphurous fumes filled the air as a puff of dark smoke shot out of the fire, simultaneously with the whooshing sound from within.

Just as the light died away an old copper kettle standing by the side of the wall, suddenly shot upwards to hit the ceiling above with a clang, as if impelled by some mysterious force. Then, devoid of energy, it fell back to the ground and lay still.

A loud scream from Clara then added to the fright of the others.

"Get off me!" she screamed. "It's RATS! One brushed against my legs. LOOK! There are rats all over the floor. OH MY GOD! What's happening in here?"

In a state of near panic Clara jumped up to stand on her improvised box seat, clutching her skirts to her legs.

Sure enough there was the scurrying sound of rats around the floor. In the dim light, seeming dimmer than ever following the dazzling effect of the explosive light, the startled visitors caught glimpses of three or four rats scurrying about the floor. At length, one by one, they found an escape route through the kiln fire-draught shutter fitted low in the wall directly opposite the fire's stoking hole. With squeals of terror they disappeared into the outside world.

"She's right," bellowed Taffy. "It's RATS! RATS! . . . RATS leaving a sinking ship! Just like they do at sea!" Taffy's background as a sailor in the Royal Navy always surfaced at times of crisis, and he sure-as-hell felt he was in a crisis now!

In the momentary silence that followed, as everybody gazed around fearfully, wondering what to expect next, the sulphurous fumes assailing their nostrils became intermingled by the addition of an extremely strong, overpowering and nauseating smell like that of rotten eggs. The combination was awful! It soon filled the room, and the silence was broken by the loudly expressed dismay and discomfort of everybody there.

This bewildering series of unexpected and frightening experiences was interrupted as the door of the Oast House opened suddenly with a bang, making the coughing and spluttering visitors jump yet again. To their relief it was due to nothing sinister, it being simply Will, arriving back. He stepped inside, having returned from his supposed visit home to see his ailing parents safely settled for the night. He stopped on the threshold of the door with an expression of alarm and astonishment on his face.

"What the hell's happened?" he asked, with great concern in his voice. "You all look as though you've seen a ghost or something!"

Then the smell hit him. "Cor, strewth!" he spluttered, with his hands to his face and his nose screwed up. "What the hell is that bloody awful smell? Have you taken your socks off, Taffy?"

This sudden return to normality evinced a laugh from his mates and brought the group back to earth again.

"You might well ask if we've seen a ghost," replied Arthur. "We've all but seen one in here tonight, if you ask me. We asked for signs that Timothy Twylock's spirit was in here and he sure gave us signs all right. By bloody hell he did! He didn't leave room for much doubt either! He didn't make just one sign. He made several, all at the same time!"

Arthur's expression changed to show sudden enlightenment—as though he had just realised something for the first time.

"Of course! That's it! He must have heard us talking. He deliberately went for our five senses! Just think back now," he exclaimed with some excitement, addressing his visibly shaken guests who were clearly still dazed and bewildered by the startling experience they had been through. "Let's check them off while we can still remember everything."

So saying, Arthur went over the events they had witnessed, one at a time.

"We certainly heard and saw something," he said. "To start with, Timothy Twylock somehow managed to re-create the sound of his own voice from all those years back. Perhaps the sounds are somehow trapped in the building forever. We heard him cry out from high up in the cowl. Then you could tell when his grip gave way and he knew he'd got no chance. You could hear him coming down as fast as fast until he was just about to hit the hops. We heard the drying platform give way, and then there was that tremendous blaze of light marking the moment he reached the furnace. And the smell too! There came that unworldly smell! God! What a stink! And it left a nasty taste in the mouth too! No question about that! A bloody awful taste!

Then—I don't know about you lot—but I certainly felt something. The hair stood up on the back of my neck! And despite the fire, I felt a chill run up my spine! And Clara felt something else too, that was caused by Timothy Twylock's spirit's presence. She felt a rat brush her legs. And think that through too. The rats bolted out of the building because their sixth sense had told them ghosts were nearby. They were scared to death. No doubt about it! Scared to death, those rats were!

And on top of all that—just to make sure and leave no doubt in our minds—he made that bloody great old copper kettle lying over there lift off the ground by sheer supernatural spirit power—against the force of gravity, as you might say—and hurled it up to hit the ceiling with an almighty bang. Then it fell back to the floor, where you see it now. That was pure supernatural spirit power at work, right in front of our eyes, that's for sure! Couldn't be anything else! Right scary to see, that was! When else had any of us ever seen something heavy hurtle *upwards* on its own accord like that? Falling upwards is exactly opposite to what is natural! Timothy Twylock did what we asked him to. No doubt about that!"

All these statements were loudly and emphatically confirmed by all those present, who were still coughing and spluttering with increasing discomfiture and milling around in the confined space in front of the fire-opening.

Clara added to Arthur's comments.

"You're absolutely right about those rats, Arthur. Those rats were terrified. Absolutely terrified! That one that hit my legs was actually squealing with fright. And it wasn't me it was frightened of either. Those rats were hell bent on getting out of the building. Taffy said it was like rats leaving a sinking ship. You're quite right in what you said, Arthur. Their sixth sense had caused them to bolt from their nests and usual hiding places in this old Oast House and race to safety outside the building. Wherever they were at the time, they didn't bolt for their holes like rats normally do when they're scared by something. They had the instinct to get outside the Oast House altogether. So they certainly knew spirits were highly active here, inside the place. Whatever scared them must have been supernatural!"

Clara shuddered at the memory of it. "I don't think I shall ever forget the feel of that rat brushing past my legs," she added. "Never! Not if I live to be a hundred!"

Taffy immediately joined in.

"You're right about the rats, Clara. You're quite right. They weren't just scared, like they might be if they saw a dog, say. They were terrified. It's their natural instinct to abandon a ship when it's in great danger. Somehow they know these things. And they certainly knew spooks were in here with us tonight. And if it's natural for them to get out of a building at such times, it's probably right for us to get the hell out of it as well!"

He looked towards their lady friends from Camden Town.

"Come on, Glad and Clara," he said with obvious strength of feeling. "I don't know about you two but I've had enough of ghosts and spirits and things for one night! Let's get the blazes out of here while we're still alive and able to. Sod this bloody awful place. I've had more than enough of Oast houses for one night."

Percy agreed without hesitation.

"Couldn't agree more, Taffy," he said. "So have I! Quite enough. The sooner we get out of here the better, so far as I'm concerned."

In immediate agreement, the ladies joined Percy and Taffy and hurried through the door to the clean, fresh, night air outside.

Arthur followed them to the door. Outwardly looking very upset and concerned, he spoke to his departing guests.

"Sorry it frightened you," he said. "I didn't expect anything quite like that to happen or I wouldn't have suggested we try it."

"No wonder our Vicar at Camden Town says people shouldn't try to contact the spirit world," commented Clara. "That's the last time I shall ever attend anything like that again, I can tell you!"

"Me too," said Glad emphatically. "I didn't really like the idea in the first place. Nobody will ever talk me into messing about like that again. Not bloody likely they won't!"

"For Lord's sake let's go and have a strong drink," intervened Percy. "I shall need half a bottle of whisky to get me to sleep tonight."

Then, turning to Arthur, he said—somewhat hesitatingly—"Thanks for having us, anyway, Arthur. It was good of you to show us round. You couldn't be expected to control the spirits, once they'd been called up. Don't suppose anybody could, except perhaps Reverend Yelman. And if he'd been here, we shouldn't have tried to contact them anyway. He'd have seen to that!"

These final parting comments to Arthur were made a little awkwardly by Percy. He felt vaguely sorry for Arthur who had, after all, taken the trouble to entertain them by showing them over the Oast House and providing them with food and drink. And now they were all clearing off, making it plain they couldn't get away fast enough.

"Poor old Arthur got more than he bargained for," Percy said to the others when they had said their goodbyes and set off up the road. "If it hadn't been for somebody mentioning ghosts in the first place we should have had a happy time sitting chatting round the fire. It was nice and cosy in there." Then, rather ruefully, for he was feeling a bit sore at being dressed down in public by him, he added, "Perhaps we should have listened to Old Motty. He certainly seems to know what he's talking about!"

"Yes," agreed Clara. "Arthur was wrong to tell us to ignore that old man. I found him interesting. We should have been content just to discuss these things, and not try to meddle with them. He was right to go home when he did, and that was the time for us to stop. Especially after the weird howling noise that frightened dog of his made!" She shuddered at the memory of the mournful sound.

"You're right, Clara," said Glad. "We should have packed up then, like he said!"

Talking excitedly, and comparing notes about what they had seen and heard, the party made their way back towards Percy's hut. As they moved off up the road, Arthur—with a wide, satisfied grin on his face—rejoined his three mates inside the Oast.

Unseen by the party, their departure was watched through a crack in the access door of the upper-floor by a man well-known to them all, but not seen by them inside the Oast that evening.

It was Bert Shrubsole, right-hand man of Ben Skinner, the Tallyman in the hop garden. A close friend and confidante of Arthur's, he had been recruited to join Arthur's team at the Oast for this special evening. Bert had a strong affinity for matters theatrical and joined them with enthusiasm. Having been told by Arthur of his plans, he had contributed several innovative ideas and played an important part in carrying them out.

Earlier in the evening, when Will had left the Oast, ostensibly to see his ageing and ailing parents safely settled for the night, he had been joined outside by Bert. By prior arrangement, Bert was waiting in the wings to join the cast for the intended entertainment of Percy, Taffy, and their two lady friends.

The two had entered the Oast by a rear door and made their way secretly to the upper floor. Once there, they collected their well-prepared stage props from a concealed corner behind the ranks of full hop pokes. Covered by empty sacks, they had been safely hidden from view amongst these bulging sacks of fresh hops.

First to be lifted out was a wire cage containing four live and hungry rats. These had been trapped over a period of two or three weeks and kept meanwhile in a rabbit hutch awaiting their debut as stage extras. They were fed just survival rations and gave every sign of being very keen to escape from their unhappy period of captivity. Bert knew that once released they would be highly active, and move to perform their intended part in the proceedings very effectively. Their job was to get the hell out of the Oast House just as fast as they possibly could!

Next to be retrieved was a pail about a quarter full of a blackish-looking, coarse-grained powder. The ingredients of this concoction were equal weights of powdered charcoal and ground-up Oast sulphur ticks, together with about six parts of weight of saltpetre. These commodities were readily available. Charcoal, sometimes supplemented by coke or another smokeless fuel like anthracite, formed the main fuel for the kiln furnace. Used on its own, about a hundred bags of charcoal were needed to dry one ton of hops, so there was no shortage of charcoal immediately at hand.

Sulphur was also used in the Oast, supplied in the form of brimstone sticks. These bright yellow sticks, looking very much like children's seaside sticks of sweet rock, were tossed on to the fire at the start of the drying of each load of hops spread on the drying bed in the kiln. The sulphurous fumes produced imparted a more yellowy look to the dried hops, enhancing their appearance, but more importantly—so some thought—improving their lasting properties.

As for saltpetre, Ben and his mates had no difficulty in obtaining some, because this nitrogen-and-oxygen-rich white powder was one of the chemicals used as part of soil-enriching mixtures to supplement natural manures in a local horticultural experimental centre.

Not for the first time Bert had made up this rudimentary form of gunpowder for stage-effect purposes. By experimenting with the proportions of the ingredients, and with the extent to which the charcoal was ground up, he had arrived at an end-product which burned in a bright, 'sparky' and spectacular way, producing plenty of smoke in the process.

To still further enhance its effects, on this occasion he had added, clipped up into small pieces, several inches of magnesium metal strip to add to the brilliance of the light.

Bert had learnt to be careful how he handled a mixture like this, and to burn it always as an exposed powder, never in a closed container, which would have been highly dangerous. Arthur had needed a little convincing, including an open-air demonstration, before he agreed to Bert using his dangerous concoction as part of his planned evening's entertainment.

The third prop to be fished out was a hand-held megaphone which was occasionally used for loud-hailing on the farm and was regularly in service at open-air functions such as village fêtes on the village green, as well as at the bonfire party held at the end of the hop picking season each year.

Finally, out from behind the hop pokes they brought a crude structure made of many thin wooden slats nailed between two pieces of timber in an arbitrary haphazard way. It looked like a crude and flimsy platform. That, in essence, was precisely what it was, except that instead of being required to bear a man's weight, this platform was designed to collapse, rather than to support him.

Using these devices, the prepared routine worked like a charm.

On the stroke of twelve, as the church clock struck midnight, Bert picked up the megaphone and pointed it upwards to the base of the cowl high above his head. In well-rehearsed tones he then shouted his lines in an anguished, terror-filled voice. The acoustics of the conical tower caused his words to reverberate around the walls and appear to the listeners below to emanate—muffled and booming—from the top of the Oast tower, not from the drying bed over the kiln fire immediately above their heads. On reaching the last word 'DIE', Bert had strung the word out in a heart-rending way, sweeping the megaphone downwards as he did so, to finish pointing it directly down towards the captive audience below.

Precisely at this moment, Will, his assistant, jumped on to the improvised platform landing with both feet squarely on the criss-crossed pattern of wooden slats. The sound of snapping, splintering wood rang out loudly, to simulate very well indeed the smashing of a body through the slatted drying-bed.

While this was going on, Bert had moved swiftly to execute his master stroke. Picking up the spade by his side, he stepped gingerly alongside the layer of drying hops to a point where a large funnel was stuck into the top of a thin piece of folded metal-plate fixed so that it was poking up through the edge of the oast mat. The other end of the improvised chute slanted downwards through the wooden slats of the drying-bed, to point towards the glowing furnace below.

Deftly Bert up-ended the pail to shoot the black powder into the funnel. A sudden brilliant light accompanied by a whooshing sound, brought an expression of delight to

Bert's face at the clear evidence of the success of his carefully-prepared mixture.

Will, meanwhile, moved swiftly to perform his second duty. On a window ledge rested a heavy, ring-topped iron weight. To the ring was tied a length of strong brown twine which passed up over a pulley fixed to an overhead beam in such a position that the twine hung vertically downwards through a hole in the wooden floorboards, about twelve inches from the wall. Down below, the end of the twine was tied to the middle of a carefully selected piece of dry wooden stick, which was inside a large old copper kettle. The stick passed from side to side across the middle of the lid-hole. Tried out and perfected beforehand, they had no fears that the scheme would not work.

Bang on schedule, Will lifted the weight and dropped it down the outside wall of the Oast. The strong twine jerked the copper kettle vertically upwards at high speed. It hit the boards above with a loud metallic clang. The stick across the lid-hole snapped immediately, and the knotted end of the twine was yanked by the heavy falling weight up through the floor, and over the pulley, to follow the weight down to the ground outside.

To the observers below, all they were aware of was the sight of a copper kettle suddenly jumping off the floor to hit the ceiling above them with a loud clatter, and then falling back to lie still on the floor. The simple piece of trickery worked like a charm. Nobody had hitherto noticed the brown twine hanging limply down the wall in the shadows. Glad said afterwards that she had seen the old kettle standing on the floor by the wall. Nobody else had seen it at all until it took off of its own accord to hurtle up to the ceiling. Its movement upwards was so fast the twine was not seen.

Bert was in position to carry out his final, self-imposed job. No sooner had the sound of the clatter of the kettle signalled its arrival back on the floor down below, than he began his task. This time there had been no rehearsal. It would have posed difficulties and was anyway judged by Bert to be totally unnecessary. This particular scheme could not conceivably fail, he had said, and he was proved right!

By the square hatch in the floor, through which the steeply-angled wooden steps from the ground floor were positioned, was tied a length of old drainpipe ending about two feet off the ground, above a thin layer of straw.

One by one he quickly shoved the rats—nose first—down the top-end of the drainpipe. In quick succession the four rats slithered down the pipe to land in the straw in a highly mobile state of terror. They took off in all directions among the startled reception committee below. The terror of the rats was not lessened by the screaming reaction of Clara, who made the first observation of their presence on the floor.

These stage extras, though untrained, nonetheless did what was expected of them perfectly. They darted around in a state of panic, and by doing what came naturally to them they made a strong contribution to the success of the evening.

Down below, as the attention of the startled visitors was transfixed by the spectacular outcome of their calls to Timothy Twylock to manifest his presence to them, Arthur had his final little duty to perform.

In his pocket he had a small paper packet provided by Bert. The packet contained five small glass phials full of a green-coloured liquid. As instructed by Bert, he discreetly dropped the packet on the floor, and ground his foot on it. The phials shattered, to release the thoroughly obnoxious odour of hydrogen-sulphide gas. Bert's 'stink-bombs', purchased on one of his regular visits to a joke shop on Margate seafront, performed very well indeed, as they unfailingly always did! One of these alone was usually enough to cause a rapid exodus from an average–sized room.

Up above, listening to the disgusted comments which floated up from below, Bert noted with satisfaction that Arthur had carried out his assigned task dead on cue.

When the visitors had left the Oast House and gone on their way, Bert descended the steps to join his delighted comrades down below. Things had gone wonderfully well, and the carefully-laid plans for the evening had run with clockwork precision. As they went over the events step by step, all agreed that as an exercise in artificial haunting the scheme had proved frighteningly convincing. So much so that Mike said it had put the wind even up him! He swore that he really did think at one stage that Poltergeists had moved in to take over!

By common consent they decided to clam up about the evening's events, leaving their visitors with vivid memories of a haunted evening at the Oast house, convinced that they really had witnessed overwhelming evidence of a ghostly visitation.

This way, as the story spread, to be told and re-told over and over again, they looked forward to hearing people talk about it themselves. They were not disappointed. In the days and weeks ahead, they gained much amusement by listening to the ghostly details being related. From time to time they were asked to confirm that the events described really did take place. This they felt able to do with a more or less clear conscience. After all, as Arthur reasoned when they discussed it, the things described did happen!

"And who knows?" Arthur had concluded, in further justification of the continued deception, "Like Old Motty has told us, the spirits can put thoughts straight into your head. It's quite possible that Timothy Twylock himself thought the thing out and put the whole plans into our heads, using us as a means of showing that he was still there in the Oast House with them."

Warming to his theme he added a further comment. "After all," he said conclusively, "he was supposed to be a very clever bloke. And it was certainly a bloody clever scheme, wasn't it?"

That little afterthought removed all trace of guilt from their minds, and secrecy was assured.

The truth was that the Oast house team, like those before them, were in no doubt whatsoever that the Oast was in fact haunted. It gave them all the creeps at one time or another. As Arthur said to his cronies, all they had really done was to make anybody inclined to disbelieve such matters much less likely in future to pooh pooh any suggestion that the Oast house was haunted.

And there was another angle to it, too. They all felt sure that Timothy Twylock, wherever he was, would be pleased that he had not been forgotten. By re-enacting his dreadful death, the memory of him was reinforced.

So the legend of Timothy Twylock was in this way destined to continue down the years. And his spirit lived on, especially in the minds of those who worked in, or visited, the Oast.

And if Old Motty were right, Timothy's ghost popped back there now and again in person, whenever his spirit got to thinking his ghostly thoughts about the Oast, and by that means transported himself there in the effortless way that ghosts have of moving from place to place.

According that is, to 'The Theory of Spirit Mobility', as propounded by Motty Marsh, Caretaker Extraordinary of Littlebrook Churchyard, as extraordinary in his specialist field as was the legendary Timothy Twylock in his.

Chapter 12

THE CARRIER AND THE
SIBERIAN WILDCAT

a happy day for three small boys
out on the road with Dan

Shortly after eight o'clock on a fine morning in late July, Cecil Elton left his woodland gamekeeper's cottage carrying one of his twelve-bore shot guns wrapped in protective sacking, to intercept Dan Hooker, the carrier. An envelope was tied to the gun addressed to Greenstock's, the Gunsmiths of Canterbury, where the gun had to go for attention. Cecil's letter explained what needed to be done to it and in addition listed some supplies, including cartridges, which were to be sent back via the carrier that same day.

These supplies would be left by Dan at the blacksmith's forge on his way home. This was one of a number of Dan Hooker's 'pick up' points, where people could leave messages and goods for him. Fred Huddlestone, the blacksmith, like others at various scattered points, acted as an agent for Dan in return for a small handling charge, or sometimes free carriage for their own goods.

Taking advantage of Cecil's intention to catch the carrier, his wife Enid had packed twelve jars of jam for her parents who lived at Rochester. This was to be taken by the carrier to Canterbury East station and sent by the Railway's Goods Service to Rochester. The rail fee would be paid by Dan Hooker, and retrieved by him on presentation of the railway receipt when he returned that evening.

Each year, from their home-grown crop of strawberries, raspberries, blackcurrants and gooseberries, Enid made a supply of jam and always sent her parents a generous gift of this via the Carrier and the Southern Railway. Later that season she would be making plum and greengage jam, using fruit from a local farm, to add to her stock. Her parents would receive a welcome package of this by the same route.

Cecil strode purposefully along the woodland paths, watchful with 'eyes all round him', as was his natural habit when he moved about his extensive territory. Behind him trotted two of his dogs, disciplined and eagerly ready to obey any sudden command from their master. Things requiring their attention often happened with little or no warning, and they were continuously alert. Unless instructed otherwise, they remained closely to heel all the way. They did not range and forage around as pet dogs usually do when out for a walk with their owners in the countryside. These were working dogs, well-trained, knowing exactly what was expected of them, and on hand for instant action.

Just before half-past eight Cecil reached the perimeter of the wood where it bordered the main road. The woodland track ended at a five-bar gate, to the side of which was a stoutly built stile, put there for the convenience of walkers using the public right-of-way along one of the footpaths that passed through the woods.

Cecil used these main paths quite a lot himself, but also had a network of private 'keeper's paths' which criss-crossed the woodlands, especially cut for his professional convenience and gamebird-breeding activities. Very precisely cut, often almost arrow straight, and in places like a tunnel cut through dense undergrowth, access to these paths was hidden from the view of people walking along the public footpaths. But their existence was known to local boys who used them frequently, although always with the utmost caution, for strictly speaking they were forbidden territory. Cecil was well aware of this usage, but was extremely tolerant of it provided his 'rules', well-known to the boys, were not broken.

On arrival at the road, Cecil stoked his pipe and leant on the gate, puffing away contentedly as he looked down the road towards the village. Just past where Cecil stood, the road swung in a gentle, right-handed turn towards the brow of Littlebrook Hill. There was no sign of the carrier as far down the road as he could see, and he began to wonder if he were in for a longer than usual wait.

In a few minutes, though, he saw that he had indeed judged it about right, for Dan's cart suddenly appeared in his field of vision, crossing the road from the left-hand side. It had been obscured by a high privet hedge and Cecil knew that Dan must have pulled in on the parking area in front of his local pub, The Buffs, where no doubt he had called in to collect orders from Old Mac, the publican. Mac kept a boldly printed 'CARRIER PLEASE CALL' notice which he put in a window facing the road when he needed Dan Hooker's services. Dan gave these notices out to regular customers, to save them the inconvenience of having to watch for his coming along the road.

Like his father, his grandfather, and his great-grandfather before him, Dan earned his living as the local carrier. Over the generations, neither the nature of the business, not the 'equipage' necessary for its commission, had changed much at all. The latter was a horse-drawn, four-wheeled covered wagon, not unlike those which later generations would be more likely to associate with stories of the Wild West than anything else.

Except in so far that it was less sturdily and heavily built, the wagon was like a lightweight farm cart in structure, with wheels of the same general form, but more slender. The heavy loads they had to carry, and the rugged ground over which they had to work, dictated that farm carts had to be very strongly built, but the carrier's carts kept to roads and transported only comparatively light loads.

Most carts in the district were made by Spindlecrofts, the local wheelwrights. Well proven principles of construction were used in them all, with the relative stoutness of timbers, and special design features that had been developed over the years, chosen in each case to match a cart with the job it had to do.

Dan's wagon was covered with a canvas hood, fastened to a hooped framework, fitted to the attractively-shaped wooden sides. Both sides of the off-white coloured hood bore the boldly painted legend **G. HOOKER & SON, CARRIERS**.

Dan's father Godfrey had added the **'& SON'** to his name, much to his own and to Dan's pride, when Dan came of age, after working with his father from the day he left school. It was then plain that Dan was committed to the business for life. By this time Dan's father had equipped a second outfit which journeyed through different villages and hamlets, to extend the scope of the firm's operation. It also did special runs to coastal towns, as occasion demanded.

When the day came for his Dad to retire, Dan took over his round and employed a man to pick up his own duties. The core business remained the same as it had been for so many years—the daily journey from his home in the hamlet of Seatonbridge, through two nearby villages and on via Littlebrook to Canterbury.

Carriers, like Dan's small firm, had over the years established a network of operations covering the whole countryside. Each village had its regular carrier passing through, forming an essential link with the nearest town and railway stations. A high proportion of goods needed in the villages and remote hamlets was collected and distributed by their local carriers.

As they journeyed inwards towards the nearest town they picked up goods to deliver when they got there, and received instructions detailing errands to bring back a wide variety of things on the return journey. By a process of gradual evolution, a widespread interlacing system had grown up, with arrangements which enabled people to send out, and receive back, most of the goods needed to keep their day-to-day lives running smoothly.

The extensive network of railways brought almost all small towns and villages within 'carrier-distance' of the Railway's Goods Service depots. This, in conjunction with canals, rivers and main roads, made it possible to send goods from one place to another, however remote the places were.

Dan's small part of this intricate network connected a handful of villages and hamlets, together with numerous isolated farms and dwellings, to the three railway stations of Canterbury. Apart from transporting goods to and from points within his own territory, it was he who formed the first link in a chain of communication which went via Canterbury to anywhere in the country, or, through Dockland Goods Centres by sea to almost anywhere in the world.

It was usually shortly after 8.30am when Dan passed through Littlebrook on his daily journey to Canterbury. As his horse clip-clopped along, Dan glanced from side to side looking for his CARRIER PLEASE CALL notices at business premises where his services were frequently needed, and meanwhile spotted individuals obviously waiting for him to come along. In a surprisingly short time, so practised was his routine, he was through the centre of the village. The last stretch was up the hill and here—as with all hills—Dan got down to walk beside his horse, holding its bridle. Both he, and any passengers riding with him, always walked up hills to reduce the loading on his already quite heavily burdened horse.

Dan occasionally took passengers with him on his journey to Canterbury, perhaps to catch a train from one of the three stations, but more often than not for a day's shopping expedition. In the latter case he would pick them up on his return journey about four o'clock in the afternoon.

During school holidays village boys would sometimes spend a day with Dan, travelling with him on his rounds and helping him in one way or another when they were able to. For Dan this made a pleasant change. He enjoyed their company, and quite often they did indeed prove a great help to him. His work involved a lot of fetching and carrying and loading and unloading, so between them they saved Dan a good deal of footwork, as well as a lot of climbing in and out of his wagon to move goods around. The rather slow-moving journey seemed to pass more quickly when he had these happy, boisterous companions with him.

On the morning Cecil waited for him, Dan had spotted one of his notices in Bill Gunston, the saddler's, window. Among other orders from Bill he had to pick up a consignment of leather from Bacon's, the leather merchants, who supplied most of Bill's requirements for his saddlery work. It was a routine task for Dan, so much so that he needed no very detailed description from Bill of the goods to be brought back. His orders came in colloquial trade terms and he knew in advance what space was involved. Often Bill would hand him his fee when he delivered the goods, without even asking him what he owed, unless the order was an unusual one. Prices for goods and services seldom changed from one year to another.

Bill's youngest son Henry, and two of his mates, were eagerly waiting for Dan that morning. Boys living in the country needed to be opportunists in seeking their holiday entertainment. It was a nice day, and when Henry saw his Dad put the CARRIER PLEASE CALL notice in the shop window he had a sudden inspiration for a possible exciting day out with two of his mates. By the time Dan arrived, Henry and his two friends were ready and waiting, complete with packets of sandwiches and cakes, and bottles of lemonade.

Bill had quite happily agreed to ask Dan if the boys could spend the day with him. The answer was sure to be 'Yes'; nobody doubted that for one moment. The only nagging uncertainty was whether or not Dan would turn up already carrying some passengers. As luck would have it he was alone, so all was well.

When Dan left Bill's shop, on the bench seat beside him, grinning contentedly, were three small boys going out on a trip to town for the day.

When Cecil saw Dan's cart coming towards him, he saw that Dan had company. He smiled to himself when he caught sight of the three boys, sitting up beside Dan on his long wooden seat, under the canvas hood that projected outwards like a peaked cap as part of the cart's structure, to give protection from rain to the driver and his passengers.

In his turn, many years before, Cecil, as a small boy, had ridden on that very

152

same cart with Dan's father, Godfrey—in fact—as he now recalled—he had on more than one occasion joined Dan himself, who was of similar age, and often liked to accompany his Dad during the school holidays.

As they drew near, Cecil recognised the three boys. They were well-known to him since they were frequent visitors to his own woodland territory. Like most countrymen, Cecil was very tolerant in his handling of the younger generation because, having grown up in the same area, he had happy memories of his own boyhood days living in the heart of the Kentish countryside.

The guidelines of what could, or could not be done, by boys ranging through the woodlands, were well-established, and known to the boys. Provided these constraints were not abused, Cecil allowed his young visitors plenty of scope for their adventurous games. When he met then in the woods they were always interested to know what he was doing. Occasionally—when he could do so without hindrance to his work—he would allow them to accompany him, and they learnt a lot about the animals and birds of the district from him. Whatever the season of the year the woodlands could be a fascinating place to roam in, and few boys would intentionally do anything to upset Cecil and jeopardise the freedom he allowed them. To them he was a valued friend.

Mentally logging the names of Dan's young passengers, Cecil nodded to himself in a knowing way as he watched them approaching. As he looked at their grinning faces he thought that whatever else Dan picked up on his wagon on this day's trip, he sure had a right load of mischief up there alongside him to start the day off.

Next to Dan, his round, ruddy, healthy-looking grinning face seeming to radiate the very essence of potential mischief, sat Morgan Thomas, whose Dad, Ivor, was a well-known regular at The Buffs, Cecil's local pub.

Like a lot of other Welsh, Durham and Northumbrian families, the Thomases had migrated from more extensive coal-producing areas to work in the comparatively small but rich Kentish coalfield, attractive because of its location in the 'Garden of England'. This had given an injection of outside blood to the traditionally agricultural communities of the Kentish villages and coastal towns in south-east Kent. In time the natural propensity of most country people for laughter and humour was enriched—and sharpened—by these other influences.

Alongside Morgan Thomas sat Bill Gunstone's youngest boy, Henry. In the left-hand corner Cecil spotted Joe Oats, son of sailor Teddy Oats, the notorious newsagent whose chief claims to fame were that he could spit further and more accurately than any other tobacco-chewing gobber for miles around, and swear more fluently, irrespective of the company he was in, than anybody else.

As the cart drew near, Cecil called out a greeting to the carrier.

"Good morning, Dan. I see you've got yourself some company today."

"Mornin', Cecil," answered Dan. "Good 'arvesting weather, ain't it?"

Then the three boys called out their greetings to an old and well-liked friend.

"Hello, Mr. Elton," they sang out in a chorus of happy voices.

"Hello, lads," replied Cecil, smiling at the boys. "I hope you're going to help Mr. Hooker today, and not plague the life out of him. Behave yourselves now, as hard as that may be for some of you!"

"Of course we will!" laughed the boys, responding happily to Cecil's cheerful greeting.

"Good 'arvesting weather, ain't it?" added Morgan, unable to resist the temptation to mimic old Dan.

Cecil grinned at this unnecessary reinforcement of Dan's observation. He knew full well, as the boys did, and it was widely known in the district, that Dan had a certain unvarying repertoire of greetings with which he met acquaintances on his daily journeys. His job, always travelling slowly through places, and meeting a succession of different people, involved him in a constant repetition of greetings. Not being a very inventive fellow, he repeated over and over again his chosen phrase of the day, according to the weather and the season.

One of the most widely-known ones was used in the early weeks of September. If it were a rainy day, he invariably called out to passers-by, with a rueful smile creasing his face, a reference to hop picking.

"Mornin'. Proper 'op picking weather, ain't it!" would be his ironic greeting.

If it were, more happily, a nice fine day, his call would be modified accordingly.

"Mornin'. Good weather for 'op picking, ain't it?" his greeting would then be.

Fine weather was very much hoped-for during the hop picking period. For this reason, irrespective of whether Dan were around or not, if it happened to be raining during hop picking time, Dan's somewhat resigned-sounding, ironic phrase of "Proper 'op picking weather, ain't it!" was frequently used by one person to another, with an unspoken but widely-recognised reference to Dan's well-known personality in this topical exchange of greetings. It was always good for a knowing smile. Dan was a well-liked local figure, and his mannerisms were known to all residents for miles around.

On such a day, if Morgan Thomas spotted 'Old Dan' coming along the road, he would invariably, with a huge grin, beat Dan to the gun and sing out to him, in a loud voice for all within earshot to hear,

"Morning, Mr. Hooker. Proper 'op picking weather, ain't it!"

Morgan's accent would be as exaggerated an imitation of Dan's voice as he could make it—so much so that his mates winced at Morgan's apparent insensitivity to its being recognised by Dan himself.

Dan, however, if he registered the unflattering mimicry, never gave an indication that he had. Beyond an appropriate response such as "Hello there, young man. Yeah, rotten, ain't it," he would pass on seemingly without noticing anything unusual or pointed in the way he had been greeted by his grinning young acquaintance by the roadside.

When Cecil had handed Dan his gun and Enid's package for her parents, with appropriate instructions, he retraced his footsteps back through the wood to his cottage to resume his normal daily routine.

Meanwhile Dan, with the merest murmur to his horse, accompanied by a slight flick of the reins, set the wagon rolling again. The road was bordered on one side by the dense woodland, and on the other, first by an orchard, then, further along, by extensions of Cecil's territory, which then lay on both sides of the main road.

A mile or so further along, the road began a gradual descent as it approached the brow of a steep hill leading to a narrow valley below. On the other side of the valley was an equally steep uphill stretch beyond which the road broke out from the woodlands into open country, with cultivated ground on one side and pasture fields on the other.

When the gradual descent began, the pulling load on the hard-working old mare eased off, with the slight downward slope giving a welcome break from the continuous strain on her bodily muscles. A little later, when the slope steepened, Dan would apply his brake gradually, to prevent the cart from rolling up behind the horse to cause it difficulty.

On the gradual slope there was a short period when the tendency of the cart to be almost able to run on its own, resulted in the mare being able to walk with very little effort, a brief respite from its hard labour which no doubt it much appreciated.

At this point in the journey, when there was a marked reduction in the exertions of the horse, the boys noticed that Dan was staring fixedly at its broad, powerful hindquarters, evidently expecting some action to take place. Hardly had their eyes joined his, when the horse raised its tail slightly. Almost immediately large dollops of rich-looking brown dung began to ease out of the large vent hole which marked the end-point of its digestive system, to tumble out in a series of plops and fall in steaming lumps on the road below.

This process was intently watched by the three boys, with obvious close interest. It was a fascinating experience to be sitting just a few feet away from the centre of activity, situated at eye level just in front of them. Living in the country, where livestock abounded, they were not unaccustomed to evidence of passing traffic on the roads, and of having to watch where they put their feet, when walking on pasture land. But this performance, commonplace though it was to Dan, was something of absorbing interest to them, and the sheer scale of it clearly astonished them.

Their inevitable sniggering triggered Dan into discussing the event with them. He had an uneasy feeling that it behoved him to restore some dignity to the matter, the boys having been committed to his care for the day, rather than to pretend not to know what was causing their suppressed laughter. It was always supposed to be better to talk frankly about things and not seek to avoid them. So this very natural function happening during their smooth progress along the road was, he thought, better treated as something quite normal. This is what Dan decided to do. He chose his words carefully.

"The old girl always unloads here," he announced abruptly.

"Why?" asked Henry with a puzzled frown.

"Well, you see," answered Dan, glad to have a lead to hang some words on, "she feels the wagon start to go downhill, so she can stop pulling so hard. Then I reckon as 'ow she can give all 'er effort to straining away to unload *erself*. If you see what I mean."

"Oh yes, I see what you mean," commented Henry, trying not altogether successfully to suppress a difficult-to-control tendency he had to grin widely at times when instinct told him he ought to be serious. "I can see that all right. That makes sense that does. It would be hard for a horse to strain to unload, and pull away at the cart at the same time, wouldn't it?"

"That's right, son," confirmed Dan. "That's quite right. Nor could we, come to that!"

While these observations were taking place, the old mare, oblivious to the incongruity of having its private functions studied so intently by four pairs of eyes in such close proximity to its person, continued its efforts.

After what seemed to the young watchers to have been an almost unbelievable quantity of steaming hot dung to be generated miraculously by just one horse, a last small egg-shaped lump plopped out to hit the road and the procedure came to an end. The horse's tail dropped, to resume its normal relaxed position.

At this point Dan, with a call of "Whoa there, girl!" reined the outfit to a halt.

A row of dollops of varying size, some in clusters interspersed with small spaces and spatterings, now extended back up the road over a distance of some ten yards or so.

"Cor, strewth!" said Morgan, awestruck by the sight. "Blimey, look at that lot!"

"Now then, lads," said Dan, in a businesslike tone of voice, "you can give me a hand here, if you please. Under the tailboard, up under the back of the cart, you'll find a bucket with a shovel in it. Help me out by trotting back to shovel that lot up for me. I never waste that, it all goes back into my garden. I feed the old girl well, and she pays me back with some right good stuff she makes from it. Wants some beating that does on a garden, 'specially round tomatoes. Nothing better, there ain't, I can tell you!"

There was no reluctance on the part of his passengers to discharge this menial errand. With great enthusiasm and a rush to be first to grab the bucket, they leapt off the front of the cart and with no little pushing and shoving, set off to do their duty.

In a matter of a few minutes the job was done. Returning to the front of the cart, beaming from ear to ear with delight, Morgan showed the bucket of retrieved treasure to Dan.

"Where do you want this lot put, Mr. Hooker?" he asked.

"There's another big old galvanised-iron bucket under the back there, with a lid on it," Dan answered. "Tip it in there, please, and hang that bucket and shovel you've got there back where you found it. She'll drop another load on the way home and I'll get you to shovel that up for me too, if you will."

"Course we will," responded Morgan, and the three of them quickly carried out Dan's instructions, then scrambled back to resume their places on the front seat. Once more Dan gave the reins a flick and they were off on their journey again.

This little episode had engendered a marked enlivening of the spirits of Dan's companions, who were loath to let the interesting subject drop.

"Cor, don't she do a lot in one go!" commented Joe, much impressed by the mare's performance.

"Well, just look at the size of 'er," responded Dan. "There's one 'ell of a big stomach upstream from the tail end. You can see that by looking at 'er. It's all a matter of proportion, that's what it is. All a matter of proportion, as you might say."

"A horse eats a lot in one day, doesn't it, Mr. Hooker?" remarked Henry, figuring that a great deal must have to go in at one end of the horse to produce all that lot at the other. And it came out more than once a day too, according to what Mr. Hooker had just said.

"Oh yes, she puts away a tidy lot in a day. She does that!" agreed Dan emphatically. "She never goes short of grub, I can tell you that. Be kind to an 'orse, and an 'orse will be good you!"

"Mr. Hooker," intervened Joe, with a rather puzzled look on his face. "Do you always collect all that stuff every day?"

"Certainly I do," answered Dan. "So long as we're out in the country, that is. Course, I couldn't hold up the traffic in a town to do it, so I always trains my 'orses to unload on a quiet road, if I can."

"Well," continued Joe, not yet finished with his enquiries, "when she starts going, why don't you call out 'WHOA THERE' and make the horse stand still, so's the lot would fall down in one heap. That would save you going back up the road to collect it, wouldn't it?"

"Cos it wouldn't work that way!" answered Dan, with some emphasis.

"Why not?" asked Joe in a surprised tone.

"Well," explained Dan patiently, "cos it would throw the old girl out, that would. She would stop moving forward all right, but she'd stop crapping at the same time."

"Can't see why," pursued Joe.

"Well, think about it," said Dan. "How would you like to get asked to do something in mid shit like that? It would stop you off too, I bet."

Morgan had been listening to this exchange with increasing delight. His mind was fired off with spectacular visions following one another in rapid succession through his inspired and vivid imagination.

"That's not the same thing, Mr. Hooker," he intervened. "Joe may be a dirty little blighter sometimes, but he doesn't walk around while he's crapping!"

There was a chorus of laughter from his friends at this remark, with Morgan, who had hardly been able to get the words out, exploding with glee at the same time.

"No one said he did," stated Dan, clearly getting a bit needled by the way the conversation was running.

"Look at it this way," he explained, after a short pause. "Just suppose somebody asked young Joe a hard question, just as he sat down and was in mid shit, still straining. That would stop him off straight away now, wouldn't it?"

"What sort of question?" asked Morgan, intent upon exploiting this opportunity for another good laugh, and probing around to see what old Dan could be induced to come up with.

Dan thought a moment or two, his mind automatically turning to his own sort of daily problems.

"Well," he said, "suppose when he'd got started his schoolmaster barked at him a question like this. 'If a railway charges two shillings to take one dozen box of apples to London, how much would they charge to take one and a half dozen boxes of apples up there, instead of just the one?' "

Dan glowered round at Morgan. "He couldn't think that out and keep straining at the same time now, could he?"

"I see what you mean, Mr. Hooker," conceded Morgan, whose fertile mind had already moved on ahead. "That might stop Joe off, I can see that. But it wouldn't stop everybody!"

"Why not?" asked Dan, walking straight into Morgan's rapidly conceived trap.

"Well," responded Morgan, finding it very difficult to suppress his laughter sufficiently to get the words out, "you take Goofy Godfrey Goldsmith in our class at school. If a teacher asks him a question, he shits himself with fear, so you wouldn't stop him off by asking him a question in mid shit. All you'd do would be to speed him up so's he'd most likely blow his guts out. He'd go off like a gun he would, just like one of Nelson's cannons going off!"

This latter metaphorical allusion stemmed from Morgan's abiding interest in the sea, later to take him into the Royal Navy as a boy entrant, heading for a life at sea with its boundless opportunities for the development of his strong, inbuilt sense of humour through the wealth of bizarre incidents and sights he would encounter in foreign ports around the world.

Morgan's last comment caused such an outburst of laughter from the three lads that no further conversation was possible for several minutes. With tears running down their faces they rolled about, clutched their stomachs and had difficulty in carrying on breathing normally. Joe developed an attack of hiccups, making it even more difficult to retain his equilibrium.

Meanwhile Dan's face bore a pained and decidedly straight expression. He was not very amused and evidently a bit put-out by being—by devious means—caught off-balance to become the butt of the joke and at the centre of the ensuing laughter. He was all too well aware that 'young Morgan' had wrong-footed him.

Spotting this and perhaps unconsciously seeking to mollify Dan's discomfiture by involving him in a more serious conversation—neatly tilted to imply some deference to Dan's superior knowledge of worldly matters—Joe, struggling to keep a straight face, and after some quick thinking, made a profound observation.

"It's not really funny, is it, Mr. Hooker?" he said. "After all, all animals have to shit, don't they?"

"Of course they do," replied Dan. Then, as if as an afterthought, he added, "at least, that's what I used to think."

Quick to pick up this enigmatic answer, Henry intervened to query it.

"You said that's what you *used* to think, Mr. Hooker. Does that mean you don't think so anymore?" he asked, looking a little puzzled.

"Not since I went up to London Zoo two years ago I don't," replied Dan, with some obviously meaningful, hidden implication.

"Why's that, then?" asked Henry eagerly, with his two mates now intensely interested in this mysterious development of the conversation. There was clearly something worth hearing about from Mr. Hooker. They watched him closely, and in silence—their laughter now quietened because they didn't want to miss anything. At this crucial point, Joe, unable to control himself, hiccupped loudly, causing Dan to look round at him, so delaying his reply.

"Shut up, Joe, can't you!" interjected Morgan fiercely. "You're interrupting Mr. Hooker and we want to hear what he says. Hold your breath or go and drown yourself, or something!"

Dan then resumed his explanation.

"Well, you see," he continued, "there's lots and lots of different animals to see up there, you know. And some very queer ones too, that most people don't know about until they go to the Zoo."

"You're telling me there are!" broke in Joe, his mind bursting with suddenly revived memories to tell everybody. "When we went up there last Easter with my Aunt Nora, you should have . . . hic—you should have . . . hic—you should have seen . . . hic—you should . . ."

"Shut up, Joe," intervened Morgan again, angrily. "We don't want to hear about you and your bloody Aunt Nora. We're trying to listen to Mr. Hooker. And the more you keep on talking, the worse your hiccups will get. Just shut up for a bit—you sound worse than our cat when it's half-choked by chewing grass. If you can't stop, go and take a mouthful out of that bucket we've just put under the tail-board—that will quieten you down a bit."

Joe, summarily dismissed and deflated by this second telling-off, sat back on the seat—but not without another involuntary loud hiccup, followed by a succession of partly suppressed ones as he tried to hold his breath to stop his uncomfortable problem.

"Yes—well—like I was saying," continued Dan, "There's some mighty queer creatures up there in London Zoo, and no mistake. When I was walking round I spotted some strange, cat-like animals prowling around behind a fence. About half as big again as our pet cats they were. I'd never seen the like of them before, that I hadn't. Very strange they were, I can tell you. So I says to a keeper bloke standing there, 'ere, I says, what are those funny looking critters in there called? They look like some kind of big cats, to me.'

'That's right,' he said. 'They *are* cats. Siberian wildcats, that's what they are.'

'Ain't they got big heads!' I says to him. 'Too big for their bodies those heads look, to me.'

'Yes," he says to me, 'they have got big heads. You're quite right. They've got bloody great heads and no arse-'oles!'

'No arse-'oles!' I says to him. 'No arse-'oles! Then how do they shit?'

'They can't shit, you silly bugger,' he says to me. 'They can't shit. That's what makes them so bloody wild!'"

The explosion of laughter which greeted Dan's last remark caused such a disturbance that a startled pheasant took off with a loud screech from the grass on the bank by the roadside, causing Dan's faithful old mare to toss her head back in alarm and break into an uncharacteristic trot.

"Ere, 'ere, steady on, old girl. Ease up now," comforted Dan. "No need to pull your guts out like that just because of a frightened bloody cock-pheasant. Quieten down,

158

old girl. Quieten down. No harm done. No need to fret. Quieten down, now."

The old mare, hearing the familiar, comforting voice, and feeling the gentle tug-message on the reins, settled down again to its normal steady gait.

"That's better," said Dan, always concerned above all else for his old horse when any untoward event upset its calm progress.

It was quite some time after that before the boys stopped laughing and repeating Dan's words over and over again to one another, a process which set the picture of this highly comical story firmly in their memories for many years to come.

Their extreme merriment caused Dan to smile quietly to himself at their reaction to his story.

But he didn't tell them that the cockney keeper at the Zoo had imparted this peculiar biological information to his country cousin with such a straight and serious face that Dan had left the Zoo not in fact knowing whether his leg was being pulled or not!

And he still didn't know really, for it happened that his mind had been to some extent pre-conditioned to accept this unlikely story. Another similarly-minded spreader of suspect seed had previously cultivated Dan's grey matter and sown some seed of like nature. So the keeper had planted his story in tolerably fertile ground!

At the back of Dan's mind he had a vague memory of hearing in his local pub one night about some strange prehistoric creature that spat its waste products out of its own mouth because it only had a single-ended digestive system.

So far as he could remember, the pundit who often entertained them with his stories culled from the depths of his vast experience over many years across the wide world, had told his astonished audience of this most unusual creature. The man was a retired old seafarer who had sailed the seas all his life, for the most part in tea clippers to the Far East. He had many fascinating stories to tell—as tall as the masts of those beautiful, many-sailed ships!

He had said that these strange animals of prehistoric times stuffed themselves with food all day; went to sleep all night; woke up next morning and spat out the accumulated waste-products that had backed-up in their guts during the night; and then stuffed themselves again all next day!

The old sailor was always going on about a famous bloke called Darwin who worked out how living things changed for the better as years went by. According to the interesting old man, in a litter of these creatures one day there was a freak, a 'double-ended' job, which, like an owl, got rid of stuff it didn't want from both ends.

This one was much stronger than the others because its guts worked better. So its double-ended young ones were all stronger than their less fortunate single-ended brothers and sisters and so, at times of food shortage, the new models ate up the old type, until, at length, there were none of these left. At least, so the old sailor had said!

Dan couldn't be sure that Siberian wildcats weren't the same sort of animals. If one lot could get by with one hole, other animals could. At any rate, he had refrained from saying anything to the keeper at the Zoo in case he made a fool of himself.

At the same time he wasn't too sure if the story about the single-ended creature wasn't another of the old seaman's apocryphal yarns dreamt up when his mind was befuddled with the strong naval rum on which he seemed to live.

So Dan reserved judgement on the truth of the Siberian cat's awful predicament and left his young passengers to make up their own minds about it. At any rate, their animated discussions on the matter, in between bouts of loud laughter, kept him entertained for most of the rest of the journey.

On arrival in town, the many jobs Dan had to attend to kept them all occupied for between three and four hours with a break of not much more than half an hour while they had their snack lunch, anticipated with much eagerness and very much enjoyed.

For this lunch period Dan drove his outfit into the yard behind a large, very ancient staging-post Inn. Many carriers from outlying villages did the same thing. This arrangement enabled them to co-operate with one another, to fetch and carry goods from one country area to another with the yard at the Canterbury Inn functioning rather like a railway junction, where radiating lines meet together.

Dan had his pint of beer and a sandwich inside the pub with his cronies, while the boys found a comfortable corner in a fodder store. Meanwhile the old mare, not forgotten, buried her nose in a forage-bag, strung round her neck by a stout rope carefully organised by Dan before he went off to feed himself.

After lunch Dan completed the rest of his scheduled calls for the day and they then set off on the journey home.

On arrival back at Littlebrook, Dan's passengers thanked him warmly for letting them ride with him for the day, and made their respective ways home, tired-out but full of stories about the day's events. Chief of these, related with great hilarity to all their young friends, was Mr. Hooker's story of the Siberian wildcats at London Zoo. This story was destined to live longer than Dan's old mare: a great deal longer.

Meanwhile, some two hours later still, Dan finally reached his home and settled in for the night. His house was very curious, one of a number of similar places owned by long-established carriers scattered about in the English countryside. It was a combination of a stable and a dwelling, built—in the case of Dan's—from a converted barn.

Set back from the road, the centre of Dan's building was an open-fronted parking place for the cart. Dan's horse could pull the cart into this undercover parking spot, turning right on getting inside to position her nose in the very entrance to her own private stable. Dan unhitched the mare, led her into the stable, and settled her down for the night. She was very comfortably housed. Then he unloaded some private goods to take into his home and made a few arrangements to sort himself out for the next morning.

Behind the cart's parking place was an area where he stored fodder for his horse. There was also plenty of room in there for him to park goods in transit and sort his gear out.

To the left of the cart's parking place was the main entrance door to Dan's small but cosy cottage. Behind the whole building was a good-sized garden where most of the vegetables and fruit his family needed, was grown.

Dan's life was a busy one. But from one day to another it brought diversions, some involving unwanted troubles, but others—by way of compensation—brought unexpected periods of joyful incidents, and happier memories. Today, on the whole, had been one of the latter. His wife, Martha, could tell this by the smile on his face when he came in to tell her, as he always did, how his day had gone.

Later that evening, two miles away in Littlebrook, young Joe, after having his tea and getting himself washed and scrubbed up ready for bed, settled down at their living room table to do some drawing. Almost always, whether on schooldays or holidays, he finished his days working away at this pursuit.

Joe had a natural artistic ability and the more he drew the better he got at it so that he gained much satisfaction from his efforts. He particularly liked drawing people and animals. His pictures were drawn with uncannily true perspective. This talent produced a quality of depth and reality in his drawings which most would-be artists have to be taught how to achieve. Many fail to master this technique no matter how hard they try. But Joe didn't even have to think about it; he just did it!

It was his habit to record in the evening anything special he had seen during the day while the memory was fresh in his mind.

After his day out with Mr. Hooker he had no problem deciding what to draw. Working away with his soft, black-leaded pencil, in a surprising short time he drew a sketch of their family cat.

Underneath it he sketched a much larger cat, intended to represent a Siberian wildcat, a picture he had conjured up in his mind from Dan's graphic description. Remembering what Dan had said, he made this second cat about half as big again as the domestic cat which he had drawn above it to give a sense of scale. He made its head abnormally large, much out of proportion to the body.

Both cats were drawn partially turned so that they appeared to be facing away from the observer. This was where his natural ability showed itself. Unlike his young contemporaries, he did not of necessity have to draw his animals sideways-on, the easy way, but could turn them through any angle he liked, and they still looked absolutely right.

In this drawing he particularly wanted the rear-end of the cats to show up clearly, while nonetheless preserving their unmistakeable identity as cats. Their faces were made to look back slightly, as though they had been walking off and heard a noise from behind them that caused them to look round to see what was what.

Joe's Dad, noticing Joe's concentration, got up from his armchair to have a look to see what his talented son was drawing. It was, however, part of Ted's nature to be reluctant to express either praise or thanks to anybody about anything. He was much more likely to find fault and to dish out criticism and complaint, more often than not with little or no justification.

Joe knew his Dad only too well, and waited with resignation for some acid comments. Out of the corner of his eye he saw his Dad lift one leg, and knew full well what was coming, for his 'old man' had an infinite capacity to generate a seemingly continuous supply of surprisingly solid spit at one end, and great quantities of nauseous surplus air at the other. A resounding fart broke the silence in the room.

"That's better," grunted Ted with evident satisfaction, and continued his study of Joe's work.

"Better for you, maybe!" muttered his busy son, a response that seemed strangely more like that from another man than a small boy.

There was no reaction from Ted to this apparent impertinence. Some boys might well have expected a clout. Joe didn't. His Dad, awkward complaining cuss though he was, had never once laid on hand on his son. Perhaps he'd seen too much violence in his time. So, at length, after a prolonged examination of Joe's work, his Dad made his first observation.

"What the 'ell are you drawing now, Joe?" Ted asked, watching Joe at work on the lower cat.

"Cats," answered Joe.

"I can see that," snapped his irascible Dad. "The top one's not bad, but the bottom one has got too big a head!"

"That's not an ordinary cat, that one isn't," said Joe defensively. "It's a Siberian wildcat, like Mr. Hooker saw at London Zoo. They have very big heads, much bigger than ordinary cats do, and their bodies are about half as big again as our pet cats."

"Huh!" grunted Ted, not impressed. "Never heard of them!"

He stood for a few more minutes, watching Joe develop the sketches. Joe worked on busily and wondered what next his Dad would find to complain about. He didn't have long to wait.

"What are you drawing that one's tail stuck straight up in the air like that for?" Ted asked. "That's not right. No cat walks around with its tail stuck up like a ship's mast."

"Why not?" queried Joe, secretly sensing that his Dad was walking right into trouble.

"Because," began Ted, with every air of having little patience with people who asked silly questions, "because it's natural for a cat to keep its tail hanging down over its backside."

"Can't see why," prompted Joe.

"To cover its arse-hole up, that's why," said his Dad emphatically. "No cat wants flies buzzing round its backside and dogs sniffing about at it, like they would do if it left its arse-hole uncovered. That's obvious, that is! I should have thought you'd know that!"

"Siberian wildcats don't need to worry about that," stated Joe, with quiet authority.

"Why not?" asked his Dad abruptly, walking slap into the trap.

"Cos they don't have arse-holes at all," answered Joe blandly. "There's nothing there to cover up."

"Don't be bloody silly," exploded his Dad. "If they haven't got arse-holes, how the hell do you think they can shit?"

Joe, with barely suppressed laughter, delivered his much savoured punch-line, carefully nurtured in his mind for just this very moment.

"Siberian wildcats can't shit, Dad. That's what makes them so wild," he said, in a quiet voice, sounding as serious as he could, but having great trouble not to grin.

Ted's face went puffy and red, but whether from anger, or difficulty in stopping himself from laughing, Joe couldn't tell.

Quick to shift the blame lest his Dad should be about to credit *him* with having thought out this little story off his own bat, Joe explained the matter a little further.

"I know it sounds silly, Dad," he said, "but it's the truth. A keeper at London Zoo told Mr. Hooker all about them. And if a Zoo keeper said so, it must be right, mustn't it?"

This apparent innocent acceptance by his son of the word of an adult in a position of authority as being beyond question, silenced Ted for a few moments. Being of cockney origin himself he could very well picture in his mind a keeper at London Zoo handing out this punch line to a hayseed like old Dan the carrier, up from the country for the day. Just right for that sort of reception, old Dan was. Ted figured that the keeper and his mates were probably still laughing up there at the way Dan had swallowed their story.

During this short period of uneasy silence Joe was acutely aware that his Dad was gazing at him fixedly, as if uncertain whether or not he was being taken for a ride. Sensing an imminent inquest, he decided to postpone further work on his drawings until later that evening when the atmosphere was safer. He got up from the table and discreetly went up to his bedroom for a bit.

His Dad lost no time in clearing off to the pub for his regular evening session there, no doubt to grumble to his drinking companions about old Dan filling his son's head with a lot of nonsense.

A little while after the sound of the door banging shut announced the departure of his Dad, Joe came quietly downstairs from his bedroom to complete his drawing.

"May I just finish my drawing, Mum, before I go to bed?" he asked.

"Yes, all right, Joe," his Mum answered. "You carry on for a bit, if you want to. You haven't got to get up early to go to school in the morning."

Joe's mother, a kindly, understanding lady, smiled to herself as she watched Joe concentrating on his drawing. She had sat quietly working at her sewing in her high-backed chair while the exchange between Joe and his Dad has taken place. She knew them both very well indeed and was a very perspicacious lady. She had listened with quite amusement as Ted had blundered into young Joe's minefield.

There was nothing she could have usefully added to the conversation between them, and Joe hadn't come out of it badly anyway. She had long ago learnt that it was better for everybody not to take sides if Joe and his Dad were discussing weighty matters, especially things as profound as Siberian wildcats, for example. They invariably argued, because it was Ted's way to nag and grumble, while young Joe had long since found that attack was the best form of defence. They were best left alone to resolve their differences on their own.

For a while the room was silent as each of them concentrated upon their own pursuits. At length Joe, with a little sigh of satisfaction, put down his pencil, got up from the table and showed his mother his finished drawing.

"That's very good, Joe," she said, as she studied it. "It's very good indeed, particularly of Mr. Hooker's cart."

On the upper half of Joe's sheet of paper were the two cats, about which she had already gleaned prior knowledge from the conversation she had heard.

Beneath them, drawn with wonderful clarity, was a picture of Dan Hooker's wagon, moving off up a road by a wood. On the tail-board, which was held up level with the floor by two strong chains attached one to each side, sat two small boys, legs swinging below their perch. They were waving goodbye to a man, unmistakeably Cecil Elton the gamekeeper, who stood by the roadside with his pipe smoking away in his mouth and two dogs by his side.

Through the inside of the cart Dan could just be made out, sitting on the driving seat with a small boy by his side.

Beneath the tail-board swung two buckets—one with a shovel stuck out of the top—the other with a lid on it.

It was the habit of Dan's young passengers to spend part of a journey, by way of a change, sitting on the rear of the cart, stretching their legs and swinging them beneath the tailboard. They liked to watch the occasional motor vehicle chug up to pass them, and to wave cheerily to the occupants. More frequently, cyclists would go pumping by, seldom without comments from the observers studying their laborious progress from the relative comfort of their tailboard seat.

Joe's drawing of the cart was angled to show it pulling from the right-hand side of the road over to the left. Just visible by this means was one side of the canvas hood. On it Joe had printed, in squashed-up letters, just as they would be seen from this oblique viewpoint:

G. HOOKER & SON, CARRIERS

His Mum never ceased to marvel over how it was that her young son could make things look so realistic, with no apparent trouble at all. Neither she nor Ted had any artistic talent, but Joe had this marvellous natural gift.

Though he remembered full well that when they had left Mr. Elton by the roadside they were all three sitting up-front, Joe's eye for a good picture composition had made him decide to put two boys on the back, and one up-front with Mr. Hooker rather than try to show four figures in a row on the front seat with their backs to the eye. It really was a splendid little picture and his Mum gazed at it with genuine admiration.

Turning her attention to the cats she said, "That Siberian wildcat is a funny looking moggy, I must say, Joe. Is that really how Mr. Hooker described them to you?"

"That's what he said they were like, Mum," answered Joe. "I put our cat at the top so I could show how big they are, compared to our pet cats."

"Yes, I can see that," commented his Mum. "That was a good idea otherwise people looking at the drawing could think it was any size they liked. I see you've put in some labels too, to show the main differences between those cats and normal ones."

Joe had indeed done just that. There was no room for misunderstanding his drawings. The first cat bore the description **OUR PET CAT 'FELIX'**. The one beneath was boldly labelled **SIBERIAN WILDCAT**.

There were three notes, in balloons, pointing by arrow-headed lines to various parts of the lower cat. The one on the left pointed to its head and carried the comment:

VERY BIG HEAD

The centre one pointed to its body and read:

BODY HALF AS BIG AGAIN THAN A PET CAT

On the right, the third arrow pointed just below the cat's vertically-drawn tail and bore the information:

NO HOLE HERE

"I don't know that I believe that, Joe," said his Mum, pointing to the third label.

"Well, that's what the London Zoo keeper told Mr. Hooker, Mum," countered Joe doggedly. "That's what the keeper said, so it must be true, mustn't it?"

His Mum made no answer, and wisely decided to pursue the matter no further. It was time for Joe to go to bed.

"I think you'd better put your things away now, Joe," she said, with a smile. "It's time you went off to bed. Up you go now, there's a good boy."

Joe carefully inserted his latest drawing into his already bulging folder, placed the folder with his toys on his corner of the crowded dresser and, with a cheerful "Goodnight, Mum", he went off upstairs to bed.

It had been an exciting but long and tiring day. He smiled to himself as he went over the events of the day, but in a very few minutes he was soundly asleep. On occasions, long afterwards, his drawing was to remind him of this happy boyhood day, and one glance at it was enough to set him smiling again at the memories it evoked.

About an hour or so after Joe had gone to bed, just after the local pub's chuck-out time, his Dad came home. He had evidently not forgotten Joe's drawing because he lost no time in picking up Joe's folder and extracting the top page. For some time he studied it carefully. His eye was caught first of all by the sketch of Dan's cart, which Joe had not started when he had left home for the pub. This he peered at closely, taking in the extraordinary amount of detail Joe had managed to convey so well.

"Pretty good this is, Mabel," he said, with somewhat grudging approval. "This drawing Joe's done of Dan Hooker's cart is not bad. Not bad at all, this isn't!"

"Yes, I thought so too, Ted," she replied. "It's very good indeed, I think. I really don't know how he does it. He's very clever at making things look just right."

Ted then spotted the labels on the now-completed drawing of the Siberian wildcat. He scowled as he read them and nodded his head up and down slowly, tut-tutting as he did so.

"That bloody Zoo keeper saw Dan coming all right, didn't he?" he muttered, in a scornful tone of voice. "Fancy the silly old sod swallowing all that load of bloody nonsense. Cor blimey! A proper bloody turnip they must have taken old Dan for!"

Looking at the contentious picture, with the cat's tail stuck vertically upwards in such a provocative manner, he inwardly winced a bit as he recalled how Joe had led him in, right up to the chop line, in their brief conversation about the controversial cat.

Not for the first time he had an uneasy feeling that his young son had somehow outwitted him. This was not a happy thought for an ex-Royal Navy man. It was too much like a destroyer outmanoeuvring a battleship. And Ted was very much a battleship man; he had served in them for many years. In the Battle of Jutland, with his close crew-mates, he had manned a fifteen-inch gun, an experience of which he had very vivid memories that would never leave him. He had the 'Big Ship' man's disdain for small ships like destroyers, which, he said, in action buzzed around like blue-arsed flies, with pea-shooters for guns, steaming about getting in everybody else's way and achieving sod all!

It happened that just a few days earlier Ted had been telling Joe, who liked to hear his Dad talk of life in the Navy, about the various ships that made up a Battle Fleet. He found himself now remembering that he had described destroyers to Joe as 'piddling little toy warships that just steamed about at high speed trying to look important.'

'When it comes to sea battles,' he had said to Joe with much pride, 'it's the Big Ships which do the real fighting and win the wars!'

'Not always they don't, Dad,' he could almost hear his young son saying, as—making a mental connection with tonight's little tussle—he saw Joe in the guise of a small ship outwitting his battleship Dad.

It was normal behaviour for Ted to relate almost all day-by-day experiences, however mundane, to life in the Royal Navy. His subconscious mind was apparently responsible for these sometimes strange connections. He had been a 'regular', not just a 'temporary war-time sailor', as he somewhat disparagingly described those who swelled their ranks when real fighting had to be done.

Like many others, Ted carried the stamp of the Royal Navy throughout his life. He was very proud of his Navy service which, he was fond of telling people, was far and away the most powerful Navy in the world, bigger—he would never tire of saying—than any other two Navies in the world put together.

Ted went to bed that night in a vaguely disturbed frame of mind. Unlike his soundly-sleeping son in the next room, he tossed and turned about a bit in the night, and had curiously muddled, confused, and decidedly bizarre dreams.

Had a psychologist been confronted with the task of trying to unravel the underlying significance of Ted's dreams, he might have found himself batting on a very sticky wicket.

It would have tested his powers of invention to come up with a logical explanation and a convincing philosophical, deeply-seated connection, between a village newsagent, a cockney Zoo keeper, a carrier's horse-drawn cart, a so-called Siberian wildcat with biological peculiarities and a proud battleship of the Royal Navy, hull-down on the horizon being chased over the skyline by a destroyer, captained by a small boy proudly directing operations, standing on the bridge dressed in the Cub's uniform!

Next morning Ted woke up from his restless night, sufficiently disturbed by his dreams to cause him to decide to leave well alone.

He made no further reference to Joe's drawing. Perhaps he had an idea he might be sunk without trace if he re-opened the engagement again. Even for a Royal Navy man there are times when discretion is the better part of valour.

His talented son Joe, young in years and small in stature, already had the measure of him and often came off best in their frequent arguments. Like the dwellers in the distant tropical countries Ted had visited in his worldly travels, growing up in a hostile environment gives those who survive a natural immunity to indigenous diseases and an acute awareness of lurking local dangers. Joe's developing intellect, honed and sharpened by the daily need to respond to incessant nagging criticism, was already becoming more and more capable of hitting back with comments that were shrewd, incisive and mature beyond his years.

Like protective armour, Joe's growing immunity to damage from attack, coupled with his developing capacity for manoeuvre, and active penetrating return fire, increasingly dissuaded his irascible ex-Naval Dad from ill-prepared verbal sorties against him. Joe's life became the better for it and his personality bore the watchful alertness necessary for survival under fire.

Meanwhile, like a token of one small victory, Joe's drawing of a Siberian wildcat remained unchallenged in his file of artistic work, and the inventive—if rather crude wit— of an unknown cockney keeper at London Zoo, was recorded for posterity.

Chapter 13

HERBIE AND HORACE
wheelwrights and coffin makers

With no enthusiasm but little choice because they had a living to earn, Herbie and Horace set off for the workhouse to do a job of work.

The twin brothers, fifty years old and unmarried, were the proprietors of Ebenezer Spindlecroft & Sons, Wheelwrights and Undertakers of Littlebrook (Est. 1823). They had inherited the business from their father, Samuel Spindlecroft, who had trained them both.

Their apprenticeship had been extremely thorough because their Dad was a stickler for accuracy and high standards of workmanship. He himself had been apprenticed as a boy to an old-established firm of wheelwrights near Ashford in Kent. This had given him a first-class background in the manufacture and repair of a wide variety of horse-drawn vans, carts, carriages and wagons, as well as hand-pushed vehicles from bakers and grocers carts, down to simple wheelbarrows. In all he had worked for the firm for eighteen years, at the end of which time he was a very competent and knowledgeable wheelwright.

Samuel then left Ashford to join his Dad, Ebenezer, who had started his own business as Undertaker & General Carpenter at Littlebrook in 1823 at the age of twenty-four, precipitated into doing so, though not unwillingly, when his own employer had died and the business closed down, leaving Ebenezer high and dry.

It had long been Ebenezer's dream to expand his business to embrace the wheelwright trade, but this involved a great deal more know-how and skills than he had himself. So Samuel eventually joined his Dad, and together they enlarged the scope of the business.

Surprisingly quickly a thriving wheelwright operation was developed alongside the established trades. In time the wheelwright part of the business became the major part, not only carrying out repairs necessitated by accidents or by normal wear and tear, but also manufacturing a range of new vehicles of the kinds used locally. Meanwhile, undertaking and general carpentry work provided a smaller, but nonetheless very important source of income.

Now Ebenezer's grandsons, Herbie and Horace ran the well-established firm with the help of two general carpenters and a boy under training.

Proudly they continued to trade under their Grandfather's name. On taking over from their Dad they had contented themselves with adding an 's' to the word 'Son' in the then-existing title, reckoning that as grandsons of the founder they could line up with their Dad, Samuel, and be embraced by this single word—'Sons'.

It pleased them to retain the original name. *Ebenezer Spindlecroft & Sons* had a nice ring to it. Their Dad Samuel did in fact live to see the 100th anniversary in 1923 of the founding of the family firm, but died less than one year later aged ninety, beating his own Dad's lifespan by five years. Ebenezer had died in 1884 at the age of eighty-five when his grandsons were just nine years old. The brothers remembered their genial old Grandad, with his bushy white beard, very well.

Herbie and Horace maintained the high standards of workmanship set by their master-craftsman Dad, and the small country business continued to flourish in their care. But there were some jobs they enjoyed more than others. They were certainly a great deal happier working on carts than coffins! However, they were philosophical about life and took the demands of their means of livelihood very much in their stride. They worked hard, were very skilled, and derived much pleasure and satisfaction from their creative crafts.

Despite their preference for the wheelwright part of their business, it was becoming all too obvious to them that the demand for these age-old skills was diminishing. Tractors were replacing horses on the farms, and motor vehicles were increasingly taking the place of horse-drawn carts and wagons on the roads. Nobody could tell how far the process would go, but the trend was evident for all to see. So, though they did not like dwelling upon it, the brothers were aware that the balance of work available to their firm would tilt away from wheelwrighting, making it imperative for them to look after the undertaking and general carpentry part of their business if they were to survive and prosper in the long term.

Their uncomfortable awareness of this fact of life didn't make them any happier about today's priority job. They never liked going to their present destination. Few people did, unless they had to. Unfortunately Herbie and Horace were among those who had to, so they set off as early as they could, to get it over with and get back home as soon as possible.

The workhouse, or 'The Union' as it was called by officialdom, and by many others who found it a less forbidding name to use, was a miserable, bleak place at the best of times. It was the more so to the brothers because the part of it they went to on their not infrequent visits was the mortuary.

Every time they visited the establishment they were very conscious as they went through the small door set in one of a pair of large, impressive, prison-like, heavy wooden doors which fronted the place, that every resident came in that way and almost all of them finished up in the small, bare, chilly, whitewashed room the brothers headed for once inside the premises.

Strict control was exercised over who went into, or came out of, the workhouse, and the twins each signed the Visitor Book, recording their time of arrival, before going off to discharge their duty. The large, arch-shaped, main double-doors were always kept securely locked and opened only to let in vehicles on official business. One such vehicle was the Spindlecrofts' hearse in which the brothers would be returning in a few days' time to discharge the second stage of their usual two-part operation.

The man in charge of the establishment was called 'the Master', an appropriate title for the present incumbent. He was a small, bumptious little man who walked about with his chest puffed out and visibly straining—or so it appeared—to stretch himself upwards to the very limit his small frame would allow. Perhaps his aggressive bullying manner was a form of compensation for his small stature, or maybe he was just born with a nasty nature. Whatever the reason, he was cocky and mean, not a nice man at all. A miserable place was made the more so by the presence of this mean and autocratic little man who presided over it.

Herbie and Horace didn't like him any more than they liked the dismal place itself. It was very much an end-of-the-road residential home for the very old and infirm. These made up the majority of the inmates, but there were some younger ones who were destitute, or, for one reason or another, unable to care for themselves in the world outside.

However, the distaste of the twins for the man, as well as for the insular world over which he presided to earn his living, in a job that afforded him great opportunities to feed his inflated ego, was mollified to some extent by the fact that they attended there on business to earn money. Attendance there also had another more subtle beneficial effect upon them as it prompted them to save some of the money they earned there and elsewhere in the hope that it would help to keep them from becoming residents when they in their turn became too old to take care of themselves. The place gave them the creeps.

Their business was concerned with the dead and—by its nature—The Union provided a steady flow of customers. So they were suitably respectful and deferential to the Master, suffering his offhand, condescending manner of addressing them without showing any noticeable offence. Their calling required of them the ability to be able to control their facial expressions and display long, sorrowful, unsmiling countenances when attending their often sad duties. If they nursed an inner desire to puncture the ego of the pompous little fellow, they didn't show it. They subjugated their desire to cut him down to size to the necessary matter of earning their living.

Today their sombre task was to measure up a tramp known locally as Wandering Willy, whose premature death had resulted sadly from his own initiative in choosing what he had thought to be an ideal place to sleep for the night.

Not for the first time in his travels, he had been attracted by the warm glow in the night sky which emanated from a lime kiln built into a bank about twenty yards off the road at the foot of a chalk hill. Previously he had enjoyed the free warmth of such places with impunity and passed comfortable nights sheltered from the wind, lying curled up by the base of the kiln. He was not aware of the inherent dangers of spending a night in close proximity to a working lime kiln.

One of the main gaseous products generated by the action of heating limestone by a charcoal, coke, or anthracite fire in order to turn the chalk into quicklime is carbon-dioxide gas. This heavy but odourless gas came off the top of the kiln and promptly sank down as an invisible cloud to surround the base like a billowing skirt. With a wind blowing, or even a just a gentle breeze, the gas was dispersed harmlessly as it left the top of the kiln and did not collect densely at its base, so nobody spending several hours sleeping there suffered any ill effects and went off with grateful thoughts of the benign nature of these small havens of comfort in an otherwise largely inhospitable countryside.

On Wandering Willy's last night, however, there was no breeze at all. The night air was still, the sky clear, and no leaves rustled in the nearby coppice of bushes and undergrowth. Willy went peacefully to sleep, and stayed asleep forever. He was found next morning looking for all the world as though he were dreaming happy dreams, deeply and soundly sleeping on while the world around him was waking up to start another working day.

To the two men who arrived to work at the kiln it seemed a pity to have to disturb him, for he looked as though he would most likely sleep on contentedly, perhaps until almost midday, if left in peace. But they had their work to do and had to get him up and on his way.

So, not unkindly, but in loud voices which broke the stillness of the quiet morning, they called out to him to 'RISE AND SHINE'.

He did not respond, so they prodded him and called again, with no more success. It was not many moments afterwards that the awesome truth was apparent to them. Wandering Willy had finished his nomadic life on earth and was away on a longer journey.

The local policeman was called, along with the doctor, and the un-paying guest of the lime kiln was pronounced dead. Shortly afterwards he was carried off leaving the two workmates to carry on with their normal duties at the kiln, their day darkened, and their spirits quietened, by this sad start to a day that had dawned so brightly.

At length Wandering Willy, who true name was unknown, was certified as having died of suffocation and transported to The Union where his body was placed in the mortuary to await the attention of the undertakers.

Meanwhile, the **DANGER** notice near the lime kiln was renewed, to discourage others from being beguiled by the beckoning warmth of the place, and perhaps meeting the same fate. People living in the vicinity of these lime kilns knew their potential dangers because, wherever they were situated, each local generation told the next of the reputation they had of being killers of vagrants who intruded upon them by night.

Such kilns were found here and there in most areas of the countryside where limestone was easily to be found, but fatal accidents were very rare and notices warning of their dangerous ability to knock out those occasional people who chose to sleep by them, tended to be neglected until their need was again highlighted by another accident.

To local people the new notice served as a reminder that Wandering Willy, for several years a regular visitor to the area, would pass that way no more. It was, in an oblique way, a memorial to this solitary, rather unkempt, bearded figure about whom nothing was known except that his home was the open road. Now it fell to Herbie and Horace to see him on his way.

It didn't really take two men to measure up one body but the brothers habitually did such things together unless circumstances dictated otherwise. And, truth to tell, neither of them ever wanted to go to the mortuary alone if they could possibly avoid it.

They were inseparable twins and made a very effective team. Unlike in appearance, they were also not identical in their natural abilities, but these latter differences developed into a positive advantage. There were some things one did better than the other and vice versa. The result was that working together over many years had caused them to use their respective skills in a naturally complementary way without any conscious effort or difficulty in deciding who did what.

To watch them at their work was impressive and entertaining, especially if they were creating something which called for both precise craftsmanship and also artistic ability. A small pony trap or a milkman's delivery cart, were examples of this. Their skill as wheelwrights was widely respected, though the scope of their business was small compared with that of their fellow craftsmen working in one of the main firms of wheelwrights found in central positions in most counties. Both were skilled woodworkers, but whereas Herbie was the more adept at the very precise craftsmanship needed for cabinet making, Horace was a natural artist. He had a good eye for shape and design— particularly in the production of the graceful curves and pleasing lines of some of the smaller horse-drawn, or pony-drawn, vehicles, and of the various tradesman's hand-carts they made. The more detailed of the paintwork on the finished products was also done by Horace.

Both of them were always a little ill-at-ease when handling the dead. It was worse if they were alone. Together their mutual bond helped them both to face up to this aspect of their work more easily.

When they had measured up Wandering Willy, they stood for a few moments gazing down at him. A tramp was a mystery. Where did he come from? What sort of parents had he had? Had there been some tragedy in his life that had driven him away from normal society to live a lonely life with no roots, sleeping under the stars on fine days, or in whatever shelter he could find in bad weather? Or was there a home somewhere that he could go back to if he wanted? It was a puzzle. Every tramp was an enigma. Nobody ever seemed to know anything about any one of them.

To the brothers the still figure struck a chord of pity in their hearts. Both of them were compassionate men of kindly disposition. He looked such a forlorn figure, somehow the more so lying dead and unknown in the bare, cold, dank, cheerless room they were in. Their job now was to go off and make him a simple coffin, of the cheapest possible construction, of the type reserved for those whose burial charges had to be met by Poor Law funds. He would then end his days in a paupers grave, buried inconspicuously in his entirely functional, simple and totally unpretentious coffin, so different, in the eyes of the professional brothers, from the luxurious attention to detail in the final arrangements made for the departure of those at the other end of the perceived scale of human importance and personal economic circumstances.

Had they have known it, Wandering Willy, whose simple instinctive philosophy had been sharpened and deepened by the luxury of endless hours of unhurried thought, living close to nature, would have seen no difference in these endings or, for that matter, of a sparrow under a hedgerow. Death could neither be diluted nor enhanced; dead was dead and that was that, the same for all, no matter what the final earthly embellishments of the empty lifeless shell. A talk with Willy before he went would have comforted them and saved them sorrow.

Herbie and Horace were struck by the strong features and athletic form of the dead man. The tendency was to pre-judge all tramps as old, or very old, shaggy, dirty, uncouth and unkempt men, plodding away the last years of life in their chosen freedom from all ties of home and family. The heavy growth of beard and side-whiskers typical of them gave an immediate impression of age, reinforced by the ragged, shapeless assortment of clothing which obscured their bodies.

This was the first tramp that had died on their patch. He was not quite what they expected. To begin with, he was clearly not as old as they had automatically assumed. Nor was his face devoid of bearing and character. Their preconceived ideas of the nature of a 'standard tramp' were dispelled by this first study of one at close hand. They were strangely stirred by this experience and left the premises feeling vaguely troubled in their minds. On their way home they were both silent and thoughtful. No words passed between them; they weren't needed. Each knew they were both pondering the same things. Disturbed thoughts do not make for easy conversation.

When they arrived back at their workshop they followed normal procedure. Coffins took priority. When they had one to do they made it straightaway, then got back to their main occupation as wheelwrights. Usually this involved carrying out repairs, but occasionally—to their greater pleasure—they were engaged in making new wheels, carts of various kinds, four-wheeled wagons, or maybe hand-carts.

Methodically they began to get the materials and tools together, in the corner of their workshop organised specifically for the efficient construction of coffins. At this stage they exchanged their first comments since leaving the workhouse about the task in hand.

"We must do what we can for that poor bloke," said Horace without preamble.

"That's what I thought," replied Herbie. "If we don't try to see him put down half-way decent, nobody else will. In a way we're the nearest thing to a family he's got. There's nobody else to bother about him, that's for sure."

So, without much discussion beyond that needed to select the wood, decide upon the model they would make and the fittings and furniture to be used, they quickly set about building a coffin for their unknown client.

A few days later, at the short graveside ceremony, the Vicar, Reverend Yelman, accompanied at his request by his two-parish 'shared' young curate—more to make up the number than for professional support—was quick to notice because of his long years of experience in such matters, that the tramp's coffin was of distinctly better quality than the standard type normally used for the burial of paupers.

As the little party moved away from the graveside, he had a word with Herbie and Horace, pacing solemnly by his side.

"Did the Master manage to locate relatives of that tramp and get them to pay towards his funeral expenses?" he asked. "If so, he didn't tell me, because so far I've had to register the man as 'of unknown name', and if the Master has found the family with the help of the police, he ought to have remembered to tell me the man's name. I reckon to tie up the Records on the day of a funeral so that the matter is fully dealt with."

The Vicar had half-guessed the answer to his question before he'd finished asking it. Knowing the punctilious nature of the Master of The Union, he would almost certainly not have failed to pass on the tramp's name if he had got to know it. That sort of administrative detail was closest to the man's heart. Truth to tell, he was more interested in keeping his books in meticulous order than in the welfare of those whose names he entered in them.

"No, not so far as we know," answered Herbie. "He just called him a vagrant, name unknown. Sad, when you come to think about it," he added.

The Vicar pursued the matter a little further. He suspected what had happened, and did not want the kindness of his respectful companions to go unremarked.

"I know of course that his coffin was not of the normal Poor Law kind," he commented. "It was considerably more expensive and better furnished. I also know that the fee you will get is fixed, no matter how good you make the coffin. Have you two done it yourselves, at your own expense, for the sake of that poor homeless soul?"

"Well—yes—we have," said Horace. "We couldn't see him go off with no thought from anybody. It didn't seem right, did it, Herbie?"

"No," confirmed Herbie, a trifle self-consciously. "We kind of felt responsible for him, as we were the last to be with him."

"God bless you both," murmured the Vicar with heartfelt sincerity. "That was an act of true Christians and I thank you for it most truly. You have sent a lonely man off with an act of real human kindness. Thank you, my friends, thank you."

The brothers made their departure, a little discomfited by the Vicar's remarks. They had done what they had done not wishing it to be noticed by anybody, except, that is, perhaps Wandering Willy himself, in whatever way it was that a departed soul was conscious of what was done for him at the end of his time on earth. It was the sadness of the sight of his lonely figure lying in the dismal mortuary that had moved them to reach out a hand of friendship to him.

As the Reverend Yelman walked away he thought for quite some time about this gesture by two of his parishioners. When he referred to furniture, he was talking of the external handles and fittings on the coffin, knowing that tradesmen habitually talked of such fittings on doors and other wooden structures, as 'furniture'.

He had not in fact looked inside the coffin. The brothers had travelled to The Union with it in their hearse, placed the body in it and screwed down the lid in the normal way. He had a shrewd idea that inside the coffin the tramp would have been accommodated in a manner a good deal better than the basic way covered by the 'going-rate' for a pauper's coffin. In this the Vicar was again correct in his supposition. Herbie and Horace had treated the stranger with gentleness and consideration. Fate had delivered him to them and they did what they conceived to be their simple duty. They made him comfortable and gave him dignity in his final bed.

On the Sunday morning, on their way into the church to attend Morning Service, they walked over to the freshly covered grave where the tramp was buried, and arranged on it, with quiet respect, some flowers selected that morning from their own garden. For some minutes they stood looking down at the simple earth mound which marked the unknown wanderer's resting place, and found themselves wondering if he had relatives anywhere who would now never know where he had ended his days. It was a sad thought.

That afternoon, out walking with Jock, their strong, eager, energetic Alsatian dog, they decided to visit the lime kiln by which the tramp had slept his last sleep. It was some two miles or so from their home and they made their way to it, not along roads, but across the countryside they knew so well. On arrival they were able to identify the sheltered nook at the foot of the kiln where he had bedded down, from the description given to them during the week by the men who found him there.

The kiln, made of brickwork and stone, was built into a niche cut into a bank. It was a convenient location because limestone could be loaded into the conical top of the kiln from the flat top of the bank, while the quicklime was taken out just above ground-level at its foot, to be loaded on to trucks and taken away along a short cart-track to the adjacent road. The kiln was heated by a charcoal, coke and anthracite fire, built in an arched-topped fireplace not unlike some bakers' ovens.

It was from this cosy-looking fireplace that the glow shone out at night. Set as it was, back into the bank, it was an attractive, sheltered corner. Though open to the sky above, on a fine night it was just about as nice a spot as a wandering tramp could rest in. Ideal indeed, except for the gently suffocating gas which insidiously settled so silently and softly to envelop the sleeping form nestled so cosily in the warm glow of the fire.

When working, the kiln was kept going for long periods, night and day, with a regular feed of limestone at the top, while the end-product of quicklime was simultaneously off-loaded regularly from the bottom. A supply of fuel was stored nearby. Tending the kiln was a routine, and it was visited at intervals each day.

The brothers were not unfamiliar with it for they had grown up in the locality, and like many boys had now and again roasted potatoes—and in their season chestnuts—by its glowing fire.

For a few moments they stood silently gazing down at the scuffed-out area against the kiln's wall, near the fire, where the tramp had obviously tucked himself in.

As always, their dog Jock was closely attending to what his masters were interesting themselves in. They looked around, taking in information with their eyes; he automatically sniffed around to discover what he could with his highly sensitive nose. He snuffled his way around the cosy nook where the tramp had lain, and it soon became evident that he had found something that interested him. No doubt he had picked up the tramp's strong scent, for the weather had been fine and dry and the area little disturbed. Perhaps, who knows, he may even have recognised it as the unusual, interesting smell his masters had come home bearing on their persons a few days ago.

Whether or not he'd encountered the interesting smell before nobody could possibly know, but it was clear by the close investigations he was making that he was on to a scent which grabbed his eager attention. At length, tail wagging and nose to the ground, he moved off from the base of the kiln and made his way, in a more or less straight line, towards a clump of bushes among which he disappeared from sight.

Shortly afterwards Herbie and Horace, still gazing down rather disconsolately at the tramp's bed, lost in their own thoughts, were suddenly jerked out of their quiet reveries by Jock's deep-throated, woofing bark emanating from somewhere in the bushes. His manner of barking told them he had found something of interest and was calling them over to see it. Without hesitation they both strode off immediately to find out what the fuss was about.

Pushing their way into the clump of stunted trees and bushes, they found Jock pulling at something pushed well under a tangled growth of bracken and brambles. He was having trouble because of the thorns on the brambles.

Horace grabbed his collar and pulled him back. Herbie got down to see what it was that Jock was after. Shoved well under the vegetation, obviously to hide it, was an old canvas satchel of the type used by the Army as a 'side-pack'. With the aid of a stick he hooked it out, much to the excitement of Jock who snuffled at it eagerly, wagging his tail furiously with satisfaction.

"This must have belonged to that tramp," said Horace, frowning a little as he examined the grubby bag. "I reckon Jock picked up his scent from the place where he bedded down and followed his trail from the kiln to these bushes."

"Yes, I noticed that myself," commented Herbie. "It looked to me at the time as if

174

he moved almost in a straight line, following the sort of path a man would have taken. You could be right. Let's have a look to see what's in it."

Returning to the clear ground by the kiln, they squatted down and undid the webbing strap which fastened down the flap. The brass buckles and side-lugs on the bag, clearly identified it as being of Army origin.

Fishing inside Herbie pulled out two tobacco tins and an old leather wallet. One of the tins rattled as he picked it up. On opening it, it was found to contain a random assortment of silver and copper coins, adding up in total to £1.7s.7 ¾d.

"If this were his," said Herbie, "it was probably all the money he had in the world, the sort of amount he would have with him to buy the odd loaf of bread, and bits and pieces he needed from day to day. They live from hand to mouth, don't they, picking up a little pay for odd jobs here and there, and now and again getting a handout from some kind souls along the way."

"What's in this one, I wonder?" murmured Horace as he picked up the second tin. It was a stronger tin of better quality, a round one with a screw-on lid which bore some partly defaced decorations on its surface and the words Balkan Sobranie Tobacco. Horace unscrewed the top and took out a chamois-leather bag which was packed tightly inside the tin. He could tell immediately what the soft bag contained, by the feel of it between his fingers. It was unmistakeably a pocket watch.

"It's his pocket watch," said Horace, as he unravelled the bag. Slipping his fingers inside the soft leather he took out the watch and both brothers gasped with surprise at the sight of it. In Horace's hand lay a shining gold watch, looking as perfect as it must have done on the day it was made. It was a 'Full Hunter', having hinged lids over both the front and the back: a familiar type of watch, recognised straight away by the brothers for the valuable timepiece it was.

On the back, in an ornate shield engraved in the centre, were the initials AAM. Hooking the back flap open by his finger nail, the inner, hinged flap which covered the works was exposed, gleaming very brightly. On it was an inscription. Horace turned the watch on the palm of his hand until they could read what was engraved on this shining surface. On it were the words:

To
Angus Alexander MacKenzie
On his
21st Birthday
19th June 1895
Aberdeen

The brothers thoughtfully examined the watch further and soon located hallmarks in two different places, showing beyond doubt the quality of the gold used for its main case-parts.

Opening the inner flap exposed an immaculate mechanism protected by the perfectly fitting case, with its precision-engineered, click-fastening front and double hinged lids at the back. It was quite evident that the watch had always been treated with extreme care. It was unscratched and immaculate. Opening the front to look at its face, they wound it up and set the hands. It worked normally and was clearly in perfect order. Carefully Horace put the watch back into its leather bag, placed it in its tin and screwed the lid back on.

They then turned their attention to the old leather wallet. Neither of them really expected there to be any banknotes in it. Tramps and banknotes didn't seem to go together, for theirs was very much a small-change, hand-to-mouth way of life, lived out in a truly one-day-at-a-time basis, with zero security as the price of freedom.

"You won't find any paper money in there, I bet," said Horace as Herbie opened the wallet to look into its various compartments. "Leastways, no Bank of England fivers, that's for sure!"

"You're right about the £5 notes, but there are two Bradburys in here," said Herbie, taking out two notes and handing them to Horace.

Horace unfolded the two Treasury notes. One was for one pound, the other for ten shillings. Both bore the plainly written signature 'John Bradbury', Secretary to the Treasury. First issued at the start of the Great War to reduce the amount of gold in circulation, the banknotes were quickly nicknamed 'Bradburys', a name which some people continued to use long afterwards, even when many of those they handled bore the name of the man who took over from Bradbury in October 1919, N.K. Warren Fisher.

"This ten bob note is out of date," commented Horace. "They ceased to be legal tender in 1920. Look at it. It's one of those early red ones, printed only on one side. I should think it's one of the first issue. He probably had it when they first came out and kept it as a souvenir or keepsake. At any rate it's worthless now, I think, except as a curiosity."

"The other one looks all right," said Herbie, taking it from Horace and examining it. "Yes, this is a current one, still in use."

The £1 note had a picture of George & the Dragon and the face of King George V on one side with an attractive picture of the Houses of Parliament on the reverse. An altogether pleasingly designed note.

"I've always liked these," said Herbie. "And the quality of the paper is much better than those first issue ones, too. Much better. The first ones were just ordinary postage-stamp type paper. Poor efforts those were!"

"There was a bloke talking to Bill Martin in The Ship the other night," remarked Horace, "who said he'd heard that the Bank of England are going to issue their own one pound and ten shilling notes in 1928, to replace all these Treasury notes. According to him, it's over a hundred years since the Bank of England last issued £1 notes. So it's taken them long enough to decide to put them out again! For years the Bank's lowest value notes have been their fivers. Perhaps they didn't want to bother with anything worth less than five pounds."

"Too hoity-toity I expect," commented Horace with a grin.

There was nothing else inside the wallet, except a rather grubby but otherwise obviously well-cared-for envelope, securely tucked away in a safe inner pocket. It was a strong manila envelope on the front of which, written boldly in black ink, were the words:

CONFIDENTIAL

To: Mr. Simon Hepplethwaite

By Hand

The flap of the envelope had never been stuck down but just tucked in, as might perhaps be expected from the inscription which indicated that the letter had been handed to the recipient directly—in fact, as it was to turn out, given to him by the writer in person.

Inside the envelope was a handwritten letter on a sheet of official War Office paper which was headed 'Royal Army Medical Corps'.

Silently the twin brothers read it over, conscious as they did so that they were looking at a piece of paper much valued by the hitherto nameless tramp, who now seemed to be taking on an identity.

The letter was brief but very cogent. Written neatly, with obvious care, in a clear hand which had a firm authoritative style to it, it read:

Shorncliffe Military Hospital
Folkestone, Kent.

Saturday 21st June 1919

Dear Mr. Hepplethwaite,

It was the dying wish of Major MacKenzie that his gold pocket watch, given to him by his parents on his 21st birthday, should be given to you in gratitude for your great kindness to him in this hospital, and your previous faithful service to him when you served together, first in the Durham Light Infantry, and later in the Royal Flying Corps.

The end when it came early on the morning of Friday the 20th June was sudden, but we know you will be glad to learn that he died peacefully. He smiled, and seemed at ease, when we promised to see that you would receive his much treasured watch. It was as though he derived great comfort from this knowledge. He valued your friendship deeply, and looked forward so much to your visits.

Yours most sincerely

Sister Gloria Summerfield.

P.S.
You will see from the inscription in his watch that he died the day after his 44th birthday. We had a little celebration at tea-time on his birthday, which thankfully he was able to enjoy.

"Just fancy that now," said Horace. "The tramp must have been an ex-soldier—and a regular too, I shouldn't wonder, by this."

"Sounds like it, certainly," responded Herbie. "It seems the two must have served together for quite some time."

"This surely must be the tramp's bag, mustn't it?" mused Horace. "Jock certainly found it at the end of a scent which started at the kiln, didn't he?"

"Yes," replied Herbie, "if you remember, the men who work here said the tramp had an old haversack by his side with some food in it, along with odds and ends of possessions. Before he went to sleep he must have hidden this side-bag he kept his valuables in, up under those bushes. I expect he had learnt to look after his special belongs in that sort of way when he was out on his own, sleeping anywhere and somewhere. If he'd just dumped it by his side with his backpack, anybody coming along while he was asleep could have picked it up and made off with it. I reckon it must have been his nightly routine to stash this little satchel away, out of sight somewhere before

177

he kipped down. That makes sense, doesn't it? Anybody coming along would think the big bag was all he'd got."

"I'm sure you're right," said Herbie. "What should we do with it now, do you think?"

Horace answered immediately. He had already figured out what they must do.

"We'll take it to the Vicar," he said. "The Reverend Yelman will know what to do. You remember what he said about not knowing the tramp's name? It may be he will use this bag to track him down and find out about him. At any rate we can't keep it, that's for sure. The Police will have to be told anyway, I expect. We can leave all that to the Vicar to sort out."

"Yes, the Police will have to be told," agreed Herbie. "There's always the chance that the watch might have been stolen, isn't there? It could be that the tramp was not Simon Hepplethwaite at all. One way or another they will have to try to sort it out, won't they? I reckon we ought to go back to see Reverend Yelman straightaway. He'll be at the Vicarage this afternoon because he's got Evening Service to think about, hasn't he? This is his busy day—he doesn't move far away from the church on Sundays."

"Sure," agreed Horace, "let's get back to see him now as we've got the chance. Better today than tomorrow."

Without further ado the brothers set off back across the fields towards the distant church, whose spire could be seen from where they stood. The Vicarage, conveniently for the Vicar, was only a few hundred yards from the church and in dry weather he could go out of his back garden and across a meadow directly to the churchyard's back entrance without going on to the road at all.

When they arrived, as luck would have it, they found the Vicar's wife, a lady they knew well, who was always much involved with local affairs, working in her garden while her husband was busy in his study putting the finishing touches to his sermon for that evening. She took them in to see him, and their finds of the afternoon were closely examined and discussed with much interest.

It did not take the Reverend Yelman long to decide what to do, and the brothers were glad to leave matters in his hands. Promising to let them know the outcome of his enquiries, he showed them to the door and resumed his important Sabbath-day duties.

He was in fact able to make a start that very evening, for among his regular congregation was a retired British Army Officer, Colonel FitzWalter, who readily agreed to take the watch, and the letter, to see what he could find out about the two men whose names were associated with them.

With characteristic efficiency the Colonel sat at his desk that evening, listed what he needed to find out and how to go about it, and losing no time, on the following Monday morning he started off on his plan of action.

Through the good offices of the Commanding Officer of the garrison at Dover, he was put in touch with the Director of Medical Services for the area, who in turn enlisted the help of his Administrative Medical Officer. From then on it was plain sailing. The A.M.O. lost no time in delving into Medical Records for the Folkestone area, and within a matter of days rather than weeks, Colonel FitzWalter was on his way to meet Sister Gloria Summerfield in person.

Now released from her Military Service, she was back working at the Folkestone District Hospital, from which she had been seconded during the War to work at the Shorncliffe Military Hospital, which was local to her home.

Sister Summerfield had a very clear memory of both Major MacKenzie *and* Simon Hepplethwaite, the Good Samaritan. She had spent many hours talking to Major MacKenzie during the several months he had spent at the hospital, to which he had been sent from the advanced base hospital in France where, for an extended period, he had first been treated.

Severely wounded, badly burnt and paralysed from the waist downwards, Major MacKenzie's days were known to be numbered from the day he arrived at Shorncliffe. That he was alive at all was regarded by his doctors as almost miraculous, and testimony to the man's great determination and unconquerable spirit. He had been shot down between the lines on the Western Front and rescued from his burning wreck of a plane by the remarkable bravery of three infantrymen who had raced out from their trenches to get him in. One had apparently died in the attempt, but the other two got him under cover until stretcher-bearers took him to the first-aid post.

Simon Hepplethwaite had turned up at the hospital out of the blue, about two months after the Major had been brought to Folkestone. His story was subsequently told by the Major. Both men had originated from the Durham Light Infantry, and both were regular soldiers in service when the Great War broke out. On active service Major MacKenzie, then a Captain, was a Company Commander when one of his men, Private Hepplethwaite, was badly wounded in the shoulder by shrapnel. When sufficiently recovered to return to his unit, he was not fit for normal duties but became a Company Orderly, and also personal batman to Captain MacKenzie.

Like others of his generation and type, Captain MacKenzie was attracted to the new Royal Flying Corps, which expanded very rapidly and had a great need for suitable men to train as pilots. It happened that from early days Captain MacKenzie had been fascinated by flying and had already had some small experience when the war broke out. In due course he decided to apply for transfer, and was accepted. When his training had been completed, and he joined an active unit by successfully pleading to the right people in the right places, Captain—later Major—MacKenzie, was able to effect the transfer of Simon Hepplethwaite to the R.F.C., to become his batman once again.

At the time Major MacKenzie was shot down, Simon Hepplethwaite was awaiting his return at a Forward airfield. He lost no time in getting himself to the advanced base hospital to visit the terribly injured Major, but of course had to return to duty until the end of the War. On his discharge he had traced the Major and as soon as he could get there, he arrived at the Shorncliffe Hospital to visit him.

The Major was clearly very moved and overjoyed at the appearance of his loyal comrade. From then on, with unfailing regularity, Simon Hepplethwaite visited the hospital to spend many hours each weekend with Major MacKenzie. When weather permitted, he pushed the Major out along the cliff-tops in a basket-work wheel chair, outings which they both enjoyed.

Nobody ever knew much about Simon Hepplethwaite. From what the Major told them, it seemed Simon had no family of his own. Very much a loner he had joined the regular Army several years before the War when he was already in his thirties. Like so many others he was discharged after the War, not unwillingly in his case, because by then he had seen all the military service he ever wanted to see.

As far as Sister Summerfield knew, Simon Hepplethwaite worked in Dover Harbour, in some temporary job, during the time he was visiting the hospital. What happened to him afterwards neither she, nor any of her colleagues, knew.

The Major had died on a Friday morning. He had been getting steadily weaker, and Simon Hepplethwaite knew that his end was near. It fell to Sister Summerfield to tell him when he arrived on Saturday afternoon, by which time she had prepared the letter for him. She told Colonel FitzWalter that it had been thought desirable to give him a formal letter along with the gold watch, to prove he was the legitimate owner of it. It was an inscribed watch and of some significant value. Clearly there needed to be a record that Major MacKenzie had personally given his watch away via Sister Summerfield, to Simon Hepplethwaite, his friend and one-time batman.

The Colonel commented to Sister Summerfield that this was a wise thing to have done at the time, and, as circumstances had turned out, the letter had proved invaluable in a totally unexpected way. It had served to identify an unknown tramp; without it no record would ever had existed about the fate of Simon Hepplethwaite. Sadly, from what the Sister had said, the man had no known relatives, but at least his grave could be named and his burial recorded properly. The Colonel determined to look after this matter for the sake of the old soldier, and also to notify his regiment, because the Durham Light Infantry would have information about his place of origin in their records. Perhaps, he thought, Reverend Yelman might then write a note to his opposite number in the man's home parish. Somebody might be around who would appreciate news of him, sad though the news was.

There was however, one point to which Colonel FitzWalter knew he must pay some attention. It was necessary to establish that the tramp was indeed Simon Hepplethwaite. He had registered what the Sister had said about Simon Hepplethwaite's shoulder wounds, and knew this was something he could check with The Union's Master. Those who had attended to his body would have recorded any distinctive features, for the very reason that he was unknown. It was a matter of routine to keep such records.

He raised this point with Sister Summerfield before he left and immediately received some additional assistance. She told him that there was a second very positive factor to help in the identification. Simon Hepplethwaite was missing the middle finger of his right hand. There was just a stump left and his forefinger was also partly deformed. Apparently the wounds were received at the same time as he was hit in the shoulder. He had been caught by flying shrapnel, perhaps by some sort of fragmentation shell.

Sister Summerfield was also able to give some more details of his shoulder wounds. She said that they had in fact extracted some fragments of metal from his back at the hospital when they had found he was suffering discomfort from his shoulder. It took quite some time for all the small fragments in such a wound to be located and removed. Gradually some bits worked their way towards the surface and could then be taken out relatively easily.

Colonel FitzWalter was quite satisfied that he had sufficient information to identify the tramp as Simon Hepplethwaite, if such he were.

He now raised the question of the gold pocket watch. Everybody seemed agreed that this should go back to Major MacKenzie's family, if his next of kin could be located. It had been, after all, a present to him from his parents to mark his 21st birthday. Apart from its intrinsic value it had a special identity, and would almost certainly be more prized by his family than by anyone else. Fortunately Sister Summerfield was able to help in this connection as well.

When Major MacKenzie had died, the military authorities had, at his father's request, transported his body to Aberdeen where he was buried with full military honours. Major MacKenzie was not married and, so far as the Sister could recall, he had lost his mother. She remembered that at the time of his death his only brother was still serving overseas in the Royal Navy. His father had been too old and unwell to travel to Shorncliffe to see his son during the months he had been in hospital there. The six hundred mile journey was too much for him, and his forlorn hope had been that his son would recover sufficiently to be shifted to a hospital in Aberdeen. Alas, it was not to be.

The Colonel was quite sure he had enough information to be able to track down Major MacKenzie's surviving relatives, with the aid of the military authorities, whose help he was well qualified to enlist. Having achieved all he could with his enquiries at

Folkestone, he returned home and pursued matters from there. In a few days' time he was in possession of the last known address of Major MacKenzie's next of kin.

He then contacted the police in Aberdeen and soon found out that Major MacKenzie's father was dead, but they had managed to locate his other son, Malcolm MacKenzie. Now retired from the Royal Navy, Malcolm had taken over his father's business. This was a small North Seas fishing fleet operating out of Aberdeen and Dundee, with its main base at Aberdeen where his father had started with a single boat captained by himself, like so many others of his day.

Before contacting Major MacKenzie's brother, the Colonel had one or two other loose ends to tie up.

To begin with he took himself off to The Union to see the Master. It was very quickly established by the Matron that the tramp's body bore precisely the same identification features as those described by Sister Summerfield, so it was agreed he must indeed have been Simon Hepplethwaite. There could be no reasonable doubt about that.

Next he saw the police. It was necessary to put things on record officially. The gold watch had, after all, been found near the body of an unknown tramp. He was now identified but there was no knowledge of his family at all. He was said not to have a family, so far as those who had known him had been aware. But it was obviously desirable to get legal clearance to pass on the watch to the Major's family.

After some delay permission was granted, but with a proviso. The gold watch could be sent to the Major's brother for safe keeping until a stipulated time had elapsed. If, during this time, a direct relative of Simon Hepplethwaite were found, or came forward to claim his possessions, it had to be understood that the rightful ownership of the gold watch would be a matter for legal adjudication. It sounded a bit complicated, but the Colonel wanted things played straight down the middle, because the matter could well create something of a legal fog. It was part of his training not to place himself where he could be shot at, when he could step to one side and be out of danger.

The Reverend Yelman and the Spindlecroft brothers were very grateful to Colonel FitzWalter for the way in which he had sorted everything out, so neatly and tidily.

Having got the facts clear, the Colonel felt that the approach to Major MacKenzie's brother should be made by the Reverend Yelman. The Spindlecroft brothers agreed with this. In a way, it seemed fitting that the Vicar should, as it were, represent Simon Hepplethwaite, whose Christian kindness to Major MacKenzie had set in motion the chain of linked events which would end with the Major's 21st birthday present from his parents going back to his own brother.

The Reverend Yelman gladly agreed to look after this final task. With some care in how he phrased his letter he sat down and told the story as it had happened. He ended by stating that all concerned felt that Simon Hepplethwaite would have wished that the gold pocket watch, obviously much prized by him, as it had been by Major MacKenzie, should be returned to the family. It remained formally to ask if his brother Malcolm MacKenzie would accept the watch, and if so the address to which it should be sent by registered post.

He did not have to wait long for a reply. A letter came by return of post. Not only was Major MacKenzie's brother naturally very pleased to accept the watch—and most grateful for the trouble taken to seek him out in order to get the watch back to the family—but he proposed to journey to Kent himself to pick it up in person. He looked forward, he said in his letter, to the pleasure of meeting the small group of people who had been associated with this strange episode.

In particular he wanted to meet Sister Summerfield to learn more about the last days of his brother's life. He had been in the Far East when his brother Angus was in hospital in Shorncliffe, and did not return to rejoin the Home Fleet until over six months after his brother had died.

Four years after the war he had retired from the Royal Navy, since when he had been busily engaged in the fishing industry.

He went on to say that after the War broke out in 1914, he saw his brother only once. They were never on leave in Scotland at the same time, but met for a brief period when their paths crossed in India, at Bombay. Angus, in the Army, was on his way back to France, while his own ship was heading for Singapore.

Somehow, so he wrote, the unexpected letter from Littlebrook—to him a remote, unknown village fully six hundred miles away down near the Channel coast—had brought him suddenly near his only brother again. He very much wanted to talk to Sister Summerfield, who had clearly got to know his brother very well after he had been sent back, seriously wounded, from France. He determined to get down to Kent, just as soon as he could make the necessary arrangements.

Two weeks later Reverend Yelman heard from him again. He was in Folkestone where he had booked into a hotel for two weeks, having decided to take a holiday. His intention was to visit not only those people whom he had primarily travelled down to see at Folkestone and Littlebrook, but also to look up two old friends, both ex-RN like himself, one at Dover and the other at Sheerness on the Isle of Sheppey. By a coincidence, they also had retained their connection with the sea. One was skipper of a paddle steamer running trips for holidaymakers, plying regularly between Dover and Southend, calling at Margate and London. The other owned a fishing-smack which he operated out of Southend.

They fixed a convenient date and Malcolm MacKenzie, brother of Angus MacKenzie, duly arrived at the Vicarage to be greeted warmly by the Reverend Yelman. By arrangement with Colonel FitzWalter, he also was there to greet their visitor.

Malcolm MacKenzie had already been to see Sister Summerfield at the Folkestone General Hospital and was going to see her again on the coming Saturday when they were intending to visit the military barracks at Shorncliffe, where Major MacKenzie had spent his time. He and the Colonel were able to discuss the information they had both gleaned from their respective talks with the Sister, and soon their conversation turned to Simon Hepplethwaite, the tramp responsible for their being together that day.

This led to the main purpose of the meeting, and with quiet dignity, conscious of the solemnity of the moment, and the deep emotions their visitor must be feeling, Reverend Yelman handed Malcolm MacKenzie the soft leather bag containing his brother's watch.

Malcolm took the gleaming gold watch out of its bag and turned it over in his hand. He looked at the initials on the back, and then opened the hinged back to look at the inscription inside. It was some moments before he could bring himself to speak.

"You know," he said quietly, "Angus really treasured this watch. He always had a thing about clocks and watches. They had a peculiar fascination for him, right from the time he was a little boy. So much so that people used to bring him old clocks to tinker with, rather than throw them away. His first watch was a large old railwayman's stainless steel pocket-watch Father bought him for a special present when he had been seriously ill, and was recovering. The doctor said it was the best medicine Father could have given him. It gave him hours of pleasure and really bucked him up. And his one ambition was to own a gold pocket-watch, like an Uncle of ours had.

Father and Mother had this one all ready for him on his 21st birthday. I remember how excited we all were to see him open the parcel that morning. We could hardly wait.

You know, it may seem strange, but I can see his face now. He was overjoyed. Absolutely overjoyed!"

With his finger nail he hooked open the inner flap and studied the immaculate mechanism, ticking away with the satisfying precision of a first-class movement.

"I've seen him gaze inside this for minutes on end," their visitor went on. "Absolutely fascinated him it did, just watching it work, and listening to it. It gave my parents a great deal of pleasure to see how thrilled Angus was with it. They would be so pleased to know it was with him to the end of his life, and is now in my hands."

The Vicar then showed Malcolm the grubby, well-worn old Army side-pack, belonging to the tramp, in which the watch had been found. He took out the leather wallet and handed the manila envelope to him.

Malcolm read the letter from Sister Summerfield to Simon Hepplethwaite and studied it for some time in silence. Plainly he was moved by its contents.

"My brother must have been very fond of the man to have wanted his watch to be given to him," he said, quietly. "What's more, he must have known that Simon Hepplethwaite would look after it and treasure it," he added. "How strange that it would find its way back to me, in the way it has. It's quite incredible, when you come to think of it."

"Yes, it is indeed," commented Colonel FitzWalter. "Of course, it was sheer luck that two men as honest as the Spindlecroft brothers found it. It was only their concern for the unknown tramp that took them back to the lime kiln in the first place. Without them the link with your brother would never have been made."

"They are very remarkable men, those two," intervened the Vicar. "I was very touched by their attitude to the tramp. They displayed what I can only describe as true Christian compassion towards this unfortunate man. Because he had nobody of his own to be concerned over his death, those two treated him with simple genuine kindness— almost as though they had adopted him as one of their own family."

Reverend Yelman then described to his visitor how the brothers had gone to no small expense and trouble, without reference to anyone else, and certainly not to gain some acclaim from others for their generosity, in order to afford him some dignity at the end of his road.

"I should like to meet the Spindlecrofts while I'm here," said Malcolm. "I want to thank them personally for what they have done, not only in restoring my brother's watch to me, but also for what they did for Simon Hepplethwaite. My brother would be very grateful to them for looking after his Army comrade. What a friend that man turned out to be to Angus. Sister Summerfield told me how selfless he had been in the way he gave up his time, to help Angus in every way he could. He did what I would have wished to do myself, had I have been able to care for Angus when he was so ill and helpless."

"Yes, I knew you would wish to meet them," responded the Vicar. "I have arranged to take you to see their workshops after lunch. Colonel FitzWalter is going to have lunch with us here at the Vicarage and then we'll go along to see the Spindlecrofts. They are looking forward to meeting you."

Early that afternoon they set off to see the brothers, but on the way the Vicar took Malcolm, at his request, to visit the grave of Simon Hepplethwaite. Malcolm had already decided on a little plan to do something on behalf of his brother. When they reached the bare mound which marked the grave, he stood looking at it and gazing around the churchyard at the other graves. Presently he spotted what he was looking for. Like most people he could not have described what it was he wanted done. But he had seen a neatly designed grave with a nicely made headstone and a simple stone edging, the surrounding ground covered with weed-free marble and granite chips.

"Reverend Yelman," he said, "I should like you, if you will be so kind, to arrange Hepplethwaite's grave to be furnished in much the same way as that one over there. We'll work out what to have inscribed on the headstone and I shall be happy to defray the cost of it myself. I know my brother would certainly wish that this, at least, should be done as a mark of respect and perhaps, in a way, as a thank-you to his old comrade. In addition, I will undertake to pay whatever annual fee is necessary to have the grave cared for to keep it in good order."

"Gladly," responded the Vicar. "I'll set that in motion straightaway. It's most kind of you and we shall all appreciate that very much."

"So will two other people I know," intervened Colonel FitzWalter with a smile. "It sounds like some useful extra work for Stony Charlie and Old Motty!"

"It does indeed," confirmed the Vicar. "It's all grist to the mill to them, although I must say I often wonder how much longer Motty can keep on grinding away. His machinery's getting pretty creaky these days. He gets more crotchety by the month, it seems to me, though he'd be the last to admit it!"

Their companion looked puzzled by this interchange.

"Who are Stony Charlie and Old Motty?" he asked.

"Stony Charlie is our local mason, our resident stone-chipper so to speak. And very good he is at it too," replied the Vicar. "As for Old Motty, he is our part-time caretaker-come-gardener at the churchyard. Some call him our 'link-man' with the departed souls whose bodies are buried here. Our resident 'liaison man', in other words!"

This allusion to local characters, who were clearly of obvious interest, sparked an immediate response from Malcolm MacKenzie who at once wanted to know more about them. The effect was to lift the rather sombre atmosphere which had clouded their meeting so far that morning, and they went on their way in a more light-hearted mood.

During the walk to visit the Spindlecroft brothers, Reverend Yelman much amused his guest from Scotland by recounting some of the many stories that circulated locally about the highly eccentric character known as 'Old Motty', his churchyard Caretaker Extraordinary, who was so well-known in and around Littlebrook.

These strange tales Malcolm stored away in his memory and nurtured over the years, so bizarre were they. He was to have occasion to meet Old Motty at a later date and learn more about his curious habits, beliefs, and reputed unique gifts of communication with the dead.

By the time they arrived they were all three in a cheerful mood. This was a good thing. The twins always reflected the mood of visitors who came to their premises—it was part of their trade to have to do so—and the appearance of three smiling faces at their workshops made the visit an assured success from the start.

Chapter 14

A VISIT TO THE WHEELWRIGHTS' WORKSHOP

the talented twins show tricks of their trade

Visitors to the Spindlecrofts' establishment usually walked straight down past the side of their house to the yard behind it. The strong, heavy, oak farm gate which could shut off the gravel driveway was always fastened back to remain fully open throughout working hours on weekdays. There were comings and goings of people calling on business each day, often with horse-drawn or hand-pushed vehicles, either making deliveries or bringing in things for repair. Various motor vehicles also visited the premises from time to time. It was only on Sundays that the gate remained shut and padlocked throughout the day.

Scattered around the extensive yard behind the house were a variety of workshops, storage places and under-cover parking areas where work could be done at any time, sheltered from the rain, if not from the wind. Usually the brothers were to be found in the main wheelwright workshop, but regular visitors got used to having a quick look round on arrival to locate one or the other of them to deal with the matters in hand.

When Reverend Yelman, Colonel FitzWalter and Malcolm MacKenzie walked down the driveway, they did not have far to look to find the twins. They were outside in the yard, having just pulled out of the workshop a spanking new cart they had recently made for their local milkman.

It really was a very attractively-designed vehicle, purpose-built for the job it had to do, quite high-sided because tall milk churns had to stand inside it. It was painted with such freshness that it seemed to radiate a clean, cool image, in keeping with the dairy products it would delivery daily. Horace had used all his artistry and imagination in his use of colours and decorative design. There was much white and yellow in the superstructure, with black along the edges and rails likely to suffer smudging from frequent handling. The two wheels and shafts were royal-blue, with bright red piping. The name **HERBERT BRISTOW, DAIRYMAN** was boldly emblazoned on the sides in attractive lettering. Loaded with its milk churns and delivery cans, it was destined to clatter its way cheerfully around the district for many years to come, pulled by Bert Bristow's sturdy little cob.

To the amusement of his customers, and sometimes the astonishment of visitors to the village, Bert's cob knew his rounds so well it didn't wait to be told what to do. No sooner did Bert step off the back step carrying his delivery can, than the cob—feeling him leave as his weight came off the step—moved off on its own to the next stop. Since, on occasions, this meant a distance of perhaps 100 yards or more, passers-by were confronted by a horse-drawn milk-cart making its way along the roads and lanes unaccompanied, as though the cob had got tired of hanging about and decided to move off wherever its fancy took it! There were two subtle advantages to this independent action, one for the man, and one for the cob.

Bert was well-known to be a lady's man. He stopped now and again a good deal longer than was necessary to deliver the milk. But his cart never advertised his presence within a house, rather it stood with its patient puller outside the next port of call. Not that local gossips were misled by this element of confusion, even if Bert thought they were.

As for the cob, local people who got to know and like the friendly horse, would go out sometimes to greet it with a sugar lump or two. This was especially true of people whose homes were a bit off the beaten track so that they had to carry their milk jugs to the road to meet the cart, and collect their milk. This involved regular stopping points at odd places, perhaps by the stile in a hedge, or a gate by a field. Perhaps the cob got to know that to stand on its own, unattended and patient, was a good way of attracting a little sympathy and some tasty morsels for its sweet tooth. Certainly it was a well-known visitor, had many friends, and was a great favourite in the area.

Spotting the visitors, the brothers responded to their smiling faces by greeting them cheerfully. The Vicar introduced Malcolm MacKenzie and for some moments the new cart formed the centre of attraction. It was much admired, especially by Malcolm, who had an eye for first-class craftsmanship.

"That's a fine-looking cart," he commented. "Was that entirely made here on the premises?"

"It was, that," answered Herbie proudly. "Bert Bristow, our milkman, has been promising himself a new cart for a long time, and he's finally got around to treating himself to one. Our Dad made the one he's been using for years. If this one does as well as that, it will see him out, that's for sure!"

The Colonel intervened, with a wry smile.

"His stout-hearted little cob will be proud to pull that around the village," he said. "The sight of that smart outfit being pulled along with no man driving it or anywhere to be seen, will attract even more attention than it usually does, especially by strangers."

Malcolm MacKenzie looked puzzled.

"You're not suggesting it does the milk-round on its own, are you?" he asked with a smile.

"You would be surprised if you saw it in action!" replied the Colonel. "It knows Bert Bristow's round as well as he does. When he gets off to deliver at one house, the cob pulls the cart along to the next one and waits for him there. People are so used to seeing the milk-cart moving about without its owner that it's only when strangers express surprise at the sight that they remember there is anything unusual about it."

"I'll tell you what," said Horace, by way of confirmation of the Colonel's comments, "if you were to stand where you are now at 8.30 tomorrow morning, you would see the cob pull this new cart straight down the driveway on its own and stop pretty well where the cart is standing now. Four or five minutes later you'd see old Bert walk in to follow it. Bert comes here when he's finished delivering at that row of four cottages just up the road. He gets off the cart carrying his milk-can at the first one, goes to the back door and walks along behind the row, going from one to another, dishing out the milk. Meanwhile the cob walks on down to our house and turns in the yard to wait for him. As regular as clockwork, Bert comes into our workshop for a cup of tea. We always brew up about half an hour after we open up and he joins us every day, doesn't he, Herbie?"

"He certainly does!" responded Herbie. "Never misses! Come to think about it, I'm looking forward to seeing the cob pull that new cart in here tomorrow. Bert is coming to collect it this evening and he says he will put it into service tomorrow morning, for the first time. I reckon he'll be as pleased as punch with this. He's had a complete new set of harness made for it by Bill Gunston, the saddler, so the whole outfit will be new. My guess is that he will give his faithful cob an extra special grooming this evening, to mark the occasion. Given a fine sunny day, he'll attract a lot of attention on his rounds in the morning. We shall certainly watch out for him. It's very satisfying to see a new cart or wagon we've just made, out on the road for the first time. It's a real pleasure to Horace and me."

"I'm quite sure it is," said the Vicar. "It's rather marvellous to think that you two can create something like this cart from trees cut down from our own woodlands. It's always a source of wonder to me."

"Well, we're lucky to have the trees we need growing almost on our doorstep," said Herbie. "There are three different types of wood in that little cart, for instance—oak, elm and ash. All of it well-seasoned timber from our woodstore over the side of the yard there."

Stacked up in a long, open-sided building that Herbie pointed to, could be seen an impressive quantity of wood, cut into planks and stored in piles, with blocks between each layer of planks to allow air to circulate freely in order to dry the wood out properly.

"Looks as though you have plenty of wood there to last you quite some time," commented Colonel FitzWalter. "You won't be buying in any more for a year or two, will you, Herbie?"

"Oh yes we shall," answered Herbie emphatically. "There are already some trees cut down for us in the woods. This winter they will be brought down here and our regular travelling sawyers will be in the yard at the saw-pit over the back there to cut it up into planks for us. That goes into store for seasoning and won't be used for a couple of years or more. There's no point in making a wagon that has to put up with hard work for years on end, and expecting it to last, unless you start off with properly seasoned wood. That's why we keep a well-filled store. It's far better to have too much in that store than not enough. Every now and again, for one reason or another, there comes a year when we can't get in the fresh supplies we order. 'Wood in the store is better than money in the bank', our Dad used to say."

"The different woods have different uses, I suppose?" queried Malcolm. "The same as they do in boat-building, come to that."

"Yes, they certainly do," agreed Herbie. "If you look at that little cart there, for example, the shafts and the frame are made of ash, the panels, the flooring and the hubs of the wheels are elm, and the spokes of the wheels are oak."

"Don't forget the rims of the wheels," added Horace. "They are made of ash. There are six sections in the rim, each carrying two spokes. We call those rim sections 'felloes'. Cutting and jointing those is a bit tricky. One of those jobs you don't learn to do in five minutes. Very proud I was when I made my first complete wheel on my own."

"Yes! So was I too!" said Herbie with some feeling. "Things had to be just right for the Guv'nor, didn't they, Herbie?"

"You can say that again!" agreed Herbie. "Nothing but the best for him. Good wheelwright though, wasn't he, Herbie?"

"He was that," answered Herbie with obvious pride. "None better, so folk around here always reckoned."

"I can vouch for that," interjected the Colonel. "Since I retired and settled here, I've heard it said many times. It's surprising how many people have shown me examples of his work, especially on the farms. I imagine he must have been a difficult man to please since he was so meticulous and talented himself. But still, it's quite obvious from that little milk-cart there, that he was successful in passing on his skills to you two. That really is a magnificent piece of work."

"It is indeed," agreed the Vicar, in support of this praise of the brothers' workmanship. "I'm sure your Dad would have been hard put to it to find any fault with that."

"You'd better ask Old Motty to check up on that," grinned Horace. "Get him to have a word with the Guv'nor and see if he will have a look at it to make sure it's up to Ebenezer Spindlecroft standards."

The Reverend Yelman smiled. He never quite knew whether or not he should join in with the half-joking, half-serious references to Motty's alleged communication and liaison with his late parishioners. But he took the opportunity to switch the attention to the purpose of their visit.

"Speaking of Motty," he said, "Mr. MacKenzie here has kindly offered to pay for a headstone and grave-surround for our ex-traveller Simon Hepplethwaite, and then commission Motty to maintain the grave in good condition. That's yet one more good thing which has resulted from your kind efforts on behalf of the unknown wanderer."

"Well, that's the least I can do," said Malcolm MacKenzie. "And that brings me to the reason I wanted to meet you both. I want to express my most sincere thanks to you for everything you have done, in particular for restoring my brother's watch to his family."

Here Malcolm took the gold watch from his pocket and held it in the palm of his hand. He was determined that the brothers should see the watch actually in his possession, in the hands of the brother of the man whose name was engraved upon it.

"You know," he continued, "my brother really treasured this watch. I think, if asked, he would always have said it was the thing he most prized in the world. That's why it is so plain to me that Simon Hepplethwaite must have meant a very great deal to him. At the end of his life there was no way he could have paid a greater compliment to his comrade and friend. So, I think you will understand that my brother would have been very sad to know that Simon Hepplethwaite ended his days as a lonely tramp, and would wish that everything that can be done to remember the man kindly, and see him buried in a known grave, he would wish me to do."

A little formally, but with obvious, deeply felt emotion, Malcolm then shook hands with Herbie and Horace.

"Thank you, my friends," he said, looking at them with his keen eyes shining with sincerity, "thank you on behalf of my brother Angus, for looking after his friend and returning his watch to me. Nothing of this would have happened had it not been for your concern for a total stranger. The world would be a better place if there were more people like you two in it. Thank you."

The brothers, a little embarrassed by this fulsome praise, and rather at a loss for words, were nonetheless very appreciative of these remarks and muttered thanks to their visitor, who had travelled so far to see them.

Colonel FitzWalter, sensitive to their discomfort, saw the need to relieve their awkwardness and intervened to change the subject.

"Have you chaps got time to let us have a quick look over your workshops while we're here?" he asked. "I'm sure Mr. MacKenzie would be very interested if you could spare the time."

"Of course we can," responded Herbie. "It will be a pleasure. Come along into the main workshops and we'll show you what we're up to at the moment."

So saying, he led the way into their wheelwright shop. Horace followed behind the three visitors to watch their progress, and in order to warn them of potential knocks and bruises which he knew from experience people sometimes suffered because of the many bits and pieces lying around, and sticking out awkwardly, in the cluttered workshops. There were hazards in a busy workshop because of the nature of the work, and the unwary needed a shepherd.

Occupying the whole of one wall were the firm's patterns of cart and wagon parts, covering the whole range of normal manufacturing work they carried out there. These wooden specimens, carved and shaped with the curves, varying thicknesses, and overall dimensions, appropriate to their purposes, had been built up over many years.

It was characteristic of the trade that know-how and information was passed down the generations in this way. There were no careful, detailed drawings with calculated measurements and the profusion of information found in precision engineering workshops.

Even the reasons for the sometimes curious and unexpected shapes and curvatures, were known only to a few people who took the trouble to enquire about them from the 'old hands'. What everybody involved was always quite certain about however, was that nothing was done which had not been found either beneficial, or positively essential.

What the brothers did have, however, were many photographs and pencilled sketches of finished vehicles, or of sections and parts of them. These folders of pictures and data, plus the array of patterns displayed on the wall, provided all the reference material they used in their constructional work.

Using this invaluable collection they were able to give their visitors a brief look at the impressive variety of carts, wagons and carriages they were capable of manufacturing, from tip-up dung carts to graceful, hay-carrying wagons with their relatively lightly-made superstructures, much seen in the district at harvest time.

Currently the twins were making a set of four wheels for a farm wagon on which they had been working, between other small jobs, for some weeks past. Nearing completion, the wagon itself was in another open-sided workshop along the yard, together with three of its four wheels. The parts of the five-and-a-half-foot diameter rear wheel still to be made were laid out on the floor, providing a convenient example of their craft for the three visitors to see.

Herbie explained to them, as he had done more times than he could remember to folks for years, that contrary to what people were inclined to think, wheelwrights didn't just make wheels. They made every single part needed to build complete vehicles, *including* the wheels. It was thought by some in the business that as wheels were perhaps the most skilled part of their trade, the word 'wheelwright' had been chosen long ago to describe the craft as a whole. The older men always said that if you could make the wheels you could make the lot. A wainwright on the other hand, was strictly a wagon-maker and not necessarily a wheel-maker.

Herbie frequently volunteered this piece of information to forestall either the question 'Who makes the carts that you put your wheels on?', or an observation—from those who spotted the answer to the question before they asked it—such as, 'Well I never, I didn't know you made whole carts as well as wheels!' People on the receiving end of tediously repeated questions or comments, especially if they carry a disparaging implication, tend to get needled. So Herbie chose to pre-empt such comments by making his definitive statement at the outset.

He pointed to the collection of parts laid out on the floor where they gave the appearance of a dismembered wheel.

"Except for the iron-work," he said, "what you see there are all the bits needed to make the wheel."

The six curved sections of the rim lay in a broken circle. Each carried a dowel rod sticking out of one end and a hole in its other end. When pushed together they would join up to make the perfectly circular wooden rim. At the centre of the circle lay the stout, barrel-like wheel-hub, around which were placed twelve oak spokes arranged in pairs, two to each rim section. At the hub end each spoke bore a tapered, rectangular-shaped jointing-tenon opposite its prepared mortise-hole in the hub. Short dowel rods projected from the other ends of the spokes to fit into corresponding holes in the rim sections.

"If you look," said Herbie, "each spoke is numbered to match a pencilled number on the hub. That's because the mortise-hole in the hub is cut at the same time as the spoke's tenon, to make a matching pair. There are slight differences in every joint, and if we muddled up the spokes we would run into trouble."

"How about the iron-work you mentioned?" asked the Vicar.

"It's over there by the wall," answered Herbie. "You can see the big iron tyre propped up there with the rest of the iron stuff on the floor."

"My word," commented the Vicar. "Doesn't that tyre look huge!"

"Yes, it's big right enough," replied Herbie, "and heavy too! It's made just over an inch less in circumference than the assembled wooden wheel. We heat it until its red hot so that it expands. Then we drop it over the wheel's rim, tap it into position, and cool it down straightaway with water so that it shrinks in size and pulls the wheel together, tightening up all the joints hard into position. We have to be smart about it too, and douse the iron quickly before it burns into the rim badly. It's a tricky moment putting the iron tyre on."

"Is the iron tyre made here in the village?" asked Malcolm.

"Yes, all our iron-work is," intervened Horace, with some pride. "Our local blacksmith, Fred Huddlestone, is a dab hand at all that sort of thing. All those bits and pieces over there, ready for this wheel, were made by him. You'd be surprised how many items there are even in an ordinary farm wagon. All the rods, brackets, bolts, hinges, chains, staples—in fact anything we need—he makes for us."

"You're lucky to have someone like him living locally, aren't you?" commented Malcolm.

"We are that," answered Horace. "Of course, in a large firm the same as the one where our Dad trained, they have their own blacksmiths on the premises. We keep Fred Huddlestone pretty busy here, but we don't have enough work to keep a blacksmith going full-time. We're lucky to have such a good bloke on our doorstep. Mind you, our Dad taught him quite a lot about a wheelwright's needs over the years, and now he's as good as they come. He's a very clever blacksmith, our Fred it, isn't he Herbie?"

"He sure is", replied Herbie. Then, picking up the question of the wheel again, he pointed to the other parts grouped by the tyre ready for their use.

"Those two broad iron bands there," he said, "fit on the two ends of the barrel-shaped hub, or 'nave' as we call it. You'll see how they fit when we look at the finished wheels outside. The other bits there are the axle fittings for the centre of the hub."

"Those spokes there," observed Malcolm, looking at them closely, "look to me as though they are curved. In fact the way the holes in the hub are cut, makes it look as though they would throw the spokes outwards, instead of straight to the rim at right-angles, the same as spokes are fixed in a bicycle wheel."

"That's right," confirmed Herbie. "When you look at the finished wheels you will see that the back ones are dished in shape. More like a saucer, rather than a flat disc."

"Why's that?" asked Colonel FitzWalter. "It's seems to make the job much more complicated than it needs to be."

"Well," explained Herbie, "the rear wheels have to be very large on many farm wagons, the larger the better really, so long as the wagon floor doesn't finish up too high off the ground. Large wheels give a horse as much leverage as possible. Not only that, but they allow the wagon to go over muddy soft ground more easily too. Their large size makes the rear wheels stick well up above the floor level. By dishing their shape the rim is thrown outwards allowing the wagon to be wider at the top of its sides than it is at floor level. That gives a bigger load-carrying capacity. If you see a loaded hay-cart going along, you will be surprised to see how much the load goes outwards beyond the wheel base."

"Now you come to mention it," commented the Colonel, "the axles are sometimes tilted too, aren't they, to splay the wheels out further, I suppose."

"Yes," replied Herbie. "On many carts and wagons, as well as passenger-carrying vehicles, there is quite a pronounced tilt. The blacksmith has to take account of that when he shapes the iron tyres, and so do we when we shape the felloes for the rim. We have to make sure we finish up with the wheels' iron tyres sitting squarely on the road's surface. If we didn't, the tyre would run on an edge and certainly wouldn't wear evenly."

"Not only that," added Horace, "the wagon wouldn't turn very well either. The horse would soon notice the difference, straightaway, especially on those deeply rutted farm tracks they have to drag wagons over on some farms. If you look down into a rut you will see it has a square flat bottom to it when it's dry."

"Yes, as a matter of interest," said Herbie, "we make all farm carts and wagons with the same distance between the wheels. If you watch them going along a rutted track you will see that they run along the ruts like a train along its rails. Somebody trying to pull a cart with a different wheel base along one of those tracks would get into a fine old mess. Farmers are careful not to buy-in second-hand carts from other areas without first checking their wheel base. A wrong one is next-door to being useless, except on made-up roads."

Malcolm MacKenzie had been listening to what the brothers said with close interest.

"There's a lot more to making a wheel than I thought," he said. "When I look at the gentle curvature of those spokes, the angled mortise joints in the hub, and the curved rim sections you called felloes there, it's remarkable to me that you can get it all so right just by eye—without apparently marking anything out from measured diagrams in the first place. No wonder it takes years of practice to become fully skilled."

"I'm afraid we all take a great deal for granted, don't we?" commented the Vicar, reverting unconsciously to his 'sermon' voice. "That's true of many things. Sometimes I look at the stonework in my church and marvel at the skill of the masons who put it up all those years ago. And as for Canterbury Cathedral, well that just makes me feel very humble. The sheer size and beauty of the place, with the wonderful intricacy of the masonry and woodwork, leaves me feeling we owe such a lot to those men of long ago."

He paused a moment thoughtfully and then continued his impromptu homily.

"Only last week I walked with an American friend round the cloisters and went into the cathedral through the doorway into the Transept of Martyrdom. We retraced the footsteps of Thomas á Becket, murdered, so it is said, as twilight deepened in the afternoon of a fateful day in late December in the year 1170. We walked from the transept into the nave and the choir. Like so many visitors we stood at the spot where the Archbishop died.

The more I look at the cathedral the more I find myself lost in admiration of the skill and artistry of the craftsmen. I must confess it makes me feel very inadequate, because I couldn't begin to accomplish even the very simplest part of it. I fancy those men grafted away for most of the daylight hours, right through their lives, gaining in skill and dexterity over the years, yet never—I am sure—being truly appreciated, or paid more than a bare minimum living wage, however much was demanded of them. So much is said, when we study history, of kings and statesmen and famous people, but so little of the countless, and nameless, ordinary men who really created these marvellous buildings, and left us such a rich heritage."

The Spindlecroft twins started to fidget a bit, no doubt thinking they were on the threshold of a long sermon, so they discreetly started to shepherd their visitors on to see more of the premises. They were aware that with a skill which bemused them, the Vicar had switched the focus of attention from the structure of a simple wagon wheel, to a discourse of the work of mediaeval craftsmen, enlivened by a passing reference to the gruesome killing of Thomas á Becket.

The Colonel, quick to read the minds of men, couldn't resist a mischievous comment.

"I expect you chaps could make a pulpit as well as a farm cart if you wanted to, couldn't you?" he said, looking at Herbie and Horace with a twinkle in his eyes. "You could put shafts and wheels on it so that the Vicar here could have himself towed around by a donkey, to deliver sermons to all those people he complains about who never take the trouble to go to church except to be christened, married, or buried!"

Reverend Yelman smiled a little wryly at this comment. The point was not lost on him. His wife was forever telling him to come down to earth when he was out and about, and not suddenly deliver a sermon to some poor unsuspecting parishioner who didn't deserve it, but could not escape, being unable—out of respect for his position—to interrupt him in full flow so that they could go about their daily business. As for the Colonel, he was fond of telling the Vicar to get down off his high horse and meet people on their own terms, at least on weekdays. Like many a zealous priest, the Vicar was none the worse for a bit of kindly straight-talk from family and friends. So he shut up.

As if to rub it in, however, the Colonel added a further remark.

"Horace," he said, with a wide grin, "you are well-known as a fellow with artistic talent. Why don't you design a horse-drawn pulpit and draw a nice cartoon showing the Vicar being towed around in it, drawn by a fine horse with a white collar, out and about on his holy rounds. Make a good job of it and I'll send it up to *Punch* and ask them to publish it."

Horace glanced at the Vicar, not sure how he would react to this good-natured banter. Reverend Yelman though, used as he was to the boisterous and often surprisingly boyish humour of Colonel FitzWalter, was smiling happily enough, so Horace responded, though in a careful, non-committal way.

"That's a bit beyond me," he replied. "I'm not good enough to design a new conveyance like that."

"Get away with you," laughed the Colonel. "If you can make milk-carts, bakers-carts, grocers-carts and carriers-carts, there's no reason why you shouldn't be able to make a sermon-cart. After all it wouldn't have goods to carry like the others. Just the Vicar and his Church Bible, that's all. What a fine sight he would make, standing up in it, holding the reins, out and about on his rounds. His only delivery load would be words. They don't weight much, do they? Maybe that's a good thing because he certainly carries a good stock of them, as we all know!"

The Reverend Yelman could not resist a return dig at the Colonel.

"Judging by your performance in here now," he commented, "you're not exactly short of words yourself. And you don't weigh them very carefully before you deliver them," he added, a little ruefully.

The Colonel laughed appreciatively at this counter-attack. But turning to Horace, he had a final comment to make.

"Well, you think about it, Horace," he said. "There could be a fortune in it for you. Once seen in *Punch*, every Vicar in the land would want one. Most of them read *Punch*, I reckon. You would be made for life. You might even get to make one for the Archbishop of Canterbury. That would make you famous the world over. Then the Pope would get jealous and before you knew it you'd be shipping a mobile Pope-Pulpit to Rome. You think it over before you dismiss the idea. What do you think, Mr. MacKenzie?"

"I think as a military man you might be getting pulpits confused with chariots," he said laughingly. "Now chariots, to go into some of the spectacular movie films they're making in America these days—those might be a more certain market proposition than horse-drawn pulpits. With due respect to Reverend Yelman here, I must say I think people would be more likely to appreciate those than mobile pulpits, however talented the drivers may be!"

Horace and Herbie were much amused by this lively, good-natured exchange, and moved off into the yard to take their visitors over to see the nearly finished farm-wagon they had been talking about before they were side-tracked.

The wagon stood in an open-sided workshop. Its two front wheels were already fitted, as was one of the rear wheels. Wooden blocks under the rear axle were supporting it at the tail-end until the second wheel was fitted.

It was a very rugged vehicle indeed, capable, Herbie said, of carrying a load of between three or four tons. He pointed out that it was constructed in two main sections. The upper section, or body, was essentially a load-carrying box, with a floor built on a strong framework of stout timbers. Its sides were planked and its ends panelled. The lower section, called the undercarriage, was very strongly built indeed and carried the front and rear axles. While the rear axle was a rigidly-fixed part of the undercarriage, the front axle was pivoted on a king-pin which passed down through the floor of the wagon and through the centre of the axle.

Seen like this the wagon looked a fine piece of craftsmanship. It was evident that the brothers did not content themselves with making just a practical, functional vehicle. There were signs of artistry everywhere. Where the size of timbers could be shaped down without reducing the structural strength, squared members were carved in pleasing curves, and edges were bevelled to give a smooth feel and nice appearance. All of this was traditional in the trade, and carried out with apparent ease by the use of their specialist tools. Herbie explained that their Dad maintained there was a reason for everything. Each cart or wagon they made had to be strong enough for its purpose, yet as light in weight as possible. In addition its edges were given a smooth feel. Sharp corners and edges got knocked, damaged and defaced. Rounded woodwork remained undamaged for longer, and looked better.

The whole of the underside of the wagon was already painted red, and the upper works were an attractive blue. This painting, with its thorough priming, undercoating and top coating, would be unlikely to need re-doing for years and years. Because of the nature of its framework, although wagons continued to look quite good for life because of their pleasing structure, they were seldom seen looking as immaculate as this one did, in its brand-new condition. More often than not they were caked with mud.

Malcolm MacKenzie had been studying the front axle with some interest.

"A wagon doesn't have much of a turning-angle, does it?" he commented to Herbie.

"Well, this one is called a 'quarter-lock' type," replied Herbie. "If you look you will see that the rims of the front wheels stand higher than the sides of the wagon, and the axle is stopped just before the wheels reach the sides. The sizes are such that in this position the wheels make a quarter turn. We also make 'half-lock' wagons for some purposes. These cost a bit more because the sides have to be waisted, and the floor structure of the body is more complicated. The two main side members of the floor framework are not a continuous straight piece of wood, like they are in this wagon. Near the front is a V structure —a sort of notch—allowing the wheel rim to turn into the waists of the sides and run slightly under the floor.

There is also yet another third kind which we sometimes have to make. These are called 'full-lock' wagons which are made with much smaller front wheels that can turn right under the floor, allowing a full turn. Wagons like that are more often used for work on all-the-year-round hard surfaces, where the problem of sinking into muddy ground never arises. Road vehicles they are, not general-purpose farm and road wagons."

"Yes," said Malcolm, "I have seen those around. In fact, on the roads I occasionally see wagons with pneumatic tyres like those on motor vehicles. How much easier they must be for the horses to pull. They run so lightly and smoothly it must be a joy to a horse to be switched from a heavy farm-cart to one of those. No wonder they trot along so happily!"

Here Colonel FitzWalter intervened. "A great many things are changing fast these days," he said. "A good many of the old trades will probably disappear in time, I expect. After all, there's not much saddler and blacksmithing needed on motor cars, is there?"

"True enough," replied Herbie. "We shall have to take a leaf out of Bill Gunston's book. Alongside his saddlery work he's already built up a good business with motorbikes and push-bikes and now he's into wireless sets. He and his mate Albert Hogshead started off making crystal sets, and now Bill is selling one-valve and two-valve wireless sets that run on batteries and work a loudspeaker instead of earphones. We bought a crystal set off him with two pairs of earphones. Good fun that is, isn't it, Horace?"

"It is an' all," said Horace. "I reckon we'll stick with that for a bit. You don't have to buy batteries for crystal sets, and anyway I'd rather listen with earphones myself. Shuts out all outside noise and makes listening more private like, than a blessed great horn speaker."

"Well, there you are, then," said the Colonel reassuringly. "As the old trades die out new ones come along. Not that you two need new trades. Your skills allow you to make all sorts of wooden things as well as carts and wagons." Then, with a broad grin, he added. "Anyway scientists may have invented motorcars, aeroplanes and wireless sets, but they haven't yet discovered the secret of eternal life. So I reckon you two chaps will go on getting a steady supply of corpses to box up! That's one part of your work that will go on forever and a day!"

"Our old Dad," said Horace, "always said that making coffins was the insurance-policy part of our business. We used to moan at having to do it, but he said that whatever else goes short, that work will always be there. So he made us learn that side of things thoroughly as well, like it or not."

"Yes," confirmed Herbie, "a bit of a sore point that was with the Guv'nor. ' You can't go through life picking and choosing just those things you like doing,' he used to say, if we tried to shy off making a coffin. 'Get on and do it,' he'd say. 'Like it or lump it but get on and do it! One day, making those may stop you from starving!'"

"Still, he made his own, didn't he, Herbie?" said Horace. "Not many people can say that!"

"What did you say?" interjected the Vicar sharply, pricking up his ears. "You surely don't really mean to tell us that your father made his own coffin, do you?"

"Sure he did," answered Herbie, with a rueful grin. "Horace is right. When he got too old to do much real work for the firm he used to potter about now and again in the workshops here when it was too wet or cold for him to be in his garden. He amused himself making toys mainly. Well, they were more than toys really. Mostly they were exact models of the carts and wagons he'd made all his life. We've still got them. Beautiful little jobs they are too. He was a fine craftsman, our Dad was. And more painstaking than anybody I've ever known."

Herbie paused a moment or two, looking into the middle-distance, obviously thinking back to the days when his Dad was around. "Not only that," he went on, "but he created a whole series of model coffins using a variety of woods, made in various styles. All properly finished they were, perfectly made with the same great care as he always did things. Those he said we could always keep as patterns, and use to show customers wanting to choose a coffin for a relative. It may seem a strange thing to do, but it was something he said he'd always thought necessary. People always find it difficult and disturbing to look at and talk about coffins. The mere sight of a real one seems to give some people the shivers. Anyway Dad reckoned the models made it easier for them."

195

Herbie paused again, as though collecting his thoughts and recalling a scene from the past which he was perhaps a little reluctant to talk about. At length he continued, speaking slowly and thoughtfully.

"Then one day," he said, "we found him labouring away making a full-size coffin. He was making it from some of the firm's old stock of beautifully seasoned and selected oak. Not the easiest of wood to work with, but the wood he liked the best of all. Of course, we asked him who he was making it for, seeing that as so far as we knew no order for one had come in. Then the Guv'nor stopped planing the piece he was working on and looked up at us with a queer little smile on his face. I can see him now, bent over his bench, and looking up over his shoulder at the two of us.

'Well, sons,' he says to us, 'I can't do much to help you these days. But I couldn't bear the thought of you two having to make a coffin for me. I had to do it for my Dad. It wasn't easy. It's hard making a coffin for your own Mum and Dad. And I know you two have never liked that part of your work anyway. So I thought to myself, I'll do the job myself and save the lads having to face up to a none-too-pleasant job!'

Of course we told him not to be so silly, but he wouldn't have any of it. He said that he'd thought about it a lot and really wanted to do the job himself to save us the burden of it. So we just had to go away and leave him to it."

"Well I never," commented the Vicar, "what an extraordinary story. A man labouring away making his own coffin. Whoever would have dreamt of such a bizarre thing happening in an undertaker's workshop. Good Heavens, I find it difficult to believe!"

"It's true enough" confirmed Horace. "What's more, he wouldn't let us help him with it at all. Not that we wanted to really. It gave us the creeps seeing him working away at that coffin. But he finished it. And when his time came he was buried in it too!"

"Tell them about the brass plate, Horace," urged Herbie. "That really did take the biscuit that did."

"Yes," went on Horace. "I don't suppose I'll ever see a better piece of work than our Dad's coffin. He made a wonderful job of it. And to finish it off he made his own brass plate for it, to screw on the top. He was clever with brass work, and very good indeed at engraving. I found him in the workshop one day when he didn't expect me in. He said he hadn't meant us to see it. He was going to tuck it away in the coffin, with a note for us, so that we would come across it when it came time to box him up. But there was a little problem with it, and in a way it turned out to be a good thing I discovered him working on it."

"What was the problem?" queried Malcolm MacKenzie, whose interest had been thoroughly aroused by this strange story.

"Well," explained Horace, "when I came upon him working on it, he was busy polishing it, having got as far as he could with the engraving. But of course, as he said at the time, he couldn't quite finish the plate because he didn't know what year he would die! So, at that time, he'd got as far as engraving:

SAMUEL SPINDLECROFT

1833 – 19

Only son of

EBENEZER SPINDLECROFT

1799 - 1884

"How old was he at the time?" asked Malcolm.

"Oh, he was 86 at the time," answered Horace. I remember him saying to us that he'd already outlived his own Dad by one year, so he thought it about time he got himself ready for the off!"

"What a weird story," commented Malcolm.

"Anyway," carried on Horace, "he lived on for quite a while after that. The day after his 87th birthday, in 1920, I found him in the workshops working on his plate again. He was busy engraving a 2 against the 19. 'I've been looking forward to putting that 2 in,' he said. 'Now you know why I didn't put 191 on there, leaving just the one figure missing. I hoped I might reach the twenties. And I've made it, so in goes the 2.'"

"Quite a character, he must have been," commented Malcolm.

"Well, I pulled his leg a bit," went on Horace. "I told him he was jumping the gun. He might easily reach the age of 97, so the 2 would mess the plate up. There was no way he could alter a 2 into a 3!

He laughed at that, and said that if he got that far he would go on to make a century, then we could scrap the plate altogether and treat him to a gold-plated one! He didn't forget that either. On his 90th birthday we had a grand party, and in his little 'thank-you' speech he said that he was aiming at a 100 not-out, to get a gold-plated name plate on his coffin!"

"Of course he died later that year, didn't he?" said the Vicar. "He was taken ill suddenly, wasn't he?"

"Yes, sadly he didn't live many months after his 90th birthday," replied Horace. "And he had the last word about the brass plate too! The night he died his last words to me were about that. I was sitting with him by his bed. Herbie and I took it in turns to be sure one of us was with him all the time, while he was so poorly.

Dad and I had been talking a bit about one thing and another, and then he said he felt very tired, and thought he'd have a little sleep. He closed his eyes, then after a few moments he opened them again and looked up at me from his pillow, for the last time as it was to turn out.

I shall never forget the expression in his eyes. It was a mixture of sadness and a very great tiredness. Then there came a twinkle in his eyes, and he gave a little smile. It was a kind of secret, knowing sort of smile. Then he spoke to me, in a soft voice—husky it was—little more than a whisper—but somehow full of care, and a deep inner understanding. And what he said was so typical of him.

'I reckon you can manage to cut a '3' for me, can't you, Horace?' he said. 'There are two of mine on the plate already. Just make sure your 3 is the same as mine. And don't forget to do the little one as well, when you get time. Mind you make a good job of them now! We must keep up the Ebenezer Spindlecroft standards, Horace, mustn't we? Goodnight then, old son. Keep your pecker up. Don't worry about me. I'll be all right. Say Goodnight to Herbie for me. God bless you both. Nobody could have had two finer sons.'

With that he closed his eyes and fell fast asleep straightaway, as though speaking those last few words had exhausted him.

He never woke again. About two o'clock in the morning he just simply stopped breathing. Herbie and I were both at his side at the time. He seemed so peacefully asleep, breathing so gently that we could hardly detect the rise and fall of his chest. Then suddenly we became aware that he was very very still. Herbie held a mirror to his mouth, but no mist formed on it. So that was that. Our Dad was dead."

"It's a blessing to end like that," comforted the Vicar, who could see that recounting the story had brought tears to the eyes of the twins. "We all have to go sometime and your Dad was granted a long life and a happy ending to it, with his two sons by his side. It would have been your love for him which comforted him and made him so peaceful, in the end. Deep in his mind, as he went to his final eternal sleep, he would have known that you two were there. I'm quite sure of that."

"Do you reckon so?" said Herbie. "Thanks for putting it that way, Vicar. It's a great comfort to hear you say that. We hoped he knew that he was not alone at the end."

There was silence for a few moments as these moving comments left the visitors aware of the deep bond which had existed between the brothers and their father.

At length the Colonel broke the silence with a question directed at them both. Looking puzzled he said, "What did your Dad mean by his reference to 'the little one'? You said he asked you to do 'the little one' too, when you had time to."

"Don't know," answered Horace. "Neither Herbie nor I could figure out what he was driving at. We never got a chance to ask him and we can't think what it was he had in his mind. We think he must have been half-asleep and mulling something over in his mind. I suppose it's something we shall never know now."

Malcolm MacKenzie found himself wondering, with a kind of morbid fascination, if the brothers had actually placed their father's body in his self-made coffin themselves. A macabre thought indeed! But he did not have to wonder for long because any doubts were dispelled by Horace's next remark.

"Anyway," he said, "I completed the plate. It was a strange feeling, almost as though the Guv'nor were standing by my side watching me do it. When we were lads and he was training us, he would sometimes stand by our side checking up what we were doing with his eyes like a hawk's. He never missed a thing. So I took especial care when I engraved in the missing 3. When we came to put him into his coffin, of course it fitted him perfectly, as you would expect. And after we'd screwed down the lid, Herbie studied the plate carefully knowing how important these details were to our Dad. And he said he thought the '3' in 1923 looked exactly the same as the 3s in 1833, so that pleased me. That coffin really was a fine piece of work, wasn't it Herbie?"

"Never seen a better one!" confirmed Herbie emphatically. "I daresay when Dad was making it he could sense his own Dad, old Ebenezer, standing by his side too. He was always telling us how good our Grandfather was. You will notice, if you look carefully, that everything we make here has the letters 'ES' stamped or engraved on it somewhere. The Guv'nor used to say it was a mark of excellence. He said our Grandfather reckoned that knowing his initials were going to be on everything made by the firm, was a good way of seeing to it that nothing second-rate ever got through. We still do it to this day.

And the Guv'nor even engraved the letters 'ES' on the bottom right-hand corner of the brass plate on his coffin. Not only that but 'ES' was stamped on the underside of the lid. This is always done by us. Dad used to say that whereas the outside got defaced with time, the inside didn't, so anybody opening up a coffin for any reason in future years, can still check where it was made.

The guv'nor said that things made to Ebenezer Spindlecroft standards were as near perfect as makes no difference. And he never let us, or men working for him, forget it!"

"Well, I must say it's been an education coming here," commented Malcolm, with enthusiasm. "I've never seen more impressive craftwork anywhere, even among the shipwrights I'm so much more used to seeing at work. And that's saying something too, because their standards are exacting enough, as I expect you know. They have to be, in that field."

The brothers then led the way into their general-carpentry workshop where their three employees were busy at work. The elder of the two carpenters, Henry Foster and the apprentice, 'young Jack' as he was introduced, were working on a sash window, built to replace one for the new owners of a local farmhouse where the woodwork had been so long neglected that much of it was having to be extensively repaired, or replaced.

When the visitors arrived, the fifteen-year-old boy Jack was busy cutting the glass panes to fit the new window. With manifest confidence he worked swiftly and easily with his diamond cutter, and snapped the edges off with a deft tap. Henry, his mentor, noticed the way the visitors' attention had been arrested by this operation. Jack made it look so simple.

"Pretty good at that for a young lad, isn't he?" he said proudly.

"He jolly well is," agreed Malcolm. "Do you know, that's something I have never managed to get the knack of doing. I'm told by the experts who usually finish up doing it for me that I'm too careful with the cutting tool and not sharp enough tapping the glass to part it. It's partly a question of confidence, I expect. But I'm afraid I'll never learn now. I'm more nervous of making a mess of it, every time I try."

"Better stay behind and get young Jack to teach you!" said Horace with a laugh.

At the far end of the workshop, in 'coffin corner' as they called it, the second carpenter, Bill Smythe, was putting the finishing touches to what appeared to be an enormous coffin. It was long, wide and very deep. A real monster.

"That's for Tubby Cornwallis," said Herbie, nodding towards the coffin and speaking to the Vicar. "Sad case that, wasn't it?"

Reverend Yelman nodded sorrowfully. "Yes, a great tragedy," he said.

"Is he the fellow whose ladder broke when he was getting his kid's kite down from that big old beech tree by the river?" asked the Colonel.

"Yes, that's him," confirmed Herbie. "They reckon he weighed nigh-on eighteen stone and stood six foot four inches tall. Too heavy a bloke to be using that old fruit-picking ladder borrowed from the cherry orchard up the lane. A rung gave way when he was nearly at the top, his foot slipped through behind the ladder and he fell backwards bringing the ladder down with him. Broke his neck and killed outright, he was. One minute he was alive and full of beans, the next minute he was stone-dead. He was a big, strong, healthy bloke, and only forty-five years old. He's left a wife and five children. According to the Doctor, although he was so big and overweight, he was very fit and ought to have been good for many years to come. Terrible thing to happen when you think of it. And all for a kid's kite."

"Sometimes people don't see obvious danger, do they?" commented Malcolm MacKenzie. "Several times in the Navy I've known men killed or seriously wounded through sheer lack of foresight. Afterwards it always seems so predictable and avoidable. It's usually due to acting on the spur of the moment instead of giving a little time to think things through."

"That coffin certainly looks a whacking big one, doesn't it?" said Horace. "When you get a tall man with a beer-belly to go with it, the coffin made for him always seems to look as though someone must have got his measurements wrong. But that one fits Tubby all right. Herbie and I always double-check on jobs like that."

"You'll need a full team of eight bearers for that one at the funeral next week, won't you?" said the Vicar. "Have you managed to fix that?"

"Yes, Vicar," answered Herbie. "It's all laid on."

Malcolm MacKenzie—perhaps fortuitously because the mood, in keeping with the subject under discussion, had become rather sombre—then made a request which led to a brighter finale to the visit than would have been the case had they left at that point.

"You have been very kind in giving up so much of your time to showing us around your most interesting premises," he said. "But before we leave, is there any chance of having a brief look at the models you said your father made? I'm very interested in model-making myself and I should love to see them, if it's no trouble to you."

"Of course it's not," agreed Herbie. "It'll be a pleasure. We love to show Dad's collection to visitors. It often seems a great pity to us that his models spend their time locked away in a cupboard. We have thought that maybe one day we'll present them to a museum. Or we have even thought of converting our old barn into a country-crafts museum ourselves. We might be able to get other local experts to lend us exhibits to display in it. In a way it would serve as a kind of advertising, apart from the interest it would create. If it got well enough known, maybe it would bring people to Littlebrook who otherwise wouldn't have found their way here at all. Come into the house and see the Guv'nors collection."

Between the workshops and their house, the Spindlecrofts had a convenient corridor, built years ago by their Dad to give a covered way to make life more pleasant in bad weather. Horace, with the permission of his Dad many years before, had made the corridor something of a personal gallery for his artwork. His work, which included pencil drawings, water colours, and also some of his own photographs of local features, caused the short walk to occupy the best part of half-an-hour, much to the enjoyment of the visitors.

At length they gathered round the large, solid, refectory dining table inside the house to study the many models which the brothers carefully took out of a long, glass-fronted mahogany display cabinet, itself a Spindlecroft product made by their Grandfather to display his collection of china, earthenware, brass and pewter objects.

Much of this collection still remained in the possession of the brothers, but was relegated in part to be stored in the cupboards below the glass-fronted display shelves. Their Dad had gradually taken over the shelf space to accommodate his models as his collection grew steadily over the years. And the brothers preferred to continue to give his own craftwork priority over the manufactured objects, attractive and quite valuable though many of them were, collected by old Ebenezer so many years before.

By the time the brothers had emptied the cupboard of models, the large tabletop was covered with them. The product of a lifetime, each one made with meticulous attention to detail, the display was of absorbing interest. There were examples of almost all the many types of vehicles and products the firm had made over the years.

Often the livery, originally painted on a tradesman's hand-pushed and horse-drawn carts, was reproduced, and in addition there were two-wheeled and four-wheeled, passenger-carrying vehicles, beautifully decorated with the glossy finishes typically found on them. Herbie explained that the latter fell outside the scope of the firm's normal work. The local demand for passenger vehicles was small, and most of the larger commercial vehicles were bought from large manufacturing firms rather than from village wheelwrights.

Nonetheless, their Dad had been scrupulously careful in obtaining details of these, either by examining them over and over again himself if vehicles existed locally, or by contacting his old firm at Ashford, or other sources, for the information he needed. His normal scale of working was one inch to the foot. This was a convenient and very easy scale to use, making his measurements simple and giving rise to models of a convenient size to handle and display.

Strange though it seemed to see them, there were also models of typical Spindlecroft coffins. These were made to a slightly larger scale because they had a dual purpose, the main one being strictly commercial.

The Vicar, perhaps because the nature of his calling made these particular models objects of special interest to him, picked one up and scrutinised it closely.

"This is incredible," he said, calling the attention of the others to it. "It's beautifully made, a real work of art. Yet not the sort of thing one would cherish as an ornament. I wonder what prompted him to go to all that trouble to make these?"

"Ah! They're not just ornaments," Herbie explained. "Like I said, the Guv'nor made those for a commercial purpose. Horace and I don't use them—but he did. When a bereaved client came in to make arrangements, he would always interview them in our little Chapel of Rest, and take some of these models in to discuss options and prices.

You can't imagine walking a grieving person along a display of full-sized coffins, arranged like pieces in a furniture shop, can you? But these small, wonderfully made little coffins could be handled and discussed easily. At least that was his idea, though I must say we've never liked it much. But you've got to remember that this, sad thought though it is, is business to we Spindlecrofts.

The Guv'nor, like his Old Man before him, never missed a trick in anything to do with business. Not that he was unkind or unsympathetic. He just saw it as a job to do, and his duty was to comfort the relatives by giving good professional advice and a first-class service.

These days Herbie and I prefer to show people photographs of coffins and samples of the wood. Some people find these little ones a bit weird somehow. Not as gruesome as the real ones, maybe, but still a bit off-putting for all that!"

While Herbie has been talking, Horace had picked up another of the miniature coffins and was examining it very closely. When Herbie had finished his dissertation on the profit-making motive of this aspect of their Dad's skilful hobby, Horace call his attention to the little polished-oak coffin in his hands.

"Herbie, just look at this," he said, with a note of wonder in his voice. "This is one we certainly haven't seen before. You know," he added, addressing the visitors, "neither of us has taken any of these out of the cupboard since our Dad died. So we've never come across it. Look, it's a model of his own coffin, would you believe!"

"Never!" exclaimed Herbie disbelievingly. "One like it, maybe, but surely not a specific model of his own particular one!"

"It is, you know!" announced Herbie emphatically. "It's a model of his all right! What's more he put the finishing touches to it sometime after his 87th birthday. Look at the dates on the lid. He's put the '2' in after the '19'!"

Everybody gathered round to have a look at the little coffin in Horace's hands. On the lid was a tiny brass plate, made exactly to scale like the rest of the job. The plate bore an inscription, complete in every detail except one. It read:

SAMUEL SPINDLECORFT

1833- 192

Only son of

EBENEZER SPINDLECROFT

1799 – 1884

"Well I'm damned!" said Herbie, with clearly unfeigned surprise. "Looks like you've got another '3' to engrave Horace. That's what the Guv'nor meant when he told you not to forget to do the little one too. He must have thought we knew all about it, but he certainly had never shown it to us, had he? That's not very surprising, though, because he was very forgetful the last few years. He often thought he'd already done something when he hadn't—and the other way round too. Not that anybody minded that. It worried him more than other people. He didn't like to think he was failing. Still, Horace, good for him! He's left us with a permanent reminder of the last we saw of him. You'd better made a good job of engraving that '3' too or he'll want to know the reason why when we catch up with him!"

The little coffin, only just over eight inches long, was passed from hand to hand to become the centre of special attention.

"My word," commented the Vicar, "it can't be easy to engrave letters and figures as small as these. But it's perfectly done, isn't it?"

"That will have been done under Dad's special bench-magnifying glass," explained Horace. "He used that a lot when doing the livery on his models, especially on those bakers and grocers hand-carts there. If you look you will be hard put to it to find fault with any of the words and decorations he's painted on those. He had a knack of doing that. Even when he was very old his hand was still steady enough to allow him to make a good job. Surprising, really, when you come to think about it. Of course he always did have a lot of patience. That was one of his great strengths."

"While we're on the subject," added Herbie, "these little pieces of polished wood here, are the Guv'nor's samples of the various woods people could choose from, for coffins."

Herbie placed out on the table several nicely-presented specimens of wood. They were each labelled and he named them as he put them down.

"We've got here elm, oak, chestnut, satin walnut, hazel pine and pitch pine," he said.

"I can't say I've ever heard of the last two," commented the Colonel. "Do they grow around here?"

"No. They're not local timbers at all," answered Herbie. "They both come from the USA. Hazel pine is actually American red gum. Now I come to think about it, satin walnut comes from the same tree. It is the heart of red gum whereas hazel pine is the sap wood. In fact some people call it sap gum. Warps like blazes that stuff does unless its property seasoned. Then it's a fine wood. Any we've got left here, though, is certainly well seasoned! Our Grandfather, Ebenezer, bought most of it. He had the chance to buy a large bankrupt stock of American red gum wood at a knock-down price, so Dad told us. There must have been a hell of a lot of it because Horace and I have never had to buy in any at all, so far as I can remember. Talk about a good investment! Old Ebenezer did well there.

As for pitch pine, that's the strongest and heaviest of the pines, that is. Just look at it. I reckon that wood with its golden yellow colour and dark red markings, is a lovely wood. Dad said that the dark red markings show the darker, denser, summer growth. Don't know whether that's right or not, but the effect is marvellous, I think."

Then he paused a moment and grinned at Horace.

"Hey, Horace," he said. "If you get the job of making my coffin you can make it out of that. I shall be quite happy tucked away in a box made of that!"

"I'll remember that," responded Horace, smiling. "And while we're sorting the matter out, if I go first you can make mine out of satin walnut. Along with the Gov'nor's oak job that will make the three of us a very presentable family if anybody digs us up!"

Their visitors were amused by this exchange although the Vicar was inwardly not at all sure that this subject—dealing with matters normally requiring his dignified solemnity—was one to be treated with such levity. As it turned out, it happened that there was to be an occasion at a later date when they were to have reason to recall this wry, good-natured bit of banter between the twins, only too clearly.

Meanwhile Colonel FitzWalter had picked up a model of particular interest to him. Probably the most complicated of the lot, it carried an incredible amount of detail. It was a model of a horse-drawn army ambulance, one of the last to be developed before the advent of motor-driven vehicles, and extensively used alongside the latter in the Great War.

Khaki-coloured and bearing a brightly-painted red cross on each side, the four-wheeled wagon must have taken Samuel Spindlecroft hours upon hours of patient work to create. Inside it the Colonel found a white card on which Sam had written some descriptive notes, again with evidence of extreme care, so neatly was it done. In very small writing, using Indian ink and a mapping pen, it read:

BRITISH ARMY AMBULANCE WAGON (Mark VI)

Designed to carry 4 stretcher cases (2 on the floor and 2 on rails resting on the seats); or 12 sitting patients; or 6 sitting at the rear end with 2 stretcher cases on rails. The ambulance as pulled by four horses. It had a crew of up to five men; the driver and his mate; an orderly on a seat in the back, and two more riding one behind the other on the outside horse of each pair.

The group studied the beautifully-made model with close interest, marvelling at the apparent inclusion of every single feature of the original. Its four, twelve-spoke wheels were fitted with solid rubber tyres so that the ambulance ran more smoothly and quietly on hard surfaces than would a wagon with iron-shod wheels such as farm vehicles used. The rear wheels were of medium size with the rims coming just up to the level of the floor. The smaller front ones, due to the design of the front-cab which was narrower than the main body, could turn through a wide angle, permitting a fairly tight turning-circle.

Working upwards Herbie pointed out some of the main features. He drew attention to the rear-carriage with its two cross-springs and two side-springs; the front carriage, equally well-sprung; the body, with its roof supported on six easily removable vertical standards; the canvas hood over the front seat where the driver and his mate sat; the braking-system controlled by a wheel by the driver's side; the side-curtains of waterproof canvas; the travelling carbide-lamps and many other details in its design. Their Dad had even built in the four lockers under the body, for the storage of surgical appliances and medical supplies. In addition there was a compartment where a ten-gallon water tank was stored.

Herbie said that their Dad had first seen one of these ambulances at the Buff's Depot in Canterbury and had obtained permission to copy it. He made many journeys to and fro recording detail after detail until he finally had a full picture of it. Because of its important purpose, it was, according to their Dad, a 'no-expenses-spared' vehicle, and the best-made wagon he had seen in his career as a wheelwright.

Colonel FitzWalter said that he actually seen these ambulances in use in Flanders during the War. He could remember seeing other types as well and could recall a Mark V, and also one known as a 'Light Ambulance Mark I'. He thought it interesting, looking back at the first motor-driven ambulances, to notice how very like these horse-drawn ambulances the quaint, early motor-driven ones were. If you looked at them side-by-side he reckoned that you could see how an engine had been put in to replace the shafts and all the associated gear necessary for the horses. Almost a straight swap to start with, until motor-driven ambulances, like lorries, started to develop along different lines and parted company, in appearance and design, from their horse-drawn predecessors.

All in all, Samuel Spindlecroft's models were very impressive. It was a collection Malcolm MacKenzie later described as the most fascinating set of 'toys' he had ever seen.

Horace commented that it was just this 'toy appeal' which he and Herbie thought would draw people to a museum for models, if they ever got round to establishing one.

"What is needed alongside that lot is a collection of models of motor-driven vehicles," commented Malcolm. "Perhaps somebody around here might be encouraged to carry on your Dad's good work. Or maybe you two will get around to making models yourselves. You certainly have the skill, that's for sure."

"You might have something there," said Horace. "We're both very interested in motor vehicles, even though they look like driving us out of business eventually!"

"Well," continued Malcolm, "I've already made up my mind to have a go at constructing model-ships when I get back to Aberdeen. It's a hobby that's always appealed to me, and seeing these wonderfully-made models you've got here has fired my imagination. There is in fact a thriving model-making society in Aberdeen and I think I'll join it. I might well get in touch with you both in due course. One thing I will certainly do is use the same scale as your Dad has. If you also decide to make models, we shall all be producing things to the same scale."

Before leaving the Spindlecrofts' establishment the visitors had a brief look at the firm's office where they looked for a while at some of Ebenezer's early records, and compared them with their father's. The development of the scope of the family business showed up clearly in these ledgers, stored side by side in a row on a shelf alongside their large, oak, roll-top desk. This solid desk was yet another Spindlecroft product. Its intriguing series of cubby-holes, drawers and other storage facilities were fascinating. Included was a cleverly built-in secret drawer which was so well camouflaged that it would be unlikely ever to be found by chance, certainly not by a casual observer or petty thief.

Finally the twins showed them into the small Chapel of Rest adjacent to the office. This room, quietly situated away from the workshops, but structurally connected, as was the office, with their private dwelling, had an unmistakeably sombre atmosphere to it.

This feeling was possibly partially engendered straight away by the bier standing ready to receive the coffin that was nearing completion in the workshop. There was a second bier stored along one wall. The room was essentially a suitable place in which a body could remain with dignity awaiting a funeral day. There was little furniture there, except for the bare essentials. But what was actually in there had been thoughtfully provided to create a quiet, respectful, and religious aura for the benefit of grieving relatives, coming in to say their last farewells before a coffin lid was finally screwed down.

Showing their visitors off the premises, the brothers said a cheerful farewell to them. And so the strange sequence of events, started by the sad demise of an unknown tramp by a local lime kiln came to an end. Or nearly so, because, in a totally unpredictable way there was to be a gruesome sequel to this happy day. It was one which the three visitors were able to comprehend, and to picture more graphically than most other people, because of their singular memories of what had passed between them and the brothers during their interesting visit.

But no hint of this strange, awesome sequel marred the cheerful mood of the three visitors, as, chatting happily, they made their way back to the Vicarage.

Chapter 15

A MACABRE END TO THE SPINDLECROFT LINE

the twins follow in the footsteps
of their father

So bizarre in its detail was the sequel to the visit of Malcolm MacKenzie, Colonel FitzWalter and Reverend Yelman to the Spindlecrofts' workshops that those hearing the story in later years found it had to believe that they were not listening to an apocryphal legend, or a tale invented by an over-imaginative writer of fiction.

Perhaps the strange events in this seemingly so-unlikely story are best described by simply reproducing the contents of a letter sent by Colonel FitzWalter to Malcolm MacKenzie, less than two short years after his visit to Littlebrook.

The following is a copy of this letter, published by kind permission of Malcolm MacKenzie and with the acquiescence of Colonel Fitzwalter.

....

> Riverside House,
> Monkton Street,
> Littlebrook,
> Kent.
> 26 – 10 – 1926

Lieutenant Commander M.M. MacKenzie, D.S.O.,
Shetlands Lodge,
Bannockburn Avenue,
Aberdeen,
Scotland.

Dear Malcolm

I am afraid I have some unhappy news for you. Sadly, the brothers Herbie and Horace Spindlecroft have both died. The very bizarre circumstances that surround their premature deaths I shall relate to you in a moment.

My first duty is to discharge an obligation which I agreed to carry out for them on the last occasion I met them shortly before they died.

The brothers had no near relatives to whom they could leave their estate. They were, unfortunately, the last of the Spindlecroft line. Accordingly, their Solicitor, following their instructions, has sold the premises and business to the very firm at Ashford where their father Samuel Spindlecroft was trained as a Wheelwright. The proceeds of the sale are, I understand, largely due to be passed to the Benevolent Fund of the Association of Master Wheelwrights of which they—like their father—were Members. But there are some ancillary bequests, one of which concerns you.

You have, I know, been in touch with the brothers over matters connected with your mutual interest in models. They told me of the work you were doing and of the 'Models Museum' which you and your friends have already established in embryonic form, in Aberdeen.

Their wish was that their Dad's collection of models, so painstakingly constructed over many years by him, and of such superb craftsmanship, should be donated to your Museum. They have also left instructions for the sum of £1000 to be made over to you, to cover the cost of transportation to Aberdeen and the provision of suitable display arrangements to ensure the safe keeping and presentation of the collection in the Museum. They stressed that you were to feel free to spend any balance arising from this money, for the benefit of the Museum, in any way you wished.

You may wonder at their request to send their collection all the way to Aberdeen. The fact of the matter was, the brothers were faced with the need to wind up their affairs quickly, and of course—as you will deduce—unexpectedly. Of all the people they had met, you were the one most deeply interested in the models, and they knew their father's much treasured work would be safe in your hands.

They did not want the collection to be split up—with one model going here and the other there—with the almost certain ultimate damage and destruction of many of them. Had they not have made this provision in their will, it is quite certain that the collection would have gone under the hammer at the subsequent auction of their personal property. They had so little time in which to determine what to do about this and similar matters. Which brings me to the circumstances of their sad departure from this world, so untimely and unexpectedly—the more so because they went together.

Some months ago the brothers—simultaneously, so it seems—both became unwell. Their condition deteriorated fast from what at first appeared to be typical of the short-lived incapacities from which we all suffer from time to time, to a continuously progressive illness which looked ominous. Our local Doctor became alarmed.

Recognising the symptoms, yet hoping they might be found to be the result of something other than the diagnosis he feared, he sent them off to the Kent & Canterbury Hospital, at Canterbury, to be seen by a Specialist. Alas, his fears were confirmed. The prognosis was not good.

Incredible although it may seem, the twins had both contracted Hodgkin's Disease, which already, at the time of the diagnosis, had progressed to an advanced stage. It fell to our local Doctor to tell them that they were suffering from this incurable disease and had but little time to live. It was no comfort to be told, as they were, that it was hoped in time that a successful treatment might be found. For them there was not hope whatsoever, beyond a miracle.

I understand nobody yet knows what triggers the illness. Doubtless it is something to do with the environment, or arising in food, or from some unknown bug invading the system. Some say there might be a factor in the make-up of certain people which makes them prone to the illness starting up. I have no medical knowledge of course, but I gain the impression that even the Specialists know only how to recognise it, but have no successful treatment to alleviate it—let alone cure it. They are all too familiar with its symptoms, and its deadly inexorable development. Not that it's all that common though. Fortunately we understand that only relatively few people end their days that way.

So, having had their illness diagnosed, the brothers were, in effect, sent home to die. What seems to have astonished the medical profession is that two people in the same family should develop that same fatal disease at precisely the same time.

The local Doctor rationalised it this way. First of all he said they were twins. This meant that they were genetically very similar, if not wholly identical. In addition they had lived together all their lives, which meant that they had always been exposed to the same environmental conditions. He also knew, having questioned them closely, that they shared the same likes and dislikes over food and drink. Day by day they consumed very much the same diets, any differences being largely of quantity, rather than the nature of what they ate. Obviously, the amounts of energy they each expended on any given day varied somewhat, according to the activities in which they were individually involved. Correspondingly, their respective appetites also presumably differed somewhat on occasions.

Be all that as it may, the fact remains—however statistically unlikely it may be for it to happen—the twins went down with the disease simultaneously. Though not identical twins so far as facial appearances were concerned, they were nonetheless of very much the same physical stature. Presumably their constitutions were very much alike so that the disease progressed at a similar rate. They went downhill side by side, so to say.

The Doctor said that insofar as it is possible for people to face their end with stoicism, the two men appeared to become reconciled to the fact that their condition was incurable. In this no-hope situation they occupied themselves with the task of trying to tie up loose ends on behalf of their customers, and also, with the help of their Solicitor, to explore the possibility of finding a potential buyer for their premises.

They seemed obsessed with the desire to keep the family firm running— not only to safeguard the future of their three employees, but also because so much of their life was bound up with it.

It was as though they felt that if the firm lived on, then in a way the Spindlecrofts also lived on. Luckily the Ashford firm, a large and prospering business already diversifying to assure its future survival, made a provisional agreement to buy out the small Littlebrook business when the time came.

What is more, they agreed to retain the name, so that the firm would still bear the title Ebenezer Spindlecroft & Sons. This gave the twins a great deal of comfort in their last days.

I now come to the most astounding part of this story of the end of their lives, a more bizarre story than anything I have ever heard—much less been close enough to witness—in my entire life. You, because of our shared experience when we visited the Spindlecroft establishment with the Reverend Yelman, will be much better able to picture the circumstances than could a stranger, or even for that matter could a good many local people, who lacked the perspective which our glimpse of the family life of these two men gave to us.

You will remember the story of their Dad's coffin which he made for himself, and indeed of the small model of it which the brothers saw for the first time in our presence. Subsequently, if you recall, they jokingly charged one another with the construction of their own coffins, each with his own particular choice of wood, selected from their family store of prime-quality seasoned timber.

Well, I have to tell you, that having been told that they were destined to die in the near future, the brothers set about making these coffins for themselves, just as their father had done before them.

Contrary to their bit of leg-pulling between one another when we were with them, each in fact made his own. If you remember, quite naturally as it then seemed, they expected that one or the other would keel over first, leaving his brother to make a coffin for him, and then, presumably, later on, when the spirit moved him, subsequently going on to construct his own. When it came to it, Fate determined otherwise.

They actually discussed this point with the Vicar. During the closing months and weeks of their lives, Reverend Yelman spent an increasing amount of time with them, doing what he could to bring them spiritual comfort. He told me that one day they announced that they had made their coffins while they still had the strength!

According to him they were quite cheerful about it, not in any way morbid. They smiled wryly when they told him. Apparently neither could face making his brother's coffin while he was still alive. They found it much easier to face up to making their own. So this is what they did!

Herbie made his of Pitch Pine and Horace used Satin Walnut. You may remember that these were their expressed personal preferences. The two then completed coffins were placed in the small storeroom adjacent to their Chapel of Rest where they kept the various appurtenances associated with funeral arrangements.

In the event it was Herbie who died first. They each had their own bedroom—or 'den' as they called them—and whichever one got up first, always started the day by making a pot of tea in the kitchen downstairs. Habitually, the one doing the honours took a tray bearing two large mugs of tea upstairs to his brother's room, and they began each day by drinking their early morning tea together.

One day Horace went down, made the tea, and went up to Herbie's room where, to his dreadful shock, he found that his brother had died in the night.

Thereafter people say that Horace behaved like a man in a trance. He set about doing what was necessary in a silent, purposeful way, saying very little to anybody. The Doctor was summoned, of course, and issued the statutory Death Certificate. Later the Vicar called, and did his best to console Horace who was obviously in a deep state of shock.

There is a lady in the village who is generally called in to do what has to be done to prepare a body for burial. She was sent for by the Doctor and carried out her duties during the morning. In the afternoon, at Horace's request, his two carpenters who were used to assisting with the rather daunting task of putting bodies into coffins, and also regularly acted as bearers at the subsequent funerals, carried Herbie downstairs to the Chapel of Rest. Herbie was duly placed in the coffin he had made for himself.

Henry Foster told me that when he and his colleague, Bill Smythe, left for home that afternoon, Horace was sitting by his brother with his face buried in his hands. It was a very sad sight, and one they say they will not be likely to forget. The coffin was resting on a bier and the two men left Horace alone with his solitary sorrow, in the quiet room where so many people over the years have said their last Goodbyes.

Malcolm, you' are going to find it hard to believe what I now have to tell you.

The following morning Henry Foster, who for the last few weeks had been effectively the man-in-charge of the premises, arrived between 7.30 and 8.00 o'clock, to open up for the day. This he did, doing his rounds to unlock the workshops and prepare for the day's work.

There was, Henry said afterwards, an eerie kind of quiet about the place, an atmosphere which made him feel very uneasy. Horace was apparently not yet up and about, and Henry supposed that he would see little of the grieving brother that day. The previous day must have been emotionally exhausting, especially to a man who was so very ill himself. Henry thought it possible that the Doctor had given Horace something to make him sleep.

However, on reflection, he thought that maybe Horace had already got up and was with his brother in the Chapel of Rest. So he quietly made his way to the room and carefully opened the door to see if Horace was there. He felt that he might be able to do something to help, even if only perhaps in making Horace a cup of tea, and talking to him for a while.

The scene that met his eyes was astonishing. A weaker man than Henry might well have been bowled over by it and unable to walk into the room.

There were now two coffins in there, not one. A second bier now stood by the side of the one bearing Herbie, which Henry had helped put there the day before. On the second bier stood a coffin made of Satin Walnut. And it was not empty. In it lay Horace, as stone-dead as was his brother Herbie. Like Herbie, he was clad in a shroud. His hands were crossed on his chest, as were Herbie's. He differed from Herbie in one respect only. On his eyes, keeping his eyelids shut, rested two pennies.

It did not take Henry long to work out what must have happened, unreal and awesome though it seemed.

When he and Bill Smythe had left the premises the night before, Horace had appeared to be in a dazed, bewildered state, hardly seeming to hear them when they asked him if there was anything else they could do before they went off home. Lost in his own thoughts he shook his head in answer to their question, looking at them in the non-seeing, distant, unfocused way people have when they are not really listening to, or indeed are not totally aware of, what is going on.

Thinking about it, Henry was sure that Horace had made up his mind he was going off along with Herbie. Never separated all their lives it seemed all too evident that Horace now wanted only to join Herbie in the next world.

He must have taken the second bier to the store room and loaded his own coffin on to it, just as they always did when making final arrangements. Pushing it into the Chapel of Rest, and placing it carefully alongside Herbie's, he must then have gone back to the house to change into the shroud.

That this is indeed what he had done was later proved, for his clothes were later that day found neatly folded in his bedroom. Apparently he had then returned to the Chapel of Rest, moved a chair near the bier, and simply climbed into his own coffin.

Knowing, as he did so well, that when he died there was a strong chance that when found in the morning his eyes would be wide open and staring—something nobody ever liked to see—he did what was often done when a person died. He closed his eyes and put a penny on each one, so ensuring that they would remain closed until rigor mortis sealed them shut for ever.

It gave Henry a funny feeling to realise that Horace had thought his way through the normal procedure, with himself as the corpse, and brought two pennies back from the house to look after this detail.

Horace's hands were closed over his chest exactly as were Herbie's in the next coffin. Having thus organised himself he must then have simply gone to sleep and died. Perhaps this is something which a human being can do if determined to do so. Decide to die, lie down—and die! It made Henry shiver to think of it.

Just before eight o'clock Bill Smythe arrived. Henry heard him come in, and went out of the Chapel of Rest to tell him what had happened, to shield him from the shock of walking into the room, as unprepared as he himself had been, for the eerie scene which lay within.

Henry sent Bill off to fetch the Doctor straight away, and also the Vicar, because he felt the brothers would like Reverend Yelman to be with them for a little while.

The Doctor, accustomed as he was to death in its many ways of happening, had never in his entire experience seen anything quite so strange as the sight that met his gaze when he joined Henry and Bill in the Chapel of Rest. He did not express any surprise, though, that Horace had apparently decided to die, and then composed himself in the coffin, and done just that. The Doctor said that, already very much weakened by his own fatal illness, now in an advanced stage, and emotionally shocked and exhausted by his brother's death, there would have been very little strength left to sustain him.

Under these circumstances dying, by decision to die, was quite understandable. With no will left to live, life was tenuous, and would soon cease.

Reverend Yelman agreed with the Doctor that he was sure Horace had lost the will to live. Having got himself ready, he just lay down and 'Gave up the Ghost'. A very apt expression in this case, I thought!

When the Doctor left, the Vicar spent some ten minutes alone in the room with his two departed parishioners, quietly praying by their side. He was very fond of the twins. They were staunch members of his congregation, and of strong Christian faith. Looking very sad, and deeply moved by the sight of these two brothers lying side by side, he left the premises.

It was time for Henry and Bill to say their final farewells to the now once more united twins, who had been their bosses, and their good friends. They had one more surprise yet to come.

Starting with Herbie, perhaps because he had been first in the queue, they put the lid on his coffin and went to screw it down. With a feeling of awe they found evidence of a last attention to detail which typified to the very end the family's meticulous care to do all things properly, a discipline handed down from Ebenezer to Samuel, and on to his Grandsons. On the lid was a brass plate, perfectly engraved, and complete in every respect. On it they read:

HERBIE SPINDLECROFT
1875 - 1926
twin brother of HORACE
only sons of
SAMUEL SPINDLECROFT
1833 – 1923

They saw at once that the year of his death was not missing its final figure. Neither Henry nor Bill thought that Herbie could have put in the '6' in 1926. Though knowing his days were numbered, he had still not given up hope, and they said it would have been unlike him to invite an end that year by putting in the '6' when there might be a chance he would live to see another one. So they were quite sure Horace had done this final service for his brother, as indeed he had done for his Dad.

But this was not the last '6' that Horace engraved. When they came to screw on his lid they discovered that *his* dates were complete as well!

Sometime during his last few lonely and terribly distressed hours, Horace had attended to even this small detail. He finished off his own plate, identical to Herbie's except for the interchange of the two Christian names of these last two of the Spindlecroft line.

You will see that they were only 51 when they died, and it was only three years after their Dad, who had lived thirty-nine years longer than they did. How sad it is that they were suddenly cut down by getting an incurable illness. Judging by their father, and their grandfather, they might reasonably have expected to live to make old bones. But there it is; I'm afraid they have gone.

They were buried next to their father and grandfather in the family plot. The Vicar had a single grave dug for them, twice as wide as normal, so that the brothers could lie side by side. This was very thoughtful of him, I think. Talking after the ceremony, we all felt that in the event it was better for them to have gone together, as they did.

A single headstone is being prepared to carry both their names. I am sure it will be an object of interest to visitors in years to come, recording as it will, the unusual circumstance of two people starting and ending their lives together. For the Doctor was certain that Herbie had died in the early hours on the morning of Thursday the 28th August 1926, and that Horace had died before midnight of that same day. This being so their birth and death dates to be carved on the headstone will be identical.

The local character Motty, about whom you heard when here, was more than usually upset by the arrival of these two newcomers in the Churchyard. Somebody said he had fixed for them to make his own coffin when his day came, and was disappointed it would now have to be made by somebody else. Motty had a great respect for the Spindlecrofts' workmanship and said he'd rather be boxed up by them than anybody else. What a weird old boy he is!

Well, I told you, Malcolm, that I had a bizarre story to tell you. And what a macabre tale it is, isn't it? Incredible! Absolutely incredible! But true in every detail nonetheless.

I expect you will come down to make arrangements over the models. Please accept an open invitation to stay with my wife and me, at Riverside

House, for a long as you wish. It will be a pleasure indeed to see you again and I shall be only too pleased to assist you with the packing of the models, if you should so wish.

Yours sincerely,

Gordon FitzWalter

P.S.
Difficult to believe, isn't it! I have just read this letter over. I must confess that even so soon after the events took place, I can scarcely believe myself that it actually happened.

I have an idea that a few years hence I shall look back and think that I must have dreamt it all! It seems like a weird nightmare.

* * * * *

Two days later, six hundred miles away in the far North of Scotland, Malcolm MacKenzie read this letter with a mixture of sadness and incredulity. Yet in his memory he carried a clear picture of the brothers Herbie and Horace Spindlecroft. It was not just a visual image of their appearances either, for he could recall the sound of their voices, the manner of their gestures, and their general demeanour as they conducted their visitors on a tour of the establishment. So astounding did he find the description of the way their lives ended that he read the letter over again, and then yet again.

At length he found the remarkable story in keeping with the characters of the players, and the background against which the curious scene was set. In this he found Colonel FitzWalter's comment to be entirely correct. Because of what had transpired during their mutual visit to the Spindlecroft workshops, and the opportunity they had enjoyed to watch the two men against the background of their work and premises, he found it was indeed possible to comprehend the logicality of the strange events which had taken place, almost unbelievably macabre and bizarre though they were.

Not without imagination, in the quiet of his study, as he sat and mulled over the contents of the letter, he could picture in his mind's eye the scene which met the gaze of Henry Foster when he had opened the door of the Chapel of Rest on that morning a few weeks ago, to find the twins silently lying at peace side by side, awaiting the final rituals that had to take place, procedures with the form of which they were so professionally familiar.

These improbable events in the peaceful village, tucked away in the lovely Kentish countryside, seemed far removed from the hustle and bustle of the busy fishing port of Aberdeen.

Malcolm MacKenzie realised, when the message of his unique legacy had sunk in, that he had been given a marvellous opportunity to bring some of the flavour of this beautiful English countryside back home to Aberdeen, where it might form a lasting link between the two so-different places.

Chance had brought him into contact with a village and a community of which hitherto he had known nothing at all. He resolved to do his utmost to justify the trust placed in him by the Spindlecroft brothers, and to ensure that the painstaking, highly-skilled work of their father would be cared for and cherished, albeit so far away from its place of origin.

213

As soon as he could make the necessary arrangements to be away from his commitments, he took up Colonel FitzWalter's invitation to travel to Littlebrook and spent a few days with him at his home.

Together they went to the Spindlecrofts' premises and carefully packed the collection of models. These were then dispatched from Canterbury West Station to begin the long railway journey to Aberdeen. Perhaps fittingly, the models were taken to Canterbury in the Spindlecrofts' large, stately hearse. This black, sombre-looking car was the best available vehicle for the task.

As he stood with Colonel FitzWalter and watched the hearse driven out of the yard by Henry Foster, accompanied by young Jack, Malcolm MacKenzie thought it somehow not inappropriate that the collection should leave the premises in this funeral vehicle. It was very much a part of the lives of the craftsman who had made them, and of his two sons. So often during their working days they rode in it with the quiet dignity its normal function demanded, and indeed all three of them had been transported by it on their last journey from their personal Chapel of Rest to the churchyard not far away.

Malcolm MacKenzie was very conscious that from now on the future of the valuable, much-prized models now making their departure from the place where they were made, rested entirely in his hands, and he was quietly even more determined that he would see that they were well-cared for.

Having completed this important task, the two of them went to see the Vicar to discuss further administrative matters with him. By appointment, the three of them went to meet the Spindlecrofts' solicitor, to deal, not only with the question of the £1000 sum associated with the model collection, but also with some other matters the twins had dealt with in their will.

One of their final arrangements was to set up a trust fund to cover the ongoing maintenance of their own, and their family's graves, in the churchyard. They were the last of the line and left no relatives around the district to care for their last resting place. Inevitably, as they well knew, if they made no provision themselves, the family plot would get progressively more neglected, especially when Motty left the scene himself. It would be extremely unlikely that in the years ahead anybody would be found who would take such personal care of his departed friends, acquaintances, and local people, as Motty did.

They went further, however, in their thoughts for the future. Touchingly, said Reverend Yelman, but not surprisingly in view of the thoughtful men they were, their arrangements embraced the care of two other graves. One was there already, the second likely to appear in the not-too-distant future.

The first was that of Simon Hepplethwaite. They knew of course that Malcolm MacKenzie had commissioned Motty to care for this grave in the immediate future. In the long-term they wished to make sure that there did not come a time after Motty had disappeared when nobody was around to watch over this stranger's resting place. So they organised that in their trust fund.

The second concerned Motty himself. They left funds to cover the entire cost of Motty's funeral, including the cost of a headstone and surround, together with the on-going maintenance costs in perpetuity. This they did because of their long association with Motty with whom their business, and his work, had 'common ground' as it were, in the churchyard.

The twins knew of Motty's concern over his own coffin, having been told of his strange but understandable reaction when he had heard of the imminent departure of the two men who had already been charged by him with the task of seeing him 'put down' when his time came.

They had fixed with Reverend Yelman to discharge the task of informing Motty of this bequest after they themselves had been buried. It had been their wish that the Vicar be sure to explain to him that there was not need whatsoever for him to leave money himself, to cover his own expenses. They knew that, like them, Motty had no family living nearby, and that he had tucked away some savings in the Post Office specifically for his own funeral. It was a matter about which he had sought their advice. The brothers wanted Motty to be able to spend this money on whatever he wished, commenting to the Vicar that they thought this to be a more enjoyable way for him to dispose of his hard-earned savings then leaving it behind him to buy his own coffin and gravestone!

Needless to say Motty was delighted by this windfall, which brightened up his immediate future quite considerably. There were things he needed that he could now buy. He made up his mind to thank them personally when he eventually spoke to their spirits in the quiet seclusion of the churchyard. He felt sure they would be in touch with him as soon as they had settled down to life in the next world.

Having completed the business in hand, the Vicar went with Malcolm and the Colonel to the churchyard, to show them the now completed grave of Simon Hepplethwaite, which Malcolm had funded, after which they looked at the new double-grave on the Spindlecroft plot.

As Colonel FitzWalter had said in his letter, the headstone was certainly unusual. He himself had not seen the completed grave, the work having been done only very recently, and he and Malcolm studied it together. Behind the names and the inscription they could picture the faces of the twins, and knowing the circumstances of their end, they, unlike future visitors from other parts, were not left with unanswered questions when they had read what was printed there. The words were:

TO THE MEMORY OF THE TWIN BROTHERS
HERBIE AND HORACE SPINDLECROFT
born 12 May 1875
died 28th August 1926

'Never separated in life
Nor yet in death
Together they journeyed
And in peace they rest'

It was a poignant message, and they stood for a few moments in silence, pondering the singular inscription and recalling the two sincere and likeable men.

"You know, somehow, looking at that and remembering the two as we saw them, it seems right they should have gone together as they did," said Malcolm thoughtfully. "If they had to die, it was surely better by far that they went together."

"Yes, I agree with you there," commented the Colonel. "But I wonder what strangers will make of that inscription. I can't remember ever having seen or heard anything like that before. I can remember brothers being killed alongside one another in the War. I suppose it's more than likely there were cases of twins killed at the same time too. But it seems very unlikely in peacetime, doesn't it?"

"We have a notebook in the church records," intervened the Vicar, "in which are recorded notes about interesting graves in the churchyard. They go back a long way too. Many many years ago an enterprising Vicar made a study of them and started the records off. Since then, over the years, anything of especial note has been added. I will make sure to write a comment about the Spindlecrofts. It's quite a fascinating book to read. It's surprising how much one can learn about bygone days by reading these true life records. This grave will surely prove as interesting as any of them to future generations."

For a few moments longer the three men stood by the graveside, lost in contemplation of the very strange circumstances which lay behind the inscription on the headstone.

There was little sound other than birdsong in the peaceful country churchyard, except for a distant, regular 'chuff-chuff-chuffing' which registered in the ears of the listeners as the unmistakeable sound of a stationary steam engine working away somewhere in the locality. A sudden blast from a steam-whistle confirmed the identity of the source.

Malcolm, the stranger to the locality, noticed this more than did the others, for they knew what it was, and where it was, so to them the sound merged into the background, as does the tick-tock of a clock indoors.

"That's a steam engine, surely?" Malcolm commented, after the sound of the whistle.

"Yes," confirmed Colonel FitzWalter. "That's a traction engine driving a threshing machine in a farmyard over the other side of the village, which you can hear. A regular event each year that is. And quite an exciting one for the youngsters around here, too. Everybody looks forward to the coming of the 'Threshing Machine'! All the children, that is, and most of the men too, come to that! I don't know many chaps who can resist going to watch it working at least once or twice while it's here in the village."

"I can well believe that," responded Malcolm enthusiastically. "There's nothing quite like a steam engine, is there? They seem to have a life and a personality of their own, something that petrol engines never appear to have. If there's time to do so, I'd love to have a look at that threshing outfit working. It's a thing I've never had the opportunity to see before."

"That's easily arranged," said the Colonel. "The farm where it's working at the moment is only about three or four hundred yards up the road from Riverside House. After we've had a spot of lunch I'll walk you along there to see it. The set-up always fascinates me anyway, so I'll be glad of the excuse to go with you and watch it again."

The immediate business of the day being concluded, the two thanked Reverend Yelman for showing them the graves and made their way along the main pathway through the churchyard towards the lych-gate, and the lane outside. As they did so they heard the sound of a small dog yapping excitedly somewhere along the hedgerow on the far side of the church. Glancing round they caught the eye of the Vicar, who paused in his stride towards the church door.

"No need to ask what's going on over there," he said smilingly to Colonel FitzWalter. "My guess is that the rat population is about to be reduced by one, any moment now."

"What does he mean by that?" asked Malcolm.

"It will be Old Motty with his little dog Pug," replied the Colonel, laughing. "One of his sidelines is rat-catching. Every rat's tail earns him one penny towards his next pint of beer. I reckon he would be far from pleased if the rats stopped breeding under that old barn over there. He's got a vested interest in the survival of that colony. The same goes for the local rabbit population as well. Their good health is also important to the old boy. In their case he either eats them himself, or sells them to somebody else to eat, giving himself a bit more beer and baccy money."

216

As they strolled home for lunch, Malcolm MacKenzie was further enlightened about life in the Kentish countryside in general, and much amused hearing more stories of the activities of colourful local characters like Old Motty about whom he'd already learnt so much. It gave him more memories to carry with him back to Scotland, about this peaceful, south-eastern corner of England, where the rich vegetation differed so much from his much loved, but starker landscape of the far north.

How strange it was, he thought, that a wandering tramp should have forged this link between two places so far apart. His own life had been much enriched by this lonely, solitary figure who had chosen to spend the last years of his life roaming the countryside of the lovely county of Kent.

But Malcolm MacKenzie could not have foreseen that this link would be extended and enriched still more, by a series of equally unlikely chance events that were to lead to a long-term friendship with some very interesting men living in California, on the far Pacific Coast of North America.

Chapter 16

"THE THRESHER'S HERE!"

an unlikely-looking machine makes its annual visit

During the afternoon, Malcolm MacKenzie walked down the road with his host Colonel FitzWalter to watch the threshing machine at work in the extensive, well-organised farmyard area of Hexham's Farm.

What he saw there he found of absorbing interest, as indeed his companion knew he would. It was a hive of activity involving closely-knit teamwork between the dozen or so men and boys busily working there.

At the centre of things, immediately catching the eye, was a powerful, relentlessly chuff-chuff-chuffing steam traction engine that was driving the threshing machine. It was tended by a grimy-faced, burly man in blue overalls with a greasy cap pulled well down over his bushy, greying hair.

Living day by day working a coal-fired steam engine which puffed out—sometimes, it seemed, angrily—a mixture of black smoke and steam into the air surrounding him for hour after hour, resulted in his oily, sooty image, an appearance providing him with a well-recognised badge of office. He was secretly quite proud of this, for it marked him out as a different breed among his farm-working contemporaries in the rural area where he lived and worked.

A steam engine driver was much respected by boys and often envied by other men, partly because of the nature of his job, but also because he was comparatively well paid. There was undoubtedly a bit of kudos attached to the job for there was an aura of awe-inspiring power about the large, complicated-looking engine thudding away so effortlessly, and to be seen to be the man who controlled such a monster was impressive. There was a certain mystique about the job that conferred a status upon him, which commanded some respect.

The Colonel identified this impressive figure as Joe Minter, known to his friends as Smoky Joe. He was an experienced and knowledgeable engine driver employed by the South Kent Wingash Engineering Company—usually referred to as SKWEC—the firm who owned all the machinery working there in front of them in the farmyard.

The entire outfit, with the driver and his similarly-qualified colleague Boris Blacklocks, was hired out by SKWEC and moved from farm to farm, threshing crops of corn for several months each year, starting soon after harvest time in September.

A well-established routine brought 'The Thresher' to Littlebrook towards the end of November each year, as it moved from place to place over a radius of some thirty miles from its home depot.

SKWEC usually had five such complete mobile threshing outfits out on hire simultaneously during the season, and could in fact mobilise six if the occasion demanded, for they normally had a spare threshing machine in reserve on standby, ready to move off as a replacement should a machine break down on-site. The traction engine itself presented no problem because they had a small fleet of the versatile engines, used for a variety of purposes. In any event, unlike the threshing machines, they seldom broke down.

It did not take long for Malcolm to observe that Joe and Boris were very much the men in charge of the operation, running the machinery and supervising the key members of the team. Boris, who was also an experienced engine driver, was easily identifiable since he was dressed in blue overalls bearing the insignia SKWEC, like Joe's. Joe was on the engine and Boris on the thresher.

Six of the men and two boys working there were employees of Hexham's Farm, but four men were itinerant labourers who followed the threshing set from place to place and made their living by picking up seasonal work of various kinds wherever they could find it. The visitors found out later that, unusually, there was an extra man there on this occasion, a self-employed pest-control expert, called in by the farmer because of a particularly bad infestation of rats around the farm. While the thresher was on-site he remained near it because the demolition of the corn ricks, as threshing went ahead, always turned out rats and mice. Normally these were dealt with by the men doing the threshing, but this year the farmer was intent upon cutting back what had became a real menace rather than a mere nuisance. He had a minor plague to deal with.

Apart from the rat-catcher, who was roaming the area of operations with his three, highly alert terrier dogs, all the activity centred round the actual threshing machine itself. It was driven by a very strong, wide, leather belt, some sixty to seventy feet long, which coupled the large, heavy, spinning flywheel of the traction engine to the much smaller-diameter, main driving-wheel mounted on the side of the thresher.

Malcolm MacKenzie gazed at the threshing machine with close interest. He had heard of them, but never seen one close at hand. It really was a strange-looking contraption, a seemingly complicated and unlikely chunk of machinery, looking very much as though it had been built up a bit at a time, as a succession of wheels and gadgets had been added to enable it to discharge an increasing number of simultaneous operations.

This in fact is how it, and machines like it, had indeed evolved. It was a logical and quite complex box of tricks which, though of curious appearance, did what it had to do efficiently and with surprisingly little trouble, so long as it was well cared for and properly maintained. It also had to be used properly and did not react well to being overloaded, or mishandled by inexperienced people. It would 'get itself into a twist', causing frustrating and expensive delays while its troubles were diagnosed and put right. That is why it needed an expert handmaiden to watch over its treatment.

Colonel FitzWalter noticed the somewhat puzzled, if not actually astonished look on Malcolm's face as he gazed at the rocking, vibrating machine. He smiled to himself at his companion's reaction.

"Looks a bit like a Heath Robinson invention, doesn't it?" he commented. "It always seems to me a wonder it doesn't fall apart at the seams. But it keeps on going and never seems to give much trouble, so far as I have seen."

"Yes," replied Malcolm, "I was just thinking it looks like a contraption that could have been dreamt-up by a Punch cartoonist! I have been trying to figure out what it's all about. One thing's for sure, it appears to keep a lot of men working non-stop, so it must be achieving something!"

Built on a four-wheeled chassis, to be towed about from place to place by its traction-engine power source, the thresher was a large, wooden, box-like construction with a platform on top, on which three men were working. Inside it and on its sides, wheels, belts and moving parts abounded, all coupled to and driven from its main, flat-rimmed driving wheel that was connected by the slap-slapping broad leather belt to the traction engine's huge flywheel, which commanded its unceasing and integrated action.

As the machine rocked, juddered, swayed and vibrated, it emitted a cacophony of sounds dominated by the quite high-pitched, humming, whining noise on which was superimposed a series of clicking, clacking, whirring sounds, all distinctly repetitive in nature and evidently emanating from different parts of the apparatus, but discharging particular inter-related purposes and functions. But for all its mechanical variety, it was in total a synchronised, organised sound, one whose pattern registered an unconsciously-recognised harmony to the two SKWEC experts who tended it. A change in its complex sound signature was immediately detected by them, sometimes with the urgency of an alarm signal, yet even then almost certainly passing unnoticed by a casual observer.

A cloud of dust, chaff and straw particles enveloped the machine and those working—for all the world like attentive slaves—on it, and around it. Malcolm took a series of photographs of the busy scene.

He was fascinated by it all, and sought to make some order out of what was obviously a flow-pattern, a form of rural outdoor production line into which its attendants were locked by a non-stop series of events.

At length he turned to his companion for enlightenment.

"Do you know how the thing works, and what exactly all those chaps are doing?" he asked.

"Well, I certainly can't claim to be an expert," said the Colonel, "but watching it work from time to time, and speaking to the men, has given me a fair idea of what it's all about.

"To start with you have to remember that its primary purpose is to take in the dried, harvested corn-stalks and separate out the grain from the straw. If you start by looking at the corn-rick over there, you will see that the two men on top of it are feeding sheaves of corn to the chaps on top of the thresher. If you watch, you will notice that they all work with a regular swinging routine, keeping up a steady rhythmic pace all the time. A sheaf is tossed across to the first man on top—I've heard him called the 'catcher'—and he passes the sheaf to the next man, who cuts the twine binding it and passes the bundle of corn to the third one of the thresher-top team.

He is the most important one up there, and as you can see from his rig he's a SKWEC man. His name is Boris Blacklocks and he is in fact another qualified engine driver. He and Joe Minter have worked as a team for years. Boris comes from a family of 'steam' men. I believe he's got several relatives in Kent involved with traction engines, steam ploughing outfits, road rollers, and even in fairgrounds. He's a bit of a lone-wolf himself, in fact very much a loner—unmarried and very dedicated to his job, so it seems.

Boris always teams up with Joe for the threshing season. When that's over, the two go off together in one of SKWEC's steam ploughing teams, driving the two traction engines that tow the plough to and fro across the fields. But for the summer season, Boris is seconded to a large travelling fairground firm—Carlo's Fairground Company, a very well-known outfit down here—with whom I understand he remains throughout each season as very much a resident steam expert. They have a great deal of steam-driven equipment, and their stuff is all looked after by SKWEC, so obviously the arrangement is a mutually beneficial one. Boris travels all over the place with them, so one way and another he is out and about with traction engines all the year round. No wonder he knows his stuff!"

"What's he doing up on top there now?" asked Malcolm. "You say he has the most important job. What is he doing exactly?"

"Ah! There's a bit more to it than you would think," explained the Colonel. "Boris is the thresher-feeder. It's his job to feed corn down evenly into the mouth of the threshing drum, the part where the actual separation of the grain from the corn-stalks is carried out. You perhaps wouldn't believe it, and nor would most people come to that, but if you took Boris off there and put somebody else in his place, Smoky Joe would know straight away, without seeing the swap-over!"

"How's that?" queried Malcolm immediately.

"His ears would tell him," replied the Colonel. "Once that outfit gets running, the engine runs at a constant speed, and the noise of the steam engine itself, as well as the pitch of the hum from the thresher's drum, remains almost unchanged for a long time. But that only happens because Boris and Joe work together. They know what they are doing, and both understand the whole operation from one end to the other.

Boris feeds the unthreshed corn into the mouth of the drum much more carefully than you would think watching him from down here. He makes sure that the drum gets a continuous, unbroken and evenly-loaded supply. The engine chunters away over there,

221

steadily and efficiently, as it is doing right now. You just listen to it now. Notice how the chimney chuffs out fairly clean-looking smoke. Joe would say that the old girl is running as sweetly as a sewing machine at the moment! That's the ultimate praise for a piece of machinery. But if Boris started mucking about, the tempo would change immediately. If he stopped the feed altogether, the speed would build up straight away. And if he started to chuck great lumps of corn into the drum—or the complete armfuls he receives one at a time from his mate up there—the outfit would begin to labour and down would go the speed.

That two-ball speed-governor spinning away up on the engine there, would try to even out the changes, but there would be a complete break in the smoothness of the whole operation. Under heavier loads the engine tends to bark because of the greater pressure of the exhaust steam from the cylinder, and very soon some black smoke appears in the steam from the chimney."

"Is that a fact?" commented Malcolm. "It seems so smooth at the moment."

"It is indeed," continued the Colonel. "I didn't know anything about that until one day I got a free impromptu lesson when I was standing watching the machine. Boris had to go off suddenly for some reason and somebody else took over. Joe got very annoyed with the man, who started just chucking whole sheaves into the thresher. Joe noticed the loading straight away and gave the fellow a good bawling-out. I heard him telling the chastened chap just how the feed had to go into the mouth of the drum, and why care was needed all the time. The man was told the how and the why of the operation in no uncertain terms—which gave me, and the other bystanders, a lesson in threshing techniques at the same time!"

Malcolm smiled at the picture of the irate engine driver and the temporary thresher-feeder which the Colonel's story evoked in his mind. It was easy to imagine the burly driver appearing a most intimidating figure if his righteous anger was roused by the misuse of his machinery. It seemed highly probable that there had been occasions when he and his colleague had been landed with the task of repairing a thresher crippled by carelessness or ignorance. The machine didn't look an easy thing to take apart.

"What happens in the threshing drum you mentioned?" he asked. "How does it work?"

"I'm never too sure about that," answered the Colonel. "Like I said, I only know what I've surmised by watching it work, and hearing the men discuss it. The drum seems to carry beater arms which continuously slap the corn-stalks against the drum's containing case, causing the grain to be knocked out, so far as I can tell. If you remember how in the old days corn was threshed by hitting the crop with flails as it lay on the smoothed ground of the threshing floor, then I think you will understand how the inventors of threshing machines were simply finding ways of making a machine bash, or maybe 'thrash', the crop in a similar way. Certainly both the chaff and the grain itself are well and truly separated from the corn-stalks in there. There's precious little corn to be seen on the straw which comes out of the other end of the thresher."

Malcolm, whose natural interest in all things mechanical was aroused, made a mental note to try and get to see the thresher when it was at rest, to have a good look at the mechanics of the drum and its associated assembly.

"There's another thing, not in any way apparent unless you're told about it, which Boris has to know about too," stated the Colonel. "It's not only the grain which the thresher pours out that's of value, but the straw which is left when the grain is knocked out of it, is important too."

"I suppose it is," commented Malcolm. "But how can Boris affect the quality of that by anything which he does up on top there?"

222

"Ah! You would be surprised," answered the Colonel. "There are two things which have to be considered when deciding how to handle the corn-crop fed into the thresher. First of all it's necessary to know what the straw coming out at the end of the process will be used for. Secondly, the nature of the type of corn being threshed has to be looked at. What Joe and Boris have to aim at, is not only the best and cleanest possible quality of the grain itself, which of course is always of prime importance, but also that the straw remaining is good enough for its intended purpose.

The straw they are most concerned about is wheat-straw, because that is used a great deal for thatching. The thatcher wants his straw as long and undamaged as possible. To get it out of the machine like that, Boris feeds the wheat-stalks sideways-on into the drum. That way the straw does not get broken because it lies along the axis of the drum. Wheat-straw intended for providing thatching for buildings has to be particularly well treated, but it's not quite so important if the straw is to be used for thatching straw-stacks, next year's corn-ricks, or haystacks."

"How about oats and barley?" asked Malcolm.

"Straw from those crops is largely used around the farm itself," explained the Colonel. "It's used both for animal feedstuff and to spread on the ground in the cattle yards and pig houses, or sometimes in bad weather just to help give a firmer footing in water-logged areas such as through cattle-gates, where the animals funnel through creating a lot of muck. It doesn't matter if such straw is broken about as it goes through the thresher, so Boris feeds it into the mouth of the drum 'end-on', which generally gives very efficient removal of the grain and chaff."

"I must say I didn't associate threshing with thatching, in any way," observed Malcolm. "Do local thatchers come along to watch the crop going through sometimes, to select it for future purposes?"

"They do indeed," responded Colonel FitzWalter. "If they intend to buy a whole stack in due course, then they can get a much better idea of the quality of the straw by watching it coming out of the thresher than by examining a whole completed wheat-straw stack after it has been built, and itself covered by thatching."

"Some larger farms have their own expert thatcher, don't they?" queried Malcolm.

"They certainly do," replied the Colonel emphatically. "This farm does. And you don't have to look far for him either. He's up on that stack over there, which some men are building at this minute from the wheat-straw now coming off the line.

If you look up there, one of the men takes the straw delivered off the elevator and hands it to the other one who lays it on methodically as he builds the stack. He's the one who is the firm's thatcher. He name is Jim Thorton. The name Thorton is synonymous with thatching around these parts. His Dad, and two of his brothers, are in business on their own account.

If you waited until the end of the threshing period you would see Jim working here after the others have all gone. He will be here thatching the row of straw-stacks they've built, replacing the corn-ricks they started off with. And incidentally he would have been the one who thatched these corn-ricks at harvest time in the first place. You could say in fact, that he handles much of the harvested crop twice, once before it's threshed and again afterwards."

"That's very interesting, I must say," said Malcolm. "Threshing is real team work, that's quite obvious. It seems the farm needs a thatcher present on the site when it's being done so that the whole job is completed in one go."

"They do," confirmed the Colonel. "Sometimes, of course, they bring in a self-employed thatcher to do the job, which then gives him a regular annual contract. No doubt many such men get involved each year at threshing times, as well as at harvest time." Colonel FitzWalter paused for a few moments to gather his thoughts. Then, well into his stride, he continued explaining the threshing proceedings to his visitor from distant Aberdeen.

"Anyway, let me finish what I was telling you about what is happening here now," he said. "Let's go back to the drum again, because there is a bit more I can tell you about what goes on around that part of the system."

"I take it that the drum is really and truly the heart of the threshing machine," observed Malcolm. "Presumably it is directly connected to that small-diameter, hefty flat-wheel which is driven by the belt from the traction engine."

"That's right," said the Colonel. "The gearing-down, from the engine's large flywheel to that smaller diameter drive-wheel, sets the drum rotating at over 1000 revolutions per minute. Eleven hundred revs I think it was that Joe told me they reckon on running at. He sets it by ear actually. The fairly high-pitched whine or hum you hear underneath the clatter of all the other gadgets is the sound of the drum spinning.

Music to Joe's ears, that is. As a matter of fact he and Boris know each of the repetitive sounds the various parts of the thresher makes, individually. If one of them changes suddenly, they pick it up immediately. Sometimes Joe gets down from the engine and joins Boris while they both listen for a bit. Then, if necessary, Joe shuts down the drive, and they get into the works to find out what's up. That way, Joe told me one day, he and Boris prevent any serious trouble happening, because they catch the problem early enough to put it right, usually without much bother.

He said it can be as simple as straw running up into a tight mass around the end of an axle, just by its bearings, creating much friction and acting as a brake on the system. Very much the same problem we all get with simple lawn-movers. Once the mass of straw is cut away the machine is back to normal again in less than no time.

Anyway, to get back to the point, underneath the drum is a shaking, grid-like piece of gadgetry—the 'riddle' I think they call it. What happens is that the crop goes through the drum and is beaten by the bars I mentioned before. The grain is knocked out of the ears and both the grain and the chaff drop down on to the shaking grid below, which sifts it out so that it falls on to a moving conveyor belt under the grid.

Meanwhile, the straw which cannot pass through the riddle is carried forward to be delivered onto a sheet of slatted-canvas which carries it off to the exit platform up at the top of the back of the machine, where the elevator is."

"Yes, I can see that," said Malcolm. "I noticed that the elevator on which the straw is being dropped, is a separate machine on its own four-wheel carriage, driven by a belt from the thresher to its own driving wheel. It clearly picks up its power from the traction engine, via the thresher. That steam engine certainly works for its living, driving that lot all day long!"

As they watched they could see a constant stream of straw falling from the thresher to lie across the broad, moving, wooden-slatted canvas belt of the elevator, where projecting spikes caught it up and ensured that it travelled upwards in an even flow instead of falling backwards to ride up in disorganised bunches.

The end of the elevator projected out over the top of a partly made straw-stack, and the straw was delivered to the two men who were busy up there building the stack, in expert fashion, as the threshing work progressed. The length of the elevator, which was now at an angle of about 45° to the ground, showed that as the stack grew in height, the elevator's angle could be made steeper until the stack reached its final required height.

"If you look along the end of the thresher," the Colonel went on, "you will see a row of grain sacks hanging there. The man standing by them collects the grain pouring out of the machine from its grain-output chute. As one sacks fills, he simply moves the chute along to the next output point, to start on another sack. If you watch him you will see that he is one of a pair of men who have the job of handling these sacks of grain. Between them they are responsible for bagging up the grain and loading it onto the farm-cart standing there, which in turn delivers the crop to the farmer's grain store. The cart runs a shuttle service all day long, from the thresher to the store.

The farm bailiff, who of course has the whole farm to run, keeps his eye on the crop arriving at the store, and from time to time wanders round the team here to check all is well, and helps with problems as they arise."

"What are those two men doing along the side of the machine?" asked Malcolm. "They appear to be handling sacks as well."

"Their job is to bag up the chaff," explained the Colonel. "If you think about it, that makes three crops being harvested at the same time—the grain, the straw and the chaff. The chaff goes off to a separate store. It is mainly used as fodder for horses. Some is retained by the farm for their own animals and some goes to the local brewery, I believe, for their horses, and every now and again a Foden steam-lorry comes up from the North Downs Riding Stables. That's a large establishment not far from Folkestone where there is a thriving training operation for a string of racehorses, together with stabling for numerous horses and ponies which are either for sale or stabled there by individual owners.

They must need a lot of fodder each year to keep that lot going, certainly a lot more than this one particular farm produces, so no doubt their Foden ranges far and wide for their supplies. Those Fodens are proper 'workhorses' themselves, a bit slow uphill but very very reliable, I'm told. I know that the one that comes here drops off a load of horse manure brought up from the stables, for the mushroom beds which another local farmer has got installed in a purpose-built extension to his main barns. It's a fast-growing industry round here these days."

"You said earlier on," commented Malcolm, "that the chaff and grain fall through a shaking-grid affair below the drum, while the straw is carried away. How on earth does the machine manage to separate the chaff from the grain then? It's all small stuff, about the same size, isn't it?"

"That's no problem, no problem at all," replied the Colonel emphatically. "It's all a question of comparative weight, not of size. They use the same method that has been used from time immemorial, from long before threshing machines were dreamt of. You must have seen pictures of people threshing corn with flails, using just their own muscle power. And you will also, I'm sure, have seen pictures of them taking the mixture of chaff and grain from the threshing floor, standing in the wind, and just tossing the lot up so that the chaff—being so light in weight—simply blew to the side, while the comparatively heavy grain fell to the ground, to be collected up and bagged."

"Of course," nodded Malcolm. "It's the age-old business of 'winnowing'. I should have thought of that. The drum in that box of tricks replaces the flail and presumably there is some sort of artificial wind created inside there, to do the winnowing job."

"Yes," confirmed the Colonel. "A powerful fan underneath there blows the chaff off the much heavier grain, so the grain goes forward on a moving belt, while the chaff is blown sideways by the air-stream into an exit pipe and finishes up going straight into those collecting sacks along the side there.

If you notice, though, a good deal of it escapes along with a lot of other light-weight debris such as thistledown and dust, to create the cloud of dust you see flying about around the whole machine. If you happen to see the team going home at night you would know where they had been. They're covered from head-to-foot in the stuff.

225

Most of them wear leggings to stop it getting up their trousers, or at least tie the trouser legs below the knee in the time-honoured way of countrymen."

"That stuff must penetrate everywhere," commented Malcolm, now that his attention had been directed to it. "This is not the sort of job people would want all the year round, then, is it? None too healthy getting that lot in your lungs, I wouldn't think. Give me the open sea any time!"

"The only men to escape that dust-bath each day are those up there on the corn-rick at one end of the system, and up on the straw-stack at the other. All of those keep pretty clean when the wind blows across the thresher from the sides, and they have a fifty-fifty chance of being lucky if the wind blows along the line of the outfit," said the Colonel with a smile. "On this subject, though, take a look at Smoky Joe's much-prized engine over there. You will see that he rigs up pieces of canvas sheeting and tarpaulins to cover as much of the top of the boiler as possible—particularly the moving parts—to keep the stuff from plastering the whole lot up.

He and Boris keep the engine looking immaculate. They're forever cleaning and oiling it. This stuff flying about in the breeze sticks on the oily metal very readily and would give them a difficult time if it clogged up the moving parts."

"I must say," reflected Malcolm, gazing around the ground, "this whole affair seems wonderfully organised to me. It's plain to see that it is a well-established routine, no doubt worked out and perfected over the years so that it all runs smoothly."

"That's true," agreed the Colonel. "Yet, as each year comes round, it still amazes me to see how quickly it is all set up and running. One day the rick-yard here is quiet and peaceful with nothing much going on at all, and often nobody about for hours on end. Then this lot arrives—usually late in the day, direct from its previous job. By the following morning, certainly by the time I pass this way at about nine o'clock, the whole lot is working just as you see it now. Usually the first many people know about it is hearing one of the village lads calling out with great excitement to his mates, **'The thresher's here!'**

That cry goes up every year without fail. And believe me there's a rush of eager youngsters to the farmyard to watch this lot at work. They are not around at the moment as they're in school. But stay here until after four o'clock and in they will come. It makes a cheerful, happy event each year, and so far as I have seen, the men here, far from not being at all pleased to see them, welcome them to the party. Just so long as they keep clear of the dangerous machinery, of course, and don't get in the way."

"I can picture the scene," commented Malcolm smilingly. "Certainly, when I was a boy it would have been difficult to keep me away from a place like this, with all this fascinating work going on. Wheels going round were always a source of great interest to me, as far back as I can remember."

"One chap here will be pleased to see them today," smiled Colonel FitzWalter. "That's our rat-catcher friend who is here on site. He'll have a bit of help at critical times, if he's lucky. When a corn-rick gets taken down, as more and more of it disappears, any population of rats and mice living snugly tucked-away inside the mountain of food there, begin to move out. When a rick is getting down towards ground level you will see it surrounded by boys with sticks—and their dogs if they are allowed in—waiting for the inhabitants to dash for safety. Naturally the rat-catcher will be happy to get some support. And there's a little vested interest in it for him too. He will most certainly be a member of the local '**Rat & Sparrow Club**', from which he will eventually pick up one penny per rat's tail. That's the going-rate for the moment, I believe!"

Malcolm MacKenzie laughed at that reference to something he had only recently heard about for the first time.

"Yes," he said, "the Vicar was telling me all about that organisation when he was talking about Old Motty and his rat-catching activities around the churchyard. I must confess that of all the clubs and societies I've come across in my time, it wasn't until I came to Littlebrook that I heard of a Rat & Sparrow Club.

That's a club with an undisguised money-making purpose if ever I heard of one. There are some areas of Aberdeen where a Rat Club could do good work too. It's a wonder somebody hasn't thought of the idea. Maybe they have, and I just haven't heard about it. The trouble is, it obviously needs people to do what the farmers down here do and fund the exercise for the mutual benefit of everybody concerned. Just another case where townsfolk could learn something useful from their country-cousins, as they call them!"

Their attention at that moment was interrupted by the arrival of a tall, hefty, strong-looking man riding a fittingly tall-framed sturdy bicycle, who came pedalling into the farmyard, calling out a greeting to Colonel FitzWalter as he passed by. He headed towards the traction engine, propped up his bike and went to have a word with Smoky Joe.

"I know why he's here," stated the Colonel. "That's Ben Skinner who is bailiff on another quite large farm around here. The thresher always moves on from here to Mansted's farm where Ben works, and he will be here now, unless I'm much mistaken, to check on the probable time of arrival of this outfit at his farm. My guess is that they will be finished here by tomorrow evening and most likely will set up in his farm the next day. The outfit has to keep to a fairly tight schedule, and there is never any time wasted in their moves from place to place."

The Colonel's assessment was proved correct a few minutes later when Ben Skinner cycled past them on his way out.

"Your turn next, I suppose, Mr. Skinner," the Colonel called out amiably, as he went by.

"Yes, it is that, Sir," grinned Ben. "They will be finished here tomorrow afternoon and are moving the thresher to us in the evening for a start first thing Friday morning."

"Let's hope it keeps fine for you," was the Colonel's parting call, as Ben went off out of the gate.

"Well, Malcolm," he said, smiling, "now you know what threshing is all about, or rather, I should say, as much as I've managed to learn about it since I retired here many years ago. Let's go back home and wash this dust down our throats with a nice pint of Kentish cider. I know you like that, and as for me, just at the moment I can think of nothing which appeals to me more than a sparklingly refreshing glass of cool cider. How these chaps can put up with this dust all day long, I just can't imagine. I've had more than enough myself for one day, already!"

"I'll second that," laughed Malcolm. "I can hardly wait to get hold of the glass!"

With that the two of them, with a wave to Smoky Joe who had acknowledged their presence earlier in the afternoon, strolled from the busy scene and out of the farmyard gate. When they turned into the road and looked back at the threshing machine, a cheerful toot-toot from the traction engine's whistle was Joe's way of signalling his good-bye as he watched them go off.

As they walked towards Riverside House, the cheerful chuff-chuffing sound of the traction engine faded away behind them, but in the still afternoon it was surprising how far they got before they could hear it no longer. Malcolm remembered though, that they had in fact had their attention directed towards the thresher in the first place, by hearing the unmistakeable sound of the steam engine and its whistle when they had been standing in the churchyard that morning. He was surprised to realise now, how far the sound had travelled in the quiet, still air of this mild November day, in the peaceful Kentish countryside. The fact that one single steam engine could make its presence known over such a wide area, was testimony to just how quiet the countryside could be. It was in marked contrast to living in an industrial area, where the normal background noise was so pervasive that the arrival or departure of one or more engines or vehicles, even in close proximity, was insignificant and would not be noticed.

Not for the first time Malcolm found himself thinking that there was a lot to be said in favour of living in a village like Littlebrook.

On Friday morning, when Colonel FitzWalter and Malcolm MacKenzie passed Hexham's Farm, they paused to glance into the farmyard. The place was transformed. All was serene and peaceful.

It was a though the scene they had witnessed had been a dream. The traction engine, the thresher, the elevator, the mobile living quarters used by Joe and Boris, and all the men, had gone. All but one, they then discovered. The exception was the solitary figure working at the top of a long ladder, busily thatching one of the rows of new straw-stacks that had mushroomed up there during the past few days.

Jim Thorton, the resident thatcher, was already well-launched into the neat thatching of the new straw-stacks. By the time he had finished, a row of picturesque, conical-topped, thatched straw-stacks would stand there, replacing the equal number of corn-ricks that also had been thatched by him, which had stood at the opposite end of the farmyard since the harvest had been gathered in. Under the deft and practised hands of the solitary expert, the traditional neat thatching evolved surprisingly quickly, even as they watched.

Somebody had already raked over and tidied up the whole area where the corn-ricks had been, ready so it seemed for the arrival of next year's crop which in due course would doubtless be stored there. Only the broad, imprinted tracks of the heavy traction engine's large iron wheels criss-crossing the farmyard, left evidence that the scene they had witnessed had actually taken place.

Malcolm MacKenzie took a photograph of this now tranquil scene. It nicely completed the series recording the threshing operation, which he took with him on his return to Aberdeen a few days later.

Meanwhile, less than two miles away, the whole threshing outfit was fully operational at Mansted's Farm, having moved there and been made ready for action, on Thursday evening—as indeed Ben Skinner had predicted when Colonel FitzWalter had spoken to him on Wednesday afternoon. Six of the team were the same—Joe, Boris and the four 'followers'—but now they were joined by seven of Ben's staff.

It was Ben Skinner's habit to remain with the thresher throughout its stay. The crop was not so varied as at Hexham's, being almost entirely of barley, with no wheat at all, and just a small acreage of oats.

There was a reason for this. Mansted's Farm was closely tied to Farmers Brewery, which was geographically less than ten miles from the farm and very much one of its main customers. Their entire crop of hops was purchased by Farmers Brewery, as was their entire barley crop. The arrangement was mutually convenient, for the Brewery many years ago had built their Malt House at Littlebrook.

So Ben Skinner—having earlier that year, in the Autumn, seen their crop of hops safely harvested and delivered to the Oast House—was now occupied in getting their barley crop threshed and placed in their grain store, ready for delivery when required, to the Littlebrook Malt House.

In due course of time, the processed barley, now called 'malt', would make its way to the Brewery, as had the dried hops from the Oast House.

Small wonder that Ben Skinner and his mates from the farm, when standing in their local pub downing pints of beer from the same Brewery, felt justified in claiming that it might just as well be labelled Mansted's beer, since both the malt and the hops used in its preparation came from their farm. In truth though, Ben wasn't too sure about this claim because Farmers Brewery jealously guarded the secrets of its products. Ben was particularly fond of their 'Extra Stout', a dark brown drink that some people preferred to ordinary beer. Ben was not sure what proportion of the ingredients came from his farm. Not that he cared too much about the origin of what went into its making; he just enjoyed drinking it! It was a softer, rather sweeter-tasting drink, then the much sharper, bitter-tasting 'normal' beer.

The Brewery management guarded their reputation as jealously as they guarded the secrets of their own special brewing recipes and methods.

Part of this quality-control extended to a very close watch on the standards of the barley and hops which they bought in. And this, in turn, had an impact upon Ben Skinner, who, as Bailiff on one of the main farms supplying the Brewery, had to keep a close watch on the growing and the harvesting of both the hops and the barley.

So Ben always stayed around the threshing operations, paying the same attention to what went on as he always paid in the hop gardens earlier in the season each year.

Samples of the barley grain were inspected by the Brewer's Buyer during the threshing process each year. There was never any question of them agreeing in advance to buy all or part of a crop, until they were satisfied with its quality.

Another pair of highly critical eyes also subsequently looked over it, ultimately more closely and thoroughly than anybody else had done before. Jack Fullerstone, the hardworking Maltster who ran the Littlebrook Malt House, had good reason to look very carefully at the barley which passed through his hands. He was held responsible for the quality of the barley 'malt' which passed out of his establishment to the Brewery. And he knew better than most that if what went into the Malt House in the first place wasn't of a high standard, then what came out certainly could never be. So he watched what came in with beady eyes.

Jack was an acknowledged perfectionist, good at his job but temperamentally not good at getting on too well with other people, especially those he found wanting in ability or unwilling to work as hard as he did himself.

Very much a lone wolf, Jack was better off alone to do any job in hand himself. Anyone offering to assist him soon found his highly critical and intently watchful eye so intimidating, that unless absolutely confident in their own ability, it was not long before his presence at their elbow caused them to flutter and fumble—making mistakes they would not normally be likely to make.

Ben Skinner knew only too well that Jack examined all barley sent to him with great care, and recorded his assessment of its quality every year. He was expected to assess it reliably and made quite sure he did so. Ben had no quarrel with this, nor for that matter did he dislike Jack Fullerstone. They understood one another, and Jack's somewhat disgruntled and often seemingly cantankerous manner, did not disturb Ben. In fact secretly Ben had a healthy respect for Jack because he was quite a talented man who could—and did—turn his hands to many things, with a skill Ben had grown to admire and envy over the years.

One way and another a good many people had been helped out of trouble by the multi-talented though largely self-taught Jack. So his rather sullen nature was tolerated by most people, and few would deliberately 'stir him up'. Some did, but beyond the doubtful satisfaction of seeing him 'needled', gained nothing from it, and were in the end more often than not the losers as a result. They alienated a potential good friend—albeit a gruff, unsmiling one—and it was far more likely they would need his help, rather than he theirs, as some future date.

The versatile Jack did much of the necessary maintenance on the large, extensive buildings himself, during periods when the Malt House was not actively working. From the tall cowls which topped it, to the ground floor and out-buildings, he tackled everything with confidence and efficiency. His employers were content to leave him alone to get on with it, for they were well aware that he treated the entire establishment as though he owned it, and nobody could ask more than that!

The task of the Malt House was to convert the barley grain into malt, the substance fermented by the Brewers to create the alcohol-containing beer. There were three stages in the process, each calling for both care and a good deal of hard work. Jack provided the expertise. He knew his job as a Maltster. Everything depended upon his experience, ability and hour-by-hour judgement. Men were brought in as needed to help with the physical labour under Jack's supervision.

First the barley grain was soaked in water in tanks called 'steeps' for several hours, until nearly half the grain's weight was water.

In the second stage the moistened grain was spread to a depth of six inches or so on the malting floor—a vast, low-pitched, dimly-lit cavern of a place—and allowed to germinate. It was turned many times using large wooden malt shovels and forks to make the process uniform throughout the layer. This process took from five to ten days. Jack had to decide when the sprouting grain was ready. The action of germination changed much of the grains' insoluble starch content into the soluble sugars needed by the Brewers.

The final stage in the conversion of the original barley grain into malt was the drying of the sprouting grain in heated kilns. This terminated the growth of the grain, in effect killing the germinated seed before its food-store was much 'used-up' by the now embryonic growing plant. This kiln work was critical. Both temperature and time had to be monitored. Flat-tined forks were used to spread the grain evenly.

After several hours of light roasting, the grain turned into a pale brown malt—the basis of most beers made. Longer periods of roasting, at higher temperatures, turned the malt a darker brown, the raw material for the darker beers called 'stouts'. Ultimately this chocolate-coloured malt, at yet higher temperatures, produced 'black malt', at which point all the sugars had been caramelised. This was used only as an 'added extra', imparting a very dark colour and a sweet flavour to a brew.

Using two kilns it was possible to produce a large quantity of the paler, lower-temperature malt, and a smaller amount of the darker malt for the darker beers, for which the demand was less.

The kilns were kept in operation night and day. In this final stage of the work of the Malt House, it closely resembled that of the Oast House, its partner in the business of providing the Brewery with the raw materials it needed for the production of beer.

As the crow flies the Oast House and the Malt House were not far apart. It is almost certain that the ill-fated crow which caused the death of Timothy Twylock—having up to that sad day habitually sat on the wind-vane of the Oast House cowl—was equally as familiar with the two Malt House cowls, as no doubt were its relatives in later generations of intelligent cowl-perching crows.

A regular local contributor to Reverend Yelman's innovative Parish Magazine, an aspiring poet who liked to use imaginative imagery wherever she could contrive to employ it, when waxing lyrical about the beauty of the countryside in the Littlebrook area had spoken of the proud cowls of the Oast and Malt Houses as having a friendly nodding acquaintance with one another. When the Vicar's wife, who edited the Magazine, read him this, the Vicar said he thought it a nice literary touch. Jack Fullerstone, when his wife read him this reference to his beloved Malt House, said he thought it bloody silly, adding curtly and dismissively, "Anyway, cowls don't bloody nod—they turn, that's all! Nod be buggered! Balls!"

Certainly it was true that each of the cowls from their lofty, dominating positions, stood high above all neighbouring local features and enjoyed a line-of-sight view from one establishment to the other, over the roof-tops, fields and gardens.

So also was it true that a crow sitting high-up on the steeple of Littlebrook church, watching with amused interest the activities of the familiar bent figure of the ancient human being 'Old Motty', with his eager little dog, messing about down below, had a bird's eye view of all the cowls and could chose—if it so wished—to fly directly to any one of them to rest commandingly on the ever-convenient wind-vanes, so invitingly there to be perched upon.

And the notoriously crafty crows were clever enough to learn that there were extended periods each year when the cowls combined both convenience and comfort in any windy, wet, cold weather, for a stream of delightfully warm air issued from them to dry their feathers and add a little welcome luxury to their all-weather lives. They could sit there in the warm, snug and dry, protected from the chill west wind which spent its energy on the broad back of the sturdy cowl.

To a crow a cowl was a coveted spot, a safe high haven, secure from the wind, and uniquely considerate as the provider of a perfect private perch, because if the wind veered, it obligingly swung round to keep the harbour for its sheltering guest in the lee of the weather. What more could a canny crow crave for, as a place to rest and recuperate between feeding forays into the surrounding fields.

But it was not a spot at which to attempt to build a crow's nest, where *all-round* vision and accessibility were necessary for the safety of the family, and as a launching pad for fledglings' first flights. A solitary tree was much better for that, a high one with open views. It was a lesson, crows noted with quiet satisfaction, that was copied by men in their ocean-going sailing ships, who placed their observation platform high-up on a ship's main mast—paying due fair tribute to their wise, land-based, black-feathered friends by calling it a 'crow's nest'.

For men have long known that crows are bright and know a thing or two.

Chapter 17

THE 'BOX'
home comforts for Joe and Boris

By Friday evening, after a full day's threshing, with no interruption other than the one-hour dinner break, a good inroad had been made into Mansted's malting-barley crop.

Ben Skinner was delighted when the brewer's buyer, making his traditional first inspection of the grain on the first day of threshing, pronounced the samples he took as being well up to standard. Not that Ben had been in any doubt that the quality would pass muster, but it was always a relief to get this first provisional acceptance of the crop.

After so many years Ben knew only too well what to look for in the barley grain. A good malting-barley grain needed to be healthily plump, of even size, have a pale yellow colour with a finely wrinkled skin, show no signs of mould or mustiness, and the inside had to be white and mealy. It must not look grey, 'steely', and compacted. The crop so far threshed met these criteria admirably, and since at harvest the barley had looked uniformly good, Ben was confident the whole lot would be well up to the necessary standard.

Unremarked by the Colonel in his discussion with Malcolm MacKenzie when they had watched the outfit working at Hexham's Farm—the Colonel may not even have been aware of such details—the threshing machine in use was a double-tier, shaker-riddle facility, which allowed any weed seeds or small-sized grain from the corn, to drop through to the second, lower, sieving stage, to be collected and bagged up separately from the main crop.

This 'small-stuff' was not thrown away, though. It was useful for cattle-feeding purposes, but the ability of the threshing machine to filter it out was one of the main factors which ensured that the bagged-up grain for the discerning customer was all of acceptable size. Uniformity of size was a mark of consistent quality, and if the machinery hired from SKWEC was not capable of 'cleaning up' the crop as thoroughly as this, then it would not be accepted next time round. There were other plant-hiring firms about, and competition was keen.

At Mansted's Farm the corn crop was stored under the protective cover of a large Dutch barn, and not in picturesque thatched ricks as used at Hexham's Farm. Although a costly investment, the end-result made it well worthwhile. It was labour-saving and good for the welfare of the crop. Mansted's barley, harvested as far as could be arranged in good weather conditions, then stored out of the rain under the wide-span roof inside this open-sided, airy, purpose-built barn, had a good chance of reaching the thresher in prime condition. In addition, a year-round supply of dry straw was available and easily accessible in all weathers, because the straw output from the thresher was fed back into the Dutch barn.

Parked alongside the far end of the Dutch barn, snugly tucked into a corner out of the wind, was the 'Box', so called because that is just what it looked like—a large wooden box on iron wheels. This vehicle was the living quarters which Joe and Boris towed around with them on their travels during the threshing season. Essentially it was a hut built on a four-wheeled chassis, a simple, sturdy, no-frills mobile caravan, necessary since they were often too far from home to go to and fro each day. Even if they were near home, it was desirable for at least one of them to be on site all night since the steam engine was kept fired-up continuously.

Unlike Joe, though, who cycled home at tea-time each Saturday and returned either late Sunday evening or very early Monday morning, depending upon how far from his home they were working, Boris never went anywhere. To him the trailer was his home throughout the threshing season. A loner by habit and preference, Boris was quite happy to make himself reasonably cosy in the 'Box', and to stay permanently on site alongside the traction engine and the associated gear, in all of which machinery he took a close interest.

This arrangement suited everybody. It was not as bad for Boris as it may seem, because he enjoyed a change of location every few days. He made for the nearest pub whenever he felt the need for company or had to replenish their stock of beer.

More often than not, however, he was busily occupied, and very happily too, with his hobby of toy and model making. Working mainly with plywood, he had his materials, tools and a 'Gem' treadle fretsaw machine, conveniently stored, some inside the trailer, and some, while they were on site, stashed away underneath it.

Inside the trailer, which had a door and window on one side and two smaller windows, one at each end, the furnishing was sparse indeed. Just the bare essentials. There were two platform-type beds which doubled during the day as seats; a sturdy table with two strong kitchen chairs; a coke-burning, cylindrical tortoise-type stove; a paraffin Valor oil-stove for back-up heating as needed; a food storage cupboard and a small, waist-high platform near the window on which stood a white enamelled wash bowl and a paraffin-burning Primus cooking-stove.

The interior was lit during the evenings and mornings by two oil-lamps hanging from the elliptically-curved roof. Each had double wicks adjusted by knurled thumb-screws. These gave out a warm, yellowish light, allowing Joe and Boris to read, or to do whatever they wanted to, during the hours of darkness. Provided the lamps were topped up daily with paraffin, and the wicks trimmed now and again, they gave no trouble. If the wicks became ragged and the flames uneven, they tended to smoke and this soon blackened the lamp-glass chimneys. If allowed to run low in paraffin as they burnt down and gradually went out, then they really did smoke, densely and nastily, causing a lot of unnecessary trouble.

This happened once when Joe and Boris were outside one evening, tying down tarpaulins over their gear during a wind that was threatening to blow up to gale force and do damage. When they got back inside they had more trouble to deal with. One of the lamps had gone out and 'smoked'. The amount of soft black soot deposited all over the room was incredible. It had penetrated everywhere. It took them both a long time to clean up, and they paid a severe penalty for this simple oversight.

The same thing applied to the Valor oil stove, except that being a much larger burner this appliance generated even more soft black soot if it were allowed to burn out: a very great deal of it. So, as with the engine outside, the oil-lamps and the Valor stove were watched over carefully and filled daily.

Water was stored in a purpose-built tank mounted outside on one end of their mobile home. At the other end there was a large storage box in which they kept tools and their necessary odds and ends.

Despite its rudimentary nature, the 'Box', all in all, was not a bad place in which to live during the working week. Once organised it was tolerable enough and—on a cold winter's night with the coke-stove going well—it had an attractively cosy feel to it. Boris had fitted curtains to the windows and put down old carpets on the floor by the beds.

At the end of their long, hard day's threshing, when Joe and Boris were shutting down the set for the night, Ben Skinner called to see them on his way home, to let them know that he had checked into the grain store just over four tons of barley that day. It was a very satisfying total and augured well for the farm's total crop that year.

Wearily, for by now they were both very tired, Joe and Boris did their last job of the day, following a regular procedure, and put the engine to bed for the night. After topping up the boiler with water, Joe placed a steel cap on the chimney, a special one made to limit the draught during the night. Meanwhile Boris banked up the fire and shut down the ash pan damper. Under these conditions the powerful traction engine slumbered quietly without trouble every night, and was never difficult or reluctant to get going again each morning, responding without fail in return for such reliable care.

Their final task was to tie down a canvas cover over the engine. It went, with a slotted hole for the chimney to poke through, over the front of the boiler, and extended back over the main moving parts and all the gearing mounted on the boiler, right back to cover the 'man-stand' area where the driver stood.

That done, the faithful engine, at all times cleaned, cosseted and well cared for, was securely tucked up for the night.

Thankfully Joe and Boris trudged over to the 'Box', well ready for a good rest. After a refreshing and much-needed wash-and-brush-up, followed by a plain but appetising supper cooked by Boris on the Primus stove, they settled down to relax for an hour or two before turning in. A large, steaming cup of hot, sweet cocoa was their preferred last drink of the day, and this they habitually made just after their evening meal. They drank this sitting chatting at the table, a ritual they both enjoyed and looked forward to during the day, when the long hours of work lay before them. Afterwards, for the rest of the evening, they followed their own pursuits until the desire for sleep overtook them.

Joe sat at the table to record the day's tally in his log-book. Then, as he had done regularly for years, he wrote a few brief notes in his diary. Joe's grain-log showed that he and Boris, now completing the tenth week of the threshing season, had turned out 243 tons of grain, clocking an average so far of just about the 24 tons per week they liked to achieve. With a tired sigh, which ran on and turned into a deep noisy yawn, Joe closed his notebooks and shoved them to one side.

Boris, busy at the table sandpapering a window frame he had cut out with his fretsaw, as one of those needed for the front of a very professional-looking, Tudor-style doll's house he was making, looked up from his work.

"How are we doing?" he asked.

"Two hundred and forty-three tons so far this year," answered Joe. "I reckon by next Tuesday we'll be over the two hundred and fifty ton mark."

"Pretty good that, isn't it?" commented Boris. "How does that compare with last year?"

"It's bound to be a bit more, I'm sure of that," said Joe. "If you remember we had that bloody awful two or three weeks of heavy rain in October when we had to pack it in for days at a time."

"So we did, an' all! I'd forgotten that for the moment," said Boris thoughtfully. "Hell of a mess that made of our trip, that did, didn't it?"

Joe reached out for his notebooks again. "I'll have a look back to see how we'd done by the time we actually left here last year," he said.

He took up his log-book and spent some time leafing through its well-thumbed pages. After a bit he found what he was looking for.

"Yes, here we are," he said. "When we finally left this farm last year we were only up to two hundred and seventeen tons. That's a hell of a lot down compared with this year. And we've far from finished here yet. What's more, the dates show that last year we were running about ten days behind this year. So we were turning out less grain and taking longer over it!"

"It was a bad year all round though, wasn't it?" commented Boris ruefully, as if by way of some comfort to them on their low performance.

"Ah well, it's nice to know we're making up for it this year," exclaimed Joe with satisfaction. "If we carry on as we are going now, we shall be well over six hundred tons by the time we've finished this season."

"How much does the firm turn out all-told in a year, do you reckon, Joe?" asked

Boris. "I think they've got five threshing outfits doing the rounds now, haven't they?"

"Yep," replied Joe. "Two this side of Canterbury, one down in Thanet, and two up around Faversham and Ashford. At the Works last year when they were moaning about things, I remember the Guv'nor saying they would be lucky to get over the twenty-five hundred ton mark by the time they totted up the lot for the year. Five hundred tons down we were then, according to him. He said the chairman of the company was very concerned about it. Mind you, that miserable bastard is always glad to have a moan about something, so it might not have been as bad as he made out. Anyway, as the Guv'nor said, nobody could be blamed for it. We were well down, though, that's for sure. But there again, the firm gets paid for threshing the crop, not for the grain there is. It's not quite as simple as it seems. They charge per half-day for the threshing outfit, not for how much grain it turns out, so if the corn is poor stuff it's the farmer who loses most. Mind you, SKWEC loses if the weather is bad and keeps us from working. That's true enough. We lost money last year that way, I suppose. But not even the chairman, for all his bluster, can control that!"

"There must have been enough barley last year, for all that," grinned Boris cheerfully. "We didn't seem to go short of beer this summer, Joe, did we?" Boris liked his beer and was secretly quite proud of his reputation for being able to put it away in seemingly limitless quantities, and to sink a pint faster than most.

"You speak for yourself," retorted Joe with a laugh. "How do you know you didn't swill down somebody else's share as well as your own, you boozy old sod!"

Boris had a chuckle at this suggestion.

"No, you needn't worry about your beer, Boris," Joe went on. "The brewer never goes short of barley. If there's not enough local stuff, they just buy it in from somewhere else. If there's a poor crop here, you can bet your life there's a good one somewhere else. The same goes for wheat grain, for that matter. When did you last go short of bread?"

"Never have! Never!" responded Boris emphatically, patting his rounded beer-belly contentedly. "Nor did the old folks go short, so far as I know. Short of a lot of things they were, but never bread and cheese. There was always a doorstep, a hunk of cheese, and plenty of spuds, no matter how hard things were. Anyway, my old grandad grew enough in his garden to feed an army. Not only that, he had umpteen rabbits and kept a pig too. I expect they could have done without bread for a while, if they had to. Not that there was ever any danger of that."

"Town people with no gardens couldn't, though, could they?" said Joe. "Be buggered without bread, they would!"

"I'd be more buggered without beer, myself," laughed Boris.

"I don't know about buggered," grinned Joe. "You'd be a damn sight thinner, that's for sure. It's beer that's causing that pot-belly of yours to grow, not bread. I'm glad I don't have to carry a lump like that around with me wherever I go, like you do. I shouldn't pat it, if I were you. You might encourage it to grow bigger still. Or burst the bloody thing. Go easy on the beer, mate, that's my advice to you, or you'll finish up looking like just a stomach with arms and legs. Your mate Sam Carlo will be putting you in his Freak Show at the Fairground!"

After this cheerful bit of repartee both men fell silent and busied themselves in their own ways. Joe lay on his bed reading his latest Sexton Blake detective magazine while Boris worked away at the table on his doll's house windows.

Before long, first Joe, then Boris, tucked themselves up in bed. Both had candles by their beds, and it was their practice for the last man to bed to light his candle, blow out the two oil-lamps and see himself to bed by the flickering light of his candle. More often than not it was Boris who was last to bed. His absorption with the practical work of his hobby tended to be less sleep-inducing than reading. Joe, however, liked nothing better than a good read, so he tended to lie out on his bed, but pretty soon became sleepy and got his head down for the night, leaving Boris busy at the table. Usually though it was Joe who got up first in the morning, so the normal routine was for Boris to put out the lights at night, and Joe to light them up again in the mornings.

Sometimes Boris, having put out the lamps and got to bed by candlelight, would park the candle conveniently by his side and spend a while reading before snuffing it out and going to sleep. Somewhat incongruously his preferred reading matter was comics, of which he always had quite a store under his bed. Some chided him over the rather childish nature of his reading matter but that did not bother him at all. The whimsical pictures he found in some of them often fired his imagination, and at times triggered off ideas for the inventive toys and models he loved to create. Mixed in his pile of copies of Comic Cuts, Chips, Rainbow and other popular comics, were copies of boys' magazines such as Magnet, Gem, and Hotspur. Like many others he liked to follow the exploits of characters such as Jack Wharton, Billy Bunter and their cronies. These, with his regularly bought Hobbies Magazine, usually provided him with all the reading matter he wanted. Occasionally he borrowed a book from Joe's store, and conversely Joe was not above reading some of Boris's comics and boys' magazines when the mood took him.

On this particular night at Mansted's Farm, however, Boris was too tired to read, and once in bed he blew out his candle and in no time at all was fast asleep.

By the time the distant church clock struck eleven o'clock, apart from the ticking of Joe's alarm clock and the gentle, peaceful snoring coming from Boris, all was quiet and peaceful in the 'Box'. The only light was a red glow from the grate at the bottom of the tortoise stove. The hinged flap which could cover it was always left lifted up, because both of them liked to see its cheerful glow whenever they woke up. Banked up for the night, the stove would still be alight in the morning, and the box remained reasonably warm all the time, unless the weather was extremely cold and icy draughts crept through the cracks around the door and the windows.

Outside nothing much stirred that night. The air was still and the weather fair. Sharp ears would have heard rustling sounds—first here, then there—as creatures of the night foraged around. Many mice were busy in the scattered rich pickings around the thresher.

Inside the Dutch barn, the prosperous-looking tabby cat which lived in the farmyard also fed well, for the work on the partly demolished barley store had disturbed many established residents. And outside, in the moonlit area between the thresher and the barn, an owl swooped down so swiftly and surely to take up a scurrying mouse, that not even his furtively feeding fellows nearby saw him plucked off the ground and carried into the sky above.

At 5.45 in the morning the peace inside the 'Box' was abruptly shattered by the clamour of Joe's alarm clock. He reached out, grabbed it, switched it off with a muttered curse and sat up for a few moments, gathering his senses before getting up.

Having lit his candle, then the oil lamps, he snuffed the candle and parked it back in its place. In a short while he was dressed and making his way by the light of their hurricane lamp around the side of the Dutch barn to the traction engine. His first task each day was to start the process of bringing the slumbering engine to life again. At this stage only two simple actions had to be taken; he lifted the steel lid from the chimney, and opened the ash-pan door. This initiated a fire-reviving draught, gentle at first but building up as the fire gained enthusiasm and drew in more air.

That done, Joe trudged back through the gloom of the early morning to the 'Box'.

Once inside, having extinguished the hurricane lamp and parked it where it lived, he lit the Primus stove to make a pot of tea. The kettle, filled the evening before, had spent the night standing on the top of the tortoise stove, so the water was already quite hot and quickly came to the boil.

Joe made the tea and while it was brewing used the remaining water from the kettle to wash and shave, but not before he had refilled the kettle from the large jug of water they kept by the door. The kettle was put back on the Primus stove for Boris's use.

Boris, by now awakened by the familiar sounds of Joe going about his normal routine, sat up in bed ready to receive his mug of tea. By chance or good management, he came to life at precisely the right moment.

"What's it like outside?" he asked without preamble.

"Still a clear sky," responded Joe. "Looks like another good day for us."

"Good," said Boris. "Let's hope it keeps fine for Sunday, too."

Joe poured out their tea. It was strong and sweet, too strong and too sweet for many people. But that's the way they both liked it.

Soon Boris was up and about. While he washed and shaved, Joe prepared their breakfast. Today, as was almost invariably the case, it was bacon, eggs and fried bread cooked in a large frying pan, over the Primus stove. Joe did the breakfast and Boris the evening meal. The arrangement suited them both, and neither of them ever wanted to swap jobs.

At 6.30am they left the 'Box' and went off to start things going for the day. They followed a regular routine, each with specific tasks which they carried out automatically and efficiently every day the thresher was working. Joe worked on the engine, Boris on the thresher and elevator.

The fire was Joe's first concern. To get at it he rolled the canvas cover back off the driver's platform and off the breast plate of the boiler, but not far enough back to uncover the working parts, this precaution being necessary because he did not want the dust he was about to create to get to the works.

He now ran a long poker into the fire along the spaces separating each bar from its neighbours. The whole fire had to be clear of clinker and he always fetched out a good deal of it, some days more than others. Just how much clinker depended upon both the quality of the fuel and the intensity with which it had been burnt. All of it he removed using the poker to lift it clear of the red hot burning fuel, and to push it on to his long-handled clinkering shovel. There being so much straw around, if the weather were dry, as indeed it was today, Joe was careful to dump the clinker on to clear ground and finally to douse it with a bucket of water. A heap of clinker could stay hot for a long time and had been known to cause problems if forgotten.

As it was Saturday, Joe used his special brush to sweep out the fire tubes which passed from the boiler's breast plate which backed the fire, right through the boiler to the smoke-box at the front. These tubes were always cleaned through twice a week, on Wednesday and Saturdays. Occasionally, if the fuel were extra smoky and the workload perhaps harder than normal, which made matters worse, the state of the tubes was such that Joe had to sweep them each day. But it was never less than twice a week because clear tubes were essential to give the strong through-draught necessary to sustain an adequately responsive fire, plus the most efficient heating of the water through which the tubes passed.

By the time Joe had finished his work on the fire it was burning very brightly. It looked healthy. Joe and Boris knew from long experience what a good fire had to look like, and how to maintain it all day.

Joe now pulled the canvas cover forward, and turned his attention to the gleaming works. All working parts were oiled every day, and the metal all around the boiler was kept very clean. No driver worth his salt could tolerate a scruffy engine. A bright, gleaming, well-oiled and well-maintained engine repaid its minder by running for year after year with very little trouble indeed. But they objected to being allowed to get scruffy, and played up those who misused them. Any engine for which Joe or Boris was responsible had no complaint in this regard. Both of them were true steam men, as indeed were most men entrusted with the management of an engine. Just a few didn't deserve the job and ultimately got found out, so lost it.

While Joe had been occupied with the engine, Boris had been equally busy doing daily maintenance on the thresher. His first job was to remove a canvas cover which was always in position over the important threshing drum section when the machine was not working. The thresher was a complicated collection of wheels, cogs, levers, belts and moving parts. All gathered dust and chaff which had to be cleaned off. Then all moving bearings and pivots had to be oiled, otherwise the smooth running of the whole mechanism could not be assured for the many hours it had to run each day.

Quite often, by lunchtime, both Boris and Joe had to repeat some cleaning and oiling already carried out first thing that morning before work had started. It was a never-ending process, but an absolutely essential one. Boris also did similar daily maintenance on the elevator.

A little before seven o'clock in the morning all this preparatory work had been completed. By this time the fire was burning brightly and the steam pressure gauge was moving up. At this stage, the hefty leather driving-belt, which was always slipped off each evening when the engine was shut down, was put back on again. There being enough pressure to run the engine, Joe set it going, adjusting it so that it ticked over quietly and pleasingly smoothly. This had the immediate effect of making the fire burn even more brightly. The exhaust steam from the cylinders, blasting up the chimney, pulled air into the fire and along the tubes. The added heat to the water from the increasingly hot tubes generated more steam pressure in the boiler.

Joe's engine, an 8 H.P. Fowler of which he was particularly fond, normally ran at 105 pounds per square inch, and at this pressure the thresher drum's speed could be maintained at around the maker's recommended rate of eleven hundred revolutions per minute.

By the time the team of men had arrived for their seven o'clock start, Joe and Boris had the machine running smoothly. It was always their practice to walk around the set together, watching the machinery and listening to it as it free-ran under no-load conditions. A few minutes only were needed, for they were quick to notice anything abnormal.

When the unthreshed barley started to be fed into the drum, Joe made his final adjustments to the engine's speed, working as always largely by ear. On this day, as on the day before, the machinery ran smoothly and faultlessly all day long.

Saturday was normally a half-day's holiday for the men on the farm. Usually they packed up at one o'clock. During the threshing period a compromise was reached. Work stopped at 4 pm giving the team three hours extra overtime on the week, but with enough time off on the Saturday to make it a little less arduous than the previous five days. It rated as an early finish by normal working-day standards, and was looked forward to because there was a long evening to be enjoyed and a day free of the work-place next day on Sunday.

There was a happy atmosphere around the thresher during the shortened afternoon. At about 3.30pm the experienced men working in the team knew, without looking at watches, that they were not far off finishing time. The fact was communicated to them indirectly by a marked slowing down of the thresher's speed. This came about because Joe, who also wanted to lose no time getting off home, started the process of shutting down the engine. Prior to banking up the fire, and to be ready for the re-start on Monday, he set the engine to take in water so as to top the boiler's water gauge up to its full level. This influx of water caused a drop in steam pressure with a consequent noticeable, though not harmful, drop in speed.

By four o'clock everybody was ready for the off. All tasks which had to be completed before leaving had already been carried out.

A cheerful blast from Joe's steam whistle signalled knocking-off time, and within ten minutes only Joe and Boris remained on site.

They did what had to be done to make the machinery secure until Monday. As for the engine, it was banked up and put to bed as usual. It suited them both, and saved them having to start extra early on Monday mornings, to keep the fire in over the week-ends. This necessarily involved Boris in a little work on Sundays, but he did not mind that. He looked forward to a peaceful day left to himself around the site, and it was no hardship to him to spend a little time tending the engine.

By 4.30pm Joe had gone off home and Boris was making himself a cup of tea in the box. Later on, after a welcome wash-and-brush-up, he cooked himself a meal. Soon afterwards he was busy at the table with his model-making.

At about 8.30 in the evening Boris went outside to stretch his legs and have a breather. The night, like the previous one, was again very still, and the starlit sky was clear of any sign of clouds. In the soft silvery moonlight the shadowy shapes of the traction engine and the thresher showed up clearly. Behind the thresher the elevator angled sharply upwards against the night sky, because when work left off, the straw level was high up under the far end of the roof of the lofty Dutch barn into which it was pointed.

As Boris glanced around, savouring the peace of the evening and enjoying the brisk freshness of the clear night air, his attention was arrested by a glimmer of light shafting out from a large old wooden barn over the far side of the farmyard, between where he stood and the rambling old farmhouse which lay beyond. It intrigued him because usually no work went on around the farm at that time of night, least of all on a Saturday.

Intent upon satisfying his curiosity, Boris strode over towards the barn to see what was going on. The large doors were pulled shut, but like most such doors they were not close fitting. Enough space was left down the sides and middle to allow for the cycles of swelling and shrinking which inevitably followed the exposure of wooden doors to all weathers. It was from one side of the doors that the shaft of light shone that had caught his eye.

Conscious that he was behaving as an inquisitive intruder, Boris moved toward the barn as noiselessly as he could. As he drew near he caught the sound of a murmur of voices from within. They seemed to come from somewhere to the left of the door. Cautiously he stepped up to the doors and peered through the gap from which the light shone.

He could see nobody in his field of vision but heard voices, then a woman's laugh from further over to the left of the door than he could see. As he stood there he thought he could hear the sound of dogs making both soft, whimpering, whining noises and growling strangely—not somehow angrily, but clearly in an excited state.

Stepping back a bit he looked to his left along the side of the barn and quickly spotted what he was looking for. A narrow horizontal beam of light shone out through a damaged or ill-fitting section of the overlapping weather boards. Silently he made his way to this new vantage point, a ready-made observation slit about five feet from the ground. 'Just right for a peeping Tom,' he thought rather guiltily.

Being careful to make no sound he bent down and peered through the slit.

What he saw astonished him. It was unlike anything he had ever witnessed before. The curious tableau, presented to him like a theatrical scene at the moment the curtain rises, imprinted itself upon his mind. Many times in the future he was to get a fleeting recall of it, like a glimpse of a photograph flashed before the eyes.

It happened that his vantage point had placed him directly opposite the bizarre proceedings which by chance were reaching their climax at that very moment.

In a clear space inside the barn stood a strongly-made, wooden work-table. Seated at it, perched on wooden stools, looking towards him from the far side of the table, were two middle-aged ladies. To Boris they looked rather formidable ladies, hefty, greying, tweedy, matronly, commanding, brook-no-nonsense, get-out-of-my-way-it's-me-coming types. Some would have described them as horsey, doggy, decidedly County ladies, who could be expected to talk in very much over-loud voices, as though loudness demanded respectful deference and special attention; they were typified by those of their kind who would barge into a village shop and bellow instructions from the door to the shopkeeper, over the heads of the patiently waiting queue of locals.

Hanging over the table, brightly illuminating the area beneath in a pool of light, was a pressure-driven, portable lamp radiating near-white light from its incandescent mantle. Because of the size of the barn, and the way in which the lamp concentrated its light downwards in a circle to what was going on below, it created an impression of a stage scene in a theatre. Beyond and all around was an area of shadowed twilight where an unseen audience could be imagined to be silently sitting watching the performance.

Boris saw immediately what was afoot. Up on the table were two dogs, each firmly under the control of one of the two masterful ladies. The dogs were in a high state of excitement. They were clearly about to be mated.

The one to the left of Boris, a healthy-looking cocker spaniel which he correctly assumed to be of true pedigree, was obviously a bitch, well and truly in heat and ready for mating. Its presenter was just finishing arranging it so that it squatted with its receptive tail-end facing down the table. She appeared to be pushing its head downwards into a submission position and holding its tail up as though in invitation. It was a position, Boris saw at a glance, that was one of maximum convenience for its intended partner and also, he felt sure, affording maximum expectation and visibility to its markedly avid observers. The bitch was in a high state of excitement, whining and positively grovelling in apparent desire and preparedness.

In the charge of the other lady was a fine golden retriever. Boris felt certain this also was of pure pedigree breed, so good did it look. She had one hand grasping and pulling back on the dog's strong, broad, brass-studded leather collar. Her other hand Boris did not fail to notice, was thrust up between the dog's hind legs holding and feeling around its red and very much 'at-the-ready' weapon.

With its nose pointed directly up the table at its target, the dog was snuffling and growling in a very agitated, highly disturbed state. His expectations had been screwed up to fever pitch by the close proximity of the bitch which was so clearly summoning him to do his duty, while he was being not only forcibly restrained from getting at it but titillated at the same time. Frustrated and highly stimulated, he looked fit to burst.

So obviously contrived and controlled was this set-up that Boris could not escape the sure conclusion that the organisers of the event were enjoying it as much as the principal players. Their facial expressions, their intently watching eyes and their state of eager and obvious anticipation, clearly betrayed their erotic interest.

As he stared through the slot with riveted attention, captivated by the intensely-charged atmosphere and the critical stage in the proceedings, the lady-controller-of-the-bitch gave a go-ahead to the visibly drooling dog-restrainer by her side.

It was perhaps their intention to control more precisely the moment of union between the two performers. If so it did not work. So intense was the pent-up energy of the rampant dog that the moment it felt an easement of the restraining pull on its collar, and was allowed to move towards its target, it became too strong for its mistress to hold back.

In a moment it was astride the bitch and Boris had time to watch both its feverish unbridled performance, and the expressions of sheer, lascivious delight on the faces of the ladies.

When the dog's energy was spent and its purpose completed, both performers were lovingly caressed and congratulated by their owners. Soon afterwards the ladies began preparations to close the theatre for the night. The one-act play was over.

Boris prepared to leave the scene as quietly as he had come to it. That it had not been the first-such covert occasion in the barn seemed certain because, as he moved away, Boris heard a hearty voice say, "Phew! Let's hope she gives a litter as fine as the last, Prissy! There is a strong demand for the cross at the moment and we ought to do very well from them. And didn't he serve her well again? He really did get right into her, didn't he? Right in hard. Marvellous! Marvellous!"

"Yes, he did indeed," said a second voice, a little quieter, less emphatic in tone. "She's a very lucky girl to have it up her as beautifully as that. Very lucky." The last two words were uttered in a wistful way. They got to Boris and set him thinking. His reaction was not unlike that of the dog to the scent of the bitch.

He walked away feeling that the two dogs had more than earned their keep. They had provided obvious pleasure to two ladies and in due course would doubtless provide them with a profit to add to their pleasure. But Boris liked dogs, and all in all he thought that those two back in the barn had nothing to complain about. They had surely enjoyed the evening themselves. Everything laid on for them! Why should they worry!

Of one thing he felt certain; they hadn't in the least bit minded being watched. He was quite sure they were single-mindedly oblivious of this circumstance. And there was something else. Watching them had probably made both those ladies hungry. The second one, certainly. It was in her voice. But there was sadness in it too. Somehow he felt sure she didn't have anybody to go home to. Somebody could get lucky there, he thought ruefully! Then, on reflection, he doubted it very much, because of her intimidating appearance. It gave a decidedly negative image. Rather different, thought Boris, from the bold message beamed out by the bitch in the barn!

She was perhaps lonely, yet wouldn't get to meet anybody, and so would stay hungry. Pity that, he thought, because he was not exactly without an appetite himself! But he could hardly go barging in there and offer to oblige her, to their mutual satisfaction!

Life was like that, Boris thought philosophically as he mooched home rather reluctantly. There were lonely people all over the place. They could pair up if only they knew one another. But they don't. They pass one another in the street without ever knowing it, perhaps brushing pass somebody with whom, given the chance, they could be very happy. Animals weren't like that, he thought. Dogs, particularly. Take those two in the barn. The bitch let everybody know she could do with a mate. If she had got out to run free she wouldn't have had to wait long before she found one. Or a hundred and one, come to that!

As it was, the golden retriever, always no doubt only too ready to serve a good cause, got himself taken to the bitch and presented to her. Boris found himself wondering how human beings had got themselves into such a comparatively disadvantageous twist. It was something he often thought about because it was not by choice that he had never married. He had just never met the right mate. Predictably, as the years went by, he had become ever more shy in the presence of women, and consequently ever less likely to pair up with one of the 'wifely' kind.

Had he but have known it, the owner of the cocker spaniel was a mirror image of himself. Formidable lady though she appeared, for all her seemingly intimidatory manner she was at heart a warm and kindly person. Her outward blustery nature and overbearing demeanour was deceptive. It was in reality contrived, but extremely convincing, because of long, unremitting practice. When it came to the crunch she was as shy of men as Boris was of women. Not that men knew it, for she was hidden behind a forbidding façade which deflected them, acting like protective armour which she did not need and which did her a disservice. With workmen she could be imperious and at times supercilious, while with men of her own circle she was off-putting and seemingly unapproachable. Predictably, as the years went by, she, underneath it all, had become even more shy in the presence of men, and ever less likely to pair up with one of 'any' kind.

So she and Boris, who would have been judged from all outward appearances, and because of the different worlds they lived in, to be far apart in the perceptions of the times, were in reality two people who had the inner potential to fill a void in each other's lives. They were equal and complementary in so many qualities that really mattered, but irrevocably separated by artificial barriers of pseudo-class and station, barriers that were certainly not built into their genes. Sadly they went their separate ways not knowing this, though chance and two mating dogs had brought them within twenty feet of one another.

The possibility that they might have been able to do something for one another had indeed flitted into the mind of Boris as a whimsical fancy, but it did not seriously lodge there. It bounced off the impenetrable wall which his years of exposure to convention and class prejudice had developed in his mind. Some things were possible, others were not. So, as he walked home across the grass, his mind turned to other things.

As for Priscilla, owner of the now smugly-satisfied cocker spaniel, she was of-course not aware that Destiny had just placed a potential partner so near her. Not that it made any difference because even had she had known of it, the mere thought of such a liaison would have been an affront to her dignity. Her first reaction would have been to dismiss the idea out of hand, even as Boris had done for converse reasons.

Until, that is, she lay in bed later that night, yearning for a partner and contemplating the entirely different conventions which allowed her faithful, four-legged friend the uninhibited freedom that had led to the deep sleep of contentment that the lucky, privileged female now enjoyed at the foot of her bed. She also, like Boris, fell to wondering if human beings had got things all wrong.

Had she indeed have been aware of his earlier proximity, she might by this time, under the pressure of extreme frustration, have got round to wishing that Boris had thrown convention to the winds, shown some determined masculine initiative, and entered the barn to join the party!

Thus set free, her imagination would have had free rein, to the greater gratification of her secret desires, albeit only in the mind. Dreams, even day-dreams, are not hidebound by conventions. These are just swept aside allowing a wonderful freedom from all unnatural restraints. If only she'd known he'd been there, she would at least not have missed these nefarious flights of fancy, although as it happened, she was not in the event denied at least these dreams, though they began a little later and not that same night. In a roundabout way, though with the astonishing rapidity that news and rumours frequently spread in a small rural community, she very soon got to hear that their private, dog-mating session in the barn had been observed by an unknown solitary man.

Somewhat incongruously, the news came to her the very next day as she walked out of Littlebrook church after the Sunday morning service, which she attended with unfailing regularity.

As an ironic twist, seeing Priscilla in earnest conversation with her dog-loving friend outside the church, Reverend Yelman was quite sure they were discussing his serious sermon on man's relationship with, and responsibility for, his fellow creatures on earth, a subject prompted by recent local news of a case of deplorable ill-treatment of domestic animals. The Vicar felt gratified by their evident intense interest in what he'd had to say about matters which he knew to be close to their hearts.

In so far as they were talking of their dog-mating session in the barn, there was a connection—though not one he would have thought of. Not that they had been unkind to their animals; on the contrary, in their book they had been extremely kind to them, an opinion the dogs would have confirmed with enthusiasm, coupled with an eager request for more of the same had it been possible to consult them. So for that matter would Boris have done.

When she got home and thought things over, it did not prove difficult for Priscilla to deduce the identity of the man it must have been. There could be little or no doubt about that.

So, unbeknown to him, speculative eyes scrutinised Boris and saw him for what he was—quite a fellow, strong and not unattractive; a virile, potential partner; a local loner; and completely unattached to anybody, so she soon established.

He proved quite an exciting man around whom to weave her erotic fantasies by day, and to dream about by night.

But alas, Boris never escaped from the lady's dreams to take a live part in the high jinks she pictured so vividly, nor was he ever even remotely aware that he was the object of her lustful imaginings.

What a very great pity! And what a sad waste! It was either a wicked waste of latent joy, or a waste of latent wicked joy, depending upon a person's point of view!

But whatever might have been the verdict of detached observers, the union was not to be. Boris and Priscilla missed out on what could so easily have been a mutually satisfying, delightfully fulfilling, on-going bit of jiggery-pokery that would have lost none of its potential joy, whatever the opinions of jaundiced, or maybe plain jealous, outsiders.

Like the happy dogs on the table, they would have been blissfully unconcerned about the reaction of any such seen or unseen observers, and just got on with the business!

Or would they? Things are not always as simple as they seem to be on the surface. There are penalties for humans to be thinking animals. Factors affect their relationships that do not in the least concern a pair of dogs enjoying their brief moments of pleasure. And sometimes, sadly, they surface too late, bringing disenchantment hard on the heels of high expectations. Apparent blissful fulfilment could turn out to be brief—maybe very very brief—as might well have been the case for Priscilla in this missed, but so temptingly possible, potential physical liaison.

For Boris, nice fellow though he certainly was, could by no means have been described as the perfect man, a personification of her deepest yearnings and secret dreams. There were flaws in his make-up, shortfalls and pitfalls in his personal behaviour patterns and job CV when measured against the requirements of her unadvertised vacancy; these, when discovered, could have so disturbed her delicate sensitivities as to destroy her longed-for experience, leaving her desperately disappointed and disillusioned.

Were that to have happened it would indeed have been a great pity. So, though she did not know it, she was better left frustrated but ever-hopeful, her expectations still high, dry and intact.

Chapter 18

WILL-O'-THE-WISPS
lights in the night for Boris

His unexpected entertainment as an audience of one at the one-act play in the nearby bar had thrown Boris's plans for the evening rather out of gear. Not that he would have missed this gratuitous show for all the world. He'd thoroughly enjoyed it, and not only that, it had given him a spicy story to tell which he knew would be listened to with close interest by his friends. So the free entertainment would be passed on to others, and he savoured the prospect of describing it.

On arrival back at the 'Box' he looked at the clock and saw that if he were to be in time to have his usual Saturday evening two or three pints of beer at the nearest pub, he would have to get a move on. He got himself ready, locked up and fetched his bike from the open-fronted, rather dilapidated old barn just across the yard where he had parked it among a variety of farm implements and clutter stored in there.

When he went to light the bike's acetylene lamp, though, he remembered at once that it had nearly spluttered out when last he'd used it and it clearly needed a refill of carbide. Grumbling to himself that he had not thought to do it earlier, he returned to the 'Box', unlocked the door again and went in to fetch the new tin of carbide he had bought at Bill Gunston's Saddlery & Cycle Shop during the week.

Using a coin he prised open the tight-fitting, push-in lid from the tall, narrow, cylindrical metal container. The sturdy carbide tin was well made and completely air-tight, because dampness getting into the can would cause degeneration of its contents.

Unscrewing the bottom section of his lamp, he shook out the damp, greyish-white, smelly powdery remains of the used-up carbide. Like a lot of people he ran his lamp until the light showed signs of going out, and then re-charged it completely. Adding small amounts of new carbide to the partly-used stuff to top it up, as some people did, only led to trouble because eventually—starved of enough carbide—the lamp would run out of gas, often just when the rider was least expecting it, out in the pitch dark somewhere, and badly needing the light.

The new calcium-carbide Boris shook out of the tin into the lamp had the healthy appearance of hard, dark-grey granite chippings, quite unlike the smelly, soft, greyish-white powder he had shaken out.

Having filled the lower section of the lamp with its fuel, he screwed it back on and turned his attention to the small water-tank which made up the top section. He took off the screw-in filler cap and topped up the lamp with water poured in from his kettle. Finally, he put the filler cap back in, pushed the stainless steel lamp back on to its bracket on the bike's handlebars, and opened the lamp's four-inch diameter front-window, preparatory to lighting the gas.

From long experience he knew just how far to twist the small turn-screw which operated a simple tap inside the lamp to release a drip-feed of water onto the carbide below. As soon as water reached the carbide a chemical reaction started and gas was forced out of the two arms of the white-topped, Y-shaped ceramic burner that was screwed into a socket inside the lamp. He then struck a match, lit the gas, closed the glass-fronted door and adjusted the gas supply to give the best possible light.

With its new charge of carbide the lamp should have been at its best, but Boris found that the two flames that jetted-out from the tiny holes on the angled, flat tops of the two arms of the Y-shaped burner, did not produce the fan-shaped, even-sided flame expected. On one side the flame was very low, but when he increased the gas supply by edging the water key on a little further, the other side got too large and became smoky. Smoke issued from the side vent holes of the rather ornate, flat-topped chimney on the top of the lamp, so he turned down the gas a little and settled for the best light he could get without the lamp smoking.

Boris made a mental note to screw in a new replacement burner the next day. He always had a new one in hand, because the heat and the by-products of combustion eventually made a burner fail to do its job properly and it had to be chucked out. Occasionally its life could be prolonged for a little while by cleaning the tiny gas vent-holes with a fine needle, but the only real cure for poor performance was a replacement.

Propping up the bike, with the lamp adjusted to give as good a light as he could make it do, Boris took the carbide tin back into the 'Box' and replaced it on his shelf in a warm dry spot near the fire, and well away from the Primus stove area where there was often a lot of steam. One tin usually gave him three refills for the lamp, provided he kept the lid securely in place and kept the carbide dry.

The tall tin was so shaped that the surface area of the carbide that was exposed inside the air under the lid above it, was at a minimum. Moisture from the air degraded the carbide and a wide, shallow tin would have exposed more of it to the air. This had led to the choice of what was a somewhat unusual shape for a storage tin, thus making a carbide tin an easily recognised and well-known object.

This much Boris had learnt one day from Bill Gunston himself. Bill had gone to get a tin of carbide from the shelf in the shop and knocked one over as he reached up. This promptly caused a chain reaction leaving twenty or more tins, some now dented, scattered all over the place. They had been ranged in ranks like soldiers on the shelf, but their shape gave them little stability. Full tins were quite heavy and got dented when they fell on something hard. Dented carbide tins were commonplace.

Bill had reacted to this little incident with a comment he often used when something suddenly annoyed him, such as jabbing a sharp, harness-maker's awl into his hand when doing his fast, double-needle stitching.

"Damn and Blast!" he'd said explosively.

"Why the hell do they have to make carbide tins that bloody silly shape?" Boris had asked Bill sympathetically.

Bill, who long ago had sought the answer himself, had passed on the reason. The one thing in their favour, Bill had added, was that the small mouth made it easy to tip the carbide into a lamp, without shooting it all over the place. It was advisable not to handle carbide because it reacted with any water on the hands, which was neither good for the hands nor for the carbide. Despite this, some people did habitually feed bits of it into their lamps using their fingers, but soon dropped it if they happened to have wet fingers because the chemical reaction immediately started up. The carbide fizzled, got hot and smelled none-too-nice on the fingers afterwards.

After this further delay, ready at last, the 'Box' once more locked up, Boris rode out of the farmyard and along the unmade road which led from the farm to the narrow country lane ahead.

His lamp, not working at its best, cast a dim light around the area immediately in front of him which was just about good enough to allow him to see where he was going, but only just. The round metal rim behind which the lamp's domed convex glass was recessed, gave the light on the ground a distinctly curved border between the lit-up area and the darkness behind it. To Boris it was like pushing the darkness out of the way by an unseen curved sweeping fender, extending outwards on either side of him in a concave arc. The jolting of the wheels on the rough, stony, uneven surface of the road caused the edge of the arc to dance up and down the bank to his left, and the rays of light gave him fleeting glimpses of the hedgerow at the top of the bank.

From the time he'd first had an acetylene lamp Boris had been curiously thrilled by them. He always experienced an indefinable sense of pleasure as he pedalled slowly along. It was something to do with the living flame, the warmth of the lamp and the nature of the light it gave out. In the still of the night he always experienced a strange feeling of absolute solitude, moving along in an isolated bubble of light through a boundless sea of darkness. Now and again he would warm his hands one at a time by cupping them over the top of the metal lamp which was comfortably hot. He was fond of his lamp and—in a way which he would not have attempted to explain—it kept him company on his solitary journeys in the nights. It was a valued friend, inanimate maybe, yet warm and alive nonetheless, provided he fed and watered it. A psychologist might have found much that was childish in Boris, when studying those things which gave him pleasure. But he was fundamentally happy, and very much a man in a man's world, for all that.

Boris was glad to reach the better surface of the lane which the track reached rather awkwardly on a bend at the foot of a hill. Turning to his right into the lane, he started to pump his way up the short but quite steep incline. As he turned, he could hear the noise of a car's engine approaching around the bend to his left. He was not far up the hill and labouring hard to climb it without getting off his bike, when the car rounded the bend and picked him up in its lights. As it started up the hill, the driver did two things almost simultaneously; he gave a loud 'honk-honk' on the hand-operated horn by squeezing its large, black, rubber air-bulb sharply—this to get Boris out of the way—and changed down into bottom gear.

The gear change did the long-suffering gear-box no good at all. Boris heard the unmistakeable sound of the driver doubling-the-clutch, but the revs were misjudged and the gear-box screamed with pain, disturbing the night by a loud, grinding, screeching noise which only stopped when the bottom gear was finally engaged.

Boris winced, for the sound of ill-treated machinery offended his ears, though he knew—in all fairness to the driver—that a change down into bottom gear on some cars was difficult to achieve quietly however hard a driver tried. Some people, he knew only too well, adopted the expedient of snatching the gear lever out of one gear and ramming it hard into the next in one swift movement, depressing the clutch pedal but not 'double-de-clutching' it. This process at best worked like a charm, and at worst reduced the gear-box's prolonged cry of agony to a short, sharp, metallic bark of pain, which was less embarrassing to the anxious driver and probably less damaging to the gears, than a long grinding squeal.

Meanwhile the 'honk-honk' was interpreted by Boris as an instruction to get off the road, and not as a warning of the car's approach, since the engine noise and the lights were warning enough. That he was correct in his interpretation was confirmed immediately, because, despite the fact that he had moved over to the extreme edge of the lane, the first 'honk-honk' was repeated by a second, sharper, more vigorously squeezed 'honk-honk'. He looked back over his shoulder and a gauntleted hand promptly stuck out of the driver's side of the car, imperiously waving him off the road.

In reality there was ample room for the car to pass him now that he was close in to the edge of the lane. Nonetheless he was being signalled to get off it altogether. Boris objected to this, knowing, as he did, that the arrogance of some car owners knew no bounds. Their pride of possession, and their rare, privileged status as a motorist, gave some of them the certain conviction that they had a high level of priority on the roads, and others should give way to them without question.

This attitude rankled with Boris, especially when he was driving a traction engine, and on principle he would never ever give way to such people under similar circumstances if they arrogantly tried to insist upon being given priority. After all, he figured, steam engines were well and truly first on the roads—after horses, that is, a fact which engine drivers never failed to remember. They could always be relied upon to be mindful of horses and would never force them to give way as they could have done so easily because of their intimidating appearance and the frightening noises they produced.

But it was a different matter on a bike. Stuck up on his massive iron traction engine he was virtually immune to personal danger from a puny motor car. On his bike though, a driver such as this one, who clearly was not too clever with mechanical things, as witness the tortured grinding racket from the gear-box, might well do him an injury. And it could easily be done 'accidentally-on-purpose' too, for all he knew. So Boris dismounted and pushed his bike a little way up the sloping grass bank out of harm's way.

The car, labouring to pick up speed up the hill, passed by him slowly. As it did so he recognised its occupants. The driver, staring fixedly ahead, was the lady in charge of the golden retriever which had performed so splendidly in the barn earlier that evening.

Her passenger, sitting bolt upright on the seat by her side, also staring fixedly out of the front window, intently watching the road ahead, was the dog itself! As they passed him the two occupants behaved quite differently, however.

The lady herself, head held high, with her nose lifted well up, presenting the snooty posture known by everybody as the 'car look', continued to stare fixedly ahead and absolutely ignored Boris. Far from giving him a wave of the hand to acknowledge his kind co-operation in getting off the road to allow her through with the road to herself, he was, he felt quite sure, dismissed in her mind as a mere cyclist, clearly a disgruntled working-class man who had to be hooted at twice to get him out of the way!

Her dog on the other hand was different. Its mouth open and tongue hanging out, it looked just about as self-satisfied and happy as a dog could look. It looked positively smug, Boris thought: as well it might! Not only that, as the car drew level, it turned its head in an inquisitive way to look at him. As it did so Boris was astonished. He gained a distinct, strong, and quite remarkable impression, which remained in his mind's eye for a long time afterwards.

In fact the more he thought about it later on, the truer it seemed to have been, or so he delightedly liked to imagine—the dog appeared to be smiling in a very knowing way as it met Boris's eye, and what's more—what so astounded him as he subsequently loved to tell amused listeners—it seemed to wink at him as it went by. A prolonged wink it was, accompanied by a knowing nod of the head, or so it seemed to the inventively incredulous Boris. By some sixth sense, Boris happily concluded, the blessed dog actually knew he had been outside the barn watching when it had done its vigorous stuff so competently on the eager cocker spaniel presented to him for his expert attention.

Passing by, it had now instinctively recognised him and was enjoying a shared secret with him in a comradely way, which excluded his mistress.

"Uncanny, bloody uncanny," thought Boris, feeling uneasy and awed by this apparently human-like, gleeful nod-and-a-wink communication from a mere dog! "It's got brains as well as balls that bloody thing has, that's for sure," he thought. "An awesome dog that one, and no mistake!"

Boris re-mounted his bike and continued his slog up the short hill. Gradually gathering speed the car, a four-seater tourer with a canvas hood overhead and completely open along the sides, chugged its way on in front of him. As it breasted the hill, where the road swung to the left, he heard it change up a gear—this time relatively much less painfully—and for a few moments, as it turned, he saw it silhouetted against the starlit sky. He caught a glimpse of its two occupants sitting side-by-side in the front seats, looking at that distance just like two people sitting under the awning of a ghostly barge drifting slowly along the sky-line.

"There is no doubt," Boris thought, "that's one hell of a contented dog sitting up there on its comfortable leather seat. And what dog wouldn't be! Fancy being driven in comfort to a welcoming, ready-and-waiting partner like that, all expenses paid and nothing to do except what comes naturally! What a life! What a life indeed!"

Smiling to himself, he could imagine the dog, respectful and behaving like a privileged servant, sighing slightly with fatigue and saying to his mistress, 'I shall be glad to get to my bed, Madam. I feel quite weary now. I put a lot into my work tonight.'

To which, thought Boris, she might well reply, in her loud and patronising voice, nodding her head up and down in full agreement with what her smug dog had said, 'Yes—yes—you certainly did *that* all right! You can say that again! You put a very great deal into your work! You ought to sleep like a log tonight. A very lucky, dog-tired log too. Very lucky. Too good for a dog—what you had tonight—I sometimes think. Much too good!'

To which her obedient servant would perhaps reply, grinning widely and hiding a happy yawn, 'Yes, Madam! Much too good! Much too good, I'm sure!' After which no doubt he would nod off to sleep as the car carried him home, like a conquering hero, to his much pampered quarters.

Amused by his thoughts, Boris lost sight of the car as it dipped down a slight incline the other side of the hilltop, and laboured his way on towards the pub and his waiting pint.

But he felt very much a second-class citizen as he pumped his way along on his old bike, and compared his lonely lot with that of the well-provided-for dog riding along in comfort in the car ahead of him.

About twenty minutes later, with just one hour's drinking time left before closing time, he was happily sitting by a log fire yarning with a small group of locals, to most of whom he was well known.

It was of course not long before he indulged himself in the pleasure of describing in detail the events which had so entertained him earlier that evening. There was much hilarity and several bawdy comments as he told his story. Of course, the ladies were one by one quickly identified.

The wistful owner of the cocker spaniel was, they said, Priscilla Mansted, the unmarried only daughter of the aging, widowed Arthur Mansted, owner of the farm, who generally looked after his affairs. As for the farm, he left the day-to-day running of it very much in the capable hands of Ben Skinner, his bailiff.

The second lady was soon identified from Boris's description of her car. It was a 1922 Morris Oxford open tourer, a dark-brownish colour as far as Boris could judge in the poor light in which he'd seen it. The car was apparently seen a lot around the area, for most of the year with its awning-like canvas hood, which had a small window in its back-of-the-car section, permanently up, but on very hot summer days folded back making the car look like an open boat. The sides of the car were always completely open, summer and winter alike.

The lady's name was Pamela Prendergast, and she lived some three miles away in a large house set back in parkland, with a driveway nearly half a mile long connecting it to the nearest road. Her husband, before he was badly injured and permanently crippled both mentally and physically in a riding accident, had for years previous to the accident been Master of the Bramlington Hunt. And quite a fellow too!

Having identified the principal players in the scene that Boris had so graphically described, and having discussed them at some length, the subject was closed by a serious-sounding comment from one of the men who worked at Mansted's Farm. He was a member of the threshing team working for a few days with Joe and Boris.

"Well," he said, with straight-faced gravity, "all I can say is, it's a bloody good job they didn't see you spying on them through that slot in the wall. You count yourself bloody lucky they didn't know you were out there. Bloody lucky!"

251

"Why?" asked Boris, taking the bait with an anxious look on his face.

"Because they would have whipped you inside there without your feet touching the ground," replied his now grinning tormentor. "And before you knew what was happening you'd have been up on that table yourself, bashing away at those two women, with the two dogs sitting on the stools with their tongues hanging out, watching you perform!"

Boris, caught with his trousers down so to speak, grinned sheepishly as those around him roared with laughter.

After things had settled down again, he spent the remaining time playing shove-ha'penny with three of his mates, and managed to down three pints of beer before the landlord called time.

There was one other incident which entertained him before he got back to bed in the 'Box' that night. The first part of his ride home took him across an area of marshland by a winding river. There was a thin mist hanging over the ground, otherwise the night was clear and the air very still.

As he cycled slowly along, turning over the events of the evening in his mind, he suddenly caught sight of a flickering flame about three hundred yards away, out on the marshes. He stopped, got off his bike, and looked towards it, but it quickly went out. He was puzzled. It looked a bit eerie, like the mysterious 'will-o'-the-wisps' he'd heard about which appear in bogs and fenlands at night.

Then another flame flickered on and off away across the marsh, diffused and ill-defined in the ground mist. Intrigued, he stared into the mist across the marsh and presently saw a flame flicker on again, this time for a bit longer. In its light he thought he saw three vague figures, and then he caught the sound of what seemed like boys' voices, coming from out there in the darkness. Concluding that it was some boys fooling around trying to light a bonfire or up to some escapade or other, he got on his bike again and pedalled home.

It was quite some time later when he learnt what in fact he'd seen. He happened to mention it to Ben Skinner. Ben smiled and explained to Boris what it was all about. Out on the marsh there were long-neglected drainage ditches now full of stagnant water. Here and there, in places, every now and again if you watched carefully, Ben said, bubbles of gas could be seen coming up from the deep mud and sludge below, and bursting at the surface of the water. It was 'marsh gas', produced by rotting vegetation deep down under the mud, and gradually finding its way to the surface.

Boys knew that it was inflammable so occasionally they amused themselves by lighting it with tapers whenever they could get near the bubbles. It was of course much more fun at night. A flickering flame in bright sunlight could hardly be seen, and was not interesting or impressive. But out on the mysterious marshland at night it produced a more spectacular, rather eerie, and ghostly, effect.

Ben said that when he was a boy he and his mates did much the same thing. It was something that had been known about for years and he expected that generations of boys had played about with it out there on the misty marsh.

He recalled can occasion when he and a friend had a fright out there one night messing about with the gas. They decided to try to collect some in a tin, and then burn it from that. They had an idea they might be able to carry it about like a lamp!

What they did was hold the open end of the can over the bubbles for a while, then stood it on the ground and put a match to it. It went off with a loud bang, and a flash of flame burnt his hand. This explosion put the breeze up them but pretty soon of course they tried to repeat it, this time using a taper to keep their hands well back. On several tries this produced nothing more than a gentle pop until—unexpectedly by now—it went off with a bang once again.

"It seemed to us," Ben had concluded, "that you needed to have just the right mixture of gas and air. Too much gas gave a little flame and a pop, too little nothing at all. In the end we gave up trying because the success rate was too small and we got fed up with mucking about with it."

This rang a bell with Boris because every now and again, when the traction engine fire was too fully banked-up at night, and the ash-pan damper closed down to give minimum draught, coal gas collected over the fire and sometimes, on opening it and giving it a poke, they got a minor explosion—and on occasions one not so minor—which they called a 'blow-back'. This caused a whoosh of soot and ash to shoot backwards out of the fire-box, smothering everything.

He and Joe were mindful of this and avoided stoking the fire to the point where a yellowy-greenish smoke, combined with the unmistakeable smell of coal gas and sulphurous fumes, warned them that there was danger of a blow-back explosion. When they saw or smelt signs of it, they quickly poked holes right down through the fire to get more air up through it, to ignite the gas it was giving off. If allowed to collect over the heaped up coal, without a flame to burn it off, there was a danger the mixture of gas and air would get to the critical point where it could explode. Most engine men learnt this lesson the hard way, and every now and again somebody would have a messy and nasty blow-back.

However, for the time being Boris's attention was diverted from will-o-the-wisps, because Ben went on to talk about something else. Telling Boris about the origin of the flickering flames out on the marsh at night had reminded Ben of another mysterious fire that had been seen out in the marshes early in November the previous year.

His Boss, old Arthur Mansted, had been roused from his bed at two o'clock in the morning by a cottager living nearby, who reported that there was a tree on fire, down on the marshes, which were all part of his land.

Sure enough, he and his daughter Priscilla, looking out of one of their attic windows, could see the tree blazing away like a Roman candle. Ben Skinner was quickly summoned and went off to investigate.

Before he got to the scene he had already guessed what tree it was. Along the edge of the marshes where a farm track ran, bordering a hop garden, there was a neglected hedgerow formed by a tangled mass of bushes and brambles, and here and there at intervals a variety of trees that had been there for many many years fringeing the marsh.

Amongst these trees, forming a well-known landmark, was the fifteen to twenty foot high remains of what had once been the largest tree along there. Struck by lightning many years ago, the upper part of the trunk had been spit asunder, and finally the whole top section of the tree was snapped right off in a gale. The remaining trunk, already partially rotted away inside, which is no doubt why it gave way to the wind so readily, died off completely.

For years the hefty stump, its broad diameter testifying to how large the tree used to be, had been a centre of attraction to boys. It was referred to by them as 'the hollow tree down on the marshes' and was frequently visited. Apart from anything else there were jackdaws' nesting holes near the top, year after year. Easily accessible to adventurous boys, they were the source of supply of a succession of fledgling jackdaws, tamed and kept as pets by boys in the neighbourhood. Some were 'good talkers', better than parrots, many people said.

By the time Ben reached the scene, the tree was well on the way to complete destruction. Apparently it had been fired from near the top, not from the bottom. Being just bone dry outside and partly crumbling, rotting timber inside, it had burned like a candle, being consumed downwards from top to bottom. When Ben arrived it was down to below ten feet, and by daylight just a charred stump remained at ground level.

It did not take Ben long to find out what had happened. The night was Guy Fawkes Night, a fair clue to him to start off with.

Some boys had amused themselves chucking lighted bangers into the top of the tree, to drop down inside it. Long ago steps had been cut into the trunk to facilitate climbing up to get inside the top of the tree. For most of its length the tree was only partially hollow but there was a completely hollow section at the top which boys had carved away at over the years to create an attractive hide-away, high-level camp up there. Below where they habitually sat there was a soft-ish wood in the core of the tree, but quite sound wood round the edge.

Firework 'bangers', lit and tossed over the top, made a nicely enhanced booming sound when they exploded. It was an interesting diversion for them during the firework evening they were enjoying.

When they were about to leave the scene, one of them saw wisps of smoke issuing from a jackdaw's nesting hole up near the top. It was clear that a firework must have gone down some distance and something was smouldering away inside there. The lads thought they had better put it out before they left.

The nearest source of water was several hundred yards away so they decided to use their own resources. They found a sizeable old tin can along the hedgerow and proceeded to piss into it, one at a time, to gather enough to quench the fire.

There were six of them and their combined efforts yielded a good canful. One of them, cheered and encouraged by his mates down below, climbed up and shot the contents of the can into the jackdaw's nesting hole. There was a satisfying, hissing noise from the tree and steam issued from the hole. Foul-smelling steam it was too, according to Ben's informant. However, there seemed to be no more smoke from the hole after the steam had stopped coming out, so off they went to continue their firework night celebrations.

The next morning, a Saturday, one of the boys was in the paper shop buying his weekly comic, when a man came in and asked Ted the newsagent if he'd heard that there had been a tree on fire down on the marshes during the night.

The lad shot out of the shop like a scared rabbit and sped around to his mates to tell them what he'd heard. Innocently they wandered down to see for themselves, and to their horror saw just a smouldering stump where the large hollow tree had been. The tree had vanished!

Nobody seemed too upset about it, though, the general opinion being that sooner or later the old tree would have had to be taken down for safety's sake anyway. Pretty soon they felt safe in telling what had happened, stressing the way they had strained to produce enough pee to put it out, and only left the tree when they were sure they had done so. This, they no doubt considered, was enough evidence of their good intentions to exonerate them from any lasting blame or punishment.

And so it turned out. Nobody bawled them out about it. Everybody seemed much more amused by their sterling attempt to put out the fire with their communally generated tin of piss. They finished up feeling quite proud of the whole affair.

Boris was much entertained by this story and subsequently re-told it himself many times.

After his talk with Ben, Boris resolved to find out what he could about marsh gas. Ben's comments about it had sparked off his interest and he determined to see what information he could dig up about the subject. It was some weeks later, however, before he had the opportunity to learn any more about it. He found a reference to marsh gas in an old general knowledge book he happened upon, the sort of book that his enquiring mind revelled in.

He discovered that marsh gas is largely methane, the same gas that plagues miners in the pits. It burns with a bluish flame. Miners call it 'fire-damp', which is highly dangerous in coal mines because it readily forms an explosive mixture with air.

Boris was reminded of Ben and his efforts as a boy with the tin can. It was evident from what he read that there was a certain critical proportion of methane and air which is highly explosive. In a situation like a mine, when gas is present, the proportion of gas to air will be changing all the time. It is almost inevitable that sooner or later the critical mixture will arise, with disastrous results if a naked flame or an electrical spark is present to ignite it. Small wonder, Boris thought, that every precaution is taken in mining operations to detect the presence of methane and guard against its potential dangers.

But what interested Boris most of all was a reference to Will-o'-the-Wisps. Marsh gas under certain circumstances, so he read, can take fire spontaneously. The mysterious lights so produced, flickering on and off away out across silent marshlands and fen-country, were widely known about down the years, largely because of the fascinatingly eerie appearance they had. Dancing about silently in the night, tantalisingly being first there and then not there, gripped the imagination of people living out in the countryside, where legends about them and similar phenomena abounded.

The very name of 'Will-o'-the-Wisp' had an attraction of its own, as did other names like 'Jack-o'-Lantern' and 'Friar's Lantern', sometimes used in other parts of the country to identify the same strange lights. Their aura of mystery was enhanced because they only appeared on very still nights, and the presence of mist across the marshes creates a silent, mysterious impression in the minds of people standing quietly looking across the flat landscape. Any wind dispersed the gas immediately it bubbled up, so lights did not appear in breezy circumstances.

Occasionally, Boris read, the lights appear to run across the ground and flit about in the distance, perhaps as a line of bubbles rising from the surface of water-logged ground got successively ignited one from the other, and briefly flared up.

Boris finished up being grateful to the unknown lads out on the marshes late that Saturday night for giving him an artificially induced display of Will-o'-the-Wisps, something he might otherwise never have seen. He could well understand the fun of making these mysterious ghostly lights, and how fascinating a pastime it must have been for the boys to hunt down these bubbles in the stagnant water and light them! In fact he privately made up his mind to go and seek some himself, to see how they burned.

He realised, having discovered the alternative name Jack-o'-Lantern for what he had always known only as Will-o'-the Wisps, that there must have been a connection between this and the game of 'Jack-Jack-Show-A-Light' which for years boys had played out in the meadows and marshes, in the twilight of autumn and winter evenings. It all linked in so well. One boy, the appointed 'Jack', would run off across the grass and disappear in the darkness. On the shout of **'JACK-JACK-SHOW-A-LIGHT'** he was compelled to strike a match, and as it briefly flared up, the others, who had scattered all over the place, watched for the light, noted its position, then set off as fast as they could run to catch him.

Jack, for his part, having shown his light, moved off as fast as he could away from any sounds of pursuit and then 'froze' somewhere. Meanwhile, he and all the others would have been counting up to twenty, because the rule was that calls of 'Jack-Jack-Show-A-Light' could only be made every twenty seconds. Quite a lot of ground could be covered in this time but inevitably, as Jack tired and the net closed, he was caught.

Then the next in line took his turn as Jack, and the one who stayed free for the most shouts won the game on that evening. Naturally some newcomers to the game would county twenty as fast as they could, and shout too soon. They were ignored by Jack, who carried on counting at the right rate until he himself reached twenty. It was supposed to be a second-by-second count, best achieved they all learnt, by counting 'ONE *and* TWO *and* THREE *and* FOUR' . . . up to twenty, with the word 'and' giving a proper interval between numbers.

At any rate the 'Jack' out running could be relied upon to observe the rules and get it about right. But he couldn't string it out if he tried; his mates were too fly for that. And if he persisted in trying to lengthen the intervals between his showing of the light he was disqualified, by common consent, and lost his go.

Though Boris as a boy had played the game using the flare of struck matches to give the 'Light' called for, as had been done for so many generations before him, he knew that boys sometimes now played the game with electric torches to give the flash of light. But this, Boris thought, took it one step away from its obvious connection with the mysterious flare of actual flames which formed the elusive Will-o'-the-Wisps that 'Jack' was emulating.

Maybe, Boris thought, if as a boy he had played 'Will-Will-Show-A-Light' he would have made the connection earlier. But nobody ever called the game by that name, and Jack-o'-Lantern was not a name he had ever heard before used to describe the eerie lights. So until then the game and the mystery of the lights of the marshes were not connected in his mind.

On reflection, though, he thought that Jack was a much sharper name to bark out than Will. The call of 'Jack-Jack-Show-A-Light' seemed to snap out across the fields, and carried a long distance in the kind of still, misty air when the game was played.

Quite often, it was the 'feel' of the night that prompted a suggestion from somebody to play this game, because on such nights it was very noticeable how sounds carried a long way. It was a special game for special nights. Often in the winter, the starlit sky was clear of clouds and the early evening already frosty. Flitting about across the grass in the twilight on such a night was exhilarating, and Boris could still recapture the excitement of it in his memory.

* * * * *

On the Saturday evening when Boris had seen the lights on the marsh as he returned from his visit to the pub, it was getting on for midnight when he finally tucked himself up in his bed in the 'Box' that night.

As Saturday evenings go, it had been a good one. He'd enjoyed it. For a while, by the light of his candle, he picked up a copy of *'Sanders of the River'*, which he had borrowed from Joe. He had delved into it before, and liked the humorous logic of the poetic justice dealt out by the young Englishman in his escapades along the African river.

It was not long though before he became very sleepy, so he blew out his candle and in less than no time was fast asleep. He slept soundly in the snug silence and somewhat spartan comfort of the 'Box', as soundly as a log.

Some three miles away as the crow flies, the golden retriever also slept like a log as his mistress, in Boris's imagination, had said he would. He lay, curled up on a soft woollen blanket, in his luxurious wicker-work basket, in his special corner by the large, black, iron cooking range in the big kitchen of the spacious country house that was his home. The banked-up fire glowed red and the room was comfortably warm. He slept the

256

untroubled sleep of a fellow who goes to bed dog-tired, with the comforting feeling of a job well done.

Upstairs his mistress lay awake. She could not sleep for she was troubled in her mind. She was not a happy lady, any more than was Priscilla. But unlike Priscilla, who could only imagine what she was missing, Pamela knew very well indeed what it was. And the dogs had stimulated her appetite.

But who should say which of them missed out the more? For a philosopher, or perhaps an experience psychologist, or maybe even a disillusioned professional provider of carnal services, might say that sometimes the practical reality does not match up to the mentally-imagined fantasy.

So it could be that Priscilla's exciting daydreams were in fact more delightful than would have been the actual experience, perhaps indeed more so than those in the memory of her friend, whose regular but maybe monotonous one-man-only experiences had ceased so abruptly some four years ago.

It is likely that this was no more than the truth when, the very next day, on Sunday, Boris—invitingly alone at night in his snug, dimly-lit box just across the farmyard—became the temporary focus of her excited fantasies, having attracted her speculative attention since she had learnt that day of his presence the evening before, outside the barn.

For there were those among the favoured few who had enjoyed the privilege of being bedded by Boris, who could have told her of his unfortunate, involuntary habit of inadvertently emitting loud and noxious, bubbly fleshy farts, at random intervals during his laborious grunting performances.

Like an unintended, loud, off-stage noise arising at a critical moment in a theatrical performance, it was an ambience-shattering sound-effect, which, coupled with the often unsavoury smell of his feet following hot, sweaty days at work, was not conducive to the enjoyment of sublime pleasure.

To be fair to Boris, this description did not represent him at his best, for his amorous adventures always seemed to follow beery nights in pubs where—emboldened by Dutch courage—he invariably picked up his occasional partners. But it is certain that were he to have produced these unglamorous 'extras' during a session with the fastidious Priscilla, her ecstasy factor on a scale of 0 to 100 would have plummeted from an expectation level of 100+ to a negative quantity.

Perhaps therefore, on the whole, she was better not to have been exposed to the risk of suffering a let-down of this magnitude. Such a traumatic disappointment could be soul-destroyingly disastrous, with dire and devastating long-term, psychological repercussions!

Better by far, perhaps, for Priscilla just to dream and wait for earthly perfection—or heaven, whichever came first—than to risk facing the cruelty of having her fragile and exquisite image of a wonderful, sublime fulfilment shattered irrevocably into a thousand fragments in a few minutes of dreadful discovery and enlightenment.

It was just as well that Boris remained oblivious of Priscilla's interest in him and did not get embroiled with her, to pose the risk of unwittingly becoming the destroyer of her idyllic dreams.

Unflattering to him though the conclusion is, she probably enjoyed the thought of him much more than she would have done the reality. Quite possibly very very much more. But nobody will ever know!

In the event, Boris was soon to leave the location, and the temptation to Priscilla, parked in such close proximity to him, would go chuffing off the premises in a cloud of smoke and steam.

In fact Boris and Joe pulled out of Mansted's Farm the following Wednesday afternoon, and by seven o'clock on Thursday morning the threshing outfit was working at full stretch some six miles away.

By the end of February they had finished their complete threshing programme for the season, having moved from place to place over a wide area of the countryside following a carefully planned route. It was a well-established routine. Those on their list knew approximately when to expect them, and were always aware of the location which immediately preceded their own. Word of the thresher's progress went out ahead of it, and as soon as it was known to be just one step away, the next farm on the line was made ready for their arrival. Except when unavoidable due to bad weather, there was seldom any waste of time and the well-organised scheme ran smoothly.

Their final move was back to their depot where the traction engine, the threshing machine and the elevator, were put in the extensive vehicle park from which they were later taken to the workshops for servicing, to prepare them for the next season.

Meanwhile, with no delay, Boris and Joe prepared for their next travelling assignment, 'Steam Ploughing'.

Had they but known it, the trip was to include one of the most memorable experiences of their lives, for by the working of pure chance they were to be at the centre of one of the most fascinating events in the history of steam ploughing. They and their team mates were destined to become known to countless people far removed from their quiet, peaceful corner of England.

Chapter 19

STEAM PLOUGHING
the five happy travellers

Early in March Joe and Boris set off, together with three other workmates from SKWEC, in a small convoy of vehicles forming a fully-equipped, mobile Steam Ploughing Team.

Both Joe and Boris were each responsible for driving and looking after one of the two traction engines which were especially designed for the job they had to do. They were bigger engines, of higher power than the ones normally used for threshing. Winding in a steel cable, pulling a plough through the soil, turning five, six, or sometimes even eight furrows simultaneously required a great deal of sustained power, and the engines were built to be able to do this hour after hour. Typically they were of 16HP to 18HP, whereas threshing machines were often driven by engines of 8HP to 10HP, and sometimes even less.

In action the two engines stood sideways-on, opposite one another on either side of a field, towing a plough to and fro between them. After each journey by the plough across the field, the engines moved along a bit. On each engine the tough steel cable, often called 'the rope', was alternately wound and then unwound on a hefty, horizontally-mounted steel drum positioned below the boiler, and driven by a vertical shaft which was connected by gearing to the engine's mechanism above.

The engines thus took it in turns to provide the power to pull the plough through the soil by winding in their cable, while the other engine was idling with its own cable being pulled off its drum by the retreating plough.

It would not have been economical for most farmers to own their own equipment for it would not have 'earned its keep'. But firms such as SKWEC were able to schedule them to go out on hire, moving from place to place, as did their threshing outfits, clocking up an impressive total of days worked per year, and making it a profitable enterprise.

There were also other activities, particularly road-making and maintenance, for which their traction engines, steam road-rollers, and other associated gear was hired out, complete with the driver and staff to use them.

Back at the depot, well-organised and expertly-staffed workshops were able to maintain all this expensive equipment. These engineering facilities and on-site expertise enabled the firm to take in work from outside, to add to their profitability. As an engineering firm they were widely respected, and their initials SKWEC were seen and recognised on traction engines, steam rollers, cranes and other mobile equipment over a wide area of Kent and Sussex.

Boris and Joe were fortunate to be a part of this permanent organisation and workforce. Each year the two of them remained together throughout the threshing season, and on for some six weeks or so of the beginning of the ploughing season.

From May until the end of the summer season, and through to early autumn, Boris however, under a special arrangement, went off on secondment to join a travelling fair. This was very much a steam-powered fun fair, and Boris had gone to them in the first place to get them out of trouble in an emergency situation. He was sent there by SKWEC in answer to an urgent appeal for help from the fairground where the traction engine driving one of their main power generators had exploded, causing havoc at the height of the season, and killing both its driver and his mate.

Boris drove a replacement steam engine there—a brand new Burrell Showman's Engine—and stayed for the remainder of the season to run it. To have a steam expert in residence on the site, after the shock of the disaster, gave the fairground proprietor a feeling of security. It was an arrangement which had been repeated each year since. To Boris it had opened up an entirely new world to him, and he thoroughly enjoyed it.

Joe, meanwhile, saw the ploughing and land clearance work right through to the end of the season, and spent some time on roadworks until the two of them met up again to start their next autumn and winter ploughing and threshing rounds once more.

Off now on their first ploughing assignment, the convoy they formed looked very impressive and people tended to stop what they were doing to watch them go proudly by. The powerful 16HP Fowler engines they were driving—originally part of a special Government contract in 1917-1918 during the Great War, for 65 complete Fowler Steam Ploughing sets to assist with home food production—made light work of the task of towing the gear along country roads to its destination.

On this occasion, and not unusually for them, they had a mixture of ploughing work, ground clearance and soil cultivation to cope with. Sometimes they also carried out agricultural field-drainage schemes, which involved towing a mole-plough through the ground, leaving behind it under the soil deep enough not to be destroyed by subsequent cultivation, a network of drainage tunnels along which water ran away to ditches at the sides of the fields.

Behind Joe's engine, hooked up one behind the other to give the appearance of a 'road-train', was a living accommodation 'Box', a large double-ended land plough and a water-tank cart. The latter was needed because the engines required a constant supply of water wherever they happened to be working, so they had to carry it themselves since water was not usually readily available close by on their work sites. Each engine also had a 200 gallon water tank which formed the lower part of the tender behind the driver's stand-plate. The open upper part of the tender carried about 8 cwt of coal.

Boris also towed a 'Box'—in this case the same one that he and Joe used when threshing. Behind this trailed a large, cumbersome, ground-cultivating machine which again—like the double-ended plough—was designed to be towed to and fro across the land by the two engines and their steel cables. If required it could also have pulled the mole-plough, were there to be a need for it in the few weeks immediately ahead. It was, however, more usual to send the mole-plough out to its location independently since its jobs tended to come up on a 'one-off' basis, rather than in a cyclic year-by-year way, as did the ploughing and cultivating work.

In one respect Boris and Joe were a little more fortunate than the other five ploughing teams that their company sent out each year, on their Autumn and Spring Assignments.

It happened that their original thresher's living-quarters 'Box', or 'Living Accommodation Wagon' as the makers chose to call vehicles like it, were intended only for two—or perhaps exceptionally three—men to live in. Later ones purchased by SKWEC were larger and equipped with more bunks and designed to take five men, which was a typical team size for steam ploughing work. They included personal lockers for each man, and the necessary cooking facilities.

But, old hands at the job as they were, Joe and Boris had turned down the initial offer by the firm to swap them over to a new van, and opted instead to soldier on with their old one. In the end it became obvious that they had been wise, for they enjoyed more privacy and more peace and quiet than their colleagues in other teams. Each year their team of five took out two of the original smaller vans, rather than one of the smarter, newer, larger ones.

When on location Boris and Joe lived in their usual Box, while the other one accommodated their three workmates. One of these was Grant Carter, the team's foreman; one was Sid Moon, an experienced ploughman; and the third was young Bob Startle who was known in the team, and by the firm, as a 'cook boy'.

Bob looked after the domestic arrangements for the team of five during a working day. In between these duties he was very much under training to become a fully fledged steam ploughing expert, so he was to be found here-there-and-everywhere, helping

261

where he was needed. Becoming a cook boy was the recognised way of starting out on a steam ploughing career.

To many men it was an attractive job and there was never a shortage of men and boys to fill vacancies with established firms. The cost of living was low, the lifestyle rather free and easy, and the pay higher than for average farm workers. Almost always the pay carried a fixed basic wage which itself was better than average, plus a bonus per acre which contracting firms found it expedient to pay the teams, because the faster they worked, the more farms they covered and the greater the return on the firm's substantial capital investment.

While Joe and Boris were the engine experts, it fell to Grant Carter to organise each job. He was the expert on soil cultivation, land clearance, and drainage. He had to arrange each contract, sorting out the sequence of work to be carried out. It was up to him to decide on the number of furrows they could plough at a time, how best to clear previously uncultivated land in order to bring it into service and also how to organise the efficient drainage of waterlogged fields. Grant was the liaison man between SKWEC and their customers.

The safe parking of the engines and the mechanics of the actual pulling of the implements was the province of Joe and Boris, but all of them had to have their wits about them to avoid nasty accidents. The peaceful surroundings and tranquil setting in which they worked could easily lull inexperienced people into a false sense of security.

Sometimes it was potentially dangerous work they were doing and things could go wrong very quickly. This was particularly true if they were reclaiming land that had been uncultivated for years, or clearing land which had not been cropped before. The smooth travel of the towed machinery could suddenly become obstructed, placing enormous tension on the steel cable. If action were not taken swiftly, something had to give. The pent-up forces spelled danger to metal, machines, and men.

A snapped cable, flying apart like a coiling, snaking, living thing, was vicious indeed, and could be lethal to anyone caught in the awesome strength of its whiplash. Experienced men watched the cable carefully, particularly the engine drivers who seldom took their eyes off it.

The one pulling in had always to be especially vigilant, for instant release of the cable could come only from him. He was aided by his ears as well as his eyes, because an increase in load was marked by a change in the sound of the engine's exhaust bark. His reaction to signs of possible danger was immediate—he disengaged the drive to the winding drum. Joe and Boris had their own means of warning one another by blasts on their steam-whistles and they had worked out a code of signals to let one another know what they were doing.

The behaviour of most steam men was conditioned by knowledge of accidents they had either seen themselves, or heard about. If asked, they could recount stories of broken bones, lacerated limbs and bodies, and of faces, hands, arms and bodies badly scalded by steam blow-outs from over-stressed or faulty boilers. Sadly, also, there were histories of fatalities down the years. Indeed, as mentioned, Boris got his fairground job as a result of the two men being killed by an exploding boiler.

Sometimes accidents came as a result of misuse of machinery, lack of regular maintenance of it, or lack of vigilance when using it. On the credit side, unrecorded and unaccounted, there were very many instances where a high level of vigilance and fast reactions by engine drivers and their mates had prevented serious and perhaps fatal accidents. Usually these went unnoticed, and those around carried on blissfully unaware that disaster had stalked perilously near them but had mercifully gone harmlessly by, thanks to the swift action of the steam men.

So silence greeted swift successful action by a vigilant, competent, steam man, but a deafening clamour of accusation and blame beat about his head if something went disastrously wrong. This being how things were, he came to know that he stood very much alone, for it was only in his own head that a fair balance sheet of his true safety record could be drawn up. Perhaps it was one of the factors which tended to make him a silent, steadfast man who stood a little aloof from others, and small wonder that steam men sometimes became taciturn and uncommunicative, well aware of the demands of their job and the constant responsibilities placed on their shoulders, but unwilling to talk much about it. But not all of them bore that stamp, and neither Joe nor Boris fitted this stereotype.

Impressive though the whole operation of their steam ploughing outfit was, if it came down to actual ploughing using the simplest, conventional horse-drawn plough, then only one of those present in the team would have been good enough to enter a Ploughing Match.

Sid Moon was the one. It was he who was the Expert Ploughman. Sid had graduated to his present job after many years' experience of horse-drawn ploughing. He had come to terms with the fact that steam ploughing, though highly efficient and comparatively very fast working, never succeeded in leaving behind it the immaculately cut, arrow-straight furrows which a skilled ploughman of the old school would proudly create, using horses and very much simpler ploughs. Control of the big, multi-furrow steam plough was far less precise. But the crops grew just as well for all that, so nobody cared very much about the sometimes less than perfect appearance of the furrow lines. That didn't stop it bugging Sid a bit, nor others like him in steam-ploughing teams.

Sid always said that the ploughman was the front-line soldier of a steam-ploughing team—the most important man in the outfit—or so he asserted to his amused team mates! All the rest, not forgetting those employed on maintenance of the gear back at the workshops, were dismissed by him as being simply his 'support staff'. His reasoning was simple. The purpose of the whole expensive outfit was to turn furrows across fields. And the bit that did that was the multiple-plough itself, under his direction! He was fond of reminding the team that he was the only expert!

He made it his business to look after the plough, just as he had done over the years with his simpler, horse-drawn ones. In essence, the active parts hadn't changed much for a long long time. It was obviously faster to cut several furrows at a time, rather than just one or two, but a furrow was a furrow and the tool which cut and fashioned it was the thing that really mattered.

Sid's first experience of a plough was when, as a small boy, he went out with his ploughman dad, to help him. His dad had told him what a plough was all about and he hadn't forgotten his simple lesson. To see how it worked, his dad had said, you needed to look at it from the front and see what it had to do as it came through the soil towards you.

Its leading edge, called the coulter, was a vertical, wedge-shaped blade, with a sharp cutting edge. Its job was to knife through the soil to cut a vertical slot about eight inches deep. Just behind it, at the bottom, was the 'share', which had the job of cutting a horizontal slot at the foot of the vertical one, forming with it an L-shaped cut in the ground. The share had a sharp leading edge to it and was angled and shaped in a backward curve so that it pulled through the soil and cut easily.

The third part was called a mouldboard, and its job was to direct the way in which the slice of soil behaved as the plough progressed forwards. It was so shaped that it inverted and buried the top soil, turning over it a 'new' layer of soil for exposure to the weather. Underneath this layer the vegetation that had covered the field was buried so that it rotted down to humus, and surface seeds were also disposed of at the same time.

As the plough moved steadily through the ground, the soil seemed to flow backwards from the coulter, curling up the side of the mouldboard and finally rolling over as it left the back of the board. When wet and shiny, this curling slice of soil looked almost liquid as it flowed out of the back of the plough to fall—'frozen' and immobile—to make one more wave in a sea of newly made furrows.

Sid kept the cutting edges clean and the whole surface of the integrated steel ploughing unit as bright and clean as he could. In use, the constant movement through the abrasive soil kept the metal shining brightly. When not in use Sid protected it from rust and himself from unnecessary labour, by seeing that the metal was well coated with oil.

On the multiple-plough they were now using, there were six ploughs set one behind the other, staggered progressively sideways from the centre line. When the soil was ideally moist and conditions were good, the clean hissing sound of the plough unit as the six furrows were simultaneously cut was testimony in Sid's ears to the good condition of the plough. He listened for it, just as Joe and Boris monitored the proper functioning of their engines by the sounds they made.

Moving across a field at four miles or so an hour, leaving behind it six shining furrows, made the action of a multiple plough a pleasing thing to watch. The appearance of a large field was transformed quite miraculously in the space of a few hours. To Sid, as to many people, a freshly ploughed field was a thing of beauty, looking for a brief period reborn and virginal. It had an attraction all of its own, evincing, to some people, a mute appeal to be left alone and unspoiled—at least for a little while—for it looked so good.

In one respect the steam plough differed very much from its conventional predecessors. It had evolved into a double-ended affair so that it could work alternative 'ways-on' as it was towed to and fro across the ground between the two traction engines. In one direction one of the engines towed it across the field while the other engine gave out its steel cable at the same rate as its partner wound in its own cable. On arrival the operation was reversed, and the two engines swapped roles. Early steam ploughs were simply turned round to face the other way at the end of each run across the field. By making double-ended ones, this turning process, always tricky and time wasting, was avoided. But provision had to be made for the end not in use, to be held above ground level.

So Sid's double-ended plough looked a bit like an elaborate see-saw, pivoted at its centre on two, large-diameter iron wheels. Between the wheels, and forming a mount for their axle, was a strong, box-framed chassis. Extending in front and behind this central section were two pairs of long, steel, girder-like chassis members, angled inwards to form V-shaped structures. Below each of these V-shaped frames were fitted six ploughs which pointed towards the large central section and the running wheels. By constructing each pointed V-shaped chassis, not horizontally, but pointing 'upwards' at an angle of about 30°, the device became a convenient two-way system. At rest, the equally weighted ends, if properly balanced, would both be above the ground, like the two sides of a see-saw.

Pulling one end down to ground level raised the other end further up above the soil. Each side carried a small, solid tail-wheel for the plough to run on. It was mounted, not at the extreme end, but a little way from the end, set on the outside edge of the V-frame, to offset the sideways thrust of the plough.

In action Sid and his partner, the team foreman, pulled the operative end of the plough down and sat on it, so holding it down. There were two seats, one at the tail-end just behind the tail-wheel, and the other just behind where the V-frame joined the central box-frame. This placed the tail-end seat adjacent to the last of the six plough-units, and the other seat just in front of the first of the six.

This second seat, up behind the large wheels, was the steersman's. The direction of the plough was controlled from this point by an iron steering wheel fixed to the end of a long iron shaft.

Sid sat on this seat and looked downwards along the edge of the ground where the already ploughed soil met the unploughed soil they were then turning. His task was to set the first plough-unit beneath his seat, to pick up the edge and maintain a straight line across the field.

Meanwhile Grant Carter, from his position on the tail-end seat, looked ahead scanning the ground they were ploughing. His line of vision, because of the way the chassis was offset from the centre, enabled him to see ahead past the outside edge of the large, right-hand running wheel, giving him a clear field of vision.

Sid, however, did not have such a clear view because the other half of the plough was raised up in front of him, obstructing his view ahead to the left. Out of this raised plough, the steering wheel that he would be using on the way back stuck up prominently and rather incongruously, at the end of its long shaft.

There was nothing very pretty about the sight of a steam plough as a machine. It was strictly a functional affair and looked both complicated and ungainly to anybody seeing one for the first time. Because of its inherently balanced design, on occasions, working in bad conditions on heavy soil, the one man seated at the tail-end was not sufficient to keep the machine down. A third man, and exceptionally a fourth, would add weight by riding the V-shaped chassis, until the difficult patch was overcome. It looked for all the world as though they were on it for a joy ride!

To obviate this difficulty some ploughs were designed to be 'anti-balanced' types. In these the central section had a degree of mobility relative to the two ends and was shifted on each run so that it was nearer the front plough than the back operative one, so throwing more weight on the tail-end to keep it down. Not everybody liked the idea. Grant and Sid preferred the balanced type they were currently using.

On arrival at the far side of the field, Sid and Grant got off, walked to the other end, pulled it down, mounted it and were at once ready for the return journey. The engine drivers signalled one another and the distant one took on the role of the work-horse, its exhaust note thudding away as it took up the strain of pulling the multiple-plough through the soil.

Meanwhile the other driver, relieved of the responsibility of controlling the plough, which demanded a high level of vigilance, now had time to look to the needs of his engine. Coal was added to the fire if necessary, and the boiler's water-level gauge was checked. An ingenious water-injector allowed the level to be topped up when needed, with the water being forced in by the device against the high pressure within the boiler. As he worked at his routine tasks the driver's ears recorded the noise of the cable drum rotating beneath the boiler as the disappearing plough pulled the cable off it. Its ratchet system click-clicked musically as the tension of the cable pulled it round, notch by notch, feeding out the cable in a controlled way. Any sudden irregularity in this sound alerted the driver to possible trouble and caused him to look up from what he was doing, to check that all was well.

It was the task of the idling engine to move forward up the side of the field by an amount equal to twice the width of ground the plough turned over on each crossing. Each engine was responsible for alternate strips and this shunting-up by first one, then the other, carried on all day long, as the powerful and well-practised system did its work.

265

Some driver teams made a practice of shifting forward immediately the plough reached them. Simultaneously with disengaging the drive to the drum, the driver shunted his engine up the field. Across the field his partner took this as a visual signal that it was time for him to start his pull. Boris and Joe sometimes did this, but whatever routine they followed neither ever started a pull until he heard the signal to do so from other engine's steam-whistle. Some were not always that careful and accidents could happen if the cable were tensioned before the plough was quite ready.

A bit of manoeuvring had to be done by the steersman just before the final few feet of a run, to swing the plough's direction sideways slightly, so that when they both got off they could pull the other end down to the ground, turning it as they did so to line up the axis of the V-shaped frame of the active side of the plough to the furrow lines for the next run across the field.

The final lining-up process was achieved by the leverage action arising as a result of the point of attachment of the cable's shackle. The pull on the cable as the tow was taken up exerted this leverage on the chassis to make the plough turn into position. Once the plough was running, the steersman controlled its precise direction using his steering wheel.

As each engine required quite a broad strip of land on its side of the field to move along, and because the plough could not turn the soil right up close to the engine, there was a sizeable strip of unploughed land, some thirty feet or so wide, each side of the field at the end of the job. This was sometimes ploughed by shifting the engines to the other two sides of the field. This left engine tracks across ploughed edges on the newly ploughed ground, so total coverage was not quite possible.

Often a ploughman from the farm would move into the field and cope with the unploughed strips, and also take out any engine tracks that had been left after the outfit moved on. If the farmer wanted to maximize the area of ground cultivated in a given time by the contracted steam plough, it made economic sense to make arrangements for his own equipment and men to do the 'engine-sides' of each field. Moving the heavy traction engines and the plough about, to pick up difficult areas, did not make sense, so headlands and awkward bits of fields were covered by the local men.

When working on a large farm with several scattered fields to do, the team chose a good central spot for their home base so that they could park the wagons and leave them there for the duration of their stay. Occasionally, with a split farm having widely separated sections, they moved the caravans about, but avoided doing so if they could.

At their present location, as with many others, they knew in advance exactly where to set up home, having been there many times before. They were in a meadow just off a hedged lane, parked by the edge of an apple orchard, by a small crystal-clear chalk stream fed with spring water which bubbled out of the ground less than half a mile away. There was nothing to pollute it and it was wonderfully refreshing to drink. Bob Startle had his brazier in a sheltered corner, and his one-gallon kettle, filled with spring water, was in regular use brewing up tea for the five of them.

Boris, the most domestically-minded of his workmates, had persuaded friends back at the depot to knock them up a simple improvised metal oven, which, parked over a narrow trench fire, gave Bob the chance of doing more varied things than were possible over Primus stoves. Boris had fixed a piece of metal, carrying a flue-pipe, over the back of the fire behind the oven. This gave the fire a good draught so that it lit easily and burnt well. Now and again, just for the joy of it, he and Bob baked some bread, which filled the area with a delightful smell. Such bread was much loved by all of them and it seldom, if ever, lived long enough to grow cold.

On working days, at ten o'clock in the morning, Bob took his mates a jug of tea and a bite to eat. What constituted the 'bite' was decided by debate. Though the choice was small, Bob managed to cater for their individual preferences fairly well.

At eleven o'clock he went off back to the vans to prepare a simple cooked meal ready for the return of the other four at half-past twelve. At 1.30pm they set off back to work. Bob went with them, but returned 'home' to bring them back a cup of tea at four o'clock. After that jug of tea Bob's domestic responsibilities ended and they all fared for themselves in preparing what food they wanted during the evening. Joe and Boris followed the same routine as when they were threshing, with Joe doing the breakfast and Boris their evening meal.

Usually the team finished work at six o'clock, but as the evenings lengthened, on nice days they often worked until much later. Putting in the extra hours jacked-up their acreage bonus and was one of the perks of the job.

When the team stopped work at night, Joe and Boris were last to leave the site because, as always, they had to bank up their respective fires and shut down their traction engines for the night, to ensure a trouble-free start the next day.

In the same way, they were always first on the site in the mornings. Joe, the early riser, was usually the one to pay a first quick visit to both engines, then open up their fire grates and take the caps off their chimneys. If they happened to be a few hundred yards from their work site, and the weather was not too good, Joe occasionally winkled Boris out of his bed when the alarm went off, to take his turn at this first chore of the day. It was not something that bothered Joe, though, because on fine brisk days he enjoyed going out in the air for a brief spell first thing in the morning.

Soon after seven o'clock they were back at their engines to attend to the fires and their normal daily maintenance routines. By 7.30am the engines were quietly turning over and the steam pressure gauges were steady on 180 pounds per square inch. This working pressure was considerably higher than that of their threshing engines which normally ran at 110 pounds per square inch.

The strong, reliable 16HP Fowler engines they were using were a pleasure to listen to as they ticked over under no-load conditions. A discerning listener could hear the characteristic sound of their two-cylinder compound engines.

Bob Startle, whose real ambition was to became a steam engine driver, spent as much time as possible with Joe and Boris, assisting them wherever he could and gleaning information meanwhile. They were both always glad of his help in oiling and cleaning the engines and were happy to teach 'young Bob' as they called him, as much as they could as they busied themselves ministering to the needs of their much-prized charges.

Bob was well aware that the engines had two cylinders and he could distinguish the sound they made from that of single cylinder machines. This was true even when they were just ticking over but was particularly marked when they were working under a heavy load. A single cylinder engine gave a pronounced staccato 'bark' when hard at it—a sound which carried a long way on quiet, still days, especially in the evenings. The exhaust note from a compound engine, though loud enough when on high-load, was more of a deep-throated, thudding sound than the sharp-edged bark of the simpler engines.

On their third day at the site, early in the morning before ploughing started, Bob was with Joe helping him with his preparations for the day and with his routine daily maintenance and cleaning. Bob was busy cleaning the boiler around the area of the cylinders.

"This is a twin-cylindered engine, isn't it, Joe?" he observed.

"It's a two-cylinder engine, not a twin-cylinder one," Joe answered, perhaps a little pedantically. "Those cylinders are not twins. Look at them and you will see they are not the same as one another. One is a lot bigger than the other."

Bob, cleaning them and looking around them, saw the point. But he soon began to puzzle about it.

"Joe," he said, "why is one of those cylinders bigger than the other one? My Uncle Tom at Sandwich has a Harley Davidson twin-cylinder motorbike-and-sidecar and both cylinders are the same size. So they are on other big motorbikes I've seen."

"Different principle, they are, from steam engine," Joe commented emphatically. "Those motorbikes have internal combustion engines. The petrol vapour and air explodes. The gas pressure produced by the explosion drives the piston down the cylinder. It wouldn't make any sense to have those cylinders of different sizes. The engine would be right off-balance and wouldn't run smoothly at all."

He paused a moment to gather his thoughts, then went on with his explanation.

"In a steam engine, there's no explosion in the cylinder. Nothing's burnt inside there at all. You just feed in high-pressure steam and as the steam expands it pushes the piston along. You let in a blast of steam, and then shut it off on each stroke. As the piston moves, the steam pressure drops. What you are doing in a steam engine is using energy given up by the pressurized steam to do the work of shifting the piston."

"Where does the exhaust note come into it, then?" intervened Bob. "I saw two single-cylinder steam engines pulling a mole-plough to and fro across a field on Romney Marshes and they were making a hell of a noise. I remember my Dad saying to me, 'Hark at those engines barking away over there, Bob. Their exhausts go off like guns when they're straining to pull that drainage plough through the ground. It's a wonder they don't blow to bits!' And that's what they did sound like, Joe. Bang—bang—bang—bang—just like guns going off. It seemed like an explosion each stroke to me."

"Oh yes!" Joe agreed. "They bark all right! But there's no explosion in the cylinder, Bob. You see, when the piston is some way along the cylinder the steam coming in behind it is cut off. In front of it is steam from the previous stroke, which the piston has been pushing out of an exhaust valve. What happens next, when the piston has got to the end and just started coming back, is that steam is let in behind it on that side of the cylinder to push it back the other way. At the same time an exhaust valve opens on the other side of the piston so that the first charge of steam is pushed out. What you hear is the blast of the exhausted steam. That steam goes into the smoke box, blasts its way up the chimney to snort out of the top. It creates a nice draught doing it, too, and that drags in a rush of air through the boiler's tubes, pulling a strong draught through the fire-grate to boost the fire."

"I still don't see why those two cylinders are not the same size, though," persisted Bob.

"Ah well, they're not quite what they seem, Bob," explained Joe. "They don't both work direct from the boiler. If they did, then they would certainly be the same size. What happens is the steam goes first into one of them, which takes some of the energy from it. Then the same steam that's exhausted by that cylinder goes straight into its mate by its side to do another job of work before being exhausted by that second cylinder into the smoke box, and up the chimney. If you listen carefully you can hear the thud-THUD, thud-THUD, thud-THUD, as the two cylinders chunter away up there one after the other. It's a two-part sound, if you listen."

"I suppose the steam from the boiler goes into that big cylinder first," reasoned Bob, "then gets squirted into the small one."

"No," said Joe, with emphasis. "No, that's just what it doesn't do. It goes into the small one and then into the big one, not the other way round. The small cylinder gets the benefit of the very high-pressure steam direct from the boiler, but the larger one has to work off the much lower-pressure steam, exhausted out of the small one. The sizes are worked out so that the two can do equal amounts of work to give a balanced stroke to the engine. Here, come and have a look at this."

So saying, Joe directed Bob's attention to the steam-pressure gauge.

"See that," he said. "Do you see what the pointer reads?"

"Yes," replied Bob. "It says 180."

"That's right," confirmed Joe. "That means the steam pressure in the boiler is one hundred and eighty pounds per square inch. That's the pressure we reckon to run these engines at normally, although we can push them higher if we need to."

"When do you need to do that?" enquired Bob.

"Not very often," replied Joe. "Maybe if we have to tow the plough up a hillside through heavy clay soil, or pull the mole-plough through water-logged fields to drain them. Those are the sorts of jobs—when the going gets hard—when we need to 'up' the pressure a bit. Anyway, to get back to the pressures. The small cylinder is fed with steam at 180 and exhausts it into the large cylinder at about 70. That's a drop of 110. So the piston in the small cylinder gets the energy given up by its squirt of steam in dropping its pressure by 110 pounds per square inch."

"Yes, I can see that," commented Bob. "That's taken quite a lot of push out of the steam, hasn't it?"

"It has that," agreed Joe. "Now that same load of steam is squirted into the big cylinder. So steam goes into it at 70 and comes out at about 20. Call it exactly 20, say. So the big piston takes the energy from a drop of 50. That's less than half the small cylinder takes out. That's why the piston is made bigger, so a smaller amount of push gives the same power from the big piston as the bigger push gives to the smaller piston."

Bob beamed with pleasure at the logic of this bit of reasoning.

"That's a good idea, that is!" he said, with marked approval. "Now I can see why it goes into the small cylinder first. But why did you say about 20 for the steam coming out? Why didn't they make it come out lower, say at 10 or something like that?"

"They couldn't, that's why!" answered Joe. "You see, out here in the open air, the air pressure we live in is just under 15 pounds per square inch. To get a blow of steam up the chimney there, you've got to let it out of the big cylinder higher than 15, otherwise it wouldn't blow at all. It does come out a bit lower than 20, I believe, but I don't know the exact figure. One of the blokes in the workshop said he'd heard it could be made to work down to about 16, but I wouldn't know if that's true.

Because these engines have two stages, people sometimes call them double-expansion engines. On ships you often hear of triple-expansion steam engines, which means the high-pressure steam from the ship's boilers goes through three cylinders in a row. But things get complicated when you move away from our sort of engines to much more powerful ones. Those often condense the steam back to water at the tail-end so you're working down to no pressure at all. But of course those don't use our simple steam-blow draught system which we need for our open fires."

"That's interesting, that is," commented Bob, with marked enthusiasm. "What you told me about our two-cylinder job, I mean", he added, frowning slightly. "I don't know about the ship's engines and that condensing business you talked about though. That's a bit beyond me. But I can see how this one works. Will you tell me some more about the steam engines we use ourselves, sometime, Joe? I want to get to know all I can about them."

"Sure I will," said Joe. "Glad to, son. I had to learn, and somebody had to take the trouble to tell me how things work. It's nice to find a youngster like you who is so interested. If you keep on picking up know-how about steam engines, I don't see why you shouldn't be allowed by the firm to become mate to a driver one day, say on a road-roller or a thresher. Then you would go on to be a driver yourself, if you're good enough."

"Hope so," said Bob, a little wistfully. "I'd love to be an engine driver myself one day."

"You will be, Bob! You will be! I'm quite sure of that, if you're really keen." encouraged Joe. "There are enough steam engines around these days. I've spent all my life working with steam engines and I wouldn't swap the job for anything. For a change though, I'm hoping to spend some time soon on Foden Steam Lorries, just for a part of each year. The firm has several of them, and other makes as well. I'd like to have a go with them. They can shift, they can, out on the open roads. Not too good at climbing hills with a full load up—then they're a bit slow—but give them a fair run on the open road and they really can get a move on!" Joe grinned a little self-consciously. "I enjoy a bit of speed myself," he added.

"Yes, and so do I!" said Bob eagerly. "My Uncle's Harley Davidson Twin can shift too. He takes me out sometimes. Good fun it is, too! It's a powerful bike and my Uncle likes to push it along hard!"

Bob's enthusiasm about steam engines was infectious, and reminded Joe of the time when he himself had been in the same position, impatient to become a fully-trained driver and thirsty for knowledge about all things to do with steam engines. He also remembered that some experienced men had been very reluctant to tell him anything at all, as though they were inwardly afraid that to spread their hard-gained know-how would somehow jeopardize their own future.

During the working day he watched young Bob with interest and pondered the problem of how to help him. When he did so he wondered, not for the first time, if the reluctance of some older men to answer his own eager questions when he was a lad, was maybe a bit of a cover-up for their own lack of a thorough knowledge about the inner workings of the machinery they used with such apparent confidence. He resolved to get his own thoughts straight so that he could give Bob the kind of help he needed if his enthusiasm were not to be blunted and frustrated. Too many times as a boy his own eager questions had been met with a stony silence by older men—no reaction at all quite often, just as though his words had not been heard. It had made him feel a nuisance, and nervous of asking. Subsequently he learnt that it was an experience shared by many boys trying to learn a trade.

That evening Joe sat at the table in the Box and carefully drew a simple diagram showing how steam was allowed into a cylinder—first on one side of the piston, then on the other—to push the piston to and fro. It took him some time to remember how to show the way in which one lot of 'used' steam was pushed out of the exhaust pipe by the action of the piston driven by the next lot of steam coming into the cylinder.

Not for the first time he fiddled about for quite a while, sorting out how the slider valve opened a steam inlet port on one side of the piston while simultaneously shutting off the steam inlet port on the other side and opening it to the exhaust passage. He got his mind in a twist trying to make sure that when the piston reached the other end of the cylinder, the reverse happened. Boris saw that he was having trouble and gave a hand. Working together and discussing it, they at length finished up with a sketch good enough to show how it all worked. It didn't do either of them any harm to clarify their own thoughts about it once again.

Standing by the engine next morning, with the aid of the sketch Joe was able to show Bob first how a piston's to and fro movement was made to turn the heavy flywheel. Then, after a bit of trouble, he managed to explain to Bob's satisfaction how the eccentric wheels on the shaft worked the slider valves that controlled the steam going into, and coming out of, the cylinders.

In the end, the effort of making his explanation clear enough for Bob to understand didn't do Joe any harm, for he finished up having a clearer idea of it himself. Bob, who really did want to know, wouldn't let go until he got things straight. That was a part of his make-up which was to serve him well throughout his life. Meanwhile, both Joe and Boris, as well as other colleagues at SKWEC, came to have a healthy respect for young Bob's intellect, because they soon realised that if he showed any difficulty in understanding anything, it was more down to their own woolly thinking and inadequate explanations than to any lack of ability on his part.

It was a salutary lesson for some people who had successfully passed as experts amongst laymen, when secretly they were not too sure of themselves. As for Bob's reaction, at length he got around to asking questions only of those he had grown to respect as men who really knew what they were talking about!

At length, for the first time, Bob—standing with Joe watching the engine smoothly ticking over—was able to see why the heavy flywheel had to be there, to keep the mechanism running between successive pushes of steam coming into the cylinders.

That pleased Bob very much, because the large, heavy flywheel, with its polished rim and massive integral spokes, was what fascinated him most. He just liked watching it go round and round. So for that matter did Joe, even after so many years. They were not alone in this. The sight of the gleaming, smoothly-turning flywheel and the flip-flopping action of the well-oiled mechanism that drove it, captured the attention of many people, young and old alike.

Drivers got used to people just standing gazing at their softly chuntering engines and understood why they were spellbound. Perhaps Boris had it right when he said to Joe one day that there was a natural affinity between human beings and turning wheels on steam engines, because the regular beat of the machinery as it ticked over so reliably, harmonised with the beating of their own hearts within their bodies. Time and time again Boris had noticed that it was when they were parked, and the engines were just simply ticking over, that people were attracted to—and seemed hypnotised by—the rhythmic, seemingly effortless action of the powerful machines.

He got round to thinking that perhaps the men who had invented them had unconsciously imitated the working of their own internal machines. After all, a man lived by the cyclic action of the taking in and breathing out of air, a process which speeded up when he worked very hard, because more air was needed. Just like the engine, he thought, which was driven by breathing in regular gulps of steam.

Bob, feeling strangely excited by the realisation that he now felt he understood how the engine worked, took the opportunity to ask another question about something that intrigued him.

"What are those two balls spinning round up there for, Joe?" he asked.

"That's the old girl's speed governor," Joe replied. "Those balls do their best to keep the engine's speed from changing from the speed I set my throttle to. If the load slackens off, the engine speeds up and those two balls fly outwards like a conker does on a string. As they go outwards those bandy-legged springs that support them, are bent outwards. That pulls the collar that the springs are attached to, up the spindle. As the collar goes up the spindle it moves a lever which shuts down the steam feed a bit. So the engine tries to run faster but is held back by this automatic valve action."

"What happens if it tries to slow down?" pursued Bob.

"Just the opposite," replied Joe. "The balls don't fly out so far and the springs straighten out a bit. So the collar slips down the spindle and the lever opens up the steam valve, which lets in more steam and makes the engine run faster. So its tries to slow down but can't."

"The bloke who thought that lot out must have had some brains," commented Bob, much impressed by the ingenuity of it all.

"You can say that again," countered Joe. "There are plenty of brains behind the design of a wonderful piece of machinery like this engine. Brains are needed in the steam engine world, that's for sure," he added, not without a feeling of personal pride and reflected kudos.

Highly pleased with himself, Bob asked Joe if he could borrow his drawing. That night, back in the caravan, Grant Carter and Sid did not hear much from Bob. He was busy at the table copying out Joe's sketch into a school exercise book and writing some notes about how steam engines work. And what's more, he got it all about right, too!

Bob the 'cook boy' was on his way.

Chapter 20

A CANNON-SHOT FROM THE PAST

for the steam men of Kent

The following morning they had a reshuffle of equipment. About one mile away the farmer had an area not previously cultivated, which he now wanted to bring into service. It comprised two adjacent pasture fields and a piece of scrubland. His own men had taken out a hedgerow between the fields and cleared bushes and trees from the scrubland.

It was a job for the team's large and capable cultivator rather than their double-ended plough. The latter was used for land which was ploughed over and over again, year after year. But for all other work their powerful cultivator, which attacked the ground with a battery of tines eleven feet wide, was much to be preferred instead of ploughs; indeed some farmers had their whole arable ground turned by it because it was faster.

The tines were vertical, wedge-shaped spikes which went down into the ground up to a maximum of one foot deep, breaking it up into lumps and chunks. It did not leave behind it the neat uniformity produced by the ploughs. Nor did it bury vegetation so efficiently. However, the ground could be raked and cropped just the same afterwards. Often, with a job such as the team now had to do, the cultivator went over the ground a second time, at right-angles to its first direction. This broke the chunks up still further, buried more of the vegetation and made subsequent working of the soil easier.

First thing in the morning, Boris and Joe drove their traction engines back to the home base, in the snug corner of the meadow. Joe towed the double-ended plough, which he unhitched and parked. He left it conveniently placed for him to pick up when they eventually left the site for their next destination.

Meanwhile Boris, with the aid of Grant and Sid, hitched up the heavy cultivator behind his engine. It weighed three tons and looked something of a monster. It was wider than the plough but a good deal shorter. Mounted between two, very large-diameter, heavy iron wheels, was a platform on which Sid and Grant stood when in action, one of them working the large, iron steering wheel which operated upon a single front wheel. Beneath the platform was the wide, hefty structure carrying thirteen tines, staggered over its eleven foot width. Its appearance bore testimony to the power needed to drag it through compacted land. It was a task needing the full potential of the 16 HP Fowler engines.

When they set off up the lane Joe led the way, towing behind him the water cart. This, together with the engine's own water tank in its tender, he had previously filled, with Bob's help, from the stream, using the engine's purpose-made water pump.

Joe stood on the steersman's plate on the left-hand side of the engine, from which point he could see exactly where his nearside wheel was positioned. If that wheel were allowed to slip into a roadside ditch, or even run on to unsound ground that dipped downwards, the engine could tip over on to its side all too easily. He knew of a driver and his mate, both of whom had lost their lives when their nearside wheel had hit the parapet of a river bridge, smashed a great hole in it and slipped over the edge. In a frighteningly brief few seconds the huge engine lay on its side like a toy in the river below. There had been no chance of the two men escaping their fate. It was all over in a moment. They were crushed.

All drivers were conscious of the ease with which their seemingly all-powerful and invulnerable engines could tip over. They were high, very heavy, and did not have a very wide wheelbase. This fact, and many others like it, had to be well and truly learnt by aspiring would-be drivers like young Bob, and he was lucky because Joe had taken him under his wing. No amount of classroom instruction could ever match this day by day experience working alongside an expert. In effect Bob had a personal tutor and nobody could have had a better start than that. He gained in practical know-how with each passing day.

Out on the roads Bob rode on the man-stand between the boiler and the tender. Standing up there with his hand conspicuously gripping a control lever, whether it was one he was actively concerned with or not, he felt very proud. Out of the corner of his eye Joe often spotted this and smiled to himself, remembering how he had felt exactly the same pride as a young boy standing up on the driver's plate.

Behind them came Boris, towing the heavy, ponderous cultivator. Grant Carter rode with Boris on his engine and Sid stood behind the steering wheel on the cultivator's platform. The arrangement of the towing shackle gave him the flexibility of being able to steer the machine off the towing-line direction if required. If they met anything and were short of road width, he and Boris could co-operate to position the wide cultivator sufficiently to the left of centre for a coming vehicle to have a through-way past them.

The front wheel, not in any way ideal for road use, was designed to allow this off-centre pull when they were in action on heavy soil. The wheel had a strong central flange which cut down into the ground, allowing the wheel to bite so that it could take a sideways thrust without sliding. Often, when running alongside a hedgerow, this enabled them to cut in close to the side, with the tow-line pulling at an oblique angle.

When they arrived on site they organised themselves with the practised ease of men who knew their job, and went about things automatically as though to a carefully pre-arranged plan. The entrance gate was in the centre of the field and Joe drove straight in, turned left, and headed diagonally across the field to position his engine in the far right-hand corner, broadside-on to the ground they had to turn over. He then backed up a bit to park the engine facing up the field from what would be his starting point—tucked as closely as he could into the corner.

Boris, following Joe in and seeing where he was heading, turned sharp left and drove along the side of the field to the left-hand corner, stopping opposite Joe. Then he, Sid and Grant, unhitched the cultivator near where he knew it had to be for its first run.

Meanwhile Bob, with a quick word to Joe that he was going over to give the others a hand, dashed off across the field. Joe understood what the urgency was all about. He knew what would happen next.

Over at the far side Boris and his mates had got the cultivator at its starting point, ready for Joe to pull across. Boris, his engine now free of the cultivator, was already getting up on to his driving position when Bob arrived by his side.

"May I take her across, please, Boris?" he asked eagerly.

"Sure," agreed Boris with a broad smile. "Up you get! She's all yours!"

Bob knew that Boris had to run across the field to pick up the towing-line from Joe's drum and haul it back to hitch on to the cultivator. The 7/8" steel cable was very heavy and there was a lot of it needed to cross right over what had been until recently two fields side by side.

Most ploughing engines carried 400 yards of cable on their drums, which was long enough for the majority of work they did. It happened that the Fowlers Boris and Joe were using, carried 600 yard lengths. The Government contract, under which they had previously been made, had specified 600 yard cables, a decision made to ensure they would cope with anything asked of them in the campaign to get more land under cultivation as part of the War effort. The situation today was one of the few occasions when the added length was necessary, because the farmer had decided upon having an extra large piece of ground as one unit. Not that they couldn't have coped with shorter cables, but a two-stage attack would then have been needed.

Once Bob was up on the steering platform holding the steering wheel, Boris set the engine rolling. Sid and Grant smiled when they saw Bob up there happily steering the engine. With a cheerful toot-toot on his whistle Boris let Joe know he was on his way. When Joe looked over he saw that he had deduced correctly why Bob had made a dash for it.

To steer, Bob was standing on the left-hand side of the engine, and Boris watched to see if he did the safest thing and made a clockwise turn as he swung in, to come up alongside Joe; but he did not interfere. He soon saw, with satisfaction, that Bob had got it worked out for he headed towards the end of the field to the left, turned to run along the perimeter, then swung round neatly, alongside Joe.

Boris adjusted his speed to match Bob's approach run and brought the engine to a standstill on arrival. On their way over the fields he had given Bob a fair burst of speed halfway across and had seen the pleasure on Bob's face as the impressive machine trundled along under his control. Boris now jumped down and helped Joe hook the shackle of his cable on to a towing bracket on the back of Boris's engine. Bob waited on the steering plate hoping that Boris would let him take the engine back. Boris did not wait to be asked; he could read Bob's mind only too well.

"OK", he said. "Take her over alongside the cultivator. Put her nose to the left of it, not on the end fence side."

With a another 'toot-toot' to let Grant know they were on their way, Boris set the engine rolling along at a steady speed, watching behind them to check that Joe's cable was running out properly.

Joe meanwhile could hear the regular clicking of the pawls on the ratchet of the cable-drum beneath his engine, and smiled as he looked at the small figure of Bob steering the softly chuntering engine on its way across the field. Joe's engine was tight up to the edge of the field, and backed into the corner as far as it could go. He was ready to make the first drag of the cultivator once they had hooked it up on the far side of the fields.

That process took no time at all. Grant and Sid unhitched Joe's cable from Boris's engine and fixed the shackle on to one of the two towing-eyes that stuck out in front of the cultivator. The 'eyes' were on the tips of the Y-shaped towing arm. The leg carrying Joe's cable was pointing straight across the field towards him. The other one pointed out at an angle towards the right of the cultivator.

While Grant was busy, Boris had taken control of his engine and run it in close by the roadside hedge, facing along the edge of the field. Ahead lay the path it would follow as the two engines proceeded to move, step by step, up the field as the work progressed. He had run out several yards of his own cable and now jumped down to join Sid and Grant. Together they pulled Boris's cable up to the head of the cultivator and fixed its shackle on to the second of the two eyes on the Y-shaped towing arm.

All was now ready, so Grant and Sid jumped up onto the cultivator's platform. Sid took hold of the steering wheel and Grant waved to Boris to indicate that they were ready to go. Boris gave the 'go' signal on his steam whistle and immediately Joe, waiting on the far side of the field, started his drum pulling. The cultivator started to move and Grant lowered the tines, which thumped down into the ground as the machine started to bite.

At first progress was marked by a series of lurches, but once the tines were fully embedded the cultivator ran steadily on, away from Boris and Bob, who watched it from the man-stand where they stood side-by-side up on Boris's engine. On this first breaking-up of the fairly hard, compacted ground, the speed was similar to that of their multiple-plough, about four miles per hour. But when they later covered the ground again at right-angles to their present direction, they would be able to travel at up to six miles an hour. The ground was not heavy clay and would then turn with little trouble, having already been well broken up. They could cover between 20 and 30 acres of such work in one day. During the summer, in favourable conditions, going over previously cropped fields, perhaps turning in clover sown for soil enrichment, they could clock up 40 or more acres in a long day.

Joe, as always, kept his eyes glued on the cultivator all the way across, ready to adjust his throttle, or stop the pull altogether, at any sign of trouble. It was always possible to hit an unseen snag beneath ground which had been either pasture land, or perhaps unused at all and allowed to grow wild for years.

As Sid and Grant advanced towards him, standing behind a rail on the large platform, between its two huge wheels, Joe was reminded again of pictures he had seen of gladiators riding chariots in ancient times. The two wheels had to be of very large diameter to allow sufficient space below the platform for the whole structure carrying the tines to be levered up above ground level when the cultivator turned after each cross, and of course as it was towed along roads on its journeys to work-sites.

On its way across the field Boris's cable, which was being towed over by the cultivator for use on the return journey, was held out clear of the machine by the Y-arm so that it could trail out safely to the right-hand side on the ground next to be turned. In this position it was pulled steadily off the drum below Boris's engine and laid out neatly right across the field.

When the cultivator reached him and had been steered half-left by Sid, Joe disengaged the drum-drive and then put it in its free-wheeling state ready for Boris to tow the cable off it when he pulled the cultivator back across the field. He now signalled Boris that all was ready.

The next bit had to be managed with care. Boris took up the slack slowly and inched the cable in very gradually. Often they were closer and he could see reasonably well exactly what was going on. In this very wide field they were now in, he could not see enough to know what was happening, but relied upon Joe to whistle him sharply if he needed to stop pulling.

As the cable tightened, the Y-shaped arm clonked round to its alternative position. As it moved, it automatically shifted the front steering wheel, and also worked a lever which hauled the tines up out of the soil, locating them in a 'locked up' position. The cable gradually pulled the front of the cultivator right round until the towing line ran straight over to Boris's engine. It was during this turning-round operation that care had to be taken. Still moving slowly the machine now began to advance in its required direction.

At this point Sid pulled a lever to drop the tines, which hit the ground with a heavy thump again. Sid gave Joe a wave, Joe in turn gave Boris the 'clear to pull' signal on his steam whistle, and the cultivator immediately gathered speed as Boris began to wind in the cable.

Meanwhile Joe noted that his own cable had begun to run off its drum beneath him and stood out well clear of the departing machine. Keeping his eye on the cable, he then shunted his engine up the field by a distance of approximately twenty-two feet—twice the width of soil turned over on each cross—to position the engine where it needed to be for its next drag.

The team was now settled into its stride and the cultivator travelled to and fro uneventfully for the next hour or so, after which a halt was called for a welcome mug of hot tea. Bob, knowing they would be too far away from their base for him to be able to pop back to the vans, had brought a Primus stove and his kettle with them and had set up a temporary base along the hedgerow, just inside the gate to the road. By mutual consent, it was to be a 'sandwich only' day, and Sid had helped Bob to prepare enough food for the day.

After the break work was resumed, but half an hour later they ran into trouble. Fortunately, because of quick action on the part of the ever-alert Joe, it did not lead to personal injuries or damage to their gear. But it did delay their progress for a while.

Boris and Joe had already identified the one possible source of potential trouble when they had walked up to look over the job the previous evening. As a result they were vigilant. And it paid off.

Wherever hedgerows which had existed for many years were removed, there was always a danger that the ground concealed buried hazards. Often old ditches ran along such hedges, and all sorts of unwanted things were found to have been dumped in them over the years. Evidence of this could be seen where the team had so far ploughed, because sundry tin cans and junk had been thrown up by the tines as they crossed what had been the dividing line between the two fields.

Both Boris and Joe always watched the machine they were pulling across very intently, wherever they were. On their present location each one paid special attention as the cultivator crossed the line of the removed hedgerow.

As Joe was pulling it across there was a sudden jerk on the cable and simultaneously the cultivator bucked and started to slew round. Sid and Grant were thrown sideways, but came to no harm. Almost as fast as if it were a reflex action, Joe slammed his throttle off and at the same time disengaged his drum's drive. The cultivator stopped dead then simply rocked back to settle unevenly on the ground. Subsequently, it also was found to have come to no harm. By pivoting on the obstruction and slewing round, it had absorbed the shock without damage.

The team now gathered round to see what was up. It did not take long to discover that the tines on the extreme right had run into something immovable about six inches down. At times like this, by long experience, the team knew that if they were not careful, their bonus would start to be eroded away fast. Digging out of the soil obstructions of unknown size could burn up time, out of all proportion to its importance.

The established drill was to mark the spot and ask the owner of the land to investigate it at his leisure. When next day they came round to turn the land, it would either be gone, or, on occasions, its presence would be permanently marked by a staked-off area. It could be an outcrop of rock, or something heavy buried there, or maybe the remains of a tree stump. Whatever it was, it was the farmer's job to decide what to do about it. In the meantime, it was in everybody's interest to press on with the ploughing up of the field.

First, however, they had to determine the extent of the obstruction, at least approximately, so that they could minimise the amount of ground not ploughed up. Sid pulled the lever which raised the tines and Joe towed the cultivator over the area to get it out of the way. They were equipped to probe and, if they so decided, to dig out obstructions within a foot of the surface. Straightaway they proceeded to investigate.

It did not take them long to discover that whatever it was down there was apparently made of iron and extended several feet along the line of the removed hedgerow. They marked out a strip some four feet wide and sixteen feet long to be avoided by the cultivator and set Bob the task of finding some improvised stakes to rope off the small area for the farmer to deal with later on.

Work then resumed and on the next three drags Grant signalled to Joe and Boris to stop just before they reached the strip, to allow him to lift the tines clear of the ground until they had passed over the area. Bob had been told to stand by the place to watch things for them until they were clear of the area, before he did his job of roping it off.

In the large area they cultivated that day, the tiny plot that was left roped-off looked totally insignificant. However, the time they would have lost had they have stopped to dig out what was buried there would certainly not have been insignificant, a fact provided that very day when four of them returned that evening to investigate.

At 5.30pm they packed up for the day and set off back to their vans to cook a meal and rest up a bit. Because they had not returned during the day, having made-do with a packed lunch, they had not taken their normal one-hour break at midday. Bob had made them all a cup of tea about three o'clock in the afternoon, and by mutual consent they had determined on what was for them an early finish.

Back in their van, enjoying their usual fry-up meal, conversation between Grant, Sid and young Bob, soon turned to the mystery object buried at the site. Sid recalled stories his dad had told him of stoneware pots containing Roman coins being dug up along the Elham Valley, and of more mundane objects he himself had turned up when out and about ploughing.

Grant pitched in with a story his grandfather had told him of a kitbag full of silver objects found hidden under a hawthorn bush down the bank of a ditch. It had been there a long time, for the kitbag was badly rotted. The Police identified the objects as church silver that had been stolen over five years before. For an ecstatic moment, when they found it, the blokes had thought their fortune was made. In the event, they did collect a modest reward for finding it, but it did not change their lifestyle very much! Since the true ownership of the silver was beyond doubt, as the 'finders' they had no legal right either to retain it or to be paid the market value of it.

This talk fired young Bob's imagination and he wanted them to go back to the field to dig out whatever it was that was buried there. His mates weren't all that keen. Grant thought it might well be an old farm implement dumped there. Sid agreed with this, having seen old, rusting machinery abandoned here and there on farms, often just inside a gate on waste land, parked where possibly it had previously lived when in occasional use, and subsequently left there discarded for good when either replaced or no longer required.

Despite their lack of enthusiasm, however, having nothing particular to do, they eventually decided—prevailed upon by the bright-eyed Bob—to walk back and have another look at it. There was always a slender chance that something interesting might turn up.

Before leaving they called in to let Boris and Joe know what they were doing. Boris decided to go with them, but Joe, engrossed in an Edgar Wallace mystery story, preferred to stay put and carry on reading.

Back at the site, armed with spades, it did not take them long to establish that it was no piece of old, rusting farm machinery lying buried there. It was a heavy metal object with a curved outer surface, which, as they dug around further, took on a marked cylindrical appearance.

Boris dropped on his knees and scratched at its surface with the edge of his spade. It was not iron that he saw; there was no tell-tale rust. He peered at the scratched surface closely. Then the penny suddenly dropped!

"Bloody hell!" he exclaimed excitedly. "I know what this is. It's a cannon! A bloody great bronze cannon!"

Now, with much more enthusiasm, they all began to shift soil as fast as they could. Very soon Boris was proved right. It was indeed a large cannon; too long and too heavy by far for them to pull out by hand.

Boris made an immediate decision.

"Don't bother to dig any more," he said. "Just burrow down in the middle of it and make me a hole to pass my cable under. I'll pull it out with the engine. That will make easy work of shifting it."

"That's a good idea," spoke up Bob eagerly. "May I give you a hand to fetch her over, Boris?"

"Yes, you can, that," replied Boris. "You open up the fire-grate and take the chimney's lid off while I pull the canvas cover back out of the way. It's not so long since we shut her down. There'll be enough steam to run her and by the time we've shifted her over here the pressure will be plenty high enough to tackle this job."

Never the lad to miss an opportunity, it was Bob who was on the steering plate when the engine chuffed over the field. Boris directed him to steer the engine about ten yards away from the gun, with the cable drum broadside-on to it.

In a matter of minutes, between them they had passed the cable round the body of the gun and fastened it back on itself to form a loop.

"Stand clear," ordered Boris, and climbed up on his engine. He then started the drum turning very slowly, and with no trouble at all the whole length of the cannon broke through the surface and was pulled clear. It was examined by them all with great interest. There appeared to be nothing wrong with it at all and it was evident that when cleaned up it would look virtually the same as it must have done when made, so very many years ago.

But the evening was drawing in and further examination of it had to be deferred for another day. It was necessary to shift it off the field and decide what to do about it later on.

Boris made light work of moving it. Disengaging the drum's drive, he made his way over the edge of the field with the cable running off its drum behind him. Because of the lateral position of his drum he had to go off at an angle so that the cable kept clear of his wheels. It needed a bit of shunting to and fro from side to side, but at length he was over by the roadside hedge opposite the cannon, in a broadside-on position allowing him to use the drum to drag it over. The cable lay snaked on the ground showing how he had weaved to and fro on his way over.

When he engaged the drive on the drum, the slack on the cable was wound in. The cable then tightened. The engine note changed as it slogged slightly to take up the load, then neatly and easily the cannon travelled smoothly across the field!

The heavy, dirt-encrusted ancient weapon from the distant past was finally left placed on the strip of land that Boris's engine was using along that side, well clear of the area not so far ploughed, so that it would not impede Boris's progress up the field next day.

Soon afterwards Boris had re-parked his engine, and with Bob's help it was quickly shut down and covered again for the night.

On their way back they discussed the strange fact of the cannon being there. From time to time objects like it were found in curious locations, often far, it seemed, from anywhere they could have belonged when in use. They immediately thought of places along the channel coast where cannons could still be seen. Dover, Deal and Walmer Castles came to mind straightaway, but there were other places scattered along the coastline where fortifications had existed, and odd cannons still remained placed about for tourists to see.

One thing was certain. The cannon they had found must at some time have been rolled into the ditch, whether to hide it or just get rid of it, nobody would ever know.

Back at their base they all went into Boris's van to discuss the matter with Joe. It was unlikely the farmer would want to be left with it on his field because once they had gone, moving it anywhere at all would be a problem for him. They thought that if they played their cards right, he might agree that if they got it away they could have it. Nobody had any idea if it had market value as an object, but Boris and Joe, being men who worked in the world of metals, were in no doubt that they ought to get it back to their depot and decide at a later date what its future should be. At the very least, even as scrap metal, it was worth shifting.

In the event, when they saw the farmer the next day, after an initial interest in it as something he could never have guessed lay under his ground, he was happy for them to take it away. As an extremely heavy lump of metal it would have posed a problem to him if they just left it dumped there. In addition, he considered the fact that they had, after all, not gone off leaving him with an awkward, unploughed strip in the middle of his new arable plot. With a wry smile, though, he did ask them to let him know if they turned up any pots of gold coins when they ploughed up the rest of the old ditch.

There was little chance during the working day to do anything other than their work, but that evening Joe lost no time in organising things. He and Boris set off for a brisk walk to the nearest local, had a couple of pints, and gained the landlord's permission to use his phone. They knew just the man to contact, and the arrangements they made unfolded with military precision the next day.

Arthur Mason, a close friend of Joe's, drove a heavy-duty 'six-wheeler' Sentinel steam lorry for SKWEC. He and his mate Terry Stokes were currently shifting road-stone to roadworks going on less than four miles from where the ploughing team were. Carrying many tons of stone each journey, the powerful lorry, which 'Sentinels', the makers, preferred to describe as a 'steam wagon' rather than a lorry, shunted to and fro from a central road-materials dump to the construction site, completing several round-trips each day. It was a simple matter for Arthur to make a detour during his dinner-hour to do his workmates from the same firm a good turn.

Shortly after midday the Sentinel lorry rumbled smoothly up the lane on its solid rubber tyres, its comparatively fast-revving engine making the well-known, deeply throbbing sound so characteristic of steam vehicles of its type, of whatever make. Arthur, like many drivers, was a 'Sentinel man'. He particularly liked the lorries which came out of this stable. To a large extent Sentinels specialised in steam 'wagons' so that amongst steam men their name was synonymous with them. Other manufacturers produced them as one of a range of steam vehicles, so design attention was not quite so focused on their singular requirements. Given a choice, Arthur was not alone in opting for a Sentinel.

With ears well attuned to the sound of steam engines, Joe and Boris had picked up the approach of the Sentinel, and when it arrived Joe was at the gate to signal it in, while Boris was by the gun to show it where to park.

As it turned into the field Joe was greeted by a cheerful wave from the two men sitting high up over the front wheels, in the cab. Joe knew they were comfortable up there, warmly seated above the fire, and with good visibility ahead through the V-shaped windscreen set not far back from the front. Beneath them, and in front of them, were the 'works', the whole design being compact and clever, occupying a minimum of space. Below and just in front of their feet, the red glow from the curved ash pan made the cab seem snug, especially with the absence of side windows, but the liberal supply of essential fresh air kept them from getting too cosy and perhaps falling off to sleep along the way.

Arthur trundled along the side of the field and pulled up as directed by Boris alongside the cannon, parking as conveniently as possible to load it aboard. He and Terry jumped straight down from the cab and walked over to examine the relic from the past which had been unearthed by their colleagues. For a minute they stood looking down at the long cannon, its formidable, hefty dead-weight being evidenced by the indentation it had made in the ground in the short time it had lain where it now was.

"Strewth!" said Arthur. "Fancy turning one of those up. I've seen some strange things discovered along hedgerows grubbed up by people making bigger fields so they can use steam ploughs, but never anything like that!"

"That looks to me," observed Terry, "very much like a cannon I've seen mounted on a proper heavy wooden wheeled-base, standing outside one of those Martello towers round the coast near Hythe and Dymchurch. It's about the same size, anyway—I'm sure of that. Somebody ought to make a stand for that one to sit on."

Terry did not know at the time but he had sown a seed that was to germinate. In due course a stand was to be purpose-built for it—a replica of the one it would have lived on originally—on which it was due to stand for a very long time to come. At the moment his train of thought was interrupted by Arthur, whose mind was on more immediate practical matters.

"Bloody good job you didn't hit that thing square-on with a two-foot deep mole-plough, Joe," he commented. "You imagine the effect of the mole-head going under it and its steel blade hitting that lump of metal. Not much 'give' there, Joe. That would have been right nasty that would. I reckon it would have shot the blokes straight over the top of their stand and rocked your engine sideways too. Something would have had to give. Most likely your cable would have snapped."

Joe and Boris nodded in agreement.

"You're right there, Arthur," confirmed Joe. "Boris said the same thing when he came back after dragging it out of the ground the day before yesterday. Most things we hit have enough 'give' to take up a bit of the shock. It always rocks the engine back on its heels and slews the plough a bit, but if we chuck the drive out fast enough we usually get away with it. It would have to be fast though—as fast as greased-lightning—to cope with a thing like that. It would act like a perfect brake. That cannon wouldn't have budged an inch if a mole-plough hit it in the middle and the engine doesn't reckon on winding itself across the ground sideways-on! Hitting that with a mole-plough would have meant a cable-splicing job for us and we'd have been lucky to get away with nothing more serious than that. Makes me nervous even to think about it!"

It was a hazard they faced with all mole-ploughing. The deep, centrally-mounted plough, with its necessarily extremely strong, vertical cutting-blade carrying the torpedo-shaped steel mole at its foot, did not argue with anything. It had no scope for sideways evasion. To make it do its work, slicing through sub-soil which was often hard and unyielding, it had to have a heavily built, stable platform above it. The whole machine was very heavy indeed and real power was needed to drag it along.

Terry, whose activities were confined to roadworks on steam rollers or steam lorries, picked up Joe's reference to cable-splicing.

"Do you mean to say that you blokes can splice one of those great thick cables yourselves, on site?" he asked, somewhat incredulously. The idea of mending a broken cable of that size, making it neat enough to wind on the drum and strong enough to carry its immense loading, seemed a job for an expert.

"Oh yes, of course we can," answered Joe. "But we don't like doing it one little bit. Apart from the job itself, which is a bloody nuisance at the best of times, it knocks out a good hour or so doing the splicing, and by the time we've sorted things out, a cable break takes two hours or more out of our day. And that's money to us."

"Not only that," added Boris, for good measure. "If you think of the strain at both ends of that tough 7⁄8" carbon-steel cable before it snaps, things on each end aren't too happy for a bit. You get all sorts of damage, depending how the cable line lies when the jerk comes."

"I suppose so," said Terry thoughtfully. "No wonder the bloke on the engine doing the pull watches the cable like a hawk all the time. I've often noticed that."

"Yes," added Joe, "you can't afford to look away for a minute, especially dragging cultivators like the one we're using here. It often bucks and jerks like a bucking bronco. On a wet cloggy clay soil it suddenly tightens up hard and you can find a great roll of clay clogging up the front of the tines. The only way to get rid of it before you're landed in right trouble, is to dish the drive, lift the tines above ground, clear off the mass of clay, and start again. You'd be surprised how the engine is rocked to and fro on its wheels when that happens, too. It's not so big it can't move. It fair jumps in its tracks sometimes!"

"Well, come on then, Terry, let's get the thing up on the back and be on our way," said Arthur, in a businesslike manner.

Working together, they dropped down the long, iron-framed, hinged wooden side of the lorry and fished out their 'shear legs' stand with its associated lifting tackle. With practised ease they quickly erected the three long steel legs of their 'shear' to straddle the cannon, and slipped a double-noose of chain from the shear's pulley block, over the cannon's nose.

They dragged the chain-noose back along the barrel as far as they could, being careful to get it beyond where they judged its balancing point to be, then started to heave it up by their high-ratio compound pulley tackle. As they pulled hand over hand on the chain, the cannon lifted off the ground with its heaviest tail-end rising up first, so that the chain's noose slipped further back and tightened around its elegantly tapered barrel. Eventually, well up above the level of the lorry's floor, it hung in a slightly nose-down position as they had intended, with no danger of it slipping out of the noose when it was swung over the ground and loaded.

Before pulling it right up, two ropes had been passed around its neck at its point of suspension. The longer of these was now taken up by Sid, Grant and Bob standing on the far side of the lorry, the other by Arthur and Boris standing on the lorry's floor. When ready to go, Terry, at the tackle, allowed the pulley chain to feed out as the others heaved the gun sideways.

As the cannon swung over, its downward slant momentarily increased, and the two men up on the lorry received a short sharp shock—Boris a physical as well as mental one—though he came to no harm. They were startled, as indeed to a lesser extent were those on the ground, because what happened was so totally unexpected.

Out of the mouth of the cannon shot a black leather bag which bounced off Boris's head to land with a thud at his feet. It was followed just a moment later by a long, metallic, trough-like object—in appearance rather like a length of crude guttering—which slithered out of the gun accompanied by a variety of small packages, all of which Arthur and Boris were able to avoid as they fell to the floor of the lorry to join the first one. Somebody said later that the old gun had fired a warning shot at Boris's thick head to give them both time to get out of the way of what was to follow.

The first reaction was an explosion of laughter from his mates at the sight of Boris's look of pained surprise when the unexpected missile bounced off his head. There had been no reason for any of them to suppose that there was anything in the barrel. What soil had been there when they had heaved it out of the ground had been idly scraped out of its muzzle by Sid using a stick, and they had all commented about the excellent condition of the gun generally. The appearance an instant later of several other objects falling out of the gun excited the immediate interest of everybody and as quickly as possible they worked together to land the cannon successfully in the lorry. A moment later they were all gathered round to examine what it was that had fallen out.

There was a period of intense concentration, highly charged with as yet unspoken expectation. Most people, at one time or another have dreams of finding treasure. For men who work the soil this is particularly true since, from time immemorial, the best way of hiding something of value was to bury it.

In the fields of Kent, especially along and behind the coastal strip where Roman remains abound, there is the added probability of historic relics being unearthed. Many ploughmen from time to time bent to pick up early English or Roman coins. It added spice to life to look for a gift from the gods thrown suddenly in their paths. The group of men around the back of the Sentinel were no exception. For a brief period there was no movement; they just gazed silently at what lay there in front of them.

"Blimey!" said Arthur, breaking the temporary silence. "Just look at that little lot. I wonder how long that's been stashed away up the barrel of the old gun. Might be something worth a bit there—could have been somebody's treasures stuffed up there. Could be they died and nobody else knew about it."

"Must have been, surely," said Joe quietly, apparently deep in thought but inwardly in a state of high excitement. "Shoved down the barrel to be fished out again later on when things were safe and nobody was about."

As yet, none of them made any move to pick anything up. They just took stock of what was there. Far from scrambling to grab things, they had already figured out that whatever was there belonged to all of them, or maybe (perish the thought) to none of them.

Grant, as the foreman, decided he'd better take charge. Except for Arthur and Boris they were all standing along the side of the lorry, leaning on their elbows, lost in their own thoughts, speculating what might be in the mysterious and tantalising packages.

"Collect it all up and shove it over here," he said, breaking the spell and addressing the two on top. "Let's have a look at it together, a bit at a time."

This Arthur and Boris quickly did. The largest item was the long piece of gutter-shaped metal. It was obvious what it had been used for. There was a partly decayed canvas bag about fourteen inches long tied in it, and another lumpy one in a similar condition, also tied in. Along the rest of the length were the remains of some rough cord showing that the other items that had fallen out separately had also been tied inside there, disposed along the trough but lying free from constraint since their retaining cord had long since rotted.

In all, now gathered together, there were six packages and as yet nobody had the slightest idea what was in five of them. The sixth, the long canvas bag, seemed that it might well contain some kind of small handgun, for this sort of form could be seen quite clearly.

Sid stated the obvious.

"Well, I'm damned!" he said. "That bit of metal was used as a push-in tray with all the things tied in it so they could be pushed up the barrel out of sight."

For the moment, attention was directed at that, deferring for a bit what they all eagerly wanted, yet were a little reluctant to do lest it proved disappointing—to open up the bags!

"That's been cut from a sheet of roofing lead," said Boris. "Whoever made it cut a strip and bent it round something like a drainpipe, to shape it like a piece of guttering so it could slide up the barrel easily. And these two handles on the ends were made of strips of lead and riveted on afterwards."

"They weren't only riveted," commented Joe, who had been looking at them. "They were fused on first—you can see how the metal melted. Then I reckon the bloke decided they might not hold so riveted them as well, just to make sure."

The 'handles' Boris had referred to were loops of lead, one at each end, which certainly would have allowed the small collection of objects to be carried easily, as if on a tray. But there was another more important purpose for the presence of the handles, which the others had already spotted and young Bob now voiced.

"I know what they did," he said eagerly. "They slid the tray in and pushed it up the far end, and well out of sight, by a pole or something. When they wanted it out they must have pulled it back by having a hook on the end of the pole to fish it out with."

This was quite obviously how the improvised safe-storage arrangement had worked. That it had been a good idea was demonstrated by the survival, for so many years, of this present little hoard of valued possessions, hidden by someone of long ago, whose name and circumstances nobody was ever to know.

"Let's have a look to see what's there then, Grant," urged Arthur impatiently. "Terry and I have got to get back on the job pretty soon now. We've been away quite long enough and will be expected back with another load before three o'clock."

"Yes, you open them up one at a time, Grant," said Joe. "We'll all see each one as it is undone."

"The first shall be last," announced Boris with a grin, pushing the black leather bag to one side. "That's the bugger that hit me on the head. Let it wait until last!"

That proposition was agreed by all with a laugh, and Grant made a start on the two rotting canvas bags which he cut free from their resting place on the lead tray with his penknife.

The long one did indeed contain a handgun, a quite remarkable one. It was a very old 'Flintlock' pistol, highly decorated and in unbelievably good condition. It had evidently been well-coated with thick grease, for though very dirty, there was no sign of decay on the metal. They all stared at this relic of the past with some awe as Grant turned it over slowly in his hands.

"Bloody hell!" he exclaimed quietly, with obvious deep feeling, his eyebrows raised and eyes wide open with surprise. "This is bloody marvellous, this is. I bet it's worth a tidy sum, never mind what else we've got here."

The use of the word 'we' and the associated reference to potential value struck an immediate resonant chord in the ears of his team mates around him. It was the first mention of possible personal spoils for them all and it sounded like beautiful music in the highly receptive ears of the intensely interested group gathered at the back of the Sentinel. For a few moments all was still, and nobody said anything as they all stared in wonder at the ornate pistol.

Meanwhile, for its part, the powerful Sentinel hissed contentedly as it softly let off steam, reminding those clustered by its side that though it was still at the moment, it was ready to be off at the touch of a lever and was not a passive pushover whose patience could be presumed upon. If it were kept waiting too long it had a habit of disturbing the peace with an ear-splitting blast of steam from its safety-valve. Impatient to be off, it would literally 'blow its top'.

At length Grant put the gun down by his side carefully, and took up the second of the two canvas bags he had cut free. Eagerly now, for the expectations of them all were well and truly raised, he quickly undid the cord that was tying it at the neck and took out its contents.

What was in it astonished and delighted them. It contained three fascinating little models carefully and individually wrapped in some kind of wax-impregnated paper which had excluded the air so effectively that the silver of which they were so obviously made, gleamed in the sunlight almost as though only recently polished.

Nobody had expected that anything so bright could possibly come out of such a dirty, time-engrained and decaying canvas bag. Almost reverentially, not wishing to put such lovely things down on the gritty boards of the lorry's floor, Grant took off his red choker and stood them out on it for all to see.

The three models, in the order in which he unwrapped them were: a tiny two-wheeled field-gun having a barrel reminiscent of the cannon that had just spawned it; a four-wheeled carriage pulled by a pair of horses complete with a driver; and a man pushing a one-wheeled hand-cart that looked rather like an open-framed wheelbarrow with a machine built into it. On close examination this third model proved to be that of a peripatetic knife-grinder.

They were truly magnificent little works of art. The group of men stood gazing with awe at these totally unexpected solid silver objects so miraculously conjured up before their eyes.

Grant now turned his attention to the four remaining packages that had broken free from their positions on the improvised tray. Three of these were leather bags, including, that is, the one that had landed via Boris's head, while the fourth was another canvas bag like the two so far opened. Grant took up the latter and opened it.

As before, what was inside had been protected by the same type of wax-impregnated paper. His audience watched intently as he unwrapped it. So potent was the atmosphere of highly-charged expectation, and so silent and intense the concentration of those around him, that Grant found his hands trembling uncontrollably as he fiddled with the wrapping. His fumbling increased the suspense, but at length he loosened the tight wrapping, got it undone, and what it contained lay exposed in his hands, once more to the astonishment of them all.

Again, the unmistakeable gleam of solid sliver appeared. Neatly tied together were two beautifully-crafted candlesticks with hexagonal bases. Their unusually designed stems had three waists, with the six-sided shape of the base being repeated up the stem and around the flanges that separated the three, gently concave-curving sections of it. They were, however, only a bare five inches tall, looking very small if they had been made as functional candlesticks and not simply as ornamental models. Candles to fit them, the group of men noted, would have had to have been only about a half the diameter of the normal candles they used every day in their caravans.

But that was not all, for the same packet had another treasure to offer up. Tied together in a little bundle were six lovely little teaspoons, more attractive in their design than anything previously seen by the wide-eyed men. They were quite obviously of considerable value and were as wonderfully crafted as the other solid silver objects that Sid now had set out on display on his red scarf.

No conjuror on a stage had ever had more rapt attention from his audience than had Grant as he proceeded to undo the first of the three leather bags he had yet to investigate.

The spell was, however, temporary broken by a muttered though good-humoured comment from Sid who—with his face screwed up in mock disgust—interrupted the proceedings by making a mundane observation, the crudity of which brought the heady dreamlike state of mind of them all, down to earth with a bump.

"You dirty old sod, Boris!" he said, in a very pained and injured tone of voice. "I thought I must be dreaming standing down here seeing Grant unpack that lot—until you let that fart go! Now I know I'm wide awake! Cor! Strewth, Boris! Do you have to treat us to that lot? I heard you easing it out, you crafty old blighter, 'cos your arse is level with my face. I reckon something must have crawled up your arse and died!"

Laughter greeted this remark but the justification for it was not lost on any of them, a confirmation expressed in no uncertain terms by some of the others. Boris, squatting on his haunches up on the back of the lorry by the side of Sid, looked decidedly uncomfortable under this onslaught, having been so explicitly denounced for his covert unsocial behaviour. There was nothing he could say. It was a fair cop!

Grant, though, benefited from this brief, if unpleasantly smelling interruption to the close attention he was giving to what he was doing.

He was able to tackle the first of the three leather bags with steadier hands, for the intensity of the concentration had momentarily relaxed. The bag was gathered at the neck by a strong cord passing through a ring of eyelets, and although the leather had hardened with age it was nonetheless pliable enough for him to be able to manipulate it by his fingers until, with the cord unknotted, he contrived to open up the neck fully. Inside was a packet, which he took out.

Once again the same wax-impregnated paper appeared, and this he unfolded, only to find that there were two separate small canvas bags inside the withdrawn packet.

The feel of these immediately revealed the presence of coins, and the attention of the watchers was again electric. When shot out on to a piece of the retrieved wax paper, the result was less exciting than the previous disclosures, for no glint of precious metals was to be seen. It was however, more in line with what they had all expected from the start, for the two piles of coins from the two bags, were clearly all bronze or copper, which they knew to be unlikely to have a really high value.

In one pile there was a variety of very ancient Roman and foreign coins, mainly of types similar to ones which all of them had seen before at one time or another since they were commonplace in England.

The second pile consisted entirely of English coins, mainly pennies but with a fair number of half-pennies and farthings. Among them there was a separate cloth bag from which Grant tipped a collection of twenty-eight George III pennies, all dated 1797 and all in perfect condition.

An interesting fact that emerged later on when they sorted them out was that the latest date on any coin of all those in this sizeable collection was 1806. It proved to be the most recent date on anything that had been hidden in the cannon and they subsequently figured out that this was the very earliest date that the tray could have been pushed up the barrel. Whoever it was that had stashed the material had done so sometime in the last 120 years. It was, however, to prove to be the only certain fact that ever emerged about the past history of the actual collection, as distinct from the origin of individual elements in it.

There still remained two leather bags. The next one lifted their spirits sky-high again for it contained, equally as well protected as the contents of the other packages, a real example of the sort of treasure they had all along hoped to be lucky enough to find buried in the ground they spent their lives working over.

It was a hoard of old English silver coins. Though not all as gleaming as the silverware objects were, because most would have been well-used when finally put to rest, they were all quite evidently made of pure silver. There were no fewer than seventy-five silver coins, made up entirely of either crowns or half-crowns. No other denominations were present. All of them were within the date-brackets of 1625 to 1685; embracing the reigns of Charles I, Oliver Cromwell as Lord Protector and Charles II.

When sorted they found 2 crowns and 13 half-crowns with Charles I on the obverse side; 8 crowns and 51 half-crowns showing Charles II and just one single crown showing Oliver Cromwell.

But there was yet another very pleasant surprise hidden in this bag. With the weight of all the silver coins now removed, Grant discovered that the leather bag was not yet quite empty! A small cloth bag had a wonderful prize to reveal. In it, to the great delight of them all, were twenty gold coins! Nineteen of them were Charles II, all dated 1663 and the other one was an Oliver Cromwell coin. They were coins none of them had ever heard of before, much sought after—so they were told later—by those few collectors who could afford to buy them. There were 10 one-guinea coins, 6 two-guinea coins, 3 five-guinea coins and the one odd one out—a gold 'unite'. These twenty coins looked to be in very fine condition, almost as though they had only just been made. They were in fact declared later on to be of the highest quality and were classified as 'top mint'.

Staggered by this absolutely unbelievable treasure shot from the mouth of an old cannon which they had so nearly left buried in the field, they hadn't finished yet, for the black leather bag that had hit Boris on the head was still lying unopened on the floor of the lorry.

Grant bent to pick it up and silence settled on the group once more.

It could have been an anti-climax; but it was certainly very far from being that. By shooting out of the gun first, and ending up being opened last, chance could not have arranged things better, for the leather bag was the buried treasure everybody dreamt of but few ever found. It was, quite simply, a bag of gold! In it was a collection of fifty-three English 16th century 22 carat gold coins of a type few people ever see outside of main museum collections that are visited mostly only by keen numismatists, who go seeking specific information.

Subsequently identified by experts were, first of all, 4 Edward VI gold sovereigns minted in the year 1551, made of 22 carat gold and having a face value not of the expected one pound, but curiously of thirty shillings. They were described as heavy, thirty-shilling 'fine sovereigns', not as might have been expected as 'one-and-a-half-pound' sovereigns.

Also present were ten coins of precisely the same description, but minted during the reign of Elizabeth I.

With this total of fourteen 'thirty-shilling sovereigns' were an incredibly thirty-nine other Queen Elizabeth 22-carat gold coins, officially listed as gold 'pound sovereigns', since these had a face value of twenty shillings. Confusion seemed to exist around the use of the word sovereign for coins of other than one-pound face value. In later generations of coins, the group were told that the word 'sovereign' came to signify one pound, and the words pound and sovereign then became synonymous.

These finer details, and much else, became known to the happy group now gleefully examining the astounding collection spread out on the boards of the Sentinel steam lorry, only at a later date. At the time they were conscious only of a bewildering array of gold and silver coinage which they thought must be worth a small fortune.

But despite the high excitement work had to go on, and a decision was made to pack the things away safely until the weekend, by which time they would have been able to determine what to do next.

Meanwhile, they had all decided not to mention their find to anybody at all. That way left them in charge of the course of events. They all knew that any hint of hidden treasure having been unearthed would bring people scurrying to the site from far and wide. There was no future in that, and nobody had any doubt that it behoved them to keep their mouths shut about it. It was a wise decision and subsequent events flowed along more smoothly than they would otherwise have done. They might have been assailed from all sides—bombarded, badgered and harassed into making unwise decisions. As it was they profited by taking it calmly, keeping their own counsel and making their own decisions after seeking confidential, expert advice.

As for the immediate task in hand, Arthur and Terry had to steam off at their best speed to make up for lost time and get their next load of road-stone shifted. The cannon remained under a tarpaulin on the lorry for the rest of the day, but during the evening it was safely deposited in a suitable out-of-the-way corner of the firm's depot.

It had been unloaded by Arthur and Terry using heavy-duty lifting gear, of a type readily available in the SKWEC yard which dealt daily with extremely unwieldy and very heavy equipment of all kinds.

Like the treasure it had contained, the cannon then had to remain 'stashed' until its destiny was decided upon. At this stage in its long history, nobody could have guessed that it had an exciting future ahead of it, and that never again would it be allowed to disappear from sight and be forgotten.

Chapter 21

'TREASURE TROVE'
seven steam men divide the spoils

Back at their home base that evening the five-man ploughing team met in Boris's and Joe's van to discuss what to do—but not immediately, because first of all they wanted to have a more leisurely look at everything they had found.

Keeping the items in their original groups, having previously decided that it might be important not to muddle things up, they laid it all out on the table. Spread out like this their newly-discovered treasure looked quite incredible. For a long time they examined it together, going over it all again piece by piece. By tacit agreement, perhaps because subconsciously they wanted to re-live the exciting experience of seeing it appear bit by bit as Grant had unpacked it, they went over it again in the same order in which it had been exposed to them before. It had been an unforgettable experience, one to savour again while the memory was so fresh.

At length they got down to business and made some decisions. They all knew that hoards of treasure had by law to be declared to the authorities, but what happened after that none of them knew. So the first conclusion was that they had to notify the Police—but not just yet.

Before handing it over they jointly agreed to seek some independent advice so that they could be sure to look after their own interests from the start. They felt they ought to have some prior knowledge of the value of the things they now had in their possession, and also the likely course events would follow after they had handed it all over to the Police. The question was, to whom should they turn for advice in the first place?

It was Sid who came up with the suggestion they adopted.

On the outskirts of Littlebrook lived an elderly, well-known, much respected, retired local doctor. He was rather an irascible man who had a reputation for straight talk and few wasted words. It was certain that his manner had evolved over the long years he had practised in the district, for his workload had been heavy with no time to waste.

Before retirement, his widespread and busy practice made his days so full that his manner to people became brusque to the point where he might often have seemed to strangers to be downright rude. Like most country doctors he ran his own dispensary adjacent to his surgery, so having diagnosed a complaint, if medicine were needed he got up from his desk and dispensed it straight away. Or if immediate attention to a wound or a physical need were required, this also he coped with there and then.

With a surgery full of people and patients spread far and wide to be visited, he could not, and did not, talk about anything except the medical matter confronting him. He was very much the complete medical man, even doing minor surgery—and sometimes not so minor—when circumstances dictated a fast response.

Perhaps the only person with whom he was never noticeably curt or offhand was Nurse Herring, the District Nurse. An Irish lady with a length of service that almost matched his own, she was quick, businesslike, highly efficient in all she did, and exuded knowledge of what she was about. She gave confidence to everybody, including the Doctor. A professional would have noted that they had a healthy respect for one another and functioned when together as an effective, no-nonsense team.

But to any person whose need was dire, their innate kindness shone through. This local people knew, and because of it they submitted without demur to a bit of military-style discipline when the pressure was on for the Doctor or the Nurse. Both of them were aware that it was said of them that they had been tarred with the same brush. Perhaps they both saw it as a compliment.

Since he had retired, though, those who had much to do with him discovered that all of his somewhat off-putting manner when at work had been just a front, worn by him as a necessary part of the job, like the white coat he wore in his surgery.

For several years Sid had looked after the Doctor's extensive garden for him on a part-time basis. It had become too much for the Doctor and his wife to maintain on their own so Sid gave them a hand with the heavier work.

The Doctor loved his garden and spent a lot of time in it after his retirement. When Sid was there they often worked together on the various tasks that engaged them, and Sid got to know him very well. When speaking of him to a mate one day, Sid paid the Doctor a compliment that would have made him smile.

"The old Doc's all right," he'd said. "He's just like any normal bloke when you get to know him. Nothing wrong with him at all!"

As a judgement of character it was as concise and unequivocal as a typical diagnosis by the Doctor of a supposed, but imagined, illness!

Sid knew the Doctor to be keen on antiques in general and had a particular interest in coins, of which he had quite a considerable collection. It was a hobby started when he was a boy, and continued off and on all his life.

Sid's suggestion that they should seek the Doctor's advice was accepted with enthusiasm by his friends, so without further ado he visited him to enlist his help. As he rightly suspected, his gardening companion was not only willing to assist but was positively anxious to see what they had found as soon as he could. A meeting was arranged, to take place at his house on the coming Saturday morning, the first convenient time they could all gather together.

The day dawned bright and clear, a cheerful day full of promise. At ten o'clock, bang on time, the five trooped down the pebble-covered drive to the front door of the Doctor's pleasant, detached house. Its red-brick walls were partly covered by climbing plants. Kept under control by Sid, the variety of trailing plants produced a profusion of blooms from springtime right through the summer until late autumn, year after year. Already, healthy green shoots were beginning their vigorous upward growth, heralding another blaze of colour to delight the Doctor, his wife, and visitors to the house in the weeks and months ahead.

Alongside the house, standing outside a neat, detached garage—which, made with the same bricks and with a corresponding attractive, red-tiled, pitched Mansard roof, complemented the house very pleasingly—stood the Doctor's maroon Austin Seven saloon car. The well-cared-for little car had to travel many miles away from where it lived before it began to pass people who did not recognise it, and greet it with a cheery wave.

Waiting in his hallway, looking through the windows of the half-glazed porch, the Doctor saw his expected visitors coming down the drive and had the door open ready for them to come in as soon as they arrived.

In a matter of minutes they were seated around the extended table in the Doctor's dining room, and shortly afterwards the treasure yielded up by the ancient cannon was unpacked, item by item, for the astonished Doctor to examine. His wife, knowing about the purpose of their visit, joined them for what was a once-in-a-lifetime experience for both of them. They were amazed by what they saw and listened with much interest to the description of how it had been stored up the barrel of the gun on its secret, removable lead tray.

Over cups of coffee and home-made cakes, thoughtfully prepared in advance by the Doctor's wife, they discussed what should be done.

It soon became evident that Sid had done his friends a good turn in suggesting the Doctor as a man who might be able to help them. He turned out to be a happy choice in more ways than one.

To begin with, his long interest in coins had made him familiar with the legalities surrounding the whole question of 'Treasure Trove'!

His avid listeners were delighted with what he had to tell them on this matter. They knew they had to make known details of their find, but had vague, uncomfortable ideas that once having done so, by one way or another, they would have kissed it goodbye. Maybe, for example, the farmer would snaffle the lot as, after all, it was found on his ground. It was true he'd actually given them the cannon, but that did not mean that what was in it would be deemed to be theirs as well. They need not have worried.

The Doctor explained that all gold and silver coins, plate or other objects made of precious metals found hidden in the soil or in a building, if the true owner was not known, had to be handed over forthwith to the Crown. Legally, it was the property of the Crown. The established procedure was that any hoards of the type they had found, had to be handed over to the local Coroner. Strangely, or so it seemed to them, it was a part of a Coroner's duty and responsibility to handle such matters. The hoard was declared 'Treasure Trove' and the only parties concerned with its fate were the Crown and the finders. Nobody else came into it at all!

In all such cases there were two possible outcomes, both of which were music to the ears of the five when spelled out to them.

"Either," the Doctor announced, much enjoying being the conveyor of such glad tidings, "the Coroner may decide, having duly thoroughly investigated and listed what was there, as well as satisfying himself that the circumstances by which the hoard was found were all above board, simply to give it back to the finders, who would then became by law its legal owners, or, if it had extreme rarity value or was of singular historical importance, it would be retained by the State, in which case the finders would receive a reward of an amount proportional to the prevailing market value of what they had found.

The Doctor later told a friend that it was as though he had pulled a 'smile switch', for as the significance of what he had said made its happy impact, the five faces staring at him so intently, hanging on his every word, suddenly simultaneously grinned from ear-to-ear. It was an experience for the Doctor that was the more pleasant because the nature of his calling had so often put him in the role of the announcer of bad news to long faces, made all the longer by what he'd had to say.

This wholly favourable working of the law of the land seemed too good to be true, and the inevitable question followed. It came from Grant, the foreman, perhaps because he could already picture the farmer's face when he heard the news and he might well be the person who had to tell him!

"Do you mean to say," he asked, with an air of disbelief, "that the farmer has no say in it? That he can't claim it even though he owns the ground?"

"That's right! That's the law!" responded the Doctor emphatically. "It has nothing to do with him at all. It's the law of 'finders-keepers', but only if the finder declares his find immediately, and only after the Coroner had made his decision. Strange as though it may seem, anyone who doesn't report such a find may be guilty of a criminal offence. For once, just for once, honesty gets its just reward!"

That further comment was enough to remove doubt from all their minds, for Grant had not been alone in finding it difficult to believe his ears. The others were also comforted by the Doctor's answer and were all glad Grant had put the question.

But his knowledge of the law of Treasure Trove was not the only factor which made the Doctor a fortunate man for the five who had gone to him for advice.

By good fortune, though not unexpectedly when they later thought it out, the Doctor knew the local district Coroner very well. He also, again because his previous day-to-day duties had brought them into contact from time to time, knew the Police Sergeant from the Kent County Police Force, who was responsible for the supervision of a small group of village policemen scattered about the area. The Sergeant's territory embraced the farm where the find had been made.

When the Doctor offered to deal with the matter for them and arrange to meet both of these key figures on the following Monday to set the wheels turning, they accepted with alacrity. Meanwhile they were able to leave their valuable collection in the safe custody of the Doctor, itself something of a relief for them in view of the low security of their living accommodation and their long hours of absence from it on each working day.

Getting nearer to the aspect of the matter that was of greatest interest to them, they then asked the Doctor his views on the way in which they ought to sell things, if, as now seemed likely, the Coroner returned all, or some of them.

On this important issue the Doctor was equally helpful. To begin with he urged upon them the advisability of doing nothing at all until they had found out a great deal about the possible value of everything.

So far as the coins were concerned, the gold and silver ones were outside of his personal experience. His interest had been in collecting coins from all over the world rather than those of known high value made of precious metals, which, in the main, he could not afford to buy and store away. Like many people, his ever present hope as he pursued his hobby was that he would discover among those coins he acquired, some of rarity and value.

His experience had taught him that sharks abounded in the world of dealers, whose abiding ambition was always to buy valuable items, such as those the ploughing team had found in the cannon, for as little as possible, trading on the ignorance of the owners.

So his best advice to them was to list the coins as accurately as they could—and in this task he offered to help them—and write to the British Museum in London to see what they had to say about them.

If they described the circumstances in which the two hoards of coins made of precious metals were found—stressing that although discovered at the same time, they had been distinctly separately packed when stored away—the Doctor was sure the people at the Museum would be very interested and might well have something useful to say about the disposal of them. He felt that though not Treasure Trove, they ought also to send details of the copper and bronze coins, for the same reason.

Finally, he offered to take the remaining items that same afternoon to show an antique dealer friend of his who ran an 'old-fashioned' business in Canterbury, to see if he could come up with any information about them. The three attractive little silver models had markings on them that were probably those of known makers. Similarly, the Doctor pointed out markings on the two candlesticks and on the six silver spoons. He was sure that his friend would be able to identify these marks and might be able to find out some details about their age and places of origin.

He was not so sure about the Flintlock pistol because, so far as he was aware, his friend did not handle such things very often, if at all. There were, of course, specialists in places like London, Birmingham and Manchester who dealt with nothing else but firearms. However, the Doctor said he would ask his friend's advice about that too, if they wished.

This offer was gladly accepted by the five of them. It was a start towards putting them in a position to make sensible decisions about their treasure. Thanking him gratefully for his ready and generously offered assistance, the five left the Doctor's house in a state of happy expectations, and set off in high spirits to enjoy the rest of the weekend.

True to his word the Doctor consulted his expert friend during the afternoon. During the evening he wrote out such details as his friend had been able to give him about the various items he had shown him. Then he carefully sorted through the coins and compiled lists suitable for the men to send off to the British Museum.

By Monday evening all the things found in the cannon were in the possession of the Coroner, and the police had full details of the find, having seen and listed it before it was passed to the Coroner.

On Tuesday morning the Police Sergeant visited the ploughing team to get all the information he needed for his official records. His visit caused the men some relief on two scores. In the first place they had become vaguely anxious lest the Doctor should be robbed of their treasure! When they no longer had it in their possession, the awful possibility that they might lose it all in some way made then decidedly uneasy.

Secondly, the whole business of the Coroner, being something completely outside their experience, had seemed so strange that when they had discussed it over the weekend it had seemed a little unreal. The Police Sergeant's confirmation that the things were now in the hands of the Coroner dispelled these nagging uncertainties and worries. He left them feeling reassured that everything was on course.

That evening, following an arrangement they had made with the Doctor on the Saturday, they all went again to his house to hear what he had found out from the Canterbury antique dealer. He had some interesting news for them.

Once more they sat around the dining-room table where the Doctor had some papers prepared for them to see.

Dealing first with the three silver models, they had been positively identified by his friend. All of them had been made in Amsterdam, though by three different manufacturers. The four-wheeled carriage drawn by a pair of horses had been made in 1749, the knife grinder in 1737, and the field-gun on its two-wheeled carriage in 1776. The dealer had never seen models like them before, but had succeeded in finding a reference to them by studying his specialised professional books.

What they had thought to be candlesticks made to take small candles, or otherwise possibly simply made as ornaments, were in fact properly described as taper-sticks. They were identified as having been made by Matthew Cooper of London in the period 1717-1718. His friend thought them to be particularly good examples of silver taper-sticks, and in fine condition.

The set of silver teaspoons he thought to have been manufactured around the year 1760.

All the silverware pieces had therefore been made in the 18th century.

As predicted by the Doctor, his friend had not been familiar with the Flintlock pistol, but was very impressed indeed by its finely-made and extremely ornate appearance. He found the date 1690 inscribed on it and also evidence that it was of Spanish origin. He felt sure that it was a rare and valuable pistol.

The Canterbury dealer was of course inwardly very reluctant to see this entire rich material pass out of the area, or more particularly out of his shop! However, he was a fair man, and indeed it was the firm's reputation for fairness that had kept them in business for so many years as respected experts in this historic city. Moreover, the Littlebrook Doctor was a personal friend as well as a valued customer, so it behove him to give his best advice on the wisest way to dispose of the goods.

This he did, and the Doctor passed it on to the five men with him. His advice was that they should pass the entire collection, or that part of it returned to them by the Coroner should he retain part of it, to a leading London Auction House. In their hands it would be property evaluated, catalogued and subsequently sold, in a well-advertised sale which brought together people who knew what things were worth in the prevailing world market, and would compete to buy.

In the meantime he had agreed with the Doctor's suggestion that they should send details of the coins to the British Museum, who would certainly be interested from a historic point of view in hearing how and where they were found. They might have some interesting observations to make about the find, and maybe advice on disposing of them. What they would not do, the dealer said, was value them. Values depended entirely upon the market place, upon who wanted what at any given time, and upon the rarity of an item. It was not part of the Museum's job to enter into this fray, except in so far as they had to do so if they wanted to buy something themselves for the Museum.

The Doctor had kindly made neatly-prepared lists of the coins for the men to send to the British Museum. He had separated them into the three groups they were in when found, giving full details of those in the two precious-metal hoards, but only outline details of the bronze and copper ones, including only such information as he considered worthy or of note.

He arranged the two important lists as shown below:

GOLD & SILVER COINS FOUND IN BURIED CANNON

GROUP 'A' (all 22 carat gold coins)

REIGN	DATE	DESCRIPTION	QUANTITY
EDWARD VI	all 1551	'FINE' SOVEREIGN 30/-	4
ELIZABETH I	various	--------- ditto --------	10
ELIZABETH I	various	'POUND'SOVEREIGN 20/-	39

GROUP 'B' (mixed silver and gold coins)

REIGN	DATE	DESCRIPTION	QUANTITY
CHARLES I	1636 1637	SILVER CROWN	2
CHARLES I	various	SILVER HALF-CROWN	13
CHARLES II	various	SILVER CROWN	8
CHARLES II	various	SILVER HALF-CROWN	51
OLIVER CROMWELL	1658	SILVER CROWN	1
OLIVER CROMWELL	1649	GOLD 'BROAD' UNITE	1
CHARLES II	all 1663	GOLD ONE-GUINEA	10
CHARLES II	ditto	GOLD TWO-GUINEA	6
CHARLES II	ditto	GOLD FIVE-GUINEA	3

In the event of the group deciding to take his advice and send everything to be sold at Auction, the Canterbury antique dealer offered his personal assistance. Having had a long business relationship with Christie's of London, a firm of Fine Art Auctioneers & Valuers established in 1766, he recommended that they choose this prestigious firm to sell it all for them. If they decided to do this the dealer offered to organise the whole transaction for them and to transport the valuable collection personally to Christie's.

The antique dealer made no secret of the fact that he would profit himself from this arrangement since he would expect to receive a fair commission from Christie's insofar as what would be his 'finder's fee'. There was nothing underhand or dishonourable about that. It was, after all, his business, and the group would certainly need a trustworthy person to act for them in a matter far removed from their own personal experience.

In telling them of this offer, so that they did not get the wrong idea, the Doctor was careful to point out that his friend's payment from Christie's would in fact come from their auctioneer's commission and would not be deducted from the team's final proceeds. He explained that the auctioneer's commission was on a fixed scale, worked out as a percentage of the selling price. That made it advantageous, he told them, for Christie's to get the highest price they possibly could for the goods they sold.

This last comment made good listening to the five seated at his table. It was nice to know that somebody would be striving to push up the price of their treasure as far as it would go!

With this comforting thought in mind, the five of them had no hesitation in deciding there and then to accept the Canterbury dealer's offer. They asked the Doctor to let him know that they would pass to him everything they got back from the Coroner for sale by Christie's in London, and thanked him for his help and advice.

Glad with the way things were turning out, they thanked the Doctor for all his assistance and returned happily to the site.

That Thursday afternoon they left the site and set off to travel to the next place on their list—but not without saying goodbye to the chagrined farmer from whose ground they had literally 'lifted' the treasure.

Earlier in the week the Police Sergeant, much to the relief of Grant who had not relished the prospect of having to break the news himself, had made an 'official' visit to the farmer to put him in the picture.

He was able to relate that the steam ploughmen working on his farm had acted entirely within the requirements of the law in passing the treasure they had found under his ground direct to the Crown, and not to him. Bitter pill though it was to swallow, there was nothing the farmer could do but accept the situation with good grace. But he didn't exactly beam from ear to ear with radiant pleasure when told of the remarkable good fortune of the men working at his expense, on his land!

The Sergeant, a keen observer of human reactions, thought that the hint of a painful smile which twisted the farmer's face when he realised he was confronted by a reality he could not change, was wrung from his reluctant facial muscles with as much resignation and acceptance of the inevitable as a confession from a poacher caught with pheasants in his pockets.

He guessed, quite correctly, that the visibly squirming farmer would lose no time after he'd left the premises in telephoning his solicitor to check the legal accuracy of what he had just been told. He also guessed, as he rode his motorbike up the lane, that the discouraging answer the farmer would inevitably have dripped apologetically into his red-flushed ear would not stop him from immediately telephoning the Coroner to make sure the solicitor was correct. And the Police Sergeant was quite right there too!

"That will push his blood pressure up a notch or two," he said to himself, "and so will the couple of stiff tots of Johnnie Walker he will sink immediately afterwards!"

The Sergeant was right again, for the third time, but—as so often happens—he had no way of knowing that his surmises were bang on the nail. That was a pity, because he was not always right. It would have done his professional morale a lot of good to learn how accurately he had read his man.

All of that personal psychological turmoil on the part of the farmer was lost to the happy steam ploughing team when they chuffed off his land. The farmer had arrived just before they were due to leave, and with as much goodwill as he could muster, thanked them for their good work in the fields and wished them well on their journey. He could not, however, forbear from making the comment that he wished *he* had ploughed the hedgerow himself, for not having done more than grub out the trees and bushes had cost him dearly.

"If I decide to remove any more hedges," he said to them with a rueful smile, "I'll see to it that we finish the job off ourselves before you fellows get here!"

So, all in all, they parted on amicable terms. When they had gone, the farmer gained some solace by thinking that if he and his men had indeed dug up the cannon themselves, there would have been no possibility at all that they would have tipped it up on end. It would either have been dumped along the side of the field, or at best simply sold off as scrap metal. This last thought set him wondering how many old guns had been dropped into a furnace, taking with them similar hoards of treasure without anyone ever knowing about it.

When the story broke, as break it did in the Press that weekend, since by midweek a number of people had already been involved in the matter, the same thought occurred to many people. All around the coastline and inland at historic fortifications, clandestine visits were made by hopeful treasure-seekers to probe deep down into the darkness of the barrels of numerous ancient cannons sitting innocently on display in many places.

Whether or not anything of value was ever found in these long-retired cannons whose privacy was so suddenly and rudely violated, is not known. There was certainly no publicity about it in the months immediately following the remarkable discovery by the steam men, so if anything were found the 'finders' kept quiet about it. This they probably would have done anyway, because too much publicity might have queered their pitch by releasing a torrent of eager treasure-seekers to clean out other guns before they could get to them to repeat their success.

Perhaps it was fitting, salt-in-the-wound though it was, that the farmer himself was the one to feel the first soft breeze of the gale of publicity that was to follow. It seems highly likely that his 'phone calls' after the Police Sergeant's visit and his baleful bleating to numerous other people that day, was the spark that lit the bushfire.

Less than an hour after the sound of the two steam engines had faded into the distance on the Thursday afternoon, a young reporter knocked on the farmer's door to ask him about the treasure. His unhappy face and obvious disquiet when asked about the episode, communicated itself to the keen-eyed young man so that the very first article on the matter which appeared in the stop-press column of the local paper next morning, bore the heading:

'GLOOMY FARMER BEMOANS LOSS OF TREASURE TROVE'

There followed a brief paragraph covering the salient facts with a promise of a full feature article the next week. The enterprising reporter, having filed his copy on

Thursday afternoon, maintained his lead because that very evening he sat with the team in one of their caravans at their new location and listened with great interest to the whole story.

A succession of reporters arrived at the farmer's house during the next few days and his telephone bell rang more times about the treasure than it ever did about farming matters. All the enquiries bounced off the farmer and descended upon the steam ploughing team, following the trail already blazed by the eager young local man who had landed his very first scoop.

In the next week a whole crop of articles was published in local papers around the towns of east Kent, as well as in the main county papers on the next Friday.

Naturally, with a story of such universal appeal, some national papers also picked it up, and the five men received instant fame, albeit for only a brief period of their lives. Their families and friends gathered articles about them avidly, and family scrapbooks bearing snip-outs were created, destined to carry the story down the years.

Once the men had been met, stories giving personal details about them, together with photographs of them with their traction engines and ploughing gear, appeared in several papers.

The feature article promised by the first reporter had a whole page of pictures, including an action shot of the two engines with the cable-drawn cultivator. Taken cleverly at an oblique angle, the staff photographer contrived to make a memorable picture of one engine in the distant background, with Sid and Grant riding their chariot-like cultivator approaching the other engine in the foreground. There was also one bearing the caption 'Conference in the Box' showing the five of them seated around the table in Boris's and Joe's van, as they had been on the evening of their discovery.

These series of articles made good publicity for their firm. To see popping up in various papers the always photogenic, powerful traction engines shining in the sunlight with the initials SKWEC embossed on their boiler name plates showing up boldly, was a pleasure to the firm's management. The description of the ploughing team at work actually brought in new contracts because the men came over as a happy, efficient team.

An enterprising national newspaper persuaded SKWEC to re-enact the moment of discovery, showing the cannon suspended with its nose pointing downwards at angle of about 45°, over the back of the Sentinel steam wagon. Boris and Arthur were up on the lorry as they had been at the time, with the others hanging on the ropes pulling the gun sideways, while Terry was handling the pulley-chain under the shear-legs.

It took a few tries before the photographer got a superb shot of the tableau, complete with the black leather bag—softly packed with flock—having apparently just shot out of the cannon, impacting with Boris's head. His assistant had practised tossing the bag on the count of three, until they got it just right. The team all enjoyed their brief experience of working on an improvised 'film set'.

The article duly appeared, given pride of place in the next Saturday edition, this being the one which sold the most copies each week of this national daily paper.

The story was headed:

'BOLT FROM THE BLUE FOR BORIS'

Under the associated picture was the caption:

'GOLDEN SHOT'
'Engine driver gets shot in the head by buried treasure'

There followed a detailed account of the whole exciting day in the lives of the steam ploughing team. The young local reporter had the satisfaction of seeing part of his own article quoted, and with it was his paper's picture of the ploughing team in action.

The account concluded with a paragraph that was to have widespread repercussions because it set off a new treasure-seeking craze which spread far and wide—not only in the UK—but also later on in many places overseas, where innumerable old weapons of war were proudly displayed. The barrel of a cannon ceased thereafter to be a safe haven for the stashing away of valuables.

The words that caused the craze were:

'It seems inconceivable that nobody else ever stored hoards of treasure in such an insecure place. Possibly, all over the world, stuffed deeply down the barrels of ancient guns, lies fabulous treasure as yet unsuspected and unfound! People have a habit of stuffing valuables out of the way when danger threatens. They do this as an individual act, not following a debate with others.

Where better to stow something away safely than down the barrel of a large ancient cannon, permanently parked as they so often are in a fixed location, and unlikely ever to be arbitrarily moved, because of their great weight and unwieldy form?

Unhappily for the secretive hoarders, they not infrequently die without ever telling anybody of their hidden treasure. It is left planted in secret places like this, where it may stay for many, many long years before some unknown person happens to chance upon it in the distant future, as indeed did the lucky men of the steam ploughing team, when they dug up the treasure-loaded cannon in a field deep in the pleasant countryside of Kent.'

After a flurry of activity and excitement over a period of two or three weeks, the fun died away and life for the team settled down more or less to normal. But there was one difference. Whereas previously they went about their daily life in the quiet rural districts in total anonymity, meeting only those people associated with the work they were doing, they were now known to a large number of people who had read or heard about them. Intrigued by the story of their good fortune, this inspired a succession of people to seek them out or contact them, more often than not hoping by devious means to profit in some way themselves. The team were, however, far too shrewd to allow anybody to break through their guard, and no outsider was to profit from these casual approaches.

While waiting for the Coroner's decision they decided to write to the British Museum, as had been suggested, describing how they had found the treasure, and in particular sending a copy of the detailed lists prepared for them by the Doctor, of the gold and silver coins in the two collections.

For good measure they also sent such details as they and he had recorded of the bronze and copper coins, although they knew already that these had no significant value. They also gave brief details of the other items, citing the information about them provided by the Canterbury antique dealer.

The reply they received, a copy of which is reproduced on the following page, had some interesting observations to make:

THE BRITISH MUSEUM,
Department of Coins & Medals,
London, WC1

2nd May 1927

Mr. Grant Carter,
Ivy Cottage,
Grove River Road,
Littlebrook,
Kent

Dear Mr. Carter,

Thank you for your letter of 25th April, the content of which has created much interest here.

We think it very likely that the two packets of precious metal coins were originally each a separate 'hoard', concealed and discovered at different times by different persons, and under circumstances the details of which we shall not of course ever know.

What is significant is that the groupings of the dates on the coins are approximately one hundred years apart, the all-gold collection being grouped in the 16th century, whilst the mixed silver and gold collection is of the 17th century. We feel certain that these two collections were originally in no way connected, each having been hidden and subsequently found, by quite different people.

Clearly, from what you say of the other objects found, the person who put them in the barrel of the cannon must have done so no earlier than the year 1806, since the most recently dated coin in the bronze collection is the George III penny of that date. We notice that you have twenty-eight George III pennies all dated 1797. We think this may be significant since this was the year when pennies of that type were minted for the first time, by Matthew Boulton of Soho, near Birmingham. Produced on new steam-powered presses, these impressive pennies created a lot of interest and are still regarded as some of the finest coins ever used in this country. They are not rare although they still attract much interest. Because of their appearance, they are sometimes called 'cartwheel' pennies.

It seems possible that the twenty-eight you have were actually purchased at the time of issue by one person, who bought them and saved them, perhaps as an investment, as people often do with new issues. Since they are all in perfect mint condition, it is evident that they have been stored away safely from the day they were purchased.

It is not inconceivable that the person who bought them may be the one whose collection of coins it was that was found in the cannon along with the other valuable objects, though we hasten to say this can be counted only as a possibility rather than a probability.

How the two hoards of valuable coins came together in the first place, and then to be in the possession of the person who finally put them into the cannon with the other objects, is a matter of pure conjecture. My colleagues and I have been much entertained in thinking of possible explanations. One cannot exclude the possibility that the two hoards may have been stolen from a common source at some time in their history, though not necessarily, one should add, by the person who subsequently hid them in the cannon.

It is of course this total lack of knowledge about the rightful owners of property such as this, which allows a find to be classified as Treasure Trove. Once the Coroner has made his decision and officially declared the gold and silver items of your find to be Treasure Trove, if a decision is made under the existing Law to allow you to keep your find, all the property will then start a new life as your legal possessions—to be retained, or disposed of, as you think fit.

We congratulate you and your colleagues on your good fortune in discovering this intriguing collection.

You intimate in your letter that if returned to you by the Coroner, you will be selling all the items discovered, in order to divide their value amongst your group. We urge you not to be precipitate in doing this. Our advice, if we may presume to offer it, is that you have it all valued by a firm of national repute, and then take their advice on how best to dispose of it. Due to the publicity which attends the finding of 'treasure' such as this, it is our experience that people in your position rapidly attract eager potential buyers, but it is seldom the case that these opportunists pay the true market value of the goods involved. We are sure you will find that a little patience in this respect will be to your ultimate advantage.

If we can be of any further assistance to you, please do not hesitate to contact us.

Yours sincerely,

S N Randigroat

Sidney N. Randigroat (Assistant Keeper)

The letter certainly confirmed that their decision to send everything to Christie's of London was the right one. Events had also proved the Museum correct about potential buyers homing in on finders of valuable things. In the interim period, since the widespread press publicity, over fifty people from all over the country had already approached them. The majority had sent letters addressed to SKWEC marked 'Please Forward', but others had done a detective job and tracked them down to wherever they were working.

Most of these visitors seemed genuine people, but a few the team didn't take to at all. These latter fell into three categories. Some were smarmy smart-Alecks; these were particularly disliked. Others were loftily condescending, addressing them as a superior being talking to 'hayseeds'—giving the impression that they were prepared, as a special favour, to spend some of their valuable time buying the things off them. The third type, recognised at first sight, were scruffy, shifty, shady, seedy, short-changing characters who might just as well have posed as the Archbishop of Canterbury as an expert in valuable antiques.

Except for these last types who were sent packing with a flea in their ear, all enquirers—postal and visiting alike—were told that everything to come up for sale would be available from Christie's of London at a future auction. No doubt this weeded out the get-rich-quick people straight away, but genuine potential buyers most probably got in touch with Christie's to be put on their mailing-list to receive details of the appropriate sale when it materialised.

In due course the eagerly-awaited decision from the Coroner's Office reached the expectant team. There was some delay because no doubt experts had to be consulted before releasing each item as having no unique value, or importance, justifying its retention by the State. In the event, everything without exception was officially given back to the finders with a document verifying their legal right of possession of the objects listed. From the outset it had been agreed among the team of five to split the proceeds seven ways. It seemed only fair to include Arthur and Terry as equal partners in the affair, since without their help probably all the treasure would still be stuffed up the cannon's barrel.

So, in official records, and in precise legal terms, the Treasure Trove was awarded in equal shares with respect to its market value, to the seven names listed. The documentation applied only to the items made of precious metals.

When the Coroner's decision was made known, Boris had already left the team for his summer season with the fairground travellers and another driver had joined Joe for the remainder of the ploughing itinerary. Joe got a message off to Boris immediately, to let him known the good news.

As previously agreed, all the collection was taken by the Canterbury antique dealer to Christie's of London. Everything, that is, except for the collection of bronze and copper coins which were not deemed by Christie's to be worthy of a separate entry in the next appropriate sale. The antique dealer valued them as being worth no more than about £10 to a dealer. Eventually, when he explained this to his friend on his return from London, the Doctor offered £21 for them, neatly priced because he knew of the proposed seven-way split, and this gave them £3 each, which they gladly accepted. It was their first pay-out from their jointly-owned treasure.

The all-important sale was to take place in July. About one month before the due date, the antique dealer kindly sent Grant a copy of Christie's catalogue listing what was to be included in the sale. He marked up in it the items owned by Grant and his colleagues. It gave them quite a thrill to see their possessions described in the impressive-looking catalogue.

Before the date of the sale the steam-ploughing round was finished and the members of the team split up. Joe went off to drive a steam-roller on some road works; Grant went with a traction engine driver towing a mobile, heavy-duty sawing bench to a woodland site where they had to saw a number of large tree trunks into planks; Sid joined a team gearing up for harvesting work; and young Bob was put into the workshops as part of his training programme. Meanwhile Boris was still enjoying life with the fair.

Because of their roving commissions, by agreement with their boss they had all given their addresses as c/o SKWEC, so that Christie's could send them their keenly awaited cheques without the hazard of letters having to be forwarded from place to place as they moved about.

When seven identical, white foolscap envelopes bearing the well-known auctioneer's name embossed on the top left-hand corners arrived at the offices of SKWEC, their Boss smiled with pleasure.

This was a job he had looked forward to, for he knew that the date they were all waiting for—the day of the sale—had passed a few days previously, and their pay-out had clearly arrived. So he took it upon himself to drop everything and set off in his car to deliver the letters personally. It was a day he thoroughly enjoyed, and long remembered, because it was unique.

He had given a bit of thought to this pleasant duty, and he had decided to go first to Grant Carter, the ploughing team foreman. He had an idea that he was going to be asked if the firm would handle the cheques by passing them through its account and paying out cash to the men—a usual favour asked by employees when they had personal cheques to deal with. Few had bank accounts, but most had various forms of savings accounts—usually the Post Office—into which cheques could of course be paid. More often than not, though, people preferred a direct cash payment from their employer, or from an accommodating shopkeeper. As yet, he did not know how much money was involved, but from the descriptions of what they had found, it seemed probable that each would get a three figure sum.

He was soon to be proved right.

On arrival at the woodland site he parked his car and was greeted by two sounds he knew so well. Penetrating the stillness and peace of the woodlands was the shrill whining sound of a large circular saw slicing its way along a heavy tree trunk. As a background accompaniment to this high-pitched whine he could hear the pronounced barking of a single-cylinder traction engine under load. He was spotted as he walked across the clearing to the site, but stood well back and waited until they had finished their cut before he went over to buttonhole Grant.

"I'd like a word with you, Grant," he said smilingly, without preamble. "Tell the fellows to have a break for ten minutes. There's something I'd like to discuss with you."

Grant's three companions were only too glad to take a breather and they sat themselves down with their backs to a pile of tree-trunk sections that were waiting to be sawn into planks. The seasoned-looking, whiskered and bearded driver up on the stand of the 8 HP Garrett engine, with a wave to his Boss whom he'd known for many years—long before he became the Boss—adjusted the regulator so that his engine settled down to an effortless tick-over, and then jumped down to join the others for a welcome rest.

Some distance away Grant and his visitor also sat themselves down on a stack of newly-cut planks.

"Got something here that might interest you," said the bringer of good tidings with a broad smile. So saying he took the long white envelope out of his inner pocket and handed it to Grant, who spotted straight away that it was from Christie's.

"Thanks," he said, his hand trembling slightly, reaching out to accept the letter. "This looks like the one we've been waiting for!"

With slow deliberation he took a penknife from his waistcoat pocket, opened it and carefully slit the envelope by running the sharp blade across it under the flap. Reaching inside he pulled out several sheets of paper folded together and—fumbling a little—opened them up to examine what was there. Grant's eyes, on a top priority mission, focused in with undisguised haste to what mattered most—the place where the amount was printed.

"Blimey!" he said, apparently startled by what he saw. "Phew—just look at that! Strewth!"

"What's up?" asked his Boss with a wide smile. "Good news, I hope!"

Grant passed the cheque to him without further comment.

Ornately printed across the top, in large imposing letters, with the heading 'Christie's of London', the cheque was made payable to Grant Carter Esq., a form of address which to Grant seemed in itself to endow the impressive-looking cheque with even greater importance. Beneath the name was the boldly written inscription, 'One Hundred and Fifty Seven Pounds, Thirteen Shillings and Six Pence' and alongside, written with an equal flourish were the figures £157.13s.6d. The cheque, which succeeded in looking more impressive than many bank notes, was signed by a director of the company.

"That should do your morale a bit of good!" said his Boss, clapping him on the shoulders. "Congratulations, Grant. That's marvellous! Excellent news!"

"Never thought it could ever be as much as that!" commented Grant, still visibly shaken."We thought it would perhaps be between £10 and £50 each. But privately I'm sure we all thought that £50 was just pie-in-the-sky wishful thinking!"

Grant, inviting his Boss to look through the documents with him, then studied the three sheets that were with the cheque.

The first was a letter explaining that the total sum payable to them had been divided into seven equal shares, as they had instructed, and that the enclosed cheque represented Grant's share. It went on to explain that the two attached documents were statements showing how the amounts were arrived at.

The top one of these listed the grand totals only, showing the total price received at the sale for all the items, treated as a group; the auctioneer's commission on this total; the net balance; and the names and addresses of the seven persons among whom this net total was divided.

The amounts shown were £1103.14s.6d as the net balance, yielding £157.13s.6d as the sum payable to each of the seven. This particular document Christie's recommended each of them to retain, as it constituted a statement indicating that the Treasure Trove had been equally divided, as instructed by the Coroner's Office.

The second statement was a detailed list of all the items showing how much each had fetched. It was something to be studied at leisure later on, not just then during working hours.

"What would you advise me to do with this?" asked Grant, just as his Boss had guessed he would. "Would it be asking too much for the firm to cash it for me?"

"We will do, gladly," answered his Boss. "But my advice to you, Grant, is to open your own bank account. Once you've got the money in there it is so easy afterwards for you to do what you like with it—perhaps buying something you want and then paying some into a Savings Account. You could then leave a small running total in the bank account and have the bank's help at your elbow from then on. I'm sure you would find it very useful. It's a much better and safer way to organise your affairs than keeping cash in the house. Much better."

"I think I'll do that," said Grant. "Now is quite clearly the time to get myself property organised, isn't it?"

"Well, I honestly think you would be well advised to open a bank account, Grant," the Boss said. "As a matter of fact I was going to suggest that you talk to your mates and suggest they all do the same. I think they would all be well advised to, and I know they will listen to your advice. If you like I will contact our bank manager and get him to come along to the office one day and meet you all. It would be simpler than you all traipsing into Canterbury, and the bank would be glad of the chance of new business anyway. That's the way they earn their living, after all! And they would certainly put themselves out to help us. SKWEC is probably one of their largest customers in the area."

"That's good of you. Thanks," Grant said. "I'll speak to the blokes about it and let you know."

"Good," said his Boss, standing up to be on his way. "I'm off now to winkle out the other six—quite a pleasant change for me. It's rather nice being the bearer of good tidings. I must say I'm enjoying the job!" So saying, he shook hands with Grant, warmly congratulated him once again then set off on his 'Fairy Godmother' journey to dispense cheques around the scattered sites where his firm's plant was at work.

Inwardly much excited, but outwardly looking rather pensive, Grant walked over to rejoin his mates, and work was resumed. He said nothing about the purpose of their

Boss's visit. So far as they were concerned Grant was their foreman, and presumably the Boss had brought some instructions for him.

Apart from a desire for privacy—at least for the time being—Grant had a special reason for not saying anything, a reason his Boss knew nothing about. The National Newspaper that had run a special feature about them had offered a fee of £35 if they would refrain from telling anybody about what pay-out they eventually received from the sale of the things they had found, until after the details had been published in their paper. It was an interesting story of the type which caught the imagination of the public, and was well worth a sequel. This £5 each for keeping their mouths shut for a few days was 'money for old rope' so far as the seven were concerned, so they had accepted the offer with great pleasure. It was just about the easiest 'fiver' any of them had ever earned in their lives.

The last of the lucky seven to receive his cheque that day was young Bob Startle. Officially cook boy and general factotum to the steam ploughing team, by common consent he was accepted by his colleagues as an equal partner in the cannon-treasure syndicate, entitled to a full share of the proceeds.

He received his cheque in the Manager's office just before he cycled home from work that afternoon. With wide-eyed disbelief he gazed at the fabulous sum of money printed on the cheque. The Manager watched him with amusement as he read and re-read what it said on the cheque. It was his name on there. Nobody else's with it. Just his!

"Is this really all mine?" he asked. "Am I really going to get all this money?"

"You've got it already," replied the Manager with a smile. "That's it, in your hands. That piece of paper is worth the sum shown on it."

"What do I do with it?" asked Bob, his facial expression a curious mixture of puzzlement and delight.

"Come and sit here," said the Manager. "I'll go through those papers with you and then we'll sort something out about the cheque. I've taken a letter like that to each of your six mates today and they have all been discussing how they are going to handle the money."

"Blimey!" said Bob. "I bet they were glad to see you, Sir!"

"They were indeed," smiled the Manager. "I've never seen so many happy faces in one day for years."

The Manager went through the papers with Bob, showing him how the sum he had received had been arrived at. He then broached the subject of what to do with the money, now he'd got it. Finding out that Bob had not, as yet, started a Savings Account in his own name, he strongly advised him to open one at the Post Office so that he could pay the cheque in rather than getting somebody to 'turn' it into cash'.

This somewhat paternalistic approach to the affairs of his young employee was typical of the Manager and traditional with the firm. It was part of the reason why, once established, men tended to stay with the firm throughout their working lives.

Bob went off home in a happy state of mind, having already determined to take his Boss's advice. By the time he had reached home, though, he had thought of a possible minor modification to this suggested plan and grew increasingly excited during the evening thinking about it.

Meanwhile when Grant got home that evening, like his mates he lost no time in looking through the documents with great care. But he also had an important duty to discharge before he could really relax. He made a summary of the salient points so that he could fulfil his promise to telephone them through to the national newspaper as soon as possible. His list read:

Prices realised at Auction   Totals

Coins: Hoard 'A'	£454	Proceeds of Sale	£1374 . 0s . 0d
Coins: Hoard 'B'	£350	Auctioneer's Charges	£ 270 . 5s . 6d
Flintlock Pistol	£170	Net Balance	£1103 . 14s . 6d
Silver Taper sticks	£185		
Silver Teaspoons	£55	Payment made to each	
Silver Models	£160	of the seven men	£ 157 . 13s . 6d

Armed with these succinct details, he then hurried out to the public telephone box outside the village's Post Office Stores and put through a reverse-charges call to the London telephone number he had been given. Explaining who he was, he then read over this information, as instructed.

Having discharged that obligation he then went back home to read the papers over again at his leisure and savour the almost unbelievable sums of money listed. And most of all he studied the bottom line, and looked at the cheque again to make sure it was all real. It seemed absolutely staggering. It was a reaction shared by his six comrades who, like him, read and re-read their documents with great delight that evening.

Grant was not alone in spotting that the sum was almost exactly what a skilled tradesman on a typical wage of £3 per week earned in one whole year. They were also only too well aware that many labourers supported a family on little more than half of this, because wages of around thirty to thirty-five shillings a week were commonplace.

Small wonder they could hardly believe their good fortune!

The next morning the national newspaper carried a brief article under the bold headline:

TREASURE-TROVE PAYOUT
'Steam Men of Kent get their Cheques'

The article referred readers back to their 'Bolt from the Blue for Boris' story, carried by the paper early in the spring. It gave a brief résumé of subsequent developments, including the Coroner's decision to allow the lucky seven to retain all the things they had found in the cannon. There followed details of the sale and the summary of the amounts of money realised, which Grant had telephoned through to them.

Picked up next day by local people, each of the group was congratulated on the news by friends, relatives, and workmates many times on that and the ensuing days. Before Friday local reporters had seen them, and each local paper, like the national one, ran a sequel to their springtime story.

And by Saturday afternoon, with the kind co-operation of the owner of the Post Office Stores, Bob Startle had a Post Office Savings' Book. The sum of money shown on the first entry was the value of his Christie's cheque, less the price of the shining new racing-bike he rode to work on the next Monday morning! He may have been the youngest member of the lucky seven but he was the first to show public evidence of their joint good fortune. He didn't believe in hanging about!

Chapter 22

A VISITOR FROM SAN FRANCISCO

for agricultural engineers in South Kent

There were repercussions from the finding of the cannon, which nobody could possibly have foreseen.

The beautifully made Spanish 17th century Flintlock pistol—'odd man out' in its way, yet having a closer affinity to the cannon than the other things discovered inside it for it too had once been a fully functioning weapon—was purchased by the American proprietor of a Military Museum at San Francisco, in the State of California, USA, who by chance happened to be on a visit to England, and was in London.

He was intrigued by the strange story of the pistol, found as it had been, hidden in an ancient cannon dug out of the ground in the historic fields of Kent, not very far from where the white cliffs of Dover look out over the English Channel to the coast of France, so near at hand. The pistol had about it an aura that was the very stuff of history.

On a sudden whim he decided to journey down to Kent to have a look at the cannon and perhaps meet some of the men whose names would now forever be linked, by the Flintlock pistol, to his fascinating museum on the West Coast of America, the windows of which looked out across the vast reaches of the Pacific Ocean to the faraway shores of Japan, on the other side of the world.

Sometimes, as he sat in the office gazing out to sea, the American, who had strong professional contacts in both Japan and Great Britain, often felt like a link-man between the two great nations. In front of him lay the Pacific, Japan and Asia; behind him lay North America, the Atlantic, Great Britain and Europe. Separated by half the world, it seemed to him that these two proudly independent *island peoples*, with their rich historic heritages, had much in common. He, in the New World, sat between the two, studied their unique histories, and sampled their military treasures. He set off now to see another.

A man drawn to his calling by an inborn sense of history and a driving urge to probe the past in order more properly to understand the present, he was conscious now of having been caught up in a time-capsule of curiously compelling circumstances. He had a tantalising feeling that he need only follow his fancy freely to find further fascinating fulfilment in his driving quest to discover links with the present times, from times long ago.

Not for the first time in his life he felt a strong sense that it was not chance but Destiny that had deliberately dropped him down at a precise moment to do his own brief duty in chronicling a singular detail of Man's unfolding story. Perhaps he was something of a dreamer, but he was off now on a journey he felt he just had to make.

So it was, that soon after Christie's sale in London, one Walter K. Richtmeyer of the United States of America, walked into the extensive premises of the South Kent Wingash Engineering Company, presented his unusual but impressive card and asked if the General Manager could spare a few moments of his valuable time.

Five minutes later, as his visitor was shown into his office, the General Manager of SKWEC rose to greet him.

"Come along in Mr. Rich-ta-my-er," he said glancing at the unusual name on the card and stumbling as he tried to pronounce it. "What can we do for you?"

The genial face of his visitor, already smiling, broke into a wider smile as he noticed the hesitant effort to get his name right.

"Walter is the name," he said. "Walter K. Richtmeyer. Call me Walter! We don't stand on ceremony where I come from."

"Glad to meet you, Walter," responded the General Manager, warmly shaking the American's hand and secretly admiring the effortless way in which the man had told him how his name should be pronounced. "My name's Richard. Richard Livingstone. You've come a long way to see us. We don't often get visitors from across the Atlantic!"

"I guess it is a long way," smiled Walter. "But I enjoy the trip on an ocean-going liner. It's nice to live in luxury for a few days. Gives me time to think! I usually come to England at least twice a year."

"A bit different from that young fellow, Lindberg, who flew over on his own in May this year," commented Richard, smiling. "Just fancy, getting all the way from Long Island, New York State, to Paris in just under thirty-four hours in that little monoplane of his—the 'Spirit of St. Louis'. What a feat that was! No wonder people have made a hero of him!"

"Yes, it was really amazing!" said Walter. "Truly amazing. A real epic, trail-blazing journey. It will certainly go down in history. No question about it! Some people think the time will come when passenger planes will ferry dozens of people at a time to and fro across the Atlantic every day. Like an airborne bus service from America to Europe, running on a daily timetable."

"Do you really think that will happen?" asked Richard. "To start with, it's dangerous to rely on engines, never mind the structure of the planes which would have to be able to fly through all weathers. It's not like a bus that just stops by the roadside if something goes wrong and waits until somebody comes along to put it right, or maybe take off the passengers in another bus. If Lindberg's 220 HP single engine had packed up on his way across, that would have been the end of him. That's what made it such a brave thing to do, apart from the sheer physical and mental endurance of remaining alert and in control all that time. Do you really think aeroplanes will get that reliable?"

"Sure thing, Richard," said Walter confidently. "Nobody in the airplane business doubts it will happen. But of course the planes will not rely upon just one engine—nor on just one pilot, come to that. No one thinks that. All the talk is of multi-engine planes with built-in, strongly-weighted safety factors and an adequate crew to cover all emergencies. In the end, those in the know say it will all come down to a question of the price of a ticket. People will choose how they travel across the Atlantic largely by the comparative cost of sea and air travel. When the service starts, as start it will certainly do, people will pay a premium for the much faster transit by air. In the long run, who knows what will develop? Maybe we shall see something akin to ocean-going ships. Airliners competing with the ships tossing about on the sea far below them, moving like snails across the water while they flash by high in the sky above!"

"That will speed up business trips like yours," commented Richard with a smile. "And who knows—maybe the time will come when people will be able to pop across from here to America on their two-weeks annual holiday! It sounds far-fetched, but I suppose even that might be possible!"

"I'm quite sure it will be," asserted Walter. "Sooner or later I'm sure it will. Just think how much progress has been made with aircraft since before the War in 1914. Who knows what we shall see in another ten to twenty years? There are exciting times ahead, I reckon."

A nice, likeable, amiable man, Walter was not unlike Richard himself, big of stature with a self-assured, confident manner. The two men hit it off straightaway; an instant rapport was struck between them as often happens when two men meet who know instinctively that they can trust one another.

Walter quickly found that he had landed among friends. Within a few minutes of crossing the threshold he'd stopped feeling like a stranger, for he slotted into the easy-going yet quietly efficient atmosphere of the rural-based engineering firm like a member of the family. When they had exchanged further pleasantries and chatted for a bit, Walter undid his briefcase and took out a soft velvet bag.

"This is what I've come about," he said. "I bought it at an Auction Sale at Christie's in London a few days ago. It has a connection with your firm, I believe."

Loosening the silken cord that tied up the mouth of the velvet bag, which, Richard noticed, bore the name of a famous London weapons dealer, he took out his newly acquired Flintlock pistol and placed it on Richard's desktop.

"I have come to see the old cannon that this has been living in for the last hundred years or more," he said, not without something of the dramatic flourish of a showman.

"My god!" exclaimed Richard, his eyes agog. "You don't mean to say that's the pistol my chaps found in that old gun?"

"That's the one!" replied Walter emphatically. "Haven't you seen it before?"

"No, I certainly haven't," answered the steam men's Boss. "You see, 'Treasure Trove' dug up in this country has, by law, to be handed over immediately to the Crown. Everything out of the cannon went to the local Coroner, and when it was officially returned to the finders they shot it off—very sensibly, I think—straight up to London for Christie's to handle. I'd no idea the pistol they found was a wonderful thing like that."

"Yep!" said Walter. "That's a real gem, that is! If I'd bought nothing else on this trip to Europe, I still would have counted my long journey justified to find a rare piece like that. It's been cleaned up this week by some specialists I know in London and they reckon it's just about the most perfect one of its type they have ever seen. In fact, in their experience, it's unique. They have seen pistols like it in form, but never one so lavishly appointed and decorated as that one."

Richard turned the beautifully made and now expertly cleaned pistol over and over in his hands, scrutinising with astonishment the fine silver inlay on the high quality wooden handgrip, and the intricate engraving on the solid silver metal supporting the barrel.

"Where was it made, do you think?" he asked.

"It's a Spanish Miquelet pistol, made in 1690," said Walter proudly. "What's more, the experts think it is a highly personalised one, made to order for somebody who didn't have to count the cost. It's quite incredible, a perfect example of a 17th century Flintlock pistol. I had to pay well for it of course; there was a lot of interest in it and I was bid up quite a bit before the hammer came down. But I still did very well. That thing will go on gaining in value for all time, I reckon. But it won't be sold, leastways not in my time. That will have a place of honour in my museum."

"Well, I must say, I don't think anybody down here in this corner of England had any idea the blokes had found anything as important as that," Richard commented. "But I saw the Christie's statement of account and I noticed it had made a pretty high price, so I thought it must have turned out to be something a bit special. The fellows passed no comment though. I think they were only interested in the total at the bottom of the page, not the detail showing how it was made up. They did very well, much better than the total the local antique dealer had estimated they'd get, so I gather."

"Then we are all pleased," said Walter with a smile. "They sure did me a good turn when they dragged that old cannon out of its resting place. Boy! What a story I shall have to tell them back home."

This brought Walter round to the purpose of his visit. A little while later he followed Richard across the extensive vehicle park, the two of them threading their way between a bewildering variety of steam vehicles and stationary engines of all types, to a remote corner of the area. Soon he was gazing down at the hefty but pleasingly elegant form of the bronze cannon he had come to see.

Walter stood looking at it for a long time, marvelling at the fact that the wonderful

Spanish pistol that now was his, had lived hidden and unharmed in the barrel of the ancient cannon for more than a century. He had a curious feeling, as softly sentimental as was the gun hard and unfeeling, that these two old soldiers should not be separated after having been together for so long. Not only that, but together they made a unique historical partnership which would enthral visitors to his museum. Pretty soon he had developed a strong desire to ship the ancient cannon back home to live in some splendour among many fellow spirits from bygone ages.

Saying nothing, but mulling over in his mind the practicalities of such a scheme, and the wisdom of it as a purely business proposition, he followed Richard back to his office. Richard noticed that he seemed preoccupied about something, but did not guess what it was that was causing him to be thoughtful, and suddenly so silent.

By the time they'd got back to the office Walter's decision was made, and he lost no time in broaching the subject. His mind now racing, already he could see the cannon, re-mounted on a carriage like the one it must have rested on so many long years ago, proudly placed in a position of honour on the green lawn at the foot of the tall white mast from which the Stars and Stripes flew each day, outside the reception hall of his impressive Military Museum. That just had to happen; of that he was now determined.

"What do you intend to do with that old cannon, Richard?" he asked. "Do you intend to dispose of it, or keep it?"

"So far as I know, nobody has given much thought to that yet," replied Richard, sensing the drift. "It belongs to the ploughing team, of course, not to the firm. We've just allowed them to store it over there until they decide what to do about it."

"Well, I'd like to buy it and ship it back to the States," said Walter, without prevarication. "Do you think they would sell it to me?"

"I'm quite sure they would," responded Richard. "I can't imagine they will have people around here falling over each other to buy it. Name what you think is a fair price and it's yours, I reckon."

"That's marvellous," Walter said, with obvious enthusiasm. "How do I get to see the men?"

"No need for that," answered Richard. "I'll introduce you to our Workshop Manager, Frank Thrushton. He will know what the chaps have in mind. They are all out, scattered about the countryside on jobs."

Glancing at the office clock, for it was now lunchtime, Richard made a suggestion.

"Would you care to have a bite to eat with us?" he asked. "Frank will be in the Works canteen now, and I could take you along to meet him."

"That's very kind of you," replied Walter. "I'd like that very much."

Walter found Frank another fellow-spirit, as indeed Richard knew he would. Over lunch Richard told Frank why Walter had come down from London to see them, and discussed the subject of the cannon. Before getting round to what would be a fair offer for it, Walter came up with another idea he had been turning over in his mind.

"Could you people here build a proper carriage for that gun to sit on?" he asked. "A replica of the kind of heavy wooden carriage those cannons were mounted on. If you could, I'd be glad to commission you to do it and then we could perhaps agree a total price for the mounted cannon, a price that would cover the cost of making the carriage, and include whatever you thought would be a fair amount to give your ploughing team for the cannon itself."

"What do you think, Frank?" asked Richard. "Could we make a mounting?"

"Yes, of course we could," he replied. "As a matter of fact I've already given it some thought. Grant told me that Terry Stokes suggested it might be a good idea to provide a carriage for it and then it would have a real market appeal. There's nothing very complicated about making one. But if it's to go into a Military Museum, then we should have to make sure the carriage looked authentic. All we would need is a pattern to study, then we could turn one out in no time. That's the sort of job that makes life interesting. Something a bit out of the ordinary. What's more I think I know where I can find out about a suitable carriage design, too."

"Chatham Dockyard, I suppose, Frank!" Richard commented with a smile. "Back to the old firm again, eh?"

"How did you guess?" laughed Frank. "Where else?"

He looked at his watch then stood up from the table. "Hang on a minute," he said. "I'll give my old mate Fergus a ring, up at Aveling & Porters of Rochester. He'll know what to suggest, I bet."

Never a man to dilly-dally over anything, Frank hurried off out of the canteen.

"You've as good as got your mounting, Walter," Richard said, with a wide grin. "If Frank and Fergus can't come up with exactly what you want, then you can take it from me nobody in the UK can. Those two are just about the best practical engineers I've known throughout my life. Typical of the Old Country's best, they are, both products of one of the finest engineering training establishments in the country, if not in the world!"

"Where's that?" asked Walter, with interest.

"Chatham Royal Naval Dockyards," replied Richard. "They run an engineering apprenticeship scheme, taking in carefully selected boys, and putting them through just about the most thorough and comprehensive training it's possible to devise. When you think of the size of the British Navy, and the wide range and complexity of the ships and equipment that goes to make it up, you can imagine the extensive facilities that are needed to maintain it all. It's a massive organisation and there has to be a constant feed of newly-trained men to sustain the workforce."

"Guess so," commented Walter. "Sounds an impressive scheme. Boys who go there must count themselves lucky, I reckon."

"They do indeed," said Richard. "There's strong competition every year for the annual intake. It's not only through retirement that the Naval Dockyards lose skilled labour, though, you know. Men who have passed through their training scheme and then spent a few years working in the system, are highly attractive to industry at large. They get poached all the time, not only by private industry, but by other Government Departments as well. That's where Frank came from of course, when he joined us at SKWEC, *and* his mate Fergus, to whom he has just gone off to speak. Fergus MacDonald trained alongside Frank, and they worked together in the Dockyards for years. He is Frank's opposite number at Aveling & Porters of Rochester, in charge of engineering workshops there. They manufacture and service steam engines of all types. Particularly steam rollers. You see them all over the place."

"I seem to see British steam engines wherever I go, all over the world," commented Walter. "Of course it all started over here, didn't it? Small wonder people look to the UK if it's steam-driven machinery they need."

"That's true enough," observed Richard. "But of course there are plenty of other countries making similar equipment now, so competition keeps the manufacturers here on their toes."

At that moment Frank rejoined them and it was obvious from the look on his face that he had some encouraging news.

"No problem," he announced. "Fergus said there is a stack of information in the Archives at Chatham about guns, going back to the year dot. Not only that, he is quite sure there is a fully restored cannon, of about the same size, with its proper authentic mounting, sitting along the seafront on the Isle of Sheppey just outside Sheerness.

Fergus agrees it would be child's play to knock one of those up for you."

"Then will you make me one?" requested Walter eagerly. "That's if the men will sell me the cannon, of course!"

"It's up to you, Frank," Richard intervened, glancing at Frank questioningly. "The decision is yours. It's quite OK by me."

"Right, then," said Frank without a second thought. "Consider it as good as done. If you buy the cannon, it will get its new carriage."

"Fine," said Walter happily. "The job's yours. Now let's get the price sorted out. I know you will want your team of men to get a good price for the cannon. Let me make you an offer. Could you fix me up with the complete thing for . . . say . . . £250 with something like £50 for the cannon and £200 for making the carriage?"

"Blimey!" responded Frank. "I should hope so. We could give the seven shareholders £10 each for the cannon and probably ship the completed job to the States for that much! About £25 between them is the maximum they expect to get, I feel sure of that. Nobody around here is out looking for a cannon to buy."

"I wouldn't expect you to pay the cost of shipping that heavy awkward thing to the States out of that sum," laughed Walter. "But that price would suit me fine. And if you can give the men £10 each out of it, then go ahead and do just that. It's worth all of that to me, that's for sure. You imagine me trying to hunt down one like that for the Museum. It would cost me a small fortune just finding one, never mind buying it, and then possibly having to get work done on it. Let me assure you, if you can provide me with the complete job for £250 I'll be more than happy."

"For that money, Walter, you will get something a bit special," agreed Frank happily. "It's a deal!"

Walter promptly wrote out a cheque for £250 there and then. He did not hesitate for a minute, just took out his chequebook and wrote it out without further ado.

"There we are," he said, handing the cheque to Richard. "It's up to you what you give to the seven men of the ploughing team. If you are sure they'll be happy to sell it, cash the cheque and pay them out as soon as you like. Naturally, if when I've gone, you have any reason to change your minds, or the men don't agree, you can post the cheque back to me with a note to say the deal is off."

Frank laughed. "There's no chance of the seven not wanting to sell it," he said. "But you certainly don't have to pay for the job before it's finished!"

"I prefer to," responded Walter. "Having met you people I would rather pay for it now. In a day or two I'm off back to California and I'd rather settle the whole thing before I go. Then you can just let me know when the cannon is ready and we'll arrange transportation."

"Well, if that's the way you prefer it," said Richard, standing up to get back to his office, "then thanks a lot! But we aren't used to people paying us in advance for anything we do over here," he added. "A 10% deposit maybe, but not the lot! People around here don't part up until they have to."

"They certainly don't," confirmed Frank with a smile, as he and Walter got up from the table.

"Would you care to have a quick look round the workshops before you go, Walter?" Frank asked, as they made their way to the door of the canteen.

"I would indeed, if you can spare the time," Walter replied. "Is that all right with you, Richard?" he added.

"Of course," said Richard. "I'll see you back at my office when you have done the rounds. Don't forget to show him the Fowler's engines and the steam ploughing gear the team were using when they found the cannon, will you, Frank? And he might like to see one of the Sentinels too, if there's one in the yard. Then he will go back to the States with a complete picture in his mind of the outfit involved in finding the cannon, pulling it out of the ground, and finally shifting it back here. It will give him the whole story of the cannon and that beautiful Spanish Flintlock pistol he's taking back with him to the States. Quite some story, that!"

"I'd like to see that pistol before you go, Walter," said Frank as he shepherded him out of the canteen. "None of us saw it here at the Depot. It went straight to the Coroner and then on to Christie's of London."

"Yes, so Richard told me," said Walter. "It's in my briefcase in Richard's office. Remind me to show it to you when we get back there."

It took well over an hour just to have not much more than a cursory look over the extensive establishment. Walter found it fascinating. Everywhere he saw signs of the long history of steam power and agricultural engineering which lay behind the impressive engineering capabilities of the place he was in and the men he met. In the machine-tool workshop there seemed little the firm couldn't do in the way of manufacturing the wide variety of replacement parts and newly designed equipment that kept them busy continuously.

Out in the vehicle park he was quite astounded at the range of steam-powered vehicles and static engines that were scattered around.

He started to dot down names of manufacturers embossed on the nameplates that most engines sported. Some, like Fowlers of Leeds, Fodens of Cheshire, Aveling & Porter from Rochester, Garrett's of Suffolk and Sentinel Wagons of Shrewsbury, he recognised. Others, such as McLaren of Leeds, Marshalls of Gainsborough, Fosters of Lincoln and Ransomes of Suffolk, were new to him. He did recognise one other in particular, though, a fine-looking, nicely decorated Showman's Engine made by Burrell of Norfolk. These he had often seen at fairs and other travelling shows and exhibitions where the engines carrying a large dynamo coupled by a leather belt to the flywheel, provided electrical power for the showground.

Perhaps it was the sight of the Burrell, standing amidst such a concentration of steam engines of so many types that sparked off an idea in Walter's mind that was destined to grow into a thriving reality in the years ahead.

"Do you know, Frank," he said, voicing his thoughts, "what I have seen around me here today has given me an idea which I reckon will bug me when I get back to the States until I do something about it. This place fascinates me and if it grips me, it would grip plenty more people back home just as much. There's a place now, I reckon, for a 'Steam Power Museum' in San Francisco, where we could collect examples such as these machines you've got all around us here, from all over the world. We all have to face facts Frank, like them or not. Most people think the days of steam are numbered. No question about that!"

"I'm sure you're right—more's the pity!" agreed Frank. "It will be a sad day for many of us when that happens. We talk about it sometimes, but it's not a happy thought. But still," he added more brightly, "I think your Steam Power Museum is grand. Perhaps you can take me along as a relic, to put alongside the engines, Walter! At least I should be among friends and could keep them ticking over for you. One thing's for sure; the way these things are made, if they are properly looked after, apart from the boilers, which need attention or complete replacement from time to time, the engines are built to last forever!"

Walter's showman's instinct was well and truly aroused. Sometimes an idea is an inspiration. This, he was already certain, was one such, just like his Military Museum had been, years ago.

"Do you know, Frank, I might just take you up on that," he said seriously. "Many of the exhibits would certainly be British. What better than a Brit for the engineer to advise us and look after all of them for us. By the time you begin to 'run out of steam' here, so to speak—or much earlier—it could be I'll be in touch with you. I'll poach you from SKWEC just like they poached you from the Royal Navy's dockyards!"

Frank grinned. "Richard has been talking, has he?" he commented. "Still, it would be poetic justice, wouldn't it?"

Now on their way back towards Richard's office, Walter's attention was attracted by something he hadn't spotted before. Over near one of the large, aircraft hanger-like workshops, stood one of the wonderful old fairground organs which belted out their unmistakeable joyous music to add an inimitable atmosphere to outside fun-fairs and shows.

"Hey," said Walter, stopping in his tracks. "Don't tell me you handle those things too?"

"Of course we do," responded Frank cheerfully. "They go wrong too, you know! Somebody has to put them right! They are clever and intricate things, but only logical machinery after all. There's nothing about them that we can't manage here. But as you know, I expect, the name "Steam Organ" sometimes used to describe them, is a misnomer with almost all of them. They are worked by compressed air. That needs a pump and the pump—although sometimes driven by a small steam engine—is more often than not driven by an electric motor which picks up its power from a Burrell, or from a similar traction engine with its own generator. You would be surprised how much fairground machinery we repair in this place. It's a bit more than just a sideline for us."

"That's a surprise to me," commented Walter. "And it gives me another interesting idea. I'll have to organise an old-style fairground alongside my Steam Power Museum with one or two of those lovely old Burrell's Showman's Engines chuffing away to power the lot. Just imagine what a collection of those fairground organs would do to pull in visitors. I reckon they would come to San Francisco from all over the States to see that lot. It would keep the average family happy for hours in a centre like that!"

Walter spoke with feeling for he could have stayed around happily himself for hours. There was so much to see of interest to him. But he knew that his new-found friends had work to do and thought it time to push off. Resisting a desire to go and look at the fine, mobile fairground organ, he set off with Frank back to Richard's office.

Inside, he remembered that Frank wanted to see the pistol, so he took it out of its case again, to show him.

Frank was a weapons enthusiast. Though Walter did not of course know it, he had created an entire double-barrelled shot-gun for himself. That included everything—the wooden stock which he carved and fashioned to look as though it had come from a professional manufacturer's factory and all metallic parts as well. With the machine tools he had around him and his thorough training at the Dockyard Apprentice School, plus the expertise that only years of experience can give, he made the whole gun, literally 'lock, stock and barrel'. It was two years later before Walter found that out, and it made his 'poaching' idea even more appealing since the restoration and repair of intricate weaponry was something with which he was constantly concerned in his Military Museum.

Walter handed Frank the pistol and Frank took it from him, his face registering surprise and astonishment.

"What a marvellous thing," he said, turning it over in his hands and examining it with great interest. "I'd no idea the pistol was such a rare and valuable thing like this. What have you found out about it, Walter?"

Walter repeated what he had told Richard earlier in the day. Frank took a watch-makers eyeglass out of his pocket and peered through it at the intricate engraving on the stock. He spotted a maker's inscription and the year 1690, engraved there. Shortly afterwards his attention was suddenly arrested by something else.

"That's interesting," he said musingly, as he scrutinised it. "Hidden in one of these scrolls engraved in the silver here, is a marking that certainly wasn't put on by the maker's. It isn't well enough done. Good, but not that good."

"What is it?" asked Walter, immediately extremely interested. "What is on there?"

"It says 'Gib.1704'. Just that," replied Frank. "Here—have a look."

"Well I never!" said Walter, peering through the eyeglass Frank had passed to him. "So it does! Nobody spotted that, either at Christie's or when the weapons experts had a go at it to clean it up for me. I wonder what the significance of that is."

" 'Gib' surely must mean Gibraltar," said Frank. "Navy blokes often refer to 'Gib'. So the inscription could mean Gibraltar 1704. It seems to me it could well be that some British naval or army chap may have obtained this Spanish pistol in Gibraltar in the year 1704."

"That certainly figures," agreed Walter. "Why record 'Gib.1704' if it didn't mean just that?"

"I don't even know if the British were in Gibraltar then," observed Richard. "To tell you the truth, I haven't got the faintest idea when it was captured. Not the faintest."

"Nor have I," admitted Frank. "I've got no idea at all."

"Just a minute," said Richard. "Let's see what it says about Gibraltar in my faithful old Historical Encyclopaedia. That usually gets me out of trouble."

He went to his bookshelves, took down a chunky, well-thumbed book and started leafing through it. After a moment or two he found what he was looking for.

"Yes. Here it is," he said. "Gibraltar. There's quite a bit about it. Hang on. I'll just glance through and see what it says."

He read for a short while and then gave an explanation of surprise.

"Well, I'm damned!" he said. "Listen to this. This is very interesting. I think we've found the answer."

So saying Richard read out a short extract. It was brief and to the point. It ran:

'Gibraltar has always been a coveted stronghold. For some centuries after 711 it belonged to the Moors. In 1462 it was taken by the Castilians and was part of Spain until captured in 1704 by a British and Dutch fleet under Sir George Rooke. The French and Spaniards tried hard to regain it in 1704-1705, but in vain, and in 1713 it was surrendered to Great Britain. In 1736 the Spaniards again besieged it without success. Yet another and greater attempt was made in 1779, when they began a siege that lasted for over three years, ending in February 1783. Since then it has remained in British hands.'

Richard put down the book with an air of satisfaction.

"Now that really is interesting," Walter said, with a keen look at his new friends. "It seemed 1704 was the first year the British were in Gibraltar. And they have stayed there to this very day. That must surely mean there is some historical significance in the date 1704 being inscribed so carefully on the pistol. Why else would anyone engrave 'Gib 1704' on it?"

"I agree," said Frank. "Most people don't inscribe things on a gun as valuable as this one unless there is a very special reason for doing so. It could be the Rock was not

317

the only thing captured at Gibraltar in 1704! Somebody got himself a jolly nice little Flintlock pistol at the same time, I reckon! And now it's yours, Walter! That is some pistol you have there. I think we've just put its value up even higher by finding that out. It will deserve a special mention on your description alongside the pistol in the museum. You're taking a bit of British history back to the States with you, and no mistake!"

Highly delighted with the way everything had turned out for him on his visit to Kent, Walter prepared to take his leave. As he stood up to shake hands he spotted a framed photograph on the wall behind Richard's desk.

It was an enlarged copy of the picture that had appeared in the press, of the seven men in the act of loading the cannon on to the back of the Sentinel. Walter saw its potential value to his museum immediately.

"Richard," he said, a little apologetically, "I hesitate to presume upon your kindness even more, but is there any chance of my being able to purchase a copy of that photograph? Back home, when the cannon gets there, a copy of that picture with its connection both with the cannon and the pistol would be marvellous for me to include in my display." Without hesitation Richard promptly took the picture off the wall and handed it to Walter.

"With my compliments," he said, smiling. "And I have another here I'm sure you would like. It shows the two engines and the cable-pulled cultivator at work, just as they were when they hit the cannon buried along the line of the old hedgerow."

Richard opened a drawer in his desk and took out a reprint of the newspaper photograph which had so cleverly included the whole outfit.

"Say, that really is something!" exclaimed Walter, clearly delighted. "Are you sure you can spare these, Richard?"

"Certainly," replied Richard. "We have collected orders for several of each and I can replace those with no trouble. The papers always offer that service. Any pictures they publish are made available on glossy prints like those, at a very modest cost. The fellows will be delighted when I tell them their pictures will be going on display in California. Another bonus for them to go with the nice little payout you have left them for the cannon."

He paused a moment, frowning slightly, then went on. "And to be fair to you, I must repeat that £10 each is far higher than anything they expected to get for it, I'm quite sure of that!"

"Well, like I said, I'm quite happy about that," remarked Walter. "I'm more than pleased with the deal. For £250 I've got myself a fine addition to my Museum. It will be a unique centre of interest and I'm looking forward very much to having it on display."

With that Walter finally took his leave, a very happy man. Frank had told him that he would be in touch once the cannon, on its mounting, was ready for shipping.

"Nice fellow!" commented Richard after Walter had left. "Like a breath of fresh sea air off the Atlantic. Makes a pleasant change from routine when a man like that sails in unexpectedly out of the blue!"

"Yes, I liked him too," said Frank. "And what's more, I don't think we've seen the last of him either. He's gone off from here with ideas in his head about setting up a new museum to go alongside his military one—ideas which could bring us a lot of business here should they materialise, unless I'm much mistaken."

Frank then told Richard how Walter had had a sudden inspiration when he stood among all the engines in the vehicle park. Having been with the man for long enough to get his measure, they both felt certain that it was odds-on he would act upon his hunch when he got back home.

They were right; he did. And in due course Frank's prediction came true, for it brought some very useful business to SKWEC and with it a long-term connection with California.

That Saturday, with the necessary vital statistics of the old cannon in his pocket, plus a quick sketch of it, Frank set off on the rugged, second-hand Douglas motorbike he'd recently bought from Bill Gunston, the Saddler at Littlebrook, and rode up to Sittingbourne where his old workmate Fergus lived. Picking him up on the punishingly hard perch euphemistically described by the makers as a 'comfortable seat for a pillion passenger', he rode across the bridge to the Isle of Sheppey to have a look at the mounted cannon which Fergus had told him about.

In the event it was a fruitful trip. The cannon, though not precisely the same as the one they had back at the depot, was of the same size and very similar in its form. Most importantly, it had the same kind of trunnions for slotting into its carriage as the one for which Frank had to design a carriage.

The two of them studied it together and left the island with all the data needed to construct an authentic-looking carriage for Walter's new museum piece. Fergus felt sure he could get hold of the thick, heavyweight oak timbers needed for its construction. The rest of it was metal work and nothing about that presented any problem at all.

Back home Frank made the necessary drawings and on Monday he was able to make a start in getting the construction work organised. It was the sort of job they did in the workshops at odd times, turning to it between important tasks when they had some time to fill in. In constant touch with Aveling & Porter's of Rochester as part of his normal routine, it was not many days before he received some chunky timber obtained by courtesy of friends of Fergus in Chatham Dockyard, and sent on one of his firm's delivery vehicles on its regular run.

Not many weeks later Richard stood looking at Frank's finished product. The cannon, cleaned up and smart, was now mounted on a wheeled carriage of extremely sturdy structure made of thick, heavy wood strengthened and framed by iron.

Now complete, the future exhibit for Walter's Military Museum looked splendid. Richard's eyes lit upon something he hadn't expected. By the side of the gun lay six cannon balls.

"Where on earth did you find those, Frank?" he asked.

Frank laughed. "We didn't," he said. "We made them!"

This unlikely announcement caused Richard to look askance at Frank, who read the disbelief in his expression immediately.

"I can see you don't believe it!" he smiled. "But I'm serious, Richard. We gave up trying to find any and decided to make our own. You'd be surprised if you tried to go out and buy some cannon balls. We all get used to seeing little heaps of them by guns around the old fortifications as part of the tourist attractions, but there are so many different sizes to start with. And nobody is in a position to sell them to you, even if you find some of the right size. We never did see any eight-inch diameter ones, which is what this gun needs—except for six by the cannon on the Isle of Sheppey that I told you about. We thought they added interest to the spectacle—in fact, a cannon without them seems incomplete—so I determined to fix Walter up with some, to put the finishing touch to his display at the museum."

Richard was now convinced Frank meant what he'd said, and that he had indeed made them. When he stopped to think, though, it was exactly the reaction he might have expected, for Frank never spent an undue amount of time looking for any replacement part needed to put something right. He just set to and made it himself.

"We don't have the facilities to cast things like that here, though, Frank, do we? How did you manage it?"

"Well, it's down to Fergus really," Frank explained. "He's got connections with a local foundry on the Medway up there. As you can imagine, Aveling & Porters, as manufacturers of steam vehicles, have links with all sorts of engineering firms. Anyway he went to see his mates at the foundry and they said if we made the mould, they would pour the metal. And that's what we did. We had a bit of a laugh though because if they'd had their way we should have finished up with six perfect, shining cannon balls. We had to persuade them to rough the job up a bit to make the end-product look right. Anyway, there they are! I can't see any visitor to Walter's museum spotting that those cannon balls are a few hundred years younger than the gun itself!"

Richard stooped to pick one up. It was heavier—much heavier—than he expected so he soon put it down again. "Good grief!" he exclaimed. "Aren't they heavy!"

"Yes, they certainly are," grinned Frank, watching him struggle. "They're not exactly overgrown cricket balls, are they? Do you know that the cannon itself weighs about 7000lbs and those balls that it fires weigh over 40lbs! Just imagine that. Fancy that thing lobbing lumps of metal about that weigh getting on for half a hundredweight. No wonder those old cannons could knock hell out of wooden ships—or anything else come to that!"

Richard grinned. "So that little lot of balls represents about 250lbs of iron, does it?" he commented. "They should be safe enough then, left parked outside Walter's museum by the side of his cannon. Nobody's going to walk away with them anymore than with the gun itself!"

"Well, what do you think about it?" asked Frank. "Do you think he will be pleased?"

"He will be absolutely delighted, Frank. And when you look at it from his point of view, it represents a good deal for him. Where else would he get an exhibit like that for £250? Guns as old as that just aren't around in America. It will attract a lot of attention, I should think."

Richard paused a few moments, looking at the cannon admiringly.

"You really have done a marvellous job for him there, Frank. It looks fine," he went on. "But now we must think of the problem of shipping it out to him."

"Don't worry about that," said Frank. "I think I've got that organised. Fergus and I have got good friends in the Dockyard. All we've got to do is get it up to Chatham. The rest is taken care of—unless something cocks things up, that is! Somebody who knows somebody with the right connections and influence got to hear about our cannon that needs to get to San Francisco. I think we are going to get some unexpected help. We have a Sentinel going to Rochester the day after tomorrow, so I'll send it on the first leg of its journey on that. The rest I will let you know about when I've fixed it."

Richard thought Frank was being a little bit less than fully forthcoming about the matter, but guessed he was up to something and didn't want to count his chickens. He seldom failed when he was 'playing the system' and using his initiative to enlist the support of people with access to the powerful and extensive resources of HM Dockyards. Frank was a man best left alone to get on with things in his own way, so Richard was content to ask no questions. He turned to make his way back to his office, but Frank called him back. He had a favour to ask.

"There is one thing I'd like to suggest, before you go," he said. "As Walter has paid such a good price for it, I should like to send him a bottle of Scotch with the cannon, as a present from the firm. What do you think?"

"Good idea," agreed Richard. "I go along with that. It would be a nice gesture, the sort of thing he will appreciate. Buy one and pass the ticket through Frank. I'll leave it to you."

From then on Richard left Frank to it. And the wheels within wheels began to turn. Frank's plan worked smoothly and easily, as what on the face of it seemed to be a formidable transportation problem was resolved with no fuss, no difficulty and seemingly—as Richard was to learn later—with effortless efficiency.

* * * * *

Several weeks later, far away in his office in San Francisco, Walter had an unexpected visitor. A smiling young officer from the US Navy was shown into his office.

"Got something for you outside," he announced, with the cheerful, open-faced directness so typical of his type. "Would you be kind enough to step outside and tell me where you want it put?"

Puzzled, although in his line of business he did get occasional visits from the Navy, Walter went out into the sunshine.

Pulled up on the forecourt was a large, US Navy heavy-load-carrying truck. Upon the back, looking truly immaculate was the mounted cannon from his friends in Kent.

"Courtesy of the Royal Navy," said his visitor, grinning happily. "Arrived yesterday on a cruiser en route to join a British fleet in the Far East. Next stop for them is New Zealand. They were invited to San Francisco on a courtesy visit and the British Captain said he did his Nelson act when somebody loaded this deadly weapon aboard! I reckon he had to do a double Nelson not to see that, though!"

The Navy truck, fully equipped with its own crane, made short work of planting the old English cannon on its prepared place by the flag-pole. Shortly afterwards they were off, leaving Walter to marvel at the authentic-looking carriage that had been purpose-built for the cannon, and wondering what behind the scenes arm-twisting had gone on back in the UK to persuade the Royal Navy to ship the gun over to him.

In the excitement he had not noticed his bonus being unloaded. By the side of the cannon he now spotted, neatly arranged on the ground like soldiers in two rows, the six totally unexpected cannon balls. These again, though he did not know it, had been purpose-built to match the old cannon.

For a long time Walter studied his grand new acquisition to his museum from all angles. As Richard had predicted, he was truly delighted with it. Pondering its strange history he was suddenly reminded of a comment Frank had made.

"We will tuck the homemade lead treasure-tray down the barrel for you, Walter," he had said. "It might add a bit of interest when you tell the story of the way your Flintlock pistol lived on that tray hidden inside the cannon for over a hundred years."

Wondering if Frank had remembered, he peered down the barrel, but quickly felt a bit silly. After all, what could he hope to see looking down the muzzle of a sixteen-foot long cannon except pitch darkness. A little sheepishly he went into the building and came back carrying a long, hook-ended pole. It was one used for opening the high air-vent windows in the museum.

There was nobody around watching him so he shoved the pole down the barrel and felt around with it until he located something it could hook on to. Pulling out gently he could hear something slithering up the barrel, and sure enough the battered old lead tray appeared at the mouth.

Dropping the pole Walter pulled the tray the rest of the way out. As it emerged he saw to his surprise—and soon to his marked anxiety—that there were three wrapped bottles tied in the tray. Hurriedly he carried the tray by its two crude handles, disappeared into his office and locked the door behind him.

He had an uneasy, yet certainly not unpleasant feeling, that his friends in England who had sent him the present had forgotten—or perhaps didn't know—about the law of Prohibition. If they had, he didn't want to land them and himself in trouble, accused of smuggling in liquor. Equally, if that's what they had done, he didn't want to lose the booze either!

The bottles fitted the curvature of the lead tray quite well and were securely tied down. He cut the cord holding the one that had come into view first and unwrapped it. His apprehension, coupled with his contrarily paradoxical hope, was confirmed. It was a bottle of Scotch whisky, bearing a famous label. Round its neck was tied a small greetings card on which was written the message:

'With the compliments of SKWEC'

Turning his attention to the next in line, he unwrapped that. It was a bottle of what he instantly recognised to be Strong Naval Rum, much favoured by present and past men of the Royal Navy—indeed part, as he knew, of their long and cherished traditions. It also carried a greetings label. It bore the message:

'With the compliments of the Royal Navy'

The third astounded him more than ever. It was a bottle of a well-known brand of Vodka. It again had a greetings label tied to it. On it was the message:

'With the compliments of the US Navy'

Lined up on his desk, in their order of appearance, Walter could not help noticing the similarity of the wrappings and the message cards. They were not identical, but it looked suspiciously as though the second had sought to emulate the first, and the third had deliberately followed the same form. It was intriguing!

Pretty soon the three bottles were locked away in Walter's safe. He alone had a key. With them out of sight and himself now in no danger of being caught in an impossibly compromising position, he was able to concentrate his mind on the curious circumstance of how the three came to be there.

The gift from Kent, he soon concluded, was no more and no less than it seemed. It was a very nice idea on the part of his friends, to send him a small gift tucked away where his pistol had come from. A little hidden treasure for *him* to discover! Of one thing he was certain; it was not put in there to avoid discovery in order to get round the Prohibition law. Walter was certain they had forgotten all about it. After all, the whole concept of the prohibition of alcohol was so alien to the British way of life, so contrary to its whole ethos, that he doubted whether it was taken seriously. He was right.

What about the gift from the Royal Navy, though, he wondered? He felt sure that Frank—and he was certain it was Frank's idea because it had his stamp about it—would not have told the Navy, or anybody else for that matter, about the booze in the barrel. That might have spoilt the fun. It was put there for him to discover, not to be told about. Accepting that premise to be true it necessarily followed that the Royal Navy had found the hidden bottle, had a smile about it, and then added to the mystery by putting in their own bottle with it.

But, and this was the important point Walter arrived at, the Royal Navy would certainly know very well all there was to know about Prohibition. So, that being true, they had deliberately run a risk of involving themselves. The fact that they had taken the risk implied that they thought the chance of the US Navy messing about looking for smuggled contraband up the barrel of an ancient cannon, was next door to zero.

That brought him to the third bottle. Why on earth had the US Navy, on accepting the comradely task of transporting the cannon to the museum, looked up the barrel anyway? But they had done—just like the Royal Navy—and decided to add to the fun and the 'spirit' of the occasion, by putting their own gift alongside the other two. This he thought, must have been a cool decision, to connive in a little harmless law-breaking escapade, just for the hell of it!

The US Navy and the Royal Navy traditionally took only calculated risks. They did not play ducks and drakes over anything. But of course they knew that they were delivering the gun themselves and no one else was involved. It was a straightforward Navy to Navy fraternal exercise to get an old cannon to a San Francisco Military Museum. The fact that it was an old weapon no doubt made it an object with which they felt an affinity, one deserving of special attention!

Walter concluded that the Nelson blind eye tradition not only survived in the Royal Navy, but had spread to the US Navy as well!

However, he took no chances and told nobody. As for the evidence of law breaking, that he destroyed in the time-honoured way of drinking it! He made the process last quite a long time, savouring his good fortune. To the pleasure of drinking it, was added the spice of cocking a snook at a pernicious law to which he and most of his friends strongly objected.

Much later he learnt that his assumption so far as Frank was concerned was absolutely right. Frank had told nobody. Only he and Richard knew about the whisky.

But Frank added a new angle and put his finger straightaway on the probable explanation of the intriguing sequence of events. So widespread had been the publicity about the treasure in the cannon, that Frank reckoned the Navy had caught the 'hunt-for-treasure-in-a-cannon' bug, and somebody among the crew had inadvertently stumbled upon the whisky.

As for the US Navy, there was no explanation for them having found the two bottles beyond either extremely high efficiency in contraband seeking or—and this much more likely—because the bug had crossed the Atlantic in advance of the cannon, which had then been eagerly probed by the first cannon-treasure-addict to spot it! By inference, the new craze had spread to the US Navy, and that is how the third bottle came to be there.

On the day of the cannon's arrival, after the museum had closed and the staff had gone home, Walter—as was his habit—sat alone in his office during the evening, dealing in peace and quiet with the various matters requiring his personal attention. He found it a productive time to think through new ideas and possible developments. The quietness and solitude were conducive to constructive thought.

Once he'd dealt with other more general matters, Walter's mind turned to his new acquisition and he started immediately to plan how best to exploit the cannon at the museum.

He decided straight away to put on a small, eye-catching display, with the Spanish Flintlock pistol as its centrepiece, telling the story of the cannon. As its backcloth, he made up his mind to have a large photograph of the cannon, as it stood now outside the museum. Above the display, in bold letters, he would have an arresting title. Something like:

WELCOME TO A NEW ARRIVAL AT THE MUSEUM!

ANCIENT CANNON COMES TO THE PACIFIC COAST OF AMERICA FROM THE CHANNEL COAST OF ENGLAND

It was Walter's practice to put together the general idea of what he wanted, and then pass the matter over to his talented young Display Manager, Pamela Thornton. She then put it all together in her own artistic way. He was pretty sure Pamela would modify his title, to start with, but knew that if she did so, what replaced it would be better. She had a positive flair for creating a maximum impact. Her influence was to be seen everywhere in the museum.

He turned his attention to the photographs that Richard had kindly given him just before he left the SKWEC establishment. These had an obvious strong impact and he decided to have large copies made of them to feature prominently in the display.

Next he constructed a concise description of how the steam-ploughing team, working in the lovely countryside of the county of Kent in England, had made their discovery. He had brought back copies of newspaper articles about it and these provided him with all the details he needed, even to some personal notes about the men involved. For his part he was able to say something about the highly interesting engineering workshops and depot where the cannon had rested temporarily until he bought it.

The project occupied him for several successive evenings, during which he thought it only appropriate to enjoy a glass or two from his strictly illegal private store of imported liquor!

At length, when he had assembled all the information, he handed it over to Pamela to organise into an attractive and logical presentation. He was more than pleased with the result. She made skilful use of the two enlarged photographs, one showing the complete steam-ploughing outfit at work and the other the gun being lowered onto the Sentinel steam lorry by the seven men.

Using these set against the backcloth of the large photograph of the cannon, with the ornate Spanish Miquelet Flintlock pistol centrally placed on the display table as a focus of attention, Pamela had contrived to describe the fascinating story without the use of too much reading matter. Early in her career with Walter she had learned the truth of an adage of his that he impressed upon her about reading matter presented alongside exhibits.

"Most people," he had said, speaking from long experience, "will read *all* of a little information but not even a *little* of a lot!" Constrained by this wisdom she had become adept at creating succinct punchy labels and comments. Walter noted with pleasure how well she had succeeded once again with his new exhibit. However, on the table-top adjacent to the display, she had provided information leaflets for visitors to take home with them, giving the full story to be read at their leisure.

Once the display was completed, Walter lost no time in calling in the Press, using well-chosen contacts upon whom he could rely to give good publicity to his new acquisition. It was a gem of a story and he knew that it was unusual enough to be snapped up by the papers.

When the story broke he was not disappointed. It attracted a welcome additional influx of visitors, at first from the local area but later, as the word spread, from further afield.

There was another totally unexpected development which ultimately led to a modest investment in this small addition to the Military Museum collection being handsomely repaid, many times over! It happened quite by chance, as these things so often do.

Somebody from the Universal Film Studios at Los Angeles happened to read a press article and saw in it the kind of whimsical story around which a short documentary film could be made. Always in demand for makeweight features alongside major films, these shorts were money-spinners.

A Producer from the Studios made an appointment to meet Walter, to hear more about the story and see the exhibits for himself.

Subsequently, sitting talking to Walter, listening to him describing the people he had met in Kent and the highly interesting time he had spent at the fascinating rural engineering firm's depot set in the picturesque countryside of England, the Producer became convinced that there was material here for an interesting film. It had a ring about it which he felt certain would do well. His professional instincts were strongly aroused and a string of successes behind him had taught him to trust his first impressions and follow them up with confidence. His film company, for their part, had learnt that backing his hunches brought them rich dividends.

He went off back to Los Angeles and Walter heard nothing from him for several months. Film studios being what they are, when films are being shot people are kept very busy and new ideas take time to germinate.

When a development did take place it came as a very pleasant surprise. Beyond saying to Walter that he thought the story would make good material for a short documentary film and eliciting his agreement to be given first refusal to do this, he had gone off about his business and not been in touch since. Walter, who saw in the idea of a film the possibility of some excellent publicity for his museum, was beginning to think nothing was to come of it.

Suddenly, wheels began to turn—and turn fast! Walter was asked if he would be prepared to accompany the Producer on an 'all expenses paid' trip to visit Kent, so that, using his established liaison with SKWEC, they could take a serious look at the possibility of making a film. The idea was to trace the history of the cannon from the moment of its discovery right through to its delivery in San Francisco by the Royal Navy and the US Navy, and its present proud position of honour—with its associated display—at the Military Museum.

There was plenty of scope in that lot to provide some first-class entertainment. At any rate, the film company felt it warranted investigation and was prepared to invest money in exploring its potential. Apart from anything else, buried treasure was always a subject that evoked a great deal of public interest.

Needless to say, Walter jumped at the proposition and found himself not so very long afterwards back with his friends at the SKWEC depot in Kent.

Things went wonderfully well. Immersed in the atmosphere of the area, meeting the people concerned, seeing the equipment involved, travelling around the countryside looking at the scenery and the picturesque buildings, soon convinced the Producer that here was rich material indeed for his thirsty industry to fashion into a winner of a film.

The film was duly made and it proved as successful as the people at Universal Studios had hoped.

Walter not only received handsome royalties from the showing of the film, but also enjoyed widespread publicity for his Military Museum. How glad he was, looking back over events, that he had stuck to his guns at the auction sale at Christie's of London, as other would-be buyers of the unique Spanish Miquelet Flintlock pistol had 'bid him up', until, one by one, they threw in the towel, dropped out and gave him best.

And of course, indirectly, so were the seven happy steam men from the Garden of England, whose share-out had been 'bid up' by these frustrated people who had sought in vain to gain possession of this most exotic item of their Treasure Trove. Not only that, but they were all paid very generously by Universal Studios for the time they spent re-enacting various sequences in the story of the cannon under the direction of the Producer and his camera team, when parts of the film were created on location: a final bonus for the steam men!

Chapter 23

A WORKS OUTING FOR THE STEAM PLOUGHING TEAMS

to the R.H. & D. Miniature Railway and a Fairground

Early on a Saturday morning in late September, Bob Startle cycled out of Littlebrook heading for his firm's depot. But he was not going to work. He was off on his very first Works outing with his steam-ploughing team mates from the South Kent Wingash Engineering Company.

In the knapsack on his back was a goodly supply of food packed by his mother—theoretically to last him all day, but unlikely to do so, as witness her wry comment when she handed him the package.

"Here's your grub for the day, Bob," she'd said. "That should last you until about ten o'clock this morning!" She knew that her fast-growing and energetic son would be into the package soon after he set out on the journey aboard the firm's transport.

In a leather purse, in the inner pocket of his sports jacket, was his spending money for the day. It had been saved week-by-week in a special fund organised by SKWEC for the firm's annual outings. He paid similar personally-budgeted amounts each week into a Christmas Club and a Summer Holiday Fund. With these essentials taken care of and after his mother had received the weekly amount he paid towards his keep, he was able to spend his remaining pocket-money each week as he wished.

About two miles out of the village Bob heard the sound of a motorbike coming up behind him and was greeted as it passed him, by a loud, rather high-pitched 'pirp-pirp' as its driver squeezed the large rubber bulb of his air-operated hooter.

It was his much-respected engine-driver mentor, Joe, on his 500cc Norton, a machine against which he had traded-in his old 250cc Cotton, having decided, with no hesitation whatsoever, to spend part of his share of the Treasure Trove payment on this much cherished outfit. In the sidecar was Grant and on the pillion sat Sid, so that briefly—in close proximity on the road—were four of the five-man, steam-ploughing team. The fifth, Boris, they would be meeting later that day.

As Joe's powerful Norton sped past, the three men waved cheerfully to Bob, pumping his laborious way up the gradual incline of the road ahead.

Bob noticed again something which had been pointed out to him before. The Norton seemed to lope along at a good speed, yet without its engine revving as highly as most bikes did at the same speed. Joe said it was 'long-legged' on the road, a characteristic which was due, according to him, to the longer-than-normal cylinder which gave it a 'long-stroke', and a higher top gear than most bikes had.

One day Bob had stood by the roadside in the main street of Littlebrook with Henry Woodman, a local motorcyclist who went grass-track racing in his spare time, and watched two motor bikes go by in succession on an otherwise empty road. There was a marked difference in the two machines.

The first was a 250cc Velocette two-stroke, which blasted by with its fast-revving engine disturbing the peace of the village and leaving behind itself in the process a cloud of blue smoke, from its evidently well-worn engine.

Its staccato, very noisy exhaust created a racket made much worse by having had its exhaust's silencer baffles knocked out by its young rider. He was not alone in liking the extra sensation of power the noise gave. But the police didn't like it at all, and had a habit of shoving a cane up an exhaust pipe to probe inside the barrel to see if the baffle were there or not. This trick was countered by some enterprising riders who pushed a ball of wire-netting into the neck of the silencer barrel, to give the inquisitive policeman something to hit with his cane, just to keep him happy!

Behind the fast-revving, noisy Velocette, pacing it at a distance of some fifty yards, followed the second machine, a hefty 500cc Norton. It sounded altogether different. Its engine gave an effortless 'thomp' 'thomp' 'thomp' 'thomp' exhaust note as it moved disdainfully along with its engine to all intents and purposes seemingly just idling, but contriving to impart a latent message that it could go like a bat out of hell if its throttle were opened up.

"Hark at that Norton," Henry had said admiringly. "The bloody thing's just ticking over!"

Henry, who had owned a variety of machines, was an enthusiast and knew a thing or two about motorbikes, both as a rider and as a skilled mechanic. He had a natural flair for getting the best performance out of an engine.

Bob admired Henry's ability and expertise. He noted the evident approval in Henry's tone of voice and felt sure that if Henry thought Nortons were good, then they must be good.

It was a high regard which Bob knew was also shared by Joe. He had not been surprised when Joe had eventually bought one.

Judging by the way Nortons won so many national and international races it was obvious they knew what they were about in the business of motorcycle engine design.

Joe had secretly long wanted a Norton, but as a man with family responsibilities he just could not afford to buy a new one. It was quite beyond him. The best he had ever hoped for was to find a good second-hand one, but that wasn't easy because they were few and far between.

His desire for a Norton had been much strengthened last year when his hero, the popular racing motorcyclist Stanley Woods, had won the Isle of Man Senior TT race on a Norton, setting a new speed record of 67.54 mph for this important event.

Stanley Woods had made his Isle of Man debut in 1922 riding a Work's Cotton in the Junior TT race and coming a commendable fifth in this, his first TT race. The next year, in 1923, he went on to win this same annual race for Cotton's, against a field of 72 entries.

Joe at this time was a 'Cotton man', and he had noted this success with much pleasure. Thereafter, he took a special interest in Stanley Woods, who subsequently went from strength to strength to become a famous rider. When Stanley Woods switched over to Norton's, Joe's ambition to own a Norton himself was finally crystallised.

Joe's share of the Treasure Trove was like the answer to a prayer. He promptly bought himself a spanking new one, complete with a sidecar. Now he was able to take his whole family out and about together, whenever he wished. His faithful old Cotton was strictly a solo machine, or at best an occasional two-seater, though Joe had for some time past not liked loading it with a pillion passenger because it had clutch-slip trouble which was exacerbated by the extra weight. In practice the Cotton was merely transport to get him to work and back. It was seldom used for pleasure.

The arrival of his Norton added a new dimension to the lives of Joe and his family. They were able to go to the coast whenever they liked instead of the very few trips each year by bus and train, to which previously they had been limited.

Watching his three friends go out ahead of him so swiftly and easily, as meanwhile he slogged his way up the long, gradual hill against a slight headwind, Bob's already half-determined intention to switch to a motorbike when he reached the age of sixteen, was reinforced. Not many boys of his age could hope to be able to buy one for many years to come. But then, not many were fortunate enough to have a share in a small fortune, dug up out of the ground, safely stored away in an ancient cannon! To back up his dreams, Bob had the comforting knowledge that safely tucked away at home was his Post Office Savings Book!

By the time Bob reached the depot a small group of men was already there, so he was cheered in by some of them as he pedalled up the roadway and turned in through the wide entrance to the vehicle park.

The occasion was a get-together of the firm's five, five-man, steam-ploughing teams, an annual event when—with the co-operation of their firm who supplied the transport—they went off to the coast for the day on an outing.

By eight o'clock, the planned departure time, they were all aboard a six-wheeler Sentinel steam lorry, with twenty-four of them sitting on improvised seats on the back of the polished-up vehicle which took on for the day something of the appearance of an open-topped holiday charabanc. Its crew, Arthur and Terry, the two who had shared in the good fortune of the Treasure Trove group, had cleaned it up and prepared it for the day.

Now they were off, all in high spirits and looking forward very much to the day ahead. Arthur drove the Sentinel. By his side in the cab sat Terry, together with Frank Thrushton, the Works Manager, who particularly wanted to accompany them on this trip. Several such groups of staff went on outings each year and usually a representative of the Management went with them if the firm's vehicles were being used.

Today these men of steam had two destinations, both close to their hearts—a miniature steam railway and a large, well-established travelling fair. For Frank the day was a mixture of business and pleasure, for he was closely concerned with both of these organisations in his SKWEC work.

In the morning they were heading for a visit to the Romney, Hythe & Dymchurch Railway, newly opened earlier that year. This fascinating miniature railway project had captured the interest and attention of many people for miles around, not least Frank Thrushton and his boss Richard Livingstone. They had already visited the railway twice while it had been under construction.

Running on track just fifteen inches wide, using locomotives, carriages and trucks built exactly to a one-third scale, it was an engineering project of great interest, not only to men who spent their lives working with steam engines like the group from SKWEC, but also to the public at large.

In the first week of August 1926, the railway received its first major publicity. It was a bonus to the owners of the railway, which arose because the Duke of York was visiting a Boy's Camp that he sponsored, situated near St. Mary's Bay, between New Romney and Dymchurch. It happened that the new railway line was due to pass near the Camp, and the Duke had become interested in the new venture. He had expressed a desire to see it while he was in the area and perhaps, if it were possible, to have a first ride on one of the R.H. & D.R.'s trains. When the time of the visit came round, the line had only just reached as far as the Camp, but there was a usable connection from there back to its starting point at New Romney.

The Duke had his wish and travelled sitting cross-legged on the tender of the locomotive 'Northern Chief' for the two-mile journey from the Camp to New Romney. He was accompanied by Captain J.E.P. Howey, the enthusiastic owner of the railway whose brainchild it was, and also by the Chief Engineer of the London & North Eastern Railway who was very interested in this fascinating new railway development, it being a serious engineering enterprise.

A small group of coaches and wagons had been assembled for the occasion, to be pulled by the locomotive, giving the train an authentic operational appearance. Several privileged guests and dignitaries, together with representatives of the Press, travelled in the coaches on the short journey. Their great enthusiasm and approval did much to enhance still further the impact of the news of the visit upon the public at large.

After being shown over the station and workshops at New Romney, the party returned on the train, in high spirits, to the Boy's Camp.

Richard Livingstone and Frank Thrushton were among those who gathered at New

Romney to see the Duke of York arrive on this well-planned excursion. In the event, behind the scenes, they learnt that it was only by a great deal of last-minute hard work that the line had been finished as far as the Boy's Camp, in time for this most welcome visit by a member of the Royal Family.

It was well worth the effort because the event received widespread publicity and brought to the attention of many people this new and so unusual miniature railway.

As men with an engineering background, whose lives were so closely associated with technical matters in general and with steam engines in particular, Richard and Frank were fascinated by this 'toy town' sized, yet fully engineered railway. Everything about it was precisely true to the form of its big brothers, but scaled down to one-third size in all respects.

Their second visit was almost one year later, in July 1927, when Earl Beauchamp, the then Lord Warden of the Cinque Ports, officially opened the R.H. & D. Railway in a ceremony at its Hythe Station Terminus.

To the cheers of the assembled crowd, he cleared the starting signal to allow the locomotive 'Hercules' to set off to New Romney, pulling behind it a long train carrying passengers in its twenty-four coaches—some enclosed, but others partly open to the weather. It was a long remembered Saturday by those lucky enough to be there. Richard and Frank were among those who travelled on this special train.

Back at their jobs at SKWEC the next week, they were sad to learn that the very next day the railway claimed its first staff victim. A twenty-seven year old platelayer was killed on the line near Hythe. He stepped sideways out of the way of a train coming towards him on the line he was working on, straight into the path of another coming in the opposite direction.

This tragic accident pointed immediately to the need to treat the little railway with as much caution and respect as any other railway of normal size. It carried traffic regularly in both directions, and a train approaching against a strong head-wind was not heard until it was almost upon anybody on the line. Winds blew strongly across the flat coastal land covered by the railway. Straying sheep faced the same danger and precautions had to be taken to avoid accidents.

On the day of the SKWEC outing, the situation was that only the first main section of the railway, from Hythe to New Romney via Dymchurch had been completed and was open to the public. The final section, from New Romney to Dungeness, was still under construction.

When finished, the overall length of the track was to be just less than fourteen miles, with dual tracks allowing for continuous regular trains in both directions, running to a proper schedule. It was a wonderful concept and destined to capture the imagination of generations of holidaymakers and visitors for years ahead.

During the afternoon the happy party of men were going to visit Carlo's Travelling Fair, at present situated in an extensive area near the Royal Military Canal at Hythe. The Fair was conveniently sited within easy reach of Folkestone on one side and Dymchurch on the other, with Ashford and Canterbury not too far away inland.

Although hitherto not on Carlo's itinerary, Hythe had attracted his notice this year because of the opening of the new miniature railway. The day of its inauguration had been widely publicised and was almost certain to bring in an increased number of visitors to that part of the Kentish coast during the year from that day on.

Not for the first time, Sam Donatello, proprietor of Carlo's Fairground Company, got it right. A shrewd business man, his decision to visit Hythe that year proved a winner. It was mutually beneficial to Sam and to the owners of the Railway, a result which led to fruitful close co-operation between the two companies in following years.

People travelling on the little railway passed right along the boundary of the fairground, which was so extensive and exciting-looking that it positively beckoned them in for a visit. The fair in full swing offered much of interest, and having had a panoramic view of it there were few of the happy passengers who could resist a visit when they got off their train at the R.H. & D.R. Station at Hythe.

Similarly, people in the fairground, seeing the fascinating little trains steaming by carrying dozens of waving passengers in its variety of small carriages, were intrigued by it and many subsequently travelled the line themselves.

Sam was a third generation fairground man. His great grandfather Giovanni Donatello, with his wife Margherita, came to England from Italy in 1838, to run a restaurant in Brighton.

Their eldest son Carlo, Sam's grandfather, went to work as a boy in a local fairground. He liked it so much that he eventually became a 'traveller' and spent the rest of his life as one.

As a young man Carlo worked for three years on a steam-operated roundabout. Called among the fairground fraternity a Galloper, it had three rows of ornate horses on which the riders sat. As they were whirled around on the moving platform, the horses continuously rose up and down so that the rider had the impression of galloping along.

Prosperity in the fairground business only came to those who owned rides, sideshows or stalls, not to those who just worked for owners. At first Carlo's parents had been none too keen on his becoming a traveller, but eventually, when it became clear that this was the life he intended to follow, they helped him to buy his first ride so that he could build a real future for himself.

He had the opportunity, at the age of twenty-one, in the year 1851, to buy a steam-driven Chairoplane Roundabout from an elderly couple quitting the business to retire. Less complicated and costly than a set of Gallopers, the riders sat in chairs suspended by chains. It was driven by a steam engine, mounted centrally in an integrated design that was reliable and well-proven. As the speed built up, the riders were flung progressively further outwards and upwards, to finish up speeding round and round about halfway between the ground and the spinning ornate top above them, from which the chains were hung.

With this acquisition, and married to Liz Matthews, daughter of a fairground family, Carlo was on his way, launched into what proved to be a highly successful career.

By the time their only son Enrico, Sam's Dad, was a young man, Carlo was the proud owner of several rides. He also possessed a Burrell Showman's Engine and, wonderful in appearance, a highly decorative Marenghi 89-key Fairground Organ which blasted out music hour after hour to create the inimitable atmosphere associated with the excitement of a fair.

When Carlo retired in 1895 he handed over to Enrico a very prosperous, well-established business. All the rides bore the name Carlo as part of their title. This was a calculated decision which had led to the development of Carlo's Fair, for instead of being the owner of one ride and travelling as a part of somebody else's fair, Carlo's ambition had always been to own the core business himself, with others contracting to travel the rounds with him each season.

Sam grew up in a palatial caravan as the son of the proprietor of a flourishing fairground company. Following typical travelling fairground family traditions, he never had any thought other than to join his Dad's business when he left school.

By the time Sam eventually took over from Enrico, his Dad, at the age of thirty-six in the year 1923, well over half the rides, shows and stalls which constituted the fair, were actually owned by the Carlo Fairground Company. The remainder were individual owners who were only too happy to be allowed to make their living by running their own particular enterprise as part of the now prestigious Carlo operation. In total it was by then a large and very impressive organisation which could command some of the best available sites in main holiday resorts and towns in Kent and Sussex.

Independent owners wishing to join the organisation to travel with it regularly each year, were vetted with great care. They needed to be compatible with the variety of rides and shows already well-established there. In addition, they had to maintain the image and good standards of Carlo's, with its wide reputation as a happy place for families to visit.

Sam always welcomed those who brought new innovations, because the greater the variety, the more popular and sought-after the fair became. The latest of these, at the time that the fair was at Hythe, was a Wall-of-Death introduced only that year for the first time. It was a real crowd-puller. A spectator show such as this attracted to it many people who then circulated around the fairground to part with their money wherever their attention was grabbed by the insistent callers who everywhere clamoured for their custom.

Many of these worked directly for Sam, on his own rides and sideshows. There were two elements to their income—a low weekly wage and a generous commission on the money they took. The right people earned a very good living, especially on major installations. But their career came to an abrupt end if they succumbed to the temptation to cheat their employer. Sam and those close to him were very vigilant and there was little they did not know about underhand ways in which the firm could be milked and swindled. A lot of cash changed hands in the fairground when it was going full blast.

People directly employed by Sam, and who earned his trust, were very well treated and enjoyed their lives. Most were seasonal, doing other jobs for the closed-down winter period. Only a few key men associated with the rides worked all the year round. These did maintenance on the equipment when it was resting in its winter quarters.

Boris was one of the seasonal workers whose services were much valued by Sam. He drove and looked after Sam's newest and most expensive Burrell Showman's Engine. It supplied power for a part of the fairground when the fair was operational. When moving locations, it towed Sam's fine living-quarters together with a heavily-laden trailer, plus Boris's own caravan. The latter, bought by Sam specifically for Boris, though small and unpretentious, was a very comfortable home-from-home for the unattached Boris throughout the whole summer season.

By good fortune the day of the outing was one of those fine September days which seem almost like a return to mid-summer, more especially so after the kind of disappointingly wet and blustery period in late August that they had recently endured. It was sunny and bright, with the sky virtually cloudless.

The journey to Hythe was very pleasant. Out on the open road the Sentinel's engine ran smoothly and sweetly, surprisingly quietly too in the ears of the men it carried, who spent their lives with the relatively slow-moving traction engine workhorses, which were quiet only when they were idling, but often barked loudly when coping with their heavy duties.

Up on the back the happy party of men spent much of the time singing lustily against the background, fast-running regular beat of the chuntering steam engine's exhaust note. It was quite exhilarating riding on the open back of the wagon, with the fresh air streaming by as they moved swiftly along. There was little traffic on the road and the journey through the open countryside and villages on route was much enjoyed on such a lovely day.

Well before ten o'clock the Sentinel reached Hythe and pulled up in the car park alongside the recently built miniature railway station, adjacent to the towpath of the Royal Military Canal. Losing no time at all the men were quickly off the back of the lorry and queuing up at the R.H & D. Railway ticket office to buy return tickets to New Romney.

Waiting by the platform, scheduled to leave in ten minutes time, was the next train. It was already beginning to fill up, so no time was lost in getting aboard to bag a seat by plonking items of luggage or coats on the seats and then clambering out again to inspect the fascinating surroundings. There were sixteen carriages to choose from, each one having two sections, in each of which were four seats. They learnt later that sometimes twenty carriages were pulled, with up to one hundred and sixty passengers being carried at a time. Larger coaches to carry ten, twelve and sixteen passengers were planned.

Everything about the station was intriguing, being an accurate scale model of the normal thing. The R.H & D. Railway was advertised as being strictly a 'miniature' one, implying a scaled-down version of the original, rather than a narrow-gauge railway which did not purport to be uniformly scaled-down in size in all of its proportions.

This was a point much emphasised by the owners, to distinguish the whole operation from the many light railways used for industrial or pleasure purposes, which were of arbitrary size and not uniformly scaled in all aspects of their equipment and installations.

This precise scaling was illustrated in a very interesting picture the Company produced, which bore the title *The Giant and the Dwarf.* It showed an R.H. & D.R. Pacific Class 4-6-2 Locomotive, with its eight-wheeled tender, standing beside a full-sized version of the same engine from the L.N.E.R. stable. This side view photograph showed how faithful an image the one was of the other. Taken from a viewpoint about six feet or so above the normal railway platform level, even their respective track sizes could be compared in the photograph, for the small engine stood on a length of its own one-third scaled track.

The L.N.E.R. engine shown was the famous No. 4472 Flying Scotsman, and its small companion was the R.H. & D.R. Typhoon. Sam Donatello, proprietor of Carlo's Fairground Company, was so captivated by this intriguing picture that he got his talented Fairground signwriter/artist to make an enlarged painting of it, in full colour rather than the monochrome of the photograph. With his usual meticulous attention to detail, this gifted man produced a magnificent painting. It reproduced the well-known L.N.E.R.'s lined green livery in which the R.H. & D.R. locomotive and tender had also been decorated. The result was not only a truly remarkable work of art, but also illustrated very graphically the underlying precision-engineering that lay behind the whole concept of the R.H & D.R. project. The painting became one of Sam Donatello's most prized possessions. It subsequently adorned Sam's luxury caravan for years to come and was much admired by friends and visitors.

The Hythe Terminus Station was examined with great interest by the SKWEC party. There were four roofed-over platforms; a signal box just up the line; a turntable to allow arriving engines to reverse their direction for the return journey; a small engine shed; and a siding for goods traffic which led out to the car park where the Sentinel now stood, content to stand patiently, hissing gently, waiting for the return of its passengers who at the moment were eagerly awaiting a ride behind its small, but powerful and extremely elegant steam-driven cousin on the adjacent railway.

The men gazed around in wonder at this unique railway, taking in the evidence everywhere of the close attention to authentic detail of those who had been responsible for designing it all.

Like moths to a lamp, the fascinated visitors were soon attracted by the operational end of the whole business—the impressive, true-life locomotive standing steamed-up, hissing and ready to go, at the end of the platform. It bore the name Green Goddess.

The driver, dressed in conventional train driver fashion with a peaked cap and boiler suit, his face smudged with soot, stood by its side, busy as always during waiting times, cleaning and polishing the gleaming paintwork. This was normal routine and kept the engines in immaculate condition.

It was part of the driver's life to expect a barrage of questions from highly-interested passengers and visitors. The arrival of a party of men whose lives were spent working with steam engines, predictably proved no exception and pretty soon they were crowding round him to hear what he had to say.

He told them that the Green Goddess was the first locomotive the railway had obtained. The second one was called Northern Chief. These were known as Pacific Class locomotives and were long, beautifully-proportioned engines, having six large driving wheels, four front bogie wheels and two bogie wheels at the rear under the cab.

The driver pointed out that this four-six-two arrangement of wheels distributed the weight of the locomotive evenly on the track, leading to a smooth ride. Known in the trade as 4-6-2s, the R.H. & D.R. Company's original fleet of eight locomotives included five of these, two 4-8-2s and one 0-4-0 TT. The latter he said, was called The Bug. It was a small shunting engine, having no front or rear bogie wheels to complement its four driving wheels, hence its 0-4-0 TT designation. The significance of the TT was that the engine was equipped with a separate coal and water tender, such 'tank tenders' being a familiar feature of normal-sized shunting locomotives.

The other three Pacific Class 4-6-2s were named Southern Maid, Typhoon and Hurricane. The two 4-8-2 locomotives with their extra pair of driving wheels were named Hercules and Samson, because of their heavy-load-pulling ability. The eight driving wheels gave greater traction than the six of the Pacific Class 4-6-2s. It had been Hercules, the driver explained, that had been chosen to pull the train of twenty coaches at the official opening ceremony earlier that year, in July.

The driver was pleased with the high level of interest shown by the SKWEC audience clustered around him, who listened with rapt attention to everything he told them. Like his colleagues on the staff, he was an enthusiast and only too happy to talk about the locomotives that he worked on.

He was busy showing them how the three large driving wheels on each side were mutually coupled, so that each of the two side-mounted cylinders thus directly drove one set of these traction wheels, when a blast on the Station Master's whistle warned them to find their seats. A call of "All aboard, please!" repeated several times, sent the men hurrying off.

In a matter of moments, on a wave of the Guard's green flag, the driver, sitting on his seat on the front of the coal tender and working the control levers inside the engine's cab immediately in front of him, set the train moving. In this position his head was just above the roof of the cab so that he looked along the top of the locomotive to the track ahead. He could, in bad weather, crouch down to keep his head under shelter, looking out of the side-windows of the child-sized cab, as do standing drivers on normal full-sized locomotives.

With a cheerful 'toot' 'toot' on his steam whistle, the driver gave the engine its head, and the train gathered speed to pull out of the Hythe Station on its thirty-five minute, eight-mile journey to New Romney, there being four stops on the way.

The party of SKWEC steam-ploughing men, some in fully enclosed carriages and others preferring to ride in the open-sided, windowless ones, were off on their first jaunt of the day.

Almost immediately they came in sight of the extensive, gaily-decorated Fairground ahead of them. As they passed along the side of it, about fifty yards from its perimeter fence, a shout of "There's Boris!" went up and several of them spotted Boris standing by the side of a fine Burrell Showman's Engine. He was looking towards the train and waving to them, having worked out that if all went well this would be the train his friends would be on. He knew the proposed itinerary of their outing and was on the lookout for them.

As the train puffed by, still slogging hard to gain speed, Boris recognised many familiar faces among the passengers aboard it. He knew they would all be back to see him in the Fairground during the afternoon.

Shortly afterwards the railway line turned to follow the coast, moving away from the Royal Military Canal which headed off across open country.

"Where does that Canal there go to, Joe?" asked Bob, as the train parted company with it. Joe sat beside him with an Ordnance Survey Map open on his lap so that he could pencil in their route, to give a rough idea of the run of the new railway which was not, of course, shown on existing maps.

It was something Joe had already checked, for the Royal Military Canal was clearly marked on the map, since it was an important feature of the area.

"It cuts across country in a loop that's twenty-three miles long in all," answered Joe. "It joins up with the River Rother near the village of Iden, at Iden Lock, near an area called the Isle of Oxney. From that point on, the river was deepened, apparently, and altered to make a continuation of the Canal so that boats could travel all the way from Hythe to where the River Rother runs into the sea by Camber Sands, not far from the town of Rye."

Joe pointed out the route of the Canal on his map and Bob studied it with interest.

"It doesn't seem to be used much," commented Bob. "What was it built there for in the first place? And why is it called the Royal Military Canal?"

Joe was used to being quizzed by Bob, who was never content until he knew exactly what things were all about.

For a few moments Joe consulted his little Guide Book covering the Romney Marsh area.

"It says here," he said, "that it was dug between 1805 and 1807 during the Napoleonic invasion scare. It's supposed to be eighteen feet deep and sixty feet wide. As well as being a defence line it was used to shift soldiers and equipment quickly from place to place across the marshes."

He paused a few moments and read on a bit, studying some of the pictures in the booklet.

"Apparently," he continued, "at the same time, between Folkestone and Seaford, all those Martello Towers along this part of the coast were built. It says here that in 1794 British troops had a hell of a job trying to capture a round tower at Cape Mortella in Corsica, so somebody thought it would be a good idea to build some like them around here where they thought Napoleon's armies would land. Seventy four were built, in all.

There's a note here which says that all along the Canal were cannons mounted in embrasures, at every angle of the bank. All those preparations must have scared them off, because they never did show up over here!"

"Don't blame them!" commented Bob emphatically.

"Can't say I do either," agreed Joe. "Seems like they'd have got a bloody nose if they'd tried to land around here!"

Settling down to its running speed of between 20 and 30 mph the train headed towards Dymchurch. On the way it stopped briefly at Botolph's Bridge Halt to pick up and unload goods which were stored in a small shelter on the platform, and stopped again at a small station called Burmarsh Road, where two local people got off and one got on. It was clear that the new railway was already being used as a local service by the few people living out in the area of Willop Marshes and Burmarsh Village.

About twenty minutes after leaving Hythe, the train pulled into Dymchurch Station. Several people got off at this popular sandy holiday resort and a few boarded, heading for New Romney.

Among those who got off were a couple with two small children from the same coach that Arthur, Terry and Frank Thrushton were in. They said that they had travelled on the Southern Railway from London to the Sandling Road Station at Hythe, crossed the town in a waiting ferry-bus to the R.H. & D.R. Station, to get to Dymchurch for a week's holiday.

In previous years they had taken a bus from Hythe to Dymchurch, but were now thrilled to have the little railway as part of their planned holiday journey. Tomorrow, they said, they were going to take the train to New Romney for the day. The three men were amazed to notice how quickly the miniature railway was integrating itself into the permanent transport network of the area, as well as being a holiday joyride facility. This was precisely what those who had planned it had intended it to do.

Within three minutes the train was off again, heading for New Romney. Five minutes later it stopped at Jefferstone Lane Station, near the small sandy St. Mary's Bay which was just ten minutes' walk away. This was the Holiday Camp stop which the Duke of York had visited when Frank and Richard had been down on their first visit the previous year.

Fifteen minutes later they were in New Romney where they all got off to go on the visit Frank had laid on for them, to the R.H. & D.R.'s Workshop facilities centred there by the owners of the well-organised new railway. From the start it had been the firm intention of those who planned the system, that though a miniature railway of limited extent, it would lack nothing necessary to ensure that it functioned efficiently and reliably with proper maintenance arrangements to enable the company to look after itself with a minimum of outside help.

While Frank went off to find an old friend of his who was going to show them around, the rest of the party had a look at the Romney Station.

The front of this new R.H. & D.R. Station was arranged rather like a small version of King's Cross terminus in London, with a drive-in crescent for cars and taxis and even a miniature clock tower on the building.

Conveniently, just across the Littlestone Road, which the R.H. & D.R. Station faced, was the Southern Railway Station. The new miniature railway now formed a link between the mainline Southern Railway stations at New Romney and Hythe, something people had long thought desirable but one which the mainline S.R. Company had not been disposed to put in.

Entrance to the R.H. & D.R. New Romney Station was through a booking office building. Inside there were four platforms, two for arrivals and two for departures.

At the buffers the tracks were arranged so that engines could be taken off one line and run on to another. Incoming coaches had to be switched from track to track and picked up by another engine, while the arriving one went off to be turned and serviced across the yard.

One of the staff said he thought the system would change when the extension to Dungeness was built. At the moment New Romney, like Hythe, was a terminus. That would alter when trains passed through New Romney and on to Dungeness, which would then form the end of the line.

Looking out of the station along the lines the party could see the familiar sight of a signal box from which traffic in and out was controlled. Beyond it, on both sides of the track, were several buildings providing workshops, maintenance facilities, locomotive and carriage sheds and also storage space for spares and equipment.

As they stood looking around, they spotted Frank coming towards them from the workshop area, accompanied by a tall, lean man dressed in a buff-coloured garage coat.

Frank introduced his friend as Bill Fordyce who had left his job at the Ashford Railway Works to join the staff of the R.H. & D.R. Company the previous year.

"Bill has kindly offered to take us on a quick tour of all the service and back-up facilities of the Railway," Frank said.

"My pleasure," confirmed Bill, who, wasting no time, got straight into his task as a guide.

"New Romney," he explained, "is the Headquarters of the Romney, Hythe and Dymchurch Railway. Although at the moment it is a terminus, when the whole lot is completed it will lie roughly at the centre, with a terminus at Dungeness in one direction and the other terminus at Hythe, where you have come from, in the other direction. This is a good place to centre all the workshop and storage facilities. If you come along with me I'll give you a quick run over the whole place. But I have to get you back here by twelve o'clock to catch your train back to Hythe, so we can't spend too long anywhere."

So saying, Bill strode off down the sidings which led to the quite extensive service area. "We will have a look at the inter-railway transfer platform first," he said. "Then we will look at the various buildings."

On the inland side of the railway he took them to a spur line which ended alongside a 250ft long platform. To their surprise, on the other side of the platform was a standard gauge railway line. The juxtaposition of the two lines showed up in sharp perspective the relative sizes of the two systems. The standard gauge line was itself a spur off the Southern Railway line on the other side of the Littlestone Road, which it crossed at a level-crossing. The neat arrangement allowed freight to be transhipped between the two railways and in effect served to integrate the miniature railway with the national rail system. For the temporary safe storage of anything valuable there was a small lock-up building on the R.H. & D.R. side of the spur line.

"There was a lot of fuss and bother about putting this arrangement in," commented Bill. "Some people didn't like the level-crossing being put in there at all. But it's a good idea. It's a direct link for freight purposes between the R.H. & D.R. and the mainline railway system. The Southern Railway can even ship us in a new locomotive here, never mind anything else!"

On the same side of the line Bill showed them two carriage sheds which would be able to contain a surprisingly large number of coaches and wagons, as the firm developed.

On the seaward side of the track was the locomotive shed, into which three parallel sets of rails led, to accommodate three rows of locomotives at a time.

Bill referred to it as a 'three-road' shed and told them that at night there could be six engines in there, 'cooling their heels' until morning. The first train on the system's lines each morning ran from New Romney to Hythe, which then placed a locomotive at the Hythe Terminus for the return journey. Thereafter trains ran in both directions for the rest of the day. A turntable in front of the locomotive shed allowed them to manipulate the engines in any way they wished, for servicing purposes, or to interchange locomotives pulling a given train if needed.

Next to this building was one of similar size which was the main workshop. Bill showed them its versatile capabilities with some pride, because he had been involved in organising it.

At one end of the workshop was a totally unexpected sight, and it soon became apparent that miniature railway engines were not the only factor which had attracted Bill away from his world of normal railways.

Parked there was a monster of a racing car, but one not unknown to the visitors by reputation, although only a few of them had actually seen it before. One of these was Sid Moon, the 'master ploughman' of the Treasure Trove team. He recognised it straight away.

"Hell's bloody bells!" he exclaimed in an excited voice. "That's old Ba-roff-ski's racing car, Chitty Chitty Bang Bang! What's that doing in here?"

Bill Fordyce grinned widely. "You're quite right," he confirmed, with obvious pleasure. "At least, it's one of them. That one was the first of the four Chitty Chitty Bang Bangs that Count Zborowski had constructed for him before he was killed driving in the Italian Grand Prix at Monza in 1924. It belongs to my Guv'nor now. Captain Howey is a racing driver too and he was a great friend of the Count's. That's how it came to be here, in the first place."

Bill paused a few moments then went on to explain.

"Count Zborowski was interested in building a fifteen-inch gauge miniature railway on that big estate of his on the Dover Road, three or four miles from Canterbury. I was asked by a friend of mine to give a hand with a small engine he'd got out there, some three years ago. I got to know him well, and helped him with his cars as well as his miniature steam engines. Captain Howey was often over there with the Count. The two of them were mad keen on the same two interests—racing cars and miniature steam locomotives." Bill looked thoughtful and a little sad. He had been fond of the flamboyant, fun-loving and enthusiastic Count.

"As a matter of fact," he continued, "the first 4-6-2 Pacific Class locomotive that was bought for this railway, the Green Goddess, was actually ordered by Count Zborowski for his own railway he planned to make. Both it and the next one on the stocks that he'd ordered—the Northern Chief, which was another of the same type—were taken over by the Captain and those were the two locomotives he started with. Of course it all turned out well for me because I was offered a full-time job over here and I jumped at it. And a very interesting job it's turned out to be too. Suits me fine."

This little discussion excited the interest of all those present. Forgotten for the moment was the world of miniature railways as they gathered round the huge, unlikely-looking car and studied it with some awe.

"Made by Mercedes-Maybach, that was," stated Bill, standing with the now silent crowd of men gazing at the huge car. "That thing's got a 23-litre aeroplane engine in it. A famous car, that is. In 1921 the Count lapped Brooklands at 108 mph driving that. Caused a sensation at the time. It was named Chitty Chitty Bang Bang because of the hell of a racket it made starting up. After that one, the Count had three more aeroplane-engined cars made following in one another's wheel-tracks so to speak, and they were all given the same name."

"I didn't know that," commented Sid. "But what I do know is that I saw that one there, more than once, pass through Littlebrook going like a bloody rocket."

Sid smiled, apparently remembering something with amusement.

"The first time," he went on, "I was outside Bill Gunston's shop looking at Bill's Harley Davidson with Henry Woodman. Henry was helping Bill do a job on it. Suddenly there was an almighty roar and that bloody great car shot by going like a bat out of hell.

338

The driver had a racing helmet and goggles on and he waved his hand as he shot by. Henry had jumped out of the way when he'd seen it coming. 'Hi-up! Mind your back!' he said. 'That's old Ba-roff-ski—if you don't watch him he'll snatch you up as he goes by and sit you on his bonnet as a mascot!' Henry said he'd watched the Count drive many times. He said the Count was one hell of a bloke on a race track, full of fun and no nerves at all in a racing car. It was too good to be true, though, to keep on taking risks like he did. Fate seemed certain to catch up with him. And sure enough, just like his Dad, he was killed motor racing in the end."

"Yes," said Bill. "It was too good to last. It shook Captain Howey up no end when the Count was killed. They were such close friends. Then of course the Captain's young brother was killed road racing near Boulogne in France last year. That was the end of motor racing for Captain Howey. He gave it up altogether after that. But he had not lost his interest in cars, or anything else that moves either, come to that. He's a real enthusiast."

"He had a rough time last year, didn't he?" commented Frank, "The day after we came down here to see the Duke of York at New Romney, you had that young platelayer killed on the track. Then, about two weeks later the Captain's brother was killed. It put a damper on things, I should think, down here."

"Yes, it certainly did," agreed Bill. "The atmosphere changed from excitement to gloom. Being such a small outfit makes us all feel like members of a family group. It seemed a bad omen at the time. Richard, the Captain's brother, was only twenty-eight years old, if I remember rightly. Much about the same age as the platelayer. But, as always, life went on and things brightened up a bit soon afterwards. And now things are going really well. The railway is running smoothly and we're all gaining confidence in its future as each week passes. It's a very exciting outfit to be involved in. Something really different from the normal run of things. I find it fascinating."

Before the party left, Bill took them into a building where his boss had several cars of various types stored. He was a true enthusiast, and though by no means as wealthy as Count Zborowski, he was nonetheless able to afford to indulge himself without the kind of financial restraints that severely limited the scope of most of those who shared the same interests.

Tucked away in the building among the others, was stored a 7-litre Leyland racing car. It was the first racing car actually owned by Captain Howey, though not the first he'd driven. He bought it in 1923 and drove it at Brooklands. By the Count's standards it was a very modest car. To the man in the street, however, it was far from modest and seemed a very impressive car indeed, standing high off the ground and with its very long, double-strapped bonnet fronted by a large square radiator.

Apart from actual cars, in the building there were many pictures of cars because Count Zborowski had had a fleet in excess of thirty of his own cars in his own private, well-staffed workshops.

He was also a founder member of the famous Aston Martin Motor Company and was very well known in the motoring world.

Also on show was a picture of the car in which another close friend of Captain Howey's, Kenelm Lee Guinness, drove at 133 mph in 1922, to break the then-existing British land speed record.

Before they left the workshop area the party of enthusiasts were fortunate enough to be addressed for some fifteen minutes or so by the man who was the technical consultant behind the entire railway project.

Henry Greenly, one of the foremost authorities on miniature railways and model engineering, was both an engineer and an architect. He had designed much of the rolling stock, the engines, the track and the buildings. They were fascinated by his talk and could have listened to him for much longer.

After he had gone on his way, Bill Fordyce told his visitors that Henry Greenly was widely known and respected not only in Great Britain but in many countries overseas. He was often called in by people seeking advice because he was able to design total systems, and not many men could do that.

By then it was just before mid-day and Frank Thrushton had to winkle his party out of the building to get them back to the station in time to catch their scheduled train back to Hythe.

With a chorus of thanks they said goodbye to Bill Fordyce and hurried to the departure platform. At 12.10pm exactly, running with the precision which Captain Howey insisted upon, their stout-hearted Pacific locomotive pulled its train of sixteen carriages out of New Romney Station. Bang on time it arrived at Hythe at 12.45pm, a journey-time of exactly the advertised thirty-five minutes.

Captain Howey was a stickler for precision, partly perhaps as a reply to those many sceptics who scoffed at the suggestion that he could run a professional service with a miniature railway.

The group who planned the R.H & D.R. had to overcome much opposition, not least from the East Kent Roadcar Company which did not much care for the prospect of having to compete with a new railway, albeit a miniature one, in an area where they had a monopoly of public transport! Captain Howey had invested a great deal of money in the building and equipping of the Railway, and most of the men working for him knew full well that these early days were critical in establishing the new venture. They gave him their full support, and worked hard to make sure that all things ran smoothly. It was very much a team effort.

On leaving the station at Hythe, the SKWEC party broke up for lunch, having arranged to re-assemble by the Sentinel at two o'clock.

In twos and threes they wandered off to have something to eat, and then explore Hythe for a while. Most of them took their packed lunches over to the nearby Royal Military Canal and sat on its banks in the warm sunshine to enjoy the peaceful scene.

Afterwards some of them went into a nearby pub for a drink before it was time to go to the fair. Among these were the Treasure Trove team, joined by Frank Thrushton.

Joe called for a Milk Stout.

"Might as well support the local firm," he said, taking a long swig of the rich, dark-brown beer. "Lovely," he added, with deep satisfaction. "You can't beat it!"

"Why did you say the 'local firm'?" asked Bob, feeling very much a man among men with his glass of beer, and smoking one of the small slender cigarettes from the paper packet of five Woodbines he'd just bought.

"Because," confirmed Joe, dealing with yet another of the endless stream of questions he was used to fielding all day long from his young workmate, "it's made by Mackeson's of Hythe. Their brewery is not far from here. Mackeson's Milk Stout is made right here in Hythe." He held his glass up to the light, looked through it appreciatively and took another swig. "Lovely drink this is," he said again, with obvious pleasure.

"I'll have to try one!" said Bob eagerly.

"Well, you'll enjoy it a damn sight better than that Bitter you've got there," asserted Joe. "It's a much softer, sweeter drink than that raw old stuff you're drinking!"

"Why do they call it Milk Stout?" queried Bob, "Is it made from milk instead of water?"

There was a chorus of laughter at this suggestion. The Landlord joined in and answered Bob's question.

"No, son," he replied. "It's not made from milk, but it does have a connection with milk. It is sweetened by a non-fermenting sugar called lactose and lactose comes from milk. They told me that when I went over the Brewery with the Dart's Club from this very pub a few weeks ago. Until then I must confess I didn't know why the name was chosen. I just thought it was because the Milk Stout has a softish taste, rather like milk does."

"I must fix you blokes up with a visit to Mackeson's," intervened Frank. "You'd enjoy that. I went round with a party from the Works a few years ago. It was very interesting—especially when we got to the Sampling Room!"

Frank grinned as he recalled memories of this visit.

"They dish out free beer in there. Visitors choose their drink from the various ones the firm brews and sample it. We helped them out by doing some sampling for them," he continued, with a broad smile. "In fact we stayed in there quite a long time 'sampling'! Of course most blokes thought they ought to do the firm a favour by sampling as many different kinds as they could. A fine old time we had in there! And we came out feeling a bit tipsy too! Mind you it didn't do the firm any harm. We got to like the stuff. I often call for a Mackeson's. It's bloody good beer!"

"Will you fix up a visit for us, then?" asked Arthur. "Sounds like a trip worth making, that does!"

"Yes, I'll do that," agreed Frank. "And I might tell you, I'll come with you all too, just to make sure you behave yourselves!"

There was a chuckle from the group at that proviso. Glancing at the pub's large wall clock, Frank decided it was time he shepherded them back to the Sentinel parked at the R.H. & D.R. Station, to move off to their second destination of the day.

"Drink up!" he called. "It's time we were off to the Fair. But I should keep off the roundabouts for a bit if I were you and give all that beer time to settle. I shudder to think what you would feel like being whizzed round and round with a bellyful of beer swilling around inside you. It would be coming out of your ears!"

With much laughter they drank up and wandered off back to the Station yard. So far the day had gone very well. The sun was still shining and they were now looking forward to spending the rest of the day at the Fairground.

At 2.30pm they were all aboard their transport and less than ten minutes later Boris, still minding his quietly and smoothly running Burrell Showman's Engine, but on the watch for his friends, saw the familiar sight of a SKWEC Sentinel Steam Wagon chuffing into the adjacent field, to park among the assortment of vehicles already parked there. It was plain to see that the fine weather was bringing a large number of people to Carlo's Fairground that day. Good weather on a Saturday was always good news for Carlo's.

Once inside the Fairground the boisterous group made a beeline for Boris to let him know they had arrived. Boris had guessed this is what they would do and knew he would come in for plenty of good-natured banter when they found him. His workmates loved to rib him about his summer job with the Fairground, which they insisted was a real soft number, just a doddle with nothing to do except drive the Burrell from one site to another and laze his days away in between. So Boris thought he would prove them right!

The men walked down the side of the field between the row of sideshows erected along the fence and the various rides in the middle ground, and when the gaily-painted Burrell Showman's Engine came in sight, those in front stopped and laughingly pointed out to those coming up behind them what they could see ahead.

Parked close to and parallel to the fence, the engine was thudding away quietly with its chuffing mixture of steam and smoke pulsing from its chimney, which was wearing its high, fairground extension to get the smoke well above the people. There was no driver on the man-stand. The engine appeared to be chugging away completely unattended, doing its own thing! Its huge flywheel was turning at an easy, unhurried rate, while the large power generator coupled to it and mounted on top of the engine, was whining away at high speed. Driven by a wide leather belt from the flywheel to its small driving wheel, the generator was well and truly geared-down so that it ran much faster than the flywheel, at the speed necessary to make it function efficiently. Once adjusted, the speed was held constant by the action of the engine's spinning 'flying ball' type speed governor.

On the grass, between the gently-rocking engine and the nearest sideshow which was some ten yards away to keep it from the fumes and noise, was the recumbent figure of Boris lying back in a deckchair with his feet resting upon a wickerwork picnic basket. His train-driver-style blue cap was pulled down with its peak over his eyes to shield him from the strong sunlight.

Boris was obviously fast asleep, peacefully far away somewhere in the land of dreams, completely oblivious of the lively activity going on around him.

Intent upon giving him a surprise rude awakening, the grinning men, given a hush sign from those leading the way, walked quietly towards him. When they drew near they could see that Boris had a notice printed on a white card resting on his chest, hanging on a cord around his neck.

They spluttered with laughter when they read the words printed in large letters across it. Small groups of fairgoers had also seen the notice and passed by, smiling at what it said as they looked at the big, burly, comfortable-looking man, snoozing contentedly in his chair. The notice said:

SHIFT WORKER – PLEASE DO NOT DISTURB

Drawing nearer, intent upon doing precisely what the notice asked them not to do—and very violently at that—his work-mates, moving quietly across the grass towards him, saw that there was a further message, written in much smaller letters, as a rider to the main request.

Gingerly they tiptoed up to read what it said. The message was rather more specific. It said:

especially if you are one of the Skyweck mob
off the Sentinel that has just steamed in

The suppressed sniggering gave way to a burst of loud ironic laughter when this message was read. Football, cricket and skittles teams from their firm had long been nicknamed 'The Skywecks'. Boris's friends knew they had scored an own-goal in this particular match and that Boris had clocked up one against them even though the odds were 27-1 against him! Tipping his cap back, he looked up at them with an evil grin. He'd successfully spiked their guns!

With much backchat and cheerful banter, the visitors gathered round Boris and flopped down on the grass to take stock of their surroundings before venturing forth on a foray around the fairground.

Boris was joined by Joe, Grant, Sid and young Bob from his own steam-ploughing team, together with their Treasure Trove partners, Arthur and Terry—crew of the Sentinel—plus Frank Thrushton, the Work's Manager, who had travelled with them in the driver's cab. Asked if there was anything in particular Boris recommended them to visit— apart from the familiar rides facing them in the central area of the fairground—he mentioned four; the Wall of Death; the Flea Circus; the Dodgem Cars; and the Fortune Teller.

The first three of these were recent innovations. 'Carlo's Dodgems' was Sam Donatello's latest addition to his already extensive set of personally-owned rides and sideshows, but the other two of these three were independently owned and joined him on a seasonal basis.

The Fortune Teller, on the contrary, was not a new attraction but had travelled with Carlo's Fair for some years. The self-styled 'Dame Crystal Star' was a close friend of Boris's and when she had heard that a lorry load of his workmates from SKWEC were coming to Hythe for their annual day's outing, she had asked him if he would drum up some customers for her from the party.

Boris had agreed to do his best but had to tell her that for most of them her line of business was not their cup of tea! He was sure, he said, that only a very few of them, if any, would be likely to spend their hard-earned money seeking her services when there were so many other attractions more likely to interest them.

However, in answer to her request to do so, he had given her a few personal details about the most likely short-listed clients, few though they might be. The rest he ruled out as positively non-starters. She had listened with close attention and asked a few probing questions about them. A lady with a disciplined mind and of no mean intellect, she tucked away in her formidable memory items of information which could be of value to her when faced with the task of peering into the future of these potential clients who might soon be sitting with her in the privacy of her den, anxiously waiting to hear from her a peep of what lay ahead for them in the coming months and years.

It was Dame Crystal Star's normal technique, by devious clever but not too obvious questioning, to elicit sufficient information from her clients to enable her to predict for them a plausible future, in line with their wishes as discerned by her from them, to gladden their expectant hearts.

Sometimes, to add to the perspective and apparent authenticity of her vision, she included for the sake of balance, some cautionary warnings of possible dangers or troubles they might face if her professional advice were not heeded. Subtle advice this, which when interpreted and stripped of gobbledegook, boiled down to pearls of wisdom such as 'don't cross a busy road with your eyes shut', or 'don't swim in deep water with hob-nailed boots on'!

But being in possession of advance information such as Boris had given her about his friends, or gleaned from gratuitous comments and hearsay, saved her time when questioning her clients, sometimes even completely obviating the need for any probing interrogation at all. Such gifts of good fortune gave her an edge and enabled her to give such a dazzling demonstration of her mysterious psychic and intuitive powers that her prestige was much enhanced by those on the receiving end, who were so deeply impressed that they subsequently relayed stories of her miraculous ability to the world at large.

So, honouring his promise of publicity for Dame Crystal Star, as he sat chatting with his friends Boris discreetly extolled the Fortune Teller's virtues, but did not say too much for none of them knew of his liaison with her, nor did he want them to.

After a while he had to attend to his faithful Burrell Showman's Engine, patiently chuff-chuffing away contentedly by their side, providing electric power for a variety of purposes on some of his Boss Sam's rides, sideshows and booths—and also for Sam's luxury caravan home. It was not the only Showman's engine owned by Sam. There were four others on the site belonging to him, one of them being a gleaming new Fowler's Showman's Engine, bought recently specifically to power his newly-purchased Dodgem

Car Installation. Its electrically driven Dodgem Cars required a lot of power when they were all in operation at the same time. On good days this full load was continuous, for the cars were popular with young and old alike. The ride had already became one of Sam's best earners and ultimately looked like giving him a good return on the very substantial investment he had made in it.

When Boris went off to get on with his work, the happy men from SKWEC dispersed to go their separate ways, mainly in small groups of close friends from their own particular steam-ploughing teams.

Frank remained behind for a while with Boris to have an expert look at Sam's nearly-new Burrell, and Boris pointed out to him what sections of the fairground were receiving power from its shining generator. Frank admired the way Burrell's had mounted the generator on a strong platform built out beyond the smoke-box and chimney, under the very front of the gaily-painted canopy. The chimney's purpose-made extension pipe, with its flanged top, complemented the attractive lines of the engine. When on the move between sites, this extension-pipe rode lying along the top of the canopy. The sideboards of the canopy bore the inscription, in bold gold lettering on a dark blue background, *CARLO'S FAIRGROUND COMPANY,* with neat, decorative scrolls bordering the lettering.

Sam Donatello was a good customer of SKWEC. Apart from his five Showman's engines used to power sections of the fairground and tow all the gear from site to site in 'road trains', there were several others among the independent operators joining Sam each season who possessed their own traction engines. In addition there were static steam engines built into Roundabouts, as part of the centre pay-box and organ structure, as well as small ones driving the air-pumps in some of the larger Fairground Organs. The owners of all of these were existing, or potential, SKWEC customers.

Having Boris employed by Sam as his resident steam engine expert every season, suited SKWEC very well. Boris was good at his job and his presence on site brought much business to the firm. Part of Frank's purpose in joining the outing that day was to scout around the fairground to see what exactly was going on there of interest to the firm, and also to discuss things with Boris. In addition he had an appointment with Sam Donatello.

After a while he left Boris and went off on his own, intending to look at the various places where steam engines were working, as identified for him by Boris who knew where everything was on the extensive site. Frank had told Boris that after visiting these he would join up again with Arthur and Terry and would be back to see him later before they all left for home.

Boris had a shrewd suspicion that Frank was also off to make a clandestine visit to the Fortune Teller. More than once, on previous occasions, he had questioned Boris about the lady's activities, and he had done so again today in the last few minutes, taking advantage of the absence of their other colleagues. Boris had discreetly sung the praises of his clairvoyant friend and done his best to channel some business her way.

Frank was known to be very interested in the occult and in matters mystic in general. It was said that his interest stemmed from the time when as a very young man he had suffered a grievous loss, and had in desperation sought help and consolation from Spiritualists. Boris knew the circumstances very well and had passed on full details of the tragic story to Dame Crystal Star, for he placed Frank high on his shortlist of SKWEC colleagues who might, just might, visit her. And in this he was right. On leaving Boris, Frank made a beeline for the Fortune Teller's caravan which was parked at a suitably secluded spot away from the hurly burly of the fairground, along the side of the site.

Dame Crystal Star's presence was well-advertised both inside and outside the fairground. The type of people who were likely to be interested in seeking her assistance could be relied upon to hunt her down, but experience had shown her that many were a bit furtive about it, and some did not care to be seen entering her caravan. So she did better by being tucked away in a discreet corner and had learnt not to be too ostentatious. Many of her clients were quiet, introspective, thoughtful people, who popped in very discreetly, having first reconnoitred the premises earlier and gone off to make up their minds whether or not to cross her threshold.

Frank was no exception. After locating her and making sure none of his staff was in sight, he approached the Fortune Teller's caravan with quick steps, hoping to slip in unnoticed. In this aim he was in fact unsuccessful, though he did not know it at the time.

By chance Arthur and Terry rounded the corner just in time to see him disappearing through the door. They smiled, but were not surprised, for they knew of his interest in what they called 'mumbo-jumbo'. It was not an expression Dame Crystal Star would have liked to think anybody used in connection with her activities! She regarded herself as a true professional, an experienced practitioner in an ancient art, with a profound knowledge of her business. At least that was the image she wished to present to the outside world.

In truth she was indeed a professional Fairground Fortune Teller, for that is how she made her living. But she was only too well aware of her weaknesses as well as her strengths and knew quite well the limitations of her actual psychic ability. So she sought to enhance in the eyes of her clients the ostensible outward evidence of this ability, in any way she could. And she was certainly talented in this aspect of her work, very inventive and very shrewd. In this she was certainly a professional!

She did her job exceedingly well, there was no doubt about that! Many people who visited her were dazzled by her performance and awestruck by her apparent supernatural ability. A few were cynical and sceptical, but she was not much bothered by these, choosing to dismiss them as insensitive people lacking in natural intelligence, who were not worthy of her gifted attention. They were very much a minority and on balance more people applauded her ability than voiced criticisms of her.

This might have had something to do with the fact that she habitually handed out more potential good news than bad, and went easy on the dishing out of gloom and doom. In the main this left her clients wanting to believe her forecasts, so that they left her presence in an optimistic mood and not looking as though they had just attended a preview of their own funeral.

As a corollary of this they were loath to countenance any suggestion that the lady was a fraud and defended her vehemently, protecting in this way their investment in their rosy future as predicted by her, for to debunk her was tantamount to casting serious doubt on the likelihood of their cherished private dreams coming true.

Chapter 24

FRANK VISITS THE FAIRGROUND FORTUNE-TELLER

and gets to feel like a bug under a microscope

The Fortune Teller's den was a solid, expensive-looking caravan. Among the flamboyant, gaily-coloured surroundings of the fairground it contrived to appear tastefully and discreetly decorated. There was nothing of the sideshow about it. On the contrary the impression was of a quiet, confidential, richly-appointed haven into which those feeling the need for a professional consultation could escape from the raucous hurly burly of the swirling, confusing world around them.

The dwelling had three rooms, the largest of which, the living room, doubled as a consulting room. Wooden steps having five treads with a handrail both sides, led up to a small platform outside the centrally positioned door which led directly into this main room.

By the door, mounted so that it was at eye level to visitors standing at the foot of the steps, was a panel carrying a bell-push alongside red, amber and green lamps. The lamps were one below the other, with an instruction shown alongside them:

       RED   Engaged. Please **DO NOT DISTURB**
       AMBER Disengaged. Please ring
       GREEN Please enter

When Frank arrived he was lucky; the amber light was on, so he pushed the bell button.

After a moment or so the amber light went out and the green one came on, so he climbed the steps, opened the door and went in. As he did so, behind him on the panel outside, the green light went out and the red came on. He was thus assured of an uninterrupted session with the lady waiting for him within, seated at a small velvet-draped table.

Dame Crystal Star, looking every inch the popular image of a Fortune Teller in dress and demeanour, motioned Frank to the seat opposite her at the table. Coming in from the bright sunlight, the small but richly decorated room seemed dimly lit and it took him a few moments to get accustomed to the change. The amount of light entering the room was restricted by royal blue velvet curtains partially drawn across the one small window directly opposite the door.

It was not only his eyes which noticed a marked difference; the harsh blare of the fairground music was also much subdued. The soft lighting, exotic furnishings and comparative quietness combined to create a vaguely mysterious atmosphere. A faint scent pervaded the room reminding Frank of the smell of sandalwood when heated by the midday sun, or freshly cut in the workshop. It was a tropical, Eastern kind of smell, increasing the impression of having stepped out of the normal world into an oasis of mysticism.

Nothing for the moment was said. Frank soaked up the atmosphere, just as he was intended to do. His glance when he sat down had registered that the dark, strikingly attractive, jewel-bedecked lady sitting opposite him, was as yet paying him no heed whatsoever, but was staring downwards into a solid glass crystal ball standing on a slightly raised, rectangular ebony platform, on the table in front of her.

Close at hand, to her right, stood a metronome. To her left was a small control-box labelled **DOOR LIGHTS**. On it were three small lamps, red, amber and green, and three switches. The red one glowed, showing him that she had put green off and red on, when he had entered.

Frank's eyes flicked around the room as he waited, keeping her under observation all the while lest he should be thought rude if caught staring at her possessions when she looked up. Though there was no way he could have guessed it since she did not have eyes in the top of her head, she was in fact perfectly well aware of his scrutiny of the room and could have told him exactly what he was looking at, all the time. She observed his interest with satisfaction, for it proved that the initial pre-conditioning phase of her procedure was working well.

There were many interesting ornaments and unusual gadgets displayed about the room. Some, he felt sure from their singular appearance, must be associated with her profession as a clairvoyant.

Dame Crystal Star seemed very still and utterly composed as she sat there, her arms resting lightly on the table with her hands clasped as if in prayer.

Round her head she had a broad black band, richly embroidered with mysterious hieroglyphics having connotations of remote Egyptian antiquity and of the occult. It was emblazoned with shining, silver- and gold-plated emblems suggestive of heraldic, mystic and astrological origins, interspersed with tiny, cut-glass prismatic ornaments which swung slightly with every tiny movement of her head and scintillated as they caught the light.

In the middle of her forehead the headband carried a large, cut-glass star at the centre of which was a highly polished, mirrored disc. It was this spectacular star, adapted by her from a much-prized heirloom, and so far as she knew, quite unique in its design, that had inspired the choice of her professional name.

Besides being highly decorative, the elaborate headband served three practical purposes, as she bent her head over her all-important crystal ball during consultations. Firstly, it stopped her long raven hair from flopping forwards—a necessary though not very scientific function. Much more important was the crystal star it bore, that played a crucial part in her proceedings. It performed two technical functions, the first of which could perhaps be deduced by an observant person, but the second not so much as suspected by even one client in a thousand.

The mirrored central disc of this impressive star, catching beams of light from the window, directed reflected sunlight down on to the crystal ball to set it afire with colour, the display changing in a fascinating way with slight movements of her head.

But this reflective property of the mirrored disc on her unique star played another much more vital—but strictly clandestine—part in her well-planned procedures. It was entirely her own invention and she alone knew about it. It gave her a distinct professional edge which she most jealously guarded and preserved. No one, not even her closest friends and confidants, were ever told of this invaluable asset. Hers was a solitary calling and her professional welfare depended entirely upon her reputation as a high-class clairvoyant. So she sat on her secrets! Except that is, for one particular one, which she shared with Boris, for he had been primarily responsible for its evolution.

That particular one had nothing to do with her crystal star, but was a most important facility which he had helped her to develop and perfect. He provided the expertise to enable her to introduce an extra dimension to her performance, based upon an idea of hers which she did not quite know how to achieve without help. But Boris enjoyed her complete trust and she knew that this particular secret was safe with him.

During this calculated period of delay, deliberately introduced to allow for the acclimatisation of her clients, Frank was suitably impressed and conditioned. At length she stirred and looked up, her large dark eyes meeting his with a directness which locked his gaze to hers.

"Forgive me for keeping you waiting for a few moments, my dear," she said in a softly caressing voice. "It is something I have to do. You came in as a complete stranger. It takes a little while for my mind to reach out for and make contact with the emanations from the spirit which fills your being. I am gifted with clairvoyant powers which enable

348

me to do this. But first I have to lay bare my mind and open my inner being to embrace your thoughts.

For normal communication people speak of person-to-person contact. In my world it goes deeper—much deeper—than that. It has to be psyche-to-psyche contact. That is a much more profound and fundamental thing. It is always difficult to achieve—sometimes impossible—but I'm glad to say that I have successfully established this with you. I am now ready. For me the outside world is now shut out completely."

She paused a moment, then continued, very quietly, but with a strange quality of tone and an awe-inspiring dramatic intensity that seemed to transcend normality. It was as though she were speaking from the far distance, her words floating in from another remote intangible world. It sent shivers down Frank's spine.

"In this room," she said, "it's as though you and I are alone in the Universe. Our spiritual selves, our innermost beings, are in intimate communion. Two spirits isolated in space, in a cocoon of complete privacy."

"Bloody Hell!" thought Frank. "This is a bit spooky!"

"You must clear your mind of any thoughts which cloud or doubt our communion," the soft voice said, as if in instant admonition for his unworthy first reaction.

"Stone the crows!" Frank thought. "She's reading my mind!"

That worried him, for her voluptuous appearance had already stirred his secret thoughts. He was uncomfortably aware that in the period of silence while he'd been waiting for her to speak, he had found himself wishing she were going to entertain him in her bedroom which he could see through the partition door standing ajar behind her, rather than tell his fortune. At what he now perceived to be his much lower level of consciousness and less lofty plane of spiritual awareness, he would gladly have swapped a bit of intimate communion of the real kind for the surreal variety with which he was evidently about to be dished out. Especially for her modest fee of fifteen shillings—that would have been a real bargain!

His slight frown and worried look, as well as his earlier speculative inspection of her person, was registered by the acutely observant lady whose face was only two feet away from his across the table. His concern would have deepened had he have known this, but he was of course unaware that his previous scrutiny of her had been simultaneously reciprocated by a more penetrating one by her, of him. Not once had she looked up, until she had done so to speak to him.

Dame Crystal Star knew only too well the effect she had on men, on *some* more than others. And this one was in the '*some*' category—of that she was quite sure.

"Don't worry, my dear," the soft voice added after a little pause. "I understand you are a child of nature, as indeed am I."

So motherly and tender was the tone of her enigmatic words as she looked deeply into his eyes that it was as though she were lightly stroking him with an infinitely gentle touch. His carnal thoughts raced out of control, then in an instant he realised why she'd said what she'd said. She was clearly aware of the unease in his mind and the precise reason for it. In a state of confusion he dropped his gaze. Somehow he had to get control of his wayward thoughts. It was one hell of a spot to be in, to have his private lewd thoughts being read. One hell of a spot!

Dame Crystal smiled to herself as his eyes dropped. Her subject was truly hers! He was in a highly receptive mental state. Not only that, she perceived with amusement that he was getting excited physically—a condition evidenced to her experienced eyes by the way he was squirming his backside about in his seat to overcome an involuntary discomfiture. It was a problem Frank had, partly due to his overactive imagination and tendency to fantasize in an exaggerated, highly inventive way, at the slightest provocation. He was, as a result of this automatic mental stimulation, a 'rapid-riser', or to use his own words, his 'Old Man' was 'trigger-happy'!

However, innocently unaware, so Frank naively assumed, of his randy physical state—even if disturbingly not of his smutty, lustful thoughts—she continued the proceedings in a comfortably normal, reassuring way.

"Now let us see what I can tell you about what lies ahead for you," she said.

Frank looked up to meet her eyes again, temporarily relieved of his growing anxiety about his wayward thoughts and randy reactions, by the normality of her voice.

She glanced sideways at a solid-looking, 'Napoleon hat'-shaped mahogany chiming clock, standing on a small sideboard. The steady tick-tock of its pendulum was the only sound in the room, except for the muffled fairground noises from outside.

"I can give you twenty minutes," she added. "My next appointment is at five past three and your time must finish when the clock strikes the hour. I'm afraid I have to run to a strict timetable, although sometimes it is not easy to do so."

"I can well understand that. I expect people sometimes get so interested they would stay all day!" said Frank, gazing at her with transparently obvious, undisguised admiration.

"And all night too, I shouldn't wonder," ran on his fertile mind secretly, until, once again, he made a belated effort to discipline his thoughts.

He realised that he had to stop thinking laterally, outside of the blinkered track he felt constrained to follow, because of the disquieting lack of thought-confidentiality there appeared to be in the place. It was a most disturbing predicament to have landed in and quite unlike anything he'd experienced previously. There was a need for continuous self-control of the normal cheerful, free-thinking run of his mind. That was something he'd never before had to achieve except, that is, for a lifelong inner compulsion to keep out intrusive thoughts when saying his prayers.

In this latter special case of mind-control he was self-disciplined, and, since childhood, if his mind strayed during his prayers he made himself start all over again. This was time wasting and he didn't like that, so by habit it became a small battle he usually won. But it was the only time he managed to rein in his thoughts. On all other occasions his mind buzzed away freely, exploring and exploiting everything of interest that attracted his attention, in much the same way that a dog sniffs away happily following its nose and diving with enthusiasm down any side track that excites its natural instincts.

Alarmingly, he knew only too well that his inner private thoughts were often startlingly at odds with the outwardly polite, professional demeanour he presented to the world at large. There had been many occasions when he had realised that if those he were talking to could hear the silent musings going on simultaneously in his wayward mind, the world would blow apart at the seams with the shock of the revelations and he would sink into the ground with embarrassment and shame.

He had sometimes wondered how many other well-respected people concealed a similarly dicey, two-track-mind duplicity, and on occasions, like him, got hot under the collar lest they were showing facial evidence of their secret abominable thoughts or—worse by far—unwittingly started to think aloud! The possibility of the presence of mind-readers added a new dimension to these concerns. It was a highly disturbing complication which henceforth he would have to remember at all times.

These considerations raced through his mind as he waited for her to continue her observations, while she in turn studied his face, with her eyes twinkling and a slightly amused expression breaking her features, seeming to him as though she were well aware what he was thinking.

"Now then," his all-seeing soothsayer went on, with a subtle change of tone, an unmistakeable nuance which made him feel he had been caught out once more, "I want you to concentrate your mind entirely on what we are doing and think deeply about that. And about nothing else! Nothing else at all! I feel very close to you now. Our minds are as one. You are a very sensitive man and I am completely in harmony with you, extraordinarily so, after so little time. But you must concentrate your thoughts on me and me alone."

"That won't be hard—except on my Old Man!" the practically-minded Frank thought, his eyes straying over her highly seductive body—a visual excursion she did not miss, swift though it was.

He knew she had spotted him, for he saw from the quick movement of her eyes that she was aware he'd given her the once-over. Straightaway this led him to wonder if his own eyes had been compelled to follow the direction of his bawdy thoughts, as no doubt picked up by her so that she'd had advanced warning of his rude scrutiny.

Or maybe, he found himself hoping, his eyes had scanned her body of their own accord, acting on their own volition under an instinctive reflex action that was entirely non-thought directed, like a blink or a twitch!

He was mentally on the evasive wriggle, reasoning that a lustful look like that ought not to count against him in the lady's book if—as she was reading his mind at the time—she knew it had been beyond his control since he hadn't thought about it first!

Frank began to feel as helpless as an ugly bug squirming under a microscope, unable, no matter what the provocation, to present a prettier profile than providence had provided.

Somewhat incongruously, his highly-perceptive examiner now turned her attention to more mundane matters. She had business to attend to. It served to ease the tension and brought him down to earth with a bump.

"First of all, though," she said, taking a small white card from a card index box by her side, "I must ask you to pay my fee of fifteen shillings. Then I want to fill in this record card. It is for my own use only," she added, reassuringly. "Nobody else ever sees these cards. I like to keep a record of clients I've seen. Quite often they come back to see me again and I like to refresh my memory of them. And, if it's a long time later, I like to find out how closely events have followed my predictions."

"I'm sure I shall come back too," Frank commented, with no hesitation, handing over his payment for services about to be rendered. There was a magnetism about the lady which he knew full well would pull him back in her direction sooner rather than later.

"I do hope you will feel you want to," she said warmly. "It gives me a lot of pleasure when people do that—especially those very few who are like you in having particularly gifted spiritual qualities that I can identify with so intimately."

Frank drank in this unexpected compliment with a psychological gulp and his attraction to her moved up several notches. The old devil in him stirred a bit more and his imagination began to work overtime. Off went his thoughts at a gallop!

"That's all right," his mind raced to think, before he could even start to hold it in check. "When I come back she can identify with my spiritual qualities and I'll identify with her physical qualities. That's a fair swap. A bit of her intimate communion of the spirits that she was on about just now, with a bit of intimate communion of the bodies that the spirits live in. A bit of the other for me and a bit of her highbrow stuff for her! What could be fairer than that? Just the job!"

Dame Crystal's eyebrows rose slightly and she smiled, seemingly tolerantly and so on cue with his thoughts that he felt sure it was a resigned, indulgent response to his sudden mental flight off track. He felt like a small boy caught eating sweets in class.

"I must fill in this card," she said with a slight sigh. "It will not take many moments and then we can get on with things."

Within a few minutes the well-organised lady knew his name, his age, his address, his job, his employer, his main interests and his hobbies.

She also knew that he was unmarried and she had discerned a note of sadness in his tone of voice when he had told her so. The name and some of the details, particularly the latter, rang a loud bell in her memory, but her facial expression betrayed no more evidence that she had picked up this invaluable information breakthrough than would that of a card sharper who had picked up a winning card.

Immediately her fertile imagination and hyperactive mind started to work away at high speed, running smoothly along the lines of her practised art, assembling and correlating data from her memory with newly acquired facts and impressions. Set in a framework of hard information, interlaced with reasonable logical conjecture, a tentative programme for the sitting clicked into place.

Backed up by a high level of natural intuitive ability, honed and developed by a lot of experience studying the attitudes, reactions and behavioural patterns of many people from widely differing backgrounds, it was a matter of only a few moments before she was inwardly satisfied that she was ready to provide Frank with good value for his money. He had come in looking for good news. She would send him on his way a satisfied customer! —but not with his head stuffed full of pie-in-the-sky predictions, as might be expected from less professional clairvoyants; his would be recognisably plausible and perfectly possible predictions.

This rapid-thinking process took no longer than the time she spent filling in the details on Frank's card. He saw her write the usual personal information—name, age, address, job, interests and so on—and then fill in a serious of letters along a line marked 'Cat.', but he could not see what they were. He would have been none the wiser had he have been able to read them. On this, her 'Category' analysis line, she had entered groups of letters: gns; hm; hf; pd; r; re; cpg; dc; vh; ss; which in her private code, recorded him as being a good-news seeker; a handsome man; healthy and fit; pleasant disposition; randy; roving eye; career prospects good; deserving case; very horny; sex-starved!

Frank would have been very amused at this accurate assessment of his character, so quickly arrived at. He would have been even more amused had he have known that among the entries against the name of the man who had sat in the chair before him, was the designation 'meb' which, not without justification, labelled him as a 'mean-eyed bastard'!

Before she put the card in her file she asked him to write his full name on the back of it in his normal handwriting and then to write his signature. This he did and she spent some moments studying his writing very carefully with a hand lens, moving it along, apparently scrutinising each single letter. Then, looking a little pensive, she glanced up at him, looked again at the card, scribbled a few notes on it and dropped the card into the box without further comment.

Frank knew there were some people who claimed they could learn a lot about a person's character by studying their handwriting. He was accordingly suitably impressed by her versatility, which was the whole purpose of the diversion—a calculated exercise in confidence building. Naturally he wondered what deductions she'd made from it, and what comments she had recorded on his card as a result.

He need not have concerned himself. She'd marked him 6 out of 10 for his handwriting, 5 out of 10 for the style of his signature and added a row of seven letters selected at random from the Greek Alphabet. She felt it necessary to be seen to be writing something and that was as good as anything! Besides, she liked using Greek letters, for in her opinion they looked pleasingly cryptic and had a certain clairvoyant class about them. For her reference she had copied the Greek Alphabet neatly and boldly on her side of the card-index box, a small measure typical of her attention to detail. Her selection was quick and decisive, as behove a confident expert. Any observant client recognising the letters assumed it to be coded information. To others they were no doubt seen as mystic emblems.

The whole exercise took only a few moments, but added to her impact and enhanced her stature by providing further evidence of her apparent wisdom in the eyes of her clients. Dame Crystal Star was no fool. She'd got things well thought-out and organised!

"Now then, Frank," she said, getting down to business and establishing an immediate personal rapport by the subtle use of his recently revealed Christian name, "I want you to reach forward and clasp those two metal knobs, one in each hand."

On the ebony board, set about eighteen inches apart, one on each side of her crystal ball, were two highly-polished brass knobs mounted rigidly on short, vertical brass stems. To Frank they looked very much like the brass knobs found on the four corners of some ornate brass bedsteads. He was right. They had once lived on her Granny's bed!

He did as instructed and grasped the knobs, the size of tennis balls, firmly, resting his elbows on the table. He noticed that the half-inch diameter brass stems screwed into the knobs passed down through holes in the ebony board. There was no 'give' in the structure so he could tell that the stems were securely fastened underneath the ebony board. What he could not see was that screwed under the board was a stout, half-inch thick brass bar into which the two stems were screwed, so connecting the brass balls into one rigid brass structure. It might have reassured him, had he have been able to see that, because at least he could have seen that he was not about to be electrocuted!

Dame Crystal now placed her hands on the backs of his, cupping them warmly and snugly over his clenched fists.

"This is cosy!" Frank thought, his heart beginning to beat a little faster.

"Just relax, Frank," she said, arresting his amorous thoughts before they could develop. "Just relax, my dear. Let your mind quieten."

Frank did his best to comply, but was disturbingly conscious of their close proximity to one another. She then continued her instructions to him.

"Now, Frank," she said earnestly, "I want you to look into my crystal ball and try to imagine that you are looking far out into the starlit sky—way out into the vastness of the Universe. Think about the immensity of it all. Try to clear your mind of all everyday things. Try to detach yourself from Earth and concentrate upon the Universe. Imagine yourself floating freely far out into the depths of space."

She paused a little while to give Frank time to settle into this dreamlike state. Meanwhile he fastened his attention on the crystal ball as directed—staring into it and doing his earthly best, without much success, to fancy himself floating freely away from his highly desirable companion sitting so tantalisingly close to him.

Her crystal ball was unusual. It was not a smooth-surfaced ball of opalescent glass, as might have been expected, but was made of beautifully clear, crystal glass, a multi-faceted, cut-glass sphere of nearly five inches diameter. There were in all eighteen flat, triangular surfaces on it, each an exact equilateral triangle with the perfect, precise, sharp edges only found in cut-glass of the finest quality.

Dame Crystal's special personal glass ball had originated in Austria and was inherited from her Grandmother. It was, like her star, one of her most prized possessions. It set her apart from her professional peers, all of whom, so far as she knew, used iridescent opaline glass balls of the conventional kind normally favoured by clairvoyants.

This sparkling crystal ball rested upon a darkened glass mirror which formed the top surface of a circular, nine-inch diameter, pivoted metal turntable mounted on her ebony platform. A light touch was all that was needed to rotate the turntable. Any movement of the crystal ball, or of the head of a person sitting viewing it, caused a constantly changing display of spectral colours inside it because of its prismatic action upon the light falling on it. Anyone looking at it soon became fascinated by the spectacular vivid colours that could be seen within.

Dame Crystal Star's clients were always treated to this display because, before beginning her proceedings, she adjusted the platform delicately, with what appeared to be extreme care. It gave a demonstration of the critical attention to detail necessary for her to employ her awesome powers.

The mirror image of the crystal ball, seen in the darkened glass surface upon which it stood, enhanced this display. As a bonus, both from the ball and from the mirror beams of coloured light were scattered about the dimly lit room as she moved the turntable, forming little blocks of rainbow colours wherever they fell. So impressive was this optical effect that many of her clients went away wondering if they could create something like her set-up back home, just for the fascinating display it produced. In the absence of shafts of sunlight through the curtains on dull days, she had an artificial light source she could use. It was a simple arrangement of a lamp in a metal box having a vertical slot in one side. This stood ready on a shelf below the window but was not in use for Frank, who enjoyed the full effect of a shaft of bright sunlight.

A clairvoyant and her crystal ball are a partnership. A factory, however skilled in the art of glass making, cannot turn out mystic crystal balls which work for everybody. What they can do is provide those with the special gifts of people like Dame Crystal Star with an object which helps them to use their own inborn mystic abilities to create mental images of scenes invisible to normal human beings. At least that is how she described the intriguing phenomenon!

A sceptic once said to her that a duck's egg would work just as well—indeed most probably even better—because of its inherently strong 'Quack factor'. Dame Crystal didn't much like that suggestion and was not amused! Like Queen Victoria, she was autocratic and disliked frivolity.

After a suitable interval, judging Frank to be ready to proceed, she continued with her instructions.

"Now, in a moment, I am going to recite some words about which I want you to think very deeply," she went on. "When I have repeated them a second time and am silent, I want you to keep repeating the words to yourself and to think deeply about their meaning as you do so."

She looked at him intently, with an earnest, serious expression on her face, as if to emphasize the points she was making.

"It is important, very important indeed, that you concentrate upon this and drive all other thoughts from your mind," she continued, staring into his eyes with such intensity that he was sure she was fishing around in his mind to seek out—and impel him to flush out—any of his usual unworthy flights of fancy. "Only if you do this conscientiously," she stressed, "will I be able to make proper intimate contact with you."

She paused a moment, to let her words sink in, then went on.

"But before I try to look onwards into your future, I first want to get to know a little of your past," she said. "You may well think what I am about to do is peculiar, because you are sitting here with me and could just tell me about your past, if I simply asked you questions. I shall probably do a little of that in a few moments. But first of all, in a mind-to-mind direct contact, I look for things which may have had a profound effect upon you. Things which, know it or not, most greatly affect your inner self and therefore to some extent, condition your probable future.

If there are any special crucial factors like these, I am able to focus in on them straightaway, without you thinking about them at all. If you were simply to sit there and tell me your life history, these vitally important matters would be lost in a mass of detail and it would take me time—maybe a long time—to ferret them out.

What is worse, though, is that people are often inclined to be reticent—sometimes I have to say, even foolishly furtive—about the very things I need to know about most, those that have affected them most profoundly."

She paused a moment, looking at him searchingly and speculatively, her gaze seeming to bore through his eyeballs into his brain-box.

"Bloody hell!" thought Frank in sudden alarm. "I hope to blazes she doesn't focus in on Fish-queue Fanny of Faversham! *She* had a profound effect upon me, that's for sure! Very profound! She bloody nearly creased me, she did!"

The stupidity of slipping into the error of thinking this stark, revealing, self-confessing thought then hit him. He gulped, frowned, set his teeth and concentrated hard to control himself.

"Glory be! Stone the crows! Saints preserve me from my stupid self!" he muttered under his breath, floundering helplessly and feeling as furtive as a flushed-out flea.

Dame Crystal noticed him suddenly tighten up and she seemed to Frank to wince. However, she carried on with her preparatory instructions without admonishing him, though he fully expected her to do so.

"Do you understand that, Frank?" she asked anxiously, with a note of completely convincing concern in her voice. "Are you quite ready to go ahead?"

"Yes, I understand," Frank replied, relieved to be off the hook and mustering all the signs of sincerity and willingness to co-operate that he could. "I am ready. I will try hard to do exactly what you say, all the time. I assure you of that. I want everything to be as successful as it possibly can be."

"I'm glad," she said, with apparent relief. "Then I'm quite sure things will go well for us. Success depends very much on a strong joint effort."

There followed a few moments' silence while she composed herself to begin her serious work and Frank meanwhile dutifully tried to do in his imagination what he had done so many times in practice during contemplative periods out on his own on bright starlit nights—look out into the vastness of the night sky and ponder its wonder and its meaning.

Then Dame Crystal, speaking slowly, with carefully cultivated dramatic emphasis, in a soft but rich and mellow voice, recited the words:

> "Worlds upon worlds rolling ever,
>
> From creation to decay;
>
> Like the bubbles on a river,
>
> Sparkling, bursting, borne away."

Frank found himself strangely moved by these words. Their message captivated his imagination.

About ten seconds later, sitting perfectly still, staring intently into her crystal ball, she went over the words again. And they registered in Frank's mind, never, as time was to tell, ever to be forgotten by him, for at meditative moments, whenever he looked at a clear night sky, they invariably came into his mind again.

Dame Crystal Star was now silent for a full minute during which time Frank repeated the words to himself and played his part conscientiously, as requested so earnestly, by his guide and mentor.

Concentrating upon remembering and repeating the words, preserving the rhythm she had set, did indeed occupy his mind to the exclusion of other thoughts. Though he did not yet know it, it also prepared him for a later, more important part of the proceedings.

Then she began to speak, slowly and hesitatingly, as if giving a commentary on a passing scene. With some relief and excitement Frank deduced that her system had worked. He stopped his mental repetition of the words and concentrated his now thought-free and wide-open mind on what Dame Crystal was saying. He listened with growing astonishment to what she had to say, his attention now completely captured by the remarkable lady.

"I see you as a little boy living in the heart of the countryside," she said. "There are lush green meadows, trees, sheep, cows and horses. It is springtime—a happy glorious exciting time, full of vibrant life. There are daises and buttercups—a sea of them right across the meadows.

Beyond a hedge are rows upon rows of apple trees—all in bloom, a mass of pink and white blossom. It is truly a lovely sight. And there is rich green grass, short-cropped, looking almost like a lawn covering the ground beneath the trees. Sheep, with tiny new-born lambs among them, are grazing there amidst the trees.

You are playing by a beautifully clear, bubbling stream with a little girl of about your own age, such a very pretty little girl with fair hair and blue eyes. How wonderfully happy you both seem.

There is a farmyard nearby with barns, haystacks and a very old thatched farmhouse. There are chickens wandering freely in the farmyard, pecking and foraging about in the straw. And I can see pig-sties along one side of the farmyard, a long row of pig-sties.

It is a lovely, peaceful, country scene, so tranquil, so wonderfully tranquil, it's like a glimpse of heaven."

Here she paused again and there was a brief period of silence, except for the sound of her clock. The measured tick-tock of her Westminster Chiming Clock spoke of the passing of time. It seemed profoundly significant.

Then she began to speak again.

"Now I see you as a young man," she said. "You are walking across the meadows with a young lady. I'm sure it's the same girl you were playing with as a child. She is now a very attractive young lady. She is wearing a pretty summer frock. She is really lovely, a beautiful girl, as fresh and sparkling as the morning dew, such a very beautiful girl."

Again she paused, as if, Frank thought later, in her mind's eye lantern slides were being changed. Then she went on,

"Now you are with the same girl, standing hand-in-hand by the doorway of a church talking to a Vicar. I have a feeling—a very strong feeling—that you are discussing your coming marriage with him.

The three of you are laughing together at something. You look so happy, wonderfully happy. And in the background, among the graves, is a very bent, old, old man with a bushy white beard, clipping the grass. He has a white terrier dog with him."

"Old Motty," murmured Frank to himself, amazed at the clarity and accuracy of her vision of scenes from the past, the first from long ago, but each of them in essence scenes from his childhood that he thought he remembered well.

Once more she waited, seemingly for the next image to appear in the crystal ball into which she was peering so intently.

Then after a bit she started speaking again. But her mood had changed and changed very profoundly. She seemed hesitant and when Frank glanced up at her, she looked anxious and apprehensive. Something was worrying her, Frank felt sure of that. It was if, he thought later on, she'd had a premonition that something was going to go wrong.

"Now you are . . ." she began hesitatingly, ". . . now you are . . ."

She stopped abruptly, as though something had interrupted her vision. There was a long pause. Her manner, previously one of marked elation, had now changed to one of extreme sadness.

"Oh! No! Not that!" she said, in a strangled, distressed voice. "I see the rolling waves of a rough sea. There is a pebble beach, a steeply shelving pebble beach. You are standing looking out to sea. There are others with you. There is a lifeboat quite a long way out from the shore. There is a great sadness about you. I feel it so very, very strongly. It is such a deep, deep sadness."

There was another long pause, during which her hands, still on his, gripped them more tightly. She seemed deeply upset and struggling to control herself.

"I'm sorry, Frank," she said at length. "I'm so sorry." She hesitated as if unwilling to go on, yet knowing she had to. Then she continued.

"The girl was drowned, wasn't she? She was to have been your wife. Is that right? You lost the girl you loved so and were to have married, your childhood sweetheart. Is that right? Oh Frank! Oh Frank, my dear, how terribly sad!"

Frank, looking down at the crystal ball, keeping his head averted and choking back his tears, confirmed that what she'd said was right.

"Yes, that's right," he replied, struggling to control himself. "My girl Mary was drowned near Herne Bay. We were swimming. We often went there to swim. But she was a much better swimmer than I was and liked to go further out to sea than I could go, into deeper water. She went too far out and got caught in a tidal flow. The lifeboat men said that when it turned, the tide where we were ran out so fast that she would have exhausted herself trying to head straight back to shore while being carried further away all the time.

They said it was like trying to swim upstream against the current in a fast-flowing river. It just can't be done. They said that maybe if she'd just let herself float with the tide, they would have followed the water's flow-line, which was outwards and down the coastline, until they found her and picked her up. It wasn't a stormy or a very rough day. But there was a stiff offshore breeze and it was a spring tide. So the current was very strong and too much for her to fight against."

He paused a moment, to control his emotions.

"But it's no good saying what might have happened," he said. "She is dead. And that is that. There will never be another girl who means so much to me. Not after Mary. There couldn't be. We grew up together. Neither of us ever looked at anyone else, nor ever could have done."

Dame Crystal was aware of a very, very profound sadness in Frank. She was uneasy. She felt she had pushed him too far and began to feel guilty. But she fended the feeling off by trying to be coldly rational about the situation. She reasoned that he had come in with the sadness, had lived with it a long time and would go out with it. It might even have helped him, she comforted herself, to have shared his grief with a stranger.

Be all that as it may, thrusting sentiment aside, her eyes on the clock, she got a grip on herself. She had to go about her business. She had a living to make and time was slipping by.

"Perhaps there may be somebody else in time, Frank," she said comfortingly. "Don't despair, my dear. Carry on pitching yourself into your work as you have done these last ten long years. You must keep you mind occupied and look after yourself just as Mary would have wished you to. Something may happen one day to make you really happy again."

Frank was startled. It was indeed ten years, but up to that moment no mention had been made of time, none whatsoever; her remarkable ability astounded him.

"Now, my dear," she said, intent upon continuing the proceedings without further delay, "I want you to try to clear your mind again as you did before and we will see if there is anything I can tell you about your possible future. I stress *possible* future. Never, ever, do I give guarantees that anything I say will definitely come true, but I do claim there is always a strong chance that it will. More than a fifty-fifty chance too, judging by people on my cards who have taken the trouble to come back and tell me. And sometimes, when I get things a bit wrong, it's probably due to my misreading what I see in my crystal ball. I have to try to interpret what I see and sometimes that's not at all easy. Things appear that are not familiar to me and quite often, in some scenes that flash on in the shifting patterns, I find it difficult to understand just what people are doing. So I can't promise anything."

"I really would like you to try, though," said Frank earnestly. "If you tell me what you see perhaps I shall be able to go away and think about it. Between us I expect we shall be able to sort out what it may mean, even if we can't be sure."

"Well, don't pin your hopes too much on it, Frank," she warned in a laudable display of seeming sincerity. "I'll do my best but I should hate you to be disappointed. You have had enough to put up with already."

"I have lived with my sorrow long enough to learn that the only thing to do is go on with life and take what comes," commented Frank philosophically. "But if there is a chance of something good ahead I'd like to learn about it now. You never know, it might stop me from missing a chance I might otherwise not see when it comes."

"That's very true, Frank, very true indeed. If Fate offers chances and people miss them, it doesn't throw them up again to be snatched the second time around. That just does not happen. Life is not like that. A chance missed is a chance lost—forever."

So saying, having finished with generalisations, Dame Crystal re-asserted her professional control over events.

"This time, Frank," she said, in a businesslike manner, "I go about things in a slightly different way. The future poses different problems from the past. Now then, are you right-handed or left-handed?"

"Right-handed," answered Frank, wondering what that had got to do with anything.

"Put out your right hand, then," she instructed, "and hold the brass ball on that side. But this time, instead of holding the other brass ball with your left hand, you hold my hand. A strong, personal physical contact is necessary, as well as our mental union."

She held out her right hand and took hold of Frank's left. He felt her give it a little squeeze, and was pleased about that. It seemed like a private message of genuine concern, not a part of the business procedure. Tiny gesture though it was, it thrilled him and brightened him up again.

"Now then, Frank," she went on. "Do you remember those lines still?"

"Yes, I think so," replied Frank. "Funny thing that. I never was good at learning to recite words from memory. I could never make myself concentrate for long enough. Or

358

hard enough. But those seem to have stuck in my head with no difficulty whatsoever."

"Then say them," she said.

Frank repeated the lines and was word perfect. "I don't think I'll ever forget those lines," he added. "I shall remember them every time I look at a starlit sky. I often wonder about the Universe and those last two lines; they seem to embrace all life on Earth, don't they? —never mind the stars in the Universe, out there in the vastness of the sky. Some people are like stars. Mary sparkled and then was gone!"

"They do indeed," agreed Dame Crystal, noting his sad but perceptive reference to his lost love. "It's wonderful sometimes, how just a very few words can mean so much and inspire our imagination. And somehow, to me, those four lines of words embrace the whole vast Universe. That is why I think they are so important in opening our minds up and emptying them of all other trivial thoughts about our own little affairs.

But this time, for what we are going to do next, it is just the last two lines I want you to concentrate upon, just those two."

She reached over and set the metronome by her side going. It was set precisely to 96 beats per minute. Its steady 'clack' 'clack' 'clack' 'clack' now dominated the quietness of the room, imposing its incisive metallic beat upon the place. It seemed to Frank as though they were gripped by the remorseless tread of passing time. It was hypnotic.

"The metronome is most important from now on, Frank," she said. "It keeps our minds exactly in step and that is absolutely vital. It took a long time to discover the precise timing needed to make my clairvoyant powers work at their best and the metronome is adjusted to exactly that rate. When we start I want you to repeat those last two lines over and over again, strictly in time with the metronome. Not aloud, but silently in your mind. You can mouth them if you like, but you must say the words very positively to yourself, putting the stress on the right words to keep you exactly in step with the metronome. Now listen carefully. It goes to the count of eight, like this,

> Like the bub-bles on a ri-ver,
> Spark-ling, burst-ing, borne a-way . . .
> . . . ONE and TWO and THREE and FOUR,
> FIVE and SIX and SEVEN and EIGHT

Have you got that, Frank?"

"Yes, I understand," Frank replied. "It reminds me of how we used to recite the poem 'Hiawatha' at school."

"That's right, Frank," she agreed. "That's exactly right."

"What's the idea, though?" asked Frank. "Why do you want me to do it?"

Quick as a flash, triggered on the instant by his own spoken words *want me to do it*, his one-track mind promptly raced off at a tangent.

"I wish you did want me to do it," he thought lustfully. "I could do you nicely to that beat:

> ONE and TWO and THREE and FOUR,
> IN and OUT and IN and OUT!"

he repeated to himself, mentally making his mating motions match the master metronomic metre. His mind was off the beam yet again, his private lewd thoughts being once again totally irrelevant to the current serious psychic proceedings.

Abruptly he was pulled up sharply, and metaphorically yanked by the scruff of the neck away from what was fast developing into a randy reverie. She knew from his glazed look that his attention had wandered.

"Frank!" she said, in a brook-no-nonsense, decisive tone of voice which seemed to presage an admonition brought on, he was sure, by his totally unacceptable, bawdy thoughts. "You must try to concentrate and do just what I ask. It's no good you asking why things work, or why I am asking you to do something or asking anything like that at all. I just don't know why. Nobody knows—nor needs to know, come to that! All I do know is that I have special personal powers—a gift, people say it is—which I have learnt how to use. If I do things a certain way, it's because it works and I get results that way—that's all that really matters.

A doctor once told me that there are regular waves of energy in the brain, steady slow rhythms, especially when we are asleep or in a trance. These energy waves can be picked up by instruments, so they are there all right. It isn't just a theory. Hypnotism has something to do with them, I believe. Hypnotists swing things in front of your eyes, or use flashing lights—things like that—to put people in a trance."

She paused a moment, seeming a bit tired and perhaps, he figured, a little exasperated by his failure to keep his thoughts on track and stop them from going mushy. Then she went on again.

"But it's no good me wasting my time even thinking about it, Frank. In fact, if I do, it throws me out and nothing works at all anymore. So I want you to stop thinking about anything else except what we two are doing right now. We must both focus our minds on that and that alone."

"Sorry," said Frank, thinking that his private randy thoughts, plus his awkward question, had thrown Dame Crystal off course and upset her a bit. "I can see the sense of what you say," he went on, eager now to please, "and I begin to see a little of what it's all about, so perhaps it's better really that I should have asked. You see I'm one of those blokes who gets on better when he knows how things tick. But I do understand that it doesn't help if I ask questions in the middle of things. So I'll try not to interrupt you again."

He made a mental effort to put things right. In effect, that part of his mind striving to maintain control turned to the randy dog department and said, 'Down, boy! Get into your kennel and stay there before you sod things up altogether!'

"Right then!" she said, more brightly—apparently pleased with his co-operative response. "Let's get on. Now I want you to say exactly what I say. I will start repeating the words with the right timing, keeping in step precisely with the metronome. I want you to pick it up and come in with me—not aloud though—but silently in your mind. That brings our brain rhythms exactly in step and they must stay so, from then on, whatever happens. That's vital. After a bit I shall stop repeating the words either aloud or to myself; my rhythms will stay locked-in automatically. But you must carry on at all costs. You must keep on. That's very important indeed. You must keep in step with the metronome."

She paused a bit to let the message sink in, and then continued.

"What happens is this," she said. "If you think of nothing but those words, your mind is empty of all thoughts and influences which would otherwise prevent me from working. Your brain rhythms are tied to mine. They are exactly in step. Meanwhile my mind, in a wonderful sort of way which I don't pretend to understand at all, is set free to move onwards into your future. Or backwards into your past, come to that, although that works differently. It's easier to go back into somebody's past because their memory and those of others all around who know them, feed in thought-energies to help me build up pictures of things that have happened. My client sitting with me has a brain stuffed full of

360

memories. Sometimes they can't get at them themselves, however hard they try, but strangely, even then, I can often see them clearly."

She hesitated a moment before going on, obviously thinking deeply about the complexities of her skilled art.

"But going onwards into the future," she said seriously, "that's much more difficult. It's a different thing altogether. There is no help from the memories of living people in looking into the future. That's not in their minds waiting to be fished out. Only the seeds of the pattern of the future are there, to help form visionary pictures."

"I can quite understand that," said Frank hopefully. "Now that you've explained it, I think I can see what it's all about."

"Right then, Frank," she went on earnestly. "This is the important thing, though. If I'm lucky I get glimpses into the future. That's all they ever are—glimpses. It's just like a picture which flashes on and off in a twinkling. I don't go travelling along, seeing things happening all around me. I wish I could. That would be wonderful. But it's nothing like that at all. I see a sudden picture—like a snapshot—than it's gone."

"Well I never!" said Frank. "How strange! I didn't imagine that at all. How very strange! It's marvellous really, though, isn't it? Marvellous to get a sudden peep at scenes in the future?"

"Yes, it is marvellous," she agreed. "But I can't guarantee it will happen now. I never can. But if it does you will be aware of it yourself. I feel a sudden surge of energy through my entire body when it happens. And at that moment, when I get a flash of inspiration—like an isolated flashlight photograph of a scene taken in pitch darkness—you will feel a pulse of energy go through me. I can't explain what it's like but you will know at the time that it's happened."

"That's interesting," said Frank eagerly, wondering what sort of exotic sensation he was about to enjoy. "I'll wait for that. Then I'll know something is working and you are finding out things for me. And I'll tell you afterwards, if I can describe it, what sort of sensation I got when you had each vision."

"Good, Frank," she said. "The keener you are and the more you try to play your part and above all keep your brain waves exactly in step with mine, then—like I said before—the more likely it is to work well. You see, the energy comes partly from you. It is as though your picture somewhere out in future time, is connected for a moment directly from your brain to mine. It's very fast though. Very, very fast. It may give your hand that's holding mine a strange tingling sensation as the message passes through. But you must not let go, either of my hand or of the brass ball. At all costs, you must not let go!"

Dame Crystal looked at Frank very intently. Clearly this was a crucial matter.

"Remember that," she said, with great emphasis. "You must not let go! It could be dangerous to let go. At the very least it would stop all contact with the future and there would be no going back. Now and then it's happened before and I have found that it's no good anybody who has broken contact in the middle of a sitting, ever coming back to try again. My mind will never tune into them again. There's a barrier put up by the sudden break and I can never get through again. Several times I've tried but never succeeded. Now I have given up trying. It's an utter waste of time, so I always make sure to make this clear to my clients from the outset."

"I won't let go, I promise you that!" assured Frank. "I want to be able to get the most out of it now, and perhaps be able to come back again another time. I'll do my best to make sure everything goes well."

"Good, Frank," she said. "I'm glad of that. And you will know when it is time to let go. You'll know when it's all over. I get a strong sensation of weakness when I lose contact with the future. It's overwhelming—almost as though I'm going to faint. You will feel my grip on your hand suddenly give way. There's no mistaking it, because I couldn't hang on any longer if I wanted to. I should tell you, though, that so far I have never had more than four pictures at one sitting, with any one person. That's the maximum. Sometimes it is four, but more often less and sometimes, occasionally, none at all. Of course, if that happens, people are very disappointed, but there's nothing I can do about it, nothing at all!"

"I don't suppose there is," said Frank sympathetically. "Nobody could blame you for that. To my mind, it's wonderful there's even a chance of it happening. Nobody could expect you to guarantee that it will."

"I'm glad you understand, Frank," she continued. "Now if I do get through to the future, the glimpses come one after another at short intervals, then stop—stop with a kind of jolt. I sometimes tell people that it seems to me as if I have been suspended, just kind of floating in the air—like being out of myself hovering above my own body, if that makes sense—and then suddenly dropped. It's a strange sensation, difficult to describe, a bit like falling out of a dream."

After this intensive build-up Frank was all attention. The lady was convincing; her manner was earnest and she spoke with a confident assurance which deeply impressed him. This was no world of pretence—of that he felt sure. This was for real! For the moment extraneous thoughts had ceased to divert his mind. She was aware of this because her randy sitter had become very still and watchful, momentarily transfixed!

"Now then, Frank, I am ready to start," she said, in a quieter but distinctly more purposeful tone of voice. "As I said, I will start saying the two lines and you must fall in with me—but silently—in your mind only. Not aloud. Keep your head perfectly still and look into my crystal ball. Keep your eyes fixed upon it and that will free your mind from all outside influences.

Repeating those magic, timeless, all-embracing words will lay a broad roadway out into the future along which my clairvoyant spirit can travel in an instant of time, being arrested at intervals, at points of powerful meaning and importance. This is my special gift which I now offer to you, and for these brief moments to you alone. The rest of the world is shut out, but remember, Frank, you must keep your brain rhythms exactly in step with mine. Say the words in step with me silently in your mind and keep it up at precisely the same rate after my voice stops. That is vital, absolutely vital. We shall then be as one—two people in intimate communion, briefly free to travel instantaneously in space and time, with your future and your Destiny guiding my spirit on its miraculous journey."

Frank got the message and felt very privileged. He sat perfectly still, staring down into the crystal ball. He could see a display of the colours of the spectrum inside it. Tensely he waited for her to start.

Dame Crystal Star now assumed her gravest and most serious demeanour. She looked fixedly down into the crystal ball, her head bent right over it. This was crunch time. She was about to begin.

After a few moments she began to recite the two lines, in time with the all pervasive clacking of the metronome,

> "Like the bub-bles on a ri-ver,
> Spark-ling, burst-ing, borne a-way —"

Abruptly she stopped. Something was clearly wrong. Still staring fixedly down into the crystal ball, a frown furrowed her brow. She was clearly disturbed about something.

"I've lost true, serious, spiritually meaningful mind-to-mind contact with you," she said, her tone of voice expressing surprise, concern and a trace of irritation. "You have stopped concentrating upon the subject of our mutual purpose. Of that I am absolutely certain. Nothing can possibly work unless you focus your mind and concentrate. That is not just very, very important, it's essential, absolutely essential!"

Unbeknown to her sitters, when looking directly downwards into her crystal ball, the optical properties of her purpose-made system gave her a direct view of the face of the person opposite. Studying their reactions was an important pre-requisite of her well-organised, highly-professional approach to her calling.

With her head bent over her crystal ball, in a perfectly normal position the star on her forehead was angled at about 45° to the table top. Looking at the mirror on which her crystal ball stood, she could see the star clearly reflected there, just behind the ball. By a simple adjustment of her head she could position herself so that the face of the sitter appeared in the reflected image down below her of the mirrored disc that formed the centre of her star.

Once there, since they were both quite still, it was simplicity itself to keep the face of her unsuspecting client steadily planted nicely in her mirror, to be studied closely as she gazed down, ostensibly studying visionary supernatural images in her clairvoyants' crystal ball. An imperceptibly small movement of her eyes shifted her line of vision from the crystal ball to the sitter's face. Mostly she looked at the latter; she learnt a great deal more from it!

The optical system did not work the other way round. Even if her client stared intently at the central mirrored surface of her impressive star, the darkened glass mirror on which the crystal ball rested gave nothing away. Only a blur of light, reflected upwards from below, could be seen in the disc. Not that any client ever did spend their time staring at her forehead, in any case.

This neat system, entirely of her own invention, gave her a distinct advantage, sometimes with uncanny results so far as her client was concerned. Now was a perfect example of this!

In the present situation she had seen Frank's eyes shift up from the downwards-slanting direction necessary for him to look into the crystal—as indeed he was under strict instructions to do—so that his line of sight was now directed above the top of the crystal ball, to a point just below her chin. She was only too aware what was happening! But the expression on her face did not betray the gleeful inner amusement she felt!

What had happened was that Frank had become momentarily mesmerized by the sight of Dame Crystal Star's ample bosom, boldly displayed just two feet from his face; wonderfully visible because of her titivatingly low-cut dress.

Dame Crystal knew that Frank had homed in on her cleavage!

No sooner did she say that she had lost serious mind-to-mind contact with him and that he had stopped concentrating upon their true purpose, than Frank realised why, and instantly shifted his ill-disciplined roving eyes to stare intently at the crystal once again.

"Oh Lord!" he thought despairingly. "She must have read my mind. She must have read me thinking what a lovely pair of knockers they are!"

He felt distinctly uncomfortable at this deduction, but his feeling of unease was ameliorated to some extent by the knowledge that she had not looked up. At least, he concluded, she did not know that he had been staring at them so rudely, as well as thinking about them. Or so he thought, because she certainly had not looked up but had been staring with great concentration down into her crystal ball all the time.

But this small measure of comfort was lost to him almost as soon as he'd lit upon it. With a feeling of hopeless inadequacy came the sickening realisation that by thinking she hadn't seen him staring at her tits, he'd automatically told her that he had been. He might just as well have shouted it to the high heavens!

Seldom in his lifetime had Frank felt so stupid. In the presence of such a gifted and superior intellect he felt as helpless as a fly stuck on a fly-paper.

As these thoughts raced and chased one another through his mind, Dame Crystal remained perfectly still, staring down into her crystal ball, trying hard, or so it seemed, to re-establish mental contact at the proper level. Frank figured that she was waiting for his mind to settle down. Meanwhile she studied his face with immense interest, seeing evidence of extreme anxiety and concern in his facial expressions as he struggled to sort himself out.

Frank reasoned to himself that he must, he just had to, take a tight grip on his mind and stop himself thinking what it would be like to go to bed with her. Words like tits and knockers—anything of that sort—must be kept out of his mind.

Then, in a state of utter confusion bordering upon despair, he realised she must be hearing him thinking what it was he had got to stop himself thinking about. So he mustn't even think about that!

He was in a twist. One hell of a twist!

The shock of this latest in a succession of failures to control his thoughts finally penetrated his subconscious mind and quelled his fertile imagination. The last untoward thought to flit through his head before his mind stilled, was to imagine what a hell of a mess his old Aunt Daisy, who was a devout Roman Catholic, would be in at Confession if she came up against a Priest with Dame Crystal Star's frightening ability to mind-read as well as listen. Perhaps it was the crushing realisation of how calamitous a situation that would be for 'Old Dirty Daisy' that finally stopped his feverishly active mind.

After this there were no further interruptions in the proceedings and thenceforth matters went ahead smoothly. He did not step out of line again and became passively acquiescent, obeying his instructions to the letter.

Much later on, when looking back at this experience, he compared his mental condition at this particular moment of his session with the Fortune Teller, with that which he'd once felt when coming out of his Headmaster's study as a severely chastised boy after having received six of the best on his backside! He was dormant, utterly subdued, and ruefully determined not to step out of line again—a condition which persisted for just as long as the memory of the moment remained fresh in his mind. As a boy the memory was kept alive by the stinging marks of the Headmaster's cane on his bare backside; as a man by the stinging embarrassment of the Fortune Teller's all-seeing eyes peering into her crystal ball reading the crude, private, innermost thoughts in his bared brain.

Neither experience was enjoyable. Both made him wince when recalled.

Although all this double-think took only a few moments, it did not seem so to him. He felt under great pressure and desperately sought to put things straight. It was clearly entirely up to him.

Remembering the metronome he latched on to that and began to count silently to himself in the hope it would lull his mind into inactivity and drive all random thoughts out altogether. His lips began to move slightly, and almost imperceptibly his head nodded in step, as he counted:

ONE and **TWO** and **THREE** and **FOUR,**
FIVE and **SIX** and **SEVEN** and **EIGHT,**
ONE and **TWO** and **THREE** and **FOUR,**
FIVE and **SIX** and **SEVEN** and **EIGHT**

Dame Crystal, watching him intently, knew full well what was happening. Almost immediately—it seemed to him again as if she had read his mind—she joined in the rhythm, precisely in step with him, but reciting the words aloud to re-start the interrupted proceedings,

> "Like the bub-bles on a ri-ver,
> Spark-ling, burst-ing, borne a-way,
> Like the bub-bles on a ri-ver
> Spark-ling, burst-ing, borne a-way . . ."

Frank, remembering that he too had to recite the words, not the numbers, fell in with her, silently going over them rhythmically in his mind.

Soon she too fell silent and he concentrated hard on continuing to go over and over the two lines, gripping the brass ball with his right hand and her right hand with his left. Her grip on his left hand tightened when she stopped reciting aloud. They were clearly now underway; the mysterious psychic performance had started in earnest.

For what seemed to Frank to be a long time, but in reality was no more than a minute or so, all was still in the room as they sat staring into the crystal ball.

There was no sound except the quiet tick-tock of her clock and the dominant, much louder, sharp-edged rhythmic clacking of the metronome. Soon this, coupled with the mental synchronism of his thinking processes with the repetitive metronomic sound his brain was locked to, began to make him feel drowsy.

Suddenly, with no warning whatsoever, Frank was literally jolted out of his tranquil sleepy state. Dame Crystal's body gave a jerk, as though her shoulder and arm muscles were contracted by a kind of spasm. She gave a little cry, as if in surprise. Simultaneously Frank received a sharp, convulsive electric shock, seemingly transmitted from her hand to his and extending right across his body to his right hand which gripped the brass ball. Unexpected and very startling, it was gone as fast as it had come. But it was a very positive, unmistakeable, physical shock with no apparent cause or origin except that of the clairvoyant's astounding psychic powers.

She continued to grip his hand and he—remembering his strict instructions and the crucial part he had to play—did not let go, but concentrated on repeating the words in step with the remorseless metronomic beat which commanded his attention.

Almost immediately he received another sharp and pronounced shock coinciding with a second spasmodic jerk of Dame Crystal's body. Again, she gave a little cry of apparent surprise, only to resume her trance-like posture a moment later.

Twice more these same events recurred, but after the fourth one there was a profound change in the lady's demeanour. Her grasp on his hand relaxed completely and she appeared to slump forward as though released from some restraining muscular tension.

Frank guessed it was all over and waited for her to speak. Anxious about her condition and bemused by the astonishing psychic experience, he gazed at her with concern and awe. At length she looked up from her crystal ball and met his eyes. She read both puzzlement and concern in his expression. Both emotions pleased her for they were the first imprint of success and rapport in their mutual experience.

"Did you feel that, Frank?" she asked, implying that she had been oblivious of his impulsive reaction to each of the four electric shocks. "I saw four pictures flash up in my mind, one after the other. As many as I've ever had at one time. Did you feel anything?"

She was looking rather strained and tired after what had evidently been an intense effort—undoubtedly, Frank guessed, a truly mentally-draining experience. The sheer energy involved, manifesting itself so clearly in the strange physical shocks he had felt, must, he thought, be a measure of the extent of her mental concentration. It was an amazing phenomenon.

"Yes, I certainly did!" replied Frank. "And I felt each one of the four. It was like an electric shock passing from your body right across mine from one side to the other."

"That's what other people have sometimes said," commented Dame Crystal. "And you say you did feel it four times? You're sure of that?"

"Oh yes! I am indeed!" continued Frank. "It was very strange. I could feel it in both of my arms and across my body. There's no mistake about that. I felt it all right! It seemed as if some power was generated in your body and came out of your hand into mine and across my body to the brass ball. A bit like the shock you get holding the brass handles of one of those little electric shock machines when they wind the wheel, but much sharper and shorter. More like a sudden jolt than the continuous tingling you get from those. Quite remarkable it was. Very strange. If somebody had told me it had happened to them, I wouldn't have believed it. I'd have thought they were spinning me a tall story. I've never experienced anything quite like that before. Never!"

"I don't suppose you have!" Dame Crystal said with conviction. "No two clairvoyants are alike. I have never heard of another who works the same as I do. Each one develops their own methods. Years ago when I was just starting to discover my powers, people told me they could feel a sudden tingling from my hands when I held theirs during 'looking-into-the-future' sessions. Then one day, quite by accident, I found that if they held something metal in one hand, it got much stronger. After a lot of experimenting I found out what works best for me and settled on the two methods we have just used, firstly for going back into the past and then secondly for looking into the future. And it works best if people hold the brass ball with their writing hand."

"Well, that's extraordinary," commented Frank. "What a bit of luck you stumbled on it! But did you see anything just now?" he enquired eagerly. "Did you get any pictures? That's the important thing for me today."

"Yes, I certainly did," she replied. "And I must try to describe what I saw before my memory fades. It's always hard to bring back all the details, even a few minutes later and after a little while, in a few hours, they fade altogether. That's why I write notes on the cards each time, as soon as my clients have gone out and before I see anybody else."

"Will you describe them to me then, please?" requested Frank anxiously. "Will you tell me exactly what you saw?"

"I'll do my best, Frank," she said. "If you bear with me I shall try to bring them back into my mind's eye one at a time, in the order they came to me. But you mustn't speak or ask questions or I shall lose focus, things will get muddled and I will not be able to recapture them clearly again. I know it would be better if I could go to and fro into the future, taking one picture at a time and coming back to tell you about it. But it doesn't work like that and the brief memories don't remain parcelled-up separately either. They come in a sequence when I see them, and that's how I have to recall them afterwards. If you listen I will describe them in their sequence, but I repeat, you must not interrupt as I am recalling them. You can commit them to memory and think them over when you get home. I advise you to lie quietly in bed with your eyes closed and think them through to see if they appear to make sense to you."

With that she stared down into her crystal ball, her hands clasped in front of her as they had been when he'd first sat at the table. For a while Frank waited expectantly, watching her closely as she remained motionless. He noticed that she was breathing slowly and deliberately, taking in very deep breaths, as does an athlete under training.

"Grasp the two brass balls, Frank," she instructed. "If you then look into the crystal ball and sit quite still, that will help me to concentrate deeply. Any movement in the middle of my contemplation can distract me."

Frank did as he was told and all was quiet and still in the room. She had switched off the metronome.

Dame Crystal, still staring downwards, adjusted her head and eyes slightly to bring Frank's face into view in the reflection below of the mirrored central disc on her crystal star. At length she started to speak, her tone of voice strangely modulated as though she were curiously detached from him, speaking about something she was seeing far, far away.

"These are the pictures in my mind," she said. "First of all I can see you standing high up on the deck of a large ship, looking down and waving to several people on the quayside. The ship is crowded with happy travellers setting out on a long journey. Most are in little groups, but you are on your own. Quite alone. It looks like a large, ocean-going liner." She paused a few moments, as evidently the scene changed.

"In the next picture," she went on, a little hesitatingly at first as though she was struggling to get things in focus and striving to study its detail, "I can see you standing on a green lawn by a white flagpole flying the Stars and Stripes. You are talking to a tall, fine-looking man with a shock of strong greying hair. He is smoking a large cigar and wearing a smart, light-coloured, well-tailored suit. He looks like an American gentleman to me.

There is a big old-fashioned gun on a four-wheeled wooden carriage standing on the grass at the foot of the pole. You both seem to be looking at it with great interest. The lawn is in front of a large, modern-looking building. It is a bungalow-type place with large windows all along it from end to end. Beyond the building I can see the blue haze of the sea and far away in the distance is the horizon. It looks a lovely setting. Things seem so new and clean."

Again she paused and Frank guessed she was now studying the third picture.

"Now I see you with the same man in a different place," she said. "It seems to me you are high up on a tower-like building, like an observation tower, looking down at a huge area full of steam engines.

Some are like the Showman's Engines we have here in the fairground. There seems to be engines of all sorts. There are steam rollers; traction engines on their own; traction engines coupled to threshers; others with road trains of wagons; traction engines with steam ploughs; steam lorries—and all sorts of engines. I can't picture in detail what they are like, for there are so many of them. It's like looking at a photograph where things are so crowded and far away that it's difficult to see just what is there. I think I can also see some very old railway engines. And in the distance there are roundabouts and swings. It looks like a fairground. Yes, it is a fairground over at the far side of the ground. I can see a helter-skelter and some large steam-organs like we have here." She paused again, this time for a longer period.

"The last picture I hardly like to tell you about in case it does not come true," she said. "You are standing outside a modern church, like some of those they have in America. You are arm-in-arm with a lady in a lovely, flowing white wedding dress. She is carrying a bouquet of beautiful flowers. There are happy people all around. You look so smart yourself too, in a grey morning suit with a big red carnation in your button hole. It must be your wedding day. You make a wonderful couple. She is a very attractive lady, with dark but greying hair. You are the same kind of age. It is the wedding day of a very happy, middle-aged couple. One of the men taking photographs is the distinguished-looking man who was beside you by the flag pole."

Frank winced a bit at the 'middle-aged' reference. But alas, he knew that he already qualified for that description, never mind what he might look like in the future if he should every join Walter Richtmeyer in his projected Steam Museum at San Francisco far away in California. Ruefully he thought that the appellation 'middle-aged' might even be a compliment to him by then!

Dame Crystal looked up and smiled at him.

"That's all I can remember from the snapshot pictures that flashed through my mind," she said. "Perhaps they mean something to you, perhaps not. But that's what I saw. Only time will tell us if they mean anything or not."

At that moment her chiming clock began to signal the hour, ringing out in soft mellow tones the well-known Westminster tune. On the strike of three, Dame Crystal reached over, switched the door lights from red to amber, and stood up. His time was up. He'd had his ration. Smoothly, with no awkwardness, her simple system showed him it was time to go.

Frank smiled broadly. "Well, I don't know if you have travelled forward into the future or just read my secret thoughts and dreams," he said. "But, except for the marrying bit, what you have pictured is very much like a private dream I have of a new life out in the States. You have a wonderful gift and I am very grateful to you for the time you have spent with me. It has been a fascinating experience and one I shall always remember."

"Before you go," smiled the gifted clairvoyant, "I wonder if you would care to buy one of my lucky charms. I make them myself out of pure amber. They are one pound each and I am told by some people who know about these things that the amber in them is probably worth more than that. It would always be a link with me," she added archly. "I should like that!"

So saying she went into her bedroom and came out carrying a tray covered with royal blue velvet cloth on which were displayed a variety of pendants and pocket charms, all fashioned from highly polished amber of differing shades from very pale yellow to a rich, dark-reddish colour. They were all well made and attractive, certainly not cheap holiday gift-shop things but decidedly professional in appearance.

Frank selected a heart-shaped pendant and gave her a one-pound note from his wallet, mentally clocking-up that this had more than doubled his expenditure on the visit. Not that he was unhappy about that, because he felt he'd had very good value for money in his consultation and was more than pleased with his lucky charm.

"I shall keep this," he said smilingly, "to hang around the neck of that lovely lady the day I marry her. And you can be sure you will be in my thoughts at the time!"

"Let's hope it brings you lots and lots of luck, my dear," she said, looking him directly in the eyes and treating him to a radiant smile which immediately re-aroused his non-psychic interest in her!

A sharp ring of the door bell signalled the arrival of Dame Crystal Star's next good-luck seeking client, so—rather reluctantly—Frank stood to take his leave. He had taken quite a fancy to his fortune-teller. And she to him, though he did not realise it at the time.

She did not miss his final swift glance of overt approval of her blatantly sexy appearance—nor that he had put a restraining hand in his trouser pocket as he stood up. She was only too well aware that she could switch him on with the mere bat of an eyelid!

Dame Crystal Star shook hands with her captivated client and smiled with inner amusement as he made his way to the door. Had he been gifted with the wonderful ability he attributed to her, of being able to read another person's thoughts, he might have been astonished at the unladylike mental observation she made as she watched him go out.

"I hope he does get married soon, or failing that finds himself a good woman," she thought. "Otherwise the pressure of that pulsating power-plant of pent-up paternity packed between his legs will probably blow his balls to bits!"

This colourful observation about his privates would not have destroyed his faith in her professional ability, despite the medical improbability of such a disastrous explosion. On the contrary he would have gone back up the steps and pleaded for relief from his dangerous state. For her part she would perhaps have been happy to oblige.

But, not possessing the power to mind-read, Frank was unaware of the decidedly earthy thoughts occupying the mind of the psychic lady as she watched his departure. So he left the premises without even knowing there was a latent possibility of a physical communion to complement their mental psychical one which had proved so successful in the comfortable privacy of the cosy caravan.

Waiting at the bottom of the wooden steps when he went out, Frank met a tall, lean, angular, straight-faced, rather severe-looking, bespectacled lady, her straight greying hair tied back in a neat flat bun. Dressed in tweeds and wearing very practical, strong, brown-leather walking shoes, he mentally classified her as a middle-aged spinster, probably a school-mistress. She was the very antithesis of Dame Crystal Star, the lady she was about to meet. She did not look a very happy lady.

"Your turn next," said Frank cheerfully. "I wish you luck."

She smiled wanly at this remark and glanced quickly around in an uneasy nervous way. Frank detected a hint of embarrassment in her manner—as though she did not wish to be seen going into the Fortune Teller's caravan by anybody who knew her. He knew the feeling! As he walked away he wondered what secret dreams she had and hoped she would come out looking a bit happier.

When he looked back over his shoulder she was still standing there waiting for the green light to come on. He guessed that the slight delay was due to Dame Crystal writing some brief notes on his record card while the memory of what he had been told was still fresh in her mind. Then, presumably, she could forget about him and focus her attention entirely upon her next client. He wondered what unlikely private thoughts would be winkled out of the head of the unhappy-looking lady. In outward appearance she looked chilly and cheerless. But was she frigid or just frustrated? Full of fears or full of fantasies?

When Dame Crystal discovered the answers, as he did not doubt but that she surely would, then maybe her look into the future would throw up a mirror-image of her client's secret dreams, dreams that would then perhaps become reality, helped to do so by inner conviction planted that very day by Dame Crystal herself.

He fell to wondering whether, by ostensibly shuffling about from the present to the past, then on to the future and back again, Dame Crystal did indeed see the future, by helping to create it there and then.

He concluded that whatever else may be true or untrue about what she did or did not do, of one thing he was absolutely certain; Dame Crystal Star was one hell of a lady! Not only that, she was one hell of a woman! Not every lady he knew qualified for that compliment.

Frank was quite right in his assumption that Dame Crystal wrote up his notes immediately he left. She also attended to another small technical matter.

Had he been in a condition to be more observant, Frank might have noticed a pronounced squeak coming from under the table, coinciding precisely with the moments when he received the mysterious jolts of psychic energy generated by the gifted lady. Dame Crystal herself had heard them and knew exactly what caused them. Lest the squeaks should lead to the arousal of curiosity and possible suspicion on the part of a future client, she decided to deal with the problem immediately. She could not risk the discovery by an alert person of one of her most important professional secrets!

Bolted under the top of her table was an old motorbike magneto, installed there by a very close friend: Boris of SKWEC!

She was very indebted to her inventive friend for this tremendous asset. Its contribution to her show was so impressive and gave her another most positive edge over others of her calling.

When talking to a client, during the looking-into-the-future routine, Dame Crystal's free hand, under the table, clutched the cog-wheel on the driving shaft of the magneto. The output lead from the magneto, which under normal circumstances went to the sparking-plug in a motorbike engine, was connected under the table to the brass bar that carried the two brass balls mounted on the ebony board above.

At the opportune moment, all she did was give the cog-wheel a single sharp twist which generated a high-voltage, sufficient in its normal application to make a spark jump the air-gap between the points of a sparking plug.

Since, at the same time, she was clutching the hand of her client, a complete circuit existed. It went from the magneto to her client via the brass ball he was holding, back through his body to her hand and via her body to the cog-wheel of the magneto that was gripped by her other hand.

The high voltage across their bodies produced a sudden electric shock. She was, of course, ready for the jolt and well used to it, though she could not suppress an involuntary jerk of her muscles. But her clients were not expecting the pleasure so received a very sharp, though brief and not dangerous, shock. They had merely been warned that they might experience a tingling sensation at the moments of her sudden 'visions'—but not a profound jolt!

Although there was no danger, Dame Crystal nonetheless avoided this part of her routine if somebody noticeably frail sat opposite her. She neither wanted to risk killing anybody by perhaps initiating a heart-attack, nor to lose her professional reputation by this decidedly non-psychic procedure becoming public knowledge following an accident or complaint.

At the other extreme, she particularly liked to give big, tough-looking men a good shaking up, and delighted in giving the cog-wheel a particularly sharp twist when she had one literally in her clutches. Enjoined as they were not to let go, she would treat them to their full ration of four visions! To maintain their macho image they, of necessity, had to 'hang on in there', for four jolts in a row!

Her immediate problem, that of the squeak, was disposed of in a matter of seconds by applying a few drops of oil to the bearings of the magneto. It was something she had to do every now and again. Otherwise the system was completely trouble-free and totally reliable.

That done, she sat down at her table again, composed herself, turned off her amber light and switched on the green one to fetch in her next victim.

Life for a professional Fortune Teller, especially that of a well-known, respected and talented clairvoyant of the calibre of Dame Crystal Star, was a busy one, though never dull and certainly not without its compensations.

She had positively enjoyed her last consultation for she had found Frank an attractive man in more ways than one and had a shrewd idea that she had not seen the last of him. Only very seldom was she able to enjoy the invaluable aid and powerful fillip to her imagination of such a fund of prior knowledge about a client. It was a rare pleasure to start off her clairvoyant deliberations knowing that she would finish the session with her excursion into the past being right on the ball and her flight of fancy into the future being immediately, at the very least, highly plausible. Her briefing by Boris had been a bonus indeed, a rich contribution which, in her highly skilled and inimitable way, she had fully exploited.

In retrospect she was to come to regard this day as a very important milestone in her life, though—despite her very considerable clairvoyant capabilities—she had neither seen the day coming, nor, having experienced it, did she predict its outcome. For Fate chooses to preserve some surprises for the soothsayer, as well as for her clients!

Chapter 25

CARLO'S FAIRGROUND

Sam Donatello's new Dodgem Cars

Frank, relieved to see none of his SKWEC party were around to see him come out of the Fortune Teller's caravan, made his way round the corner towards Sam's New Dodgem Cars. Unhappily for him his assumption that his visit to Dame Crystal Star had been unobserved was soon disabused.

Standing watching the antics of the cars was a small cluster of his Company's men, Arthur and Terry among them. They spotted him, waved and called him over to join them.

"How did you get on, Frank?" asked Arthur with a sly, knowing grin. "Did you get some good news?"

"Where?" stalled Frank, fearing the worst, but momentarily clinging to the hope that Arthur was referring to something else. It was a vain hope.

"At the Fortune Teller's," replied Arthur. "We saw you sneak into her den!"

"Yes," chipped in Terry, "we were a bit worried about you. You have to be careful with Fortune Tellers. Some of those ladies practise magic. Witches, I reckon some of them are! We thought you might get a bit fresh with her and get yourself turned into a randy horny old toad or something!"

There was a chorus of laughter from the group around them. The unattached Frank was thought to be a bit of a womaniser who reputedly took his opportunities wherever by good fortune he found them—a reputation not uncommon for men of his age-group who had survived so long without being hooked. They were ready game for this sort of leg-pulling.

Frank had a shrewd idea that some of his married friends who had been tied up for several years, actually envied him his freedom and that their highly imaginative accusations reflected their fanciful notions of what their lives might be like if they were an unattached 'free-ranger' like him. So he often played up to them and sometimes twisted their tails a bit.

"You needn't have worried," smiled Frank, making the best of a bad job. "I survived—just! I behaved myself and got out alive and unharmed."

"What was it like, though?" pressed Arthur. "Was she good?" Arthur contrived, by facial expression and tone of voice, to make the word 'good' seem loaded.

"Oh yes! She's good all right! Make no mistake about that!" responded Frank positively. But quick to pick up the double-meaning implication of Arthur's question, he determined to concentrate only upon her professional ability and say nothing about her physical attraction. He was conscious that if he were not careful another highly colourful story would quickly be invented, to add to the store of apocryphal adventures with which he was already credited.

Sometimes he was ribbed unmercifully about these largely fictional episodes. On occasions, in some company, he squirmed like a fish on a hook, especially if comments were a bit too near the bone for comfort. Boris came in for the same kind of treatment. Neither of them enjoyed it much; they had to tolerate it and put the best possible face on it. To show sensitivity to it only served to stoke up the fire. To be needled was to be defeated; it was an open invitation for those wielding the needle to prick them without mercy!

In this respect Frank and Boris were quite unlike their mutual acquaintance Taffy Thomas, the local, ageing, unmarried woodcutter whose notorious sexual adventures were widely discussed. He seemed to glory in the fame of his reported personal conquests, real or imaginary! It was impossible to needle him. There was no pleasure in that; he was needle-proof. The pleasure to be harvested from him was simply to feed his eager ego by denouncing him in public for the unashamed womaniser he was, and stimulate him to entertain those present with lurid details of his adventures. Frank and

Boris were always pleased if he were present at convivial gatherings because they were able to shelter under his umbrella, for the spotlight was on the star turn. They, by comparison, were small beer.

Under the present circumstances, conditioned by this background, Frank played his hand carefully.

"Dame Crystal Star is a very impressive lady," he continued. "Very clever, she is. It's a battle of wits in there! I pity anybody going in with the wrong ideas, or carrying a guilty secret. She can read anyone's mind as easily as reading a book!"

"Count me out, then," laughed Terry. "She might pass on to my wife things I'd rather she didn't know about!"

"Did she have some good news for you, though?" repeated Arthur persistently, inwardly not at all sure he wouldn't pop along quietly himself later on to see if he might perhaps be going to win the Irish Sweepstake, or have something equally as welcome and exciting lying ahead of him in the future. He was an inveterate dreamer, very much a 'pie in the sky' man—a fact well-known to Boris who had accordingly placed him on his shortlist of potential customers for Dame Crystal.

"Yes, she did indeed!" countered Frank, wanting a quick way out of an inquisition and spotting a way to turn it on its head.

"What did she say, then?" asked Arthur eagerly, taking the bait—the serious and unsmiling Frank having infuriatingly stopped short of telling him.

"She had some marvellous news for me," answered Frank, quietly and portentously. "Wonderful news! She told me there is a fortune waiting for me to pick up if I like to take the trouble to go after it!"

All eyes were now on him and he paused again, as if he had dramatic news to impart, but was reluctant to tell.

"What did she mean?" queried Arthur, intent upon prising the information out of the cagey Frank. "How do you have to go after it? What do you have to do?"

Frank relented. "I suppose there's no harm in telling you," he said, hesitatingly. "What she said was, that if I go digging around the fields near Dover long enough," he went on, speaking slowly, conscious that they were all hanging on his words, "then sooner or later I'll unearth an ancient cannon with a fabulous treasure stuffed up its barrel!"

This punchline brought a loud laugh from the group of men listening to the exchange between the three and successfully brought an end to the conversation. Frank had escaped comparatively lightly, and in any event their interest was quickly switched elsewhere.

Their attention was diverted by an extra loud bang from two cars meeting in a head-on crash out in the middle of the floor, followed by an angry shout from the man in charge who was standing by the Pay Box at the far end. It was Alf Butcher, Sam's Dodgem Car Manager. He switched the power off, bringing all the cars to a sudden standstill and strode angrily across to where a bit of a rumpus was going on between the occupants of the two cars.

In one sat two outraged girls whose progress had been abruptly halted by a ginger-headed youth who had driven his car quite deliberately slap-on in a nose-to-nose crash with their car.

The girls were not amused! The impact was too violent and uncomfortable to be regarded as fun and they told him so in no uncertain terms, firing off forceful, four-letter Anglo-Saxon words in a furious stream of unladylike invective that made the atmosphere fairly crackle with female fury. Their vocabulary clearly shocked some of the bystanders, but their fierce reaction was welcomed by some of their fellow car-riders who'd had more than enough of the young man in question and were equally keen to see him off.

"That's it!" shouted Alf to the offending youth, obviously very annoyed indeed. "You can get out of that car and sling your bloody hook. I've warned you twice before and that's enough. Get the hell out of here and don't come back!"

The ginger-headed youth made no move, but just sat and looked up at Alf speculatively, sizing him up. 'Ginger' was obviously a troublemaker, defiant and bloody-minded, a typical spoiler.

"Who is going to make me?" he asked insolently, seeing an opportunity to show off in front of the girls by defying the irate, ageing man glowering down at him as he sprawled back in the car's seat.

That was too much for Alf who signalled his two assistants, pointed a finger at the arrogant youngster, jerked his thumb sideways towards the exit and gave the two men an unequivocal instruction.

"Get rid of this big mouth!" he stated sharply. "Chuck him out and don't let him on again."

Seeing the two, tough-looking men moving purposefully towards him, the tousle-headed nuisance beat a hasty retreat. Had he not done so, Alf's assistants would happily have carried out his instructions literally and with alacrity. He would have gone out ignominiously on his neck—not least because there was a commission element in their wages and time wasted was money lost to them. Sam Donatello had fixed their terms of contract to encourage the maximum through-put of punters on his new ride. Not only that, damaged cars also cut down the takings, as well as costing time and effort of staff in putting them right. It was in everybody's interest to keep the whole stock of cars fully operational.

Having put a safe distance between himself and the advancing men, the young troublemaker bellowed a final defiant "Stuff your bloody Dodgem Cars!" at Alf, thrust two fingers up at him in a rude, insolent gesture and disappeared off the scene.

Power was then switched on again and one of the men drove the abandoned car to the side out of the way. The second one rode standing on its fender, holding the vertical pole which carried the electric cable up to the robust spring that picked up power from the grill above. Jumping on the bumpers and riding cars like that was their normal way of communicating with the riders, sometimes to take money or deliver change, or maybe help the riders out of trouble. People sometimes got themselves in a twist and needed help to extricate themselves from difficulties.

The rest of the cars now resumed their bumpy buzzing around the track, with more fun now that the ginger-headed menace had been ejected.

"He's been asking for that!" commented Arthur, who had watched the winkling-out of the pest with some satisfaction.

"What's he been up to?" asked Frank.

"Well, the rule is that all cars must flow round the area in a clockwise direction," explained Arthur. "They dodge in and out and bump one another as they go, that's half the fun of it. But turning back and driving against the stream is forbidden. The cars can stand plenty of bumping when they're all going more or less in the same direction. With the sprung rubber-covered fender all round them that's what they are designed for. But that little twerp has several times turned right round and driven full tilt into an oncoming car. Nothing can stand too much of that kind of punishment and the cars suffer, never mind the people in them who could be injured by the sudden jolt."

Arthur continued, "Boris was telling us that this Dodgem Car installation, together with the Fowler traction engine that powers it, has cost Sam Donatello a small fortune, apart from the cost of staffing it. Sam apparently gets hopping mad if his men allow people to knock all hell out of the cars in head-on crashes. They're under strict orders to stop that from happening. He reckons they've got to last four or five years before he gets his money back on his investment and starts to make a real profit on his money. It's not the easiest of rides to maintain in good working order. A few stupid blighters like that youngster could soon put half of it out of action. But I marvel at the punishment the cars can put up with. Even when people are driving them properly, keeping to the rules, they still get a fair old bashing!"

"We've been talking to those two blokes over there," said Terry, referring to the two burly assistants. "Those two tough nuts and Alf Butcher, plus the bloke running the Fowler Showman's Engine, work full-time on this Dodgem Car set-up. And two more of Sam's men work part-time to relieve those two to give them a few hours off each week. They reckon this outfit often works ten hours or more non-stop on some days, especially Saturdays and Bank Holidays. The cars have to be pretty rugged to put up with that bashing, even when they are used sensibly. You can understand Sam being worried about them."

After watching the proceedings for a while, Frank thought he would take himself off to have a word with the man responsible for driving and looking after the Showman's Engine that was working continuously to provide the power to keep the whole lot going.

The strong smell of ozone in the air, caused by the sparking contacts above and below the cars, was testimony to the substantial current needed to run all the cars simultaneously. It also indicated to Frank that continuous maintenance routines must be necessary behind the scenes, to keep them all running efficiently.

The nearly-new Fowler's Engine, positioned along the edge of the fairground adjacent to the ride, with power cables from it strung overhead to the Dodgem Car's junction-box and control gear inside the Pay Box, was running smoothly and sweetly, driving its large generator. It was attended by a watchful, competent-looking driver, judged by Frank to be a man in his late forties who had probably spent his working life with steam engines. He had that sort of look about him; he and steam engines seemed to go together. He looked confident and capable to Frank, a first judgement which subsequently turned out to be a correct assessment.

Frank introduced himself and was not surprised to learn that the man was well acquainted with Boris and knew of his association with SKWEC.

His name was Bert Crossley, a North Countryman, born in Burnley, Lancashire, who had previously been responsible for working a similar engine in an installation of the same kind at a funfair in Blackpool. Sam, setting up his outfit for the first time, needed an experienced man to look after it and was lucky enough—through the agency of the manufacturer of his installation—to find Bert Crossley, who wanted to move south.

It was not long before Sam decided he had got himself a winner. Bert really knew his stuff, not only about steam engines, in which field he had served a full five-year apprenticeship with an engineering firm in Manchester, but also about the electrics of the Dodgems.

Sam paid Bert Crossley very well because the whole outfit depended upon him. He hooked up and looked after the power supply on site, and advised upon, as well as assisting with, the maintenance of the cars to keep the whole outfit functioning properly. In addition he supervised the loading and unloading of the entire installation when they moved sites, and of course drove the engine with its train of heavily-loaded trailers on the journeys. It was a responsible job and Sam had been fortunate enough to find a man who was tailor-made to fit it.

Interested in the mechanics of the complicated business of assembling and dismantling the entire outfit each time they moved, Frank asked Bert what the routine was for shifting the installation. It seemed such a complicated and formidable job.

"There has to be a strict system," pointed out Bert. "The secret, as with all fairground rides, is in loading and unloading the trailers methodically in a carefully-numbered sequence. The last item loaded is the first one needed at the next site. Once worked out, the system has to be followed faithfully as a repetitive routine—much like a military drill. If that is done, it is surprising how quickly the entire outfit can be taken down, loaded and towed away behind this Fowler traction engine."

"How many trailers are there?" asked Frank.

"Three," answered Bert. "One takes all the cars and also parts of the super-structure. The second takes the rest of the upper structure and the flooring. The third is our living wagon which carries our personal belongings."

Frank was aware of the slick efficiency with which a travelling fair could materialise as if by magic overnight, and disappear equally as quickly at the end of its stay. He was intrigued by the carefully worked out organisation this implied and wanted to get a picture of it in his mind.

Inspired by Dame Crystal Star's so recent predictive visions, he was already thinking ahead of the time when technical information about fairgrounds might be useful to him should he ever work for Walter Richtmeyer in San Francisco. The sharp electric shocks he had received from her body, marking the moment of appearance of her visions, plus her confident, assured manner, was convincing evidence to him of her mysterious psychic powers. As yet he had not had any time to dwell upon the likelihood of there being any jiggery-pokery behind the manifestations of these curious powers, and, truth to tell, he was as yet ill-disposed to doubt them because he liked the content of the pictures she had provided! At the moment he was pushing the possibility that there might be some hidden hanky-panky in her powerful performance well to the back of his mind. There it could remain for the time being, stewing in his subconscious!

That there was a possibility, and a strong one in his optimistic judgement, that he would indeed land up in San Francisco, was not in doubt. Dame Crystal's efforts on his behalf had brought his cherished dreams swamping back into the forefront of his mind; that was the dominant fact of the moment. As a result he was somewhat elated and excited by the thought that he could here and now begin to strengthen his personal background and start to prepare himself to embrace wider responsibilities. He saw himself *ready* to embrace wider responsibilities. He saw himself as the Resident Engineer in charge of Walter Richtmeyer's ambitious and visionary new project out in California.

So with springs in his heels and expectation in his heart, from now-on-in he intended to gobble up as much information as he could to equip himself for the big job ahead. The unsuspecting Bert Crossley was swept up in this freshly stoked-up burst of enthusiasm to make Frank's dream come true and was about to be asked to make a contribution by having his brain picked!

"Tell me, what you do when you arrive on a site, Bert?" Frank requested. "Looking at that complete Dodgem Car set-up as it stands over there now, tell me how you put it all up."

"To start with," grinned Bert, "we need some muscle men. Those two over there with Alf are key men, with two others from Sam's staff to assist them. Working with those four men, I supervise the unloading and Alf the erection, of the entire ride."

"Is it asking too much to tell me the routine?" asked Frank. "Could you run over it briefly step by step with me? I'm interested to learn what's involved."

"Sure! Glad to," agreed Bert, good-naturedly. "But you're not thinking of starting up a set yourself, are you?"

"Not likely!" answered Frank. "I don't have that sort of money, I'm afraid. I'm always interested to see how things tick, though. With steam engines being ousted all over the place by petrol-driven vehicles, firms like ours have got to diversify in the coming years. And there's nothing I can see about this Dodgem Car outfit that SKWEC couldn't manufacture, from scratch. We already have a strong connection with fairgrounds and maybe we could extend the scope of it. If you can spare the time I'd like to know how it all fits together. That will tell me what is involved in the entire outfit."

Frank forebore to mention his American ambitions, but was quite serious in his suggestion that SKWEC might in future interest themselves in manufacturing fairground rides, as a new venture.

"OK, then," said Bert. "Here goes. This is what happens. When we arrive on a site, like this one at Hythe, Sam Donatello has already worked out where everything has to go. He prepares a master plan of the entire fairground. So we drive in and are directed straight to our pitch. Alf, with his two assistants, quickly measure out a rectangle, marking the four corners with pegs and stringing lines all round. Then, off the first trailer, they unload those hefty beams, like railway sleepers, that the floor is built on. These, which are all numbered, are laid in sequence right round the rectangle, regularly spaced. Where necessary, on uneven ground, they are raised on a series of wooden blocks of varying thicknesses, which are used to level the beams. Another line of similar beams is laid down the middle. Alf has to be very careful with that job and goes round it with his two mates using spirit levels, adjusting the blocks until they get the whole lot right."

"Some job that!" commented Frank. "And they've got to be absolutely level, by the look of the installation."

"You're right there!" agreed Bert emphatically. "It's the most important job of all, and has to be done very carefully. But once done, the rest—though bloody hard work—is straightforward enough. If the beams are not precisely level the whole lot goes wrong. Both Alf and I have seen the chaos that an off-level floor causes with the rest of the erection, so it is never allowed to happen with this outfit. Sometimes we have to use sharp spades to cut away soil under the beams in various places, to get them slotted down a bit and level. But Sam does his best to find good level ground for us, to avoid having to do too much of that sort of thing, because it holds up the job and creates a lot of aggro all round."

"What happens next?" asked Frank.

"Well, next off the trailer are the flooring rafters," continued Bert. "These lie across from one side to another, bolted in pairs to give enough length. The joints of the paired-rafters lie side by side on the centre row of beams. This central support strengthens the floor and stops floor-bounce. That completes the floor framework and on it is laid the steel plates which form the electrical earth-return path connection for the cars."

"They must be heavy," observed Frank, who had noticed when he stood watching the cars that they ran on a well-fitting steel floor, with sliding contact springs underneath them sparking away like the springs on the metal grill up above them.

"Yes, they're heavy all right!" confirmed Bert ruefully. "That's the toughest job of the lot in terms of sheer hard work. Each plate is about six feet long by three feet wide and weighs over a hundredweight. Two men up on the trailer hand one at a time down to their two mates below, who carry it across and fit it. There are 120 of them in this outfit and that's a total of over six tons of steel the blokes handle each time we put down or take up the floor. The pairs of men change jobs every ten plates, otherwise the ones below would flake out. On the floor Alf sees that each plate is correctly placed. He moves them into their final position with a crow-bar. The floor measures about sixty feet by thirty-six feet, overall."

"Alf must be busy, then," said Frank. "I imagine squaring-up and properly locating one hundred and twenty steel plates is pretty tiring work!"

"It certainly is," agreed Bert. "The plates are the hardest job of all, shifting this outfit from site to site. We always have a break, though, after we've shifted half of them. Sam has a barrel of beer on site every time we are putting up or taking down, and boy do we need it! That Dodgem Car floor, with its foundation beams, flooring rafters and steel plates, is pure hard graft!

Anyway, once the floor's down the rest is easy. The Pay Kiosk, and the side supports for the roof-grill are erected next. Then the strong overhead metal grill itself, that the cars make contact with, is put in. That has to be done carefully to keep the mesh tight so that the contacts run smoothly over it, as the cars turn and twist about below. But all that's light work compared with the floor. When the grill mesh is in place, the canvas canopy is tied on to keep the rain off the whole outfit. Last of all, the headboards with the wording and decorations on are put up to pull the crowds in."

"I suppose you then hook up the electrics?" queried Frank.

"That's right," said Bert. "While the others are getting the cars unloaded off that second double-tier trailer you can see over there along the fence, I wire in the power. By the time they have all the cars in position, with their canvas hoods off and lined up ready for testing, I have the engine running and the power on. As for the lighting that makes the place look so attractive at night, that all goes in as the grill and sideboards go up. It is permanently fixed and simply needs inter-connecting."

"You have certainly got things well organised," complimented Frank. "You make it sound easy, but looking around this field full of fairground rides, sideshows and booths, it is difficult to imagine the whole lot being dismantled, loaded and back on the road in a matter of a few hours."

"Well, that's the heart of the fairground business," said Bert. "It's all very slick, using systems developed over donkeys' years. If you look at Sam's largest set of Gallopers you will see that's a hell of a complicated set-up. But of course the mechanics of Roundabouts like that have been perfected over far more years than Dodgem Cars and the machinery is really ingenious. You can only see clearly how it works when you watch it being built up or dismantled."

"Then there's the switchback," observed Frank. "That looks like a glorified set of Meccano parts. It must be quite a job to get that put up and taken down quickly!"

"It's not too bad," said Bert. "Again it's straightforward if all the parts are numbered and handled in a strict sequence."

Frank turned his attention to the relentlessly softly-running engine and stood looking at it for some moments. An engine turning over at a moderate speed, always, he felt, looked at its best. Watching the mechanism reminded him of a long-distance runner loping effortlessly along. It seemed to work easily and tirelessly.

The engine looked highly decorated compared with its brothers working on the land and the roads. The curved-surfaced canopy that extended right over the engine from end to end to protect all the machinery from the weather, was colourfully painted, with its vertical, twisted-metal supporting rods attractively gilded.

Along the canopy's curved-edged side boards, were emblazoned the words CARLO'S DODGEM CARS, with the letters standing out boldly against an artistically-painted background of bright, gaily-swirling colours. Frank knew from experience how fascinated people were by the striking appearance of a travelling fair on the road. He admired the enterprise and ability of the fairground folk who knew how to pull in the crowds by the magnetic attraction of their gaily-painted convoys as they passed through the countryside on their way to their next well-advertised stopping place.

The signwriting and decorative painting was done by some of their number who seemed to inherit a natural artistic ability and found endless opportunities to develop it around the rides and side-shows of the fairground.

Sam's two sets of Gallopers showed fine examples of their work. Not only were the horses and ostriches that people rode on painted very attractively and cleverly, but the artwork on the headboards and around the overhead canopy included some fine paintings. One of them showed a series of animals racing at full stretch around the overhanging sides of the canopy. Amongst these were three lions that were truly striking works of art. Most people admiring them were totally unaware that some of the often rough-and-ready-looking men seen working around the fairground had done this work during winter months, and assumed that skilled sign-writers or professional artists must have been commissioned by Carlo's to paint them.

A further outlet for this artwork was in the production of posters advertising Carlo's Fairground. In advance of the arrival of Carlo's Fair at each site, fly-posting teams covered the surrounding catchment area with highly colourful posters. This was a night-time activity, and the ubiquitous fly-posting people from Sam's staff flitted surreptitiously around towns, villages, hamlets and farms, pasting their posters on noticeboards, telegraph poles, pub walls, fences, garden walls, and anywhere else where they could conveniently brush them up quickly and then disappear into the night.

Exorbitant claims and lurid descriptions, with the free use of extravagant terms such as magnificent, colossal, gigantic, unrivalled, astounding, heart-stopping, unbelievably thrilling and death-defying, were a feature of these posters, with their itemised lists of what marvels were shortly coming to the local site.

Dame Crystal Star was modestly described as the 'Greatest Clairvoyant in the World', which gave her a useful apparent advantage over any rival Fortune Tellers who might be around at the time, or who, by their mediocre performances, may have disenchanted customers in the past.

Whether because of these posters, or by people seeing the long convoys of intriguing, brightly-painted vehicles pass them by somewhere en route, or by dint of enthusiastic word-of-mouth recommendation, or maybe as a result of happy memories of previous visits, CARLO'S FAIRGROUND always attracted crowds of visitors from far and wide, wherever they went. Only a prolonged spell of dismal weather ever dented the profits. Sam Donatello went from strength to strength, and his travelling business grew better by the year. Those working for him, there by choice because they liked the travelling life, had permanent carefree jobs.

As for the independent owners of rides, side-shows, or stalls travelling with him from place to place, the majority also flourished, bringing further profits to Sam. Those who failed disappeared, without harming him in any significant way.

All in all it was a time of ever-growing prosperity for Sam, and even the short-lived General Strike in May the previous year, and the much longer Miners' Strike which went on until December, made little or no difference to his thriving business. On the contrary Sam had more than a suspicion that strikes and industrial upsets were a bit like Bank Holidays, and swelled the numbers of people thronging the Fairground. Sam was a happy man, and had good reason to be.

Frank was conscious of the thriving prosperity of the Fairground as he stood admiring the new engine in all its splendour. Somehow the uninterrupted, purposeful yet relaxed motion of the well-oiled machinery seemed to epitomise the strength and comfortable security of Sam's outfit. He could well understand how Boris and Bert were happy to work for Sam Donatello. Their knowledge of steam engines and their general engineering expertise was usefully employed in cheerful surroundings but set them apart as very much the resident experts, and made them virtually their own bosses.

A sudden change in the sound of the generator and the engine indicated to Frank's experienced ear that there had been an abrupt change in the electrical loading on the generator. He automatically glanced at the governor and noticed the two balls swing out further as the engine gathered speed, only to sink back again as the steam valve operated by the governor reduced the steam input to bring the speed back towards its normal level.

"Notice that?" asked Bert. "That was Alf switching off the cars at the end of the six minute run. Any moment now, as soon as the next load of riders jump into the cars, you will hear the generator's whine change again when Alf eases his starter handle over and brings the power back to maximum to set the whole lot moving once more. When the crowds are piling in, as they are today, it takes them about three or four minutes to move the next lot in and Alf aims to run six or seven sessions per hour. Listening to the ups and downs of the engine, I could almost check the money they take in a day. Going well they can clock up around seventy sessions in a day. Gives the old girl something to think about," he added with a grin, patting the Fowler's boiler affectionately. "Stops her dozing off to sleep, and as long as I look to the fire now and again the whole thing runs without a sniff of trouble, all day and every day."

"Yes, it's an impressive set-up," commented Frank admiringly. "It certainly runs smoothly enough. I can't see much going wrong with this outfit if it's cared for properly. No wonder Sam is pleased with his new toy."

"It should earn my living for several years to come, provided the punters keep rolling in," smiled Bert with satisfaction. "Suits me fine, running this show. With luck it should see me out all right!"

A momentary dip in the lights around the canopy of the engine and a change in the generator's whine indicated that Alf had started the cars rolling again.

Almost simultaneously Frank was joined by Arthur, Terry and 'young Bob', who were leaving the Dodgem Cars and heading for their next port of call. They were off to the 'Wall of Death'.

"Are you coming with us, Frank?" asked Arthur. "We're going over to have a look at the Wall-of-Death. You said you'd like to see it and young Bob has just been to check up. The next show is due to start in fifteen minutes' time."

"Too true I am!" replied Frank. "I'll join you. I really want to see that. It sounds very interesting. Boris said the fellow running it brought it over from America earlier this year. It should be well worth seeing."

"It sure is!" commented Bert Crossley emphatically. "Blow that game for a lark, though. Too bloody dangerous for me, that would be. Talk about dare-devils! A dicey way to earn a living, that is! I don't reckon the blokes riding that will live to make old bones. It puts the breeze up me just watching them!"

Encouraged by these remarks emphasising the dramatic nature of the new show with its decidedly bleak name, the four of them went off, leaving Bert to carry on tending to the needs of his immaculate Fowler Showman's Engine, and made their way eagerly across towards the far side of the fairground where the Wall of Death was situated. In recent months they had heard a lot about this new show and looked forward very much to seeing it for the first time.

They were not to be disappointed. The spectacular new show more than lived up to their high expectations.

Chapter 26

THE 'WALL-OF-DEATH'
a death-defying display by daredevil riders

Frank, Arthur and Terry could hear evidence of the Wall-of-Death before they rounded the corner to see it, and thought they had missed the start of the show because plainly to be heard was the staccato roar of unsilenced motorcycle engines. However, when they arrived they were relieved to find that they were well on time. The racket came from two motorbikes ridden by attractive young ladies, seductively clad in close-fitting, soft-leather racing gear.

About four feet up on a platform fronting the Wall-of-Death building they were crouched over the handlebars of their roaring machines, riding flat-out if the sound of the engines was anything to go by, but in reality getting nowhere fast.

The bikes were each on separate roller-beds, one behind the other. With the engines barking away the back wheels of the machines were spinning at high speed, making the steel rollers beneath them whizz round at a great rate. It was an unexpected sight and quite impressive to see. Designed as a crowd puller it was certainly doing its job.

Hearing the noise, people were drifting along in a steady stream to see what it was all about. After watching the girls and reading the notices about the show, a fair proportion of them promptly paid their dues and climbed the exterior wooden stairway to find a place on the viewing platform which ran round the perimeter of the top of the cylindrical wooden tower that constituted the actual Wall-of-Death.

For a while Frank and his companions stood and looked at the girls. The steel rollers of the two eight-foot long beds were about two feet wide, with the rollers spaced to fit the profile of a rear tyre snugly so that it spun them, rather than rode over the top of them. As the girls rode they contrived to sway to and fro a little, so that the back wheels moved sideways over the width of the bed, giving the impression that they might hit the side at any moment. It didn't need much imagination to picture what would happen if the spinning wheels should leave the rollers to reach the side above the wooden platform.

Spotting the inherent danger, Arthur, Terry and Frank prudently kept to the side of the platform that was well out of line of the direction a bike would take if it shot off the floor like a projectile—as it surely would do if anything went amiss.

Had they have known it, their instinctive precaution was not without justification, for the sister of one of the men they were to see riding the wall had been seriously injured in America in just such an accident when her machine took off from the platform.

"I reckon those bikes would be doing forty or fifty on the flat," commented Frank. "It makes me squirm to look at it. I keep picturing those rollers suddenly seizing up tight. Strewth! I should want to have a good look at their bearings before I had a go at that lark!"

As if having heard his doom-laden remark, one of the girls opened her throttle wider still, then took one hand off her handlebars and waved laughingly at them— casually maintaining her in-line direction in what appeared to be a highly dangerous way.

"Blimey, look at that!" said Terry. "At those revs I reckon she would be doing over sixty miles an hour on the road now—never mind your forty to fifty, Frank. Bloody dangerous that is, if you ask me! Let's get out of the way before she takes off!"

Laughing, the three of them waved back, joined the queue of people, paid their entrance fees and mounted the stairway.

Up on top they walked along the platform, which ran waist-high around the top edge of the riders' vertical wall, to join the others of their group. Joe, Grant, Sid and young Bob, had reserved space for them. The platform they were standing on was built out from the wall, just below its top. Behind them were safety rails to prevent anyone taking a fatal step backwards. In front of them, jutting out on stand-off brackets round the top inside edge of the wall was a safety cable to help prevent a rider from allowing his front wheel to run up over the edge. This, together with a broad, black-painted band right round the wall about one foot down from the top, indicated to the riders as they sped round, how near to the top they were.

Looking over the edge the seven spectators from SKWEC studied the structure with interest. The wooden wall, made in sections which bolted together, formed a large open-topped cylinder. At its foot a sloping ramp ran right round the bottom to allow the riders to make the transition from riding round and round on the flat floor to their hazardous, unnatural position speeding around the vertical wall, stuck out at right angles to it, seemingly defying the laws of gravity.

The structure was not unlike a thirty-foot high, circular wooden fence standing around a saucer-shaped bottom. Frank had noticed when they were down below, that the building rested on a strong base made of beams like railway sleepers, carrying rafters in much the same way as did the Dodgem Car outfit he had just been studying. No doubt considerable care had to be taken, using spirit-levels, to ensure the base was level, before the floor and the sectionalised wall panels, were installed.

As they stood there the viewing platform was rapidly filling up. All the favoured front positions were now full and people were forming a second row, slotting in to peer over the shoulders of those along the edge.

"There are well over two hundred people round the edge up here now," announced Arthur, who had been doing a rough count. "With those behind there must be nearly three hundred people all told. I shouldn't have thought they would allow many more to squeeze in or this viewing balcony could collapse!"

This remark prompted his friends to have a quick anxious glance at the floor they were standing on, to assess its strength. Frank, ever watchful over technical standards, made a more searching scrutiny of the balcony's construction, and pronounced judgement.

"It's safe enough," he said, reassuringly. "So long as the bikes don't run up over the top and knock us off our perch, we should be OK!"

A young Royal Navy sailor standing nearby, whose hat-band—no doubt to his great pride—bore the illustrious name HMS Hood, overhead this remark and chipped in with a comment which did nothing to improve their confidence.

"That's not as unlikely as you might think, either!" he remarked knowingly. "Out in San Diego when we were there, a girl rider went right over the top, straight through the people standing up there, smashed through the rails and shot out down the outside. Killed outright she was!"

"How did that come to happen?" asked Frank. "And how did she cross this safety cable?" he added, putting his hand on the cable that ran round the top.

"I can't remember there being a safety cable," replied the sailor. "Nobody could figure out quite what happened. They reckoned she was travelling faster than normal, lost her concentration for a moment, and just went over the top. She was spiralling upwards and just kept on coming. The funny thing was the engine roared flat out until the moment she hit the ground. Somebody said that maybe her throttle got stuck fully opened-up. That would certainly explain things. It all happened so quickly."

"Anybody else get hurt?" asked Terry.

"Not badly, fortunately," said the sailor. "She bowled over three spectators up top, but apart from bruises and the shock they were all right. She must have caught them a glancing blow or they would probably have been carried straight through the safety rails as she shattered them. And down she fell, behind the building, on empty ground. It was concrete, so she didn't have a hope, but at least nobody else was hurt or killed, as they might well have been had she gone over the front instead of the back."

After that cheerful little anecdote the group was silent for a few moments.

"Maybe it was after that nasty episode that they started putting a top safety-cable in," suggested Frank. "With shows like this I expect they learn the hard way—by experience! They haven't been going long, have they?"

"Not over here," said the sailor. "But they've been around for quite some while in the States, I think. That's where this outfit came from. It's run by an American. I've a photograph with me that I've brought along to show him. He might know the bloke on it. There can't be all that number of them and it seems from what it says on this picture that they have formed some sort of association for riders. Here—have a look," he added, taking a photograph out of an envelope and passing it to Frank.

The picture showed a rider sitting on the tank of his motorbike with his legs across the handlebars and his feet on extra foot-rests sticking out from the axle of the front wheel. He was riding the machine with his hands stretched out to the sides, as though he were doing a balancing act. He was up near the top of the wall, just below the black line. A row of very American-looking men, many wearing broad-brimmed, cowboy-style hats, could be seen along the rim of the wall, peering down at him as he rode by just below them. Frank and his friends passed it round and studied it with interest. In one corner it bore the inscription:

AMERICAN SILO-DROME RIDERS' ASSOCIATION

presents

"THE WALL OF DEATH"

"This couldn't have been the one the girl was killed on," said Arthur, looking at it closely. "Look—you can see a wire safety-cable sticking out a little way at the very top of the wall."

"So you can," said the sailor. "I must say I hadn't noticed the cable before. But it isn't the same wall anyway, that's for sure, because the wall in this picture is made of a different material. The one she was riding was a sectional wooden one just like this one we are standing on. But, like I said, I can't remember whether or not there was a cable."

"May I have another look at that, please?" asked Frank, as the sailor was about to put it back into the envelope. "I've just thought of something interesting."

"Sure," agreed the sailor, handing him the photo.

Frank took a small folding magnifying glass from his pocket and scrutinised the picture closely.

"Well I'm damned," he said. "I reckon I'm right. The wall sections on this photograph certainly don't look like wood at all. You can't see any signs of vertical planks like this one we're on has. These sections could be concrete or even galvanised metal—not wood, I'm sure of that. It's the word 'silo-drome' that interested me. I wondered why they gave themselves that particular name. I think I may have the answer."

"What do you think, then, Frank?" asked Joe, who shared Frank's enquiring mind. "I thought myself that it was a rather strange name for them to choose."

"I wouldn't be at all surprised," answered Frank, "if this whole business of 'Walls-of-Death' didn't start off by some mad-headed Yanks out on the farmlands messing about with motorbikes in some of those large silo-towers they have out there for making silage from fodder. Early ones were made from wood, but now they mainly build them from concrete or galvanised iron. You just imagine young blokes with motorbikes, latching on to the possibility that a silo-tower might be a place for a bit of dare-devil fun.

385

I bet somewhere a bloke involved in building one, or maybe seeing an empty one, suddenly got to wondering if he could possibly get up enough speed to belt round and round the wall fast enough for the centrifugal force to keep him from falling off. The same way a bucket of water can be swung up and over without the water coming out.

Come to think of it, I know a good many mad characters who wouldn't think twice about building a sloping ramp round the floor of one of these and having a go at getting up the vertical wall!"

"I bet those two mad-headed motor-bike maniacs from Littlebrook who call themselves Hurricane Henry and Belting Bill would have a go, given half a chance," said Joe with a smile.

"So do I!" interjected young Bob Startle with obvious conviction. "Henry Woodman and Bill Turner—the grass-track riders you mean, don't you? I know them both. *They* would have the nerve, I bet!" he said admiringly. They were great heroes of his.

"That's them," confirmed Joe. "I've seen them ride on the track. Very good they are, too. They're a couple of mad-brains, they are. I saw them belting round the old gravel pits one day. They were riding as fast as they could up a mound, taking off at the top and seeing how far they could travel before landing. Beyond the ridge the ground fell away quite sharply and they were truly airborne for a time. It looked bloody dangerous to me. They would try anything, I reckon."

"Yes, and so would that garage owner chap Tommy Carter, who runs the Dover Grass Track Racing Club's circuit near his agricultural engineering workshop out in the country—just outside Dover, on the Canterbury Road," added Sid. "He and his brother scare me, the way they belt round that track. They both take a lot of beating. Neither of them seems to know the meaning of fear. They do a lot of work on motorbikes in their workshops, so you can bet your life they ride very good bikes themselves. They could soon fix up machines suitable for the Wall-of-Death if they wanted to, I imagine. Perhaps they will start one up near their grass-track, once they've seen this one. Hope so, anyway. It would be nice to have one on our doorstep."

"How big are silo-towers in the States, Frank?" asked Joe. "Those I've seen around here are much smaller in diameter than this place we're in now. Too small to ride a motorbike in, that's for sure."

"They vary a lot," replied Frank. "It depends upon the amount of silage they handle and of course that depends upon how many animals the farmer has to feed. Those you've seen locally are fairly small, in the main. But even over here they can be anything from about fifteen to thirty feet in diameter and forty to seventy-odd feet high. Usually they are about two and half times as tall as they are wide. We've done some work on mechanical loading-gear for silo-towers, at the firm."

"Well, the bottom sections of a silo that's twenty-five to thirty feet in diameter could make a pretty good Wall-of-Death then, I should think," concluded Joe. "Perhaps the stunt-riders adapted some silos to make them easy to erect and dismantle, and then started to travel around with them as mobile shows."

"Seems more than likely to me," agreed Frank, handing back the photograph to the young sailor. As he did so he glanced at the sailor's hat and smiled. "Some ship you're on," he commented. "My Uncle served on that, at one time. He's out of the Navy now, but never stops talking about it! They call her a Battle Cruiser, don't they?"

"Yes, she's a marvellous ship," said the young sailor proudly. "She was launched in the last year of the War. She can do 31 knots; armament eight 15-inch and twelve 5.5 inch guns; 42,100 tons displacement; armoured plating on the belt 12-inch maximum, 6-inch minimum. She cost just under six million pounds to build!"

Frank smiled at the way these vital statistics were rattled off and had heard his

Uncle do exactly the same, with equal pride at being a member of the crew of such an impressive fighting ship. A strong pride in their ships by the men who served in them was a traditional part of the long history of the Royal Navy. It was something with which Frank, with his background of training at the Royal Naval Dockyards at Chatham, and strong RN family connections, was well familiar. He was glad that chance had brought him into contact with the young sailor and resolved to find out all he could about the origins of the Wall-of-Death in America.

He had an idea that the growing popularity of aerobatic and stunt-flying shows on aerodromes over there might have inspired the motorcycle 'ground level' dare-devils to come up with the word 'silo-drome' for this fascinating new addition to their well-known stunt-rider shows.

He quickly got round to wondering if there might come a time when he had one of them as part of the historic Fairground display which Walter Richtmeyer had said he might develop alongside his Steam Engine project. If Frank ever did get to California to join the business, Walter was not going to find him short of enthusiasm and good ideas.

While they had been talking, things had been happening down below and it was evident the show was about to begin. A panel had opened at the foot of the wall. People who had been wondering how the motorbikes and their riders got inside the closed cylindrical structure could now see the answer; a section of the curved wood wall was hinged to form a door that opened outwards. It was fitted with strong bolts and a cross-bar outside to hold it securely in place when shut again, since it then formed a part of the wall the riders rode up.

The billing for the show named three riders. Each of these, prior to devoting their time to the Wall-of-Death, was said to have had a previous history of stunt-riding, road-racing or of speedway riding on grass-tracks and the newly developing experimental cinder-tracks.

The names listed were:

1. **'Reckless Rudy Ritter'** the world-famous Wall-of-Death rider from the United States of America
2. **'Daredevil Dougy McDougal'** from the Highlands of Scotland, a racing motor-cyclist who has ridden in the Isle of Man TT Races for the three years 1924, 1925 and 1926
3. **'Fearless Francis Fox'** the well-known stunt-rider from Southend-on-Sea.

They rode under self-styled names which had an appropriately exciting ring to them.

Rudolph Ritter used the fate-taunting title of 'Black Death'; Douglas McDougal called himself the 'Red Devil'; and Francis Fox had given himself a name with a gladiatorial ring to it, calling himself the 'White Knight'.

These names were boldly stencilled on the backs of their close-fitting riding jackets. They wore riding breeches laced below the knee, and calf-length riding boots. There were no loose ends, flaps or frills anywhere on their gear, because something caught up in their machines could have fatal consequences when they were perilously defying the force of gravity, riding the infamous wall. Even a slight, unexpected jerk was potentially dangerous.

At the Pay Kiosk each visitor was given a leaflet on their way in which gave these brief details of the riders and also listed the programme of events.

In bold letters, at the foot of the leaflet, were the words:

NO INSURANCE IS POSSIBLE FOR OUR INTREPID RIDERS IN THIS DANGEROUS SHOW

PATRONS ARE INVITED TO MAKE A CONTRIBUTION TOWARDS OUR OWN 'RIDERS-SUPPORT-FUND' TO HELP THEM SHOULD THEY BE INJURED AT WORK

PLEASE TOSS A COIN INTO THE CATCHING-SHEET YOU WILL SEE BELOW AT THE END OF THE SHOW

THANK YOU

The watchers up above gazed down expectantly, finding it difficult to believe that motorbikes were going to be ridden up the vertical wall to whizz around just under their noses.

Their programmes showed that the first three events were solo rides by the three men in turn. As they watched, through the opening in the Wall stepped one of the two girls who had been riding the machines on the roller-beds outside. She waved to the spectators above and held up a large placard, turning so they could all read it in turn. On it was printed in bold letters:

Presenting

'THE RED DEVIL' · 'THE WHITE KNIGHT' · 'BLACK DEATH'

Meanwhile, from outside came the sound of an engine being revved up. Standing to one side the girl waved the rider in and then went out quickly, the door being at once made fast behind her.

Attired all in red, as his name would suggest, the rider waved to the crowd above as he rode a few times round the floor below. Then, gathering speed, he started to circle the foot of the wall, riding the banked base, leaning over at an ever increasing angle.

Abruptly, he then made the trickiest manoeuvre—to move on to the wall itself—in effect treating the wall like a continuous corner with the surface banked at the seemingly impossible angle of ninety degrees.

Round and round he roared, moving further and further up the wall all the time, until he was soon tearing around just below the noses of the startled people peering at him apprehensively over the rim. For a time it was entertainment enough for him merely to ride round and round. To the spectators, some of whom became dizzy watching him, it looked awe-inspiring and highly dangerous. Did they but know it, however, they became giddier watching him than he did riding. Whereas his eyes were directed steadily at the boarding in front of his front wheel, as though riding an ever unfolding road, they tended to turn their heads continuously to keep him in view, while simultaneously looking downwards. The combined effect of this unusual experience caused some watchers to suffer a slight loss of balance.

Suddenly there was a gasp from the spectators, for the rider let go of his handlebars and sat bolt upright on the machine with his arms stretched out sideways. Not content with that, he then slowly raised himself off his seat until he was standing on his footrests, gripping the petrol tank between his knees.

Then, having sat down again in the normal riding position, he proceeded to shift his feet over the handlebars until he had planted them on footrests mounted along the line of the axle of the front-wheel and was now sitting on the tank rather than the bike's saddle. He appeared to control the bike with his legs, which were bent over the straight handlebars, because he let go of the hand-grips and once again raised his arms sideways. Not satisfied with that, he presently lay back along the top of his bike as though taking a quiet nap for a while. The bike, with its engine roaring at a constant speed, behaved as though it were stuck in a groove in the wall, so steady was it in its stance at right-angles to the surface.

After a period going up and down the wall and carrying out a series of variants in his repertoire of unusual and highly perilous-looking riding positions, The Red Devil finally spiralled down towards the bottom. When he was well down he cut off his engine and coasted down the last few feet to reach the inclined ramp, and finally the floor.

Coming to a halt he waved to the crowd above, and their outburst of clapping and cheering was the signal for the girls outside to open the door to let him out and the next rider in.

First the White Knight, suitably attired all in white, then the gruesome-sounding Black Death, rode the wall with their own demonstrations of a variety of highly dangerous-looking postures on their bikes.

Black Death finally astonished the observers by calmly contriving, as he sped round high up on the wall just beneath them, to climb up on his seat, stand on the saddle and ride the machine with his arms stretched out either side of him—rather in the manner of a tight-rope walker balancing on his high-wire in a circus. Many stomachs just above him rose up in the throats of their owners when they started to think about his impossible position. His bike was stuck out at right-angles to the vertical wall, and on its saddle stood the rider, travelling round and round, sideways-on to the floor a long way below him. It seemed unreal, and fraught with disaster. It made some of those watching turn away feeling positively sick with apprehension.

The black-clad rider had well named himself Black Death, for if ever a man diced with death he for sure seemed to be doing just that, only a few feet away from them.

When at length he took his bow and left, the White Knight came in again to give his second display, but before the door closed behind him one of the girls slipped in— seemingly unnoticed by him as he sat preparing to start his ride. As he rode round on his first circuit he was confronted by her standing on the floor at the edge of the sloping ramp laughingly 'thumbing a lift'. He stopped and they exchanged a few words, she ostensibly pleading with him earnestly and he shaking his head in adamant disagreement.

But the girl was clearly not disposed to accept No for an answer and continued to badger him vehemently. After a little while, with a shrug of his shoulders, a shake of his head, hands held out palms upwards in a worn-down 'OK! I give up!' gesture—an altogether well-manufactured air of resigned but reluctant acquiescence—he then proceeded to help her up on to his machine. There being no pillion seat he organised things so that she sat in front of him on the petrol tank with her feet on his footrests, while his feet were placed behind him on two more rests located at the hub of the back wheel.

Once settled to his satisfaction, he set the bike in motion again and shortly afterwards they roared around the ramp several times, after which he appeared to shout a question at her. She nodded her head vigorously and eagerly, then tensed herself, at which point he promptly rode the bike from the ramp on to the wall. For several circuits he kept his bike low down on the wall and then, evidently satisfied by her plainly nodded assurance that she was all right, he began to spiral his way upwards until they were near the top, close to the intently watching people looking over the rim.

389

The girl, laughing with pleasure, raised her arms sideways and they sped round just beneath the black line. Then he too raised his arms sideways with his hands stretched out, and they continued roaring round the wall 'no-hands'—the bike apparently being steered by the rider's knees.

When he once again took hold of the rubber hand-grips, she lazily lifted one foot over the handlebars, placed it on a small rubber-covered platform built out over the front forks, and then nonchalantly lay back against him, to all intents and purposes lolling back, comfortably enjoying the ride.

At length she sat back and resumed her 'normal' position and they spiralled down to the floor. The White Knight got off and went to assist his passenger off the tank. Ignoring his proffered hand, to his apparent indignant surprise she slid back off the tank to sit on the saddle, revved up the engine and started to circle him, riding round and round the floor laughing happily.

As if on a spur of the moment whim she suddenly accelerated, drove on to the raised banking and sped round, leaning over, looking every inch the racing motorcyclist to the consternation of the anxious White Knight. Evidently nonplussed and extremely worried over this wayward behaviour on the part of his partner, he waved her to stop; but she took no notice.

Then, as if suddenly making up her mind, she braced herself, leaning well down over the tank, looked very determined and steered off the sloping track straight on to the wall.

In no time at all, riding with calm assurance, she drove round and round the wall heading towards the top, until, to the astonishment of the spectators she reached the black line and sped round just below them, obviously thoroughly enjoying herself. Way down below, standing in the centre of the floor, the White Knight, looking very worried indeed, gazed up at her, beckoning her down.

There was no mention of a girl rider on the programme, nor did anybody expect there to be, for even with grass-track racing, never mind this awe-inspiring Wall-of-Death, such things were essentially a man's game!

This diversion, slipped in as a surprise, always went down well with the spectators. When she eventually rode down to join her companion waiting below, she received enthusiastic applause from above as she and the White Knight made their way out, waving happily as they pushed the bike through the opening in the wall.

No sooner had they disappeared than in came the next act, a motorcycle and sidecar with Black Death driving and the Red Devil as his passenger. The sidecar, like the bikes, was a rudimentary affair consisting of just the bare necessities. It was simply a one-wheeled, wooden platform with a steel frame made to provide what was, in effect, a handrail all round. The rail was not only there for safety reasons but also to provide a grip to facilitate various acrobatic feats which the passenger could execute as the machine roared round the wall.

After several breathtaking exercises the ride culminated with Black Death standing on his footrests, driving 'no-hands' with his arms stretched sideways, while his passenger was doing a hand-stand, gripping the side rails of his narrow sidecar. The people above were not sorry when the two of them resumed their 'safe' normal seated positions, and then rode down to ground level.

On arrival there the passenger got off and banged a signal on the hinged section. This opened to let him out and in walked one of the girls leading an Alsatian dog, which didn't wait to be told what to do but promptly jumped up on to the sidecar and stood, tail wagging, facing the front, seemingly with excited anticipation of what was to come.

When the girl had left and the door had shut behind her, the motorbike and the sidecar gathered speed to circle the floor, with the dog standing perfectly still looking fixedly ahead. To the amazement of the spectators the machine then travelled on to the wall and whizzed round and round, climbing all the while until Black Death and his four-legged passenger were just below them. They noticed that the dog's legs were slightly splayed out, and his paws somewhat spread, looking a little abnormal for a standing dog. This was, however, not surprising because tearing round the wall created a centrifugal force that was so great that the dog was in reality braced against a very unnatural pressure tending to flatten his belly to the floor of the sidecar.

This same force, unbeknown to the viewers, caused some considerable discomfort to the Wall-of-Death riders since it pushed their backsides so firmly down on their seats that they invariably finished each day aching and bruised by the pressure. Their hands and feet also felt the strain.

The saddles, like the bike frames, were devoid of springs. To give maximum safety on the wall, the machines were just rigid frames, specially constructed for their task by modifying road machines. They had no brakes, no mudguards, no front-fork springs and no gear-change. Everything that could be done was done to prevent any variation in what had to be a firm, fast ride with no interruptions and no bouncing. This made for the safety, not the comfort, of the riders.

Those performing on the wall were very conscious when riding, of the very high 'g' force they were subjected to in order to be able to carry out their spectacular rides on the vertical wall. It took a lot of courage to start doing it in the first place, and a lot of stamina to put up with the physical strain of carrying out several performances each working day. It was an exciting, but physically and mentally exhausting way of earning a living.

When the machine finally reached the floor again, the dog showed no inclination to get off its perilous platform but stood there happily wagging its tail when the machine came to rest and all was still. He received much appreciative cheering as the girl came in to collect him and lead him away. Black Death then re-started his engine and drove the machine up the ramp and out through the opening.

The last item listed on the programme was called the 'pursuit-race', and the watchers waited expectantly to see what this was all about. It turned out to be an exciting event, bewildering to watch and seemingly fraught with danger to the riders.

The three riders entered the place one after the other and parked side by side on the floor, engines revving, creating a very noisy chorus of three, barking, unsilenced exhausts, while the door was securely fastened behind them.

Then they began to circle the floor, one after the other. The first away was the White Knight, who started to go up the wall followed shortly afterwards by the Red Devil, and lastly by the grim-looking Black Death. The harsh, combined staccato noise of their engines funnelled up the wall to blast the ears of the spectators above.

From the start attention quickly focused on the Red Devil who was obviously gaining fast on the White Knight as they made their way up the wall. Very soon they were neck and neck, very close to one another—dangerously close—with the White Knight about a third of the way up the wall and the Red Devil just below him. After a few more circuits they were neck and neck, and very soon the Red Devil was a length ahead of the White Knight and just below him.

The crowd gasped as the Red Devil turned to cross the path of the White Knight. It looked frighteningly dangerous.

In reality, it was a well-rehearsed drill, and the White Knight actually descended a couple of feet at the crucial moment so that the Red Devil finished higher up the wall, and out in front of him.

Meanwhile Black Death was gaining fast on the two of them and in no time at all he too had passed the White Knight in just the same manner. About six feet down from the top of the wall he was neck and neck with the Red Devil and gradually went ahead of him. The noise was ear-splitting to the watchers just above them, and the scene bewildering as the three bikes roared round high up on the wall.

The crowd heaved a sigh of relief when Black Death eventually pulled in front of the Red Devil. Because they had appeared so close there was a danger of them colliding.

Once again the faster machine appeared to gain enough edge in speed to be able to pull up higher in front of its competitor to take the lead. Although nothing could be seen to reveal it, the drill was worked out with military precision and split-second timing. When a mutually understood signal passed between them, only then did the one who had to take the lead move slightly up the wall while the other unostentatiously shifted downwards by a vital foot or so to allow the 'winner' to pass.

Experience showed that all eyes tended to be on the machine climbing to go out in front, and few, if any, observers spotted the 'let by' co-operation of the rider being passed. But, even though not everybody was convinced by the deception that it was indeed a race, the fact remained that they *did* pass one another going up the wall, and that was achievement enough. It was dangerous, needed steady nerves, and took a lot of practising to make it 'safe'.

Having clearly 'won' the pursuit race, Black Death rose up on his footrests and held his arms triumphantly above his head while he roared around the wall right up near the rim.

The show was now over and the three riders, one after the other, spiralled down to the bottom, cutting their engines and coasting the last few feet as was their normal habit. They were able to use the slope of the ramp skilfully, once down, to bring their machines to a halt under close control, so allowing room for the three of them to get down safely.

Once the engines were quiet the riders waved cheerily to the applauding spectators up above them, and simultaneously, with no time lost, the door panel opened and the two girls came in carrying a folded white canvas sheet.

The three riders with their machines left the arena, and the girls lost no time spreading their money-catching sheet over the centre of the floor. They got it down smartly, to be sure it was there before the spectators had a chance to start making their way down. It had been made from a shop sun-blind and was stretched out by ropes through brass eyelets around the edge.

When spread out those above could see the large words stencilled on it which read:

WALL-OF-DEATH RIDERS SUPPORT FUND
PLEASE GIVE GENEROUSLY

As the girls stood back smiling against the wall, a shower of coins came down to fall on the sheet from the spectators above who were much inspired to be generous because of the bravery of the riders who had entertained them so breathtakingly.

Frank and his SKWEC colleagues were full of admiration for the riders and left feeling very glad they had not missed the opportunity to see this daring and exciting show which had reached England from America for the first time only so very recently.

Sadly, just how dangerous a game the Wall-of-Death could be was demonstrated later that same day. The show fully justified its dramatic name in no uncertain way.

As the SKWEC men chugged home happily during the late evening, back at the Fairground a dreadful calamity occurred about which they knew nothing until a few days later when news of it appeared in the Press.

Francis Fox, the self-styled White Knight, was killed during the last show of the day.

Apparently, when high up on the Wall, riding his bike sitting on its tank with his feet on the footrests which extended out in line with the axle of his front-wheel—arms stretched out sideways just as the SKWEC men had seen him do earlier—the roar of his engine stopped dead instantaneously. There was no warning stutter of impending trouble. None whatsoever. Later examination showed that there had been a catastrophic failure of the big-end bearing which jammed the engine solidly, stopping it dead and locking the back wheel.

Spectators said they could not distinguish between the moment of cessation of the loud exhaust noise and the plunge downwards of the bike and its rider.

In effect the life-saving centrifugal force which kept the bike pinned to the Wall was switched off instantaneously, and the machine plummeted downwards to smash on to the floor below. It came to rest partially across the crumpled body of its rider who lay there with his head twisted sideways in a grotesque, unnatural manner. His neck was broken and his life ended only seconds after his bike's engine had stopped.

According to the newspaper report an eye witness said that one minute there was the ear-splitting noise of the bike as it tore round the Wall. Then there was an abrupt silence followed by a shattering crash as the bike hit the floor. For a few moments afterwards there was an eerie, stunned silence as the horrified watchers gazed down at the wrecked bike, and the twisted body of its rider, who a moment ago had been riding by them just below the black line, laughing with daredevil delight as he performed his breath-taking stunt.

Under the same circumstances, when riding on the ground, the sudden locking of the back wheel would have caused the bike to skid along the surface. On the Wall there was no question of it skidding at all. When its speed abruptly fell at the moment of engine failure, at that very instant the omnipotent force of gravity—hitherto thwarted by the much larger centrifugal force acting upon the bike because of its high-speed circular motion—simply plucked the bike off its impudent, gravity-defying position high up on the vertical Wall and pulled it mercilessly vertically downwards to the ground.

As for the rider, the sudden jerk when the bike stopped, threw him forwards so that he was separated from the machine, and his body described an arc—actually impacting with the Wall on the way down. He hit the floor headfirst in the central area and the machine hit the ramp and tumbled on top of him. Doctors said he must have died instantaneously at the moment he hit the floor.

The newspaper article went on to say that, perhaps surprisingly, their enquiries since the accident had revealed that despite the highly dangerous nature of the sport, there had in fact been relatively few fatal accidents recorded in America. There had been a good many injuries, particularly broken arms and legs, but few fatalities. Sometimes the accidents were due to mistakes on the part of the rider, or loss of speed due to engine troubles. Often though, the rider—if not too far up the Wall—could put his bike out of gear and use his momentum to spiral rapidly down to ground level.

Total engine failure combined with a jammed transmission system was, so it seemed, rarely heard of. A broken driving chain which had jammed the rear-wheel was the only example their correspondent's American contact could recall, that had led to the death of the rider.

And, far from dissuading people from going to see the Wall-of-Death, due to the perverse nature of the public, the widely-reported fatal accident at Hythe had the reverse effect, and seemed to enhance the attraction of the awesome-sounding show.

The report of the accident managed to find something to be grateful for. The show's programme, in the sequence as seen by the SKWEC party, indicated that the next time the bike was due to be used that evening would have been when the White Knight took his devil-may-care girl companion with him on her begged-for joy-ride. Engine failure then would almost certainly have killed her as well, and to this extent the team working the show, and their friends at the Fair, felt a reason for some consolation.

Continuing the theme, had the bike survived that act—so the logic ran—then a little while later it might have failed when the White Knight was highest up the wall during the pursuit-race, with the other two machines just below him. Failure might then have involved all three machines and their riders, with awful consequences.

None of this convoluted thinking made poor Francis any the less dead.

At a subsequent enquiry the authorities, with the unctuous, self-righteous wisdom of hindsight, loftily and blandly concluded their findings with the declaration that 'It was an accident waiting to happen!'—a nonsensical cliché that helped no one.

However, the death of Francis Fox did give rise thereafter to more vigilance in the care of the bikes, and a more rigid control over safety factors. After the accident the machines were stripped down and thoroughly checked for incipient wear more regularly than had been the case before.

But the Wall-of-Death remained what it so obviously had always been, and always would be—a decidedly dangerous form of entertainment. Not that it was alone in that. Many sports involved an element of danger and there were those who argued that it was this element that added spice to the excitement and made them what they were.

The Vicar of Francis Fox's Parish Church in rural Essex, a few miles from Southend-on-Sea, could not forebear to observe in an article recording the sad event in his Parish Magazine, that it was a pity some people had to risk—and on occasions such as this actually to give—their lives, in order to entertain members of the public who relished the sight of others risking their lives and limbs.

This observation, like the fatuous pronouncement of the accident enquiry panel, did nothing to help the grieving members of the young dead man's family, nor did it in any way curtail the pursuit of this or any other similarly dangerous activity. Francis hadn't *had* to do anything. Up to the very moment of his sudden end he had been a very happy, 'devil-may-care' young man, and his Mum and Dad clung to that comforting thought, leaving the Vicar and others to pontificate or prattle as much as they liked.

Francis Fox's Dad had another perspective on the loss of his son. He himself, sole survivor in his family of four brothers and two cousins who had all been summoned to the Army during the Great War, had miraculously come through four long years of dreadful carnage on active service with the British Expeditionary Force in France. He had seen countless young men die in the terrible muddy squalor and unimaginable, nightmarish, blasted battlefields of Flanders, cut down, mangled and torn to pieces, in hellish misery and abject fear. Lives were brutally and callously thrown away, often, it seemed, sacrificed by being sent into hopeless attacks by incompetent and uncaring leaders indifferent to the dreadful slaughter that followed their inflexible, ill-judged orders. Strangely, the stark memory that would remain with him forever of those terrible days, brought him some solace in his grief now, at this latest period of personal tragedy.

Young Francis, his much-loved, only son, had died when gloriously happy and his Dad carried the image of his tousle-headed, blue-eyed, devil-may-care son, so aptly named 'Fearless Francis', in his mind for the rest of his life. He was proud of his son and felt no resentment against the Wall-of-Death which had killed him. The lad was never happier than when riding his beloved motorbikes, whether belting around grass-tracks; stunt-riding at village fêtes and outdoor events; or following this, his latest craze, of riding the challenging Wall-of-Death. Francis had known full-well the risks of his daredevil pursuits, accepted them, and finally paid the ultimate price for enjoying the thrills and challenges of his death-defying choice of life-style.

His Dad contrasted this sudden extinction of the life of his young son in the midst of a happy, laughing life he loved, with the awful end of all those young men of a similar age, including his own three brothers and two cousins, in absolute unimaginable horror and misery during the most terrible war mankind had ever known. If Fate decreed that Francis had to die young, then how much better it was that he should go instantaneously when gloriously happy.

In the years ahead, like so many men of his generation in whose minds the indelible horror of total war was forever stamped, Francis Fox's Dad drew increasing comfort from the simple words of the poet, Lawrence Binyon, which spoke so deeply and movingly of the eternal healing power of time:

> 'They shall grow not old,
> As we that are left grow old;
> Age shall not weary them,
> Nor the years condemn;
> At the going down of the Sun;
> And in the Morning;
> We will remember them.'

Gradually, as the years passed, the image of his son merged with the sea of faces of his young comrades and of his brothers and cousins, who died at very much the same tender age. And every now and again, at quiet moments when his thoughts turned to the inexorable passing of time, he had fleeting glimpses of the meaning, significance, and awesome reality of Eternity. He came to feel that against its boundless enormity, the brief life-span of the overlapping generations brings them together when leaving this life, to arrive virtually simultaneously to stand united at the beginning of the endless end.

In this perspective he came to believe that the heavenly spirits of everyone were ageless and timeless. He could not believe that a tiny baby who died, remained a helpless baby for all eternity, nor that a man or woman who died when very old and infirm, would remain so for ever and ever.

Gladly he embraced the belief that the age at death of the earthbound body was of no significance to the spirit then set free. In the fullness of time he knew his own day would come when he would leave his ageing body to cross the Divide, whatever unimaginable forms it took.

But he found his mind grew tired if he tried to capture and comprehend these fleeting glimpses, or to contemplate the significance of the concept of Eternity.

In time he gave up trying, and was left with an abiding comforting awareness that all was not lost when a loved one could no longer be seen around in this so transitory moment of eternal time. And in this he found warmth and true solace.

One day he would be with his beloved son again.

Chapter 27

FRANK VISITS SAM DONATELLO

and hears of Dame Crystal Star's
free amber supply

On leaving the Wall-of-Death, blissfully unaware of the tragedy Fate had in store for the place later that day, the SKWEC group split up to go their separate ways, intent upon packing all they could into the time they had left before they were due to assemble at the Sentinel to travel home.

Frank went off on his own to keep an appointment with Sam Donatello in his luxury caravan, while Grant, Sid and young Bob set off to enjoy a few more goes on the various rides in the central area of the fairground.

Showing an altogether different preference, Joe, Arthur and Terry shared a quirkish desire to go and see the newly introduced Flea Circus where they were anxious to study the alleged acrobatic and amazingly versatile ability of the widely-advertised 'World's Most Highly Trained Performing Fleas'. This description intrigued them and, like a lot of other people, their curiosity was sufficiently awakened to persuade them to pay to have a peep at what it was all about. Boris had thoroughly recommended the show and said it was very popular—not least because of the entertaining ways of the strange eccentric bloke who ran it.

Joe had been a prime mover in persuading the others to go with him. He said people were always bleating about 'live theatre' being a cultural activity which everybody should support—not let die just because of the coming of the Cinema—and he made the point that there could hardly be anything more 'live' than a flea with its guts bloated by human blood! In any case he reckoned that going to the Performing Flea Show was a more fitting activity for men of their staid, respectable status, than being whirled around on Sam's Gallopers, hurtling up and down a Switchback or whizzing down a Helter-Skelter sitting on a coconut-fibre mat.

Apart from feeling a bit past these things, Joe, Arthur and Terry were only too conscious of the fact that their bellies were bursting with beer. They were too topped-up to risk taking part in vigorous activities, a lesson they seemed to learn to their extreme discomfiture and cost on every successive annual outing, but often forgot before the next.

As the three of them ambled slowly towards the famous fleas, they determined that after attending that highbrow, culturally uplifting show, they would do nothing more punishing to their queasy digestive systems than things like potting at targets with air-rifles; gambling with pennies on Penny Roller stalls; throwing darts at a display of playing-cards aiming at various designated prize-winning spots on them; gambling on simulated horse or motor racing events; hooking toy floating ducks and fishes out of the swirling waters of the 'Fish Yourself a Prize' stall, and maybe—if their condition permitted it—throwing balls on the coconut-shy to win one to take home as a trophy to their families.

Meanwhile, following directions given him earlier by Boris, Frank arrived at the quiet corner of the fairground where Sam Donatello—the boss of the entire sprawling concentration of vastly varied entertainments and attractions—had chosen to position his sumptuous caravan.

A little while later, safely ensconced in Sam's luxurious mobile home, seated in a comfortable armchair sipping a glass of Scotch whisky and feeling very much at peace with the world, Frank discussed for a while Sam's requirements for the servicing during the winter months of his various steam engines and other fairground equipment.

Sam owned a country estate a few miles from the coast behind Sandwich and Deal, not far away from SKWEC's workshops, and this provided winter quarters for his entire outfit. It was no accident that Sam's home base was situated at so convenient a point for the off-season winter servicing of his equipment. Some years earlier his father Enrico, when selecting a new home for his fast-expanding business, had been influenced

397

in his choice of a suitable geographical location, by the need for easy access to the professional engineering facilities that were essential for the regular maintenance of his many machines.

Liaison between Carlo's Fairground Company and SKWEC had been close for many years, to their mutual advantage. Frank had always got on well with the Donatello's, both with Enrico before he retired and now Sam. He enjoyed his occasional meetings with Sam, a man of about his own age with whom he shared common interests, for there was a great deal of engineering technology concentrated in so extensive an establishment as Carlo's Fairground Company.

Once essential business matters had been dealt with, conversation turned to the present visit of the Steam Ploughing teams to the Fair. Sam was interested to hear how they were enjoying their day, and Frank told him of their visit during the morning to the Romney, Hythe & Dymchurch Railway. The development of the miniature railway had been watched with close interest by Sam. He was very well informed about the present situation and the future plans of the R.H. & D. Railway Company. Frank also told Sam what they had been up to since reaching the fairground that afternoon.

Suspecting that Sam would sooner or later hear that he had visited the Fortune Teller since he quite rightly suspected that he was not yet through with having his leg pulled about it, Frank decided to tell Sam himself. That way he was sure he would come out of the matter looking less of a green and gullible goof than he might otherwise appear to be! He knew that the very best construction his mates would be likely to put on his session with Dame Crystal Star, was that he had gone in pretending he wanted his fortune told, but in reality looking for an 'easy ride', and had got thrown out on his neck as soon as the lady rumbled him for the randy old reprobate he was.

So Frank told Sam he had heard that Dame Crystal Star was a very talented Clairvoyant and went along—motivated by sheer curiosity of course—to see what her Fortune Telling was all about. He gave no specific details of his experience, but confined himself to saying that he thought her to be a very unusual and remarkably gifted person.

If Sam, knowing Dame Crystal as well as he did, thought this a somewhat naive assessment of her ability from so practical a man as Frank, he did not betray the thought by his reaction. On the contrary, he agreed with Frank, making the comment—albeit a cryptic one expressed with a suggestion of a mischievous twinkle in his eyes—that, "Yes, she's unusual all right—you can say that again! In fact I'd go further. I'd say she's unique! The best in the business, in my experience!" Then, as if as an afterthought, he added, "She's pretty good at her sideline, too!"

"What's that?" asked Frank, with such an immediate and obviously eager interest that Sam wondered if Frank had jumped to the wrong conclusion. Frank wouldn't have been the first to show an amorous interest in the strikingly attractive and provocatively dressed Fortune Teller, and Sam thought that maybe he was hoping to hear something that would raise his expectations in that direction.

Sam was right, for Frank had detected the twinkle in his eyes, and suspected from his tone that there was some depth and hidden meaning in his comments. However, Sam always made a practice of not discussing the private love lives of his Fairground friends and associates, so his reply was strictly confined to straightforward business matters.

"Oh! She's a very creative lady," he explained. "She has a lucrative second string to her bow. She makes lucky charms to sell as part of her summer fortune-telling operation. And she also makes pieces of costume jewellery using semi-precious stones, as well as a variety of small ornaments and that sort of thing, which she sells to traders. That's how she keeps herself busy all through the winter, when the Fairground is off the road."

"Yes," said Frank, reaching into his pocket, "as a matter of fact she sold me this." So saying he handed Sam his newly purchased lucky charm to look at. "According to her, that's made of pure amber," he added, with perhaps a hint of disbelief in his tone of voice.

"That's amber all right," confirmed Sam. "There's no question about that. All her lucky charms are made of it. She's quite an expert on amber. She's made a study of it, and knows what she's talking about. And apart from its market value, according to her, after she's handled it and done her special, secret, sorcery stuff on it, the amber carries with it everlasting mystic properties. It becomes a lucky charm!"

Sam went on to tell Frank a little bit more of Dame Crystal's winter activities. Her raw materials, he explained to Frank, were gathered throughout the year, whenever she had the opportunity. They came mainly from the seashore during the travelling season when the Fair moved from place to place. She collected coloured pebbles and chips of rocks, together with sea-shells and fragments of coloured glass. There were also disused gravel-pits where she dug about for stones she wanted. During winter months, with her caravan parked in the garden of her cottage home near Whitstable, she went into production.

Equipped with gem-cutters, a trim-saw, a tumbler-polisher and a grinding-wheel, she produced a wide range of highly-polished pieces of minerals having a variety of colours and textures. From these she made personal trinkets and household ornaments. Most of her production she sold to Fairground and Market Traders and to her travelling friends. The rest went to seafront holiday gift shops where people were always looking for unusual small presents to take home to their families or friends.

The amber ones, however, she retained to sell to her clients at Carlo's Fairground. These, Sam said, she apparently regarded as something special, and very different, because amber to her was a mystic substance which had a living origin and was not just another piece of mineral rock from the earth. She believed that some trees possessed a mysterious spirit of their own, and that amber carried within it a 'tree-spirit' influence, passed to it when it was exuded as a resin from trees which grew in the far North of the World, millions of years ago. And that, to her, made it a very different substance from a bit of rock dug out of the ground.

Frank was intrigued by this. Deeply interested in matters mystic himself, anything of this nature always alerted his attention.

"Where does she get her amber from, then?" he asked. "I thought amber was quite valuable, far more so than a piece of rock or a pebble off the beach, however pretty they may be. You could hardly expect to be able to flog one pebble off the seashore, but a piece of amber the same size would have a definite inherent value of its own. At least that's what I always thought."

He turned his lucky charm over in his hand as he spoke.

"There can't be much of a profit margin in a thing like this," he said. "She only charged me a quid for it. She must have paid the best part of that for the amber!"

"She didn't, you know! commented Sam with a grin. "I asked her one day about her source of supply of amber. Like you I wondered how she could knock out her lucky charms as cheaply as she does. Her answer surprised me. The amber costs her nothing! Nothing except her time, that is. She finds it, believe it or not, on the seashore along the North Kent coast. Much of it she has found between Birchington and Herne Bay. She told me she catches a train to Birchington, then walks back along the beach from Minnis Bay to Reculver Towers, looking for it along the tideline and up on the beach. At various points she has found places where high tides of bygone years have washed it up and deposited it in groynes and shingle banks."

"Well I'm damned!" exclaimed Frank. "I've lived in Kent all my life and nobody before has every mentioned to me that amber can be found on the Kentish coast. Never!"

"No, neither had I ever heard of it until she told me," said Sam. "It's one of those things that the true travelling fraternity, like Romany Gipsies, know about, but of which most people never hear, even if they spend their lives in a place. Crystal has lots of contacts in her business as a Fortune Teller. You'd be surprised how much she knows about the countryside, especially about the properties of herbs, plants, trees and animal-derived substances. She's absolutely steeped in Gipsy lore, and very interesting to talk to. Mind you, like a lot of her friends, she doesn't volunteer a lot of information. She's pretty loath to divulge secrets of her fraternity. They all are! It's a bit too loosely connected with the way they earn their living!"

Frank found his interest in Dame Crystal Star growing by the minute, and inwardly determined that he would visit her again as soon as he could. Meanwhile, he had another idea.

"I'll tell you what, Sam," he said, his face lit up with enthusiasm. "As soon as I get home, with a bit of time to spare, I'll go and do a bit of beachcombing myself!"

Sam laughed. "You won't find it easy, Frank," he commented. "She has developed a nose for amber, and every time she goes looking for it she seldom ever fails to find a few pieces, sometimes a surprising amount. But you try it yourself, though. It will surprise me if you find any at all!"

"Why is that?" asked Frank. "If she can find it, why can't I?"

"Well, maybe you'll be luckier," answered Sam. "But when we were at Herne Bay with the Fair, two blokes spent all one Sunday hunting along the coast for it, right back as far as Birchington. They came back with a great bagful of what they thought was amber!

But when 'Her Ladyship'—as they call Dame Crystal Star—looked all through it bit by bit, there wasn't one single piece of amber in the whole lot of it. Not one small bit. All they had was brownish, yellowish or reddish mineral rocks, just like a lot of stone chippings and pebbles you often find in quarry ballast, or in a pile of road-stone! They were very disappointed, I can tell you. They thought they were onto easy money. It's all too easy to be fooled by appearances, it seems. It's like anything else, you've got to know what you're doing. And my blokes didn't know, that's for sure!"

"How the blazes does she tell the difference between what is amber and what isn't?" asked Frank, his curiosity at once aroused. "Surely, if she can sort it out, other people could learn to do so as well, couldn't they?"

"Well, at least we learnt a bit about that," laughed Sam, "after their disastrous failure. Not that she needed much more than a quick look at most of what they brought back, before she just chucked it out as nothing but stone. She is so used to it that she didn't need to do more than just look at it and in some cases feel it, in order to reject the lot out of hand as useless! She spent a little longer over one or two pieces they'd got there, but there was nothing of interest in the end. No amber at all amongst the whole lot! Anyway, I asked her how she could tell the difference, and she told me that there are four or five tests you can make to prove if something is amber or not."

"Did you ask her what they are?" asked Frank. "That would be something useful to know."

"Yes, I did," replied Sam. "Like I said, she herself is so used to the stuff that she seldom needs to test it at all. But until she got to know a lot about it and got used to handling it, she told me she carried out all the tests to make quite sure she didn't finish up swindling somebody by calling a lucky charm amber, when it was nothing of the sort."

"What were the tests she described them?" queried Frank, impatient now to get down to something he could latch onto, so that he could have a go at finding some amber for himself. He was fast reaching the conclusion that the reason why nobody else could find it was that they probably couldn't be bothered—or maybe hadn't got enough savvy—to enquire into the matter deeply enough to learn what it was all about. It seemed apparent that there was a great deal of stuff on the beach that looked like amber, but only a very little actual amber. The key to success was obviously to learn how to test to distinguish the one from the others.

"Oh! The tests are simple enough," answered Sam. "Nothing to it at all really, once she'd explained them to us. She showed us by using a piece of amber from her store, and comparing it with typical bits of other materials found on the beach that look very much like it.

First of all she scraped it with a penknife. Amber is soft enough for you to be able to pare it away with a sharp knife. She just shaved the surface with her knife. That test alone knocks out most of what you find.

Next she held it to a flame. Just candle flames, or a match, mind you," he laughed. "Not one of the blowlamps you're always using in your work! A little spirit lamp would be best, I reckon. Amber melts a little in a gentle flame and gives off a very distinctive aromatic smell. Rather a pleasant smell it is too. One you would get to know and recognise . . . so that's three tests so far, already, isn't it! You can pare it with a knife. It melts easily, and it has its own particular, pleasant, aromatic smell when heated."

"What else can you do?" pursued Frank, intent upon gathering all the information he could.

"Well, another important thing is apparently its weight," said Sam. "It's much lighter in weight than most of the bits and pieces you pick up that look like it. There are one or two notable exceptions—wax and pieces of glass, for example. But all bits of stone and pebbles are noticeably heavier. Amber is only just heavy enough to sink in water. In a jar of sea-water it almost, but not quite, floats.

So if you put a bit of amber in a tall jar of sea-water or strongly-salted tap-water, together, say, with a pebble or stone chip of similar size, the pebble or stone drops quickly to the bottom, leaving the amber at the starting post! The amber just gently sinks slowly down the jar—it drifts down lazily.

It seems that amber is only just marginally heavier than sea-water. Crystal is so used to it she can toss about in her hands anything she finds on the beach and throw out bits that couldn't possibly be amber straightaway. That gets rid of most of what she picks up. One thing's for sure; she certainly doesn't arrive home with loads of junk and then has to spend a lot of time sorting it.

Then, apparently, there is the 'feel' of it. Amber is warmer to the touch than stone. Mind you, Dame Crystal Star's fingers are much more sensitive than those of an old fairground worker like me!" Sam grinned. "I was hard put to it to feel the difference. But she certainly could. She says that it is kind of 'soft' and 'warm' to the feel. My hands are too coarse to be any good at that sort of test. But certainly, you can sense that it feels warmer than stone. That of course is because it doesn't conduct heat away from the hand as fast as stone or metal, not really because it is warmer to start with."

"All that makes sense so far," observed Frank who had been all ears, intent upon finding out all he could. "Is there anything else?"

"Yes, there is indeed!" replied Sam. "Something I found interesting, although from what she said it is not something she bothers much about unless she's really in any doubt. It seems if you rub a piece of amber on fur, or even maybe on the short dry hair

401

at the back of your head, it becomes charged up with electricity. You can pick up tiny pieces of tissue paper with it. She had little bits of paper jumping off her table when she showed me one day. According to her, that's where the very word 'electricity' comes from. The ancient Greeks, among others, found they could make rubbed amber pick up lightweight pieces of material, particularly the soft dry pith from the core of a stick of wood such as elder wood. Apparently the Greek word for amber is 'electron', which seems to tie up nicely, doesn't it?"

"Well I'm damned!" exclaimed Frank. "It gets more interesting by the minute. Is there anything else she told you?"

Sam smiled. "You really are an eager-beaver when you get your teeth into something, Frank," he remarked. "It seems to me you ought to go and have another session with the lady and get her talking about her precious amber! But there is something else that comes to mind . . . she pointed out that much of the amber is translucent. Hold it up to the light and it lets some light through, especially when it's been well cleaned and polished. Some of it is even fully transparent. That's part of the attraction it has in some jewellery.

You may not get much light, if any, through some lumps of it, though, so don't go throwing away pieces of what you're testing on that account only. But it's clearly something useful to know. She has some lovely-looking pendants made from translucent pieces, some pale yellow, others a deeper yellow, or orange—indeed a variety of colours shading into reddish browns and quite dark browns. I remember, too, that she also said that though very, very rare, there are occasionally pieces of amber which are distinctly greenish and blue in colour, though she has never found any herself."

"There's quite a lot to go on, then, isn't there?" responded Frank. "I reckon I could get a lot of fun trying to find some amber for myself. In time perhaps I would get to know it well enough to pick it out from all the stuff around it, like she does. Without that knowledge, it seems looking for it could involve a lot of wasted time gathering worthless pieces of stuff and spending ages carting it home and sorting it all out and perhaps—like your blokes—in the end finding none at all!"

"Well, I do know that what she actually carries home is almost always amber," said Sam, encouragingly. "She told me that now and again she gets fooled by, say, a piece of beeswax. That is lighter in weight and warmer to the touch, than pieces of stone. And of course you can pare it away with a knife, *and* it melts in a small flame.

She says that the confusion arises because many pieces of amber get encrusted and mucky looking, much like a piece of beeswax. But of course beeswax gives off a different smell in a flame. And not only that, it doesn't polish up and shine as much as amber does. I think attempting to polish it soon gives the game away. But it doesn't take her long to sort it out when she gets it home. As far as I could see, that was about the only small trouble she has. Otherwise she seems to do her sorting on the beach very quickly as she goes along.

Mind you, I think there's quite a bit of expertise in cutting, shaping and polishing it. She is very careful how she handles it and spends a lot of time getting a high polish on it. Apparently you have to be careful what you use because spirits dissolve it, and some cosmetic sprays attack its surface too. She says that once polished, it should only be cleaned with warm, soapy water. Some spirits, if used on it, will destroy the high polish very quickly, so you have to treat it carefully. You ought to persuade her to show you her collection of amber. It's surprising what a wide variety of different colour, shades and textures you can get with it."

Frank had already decided that seeking information about this fascinating subject would provide a perfect pretext for him to return to see the attractive Fortune Teller. His mind, as always, was ticking along, occupied with the lateral thinking that was automatic in his make-up.

"It all sounds straightforward enough to me," he said. "I expect it's like everything else, just a question of experience and practice. I think I shall certainly have a go myself. It must be a thrill to pick up something quite valuable off the beach. I'm all for getting something for nothing!"

"Well, Crystal told me she hardly ever fails to find some whenever she really hunts for it," Sam said. "Mind you, she seems to know where there are pockets of it. But naturally she won't tell anybody where her favourite places are along the coast. It's part of her livelihood, and I expect it took her a long time to discover the most likely places to find it."

"But where does it come from in the first place?" asked Frank. "And why the North Kent coast, rather than any other coastline?"

"That puzzled me too," said Sam. "Apparently amber is a resin which oozed out of certain coniferous trees that grew far away up North, in the Arctic Circle, millions of years ago. When the forests became submerged, bits of amber, being light in weight, got carried along in the waters of the North Sea and the Baltic for countless years. Eventually some of it got washed up on the north-facing coasts of Europe, and presumably still does, and no doubt will continue to do, forever and a day.

Of course it doesn't wash up on the shore as highly-polished, almost transparent amber. It's translucent at best, but more often it's roughened and encrusted, so no wonder it takes a bit of finding. That's where the skill comes in—recognising what you see for what it is among the masses of stones and pebbles on the beach. It's only when you polish it that its beauty is revealed.

As Dame Crystal Star says, every tide rolls the beach over and over. Some bits must be washed ashore and then carried back out to sea again and again until perhaps, on a strong Spring tide, coupled with an inshore gale, it gets carried far enough up the shoreline to stay put for good.

She says that if you watch the edge of the water on the tideline, especially on a sandy patch of a mainly pebble-beach shore, you can see how the various different substances tend to get separated out, with the heavier bits sinking first, and the light-weight, floating pieces, getting carried further up the shoreline. Not only that, she reckons she has a sixth sense about it! Something tells her, on occasions, of its near presence, so she says! So she just stands there and the sea delivers up pieces at her feet! Quite a privilege, that! But you have to hand it to her—she certainly finds the stuff and goes on finding it!"

The more Frank heard about this subject the more interested he became, and he resolved to work at it until he too could harvest this free gift from the sea. Then Sam told him something else which increased his enthusiasm still further.

"Sometimes," he said, "just occasionally, pieces are found with complete insects embedded inside. The story is that the insect must have settled on the tree, got stuck in the resin, and then became enveloped by it as it oozed out. These specimens of insects are quite often in absolutely perfect condition, preserved in a chunk of amber so that they look completely undamaged. Every detail, however fine, can often be seen—wings, legs, antennae, body, head, eyes—everything locked forever in a capsule of solidified amber. When the amber is polished, you can see them perfectly. It seems incredible that there in your hand is an insect which flew on to a tree trunk millions of years ago and still looks exactly the same as it did when it landed and got stuck in the resin. It seems that the slow oozing of the resin caused it to flow so gradually all over the insect, that it did so without damaging it. Once fully covered it became protected forever from the effects of air and water. That to me is the most fascinating thing about amber. You can have a perfect insect in a transparent block of it!"

"Has Dame Crystal ever found one?" asked Frank. "They must be very rare finds indeed, surely."

"Oh yes," replied Sam. "More than once, too, I've seen them. She has three or four beautiful examples tucked away at home. But she won't ever part with them. I've tried to buy one off her, but she just will not sell them. She reckons that they have got special mystic powers which assist her in her work as a Clairvoyant. They form a direct connection, so she says, with life on Earth millions of years ago. She says they help her to come to terms with the passage of time, and link her directly to times of long, long ago. They form some sort of ley line, so she says. A kind of time pathway she can pass along.

To tell you the truth, Frank, when she started to talk about time as a dimension she pretty soon lost me. I couldn't understand what the deuce she was talking about. But she seemed to talk coherently, and with conviction. So I suppose *she* knows what she's talking about! But one thing is for sure. Those specimens are very precious possessions of hers. There's no mistaking that. Even her good friend Gemstone George can't persuade her to sell one to him, no matter what he offers her!

George told me that Crystal Star believes that once having been delivered by Destiny into her hands, to part with one would bring her bad luck, and perhaps rob her of some of her mystic powers. She says it would be a 'Breach of Faith'. According to her beliefs, Fate has ordained that the privilege of receiving some of these rare specimens has been granted to her to provide a definite link in the unfolding mystery of life. It may sound far-fetched, but that's what she believes.

And when she says they have been 'delivered by Fate', she means it. She says her ability to find amber easily, when others fail, is because she is guided to it by some kind of sixth sense—something, she says, that is akin to instinct. Maybe she's right, too, because I've heard of people finding odd bits of amber now and again down on the beach there, but not very much. And certainly nobody else that I know has ever found a piece with an insect inside. Most get tired of looking for amber and give it up before they have found any at all, never mind a piece with an insect in it. I sometimes wonder how many times I have picked up an encrusted bit of amber without knowing it— perhaps a chunk that if polished would reveal a perfect insect encapsulated within! Who knows!"

"Who an earth is Gemstone George?" asked Frank with a grin.

"Oh! He's the bloke she caught the pebble-polishing bug from," smiled Sam. "George Rodway is his name. He taught her all she knows about it. Now he supplies her with all the bits and pieces she needs, like mountings and fittings for brooches, bracelets, earrings, necklaces, cufflinks—all that sort of thing. He also gets her plaster casts for ornaments, rubbers moulds, proper cement for sticking precious stones on with, and also various minerals and shells from abroad—things that can't be found in this country. Most of what she makes he then buys from her to sell on his stall in the Fairground here during the summer, and at market places in the winter."

"Do you mean to say he has a stall in this Fairground now?" asked Frank.

"Yes, he certainly has," explained Sam. "I wonder you haven't spotted him before. Of course," he added with a broad grin, "there are no steam engines in his outfit! George is not steam-driven—so there's no SKWEC interest for you in what he does. He doesn't need the help of steam power. His stall is a proper money-spinner. No question about that. He's got a bob or two, our George has! He's no fool. He has a good head for business and is full of new ideas all the time. He and I have been close friends for years."

"Whereabouts is his stall?" asked Frank.

"Right over the far side of the ground," replied Sam. "He has a big, open-sided caravan with a red, white and blue-striped awning. Right across the top is his headboard. Nicely designed it is too. Quite striking. Painted on it in large letters you will see:

GEORGE'S GEMSTONES
Come Here for the Bargain of a Lifetime!

He sells something and everything over there—the sort of things holidaymakers take home for presents, or treat themselves to—costume jewellery, ornaments, cheap watches and alarm clocks, penknives, sheath-knives, trinkets and all sorts of knick-knacks that don't cost too much and take people's fancy. Then he also has stuff for holidaymakers and children to use on the beach—hats, balls, buckets, spades, kids' hand-held coloured windmills, dirty postcards to send home—all that sort of thing. A good businessman, George is. He spots what people want and he 'buys well and sells well' as the saying goes."

"I must go and have a look at his place later," said Frank.

"Yes, you do that, Frank. You will find it quite an impressive set-up," said Sam. "He's next to his wife's 'Wheel-'em-In' stall. That's a nice little goldmine too. You will see her headboard welcomes punters in to win a fortune. It reads:

LILY RODWAY'S PENNY ROLLERS
Wheel Yourself in a Pile of Pennies

George takes care to give his customers plenty of pennies in their change and they often go straight to Lily's stall where they promptly roll them all down her Penny Roller chutes, to be raked off the numbered chequer-board to go back full-circle into the family kitty again! A good partnership those two make. Mind you, old Lily Rodway would never make a fortune left on her own," he added laughingly.

"Why's that?" asked Frank.

"She's too kind-hearted, that's why!" explained Sam. "George says that if he ever left her to run his stall on her own for a few days, by the time he got back she'd have given the lot away to people she felt sorry for. A real soft touch, our Lily is!"

"She sounds a nice person," commented Frank. "Not that you can afford to be too kind-hearted running any sort of business."

"True enough," agreed Sam. "But it's nice to have a few people like her in the world, all the same. They have an instinct for spotting people who need help, or who are having a miserable time for one reason or another, and quietly doing something to help them on their way."

Sam paused for a moment reflectively, as though mulling something over in his mind. Talking of Lily had reminded him of a little scene that had stuck in his memory. He told Frank what it was.

"One day I saw a little incident which I have never forgotten," he said. "A runny-nosed, scruffy little lad went up to her Penny Roller with his sixpence pocket money. It was all the money he had in the world at that moment, that's for sure. He asked Lily to change it for pennies. So she promptly counted him out six pennies then threw him down an extra one. 'That one's for luck', she told him. She knew what he was about. The boy had been watching people play the boards for quite some time and thought he could turn his sixpence into a nice big heap of pennies. It looked easy, and he'd been mesmerised by seeing Lily counting out several pennies every now and again and rolling them down her little chute to people. But of course he did not notice how many pennies any one

405

punter lost as they played. He just saw pennies rolling down, back from Lily to the players, first to one, then to another.

So he started to play. And Bingo! The first penny he rolled down his chute landed plumb inside a '3' square. He grinned happily at the sight of that, and Lily rolled him back three pennies. So now his little heap was nine—half as much money again as he'd started with. His next two pennies landed on lines, so he lost them. The he won four and was back in profit again. He counted out his kitty carefully and now had a nice little pile of ten pennies. He beamed from ear to ear—he was well on his way to unlimited wealth!

Well, you know how it goes, on those games. He carried on playing for some while, losing some then winning some, but of course going downhill in the long run as always happens. The odds are heavily loaded against the punter, and the trick—if trick it is—is to bail out as soon as you're in profit. But who does? The lad couldn't let go, any more than most adults can. So he played on until he'd lost the lot."

"Yes," interrupted Frank. "I know how easy it is to do that. I've done the same myself on many of those stalls. What you're really doing is paying for the fun of playing. It's a real money-maker for the stall holder, that racket is!"

"Anyway," continued Sam, "he lost the lot. He looked pathetic standing there. Kind of puzzled and disappointed. He hung about a bit looking dispirited, and I saw Lily watching him. After a bit she called him over and chucked him down two pennies. 'Here you are, kid,' she said to him, 'try your luck again.'

Well, he rolled the first one down and it landed on a line, so he lost it. Then the second one did the same, but old Lily smartly gave it a quick shove with her coin rake and pushed it nice and tidily inside the most difficult-to-get spot on the board, the top of the house '10' spot! That's actually a diamond shape inside one of the squares. It's very *very* seldom anyone ever gets a penny in that one, without touching a line.

'Well done, kid' she said giving him a knowing wink, and solemnly counted him out ten pennies. 'Now take your money and go, before your luck changes,' she said to him. 'You won't get another one in there for a long, long time, so give up while the going's good!'

So the little lad went off beaming from ear to ear. Typical of Lily Rodway, that was. But a few minutes later he came back sucking a penny bar of Sharp's Toffee out of Gemstone George's penny-in-the-slot vending machine, and handed one like it to Lily. 'This is for you, Lady,' he said with a shy smile and pushed off quickly, leaving Lily looking after him with tears in her eyes clutching the bar of toffee.

'Thanks, Kid', she called after him. 'I shall enjoy that. I love Sharp's toffee'. As he wandered off back past George's stall she said to me, 'His heart's in the right place, Sam. When he grows up I bet his kids won't walk around as ragged-arsed as he is. Poor little sod—just look at him. Look at his clothes and his boots. Just look at them, Sam!'

Well, he certainly was a very scruffy-looking little bloke, Frank. You know how many kids look totally neglected. Lily was quite incapable of taking money from a kid like him. That's absolutely typical of her. They don't come any better than our Lily. A heart of gold, she has!"

"Reminds me of my mother," commented Frank. "She was just like that. In the village where I was born anybody in trouble always seemed to turn to her. Everybody liked her—not just for what they could get out of her—don't misunderstand me. She was just a very, very nice lady."

"It's the same with Lily Rodway around the Fairground community, Frank," Sam said. "She's everybody's friend. But that's not to say people always take advantage of her. They don't. It's just nice to have somebody like her around the place. 'Lucky Lily' they call her, in the Fairground.

"Why's that?" smiled Frank. "Does she bring people luck, or something?"

"No, it's not that at all, Frank," Sam replied. "It's one of those strange things that can happen. If we run a raffle around the place, or maybe our own sweepstake on the Derby or the Grand National—you know the sort of thing, where you all draw lots for horses—a lucky dip in other words—then time and time again our Lily's name is on the winners' list. In fact if her name is not there people say, 'What's happened to old Lily? Has her luck run out at last?'

You know, Frank, I've noticed that happen time and time again with competitions. Some people always appear to win and others never ever win a bean. Strange that! Unfortunately, it's not always the nice people, like Lily, who win. Sometimes the most miserable bugger around always wins. You know how it goes."

"Why don't you ask Lily to pick you the winner in the Grand National and the Derby next year then, Sam?" laughed Frank. "It sounds as though she might do a lot better than the tipsters in the newspapers."

"Don't worry, that's been tried before!" grinned Sam. "Gemstone George has tried all-ways-on to use Lily's luck on the horses. He loves a bet. But it just doesn't work. She will pick a runner, but it never wins. He even tried the dodge of putting all the horses' names in a hat and getting Lily to draw one out. That way he figured her natural luck would work its way through, whereas picking a name from the list didn't work. But that didn't do any good either. Yet she still goes on winning the Fairground raffles!"

"It's one of those strange tricks that Chance plays in life, I suppose," observed Frank. "Like when some of our blokes turned up that cannon full of treasure with their steam plough one day! That was in the stars somehow. But I doubt whether it will ever happen again! In fact I'm bloody sure it won't!"

On that philosophical note Frank took himself off to continue his last look around the Fairground before saying goodbye to Boris and rejoining his colleagues for the homeward run.

One way and another he had thoroughly enjoyed his day. He'd seen a lot and learnt a lot—especially from, and about, Dame Crystal Star who—in more ways than one—had made a lasting impression on him. He looked forward very much to meeting her again, and in the not too distant future too, armed, as he now was, with a good excuse to call and see her.

Meanwhile he set off to make the acquaintance of Gemstone George, to have a look at his interesting-sounding Emporium, and also to meet his kind-hearted wife, Lily Rodway, on her Penny Roller stall.

Chapter 28

FELIX FODEN'S FLEA CIRCUS
a flea-bitten ex-P.O.W. makes good

Larry Smith, a true-born Cockney, got interested in fleas when incarcerated in a German Prisoner-of-War Camp during the 1914-1918 war. They forced themselves upon his attention; it was certainly not an association he had sought voluntarily. He didn't know why he was so favoured by the fleas, but for some reason he was more flea-bitten than any of his comrades. One day he made the mistake of saying so, and a generous-hearted fellow prisoner with a logical mind, doing his best to be helpful and to appear pragmatic but dispassionate, suggested it was no doubt because he was filthy dirty and stank to high heaven!

Not wishing to offend Larry by this rather personal observation however, he hastened to mollify the remark by adding that it was a blessing in disguise for the rest of them, because their own fleas migrated to Larry, finding him a far better home. In this, he went on, the fleas showed how intelligent and discerning they were.

From then on it was inevitable that Larry and fleas were forever associated, and his leg was pulled as unmercifully by his mates as the fleas that bit his person. Somebody pinned a card to his bunk-bed bearing a not very complimentary or subtle notice. It read:

Larry Smith's Flea-Pit
DANGER!
Beware of Bubonic Plague

He never bothered to remove it, figuring that its presence probably increased his very limited privacy.

To wile away the hours, men interested themselves in a variety of activities. Larry turned an unwelcome partnership with fleas into an absorbing occupation, providing a shining example of the triumph of the human spirit over adversity!

He had heard of performing fleas and took to making tiny models which, with their truly phenomenal strength relative to their weenie size, fleas could work. He became ever more inventive and eventually he was able to entertain his comrades with impromptu shows, when he demonstrated his well-trained team of fleas doing a variety of fascinating things. Backed up by his natural Cockney wit and sense of humour, he finally made a virtue of his affliction and was much in demand. Provided he kept himself and his talented performers at a safe distance, far from being shunned Larry was in fact much sought after as a source of amusing relief from the depressing tedium of prisoner-of-war camp life.

Some years later, safely home from the War, but fed up with menial labouring jobs—and, like many other ex-servicemen, demoralised by intermittent unemployment— one day he had an inspiration. He decided to use his wartime experience as the basis for an entirely new life for himself. Fired with enthusiasm he set about organising a one-man travelling flea-show which he could set up at various suitable places and functions. Thus it was that with no attachments and responsible only for himself, he gradually prospered.

Eventually he had a mobile show which earned him a good living. At length he moved out of London down into Kent, moving from place to place as the fancy took him. Often he did well at outdoor events which cropped up here and there throughout the spring, summer and autumn months. In between such events he spent much of his time along the coast, moving from one holiday resort to another. At an Amusement Park in Ramsgate he met Olive Gandy, a fellow spirit and daughter of a family of Travellers, who became his wife. She proved a powerful partner and together they organised a happy, contented life. And it was all down to fleas!

At outdoor events where various widely different attractions competed for attention, Larry discovered how important it was to have a good name for a show—one that caught the eye and slipped easily off the tongue, so that people tended to notice and remember it. So, poaching the maker's name off the ageing lorry he used for transport, he came up with:

FODEN'S FLEA CIRCUS

For good measure he decided to call himself Felix because he liked the sound of 'Felix Foden's Fleas'. Then, entering into the spirit of things, his wife Olive said she would be called Fanny. Thereafter, to all new acquaintances met during their travels, they were known only by their adopted names and were spoken of as Felix and Fanny Foden, the Flea people.

Eventually he decided to incorporate his new Christian name into the title of his show, and in later years when **FELIX FODEN'S FLEA CIRCUS** was well-known in Kent and Sussex, Larry became certain that he would not have done so well had he continued to use his originally chosen show name of 'Larry Smith and his Performing Fleas'. It didn't sound anywhere near so good or professional. His new name had precise and immediate impact.

One person whose attention was arrested by it was Sam Donatello.

It happened that Sam caught sight of their boldly printed headboard, **FELIX FODEN'S FLEA CIRCUS**, at an Agricultural Show in Maidstone, and—on a sudden whim—went in to see the show. He was so impressed by its originality and by the happy reaction to it by those gathered around watching the bizarre spectacle, that he at once thought it would be a useful extra attraction to Carlo's Fairground.

At an opportune time later in the day, Sam introduced himself to the proprietors and broached the subject with them. Felix and Fanny responded enthusiastically to the prospect of a regular seasonal commitment with somebody else doing all the worrying for them about the main itinerary of their annual programme. They jumped at the chance and the next season they threw in their lot with Sam's outfit. It was to prove a long and happy association.

By the time Carlo's reached Hythe, towards the end of their first season, the Flea Circus had slotted nicely into Sam's organisation and he was pleased with the reception they got. It was yet one more attraction added to his already extensive Fairground. Something new always paid dividends, not only in bringing in new punters but also in maintaining the interest and support of old customers who patronised his Fairground each year when it was in their locality on its annual visit.

Joe, Arthur and Terry came into this latter category for they always looked forward to at least one visit to Carlo's each year, though in their case not always at the same location, because a number of the Fair's regular places of call around the South Kent area were well within reach of Littlebrook. When the three of them reached Felix and Fanny's sideshow they were lucky enough to arrive just as the tail-end of the small queue forming the next audience filed inside, so they were able to slip in before the door closed thus losing no time waiting for the show to start.

Because of the smallness of the performing livestock, the number of people who could fairly be admitted to each show and given a good view of the proceedings was very limited. Twenty or so was a good convenient number to aim at, and usually Fanny closed the door when she had admitted an audience of about this size. An entrance fee of two shillings generated an income of around £2 per show. Each show lasted about thirty minutes and this provided an income of around £4 per hour as their takings—though mostly at times when the Fairground was well attended and they were running continuously. Although never likely to get rich on that sort of maximum turnover, Felix and Fanny were happy enough in their independent travelling life. Compared to many they considered themselves to be doing very well.

Their portable show was staged in a bolted-together sectional cabin made of marine plywood, built very much like a large garden shed or workshop, and had been specially made for them by a manufacturer of such easy-to-erect garden buildings. It was transported on the back of their lorry, and they were very slick at putting it up and dismantling it as they moved from site to site. Behind the lorry they towed a small but comfortable caravan as their living quarters.

This complete outfit, modest though it was compared with some of the other independent operators travelling the roads with Carlo's, was a substantial improvement on the outfit Larry had when first he moved to Kent. His show had then been conducted in a frame tent of striped canvas which, augmented by a camping tent to sleep in, had doubled as his domestic accommodation. His transport was at that time a motorbike and box-type sidecar.

He still had the frame tent which now served to house some of his show equipment, but—more importantly—provided sheltered accommodation for the animal assistants whose presence helped him to have available sufficient fleas for his requirements throughout the season.

Inside the cabin Felix had arranged things so that the spectators stood along a thick white rope behind which he had organised his display area and stored his various props. Experience had taught him to keep nosey people from peering too closely at his trade secrets, so he defined where they should be standing and left himself plenty of operational and storage space, ensuring that he could dictate what could, or could not, be seen. The rope, looping between numbers of free-standing posts on heavy bases, curved in an arc from one end wall to the other, leaving him inside a semi-circle, an arrangement emulating partially the way in which people in a circus sat around a central area where the entertainers performed.

From this position the spectators were confronted with a large rectangular table, covered like a billiard table with smooth green cloth. At one end stood the miniature circus ring where some of the action they were to see took place. The fleas' circus ring was just under three feet in diameter. It was made of white-painted wood, edged with a one-inch high rim which was there to keep performers from leaving the arena without permission. Had they not been so 'dedicated' to, and it must be said physically 'attached' to, their own individual pieces of apparatus, they would of course have jumped over the wall with the greatest of ease. But they couldn't, so they didn't even try, having—as Felix put it—too much commonsense ever to attempt the impossible. This was a trait of a flea's character which Felix often had occasion to mention. From a flea's point of view, the supreme irony of this assertion was that had they not have spent their entire life as performers doing exactly that—i.e. attempting the impossible—the whole show would have been as dead and dormant as a natural history museum. For the truth was, their struggles to get free provided the motive power of their performances.

Once the spectators were all inside and the door closed behind them, their attention focused automatically on the brightly illuminated circus ring, and Felix lost no time in getting the show started. The three friends from SKWEC watched him with amused interest.

"The performing fleas you are about to see," he said to his new audience, with an air of complete self-confidence and contriving to imply they were privileged to be present, "are probably some of the best-trained and most talented fleas in the world. Presently I shall tell you a bit about them, but I'm sure you will want to see some of them in action straight away. For a start, just have a look at this little character."

From a shelf behind him he picked up a small black ebony box of a type made in the Far East, with an ornate inlaid lid and containing several small, neatly partitioned internal compartments. It was a luxurious-looking box, a fitting home for fleas ranked by Felix Foden as being amongst the finest and most famous in the world.

With a pair of forceps he extracted from it his first exhibit and placed it in the centre of the ring. As soon as he let it go, it moved off of its own volition. The astonished watchers saw a tiny, beautifully-made little two-wheeled carriage, rather like a Hansom Cab but having a single shaft, being towed along by a flea tethered to it by a slender, springy, brass-coloured wire that projected out from beneath the front of the carriage. This thin wire shaft formed an arc, curving upwards then down again to terminate behind the head of the flea to which it was attached by a loop round the flea's neck. For some moments everybody watched intently as the tiny carriage rolled steadily around the ring.

"That's young Alf on the end there, pulling that," announced Felix, with apparent pride. "He's only four weeks' old next Tuesday and one of the fastest learners I've reared this year. He's going to be a real champion. Just look at the size of him, and then look at the vehicle he's pulling! Alf is less than a sixteenth of an inch tall and the carriage is about five-eighths of an inch high from the bottom of the wheels to the top of the hood. That's between ten and fifteen times as tall as he is. Just think what that means. A man six feet tall would have to be pulling a carriage between sixty and ninety feet high to equal that! You imagine a man harnessed to a two-wheeled trap that was as tall as a church. That will give you some idea how strong this little fellow is!"

This unlikely piece of imagery caused the people to look closely at the tiny vehicle. Every now and again, if it approached the rim, Felix gently diverted it back towards the middle. The flea looked like a small, dark-brown, oval-shaped bead on the end of the wire, yet it evidently pulled the carriage with ease because it showed no sign of tiring. Its body, being flattened from side to side like a fish, made it look narrow and humped, rather like a tiny horse. This was a good shape for fleas to have since it enabled them to slip easily between the hairs or feathers of their host. Dangerous 'back-sliding' was prevented by backward-slanting spiky hairs on their bodies.

"We'll let him enjoy himself," said Felix, "and I'll put out a few of his mates to entertain you. That will please Alf too, and make him easier in his mind. These performers get to know one another and are close friends. They all suffer a bit from stage fright when they first come out in the ring to face an audience, but they're a lot less nervous when they are with a group. It's natural enough, I suppose."

Felix seemed quite serious as he made this comment. He said it with such aplomb that those watching him suppressed a tendency to giggle. He seemed to mean what he said, an impression he maintained with studious intent throughout the show. The more outrageous his assertion, the more earnest was his manner in making it.

He now used his tweezers to lift out of his black box a whole succession of tiny wheeled-models, all of which were immediately mobile as soon as he put them down, and each setting out—or so it seemed—in hot pursuit of Alf. Each of these had its wheels so set that all the models tended to move in a circle. This minimised the number of times any one of them reached the edge and kept them all on the move. Every one created much interest for they were all very well made. They were intriguing, natty little vehicles.

There was a car cleverly made to give a fair representation of a Model T Ford; an adult's-style tricycle; a London Tramcar; a Carrier's Cart; a Fire Engine; and a Baker's Delivery Van. These six models were each towed by a flea tethered to pull it in the same way as the first one they saw, but unlike it, the weight of them did not bear down on the tireless fleas because each model had more than two wheels. This meant they could be relatively heavy provided they ran easily. It was the springiness of the wires that kept the fleas' feet on the ground in all such models, not the weight of the vehicle on the shaft.

The seventh model in this group raised a laugh when Felix put it out. It was a four-wheeled farm cart complete with a driver. Sitting sedately in the cart was a wasp. It couldn't help sitting sedately because it had been permanently sedated by being drowned in Felix's wasp trap—a jam jar smeared under the lip with jam and nearly full of stale beer—and it was stuck down with its backside in a drop of candle grease. The cart was pulled by a pair of fleas, with their wire supports looking like the two shafts of a farm cart. To complete the appearance, a cross wire fixed between them, just behind their heads, carried reins made of black thread 'held' by the wasp. Felix was fond of using insects as passengers, and at this time of year made use of the usual plague of wasps which delivered themselves to his trap in abundant numbers.

Bluebottles also made attractive passengers. They were very smart and had a certain class and dignity about them. There were two of these sitting side by side in the eighth and last of the towed vehicles that Felix put in the ring. It was a model of an American Buggy having the characteristically large rear wheels and much smaller front wheels that typified these easy-running vehicles. Neatly inscribed on the side was the name **John Quincy Adams**, and on the back was printed **Boston U.S.A. 1826**. Due to the portly physique of the posh passengers being pulled, Felix once again used a two-flea team. The Buggy rolled along smoothly, running lightly and easily.

When asked who the passengers were supposed to be, Felix said they were the President of the United States and his bodyguard, disguised as bluebottles for security reasons, going off into the country to pot jack rabbits because the President needed target practice with his cowboy six-shooter.

"Was he a good shot?" asked the man who had put the question.

Back came the reply, faster than a shot from the gun of one of the legendary quick-shooting heroes from stories of the Wild West.

"Afraid not!" answered Felix regretfully. "He shot the bodyguard's balls off and nobody would go with him after that so he never did get to be a good shot."

There was loud laughter from the onlookers at this sudden unexpected interruption in the quietly serious business of studying the exhibits and it was a little while before they settled down again.

Fanny was not always happy about the off-the-cuff remarks Felix often made. But it was born in him. His wits had been sharpened by having been brought up in the East End of London and the Cockney rapid-fire repartee was automatic. This was in fact a great asset because not only did it result in much hilarity, but also—due to the unpredictability of audience reactions—no two shows were alike. Already people had started to return to see his show over again, bringing friends with them—not only to see the fleas—but to delight in the po-faced pronouncements and razor-sharp back-chat of Felix.

A very, very small minority took exception to the Flea Man's coarseness and left, muttering about his disgraceful comments, vowing never to come near the dreadful place again. These were the ones who made Fanny uneasy. On the contrary though, Felix was not unhappy to needle anyone having the manner of a prude, and the verbal interplay that resulted between such a person and himself, following any adverse comments they threw at him before leaving, created a little diversion enjoyed by everybody else. He always had the last word, usually after they had already gone out, and the sound of loud laughter they heard emanating from the cabin as they walked away left them in no doubt who had won the brief skirmish in the opinion of the rest of the audience!

At this stage in the show—picking the models out one at a time, using his forceps—Felix cleared the ring, with the exceptions of the wasp-driven farm-cart and the

President's Buggy. These he left there for a bit longer to hold the attention of the audience while he got himself organised and prepared the next part of his show.

The eight models seen so far were all pulled by tethered fleas 'walking out in front'. The next were rather different. They were driven by what Felix called his 'flea-motors'. These were his own adaptation of a well-known method of making a flea move things about. Using this principle a flea was suspended by a wire so that its six feet could just reach a tiny pivoted drum. Its training didn't take long because it moved its six legs continuously in the way it was accustomed to do when it wanted to go places, and in so doing rotated the drum at a fair rate.

The first model Felix had made using this system was a motorcycle and sidecar. The drum formed the wheel of the sidecar and the flea rode the machine on a wire which stuck it out over the side so that as it busily worked its feet on the drum, the machine ran along at a pleasing speed. This, however, seemed too crude for Felix, and he later modified the machine so that it had a normal sidecar-wheel connected by its axle to a drum pivoted inside the sidecar box. This much improved the model because the flea was fixed above the sidecar, and the outfit looked altogether more realistic. The only abnormality was that the passenger—instead of sitting still enjoying the ride—had to work vigorously to provide the motive power!

After making a variety of drum-driven models Felix had hit upon the idea of making a standardised, separate flea-drum unit which he could then fit into any of a number of models designed to accommodate such a prefabricated 'flea-motor' unit. This system enabled him to have a ready reserve of these 'flea-motors' that he could pop into his models to replace engines which stopped because their flea had 'kicked the bucket', as he put it. In its way it was a very ingenious little gadget, simple, convenient and very versatile, once he'd perfected it.

Similarly, all his towed models could have their motive power replaced quickly because he so designed them that he could effectively 'plug in' a wire-suspended flea from a prepared back-up replacement stock.

Felix and Fanny regularly made up these two types of spare flea-power units, working after hours and during their spare time on quiet or rainy days when customers were thin on the ground. This enabled them to keep the show running smoothly without being inconvenienced by having tedious work to do during busy periods.

Before adopting this efficient system, if a flea died on them they had to unfetter it and wire in another. Fitting a tiny noose around a flea's neck and fabricating a wire support, was tricky enough anyway, when done in the first place and at leisure. Replacing one flea with another, using the same wire and noose as Felix used to do, was much more difficult, more especially so if done in a hurry.

There was another less obvious advantage of their present system; it was easy to keep the ready-prepared mounted fleas well fed, and fit for immediate action. Previously, they first had to hunt down a flea from its host, and then wire it in straight away. This had to be done on an 'ad hoc' basis to fill an urgent need. Fleas could not be collected in advance and kept healthy for long, because a flock of fleas was difficult to feed. When placed on a host a free, unrestricted flea promptly scarpered very smartly, showing a marked preference to hide away in private before settling down to feed.

A mounted flea, on the other hand, was easy to handle and could be allowed to dine while still being securely held captive.

This was a procedure which Felix always demonstrated to his audiences, much to their amusement. It was a memorable part of his act. What he did was to roll up his sleeve revealing an area decorated with numerous flea bites, pick up a model with his forceps and hold it so that the captive flea could pierce his arm with its beak-like mouth and take a refill of his reservoir of life-sustaining blood. No circus animal could ask more of its master than that!

As with any other well-run business requiring a constant reliable source of new stock, Felix and Fanny had a nicely-organised system running. Their performing livestock fell into three categories. These were the actual current performers already wired on to their models; then the first-line reserves of both prepared, tethered 'towing-fleas' and mounted 'flea-motor fleas'; and finally a small supply of the most recently captured fleas kept in labelled storage pots, ready to be wired-up or otherwise dedicated to a special purpose.

On being captured, the latter—with the exception of some selected specimens destined to be trained as long-jumpers—had to live on their existing bellyful of blood until wired-up. Once wired-up these new arrivals from then on followed a regular feeding routine—as indeed should all properly cared-for circus animals deprived of their freedom to fend for themselves, in order to entertain well-fed, gawking human beings. The unfettered potential long-jumpers were fed in groups on prepared patches of their hosts' bodies, by a neat method devised by Felix.

Whereas the necessary supply of animal fleas was assured by their resident staff of specialist hosts, true human fleas posed more of a problem to Felix and Fanny, so special arrangements were needed to acquire them. People tended to have a flea at arbitrary times and certainly didn't want it when they'd got it, so didn't keep it! As a result nobody could provide one to order.

On feeling the itch resulting from its covert bite, most people did their best to catch the flea immediately, and squash its tough little body without mercy to prevent it from ever biting anybody again. Few people, however hard-up, could be persuaded to trap them and flog them to Foden's Flea Circus. But there were exceptions, and Felix was used to identifying and seeking the assistance of such people. He could usually smell them a mile off!

Since joining Carlo's, Felix had got himself well fixed up. He had appointed a 'Flea Agent', one *Jumbo Pulex Orwell*, whose pig-keeping father George had scratched his head long and hard in order to come up with an unusual and distinctive name for his own son.

Jumbo was one of a number of the group of fringe members of Sam's extensive travelling fraternity. They were employed as seasonal labourers and followed the circus around, fending for themselves, but being on hand when needed. Some were none-too-clean in their personal habits, making them attractive hosts for homeless fleas.

Felix paid Jumbo half-a-crown for ten fleas, and gave him a standing order for twenty per week. This was an adequate number for Felix and allowed for those unfortunates who gave their lives undergoing rigorous training regimes, or in experimental, untried, new apparatus. Jumbo met this commitment unfailingly, buying them in from his cronies with seldom any difficulty in meeting this quota, with the willing co-operation of his flea-bitten friends.

It might be supposed that the number could have been made up fraudulently with sundry more readily obtained cat and dog fleas, especially as some of these were not averse to plaguing human beings as well as their preferred hosts. But Felix was far too discerning to be caught out in this obvious way and knew human fleas from all others at a glance—with the possible exception that is, of one that had originated on a pig.

Felix had become aware, as a result of a discovery by his pig-keeping Dad, that due to a curious limitation in its intellect— highly-trained though it is in most things — a human flea does not seem able to tell the difference between a pig and a human being. His Dad had found that many of the fleas on his pigs were human fleas, presumably having migrated to them from humans. Though he claimed no expertise at all on the matter, Felix's Dad had picked up information from his son and was able to identify a human flea from others when he saw one. Yet previously Felix had always told him that human fleas were in a class of their own, and fed only upon humans.

It was a point which troubled Felix, for on studying his Dad's pigs he had found that what his Dad said was true. There was no question about it; there were indeed some human fleas on them, and look as he might he could find no others. It was a worrying discovery!

However, Felix was careful not to tell Jumbo of this curious mental blockage on the part of human fleas. He most certainly did not want his stock of human fleas adulterated by an influx of fleas fleeced from fat and fatuous pigs. There were too many friendly pigs around the countryside that would be only too happy to part placidly with their fleas in exchange for a small bribe of something good to eat, given to keep them still while they were being de-bugged.

Felix had an uncomfortable suspicion that a flea which had spent too much time on a pig would not be mentally as bright as one that had pure human blood in it. Not only that, he figured that its presence on the pig in the first place might be due to a degree of mental deficiency on the part of the individual flea. An influx of such fleas could easily give rise, by interbreeding, to the spread of fleas of low IQ among his performing stock. This possibility worried him.

Apart from this one weakness of species identification, human fleas stuck to humans as hosts. Or so Felix thought. He was blissfully unaware of any other cause for anxiety over the origin of his human fleas.

Under the expert tutelage of Felix, Jumbo became very adept at distinguishing one flea from another, and he filtered with great care the fleas passed to him by his enterprising suppliers. In this he was very successful, and Felix was more than pleased with the high quality, and pedigree characteristics, of the fleas Jumbo sold him. Felix was sure that their strength and robust good health was due to them having had as hosts, tough, strong, young men who lived an active outdoor life, providing their fortunate fleas with good, rich, wholesome blood.

Despite their vigilance there had, however, been a recent occasion when, unbeknown to either of them, their security net was penetrated in a totally unpredictable way. At a previous location it happened that some Gypsies, staying for a few days in the vicinity of the Fairground, got to hear that Jumbo bought human fleas. Living much closer to nature than the Fairground folk, they knew things normal people didn't know. Fleas plagued them viciously because of their lifestyle, but they had their own ways of dealing with these unwanted fellow-travellers and did their best to keep them at bay.

However, they were very well aware that both foxes and badgers carry fleas of the same breed as those that enjoy preying on human beings. It was not something generally known, since these animals kept well out of the way of human beings, and avoided social contact with people, all of whom they by instinct regarded as potentially dangerous creatures, not to be trusted.

But Gypsies saw more of them, understood their ways, and now and again captured them. By chance, the group in question had come across a small badger sett nearby and—for their own commercial, cosmetic and culinary purposes—dug it out, capturing a healthy female badger and two young cubs. There were no better hairs for shaving brushes than badger hairs so these had a market value. Rendered-down badger fat was much favoured by the Gypsies for smearing on their hair, and healthy badger flesh was considered by them to be very good to eat. On this occasion though, they had an unexpected bonus.

From the three badgers, and from the nest itself, they collected a grand total of forty-five fine fleas, all in good, lively shape. These they sold to Jumbo, telling him that they had all scoured their own bodies and their beds to harvest for him this wonderful bounty of human fleas.

Jumbo was truly delighted with this sudden influx of stock. He divided them into two groups, storing them as was his custom, in jam jars. Twenty of them went to Felix on the next due delivery day, and meanwhile Jumbo was able to take things easy, allowing his cronies a respite during which the stocks of fleas on their own bodies, and in their bedding, were able to multiply fruitfully.

Unfortunately, during the second week, some of those remaining began to die. When six had handed in their chips, Jumbo began to panic and concluded they must be starving, although he knew that well-fed fleas can often go a long time without a meal. He figured that their Gypsy hosts must have been undernourished and thin-blooded.

The emergency situation called for special measures. Jumbo's first step was to shave the dark hair off a suitable area of his belly. This done, he put a postcard over the top of the jam jar in which the remaining nineteen fleas were stored, lay on his back, up-ended the glass jar on his belly, then—with a swift movement—yanked out the card, allowing the fleas to jump or fall onto this temptingly soft source of nourishment. As bellies go, Jumbo's was a good one.

Almost immediately his suspicion that they were short of fuel rather than desperately ill was confirmed, for he felt a succession of bites as the captive livestock gratefully got stuck in ravenously to a most welcome meal. In due course, when Jumbo with his expert knowledge judged their appetites to be replete, he pushed the card carefully under the lip of the jam jar to edge the fleas off his belly on to the card and then swiftly inverted the jar to trap them once again inside it. This was Foden's standard procedure for taking a flea off a surface.

The nineteen all survived, and Jumbo added one caught off his own person to make up the statutory twenty. He had a tolerant attitude towards an odd flea or two dwelling on his body, being ill-disposed to destroy marketable stock that was so readily to hand if needed. The nineteen fiery red bites forming an angry cluster on Jumbo's belly, which he had counted with smug satisfaction, bore testimony to the fact that these newcomers all started their professional careers on Foden's staff, having first enjoyed the benefit of a stomachful of his high-grade, well-proven, rich and tasty blood to launch them on their way. He delivered his package of twenty on the next due-date, and thereafter resumed his normal sources of supply.

Jumbo was the innocent dupe of the Gypsies, but Felix never knew the difference anyway, so no harm was done. And, as is their way, the gypsies stayed tight-lipped about the episode and kept their expert knowledge to themselves, simply looking forward to the next time they could enjoy a similar windfall.

Jumbo took his responsibilities seriously, and certainly would not have knowingly pulled a fast one over Felix, for he valued his part-time job. It was not just a matter of supplying fleas. He had other duties including one that he did not advertise. This was a most important task, indeed none more so.

This particular duty involved feeding the stock of all wired-up human fleas—both current performers and those in the first-line reserve—once per week on his own person. He fed them on his upper arms, his thighs and—less often because it was physically more difficult and inconvenient—on his stomach. He spread the diners around so as not to over-concentrate the flea-bites per unit-area in these feeding fields. Naturally, this duty was not something he talked about. It was a bit like being in the Secret Service and made him something of an unsung hero. But he didn't mind his heroism going unremarked. He was, when all's said and done, by nature a modest man.

Apart from the proprietors Felix and Fanny, the total staff complement of Foden's Flea Circus now comprised a shaggy little black and white terrier dog; a tabby cat; a female rabbit with long, soft, brown and white fur; a mole; and of course the all-important current team of highly-trained performing fleas, backed up by others held in reserve—some already under training and others just arrived.

Of this staff, the dog, the cat, the rabbit and the mole, were employed as flea keepers. The first three of these were permanent members who lived with Felix and Fanny, doubling as pets throughout the year. But the mole was a temporary visitor only, being ill-disposed to becoming domesticated.

As for the performing fleas, most of them—though showing no signs of being unhappy with their environment—only remained stars for short periods. With few exceptions they were on the active staff for just a few weeks—sometimes, sadly, only a few days. The trouble was they were workaholics and tended to overdo it, so that all too often they became totally exhausted and turned up their toes prematurely, despite the fact that Felix did his best to ensure they had little option but to rest between shows.

There were, however, remarkable exceptions, particularly among those fortunate fleas whose duties did not require them to be permanently attached to a piece of apparatus.

The latter were, in the main, competitive jumpers. Very occasionally a few of these worked for a whole season, and one or two—but this extremely rarely—actually survived to work for part of the next season as well. These super-fit fleas were usually carefully cosseted by Felix, having been singled out as having stirling qualities, outstanding ability, and admirable temperaments. Had there been Olympic Games for Fleas these would have been the potential Gold Medal winners.

Fleas of outstanding ability were often marked by Felix with a dot of quick-drying paint, for ease of identification. He felt he had a special rapport with these few elite fleas, a rapport enhanced perhaps because he fed them personally on his own arms so that they shared his blood, which established a strong bond between them. Fanny was aware that her husband, without wishing to appear big-headed, felt that his blood contributed towards their exceptional prowess because of his strong affinity with fleas. Her blood, he told her, was the next best thing in his absence, though it was not a duty she liked discharging. She did not like flea bites, not one little bit, despite the fact she owed the greedy little biters her living.

Returning to the subject of their flea hosts, the mole was in a category of its own. A visiting mole soon became dispirited and had to be returned to the wild, to be replaced by another, for it is not in a mole's nature to wish to remain in a restricted space for very long. A mole is a very keen tunneller, gaining much joy and personal satisfaction from this activity, being exceptionally well-equipped to bore its way along under the surface of the soil. It is very strong indeed, with powerful front limbs bearing sideways-on, spade-like hands, having sharp thick claws capable of tearing away the soil in front of its pointed snout with astonishing ease.

This specialised anatomy enables a mole to burrow its way along in a highly efficient manner, the neat heaps of finely-broken-down powdered soil pushed up to the surface out of the way to form its molehills, being testimony to its engineering ability. Its firm, tubular-shaped body leaves behind it a well-designed tunnel having strong walls of compacted soil. Its dark but extensive subterranean lifestyle, with its three-dimensional freedom of movement, is not one that can be reproduced in a small box.

Felix had tried hard in the past to establish a lasting friendly relationship with a mole so that it would stay on the staff. But even when fed with a regular, very generous supply of high quality worms to eat, delivered to it without it having to move a claw to get them, he found that a mole was just not happy to remain in a small space with nowhere to tunnel. He had hoped that, treated with kindness, one would settle down and develop the contented disposition of his cat, his dog and his rabbits. But none would, so he gave up trying.

Nonetheless, having a mole available, even for a temporary period, was a pleasure and an asset to Felix, because on the body of a mole were to be found the particularly impressive 'mole fleas'. These were larger by far than any other fleas available in the countryside. They really were whoppers and it was always good to have a few around as centres of special interest in his show.

There had been occasions when Felix was left with mole fleas but no mole to nourish them, the host having either died or been set free after letting it be known that it would pack up living if kept restricted any longer. He had heard that similar fleas were sometimes found on shrews and small rodents, having perhaps migrated to them in an emergency. This gave him an idea, and he succeeded in keeping his orphans alive for some while by allowing them to feed on the plump bodies of the pet white mice which Fanny delighted in breeding. The mice were not a part of the flea circus staff, but were a hobby and a profitable sideline. They sold them in cages which Felix made during the winter months, to people who saw them at their show.

Occasionally, for added interest, Felix employed another four-legged member of staff: a hedgehog. They were readily available during the working season and could be kept for a while in a small, outside, wire-netting pen, with a built-in, snug, rain-proof shelter. A prolific source of fleas, and very undemanding on its diet, a hedgehog was a co-operative assistant, but didn't like to stay overlong.

If pushed too hard and over-persuaded to stay longer than it really wanted to, then—like a mole—it showed its displeasure by dying. Though by nature a loner, it nonetheless had strong family ties in its local home neighbourhood, and not only that, it liked nothing better than roaming around its territory freely, especially by night, and even more particularly in bright moonlight, which it loved. So, recognising signs of unhappiness in a hedgehog that had been his guest for a while, Felix would release it and swap it for another involuntary assistant every few weeks. Like his natural affinity for fleas, Felix was fond of his fellow creatures of the countryside and preferred them to stay in the land of the living.

The people now standing watching the farm cart and the American Buggy moving around the circus ring while Felix prepared his next exhibits, could see some of his animal assistants behind him along the wall of the cabin.

On a trestle table, each with its own wickerwork basket 'bed', was Fido his dog and Liz the cat. They each wore leather collars and were prevented from wandering off and not being there when wanted, by lightweight leather leads clipped onto their collars and hung over hooks on the wall just by them. They lay on comfortable pieces of old woollen blankets, none-too-clean, for good reasons, because this sleazy bedding had its part to play in the organisation of the business.

It is the habit of fleas to drop off their hosts, lay their eggs in an animal's nest and then hop aboard again. The little white eggs, which look like tiny pearls, hatch into larvae which feed greedily on the rich supply of food deposited there most conveniently for them. Their diet of skin debris from their hosts and coagulated, unused blood, plus partly digested food, is highly nutritious. Fleas gorge more blood than they need for personal survival, so the excess finishes up being excreted from their system—a neat way of providing nourishing sustenance for the next generations. Felix thought this to be just one more example of the superior intellect of his chosen friends. He watched his animals scratching, with much amusement and satisfaction. The very act demonstrated the cunning of his fleas, because the itch which the scratching was attacking was itself all part of the fleas' well thought-out system.

Their technique, so he had figured out by long observation of their habits, was to take a bite to fill their stomachs, then, just when the resulting itch that was a deliberately built-in reaction to their skilled bite, began to irritate their host severely—to step smartly out of harm's way while their benefactor and source of survival scratched vigorously with their claws, sending down a shower of skin debris to build up a basis of food in the larder for the future members of the fleas' own young families. To add insult to injury, they subsequently sent down neatly packaged little dollops of their host's own blood in their personal droppings, to mix with, and add a wonderful richness to, the nursery food store.

Safe in the warm and luxuriously mucky nest, their lovely little legless larvae fed greedily—moulted two or three times until fully grown—then spun fine cocoons inside of which they turned into pupae. At length, emerging as fully-fashioned adult fleas, they happily jumped up on to their generous host to join the foraging, scurrying members of their tribe.

By this automatic natural process they helped Felix and Fanny earn their living, and everybody was happy, except, that is, for the comparatively small inconvenience to their hosts, of the itching bites. But Felix reasoned that when all was said and done, an itch or two between friends is a minor detail. He himself, regularly and with coolly calculated intent, allowed his own person to be afflicted with a fair share of itches. It was, he reckoned, par for the course and demonstrated to his four-legged colleagues, and to the community of fleas that he administered, the even-handedness and fundamental fair-mindedness, of their boss.

On an adjacent trestle table stood a comfortable rabbit hutch inside of which Felicity, the healthy-looking brown and white female rabbit, squatted, happily munching away at a carrot. At intervals decided by Fanny, who now and again popped Felicity's lustful mate 'Ben the Buck' in with her as a welcome treat for them both, Felicity produced a litter. At these times her complement of fleas joyfully joined in the spirit of the occasion and dropped off her body into the nest to lay their own eggs. After this delightful and exciting job, they jumped back aboard their congenial host to resume their comfortable lifestyle.

Meanwhile, in the warmth and safety of the nest, the newly-developed young fleas which subsequently made their appearance, started their parasitic lives by relieving the beautifully tender-skinned baby rabbits of some of their rich blood, before, in due course, jumping up on to Felicity's wholesome body to join their parents.

Curiously, by some miracle of mutual communication and understanding, the fleas only bred when their host produced young. This was the most opportune time for them to raise their brood. Felix was aware of this, which was why Felicity, and not Ben, was the more favourably treated of the two rabbits. His was a back-room job, his task merely to start the cycle of events after which he was kept out of the way. Felicity meantime spent her days where the action was in full view of the public, and the family of rabbit fleas lived with her.

Felix could only marvel at this ability of rabbit fleas to synchronise their breeding with that of the rabbits. In this respect, so far as he knew, they were unique among their kind, at least in his experience. They had another special ability which he liked to demonstrate if he had time. They knew a rabbit when they saw one, and were not easily persuaded to live on other creatures.

The same could not be said for his cat or dog fleas—or for most other breeds for that matter. None of them was anywhere near so particular and discriminating. They would jump on anything with blood in it, so it seemed to him. Felix put this down to one of two things—either sheer greed or plain stupidity. But either way it gave his rabbit fleas an edge over the rest, because they kept their blood strain pure. Mixed blood never did any flea any good, in Felix's judgment. So rabbit fleas ranked next to human fleas in his book. But he was always at pains to point out that human fleas were a race apart. They had a natural intellectual ability derived from their hosts, which put them in a class of their own. This, he asserted, affected their work in the circus, because everything they did was well thought-out in advance.

All in all, this nice little set-up with the rabbits worked very well. The system ran smoothly and faultlessly without much bother to Felix and Fanny, who merely supplied the rabbits with food and changed the straw in their hutches, at reasonable intervals.

The rabbit fleas even co-operated still further with the management by congregating in the main, safely tucked away in, on, or behind Felicity's ears, where the flesh was easily accessible but where they were out of reach of Felicity's powerful, scratching back feet—not to speak of her vicious nibbling mouth, equipped as it was with a set of fine prominent teeth that were more than capable of ending their fun very efficiently. Their presence in these known locations made it easy for Felix and Fanny to collect new recruits whenever they needed them, with a minimum of trouble.

Also on this table, by the side of Felicity's hutch, was the mole's box. But the mole could not be spied upon because—to preserve and respect its habitual desire for darkness, privacy and anonymity—its box was covered with a black cloth.

Separated from these members of staff, placed prominently on a shelf alongside the tables, was a well-made, white mouse cage. In this a happy white mouse, inside its much loved tread-wheel, was busy endlessly trying without success to run up the parallel stainless steel wires, so keeping the wheel spinning away merrily. A notice on top of the cage read:

PET MICE FOR SALE
White, Black, Sandy and Mixed Colour
CAGES & ACCESSORIES FOR SALE (or made to order)

Fanny looked after the stock and took complete charge of the breeding. She maintained a purebred white strain, and also, by random cross-breeding, contrived to produce unpredictable, interesting variations of colours to add attraction to the range of those she had for sale.

Felix, as well as making a stock of cages in the winter, also carried with them on their journeys pre-cut, three-ply and five-ply wood panels for the floors, sides and hinged tops of his range of cages, so that he could make up further cages when needed. He made both glass-fronted cages, and cheaper ones with fine-mesh, wire-netting fronts.

Since joining Carlo's he had found a mouse-keeping fellow-spirit and useful ally, in Boris of SKWEC, who made up for him both cages and mouse-wheels if he ran short or wanted anything special. Boris, with his fret-machine and his considerable practical ability, was a source of strong backup help when needed.

Ready now for the next part of the programme, Felix lifted out the two remaining models from the ring, placed them carefully in their compartments within the black ebony box and shut the lid. The bottom of the box was lined with felt, and there was no room for movement in their individual dwellings. Once inside the fleas dug their bristled feet into the felt and when the lid closed all activity ceased. The weary performers rested up in the snug darkness of their comfortable homes, quite content to relax until it was time to be brought out to perform again.

Felix now opened up another similar box, and all eyes watched with interest to see what next he would put into the ring.

"You might be surprised to know," he announced, "that the next flea you are going to see is Alf's grandfather."

This immediately caused a delighted laugh, but Felix did not smile. In fact his rather pained expression seemed to show that he was not at all pleased that this statement had not been taken seriously. The laughter subsided very quickly, for his displeasure was evident to all.

He paused a moment in what he was doing, to give a word of explanation, but was sharply interrupted by an unsolicited remark from the audience.

"Alf's Grandfather my arse!" commented a rough, burly man in the back row, in a loud, scornful voice.

"Thank you for your erudite contribution," retorted Felix, glancing towards him appreciatively—a totally unexpected response that effectively silenced the would-be trouble maker and much amused the assembly.

Felix then continued what he had been about to say, exactly as he would have done if the interruption had indeed been deserving of his appreciation. But the rude remark rankled in his mind and he determined to rock the loud-mouth back on his heels when he'd finished his present observations.

"You obviously don't know much about fleas," he said, in an understanding tone of voice, looking around him at the audience, now quiet and attentive. "Fleas' families aren't like ours," he explained. "There may be umpteen generations living together at one time. Presently you'll be seeing Alf's Grandfather's Great Grandfather's Grandfather Tom, doing a long-jump. And I must say that, good though he is already, young Alf can't beat old Tom at jumping, and I doubt if he ever will. Mind you, to be fair to Alf, Tom is exceptional for his age and not only that, Alf is in the wrong generation. Champion long-jumpers only come up every second generation in Tom's family. When Alf has a son, he like as not will be able to out-jump old Tom when he's only as old as Alf is now."

Despite the serious face of their instructor when he made this definitive statement, the people around him burst out laughing at his bizarre assertions. Felix lifted his eyebrows, shook his head and shrugged his shoulders in apparent resignation at this display of ignorance. His preposterous statement was clearly intended to be accepted as factual, not as some kind of joke! Or so it seemed to his bemused listeners. His demeanour was that of a sincere man, the truth of whose earnestly-expressed statements had been received by a scepticism that plainly cast doubts upon his integrity and honesty.

"I suppose it does seem funny to people like you who know bugger-all about fleas," he conceded, with a display of tolerant understanding, but contriving to look a little hurt. "But you wait until you see Tom. The thing is, I breed fleas like some experts breed horses, and keep records too. Alf is so clever because he comes from such a good pedigree stable. His talent is bred into him, you see. Anyway, like I said, the very capable little fellow you are going to see really is Alf's Grandfather, Wilfred. If you look carefully you will see the family likeness. He's a fine, handsome flea, with the heart of a lion. A really nice bloke—

—and if I may say so without being offensive," he added, glancing from one to another of his congregation like a parson in a pulpit about to pontificate about a pertinent point, "Wilfred has got nothing to do with the stinking arse-hole of that bloody ignoramus up the back there who opened his big mouth just now! Alf's Granddad wouldn't be seen dead near his fat arse, much less suck his blood. Nor would any self-respecting flea for fear of catching a dose of his painful ignorance. Well-bred, cultured fleas detest ignorance. Especially the serious strain he suffers from! It scares the living jumps out of them!"

Having administered this none-too-gentle rebuke to the now quite flattened, flabbergasted and speechless heckler, Felix picked out of the box a model which immediately grabbed attention and left the loud-mouth to nurse his wounds in sullen silence.

It was a replica of the first drum-motor model Felix had made, a motorbike with a box sidecar. As soon as he put it down, off it went at a startling speed. Wilfred had made a dash for cover at the first whiff of freedom—his legs working furiously, running on the tiny drum beneath his feet, propelling the neatly-made little machine smoothly and easily. It ran wonderfully well. The front wheel was set at a slight angle and the smart, lightweight model went round and round the ring watched closely by everybody.

"It took me a long time to train the first flea to work one of those little drum-motors," Felix said proudly. "I made a little treadmill and tried several fleas on it, but none seemed to get the idea. Then I had the idea of trying one out that I caught under my own armpit. I knew it was pretty bright because it had been living in my vest for two or three days and I hadn't been able to catch it. That one turned out to be a natural and got the message straight away. Of course it had a bellyful of top-quality, friendly blood, and was fired up with enthusiasm picked up from the blood. It's in the genes, as they say.

Well, after that it was easy because that flea showed others how to work the machine. Fleas copy one another, you know. And they can talk, in their own special way. So you find a bright one and teach that one new tricks, which the others then copy. Then of course, the talent gets bred into the family strain. It's easy, once you know your fleas!"

People grinned as they studied the captive flea treading away at the tiny drum, and contemplated Felix's story: so unlikely, yet spoken with such confident conviction and assurance!

"Wilfred loves that bike," Felix said. "A born motorcyclist he is. I gave him a go on my steamroller thinking that would give him a thrill, but he took no interest in it at all. Just sulked he did. Most unlike him. Went off his food and sat up on the machine under the canopy, moping all day. So I shoved him back on his motorbike again and off he went like a rocket. Full of beans again, he was. Happy as a king. And pretty soon he was as hungry as hell. He got stuck into my arm as though he were starving. Raised bloody great corker of a red spot too. His guts must have been nearly empty. I reckon he would have just sat up on that steamroller and died if I'd left him there. I'd never have forgiven myself."

Felix paused a moment or two, meditatively, then went on.

"Funny that, you know. Unusual. Most fleas get a buzz out of trying out other rides. Especially the steamroller. That's very popular with my fleas. Most people like steamrollers; they've got something about them that people like. So do fleas. Human fleas, that is. Hedgehog fleas are scared to bits by them. It's in their blood you know, that fear is. Handed down from generation to generation, it is."

The logic of this statement was clear and most people laughed loudly at it. But some—perhaps more observant than others—didn't, and laughed only timorously, if at all. They were watching Felix closely, and noticed that he was not smiling. He appeared to mean what he said and they had no wish to offend him by treating too lightly a matter he took so seriously.

Felix opened his box again. "Here's the steamroller I was talking about," he said. With his forceps he picked out an attractive, whimsical-looking little steamroller. Its tiny boiler was painted green, and its flare-topped chimney was black. Its driver, contrary to what might perhaps have been expected, was not fixed, so that it used the roller itself as a treadmill. The driving drum was inside the engine under the canopy, between the large back wheels which were mounted on the drum's axle. The flea was riding under the canopy where a driver would be expected to be.

When put down, the steamroller moved forwards and started following the motorbike and sidecar round the ring, but at a slower speed. After a bit the bike overtook the steamroller, 'lapping' it and going off in front in a most realistic way, as a motorbike would pass a steamroller on the open road.

The men from SKWEC were particularly amused by the tiny steamroller. Joe, who possessed a motorbike and sidecar and had driven many a steamroller, had a special interest in both models. They captured his imagination. He noticed their relative speeds with interest, and compared the tasks of the two, hard-working fleas. The one on the steamroller had the advantage of the large driving wheels which made his a high-geared job. Wilfred's superior speed, Joe concluded, was a result of the comparatively very light-weight of his motorbike and sidecar. And the gearing of it was more suitable he thought, to the physique of a flea, the high-gearing on the steamroller making it hard going for the patiently-treading driver up under the canopy.

But Felix evidently thought there was more to it than these mere mechanical considerations.

"Just look at Wilfred whizzing round that ring," he said admiringly. "You've got to hand it to the little bloke—he's a damn good rider, there's no doubt about that. He really can ride! Remarkable he is! He's a natural! Comparing him with an average flea is like comparing an Isle of Man TT rider with a bloke riding an old motorbike to work. He's got class, he has. Real class!"

No professional rider could have wished for a better talking-up from his Publicity Agent than this, and Wilfred responded by continuing his impressive speedway ride around the ring.

One of the audience then put a question to Felix.

"You mentioned hedgehog fleas being scared of that steamroller," he said. "Does that mean you use animal fleas as well as human fleas to drive your models?"

"Not usually. No," answered Felix. "Only when it's a job an animal could be expected to do. Anything needing intelligence has to be done by a human flea. But, to give you an example, I am working on a dog-sledge pulled by a team of six fleas. I'll soon have it ready to include in the show. It's coming on nicely. Now that sledge is pulled better by dog fleas than any others. It's in their blood you see. Something dogs have done for years and years—especially for the Eskimos. So I shall harness-up dog fleas to pull that model when I put it on show."

"I can understand that," observed his questioner, smiling quizzically. "That would seem to be a natural thing to do, if, as you seem to suggest, animals pass on to their fleas, their own particular characteristics, carried in some way in their blood. You ought to try to get some fleas off Husky dogs—they'd get your sledge moving nice and fast!"

"I'm sure you're quite right there," agreed Felix. "But when it comes to models that have to be driven, rather than pulled, I use human fleas. They have plenty of commonsense as well as strength and staying power. Most road vehicles running on flea-motors are driven by them because driving comes naturally to human fleas, and they have built-in road sense. Not only that, they get to know me and listen to what I have to say. They're keen you see. Driving is in their blood, especially if they have been living on somebody who does a lot of driving. Being an experienced driver myself I always feed the best drivers on my own blood—so they're pretty good, even if I do say so myself!"

This explanation, dubious or not, seemed to satisfy the questioner, who did not pursue the matter further. But someone else—a thoughtful, sincere-looking little man— did.

"Why don't you use horse fleas to pull your wagons?" he asked.

"Horses don't have fleas," replied Felix. "That's why. You imagine a flea trying to poke its beak through a horse's hide! Snap off, it would! Can't be done! Fleas can penetrate normal skin, but not leather. Even if they could, horses don't have the right kind of bed for the youngsters to hatch out and feed in. A good question, though," he added encouragingly. "A very good question you've put there. If horses had fleas they would certainly be good pullers. There's no doubt about that. It was clever of you to have thought that out."

The little man looked pleased at these words of praise from the expert, and nodded appreciatively to show he understood the reasoning. Felix had made a friend and an ally.

The next exhibit Felix took out of his box was a model of an early motorcar of a fine, classic, vintage style. He had used as the basis of his idea a picture he had of a 1903 Mercedes Tourer, and had succeeded in producing a really smart, attractive version of it, tiny though it was. It had a high back seat in which sat two flies as passengers—a bluebottle and a somewhat smaller greenbottle. Fanny had contrived to fit the green-bottle with a tiny bonnet, and the bluebottle with a little grey topper. These details, together with white ribbons which bedecked the front of the car, showed that the occasion was a happy one.

The front section of the car was occupied by a flea intended to represent the chauffeur, but providing the motive power of a one-flea-power engine at the same time. He was suspended over his flea-motor drum which had the two front wheels of the car on its axle ends. Life was difficult for him. His dual role was too demanding and he was in trouble from the start.

The car only just managed to run at all. It stopped and started in a jerky fashion. Once or twice Felix had to help it along. The driver was rather too heavily loaded and Felix knew he would have to modify the model to make is successful. It was all right when rolling along at a fair speed, but the flea needed a push to start the vehicle off and was clearly having to struggle hard to keep it going. It was a borderline case.

"The old car's having a bit of engine trouble," he explained. "Not surprising when you remember that it's getting on for twenty-five years' old. It's the 1903 Mercedes Tourer that used to belong to the German Kaiser. You can't expect it to run like a modern 1927 model, even though it's a Mercedes. I bet the old Kaiser belted the guts out of it too, when he had it!"

As it made its hesitant way around the ring, aided now and again by Felix who pushed it with a knitting needle he kept by him to prod stalled vehicles or reluctant fleas into action, the audience laughed when it turned to show its back. A 'JUST MARRIED' sign could be seen hanging on the back of the high rear seat.

Suddenly the car stopped yet again, but Felix did not prod it to move it on. Something had attracted his attention because he was peering down intently at the car.

"Hey! Wait a minute! What the hell's this?" he said explosively. Snatching up his forceps, he gingerly poked about with them inside the car under the driver and took out a tiny little object that looked like a flat brown bottle. "This explains it," he went on, frowning with annoyance. "The bloody driver's pissed! He must have nicked this bottle of whisky at the wedding reception. Well, I tell you, that's the last time he'll drive for me!"

Without further ado, oblivious to the laughter of his audience, he picked up the model with his forceps and put it back in his box. He seemed genuinely annoyed, and some people wondered if he'd lived with his fleas so long in his make-believe world that he had got round to believing what he said about them, himself! Perhaps, some of them thought, he was screwball, and had lost touch with reality! The thought only added to the piquancy of the proceedings, and they watched him with increasing fascination. He seemed lost in a world of fantasy of his own creation.

The fourth and last of the drum-driven vehicles that Felix picked out of his box was a model of an early 'Puffing Billy' type of locomotive. This he had managed to make very light in weight and it ran quite fast around the ring as soon as he placed it down. The pair of front wheels was smaller than the rear ones, and the little model looked attractive as it chuffed around.

Acting now in the manner of a ventriloquist, Felix produced the chuff-chuffing noise as a sound-effect, thrown in for no extra charge. The engine normally pulled a tiny coal tender, but this had got damaged so Felix had to content himself with holding it up with his forceps to display it to his audience, explaining that it had got to go to the Ashford Railway Works for attention.

Felix glanced at the large face of the clock on the wall behind him. He had to discipline himself to keep the show rolling steadily, and did not like to exceed thirty minutes too often because it soon cut into his takings. It was all too easy with so much to interest people, to get involved in discussion and overrun his target time. He still had a great deal to get through with his present audience.

He now cleared the ring, carefully picking up each model and replacing them in their compartments in his second black box. With Fanny's help he then prepared for the next part of his show.

Fanny bent down behind the table and opened the doors of a small cupboard parked underneath it. When Felix was ready, she handed him up something quite different, which he placed in the ring.

"This is a flea's tightrope," Felix explained. "Fanny trains fleas to walk the tightrope. You may be surprised to know that we have found cat fleas make by far the best tightrope walkers. But in fact that's just what we expected. Cats are good climbers and have a fine sense of balance. So this is in their blood and gets passed on to their fleas. It's obvious when you think about it." This last emphatic assertion brooked no denial.

The apparatus was mounted on a wooden board some eighteen inches long. At each end were fifteen-inch-high, vertical dowel rods, painted bright yellow and topped with red caps. Just below the tops each rod had a hole through which passed slender brass bolts, held in place by small wing nuts. Stretched between the ends of the bolts was a thin white cord. This was held taut by adjusting the wing nuts. There was a glass bead at each end of the cord so the tightrope was terminated by these. Their purpose was soon to be seen.

Fanny had a small, screw-top glass jar in which a number of fleas could be seen hopping about rather clumsily. Their natural movements were somewhat impeded because each had a tiny piece of thin coloured card cemented to its back along one folded edge of its card. The cards were of different colours, and stood up like flat, vertical spines along the fleas' backs.

Using flat-nosed forceps Fanny picked up one of them by its yellow card and presented it upside down to the end of the tightrope. It clung to this, and when she let it go it was left hanging below the taut cord. Immediately, following its nose, it set off along the cord. Unlike its human counterpart, the flea tightrope-walker walked under, rather than on top of, the rope. Without a label it would have been difficult to see, but wearing it people were able to see the tiny yellow label proceeding across the tightrope.

On reaching the far end its progress was blocked by the glass bead. Though able to cling to the cord without difficulty, its feet could not grip the shiny glass bead, so—looking puzzled—it stayed at the end. There was no point in reversing, even if it were able to, so quite sensibly, it didn't appear to bother to try.

Standing at the front, as near the table as he could get, was a short, tubby, genial-looking man, obviously with very poor eyesight, for he was peering at the flea through thick pebble-glasses, bending forwards studying it intently. Beaming from ear to ear, he put a question to Felix about the performer.

"Why does that little fellow choose to walk underneath the tightrope instead of on top of it like proper tightrope-walkers do?" he asked, in a jocular manner.

Felix looked at the questioner, mentally logging him as a good-natured Friar Tuck-type, for he had a bald pate fringed all round the edges with frizzy grey hair and his round ruddy face had a happy look about it. The man's enquiry, Felix judged, was a serious one, and not just an attempt to be funny. He had a ready answer to this frequently-asked question.

"All my fleas prefer walking the rope that way," he replied. "That's to prevent them getting giddy and falling off. Just look how high they are compared to their size," he went on, looking admiringly at the intrepid flea. "A man would have to be about six hundred feet up to face an equivalent drop, and I reckon the best tightrope walker in the world would get giddy at that height! So you can't blame the fleas for preferring to walk under their tightrope looking upwards, instead of on top of it looking downwards. They're a hell of a long way up, size for size. It must be frightening for them!

I've seen pictures of men heaving themselves along under ropes stretched over canyons. Nobody would expect them to try to walk across looking down. Only a very few would attempt that. And then they would have to carry a long pole to keep their balance. You've got to give credit where credit's due. That little bloke in front of you had to pluck up his courage to go across that tightrope at all—upside down or not!"

"Yes, of course! I take your point," said 'Friar Tuck', the chubby-faced man. "We've got to look at the world through the flea's eyes, to judge its achievement. It's easy to forget that. Yes indeed, that's a plucky little fellow up there on that rope. A plucky little chap to be sure!" he chuckled.

Fanny now sent a series of fleas along the cord to follow the first one. At length a column of six fleas was formed up in line astern at the far end, easily counted by the six different colours of their cards: yellow, white, red, green, blue and orange.

Felix announced that they had a six-wire track under development. The six wires would be parallel to one another, separated by two inch spaces. The intention was to run races and take bets, by colour, on the fleas. When asked how he would be able to start them fairly, Felix said that they had already solved that problem. They had a slotted card which fitted over the six wires forming a barrier in front of the fleas at the start end. On the command 'GO', he explained that the card would be lifted off, releasing all the fleas simultaneously. They would all have their noses to the card at the start, each one having already automatically moved along from its tail-end bead, until it could get no further.

Some people on previous occasions had already told Felix that they would like to see this, and have bets on the fleas, but he had not yet worked out how to administer the bookmaking and fit it into his routine. It had occurred to him that they could probably successfully run a separate 'Flea-races' operation, maybe two or three times a day, pulling back interested people who had been to the show that day and were still around the Fairground. It could prove a paying proposition, and sounding out his clients he and Fanny had already concluded they could look to run at least three sessions a day: morning, afternoon and evening. People tended to spend a half day, or an evening, at the Fairground, and it seemed certain they would be able to recruit three groups of race-going punters per day.

Felix had built a prototype for this 'High-wire' race and the system worked. It was now a matter of refinement and organisation.

The people standing there now, especially those who liked having a flutter on the horses, were even more interested when Felix told them he had previously run chariot races using cat, dog, rabbit, mole, hedgehog and human fleas, all pulling two-wheeled chariots along a special racetrack. This he had abandoned because it took up too much time when made a part of his normal show. People wanted to gamble on them and frequently started to lay bets with one another, and wanting him to have race after race! However, the seed had been sown. Clearly there was money to be made.

What he now had in mind, he explained, was to organise multi-sport race meetings, using the tightrope walkers, chariot-pullers and paddle-boat drivers. Mention of the latter immediately gave rise to further questions and Felix told his interested listeners that they would shortly see a model paddle-steamer working. Their reaction once again pointed to the almost certain success of his new proposed venture.

In the meantime, while Felix had been discussing his future racing plans, Fanny had put out another performer in the circus ring—a flea juggler. She had stood a small, flat-topped, cone-shaped stand in the ring. On its top, lying on its back with its feet stuck up in the air was a large flea. It was nearly a quarter of an inch long! A real big fellow!

Felix now turned his attention to the newcomer. He pointed out its monstrous size and explained that it was a mole flea, one of a family that had a long history of juggling. It was, he said, not at all easy to train a flea to lie on its back—never mind teach it how to juggle. But Fanny, he told them, with evident pride, was gifted when it came to communicating with fleas. She had patience and understanding and had developed a knack of teaching them this particular juggling discipline. Though he did not of course divulge her trade secrets, she actually accomplished this difficult task by sticking down the hapless fleas on their backs, with sealing wax. This reinforced their self-discipline, and enabled them to stay put indefinitely.

The one on display now was ready for action. Fanny picked up with her tweezers a small coloured ball. It was about half-an-inch in diameter and not unlike some popular rubber beach-balls in appearance, for it had segments of various bright colours. It was very light in weight, having been made of pith taken from an elderberry bush. Carefully she lowered it on to the flea's flailing legs. It immediately grabbed the ball with its feet—pleased at last to have something to hang on to. Life without a floor for its feet was not natural, and so far as it was concerned it was a relief to have a floor presented to its air-borne feet. The ball dwarfed the flea and looked a truly enormous thing for it to carry. But it was as nothing to the powerful performing flea, being by its standards just larva-play. Happily it strove to walk on its new-found surface, and the ball started to rotate pleasingly, the coloured segments allowing the audience to see how cleverly the flea spun the ball.

Felix told them that fleas of other breeds were by no means as good as mole fleas at this skill. He reckoned it had something to do with the fact that moles lived in the dark and got especially good at feeling their way about using their feet and their snout. This extra ability, he explained, was in their blood, and got passed on to their fleas which were therefore really clever at controlling things by their sense of touch. Their eyes weren't too good, because they didn't have a lot of seeing to do where moles lived.

In addition to that, he elaborated, they were used to being upside-down because most of them lived under their host's belly. When riding on its back, they were in constant danger of being brushed off, as the mole shuffled its way along its tunnels that were tailor-made to fit its body closely. This was a fact of life, passed on by word of mouth, from one generation of mole fleas to the next.

There were thus two logical reasons why mole fleas were particularly suitable for this special circus act.

At this point in the show Felix reckoned to be roughly half-way through his routine. Fanny helped him to clear the ring, to prepare for the next event. She quickly retrieved the six tightrope walkers by the simple expedient of holding the jar under each in turn, picking it off with her forceps and dropping it into the jar. Then she screwed on the lid and stowed the jar away in the cupboard, the six performers now being left to rest up until the next show.

The mole flea was not detached from its pedestal but stored away as it was. At the moment it was industriously turning the ball round and round. It was destined to spend the remainder of its life upside down on the little conical stand, being permanently stuck there. It was fed at regular intervals on the body of its host, or on a fat mouse if time were short, or no host-mole available.

Felix and Fanny had well-organised methods of presenting their performers to shaved patches at suitable access points on the bodies of their respective hosts. The precise positions of these patches were changed at intervals to prevent any one place on the skin being punished unduly. Sometimes, if the patches were too conspicuous, the dog and the cat when released from their duties and out and about, wore neat, tie-on body coats fashioned by Fanny, which served the additional purpose of advertising FODEN'S FLEA CIRCUS—the words being boldly displayed on their sides.

Felix picked up the mole flea on its conical stand and passed it to Fanny. She used her tweezers to lift off the coloured ball from the feet of the highly-skilled juggler, and bent down to place the performer with its ball into a small storage box in the cupboard under the table.

A lean, angular, rather severe-looking lady, who was watching these actions very closely, directed a sharply-delivered question to Felix. He could tell from her manner and tone of voice that he was in for a little tussle.

"You're not going to leave that poor little creature lying upside down on the top of that stand until you need it again, are you?" she asked.

"Why not?" replied Felix. "That's one of the happiest performers in my show, that juggler is. It would break his heart to take him off that stand. Anyway, he'd get off if he didn't like it!"

"I don't believe it," she said emphatically. "In fact I think you've actually stuck the poor thing down on there!"

"You know nothing about fleas, that's obvious," Felix countered, choosing to ignore the suggestion that the flea was stuck down. "That flea would stop feeding if it didn't like its job. They always do. It's their way of complaining."

"Well, it seems to me the whole business is cruel," the busybody continued, getting up steam and intent, it seemed, on getting her teeth into Felix. "You just fasten fleas into your models permanently, wherever you want them. There's no question of them being able to get out!"

"Yes there is," responded Felix, looking a little hurt at the implication of cruelty in her remarks. "In fact they don't have to ask to come out—I take them out regularly to feed them!"

"But they don't stay out, do they?" she persisted.

"Of course they don't. They don't want to," replied Felix a little heatedly. "All they want to do is have a quiet kip when their guts are full of blood. There's nowhere they want to go once they've had their nosh. A flea on a cat or a dog only roams about a bit to find a good place to feed. Then afterwards it tucks up somewhere and goes to sleep. On a rabbit they don't bother to move much at all. If I had time I could show you a family of them now, all asleep this very minute, up behind Felicity's ears. You've got the wrong idea about fleas. They move about to feed, that's all. Then they sleep. Mine don't have to move about. They've got a cushy life, they have. I move them myself, and not only that I put them smack on the right place to feed. My fleas live on Easy Street. Don't you worry about them!"

"Well, I still think it's cruel to fix them on a model," she said, her thin-lipped, turned-down-at-the-corners mouth set in a grim line.

It was not of course the first time this comment had been made by visitors to his show, and Felix had a number of well-tried counter arguments, most of them based upon the well-known axiom that attack is the best form of defence. The reference the lady had made to his mole flea being stuck down had already inspired his strategy.

"Do you allow flies in your house to roam about over food you're going to eat?" he asked his critic, apparently inconsequentially.

"Of course I don't!" she replied. "Of course not. What's that got to do with anything? Nothing at all, so far as I can see."

"But you must get flies in your house," Felix continued. "Everybody does. Nobody can keep them out altogether."

"Of course they can't!" she retorted, sharply and angrily. "I'm not suggesting they can."

"Well, what do you do to them, when they do come in, then?" asked Felix. "Make pets of them, or just ask them to leave?"

"You know very well what people do," she said. "Swat them or drive them away."

"So you swat them and kill them, do you?" pursued Felix. "That can hardly be described as being kind to insects, that can't. Bashing flies into pulp with a fly-swatter isn't very kind, is it?"

"I don't see what that's got to do with anything like I just said," she snapped. "You know very well flies mustn't be allowed to settle on food."

"When you're out of the house, I bet they do, though," Felix went on relentlessly. "I expect without you knowing it, flies are walking around your house leaving germs and mess all over the place. A fly can be walking on a lump of dog's shit one minute and plodding about your house the next, maybe leaving some on a plate you're going to use or on the rim of a cup that will soon be in your mouth. You wouldn't even know about it. There's nothing you can do to stop it."

"That's where you're quite wrong," she stated firmly. "Absolutely wrong. I'm very strict about hygiene in my house. Just inside the doors of my house, and most certainly in the kitchen, I have always got flypapers up. Always. Not many get past those, I can assure you. They are highly attractive to flies, more so than anything else that may be around. So they go to those."

Felix could hardly believe his good fortune. She had walked right into it. But he was after the last ounce of advantage from his now unassailable position.

"How do you know they don't get past them when you're out?" he asked.

"Because the flypapers are covered with them, of course," she snapped.

"Are they all dead, then?" Felix asked, innocently. "If they're dead, then they are most likely yesterday's, or the day before's. I don't see how you can possibly know they've been caught while you were out. How can you tell?"

"Because they're still alive, that's how!" she replied angrily.

"Oh!" said Felix, looking shocked and astonished. "So when you get home there are flies stuck on the flypapers, still moving their legs about, trying their very hardest to get themselves free so they can go home too. That seems very, very sad to me. Sad and terribly cruel. They just have to stay stuck there until they die, I suppose. What a sad end to their lives. When they get to heaven I don't suppose they will look back on you with much pleasure. They will remember you as the lady who tricked them into being stuck down on pretend food and left to die of starvation."

"Flies are dangerous," the lady said, defensively. "They have to be killed."

"Agreed," said Felix. "Agreed. So are fleas dangerous. It was fleas that caused the Plague of London. You can't get much more dangerous than that! A flea can move from a filthy-dirty, diseased rat and straight onto your body. At least a fly doesn't stick his mouth right through your skin into your body, and suck your blood after it's just sucked some out of a disease-ridden rat!"

"What are you trying to prove?" asked the lady, looking thoroughly confused because the Flea-man had now apparently turned against fleas which clearly earned his living for him. It was not a response she expected.

"I'll tell you what I'm trying to prove," answered Felix, now feigning genuine hurt feelings over having been wrongly accused of cruelty. "I object to you saying I'm unkind to my fleas. Just think about this. I put my fleas on my models giving them a job to do which they thoroughly enjoy. I keep them in warm, snug surroundings, safe from normal dangers and disease-ridden rats and no longer having to fend for themselves. I feed them regularly on rich, healthy blood, and leave them to sleep away in peace when they're not working.

Compare that with what you do to your flies. You stick your flies on a sheet of glue, tempting them into thinking they are going to have the feed of a lifetime, but tricking them into being trapped, to die of awful hunger. Once you have stuck your flies down, you never feed them at all. Lady, don't you ever come in here again accusing me of being cruel to my fleas. My fleas are my life, and no flea ever had a better home than he gets in Foden's Flea Circus. There isn't one of them that would change places with your flies, stuck down on one of your horrible flypapers. What a dreadful death you inflict upon them!"

The irate lady had nothing further to say. There was an awkward silence in the cabin as people contemplated the curiously twisted logic of Felix's case. His counter-attack had seemed confusing and tortuous, yet in the end strangely compelling. And some thought that when they got home they might discreetly take down their own flypapers. Most of them had watched trapped flies dragging at their feet helplessly, and struggling, with never a hope of success, to get free of the dreadfully sticky mess they were stuck upon. It was not a nice thing to see!

After listening to Felix, some now began to feel a bit uneasy and guilty. Certainly it was not a very kind end to inflict upon an unsuspecting insect. It was a hard way indeed for a food-foraging, fancy-free fly to finish its final flight. Not pleasant at all!

Meanwhile Felix and Fanny quietly prepared for the next part of their show, leaving their audience for the moment with their own private thoughts on these weighty philosophical matters.

And Felix, they noticed, looked pensive and troubled. Once he glanced towards the lady and shook his head sadly from side to side as though finding her devilish behaviour towards innocent insects hard to understand and almost beyond belief. She glared back at him, looking set-faced and angry, but had no immediate answer to his infuriating, tail-twisting counter-attack.

Felix registered with quiet satisfaction that she was stewing nicely in her own juice, and at the same time Fanny too saw the lady 'cooking' and secretly admired her husband's psycho-culinary abilities. She was used to him putting acidic people to one side

431

to stew, having first stirred them up in his own inimitable, devious ways. But she was uncomfortably aware that now and again he overheated them so that they suddenly boiled over and blew their tops. She hoped that the angry lady would cool down, for rows bothered her and upset the normal tranquillity of their flea-centred miniature world of make-believe.

She had her own way of warning Felix to lay off, when, as a detached observer, danger of a boil-over became evident to her. Unobtrusively she reached under the table and took out a rather ornate looking egg-timer which she placed, without comment, on the table, inverting it to set the sand falling. People watched it and wondered what purpose it was to serve. It actually did its twin job very well—Felix took the message and said no more, and meanwhile eyes were diverted from the simmering source of explosion. This dual effect reduced pressure on the victim.

Fanny's hope always was that the show would then proceed happily, with peace restored to the cabin.

It is certain that many people, thinking afterwards about the strange things they had witnessed, were left wondering what part the egg-timer had played in the proceedings. Neither Felix nor Fanny appeared to pay any attention to it, nor did they mention it. If asked, Felix simply said that it was a flea-performance timer-monitor—one of his regular standards-checking procedures, but not part of the show.

This clever little ploy of Fanny's almost always bridged the gap very successfully. By the time the sand ran out the next events in the show had captured the attention of the audience and tension was relaxed once again.

Chapter 29

FELIX HAS HIS PATIENCE SORELY TRIED

by an unpleasant heckler who
seeks to debunk him

Felix now placed in the ring a shallow, stainless steel roasting tray into which he carefully poured water from a kettle, so creating a convenient miniature boating lake. He then opened the lid of a polished mahogany box and picked out three, very nicely made little models of paddle steamers. These he launched in the water near one end of the tray. Though he had done his best to keep the water smooth, it was a bit choppy at first and took a few moments to settle down. However, after bobbing about a bit, the boats began to move forward under their own steam.

The watchers studied them carefully. Looking very realistic, each had twin paddle wheels turning under arched safety guards like those fitted over the large paddle wheels of steamers plying around the coast from one holiday resort to another. A round trip between Margate and Southend piers, with a few hours ashore at Southend was a favourite outing for the SKWEC men, and they looked at these tiny models with amused and nostalgic interest.

Between the pairs of paddle wheels in each boat, neatly placed in the centre of the hull, was one of Felix's flea-motors with its captive flea busily treading away at the drum. The gaily-painted little boats, with neat striped awnings over the seats in their sterns, looked very attractive as they moved along with their paddle wheels churning up a little wash behind them.

It was easy to imagine how an exciting race could be arranged using such boats. Felix had found that in perfectly calm water, the craft, using a simple rudder, kept a tolerably straight course and first one, then another, would take the lead. He had great hopes for his racing-fleas project as a sideline to his established business.

Watching the steady progress across the water of the tiny vessels and the faces of those now looking at them so closely, Felix felt quite sure that if he did manage to get the project going, the racing paddle steamers would excite a lot of interest.

He planned to make a larger, shallow, glass-bottom lake, standing on a board painted pale blue and perhaps decorated with flags and bunting to create an authentic, holiday race-meeting atmosphere. The close interest being shown by his present customers encouraged him to believe his idea would be a winner. In his mind's eye he pictured people cheering on the paddle steamers as they travelled across the sunlit blue waters of his lake.

Felix was a dreamer and had created around himself his own private, dreamlike world in which, to an acute observer, he appeared to move almost like a sleepwalker in a part-real, part-imagined, miniature world, so absorbed by it was he. People listening to him and watching him closely, sometimes had a strange feeling that they had caught tantalising glimpses of his surrealistic world, almost as though they were aware, for a fleeting moment, of the existence of an Alice in Wonderland-type place—a detached dream world with Felix as their link-man and guide. He had the unusual natural ability of providing, with no apparent effort on his part, a window to his fertile imagination, so that others were able to share his fascination and become infected by his enthusiasm.

There had been silence for a few moments, Felix having been temporarily lost in this private contemplation of his future plans. A thought now evidently struck him for he looked up and spoke directly to the little man who had put the 'horse' question.

"This will interest you," he said. "Those fleas in the paddle steamers are an exception to my rule of always using human fleas to drive mobile models. They are dog-fleas turning those engines. There's no steering to think about, you see. Just treading the drums. That's all. They were taught by watching a human flea. I was short of human fleas at the time and the idea came to me when I made the first boat. Some dogs love water. My dog Fido over there," he added, pointing to his terrier in its basket on the table behind him, "he loves swimming. So I tried his fleas out in the boats and found they could cope very well. What's more I could see they thoroughly enjoyed it. So I've given Fido's fleas those three boat-jobs. It's turned out very well."

Fido, hearing his name mentioned, had stood up in his basket and was looking towards his master, wagging his tail eagerly. "There you are," said Felix, pointing to Fido. "He's backing up what I say. Fido's proud to know his fleas are working the boats. Fine fleas I get off Fido. He looks after his family very well for me."

At this further mention of his name, Fido's excitement increased and he gave a joyful little bark.

"He's nearly human, that dog is," exclaimed Felix, as Fido's tail thumped to and fro. "No wonder his fleas are bright. You can teach a clever dog like him to do all sorts of things. When you think about it, a clever dog's fleas are also found to be intelligent. It stands to reason."

With that profound statement, confirmed by Fido with another sharp bark before he resumed his prone position of watchful rest, Felix picked the three paddle steamers out of the water and placed them back in their box. He did not put the improvised lake away for the moment because he had another function for it to serve before he took it off the table.

Being careful not to spill the water, he picked up the metal tray and placed it alongside the circus ring, positioning it so that one of its long sides was against the edge of the ring. Its flanged edge was then overhanging the rim of the circus ring at the point where they touched.

Fanny then handed him a little device which looked very much like a diving board when he put it in its place. Made of wood, its base stood in the ring adjacent to the edge of the tray, and from its top a small plank stuck out over the flanged edge of the tray to reach out a few inches over the water. Except for the fact that it had side-pieces like a water chute, which were fitted there to act as blinkers to make sure the fleas looked and moved to their front, it was indeed so much like a diving board jutting out over the water below, that somebody laughingly asked Felix if that was what it was.

"No, it's certainly not," replied Felix, a little disdainfully. "Fleas are not fond of swimming, any more than cats are. Some animals like swimming and some don't. Dogs do but cats don't. And fleas don't. But you'll see what this is for in a minute. It's a long-jump take-off board. That's what it really is. I've taught fleas to jump off this, right across the water, to land on the green cloth on the far side. They love to compete with one another to see how far they can go! There's nothing a flea likes more than a good jump. There's never any shortage of volunteers for this sport. They love it!"

This statement raised a laugh but Felix did not smile. Once again he was clearly serious, so they quickly quietened down.

Fanny moved to the edge of the table, to the far side of the water, and placed there a small tray bearing six, empty, glass, fish-paste pots. These stood upside down on the tray and the bottoms were seen to be painted in six different colours. The pots, which were about three and a half inches high and one and a half inches in diameter, had no caps on—these were laid out on the tray ready for use later on and were identified by the same six colours.

Felix meanwhile had collected from the cupboard a similar tray of paste pots but these stood the right way up and were capped. The caps and the bottoms bore the same six colours.

"These pots," announced Felix, without further ado, "each contain teams of specially selected fleas. They're all trained long-jumpers. The colours show what breed of fleas they are. This card," he added, propping up a white card in the ring, "shows what colours the fleas compete under." The card read:

435

```
┌─────────────────────────────────────────────────────────┐
│                                                         │
│     TEAM COLOURS FOR FLEA LONG-JUMPERS                  │
│                                                         │
│         WHITE      .......... human                     │
│         RED        .......... dog                       │
│         BLUE       .......... cat                       │
│         YELLOW     .......... rabbit                     │
│         GREEN      .......... hedgehog                   │
│         BLACK      .......... mole                       │
│                                                         │
└─────────────────────────────────────────────────────────┘
```

"Everybody knows that fleas are good jumpers," Felix went on. "All of them can jump, just like frogs can, but fleas are much better than frogs, size for size. You will be surprised how far these specially-trained fleas can go. That's if they have a mind to, and put all they've got into it. That's where training and discipline comes in. Even an ordinary untrained flea can easily jump two hundred times its own length if it puts its back into it. You imagine a horse jumping over two hundred horses standing nose to tail. That shows you how good fleas are. But people don't stop to think how clever they are—they just belly-ache about being bitten by the bastards! Fleas are special. Deserve far more credit than they get, fleas do!

But watch these trained ones carefully now. Keep your eyes on them. They're really keen. They don't hang about. Like all good athletes, they're all hyped-up and ready to go when faced with an important competition. I'm going to jump them off one at a time and see who can jump the furthest. In case you should wonder how I decide who goes first, I must tell you that to be fair, for each competition I change the jumping order for the six teams. You can't be fairer than that. This time the rabbit team has first go."

So saying, Felix picked up the yellow-capped jar, took the lid off, and prepared to extract one of the fleas. He had his own special way of doing this. At one time he used to use a small glass tube with a rubber bulb on the end, originally designed to drip a catarrh-clearing fluid into the nose. He sucked a flea into it then blew it out where he wished to place it. But it was not entirely satisfactory. Often he had trouble making it work first time and had to fiddle about a bit. It only had a small bulb to squeeze and to use his own words, "It didn't have enough suck!"

Then by chance one day he happened to see a pipette in use in a chemist's shop. This gadget gave him an idea. He persuaded a clever glass-blower on Margate seafront, who worked in a small cubicle blowing glass tubing to make ornaments which he sold to holidaymakers who stood watching him work, to design and make him a purpose-built pipette to suit his unusual requirements. It worked wonderfully. All he had to do was place its slightly flanged end over his chosen flea, suck it into a small central bulb half-way up the tube, and carry the flea wherever he wanted it to be. A sharp blow of air down the tube delivered the flea, unharmed, though perhaps somewhat bewildered, just where he wanted it placed.

Using this invaluable aid he now sucked up one of the rabbit fleas and took it to the jumping platform.

"Watch carefully, now," he repeated. "These blokes move pretty fast. You don't want to miss the action."

Putting the end of the tube just over the jumping-board, he gave an expert little puff and out shot the flea to land near the open end of the board. It was neatly done, for

436

Felix was well practised and much rehearsed in the use of his special device.

For a brief moment the flea appeared to take stock of its surroundings. Behind it was the pipette it had just escaped from; to the sides were the constraining walls of the chute; but ahead lay bright open country. Its escape route was clear. The wide open world and freedom beckoned in front of its nose.

Losing no time it moved to the edge of the board, paused momentarily in a purposeful squat, stoking up energy in the powerful, muscular, jumping system beneath its body, then immediately took off in a phenomenal leap, easily clearing the water, to land up the green fairway about fifteen inches away from the tray.

Its freedom was short lived. Quick as a flash Fanny plonked the open-topped, yellow-bottomed paste-jar over it, trapping it precisely at its point of landing. The pot neatly marked the rabbit flea's achievement and in due course would provide it with free transport to its home base.

"How about that!" exclaimed Felix proudly. "Did you see what it did? It took one look down at the water, knew there was no future down there, so decided straightaway to jump over to the far side of the lake. The sight of that water reminds a flea it has got to jump and not just hop. Not a bad jump either, was it? But by no means the best jump we shall see today, unless I'm very much mistaken!"

The spectators were clearly much impressed by this highly agile performance and craned forwards eagerly to see the next competitor.

Next to jump was a cat flea. This proved how right Felix was in his expectation for it shot at least four inches further up the table than the first jumper. It was trapped, with equal alacrity, under the appropriate blue-bottomed jar by the swift, well-practised action of Fanny.

"By bloody hell, can't they jump!" commented a man standing near the table opposite where the flea landed. "They look like they're fired from a gun. There's no running up to the jump-line for them, like our long-jumpers do. That cat flea just took off from a standing start. I saw it. I didn't see the rabbit flea go—reckon I blinked and missed it or something. But I kept my eyes on that cat flea all the time. One minute it was squatting there absolutely still, then it just shot up in the air. It's uncanny that is. I wonder how they do it?"

"Yes," agreed Felix, "it's amazing when you watch them closely. You certainly can't see them getting ready to go, gathering themselves up like some animals do to spring on their prey. They just go! It's got something to do with them being able to store energy in their bodies in the flat pads they have, made of a special, muscle-like material under their hard body cases. A bit like energy stored in a coiled spring. At least that's what a Vet told me who came to see Fido when the poor little bleeder had the shits."

He was interrupted by an eager bark from Fido, who, ever alert and watchful, had evidently heard his name mentioned and thought a comment was called for.

"It's all right, Fido! Lie down, boy! There's nothing to get excited about," Felix said, looking at the tail-wagging little dog reassuringly. "And I'm sorry if I embarrassed you by being too personal. Lie down, boy!"

Fido did as he was told and Felix resumed his comments.

"One thing's for sure," he said. "Fleas have got the edge over us when it comes to jumping. That Vet reckoned that if a man could jump as well as a flea, taking off from a standing start like they do, then—size for size—he could jump over Canterbury Cathedral. Or land 235 feet up on top of Bell Harry Tower if he wanted to! He could be right, when you come to think about it. A flea takes off like a bat out of hell. It's anybody's guess where a man would finish up if he were as good as a flea!"

Getting back to the contest after imparting this mind-boggling suggestion, Felix now announced that it was the human-flea's turn to jump, and took up the white-capped pot. Taking off the cap he appeared to study the occupants with care before selecting the one he wanted and sucking it up into his pipette.

"This is old Tom I told you about earlier on," he said. "You remember—he's one of Alf's ancestors. He's actually the oldest living member of Alf's family now he's lost his own Dad, who died last month. He jumps for the team once each day, like the others do. Mind you, I can't pretend he's anywhere near the best in the team now, because he's knocking on a bit. But he's still pretty good and well worth his place in the team. He'll stay with them until somebody beats him in a jump-off, when we run our regular team selection trials."

These were measured words. Felix had long since learnt not to make over-confident predictions about an individual flea's imminent performance. His caution was justified in this case because 'Tom' landed quite a bit short of the other two. Felix was secretly annoyed about that because he'd picked out what he judged to be the best prospect from the random assortment of human fleas in the pot, although ostensibly at the time he had been seeking out 'Tom'—a particular flea he apparently could recognise in a crowd!

"That's disappointing," commented Felix, as Fanny plonked the white-bottomed pot over Tom. "He usually does better than that. In his round yesterday he came second—just behind the mole flea. Still, they're like all athletes. Some days they're out of form. But I must say that's a poor jump for Tom. He must be under the weather. I'll put a reserve in the team and give him a holiday for a few days."

"Send him to Blackpool for a week. That will put him right," laughed a lady with a strong Lancashire accent.

"No! I'll do better than that," responded Felix, for once with a wide grin on his face. "I'll shove him inside Fanny's pants for a couple of days. Roaming around feeding on her lovely backside will be real luxury for old Tom. Much better than anything Blackpool has to offer, and smelling a hell of a lot better to him than any amount of sea air!"

Fanny, not at all pleased at being the butt of the laughter that followed, struggled to force a tolerant smile on her face, after momentarily looking daggers at Felix.

Now, unfortunately, things started to go wrong, as much more serious disappointments than Tom's lack-lustre performance lay ahead.

Next out of its pot was the mole flea. Looking twice the size of the others it was expected to out-jump the lot. It didn't! It appeared to amble thoughtfully up to the edge of the jumping-board, paused a little—shuffling around with its nose over the edge—then gave a pathetic hop, only to land with a tiny plop in the water below. There was a howl of laughter from the spectators.

"The dozy sod!" Felix exploded, with apparent disgust. "What the hell's got into him?"

Quickly, using a fine-meshed tea-strainer, he did a life-saving job and fished the unhappy failed-performer out of the water. Fanny took the strainer from him and dropped the bedraggled flea into the black-bottomed pot which she had had in her hand ready to trap him in when he landed. Placing the black lid on it, she stood the pot on the table alongside the lake, opposite the point where the flea had hit the water.

"Eyesight problems! Must have forgotten to open its eyes again!" explained Felix succinctly. "The trouble with mole fleas is they often forget to open their eyes because they're so used to seeing nothing with them when they do so. They kind of forget about seeing, living down there under the ground. Pity that. I'd like you to have seen just how far they can jump. I've seen them clear over thirty-five inches many times. It's only a matter of time and training before one hits the forty-inch line. No doubt of that at all! Cuthbert, the one that pipped Tom yesterday, reached thirty-four inches. And he's not the best in the current mole flea team. But fair's fair. This one's first jump must stand. Those are the rules. He can't expect to win any gongs going round with his eyes shut!"

"What's his name?" enquired 'Friar Tuck', his eyes twinkling with amusement as he listened to the po-faced Felix and watched the proceedings with close interest.

"Don't know, to be honest," answered Felix without hesitation. "I must say I just picked one out without clocking his name. Who is he, Fanny?"

Fanny took the cap off the mole's pot and peered inside. "It's Archibald," she said, after studying the failed competitor for a few moments. "You put him in the team last week."

"Well, we shall have to watch him for the next few days," commented Felix. "It's early days yet but if he sods about like that again we'll have to chuck him out."

Frowning a little, not too pleased with this abject failure, Felix consulted his jumping-order list and picked up the green-topped pot.

"It's a hedgehog flea's turn next," he announced. Using his pipette expertly, he sucked up a waiting competitor out of its glass rest-room and deposited it near the end of the jumping-board. It sat there without moving. Puzzled, Felix poked it up the backside with a knitting needle to encourage it to jump. It didn't. It just shuffled about a bit and then sat there impassively.

From long experience Felix recognised the inevitable when he saw it. The flea was on its last legs; it was on its way out. There was no question of it having been in the pot too long without food. That was impossible. It was their practice to gather enough competitors for the day first thing each morning, returning them all—both those that had been called upon to jump and those that had not—to their respective hosts at the end of each day. Fanny took charge of this operation. Her first job each morning was to go round the animals and harvest the necessary fleas. So the flea certainly had not been starved. Even if it had been used yesterday, which was statistically doubtful, it had at the very least sat on a mountain of food all night!

"Something's wrong with this one," Felix stated, after a further abortive poke at it with his knitting needle. "I'll test it."

The audience watched him attentively. First he took a folded piece of tissue paper from a flat box of interleaved toilet paper. Then he sucked up the flea with his pipette and blew it out onto the paper. Quickly folding the paper over the flea, he trapped it between the thumb and forefinger of his left hand.

With his right hand he took up a small, ornate wooden mallet which some of those present recognised as an Auctioneer's gavel, placed the folded-in flea on the table and gave it a sharp clout with the mallet. Unfolding the paper he then studied the squashed remains of the flea with an expert eye.

"Thought so," he said, authoritatively. "There's no blood in its guts. None at all. Not a drop."

"There's not much in the wall of that glass jar for the poor little bugger to suck out, is there?" interjected a smart aleck amongst the audience, raising a loud laugh from everybody.

Felix was not pleased, and he showed it.

"No, Clever Dick, you're quite right," he snapped. "But there's plenty in the hedgehog this bloke was on all last night. He just stopped feeding, that's what!"

"Why would that be?" countered the speaker. "Gone off his food, had he? I wonder why?"

"Could be a number of reasons," answered Felix. "Gone bolshie most likely. On hunger strike for better conditions. Or maybe upset by an argument with his wife!"

This raised a bigger laugh, and lightened the atmosphere a bit. But the matter was not yet closed.

The little man who had clocked up some credit with Felix, not only by his thoughtful horse flea question, but also by the respectful way he had spoken to him, now put a further question. His brow was puckered and he appeared anxious and rather uneasy.

"Excuse me, Mr. Foden," he said to Felix politely. "When you put that flea in the piece of paper, you said you were going to test it. You didn't know it would have no blood in it then, did you?"

"No, I didn't," replied Felix. "Of course not. That's why I tested it!" He was about to say he didn't have X-ray eyes, but forbore to do so. The little man looked worried and was a nice little bloke. Felix didn't want to make a joke at his expense. "Why do you ask?" he enquired in a kindly way.

"Well, I just thought it seemed a pity to kill it in order to test it," the little man answered rather diffidently, his manner showing genuine concern. There was a chuckle from the audience at this logical observation.

"Oh! I see what you mean," said Felix, in an understanding way. "No, you needn't worry. I know my fleas. When a flea decides it's time to die it stops eating and sits around moping all day. I just put the little fellow out of his misery, that's all."

The Clever Dick thought it was time for him to put his spoke in again.

"That's all very well," he intervened. "But suppose when you clouted it you had found it full of blood. You'd have killed a good flea finding out there was nothing wrong with it, wouldn't you? That doesn't seem to make much sense to me! That's not very clever, surely? And pretty unfair to the flea, I'd say! It amounts to you dishing out a death sentence to a flea because it refuses to jump! A little bit harsh, wouldn't you say?"

Felix visibly bridled at this cutting remark. The biting heavy sarcasm got right to him, deeply.

"That's where you're wrong. Absolutely wrong." He said emphatically. "If that flea had been sitting up there on the jumping-board with its guts full of blood, but not attempting to jump, it would have been an idle, good-for-nothing little sod! It would have been a dead loss to me anyway. I can't afford to carry passengers in this business. Either way it deserved the chop!"

Then remembering the little man's honest concern, Felix directed his final comment to him.

"Sorry, mate," he said sympathetically, with a pained expression on his face. "I'm afraid that's the way it has to be in this job. But don't worry about it. No flea suffers when I clout it hard like that."

"Of course not. Of course it doesn't," confirmed the smart aleck, butting in again jeeringly. "Quite enjoys it, I expect. It must be a very pleasant, once in a lifetime experience for it, being smashed to pulp like that—especially with an Auctioneer's hammer. Going! Going! GONE! And gone for bloody good, too!"

Felix ignored this latest dig from his leech-like persistent heckler, and waited for the ensuing loud laughter to subside. When it did so, however, Joe from the SKWEC group, made a wry comment which caused another burst of laughter.

"It's what we in the engineering world describe as 'testing-to-destruction', he muttered quietly, but nonetheless loud enough for all to hear in the momentary silence.

"That's as maybe," countered Felix sharply. "But I don't see much connection between lumps of bloody metal and my fleas. These are living creatures I'm working with, and much more complicated than any machine *you* may mess about with."

440

Suitably cut down to size by this enlightened comparison, Joe wisely shut up.

"Are you going to put another hedgehog flea up there to have a go?" asked Arthur, in an attempt to re-establish a better atmosphere and divert the flea-man's attention from his friend Joe.

"Certainly not!" replied Felix abruptly. "That last jumper was disqualified. He . . . "

"Not only disqualified, he was summarily executed! Clobbered with a wooden mallet and mashed up to pulp!" interrupted Felix's tormentor before he could get another word out.

Once again Felix ignored him and waited until the inevitable chuckling subsided. Then he continued his answer to Arthur's question.

"He was put there to represent his team and he chickened out," he said. "No! I don't allow them to mess about like that in a competition. Rules are rules. He's blown the hedgehog team's chance in the contest. There's only one more competitor to jump now. That's the dog flea."

Intent on catching up on lost time, Felix quickly took up the red-capped jar, sucked out one of the fleas squatting in there patiently waiting their turn, and delivered it expertly to the jumping platform.

This time there was no snag. Without a moment's hesitation the flea discreetly gathered its hidden formidable muscles and took a mighty leap over the water, landing well out in front of the rabbit's marker-jar, to win the contest handsomely.

Fanny smartly planted the red-bottomed glass jar over the successful flea and joined Felix in clapping hands to applaud the winner.

"Well done!" she said. "That will please Fido!"

A sharp bark from Fido, who never failed to hear his name mentioned, confirmed his pleasure in the success of his representative.

Felix then measured the dog flea's jump with his tape and announced the winner's overall distance.

"Thirty-one inches," he said, with obvious pleasure. "That's made up for the balls-up by the mole flea and hedgehog entries. You've seen a bloody good performance there, I'm glad of that."

Fanny now secured the competitors inside their pots. Her method was to slide a postcard under the pot to edge up the flea onto the card; invert the pot; give the card a sharp tap to dislodge the flea and propel it to the bottom of the jar; then finally, promptly put back on the pot's coloured cap.

The gathered-in competitors were then tipped into her series of flea stock jars where she stored her daily harvest of fleas. The stock jars were colour coded using the same colours as the jumpers' paste pots. If business was exceptionally good, Felix's competitor pots would sometimes empty before the last show, in which case Fanny dished out some more.

Regularly, at the end of each day, she emptied the stock jars by tipping the contents back on to the long-suffering hosts, but with one exception. The jar of human fleas was taken care of by Felix who fed the performers on himself by the jam-jar-on-the-body technique, or sometimes—if nobody was around to witness his perfidious behaviour—he fed them on one of his stoical animal assistants.

Though he would not have condoned this lazy behaviour by anybody else, he figured that an occasional feed of non-human blood would not harm his flock. His conscientious collector *Jumbo Pulex Orwell* would not have dreamt of breaking the rules in this way.

While Fanny was looking after the livestock, Felix busied himself clearing away the artificial lake and making ready for the next part of his show.

441

During this brief interval, a lady of large and bustling appearance put a question to him.

"I'm interested in breeding pedigree dogs," she said. "Were you serious when you said earlier on that champion jumpers only turn up every other generation with your fleas? That's a most unusual trait in a breeding line—the regular missing of a generation like that. Most unusual!"

"They do in Tom's family," stated Felix emphatically. "No question about that. Regular as clockwork. I'll tell you how they run, from Tom downwards to Alf.

Tom's grandson Pete is a champion, but none of Tom's sons are. Pete's grandson Noble is a champion, but none of Pete's sons are. Noble's grandson Jake is a champion, but none of Noble's sons are, including Wilfred whom you've met. Alf is one of Jake's sons and is not a champion. Wilfred is Jake's dad of course. I expect with your experience with pedigree family trees you can follow all that easily enough. You will be used to running down a family's generations, I'm quite sure."

"Well . . . yes, I suppose I can," confirmed the lady hesitatingly and more than a little doubtfully. "It's a most extraordinary fact, though, I must say."

Felix had rattled off these names with no hesitation, too fast by far for most of his audience who lost track halfway through the strange sequence. He was well-rehearsed because somebody often queried his Grandfather's Great-Grandfather's Grandfather bit. His smart aleck tormentor in the audience saw another opportunity to have a sly dig at him.

"How do we know all that tripe is right?" he exclaimed contemptuously. "You invented all those names off the top of your head as you went along, I reckon!"

Felix looked angry. Bending down to his cupboard he took out a large, stiff white card on which he had set out in bold black letters a family tree.

"You're just bloody rude, you are!" he stated angrily, glowering at the speaker and addressing his words directly to him. "Just take a look at this," he went on, holding up the card. "This is Tom's family tree. The last name on there is Alf. Now look upwards above Alf. Alf's Dad is Jake and his Grandfather is Wilfred, Wilfred's Dad is Noble; his Grandfather was Claude, and his Great Grandfather is Pete. Pete's Dad is Sam and his Grandfather is Tom. So Tom is Alf's Grandfather's Great Grandfather's Grandfather, just like I said. You can see that's true. Even a bloody twit like you can see that!"

Felix paused a moment looking daggers at the quibbling questioner, then deliberately turned his attention away from the man and addressed his remarks to the audience as a whole, pointing out some further details shown on the card.

"Now that I've got this out to show that ignorant bugger over there," he said, "there are one or two things on here that might interest you.

You will notice that Tom's son, the one that's Pete's Dad, is called Sam. I named Tom's first son Sam, after Sam Donatello, when I first joined Carlo's Fairground early this year. Tom was with me when I came here, and all the others on that card are still alive and with me today—all except for Claude, Wilfred's Grandfather. That poor little sod was pecked up by a blackbird that flew through the door and whipped him off the table when we were trying him out as a jumper."

The reference to the sad fate of Claude raised a laugh among the spectators and lightened the mood somewhat. There was, however, no smile on Felix's face. The loss of one of his family under such tragic circumstances was clearly something which gave him no cause for amusement.

Looking a little pained, he propped up the card on the table, so that they could all have a look at it. It read:

FLEA FAMILY-TREE OF TOM (1927)		
GENERATIONS	**CHAMPION JUMPERS**	**Alf's link with Tom**
TOM	TOM	**GRANDFATHER (of Pete)**
Son (Sam) +		
Grandson (Pete)	PETE	**GREAT-GRANDFATHER (of Wilfred)**
Son (Claude ++ R.I.P.)		
Grandson (Noble)	NOBLE	
Son (Wilfred)		**GRANDFATHER (of Alf)**
Grandson (Jake)	JAKE	
Son (Alf)		**ALF**
(grandson)*	(GEMSTONE)**	**Alf's ancestors; read upwards (all living except Claude)**

LINEAGE OF FLEA LONG-JUMPING CHAMPIONS
FOR SUMMER SEASON 1927

This chart proves that:-
(a) Champions come every other generation
(b) Tom is Alf's Grandfather's Great-Grandfather's Grandfather

NOTES ON ENTRIES MARKED WITH SUBSCRIPTS:-

+ named after Sam Donatello * expected soon
++ killed in action   ** name for next champion

CERTIFIED CORRECT AS AT 31.8.1927
Signed: *FF* Felix Foden, qualified Flea-breeder, est. 1921

For a few moments the audience studied the card in silence. The little man with whom Felix had established a friendly rapport watched him anxiously, for he was uneasy. Felix looked sad and the compassionate man felt sure that the unseemly laughter about the death of Claude had upset him. He clearly thought the world of his special pedigree fleas so painstakingly reared, and was no doubt struggling with his emotions. So he put a thoughtful question to Felix to divert his mind from the tragedy and help him over the hump.

"I see you have pencilled in another champion called Gemstone, as Jake's grandson," he commented, referring to the chart. "Does that mean you've got him under training and he's set fair to become a champion?"

"Well, no, not exactly," Felix replied. "But Alf's wife is expecting, and I'm sure his first son will be a champion. Certain of it. And Fanny and I have decided we shall call him Gemstone, after Gemstone George who has been such a good friend to us since we joined Carlo's. I expect you've seen Gemstone George's gift stall over the other side of the Fairground, next to his wife Lily Rodway's Penny Roller outfit."

"Yes, I've seen it," confirmed the little man. "He's got some good stuff over there. And if Lily's his wife, then he's a lucky man. He's married to a real lady. I liked her. She seems very kind—a really nice lady."

Clearly, Lily Rodway had made a deep impression on the little man.

"She is that!" agreed Felix. "One of the best, she is. Everybody likes our Lily. She's everybody's friend around the Fairground."

This little exchange appeared to brighten up Felix very noticeably, but the improved atmosphere was not to last. The spoiler hadn't finished with Felix yet. He had been studying the card with a cynical smile on his face and could not resist having another dig at Felix. Maliciously he stuck his barbed needle in again.

"All that bullshit written out there doesn't prove anything, though, does it?" he said, in a sly, know-all way, his voice heavy with sarcasm. It was plain to everybody that his intention was to put the skids under Felix and embarrass him as much as he could. But he got rocked back on his heels!

"Of course it proves it!" countered Felix emphatically. "What kind of an idiot do you think would take the trouble to write that lot out if it were not true?"

Felix fixed the unpleasant interrupter with angry eyes. The question was obviously a direct challenge and the atmosphere within the cabin was suddenly highly charged. The gauntlet had been thrown down in no uncertain manner. There was only one answer to the question and without doubt it carried a high risk of repercussions if spoken. Felix was clearly very angry indeed. So the man, whose mouth was louder than his courage was strong, stayed silent, and the moment passed, leaving Felix as having had the last word.

Fanny was pleased the nasty man had backed off. She had listened to the exchange with mounting apprehension because—on very rare occasions—she had seen men needle Felix until he lost his cool, jumped over the rope, and slung a cynical sarcastic sceptic out on his over-extended neck. It was not something she liked to see happen.

Felix was a strong man, and sometimes Fanny wondered if the result of his having been bled over the years by countless hungry fleas might perhaps have had a beneficial effect upon him, in the same way as, according to what she had read, leeches are said to do. So far she had never seen Felix bested by aggressive customers, partly she thought, because fortunately Clever Dicks were so often cocky, bumptious, *little* men who made up for their lack of size by making a lot of noise. But she didn't like the happy atmosphere of their show being upset by troublemakers and she tried to encourage Felix to ignore them.

To give Felix his due, he did try hard to follow this advice, but Fanny knew that the present pest was pushing his luck.

However, all was now quiet again, and without further comment Felix put away the card, cleared his artificial lake off the table and was ready to get on with the next part of his programme.

"You're going to see something new now," he announced to the expectant audience. "I've started a brand new idea this year. I'm forming a new team of flying fleas. I got the idea at a flying display on Manston aerodrome last summer. I'd got my show down there amongst the sideshows, and some RAF flyers came in to see it.

One of the pilots was scratching about under his shirt and picked out a fine-looking flea. Of course everybody laughed at him, but he enjoyed the joke as much as they did. It's the first time I can ever remember somebody with an itch actually catching a flea during one of my shows. Trust the RAF to clock-up a first, even in a flea show!

Anyway, he asked me if I'd like to have it, and of course I accepted it gladly. Jumped at it, as you might say! It really was a grand-looking flea, a real top-notcher. Mind you, I would have expected that. Those young pilots are in the pink of health. They have to be, to do their job. A wonderfully healthy home for a flea one of those pilots makes. It would be hard to find a better one.

Well, that pilot told me the flea had been tormenting him for weeks. He said it was a crafty little blighter and he hadn't been able to catch it. It seemed the flea only bit him when he was airborne, so he could never get at it. When he got down to ground and stripped off, try as he might he couldn't find it, either on his body or in his clothes.

Then he had finally figured out what was happening. The flea was living in the lovely warm woolly lining of his leather flying jacket, buried deep in the wool, as free of being found as a fortunate flea could possibly be.

It was evident that the flea could tell when it was airborne, but how it determined this the pilot did not pretend to understand! But it obviously did know when it was off the ground, because when the pilot took off, the flea came out of the flying jacket, popped under his shirt for a good feed, then nipped back into the wool again when the plane came in to land.

Up aloft, the pilot could not possibly undress to ferret the flea out, and back on land the crafty little bloke was deeply hidden in the thick woolly lining. A very nice set-up from the flea's point of view: a comfortable home and top-class food! But it was no joke to the pilot. Got up his nose, it did, to be beaten like that. Bugged him something chronic, it did!

Anyway, he finally ran him to earth in my cabin. A fitting place for such a shrewd flea to be found—in here, among all my highly-talented fleas. The pilot reckoned the flea had slipped up that day at the Air Show because he had been taking off and landing, over and over again, so that the little perisher must have got thoroughly confused and didn't know whether it was arse-hole or breakfast time! He had everybody in the cabin in fits of laughter, telling them about the antics of his artful flea!"

Felix paused a moment or two and looked around the attentive faces of his patrons, who had followed his recollections with amused interest. Then he went on with his apparently true story of his encounter with the flea-bitten young pilot.

"When the pilot handed the flea over to me," Felix went on, "he said 'Here you are, Mr. Foden. You're welcome to him! He's yours and he comes with a full tank of fuel—he's just filled up from me this minute. He's bitten the hell out of me on my chest, under my arm!'

All the people laughed as he scratched about under his arm to relive the itch. A good sport that young pilot was! A real nice young bloke.

445

The he said something I thought was very interesting. He said he doubted whether the flea would settle down to life in my outfit because it had developed a passion for flying. And it had got a natural ability to tell *up* from *down*! If fleas had an Air Force, he reckoned that little fellow would make a first-class pilot, and probably, in time of war, become an ace Fighter Pilot.

He said what amazed him most was that the flea seemed to be immune from the effects of 'g-forces', as he called them, because it bit him when he was looping-the-loop; bit him when he was pulling out of a high-speed dive; and bit him when he was taking the tightest turn he could possibly do in his fighter plane! He just couldn't shake him off, no matter what he did. Everybody laughed at what he said. He made it sound like a war-time dog-fight between two fighter planes.

Anyway, he went on to say that when he was telling his mates in the Mess about the flea plaguing him, one of them said that he was not surprised the flea took no notice of the g-forces generated by their aerobatics, because he had read somewhere that when a flea takes off on a jump it generates an acceleration of over 200g!

I must say I didn't understand what he was talking about—for all I knew one 'g' could mean half a horse—but some of the people in the cabin seemed to know and they could hardly believe it. One know-all sort of a bloke said he certainly didn't believe it, because he thought a flea would black-out if it were fired off at 200g and be unconscious when it arrived. He reckoned it would hit the ground and ricochet off with a whine like an airgun pellet. But another young chap there, who struck me as knowing what he was talking about, said that watching the way my fleas jumped, and how far they travelled, he wouldn't be at all surprised to learn that the acceleration was as high as the RAF man had suggested.

I wouldn't know about any of that. But it set me thinking and gave me a good idea. I decided to make some flying machines for fleas to fly in. And I bred from that special ex-RAF flea with flying experience, using one of my very best woman fleas. A real flighty bit of stuff I chose for him, too. And he sure got stuck into her all right. Fair pounced on her he did. Truth to tell, he was probably sex-starved in that flying jacket. Hardly likely to have been any women in there for him to knock off. He'd have been the only flea in it, that's for sure.

They've done me proud, those two have. They've already raised me a small Air Force. Believe me I've started something exciting in the flea-show world. Mind you, it's early days yet. But what I've got at this early stage will surprise you, I bet!"

With that, Felix went to another cupboard under the table to bring out his first aircraft exhibit. As he crouched down he made an announcement.

"I thought I'd start with some of the early flying machines," he said. "The ones that have done something special. This one is a model of Bleriot's monoplane in which he crossed the Channel, back in the year 1909. Some of you, I expect, have been to see the place where he landed, up on the cliff tops near Dover Castle. Anyway, this is my Bleriot model."

He squatted down on his heels, took out his model, and got up to stand it with much pride on the green, cloth-covered table top. For good measure he had a picture of Bleriot's aeroplane actually in the air, taken as it passed over the seashore as it left France for England. The picture had been reproduced by a newspaper for sale to the public as a special feature, at the time of the historic flight.

Felix's model was remarkably like the photograph of Bleriot's No. XI monoplane. The very simple structure of this famous little plane with its 25 hp engine made it an ideal thing for Felix to craft. He built its slender, box-sectioned fuselage from fine-gauge silver wire, aided by his new-found friend Gemstone George. George had had a great deal of experience over the years in the delicate work of making brooches and costume jewellery for sale on his popular stall. Felix had much to thank him for, as was evident by his choice of Gemstone as the name of the next in the line of his long-jump champions.

The front half of the fuselage, the single wing, the tail and the rudder, were covered with doped fabric, the back section of the fuselage being just a skeletal open structure with its tapering four, longitudinal corner wires held in place by a series of wire-squares of diminishing size.

Underneath, set slightly back from the front, was the simple undercarriage with two wheels like tiny bicycle wheels. A similar, but rather smaller tail wheel, was positioned about one-third of the way along the fuselage from the tail-end, well clear of the tail plane.

Sitting in the cockpit—incongruously, but bearing the unmistakeable mark of the model's quirkish maker—was a grasshopper serving as a pilot. Its green body, leaning slightly forward, was rigidly stuck just behind the trailing edge of the wing. Its posture seemed to be one of intense concentration.

In front of the pilot, with its axle mounted dead-centre inside the fuselage, was one of Felix's flea-motors. Necessarily, in order to mount the propeller on the front of the motor's shaft, the flea's tread-drum had to lie along the axis of the fuselage. This meant that the flea itself was sideways on to the pilot—not a matter of great importance although Felix would have preferred the flea to be looking towards the front, rather than sideways along the wing. Not that it really mattered since the flea was part of the engine and not the pilot!

So far in his development of flea-motors, Felix had not yet managed to solve the problem of providing a mechanism to drive a shaft at right-angles to the axis of rotation of the drum. All his attempts had been frustrated because they introduced too much friction, so that the added load on the flea left it either helplessly immobile, or at best needing a push-start, even when fitted in a machine of very light loading.

A flea would only 'run' if its legs felt relatively free from restraint. In discussing this problem with Fanny, when she had been watching him experimenting, trying to devise a satisfactory system, Felix had explained that a flea had too much common sense than to risk a heart attack by struggling too hard to push a drum round. A flea, he said to her, was very well aware of its own limitations and in this respect had the edge over most human beings.

With a call of 'chocks away', Felix pulled a little stop-wire brake away from the drum. Immediately he did this, the freeing of the drum under its feet prompted the flea to start 'running forwards' as fast as it could go so that the little propeller began to turn very pleasingly at the front of the aircraft.

Felix had the monoplane suspended by two lengths of thread attached to a small brass ring, which, with the coiled thread, was stored in the fuselage. He picked up the ring and lifted the little aeroplane in the air, contriving to move his hand forwards as the plane rose up, to simulate a take-off. The two threads were attached to the fuselage either side of its centre point so that the aircraft hung level. He then gently caused the plane to swing in a circle on the end of the threads, so that it flew round and round, with its propeller spinning quite fast as the captive flea worked away tirelessly at its important task.

"There we are," said Felix, with obvious satisfaction and pride. "That's how Bleriot looked when he crossed the English Channel on the 25th July 1909. I was twenty-two years old at the time, and went down to Dover from London by train to look at his aeroplane before it was taken away.

"He wouldn't thank you for saying he looked like a bloody grasshopper!"

447

commented the smart aleck, bouncing back yet again in his supremely insufferable way.

This time his remark was greeted by just a few sniggers and was totally ignored by Felix, winning another silent inner battle to restrain himself from clouting the big-mouth to shut him up once and for all.

"Not many people actually saw that plane," he went on. "It was a marvellous little thing. I'm rather proud to think I was one of the few who got near enough to have a good look at it. It was the first aeroplane of any kind that I had ever seen, never mind the first one to fly across the English Channel."

"The same goes for me," commented Arthur from SKWEC. "I cycled with two mates from Littlebrook down to Deal, and along the cliff-top road to Dover Castle to have a look at it. It looked a very flimsy affair to me at the time. We thought the man must have had a lot of courage to cross the sea in that thing. As a matter of fact I've a copy of that photograph you have there at home to this day."

The fascinating little aeroplane attracted much attention from the audience as it flew gently round, manipulated by Felix on its thread.

Felix's grasshopper pilot added a whimsical touch to the appearance of the well-made model. Many of those watching that day were to carry with them for many years to come a picture in their memories of this bizarre miniature aeroplane, piloted by a grasshopper, powered by a flea, and proudly presented to his public by the po-faced, eccentric, beguiling proprietor of Felix Foden's Flea Circus. So unlikely were the memories that to some it seemed they must have imagined them in a dream long ago.

At length, watched in silence by those in the cabin, Felix, manipulating the two threads with his fingers to angle the aircraft downwards, brought it down to land gracefully on the green-topped table and taxied it expertly across to the far corner where he parked it—with its propeller still spinning—facing the audience.

Curious though its occupants were, it looked strangely realistic from a distance, parked, for all the world like a real aeroplane, on the perimeter of the mowed grass of a typical airfield.

Unexpectedly, it drew a spontaneous clap of appreciation from the crowd, something quietly noted with pleasure by Felix, who had spent a long time on this, his first model of a flying machine.

"We'd better save petrol where we can," he said after a few moments, and bent down over the machine to apply the simple brake to the flea's drum. This gave the stout-hearted living engine a period of enforced rest, and ensured that it would function just as well in the next, and probably last, show of what had been a very busy day for it.

"The next aeroplane is another historic one," announced Felix, bending down to his storage cupboard. "Let's see if any of you recognise it!"

His confidence to make this virtual challenge was based upon his experience so far of the reactions of his patrons in this first season of including a small display of flying machines in his show.

On the table he now placed an equally well-made but considerably larger and more complicated little aeroplane. It was a twin-engine biplane. Irrespective of the 'flea connection', the model itself immediately commanded the applause of his audience for it was cleverly crafted and looked very realistic. It had not been there more than a few moments when somebody in the audience correctly identified it.

"I reckon that's a model of Alcock and Brown's Vickers-Vimy Transatlantic aeroplane," he stated confidently. "The one in which they crossed the Atlantic in 1919, making the first non-stop flight across the Atlantic ever made by an aeroplane. It was a converted RAF Bomber, surely?"

"Got it in one," confirmed Felix, secretly delighted that once again his model had

448

proved realistic enough to be recognised for what it was intended to be. Consulting a card which he kept with the model, he read out some information about the flight.

"The plane went from St. John's Newfoundland, to Clifden, County Galway, Ireland, on the 14th to 15th June 1919, piloted by Captain John Alcock and navigated by Lieutenant Arthur Whitten Brown. Distance 1890 miles; average speed 118 miles per hour; total time 16 hours 27 minutes. They won the Daily Mail prize of £10,000 for the first flight across the Atlantic in a heavier-than-air machine. Both men were knighted shortly afterwards, but sadly Sir John Alcock was killed that December in an air crash while flying from London to Paris."

Felix read this piece of aviation history with evident personal pride as though, through his production of a flea-driven model of the award-winning biplane, he identified himself with the famous pair of pioneers.

Unwilling to allow Felix to get away with any reflected glory from this reported triumph, remote though Felix's connection with it was, his sneering smart aleck critic felt it necessary to intervene.

"Yes, they may have been the first to fly non-stop across the Atlantic in an aeroplane rather than an airship," he said, apparently reluctant even to acknowledge the event, "but they came that side to this, with the prevailing wind behind them, don't forget. All they had to do was sit there in that string-bag and get blown across!"

This was too much for Felix to stomach and he was quick to register his extreme annoyance at this small-minded, quibbling attempt to belittle the achievement of his newly adopted, brave British airmen. He couldn't stand mutely by and allow his fellow flying experts to be debunked in this way.

"What a miserable little bugger you are!" he said with obvious distaste. "So they had a tail-wind part of the way. They also had some bloody awful weather and were lucky to survive. It took guts to set out on that journey. And they *were* the first to achieve it. Blokes like you get on my wick. You never do anything yourselves but you spend your time sneering at other people. If I didn't have a touch of gout I'd help you to create a new record yourself!"

Felix paused a moment, glowering at the man, weighing up what best to do with the pest if he were able to boot him up the backside without pain to his highly sensitive right foot. The decision made, he then went on to describe an appropriate penalty kick.

"I'd like to grab you by the scruff of your neck," he said, speaking slowly and deliberately, "frog-match you to Land's End, and see if I could kick you up the arse hard enough to get you across the Atlantic against the prevailing wind. That would make you the first lump of shit to fly solo non-stop across the Atlantic from East to West. At least if I failed I'd have the satisfaction of drowning you and shutting up your big mouth once and for all. A lot of people would be pleased about that, I bet."

This very annoyed reaction from Felix was greeted with a laugh and a loud ironic cheer from most of the audience, who were conscious of the fact that the rather nasty, cocky, carping, creep of a man seemed to resent the success of the flea-man's show, and was losing no opportunity to debunk and needle him. They were getting fed up with the way he kept upsetting the smooth running of the show.

But Fanny was not very happy about the unseemly nature of her husband's comments, though she knew full well that the man was making Felix's work hard going and he deserved to be slapped down.

However, the attention of everybody was soon diverted back to the newly-introduced biplane, because Felix began preparing the plane for takeoff, and they examined it with interest.

The aeroplane was much larger than his Bleriot model, and was fitted with two of

449

his flea-motors driving four-bladed propellers set back one on each side of its broad projecting nose, which stuck well out in front of the wings.

Side by side in the cockpit sat the pilot and his co-pilot/navigator. The tiny figures, representing Alcock and Brown, had been fashioned by Fanny from small birthday cake wax candles. These she had spent a long time carving, painting and partially clothing, down to the waist, in an attempt to make them as realistic and as in-scale as possible. Like Felix she had worked from newspaper photographs of the plane, reproduced in books about this and other famous flying machines.

Felix, though grateful to Fanny for making this contribution to the new model, was secretly not all that happy about it. As a showman he favoured his habit of having insects as representatives of humans in his models. Apart from their whimsical appeal to the audience, he had a feeling that his insects had the edge over modelled human beings because they were creatures that had once lived before being permanently taken out of circulation and petrified in a coating of clear varnish to man his models.

Perversely he was also sure that his fleas derived some psychological comfort from the presence near them of other members of the insect population. Naturally he did not voice these reservations. It would have been churlish and hurtful to have done so, and that would have been out of character, for—despite his free use of euthanasia on failing fleas—he liked to think that he had the reputation of being a kindly man who wouldn't hurt a fly, much less a fully-functioning flea, and certainly not his wife Fanny who was cherished by him even more than his fleas, albeit only marginally so!

As with the Bleriot plane, the flea-drums had to be in line with the propeller shafts, so placing the suspended fleas treading them at right-angles to the fuselage. This left them looking along the wings, which he couldn't help feeling was rather unfair to them since they were the stars of the show.

The broad, fabric-covered, rectangular-shaped pairs of wings were supported by four pairs of taper-ended struts each side of the fuselage, with bracing wires connected in the form of a series of X-ties along the front and back of the wings. Curved-ended ailerons were mounted on the backs of the wings, projecting out a little further than the squared, leading edges of the broad wings.

The four-bladed propellers on the ends of the flea-drum axles stood out in front of the hexagonal grills that Felix had fitted to simulate the ends of the engine cowlings. Between the wings the two fleas could be seen patiently waiting with their feet on the two drums—perfectly still because the locked drums prevented any productive, forward-walking movement of their feet.

Beneath the wings, and positioned directly under the engines, were pairs of sturdy black-tyred wheels, neatly mounted on simple undercarriages. These were so placed on the Vickers-Vimy biplanes to support the weight of the aircraft at the optimum points.

Under the box-shaped tail, with its two tail-planes and two vertical rudders, was a skid rather than wheels. The tail on these planes quickly lifted as the crafts began their take-off runs, and conversely sat back on the ground again only just before they came to a standstill on landing. Skids were found perfectly adequate for practice. Despite this, Felix had been tempted to fabricate his own design of tail-wheel because he preferred a wheel rather than a skid, but thought better of it in the interests of preserving the accuracy of the model. However, because of its long protruding nose, the plane was fitted with a nose wheel and this he had faithfully reproduced.

Again, as with his Bleriot model, Felix had fitted suspension threads tied to a brass ring so that he could lift the aeroplane and keep its stance under control. With this larger plane he had found it better to have three lines to his lifting thread, rather than two as with his Bleriot.

One of these three was attached to the tail-end of the fuselage and the other two at the tips of the upper of the biplanes' main wings.

Ready now for the off, with calls of "Start the port engine," then "Start the starboard engine," Felix pulled out the drum brakes from first one engine, then the other. Simultaneously with the freeing of the drums beneath their feet, the two fleas started 'running', so that the two four-bladed propellers, one after the other, began spinning away merrily.

Then, with his customary call of "Chocks away", Felix—manipulating his threads skilfully—ran the aeroplane forwards along the green surface of the table, lifted its tail off the ground, and made a realistic takeoff. He had watched enough aircraft take off during displays at Manston aerodrome, on the Isle of Thanet, to be able to make his efforts look good.

Once airborne, he did as he had before, and made the plane fly in circles about the table-top, even, on this occasion—by dint of his three-thread suspension—contriving to make the little aircraft bank as it turned. It made a captivating sight.

After a little while he brought the machine in to land, making a touch-down near one end of the table and controlling the plane so that its nose-wheel reached the surface just before the four main wheels. Then, slowing down, he allowed the tail to drop and taxied the plane over the airfield before bringing it to a halt, where it parked professionally alongside the smaller Bleriot model monoplane. He let the propellers continue to turn for a few moments and then finally stopped the engines by inserting his simple drum-brakes.

This impressive performance brought a round of spontaneous applause from the audience again, something which once more gave Felix a great deal of pleasure because his venture into the world of flying-machines was very much a new, untried field of interest. To him it seemed that human fleas, like their hosts, were taking to the air with enthusiasm, and were serving him well.

There was one more model in this new category of flying machines he had tucked away to show his appreciative audience. He had kept it until last because he knew from experience that it aroused a great deal of interest and amusement.

Ducking down behind the table again, he came up with a plywood building, unmistakably an aircraft hanger, not only because of its typical proportions, but because it stood on a green-painted baseboard in the corner of which stood a wind-sock, stiffened internally by a wire frame to make it appear as though it were blowing out in the wind. Painted matt black, as were so many hangers, especially on military airfields, the building measured about two feet by one foot; standing some fifteen inches high at the highest point of its shallow-pitched ridged roof.

"This will surprise you! I think you will like this!" announced Felix, without preamble, lifting off the ridge roof and placing it out of the way under the table.

Projecting through the long side facing the audience, two dowel rods could be seen passing through half-inch holes near the top. They were positioned about one-third of the way in from each end.

Felix put one hand inside the building, apparently holding something down, and then pulled out the two dowel rods from his side of the hanger. Then, looking towards the intensely interested audience to study their reaction to what they were about to see, he took away his hand to release what was inside.

To the astonishment of the watchers, out of the building rose a model airship, a lighter-than-air flying machine which gradually ascended to the accompaniment of a regular clicking noise coming from inside the hanger. To some of the audience—certainly to the ears of Joe, Arthur and Terry from SKWEC—it was evident that the thin tie-cord attached to the rising airship was unwinding from a ratchet-controlled drum, for the sound was clearly that of a spring-loaded pawl riding on a toothed wheel.

Under the tightly inflated, cream-coloured, cigar-shaped body of the airship, suspended by a number of threads attached to both sides of the envelope, which had its underside covered from end to end with a stuck-on, fine-meshed net, was a rod boom made from a strong wooden knitting needle with its ends cut-off. The net was recognised by some of the ladies present as having been made from pieces of hair net, for it had a mesh plainly typical of these.

Beneath the boom, which was nearly as long as the inflated envelope itself, was fixed the crew and passengers' cabin, looking on this model rather like a long, open-topped boat.

Towards the front end of the boom, fastened beneath it, was one of Felix's flea-motors driving a propeller facing forwards—though not at present turning. At the tail-end of the boom was a rudder, and between this and the cabin was a second flea-motor. Curiously, at the moment, the propeller driven by this one faced sideways towards the audience. Like the first motor it was not at present running.

Side by side at the front of the cabin sat two leather-helmeted wasps, bending forwards slightly and clearly intently engaged in the business of controlling the airship's flight. Behind them, sitting in pairs, were six honey bees wearing tiny, flat-topped, navy blue Royal Navy sailors' hats made by Fanny.

The tail-end of the airship had a fabric-covered end-piece contrived to look like tail fins. Its primary purpose was to conceal the tied-up end of the long, snub-nosed, inflated rubber balloon, which otherwise would have spoilt the realistic appearance of the airship.

As for the problem of filling it with gas, Felix again had his friend Gemstone George to thank for solving this. George sold gas-filled balloons on his stall, having equipped himself with the necessary pressurized gas-cylinders to enable him to sell a variety of multi-coloured balloons, which children loved to have because of the novelty of being able to carry around lighter-than air balloons that strained to escape up into the air from the string by which they held them. Many were subsequently let go to fly high in the air and disappear into the distance, carrying self-addressed labels bearing a message which requested the finder to return them stating where they had been found. Some came back from across the sea, a great thrill to the young owners who had released them.

When the airship had risen to a point where the cabin was level with his face, Felix reached down inside the hanger and stopped his homemade Meccano winch from turning. Then he removed the drum-brakes from the two flea-motors, and immediately he did so the two propellers started to turn, in the same way as had happened in the two aeroplanes seen before. Having set the engines going, Felix reached down and released the winch to allow the intriguing-looking airship to rise higher until it unwound all the twine on the winch. This left it hovering about eighteen inches above his head.

So far Felix had made no comment about the model, leaving the silent people to gaze at it with obvious fascination. On the side of the envelope, near the front, painted on it in bold black letters was:

ROYAL NAVY H.M. AIRSHIP SS MkII

This prompted the first question about the model from a member of the audience who wanted to know what SS stood for.

"She's a model of an early experimental airship built during the war as a Submarine Spotter," Felix explained. "Built to the design of a well-known Airship Maker from Cardiff in Wales. Perhaps you have heard of him. E.T. Willows was his name. Ernest Willows. He was killed last year in August 1926 flying a captive balloon at Kempton, Bedford. You may have read about it in the papers. He had been taking people up for rides at two shillings a go, to a height of 600 feet, tethered to an anchor line.

On his last ride the wind got up suddenly when he was at about 100 feet and the trailing line snarled up in a tree. The force ripped part of the balloon's net apart and Ernest Willows with his four passengers crashed to the ground. They were all killed. Two married couples were in the balloon's basket and Ernie Willows was riding on a hammock seat above the basket. The balloon broke free from the netting, blew away and disappeared."

"I remember reading about that," said a lady in the audience. "What a tragedy it was to die like that. After all the dangerous things he'd done developing airships, then to be killed in a balloon giving people joy-rides. What an ironic twist of fate!"

"Yes," agreed Felix, "It was very sad for such a gifted, brave man and four other people to die on a simple joy-ride like that. Fanny's brother, who lives in Cardiff, sent her a local paper at the time, and I read a lot about his early pioneering work with simple airships. It gave me the idea of building this model based upon some of the pictures he sent us. It seemed a simple one to start on."

"Were they really like that?" asked Arthur of SKWEC. "Seems pretty crude compared with modern ones, doesn't it?"

"Yes, that's a fair model of the original," Felix assured him. "That simple idea of a boom to hang the cabin on—or car as some people call them—made it easy for me to copy. But next I'm going to build a model of H.M. Airship R.34, which was the first lighter-than-air craft to cross the Atlantic from Scotland to Long Island, America, in July 1919.

But that's a bit more complicated. It was a rigid airship, whereas the Willows ones were non-rigid, and I could make a model, like this one here, simply by blowing up a sausage-shaped balloon."

At this stage in the serious discussion there was a sudden note of great hilarity introduced into the proceedings, initiated by a loud comment from a voice at the back.

"I don't know about a balloon," he was heard to say, to his mate standing with him. "That's no kid's balloon he's got pumped up with gas there. It's a bloody French Letter!"

There was a howl of laughter at this clearly audible observation, which put a temporary stop to the serious proceedings. The truth of the categorical statement was plain to see, and indeed others had spotted it before and were quietly smiling at the improbable sight they were witnessing, when the loud announcement from behind released them from their politely suppressed amusement, to join in the general laughter.

It had been the ever-practical Boris from SKWEC who first had suggested to Felix that he would do better to replace his original, brightly-coloured, sausage-shaped child's balloon, with this much more durable, much higher quality, and quite fortuitously much more appropriately-shaped and proportioned, device.

Felix, maintaining his po-faced profile, neither acknowledged nor denied this unsolicited observation; indeed he showed no sign of having heard it at all. He just busied himself making corrective adjustments to the model by slipping small hanging bags of leadshot sideways along the boom to get the aircraft nicely horizontal, instead of flying inclined slightly nose downwards, as it had been before. It was a system of levelling that he had read about in his study of early airships.

It was some time before the merriment subsided. Once the unrestrained laughter had started, the sheer incongruity of the bizarre model hovering in front of them, gave some of the fascinated audience a difficult-to-control, extenuated attack of the giggles.

At length the laughter died down, but not for long. Felix was just on the point of picking up where he'd left off when a question innocently put by a middle-aged man still grinning widely at the blatantly obvious true nature of the model Willows airship he was gazing at as it drifted lazily in the air above Felix's head, drew an answer which caused an even greater eruption of laughter and which was a long time dying down again.

"Who are those two blokes sitting up front supposed to be?" the grinning man asked.

"The one on the left is Captain Condom, the pilot," Felix informed him, pausing a little for his words to sink in, his face utterly bland and expressionless, "and the other one is Flying Officer Spunkstopper, co-pilot and navigator."

Mention of the Captain's name led to a suppressed, stifled snigger of delight from a small number of those present, though why it should do so the rest did not know, for they did not recognise, nor see anything funny in the unusual name. It was not a word that enjoyed common currency in the locality. But the introduction seconds later to the Captain's companion led to an immediate roar of laughter from almost everybody there, allowing the self-conscious but more word-wise sniggerers to enjoy the release of a hearty laugh. The 'flypaper lady', though, was not amused. She winced with embarrassment at the first name and nearly choked with horror at the second. But for the moment she held her peace.

Felix, his brow furrowed, contrived to look puzzled—even a little hurt—by this explosion of laughter, demonstrating yet again his capacity for enigmatic and unpredictable behaviour.

Disdainful and unsmiling he managed to convey an air of superior, lofty disapproval, if not indeed of parental-like, pained disappointment at this unseemly reaction both to the origin of his airship's envelope and the names of its experienced flying crew. He clearly wanted no part in this low-minded levity.

So successful was he in displaying this detached superior demeanour, and so convincing were his reactions, that a dignified, professional-looking man, a solitary figure standing alone behind the gathering, had the capricious thought that somebody could well have scripted part of Felix's show for him, writing in an almost malicious exploitation of the flea-man's ingenuous character.

Either that, reasoned the discerning man, or Felix had a talent which could have won him a highly successful stage career as a serious actor had his natural ability been spotted at an early age by somebody capable of recognising an infant prodigy, of exceptional latent potential, when they saw one!

On balance, he favoured the latter conclusion and subsequently the more he saw, the more convinced he became, that Felix had profound hidden depths.

The observer was not the first person, nor would he be the last, to be thoroughly confounded by this strange mixture of a man who seemed to combine coarse crudity and incredible naivety with a hidden, penetrating, intellectual ability which seemed to enable him to play with his audience's reactions with the subtlety of a gifted conductor of music, capable of cleverly conjuring his own unique response from an orchestra.

Incongruous though it may seem in those surroundings, the visitor was a Dean of the Church of England, though very much at present a man in mufti, most certainly not wishing to be recognised.

A student of human nature, the Dean was a successful novelist, but as such known only by an unlikely pseudonym, except to his publisher who had been a staunch friend since their University days together at Oxford.

The thoughtful visitor had chanced upon Foden's Flea Circus, and, ever ready to discover new material, entered the show on impulse. On holiday from his responsibilities in the industrial North, and staying in Folkestone, he was doing what he enjoyed most, snooping around incognito, free of the restrictive influence normally imposed upon him at home by his clerical garments and high-profile religious office. He spent his time seeking new slants on everyday life to inspire fresh ideas to fuel his imaginative writings. The County of Kent was a favourite hunting-ground for these anonymous covert wanderings.

There was a second compelling reason why he often visited this south-eastern corner of England. He loved the Cathedral at Canterbury, but when there he again always preserved his anonymity, merging unnoticed with the throng of tourists. He nursed a private ambition to reach what would represent for him the ultimate fulfilment in his ecclesiastical career, by landing the job of Dean of Canterbury. It was more than just a possible dream, for, by the devious workings of the Church of England's grapevine, he had good reason to believe that the post might well be his in the not too distant future.

Meanwhile, for these brief holiday periods, he enjoyed the best of both worlds. He was well aware that this presence in the Flea Circus show would not exactly endear or recommend him either to the Archbishop of York, whom he knew so well, or the incumbent Archbishop of Canterbury who was a formidable, starchy figure—too remote and absorbed in his theological world even to know there were human beings whose lives were devoted to making lowly fleas perform bizarre tricks for the entertainment of members of his Christian flock.

Strangely, in stark contrast, the Dean, a man of singularly unlikely personal interests, philosophical beliefs, and political convictions for one of his profession and standing, felt quite at home in his present surroundings. He did not sense any personal feeling of incongruity in his being there. On the contrary, he was thoroughly enjoying it, rather different though the proceedings were from the solemn ceremonies and dignified happenings that were normally his daily concern!

In Felix, the Dean had in fact discovered a fellow spirit, a truly eccentric-eccentric, and though Felix did not know it, nor was ever to learn of it, in this particular show his actions and behaviour underwent a searching scrutiny that far exceeded any individual attention to which previously he had been subjected during the whole of his accomplished career as a flea expert.

The man of God and the man of Fleas shared something in common, a bizarre and sometimes outrageous sense of humour, often coupled with a wilful disregard of propriety.

Neither the Archbishop of Canterbury, Primate of All England, nor Sam Donatello, Proprietor of Carlo's Fairground Company, witnessing the two from such totally different viewpoints, at opposite ends of the social spectrum, would ever have considered in their wildest dreams that two such different men, of two so remotely different professions, could possibly have anything in common except that they both itched when bitten by fleas. But now, in close proximity, the one watched the other with growing respect.

Having established—much to the amusement of everybody—the identity of the two intensely-occupied figures riding in the front of the airship's car, the questioner then enquired about the other passengers sitting bolt upright in pairs behind the impressive two-man crew. The Dean listened with great amusement.

"And who are those blokes sitting behind Captain Condom and Flying Officer Spunkstopper?" he asked, causing another ripple of gleeful laughter by his carefully precise enunciation of the two names. "They look like sailors."

This second bold pronouncement of the two names was too much for the flypaper lady. Still smarting with resentment at her public dressing-down by Felix, and smouldering with suppressed indignation at the brazen effrontery of the crude man in introducing such sleazy, distasteful references to unmentionable sexual devices and practices, she could contain herself no longer. She blew her top!

"Oh! Oh! Really! This is too much! This is absolutely disgusting! I can't stand any more of this filth! You . . . you . . . you should be downright ashamed of yourself," she exploded, glaring with fury at Felix who had been on the point of answering the man's enquiry, but now studied the red-faced, blustering lady with his eyebrows raised questioningly—his expression one of mild interest rather than showing surprise or concern. To the watchers he seemed to be looking at her in much the same way as a scientist might be expected to regard an interesting specimen. She also registered this, and up went her blood pressure another notch or two.

"To think," she continued, winding herself up into a state where she seemed to have difficulty in controlling herself and getting the words out, "to think that you charge people money to come into this . . . this . . . this awful place, to listen to this . . . this . . utter depravity . . . really . . . really . . . you should be locked up! I am not going to stay in this awful place a moment longer! This is dreadful! . . . dreadful!"

All eyes now on her, the room in silence except for her huffing and puffing, she now tossed her head back, assumed an expression of utter outrage and flounced her way to the door.

As she opened the door, Felix called to her so that she paused on the threshold to look back at him.

"Excuse me, Madam," he said politely, in a mild voice so totally at variance with her own that she thought she was about to receive a public apology. "May I suggest you use warm soapy water?"

"What an earth do you mean?" she snapped. "What are you talking about, for heaven's sake?"

"You'll be wanting to save the lives of those poor flies struggling to escape from your 'death-by-slow-starvation' system," Felix said helpfully. "When you have picked them off, may I suggest you try bathing them in warm soapy water to remove your diabolical glue?" He hesitated a moment, his brow furrowed by seemingly genuine concern, and then added. "But if you can't get them free, I beg you to be kind to them like I am to my dying fleas, and clout them with a mallet. Please don't just leave them there to die, like you have been doing! That would be too cruel! I couldn't bear the thought of that!"

For a few moments the outraged lady stood open-mouthed, transfixed and speechless in the doorway—spluttered as if to reply—gave it up as a bad job—and slammed the door shut so that the flimsy cabin shook.

"Goodbye, Madam," called Felix. "Peace be with you. And with your flies! Poor benighted little bastards!"

There was a good deal of laughter from his astonished audience at this little exchange of pleasantries.

"She must be sickening for something," commented Felix sympathetically. "I pity any flea that sucks up a gutful of *her* blood! It will pickle its liver and poison its poor little piccaninnies!"

So saying, he returned to the business in hand and answered the man's question.

"You asked me about the six passengers in that car," he said, addressing himself to the questioner. "You are quite right. They are indeed sailors. In fact they are carefully selected Royal Navy matelots with exceptionally good eyesight and a good head for heights, under training as Submarine Spotters. That makes eight pairs of eyes up there, all searching the sea for Submarines!"

He looked around at the audience, waiting for this impressive piece of information to sink in, and then added a further military comment for their edification.

"Not much escapes that amount of eyeball power!" he said emphatically. "Put the wind up the Jerries, that did, knowing that when they came up for air there were all those eyes up above to lock in on them and call up the Bombers and Destroyers to blast them out of the sea. It buggered up their little game nicely, that did!"

After delivering this brief talk on naval anti-submarine tactics, Felix directed attention to some features of the Airship itself.

"These two engines are interesting," he said. "The one in front gives most of the power to move the ship through the air. But, if you look, it can be tilted up or down by quite an amount too. That enables the Pilot to give extra lift to the airship to make it climb faster or higher, or when swung the other way it helps it to come down again. Neat that, I think."

Felix then demonstrated this facility by carefully twisting the suspension carrying the front flea-motor. He had devised a simple way of giving the mounting this freedom of movement in the vertical plane.

"How about the rear engine?" somebody asked. "That's pointing sideways. That seems odd!"

"That's another Willows special," explained Felix proudly. "That engine is called a steering engine. It helps to change the direction the airship is pointing in, especially when it is not going fast enough through the air for the rudder to have much effect. The Pilot has control of the direction the propeller points, and that causes the tail to swing round."

Again Felix had been able to make provision for the flea-motor to be twisted manually on its mounting, this time in the horizontal plane, and was able to demonstrate this to his audience.

"If you keep still, and don't blow on the airship," he explained, "providing there's no draught in the room, even that tiny little flea on the rear-end motor can set up enough power to twist the airship gently to make it point another way. Have a look. I'll see if I can show you."

Felix asked those nearest to the table to move back a bit, so that breathing—or worse still discreet deliberate blowing—didn't affect the action. He had known bloody-minded people to upset the performance by slyly blowing the airship about. On occasions he had known cigarette or pipe smokers who had craftily employed their innocent puffing to make covert attempts to concentrate the direction of their puffs to see if they could make the airship go the opposite way to that in which he clearly meant it to go. Watchful for these potential acts of sabotage, Felix gently prepared the airship for his demonstration of flea-motor turning power.

Holding the airship with one hand to steady it, he twisted the flea-motor's mounting through 180° so that the propeller now faced away from the audience. While doing so he gradually twisted the airship slightly so that it was no longer in line with the table-top but had its nose pointed to the rear corner of the cabin. This wound up the vertical suspending twine a little bit, an unobtrusive way of helping his tail-end steering flea to perform its duty!

All now being ready, he asked everybody to hold their breaths for a moment or two while he let the airship go. Slowly it turned back to its original position and overshot it a bit, bringing its nose round towards the audience. Before the natural untwisting action of the twine made it turn back again—which would have demonstrated all too clearly that the flea was not achieving much beyond exercising its muscles—he reached out to hold the ship still with one hand, so marking the end of the turning operation.

Then he rotated the steering motor to make the propeller face forwards, and as he did so, unnoticed by his audience, he quietly took the opportunity to twist the airship so that it was once again square on to the table.

"When the Pilot turns the steering propeller this way using his control cable," he explained, "the steering motor can help the front driving-motor to pull the airship along."

Then, rotating the steering motor to point the propeller backwards, he added, "And this way round the Pilot can use it to work against the front propeller, and in light winds, with practice, he can balance the two propellers to make the airship stand still so that its observers can keep a watch on the water below, waiting for a submarine they know is down there to pop up to the surface. If you notice," he added blithely, "Captain Condom is doing just that right now. The airship is hovering in one place, just like I said!"

His claim was indeed true, for the model was quite still, pointing along the table as it had been when it had first risen from its hanger with both its engines switched off.

The airship was truly enormous compared with the tiny fleas powering its engines, and in reality the slightest draught prevented them from in any way influencing the behaviour of the floating model, which moved about arbitrarily in the breeze, however hard they pedalled their drums.

But Felix was not without hope. He had found that when the air was utterly still in the cabin, the spinning propellers could in fact create enough airflow to affect the airship very slightly. He had a fair idea that if he used a series of five, two-flea motors mounted underneath his proposed new model H.M. Airship R.34, employing a total of ten flea-powers, he might be able to make it fly quite well. Anyway, he reasoned, there was no harm in trying. If when built it didn't work, he knew full well that he could make up for its deficiencies by the judicious use of his well-developed sleight-of-hand. Over the years he had become quite an accomplished conjuror in cunningly helping his tiny performers achieve the seemingly impossible. But to give them their due, they were phenomenally strong for their size and could work wonders without any help from him at all.

Even if his 10 F.P. ship, the R.34, did need a small contribution of manpower to aid its ten flea-powers, he knew it would look fascinating once he'd got it finished and flying, with five propellers proudly spinning. He and Gemstone George had already inflated the envelope—the largest one available in the range sold very discreetly as a profitable sideline in a local barber's shop. The barber had referred to it as his buck-Matelot Mk.II OS Special, an ultra-strong model of long-proven pedigree and performance.

It was an impressive-looking beast, and they were currently busily engaged, when they could spare the time, in marking out on its surface a lattice network of horizontal and circumferential lines to simulate the typical framework of a rigid airship. The presence of this framework could often be seen from the outward appearance of such airships, since the long, cylindrical, gas-containing body of these more sophisticated airships was made by doped fabric stretched so very tightly over the inner lightweight structure that its form was revealed.

To establish a rigid, non-floppy airship looking more like the real thing, they were going to cement three stiff rods along the underside of the envelope, one central and the others suitably spaced either side of centre. This would also provide the means of attachment necessary for the suspension of the cabin and the five, twin-flea motors driving the propellers.

Before finally committing themselves to the fitting of this superstructure, they intended to try out a suggestion made by Boris that they deflate the envelope, turn it inside out, and re-inflate it. This would put their perfectly symmetrical, black framework lines inside the rubber—perhaps making the airship look even more realistic, provided their Indian ink markings showed through adequately. Though not imperative it seemed worth a try, especially as Felix intended to make others in the future and wanted them to look as realistic as possible. There was something about models floating in the air which seemed to hold a special attraction to his audience, one which he himself very much shared.

It was time to put the R.N. Submarine Spotter type SS Mk.II away, and Felix prepared to do so. He reached inside the hanger, reversed the ratchet on his winch to its wind-in position, took out a long-shafted handle which he inserted through a hole in the rear wall of the hanger to locate in a socket on the winch, and started to wind down the airship. The spring-loaded pawl on the winch clicked away sharply as he did so, and when he stopped winding, having got the ship down to eye level, the ratchet device prevented the twine from unwinding so that the airship stayed still just in front of him.

"You did a good job there, fellers," said Felix to the two fleas who were still working away at their drums, "but it's time you came down for a rest."

With that he stopped the motors with the drum brake-rods, and wound the model down until it disappeared inside the hanger. After inserting the two dowel rods to hold the airship down, he took out the winding handle, set the winch ready for the next flight, reached down beneath the table to pick up the hanger roof, and slotted it into place. Fanny then helped him to replace the building, on its self-contained base, into its storage place under the table.

Now approaching the end of his main programme, Felix glanced at the clock to see what time he had left before deciding what else he would show his appreciative audience. On busy days there were those amongst the showmen in the Fairground who were all too ready to cut short the time devoted to each group of punters in order to whip as many through as possible to cash in while the going was good.

Felix could never be accused of being one of these. If anything he inclined the other way and appeared reluctant to call an end to a session when he knew he had captured the keen interest of those watching him. In the long run this probably worked to his advantage, for it was generally agreed by people who had been to his show that he gave very good value for money, and the word spread.

One thing was certainly true. People left Felix's cabin with plenty to talk about, and he probably contributed more to the sum total of their Fairground memories than any other individual show or experience, with the exception perhaps of the much smaller number of those very deeply impressed by their experience with Dame Crystal Star. The Flea-man and the Fortune Teller were both, in their fields, rather special practitioners of their learned professions.

Fanny, aware of his tendency to over-run his time, kept a watchful eye on things and made a habit at about this stage of the proceedings of having a look outside to check if a queue was building up, waiting for the next show.

She did this now and signalled unobtrusively to Felix that so far there were only seven people waiting outside. This gave him a bit of leeway and left him free to carry on for a while, without hurrying too much through the tail-end of this present programme.

His audience waited expectantly to see what next he would be conjuring up out of his cupboards, with which to entertain them. So far his fascinating show had been a succession of surprises and they were loath to see it come to an end.

Chapter 30

FELIX WINS THE SILENT ADMIRATION
of a Dean of the Church of England

As well as his growing collection of mobile models, Felix had a number of static ones which he activated and introduced in turn, one or two at a time, to give variety to his show. Each involved using fleas to provide the motive power for any moving elements or machinery in the model. When he decided to use them he simply inserted the necessary fleas.

His present stock of miniature models, to which he was adding all the time, included a primitive, treadmill-type water wheel used for irrigation purposes and still in use in remote parts of the world; a cider maker's apple crusher of a type worked by a horse walking in a fixed circle attached to a pivoted pole that drove a simple machine at the centre of the area—a system Felix had seen on a small farm in Somerset, and immediately saw as very suitable to be worked in model form by a tethered flea; a children's roundabout using hanging chairs, based upon one Sam had on site; a windlass for drawing water from a well; three different types of cranes; and a recently completed windmill.

At present the windmill, one of the cranes, and the apple crusher were operational. He decided he had time to show the present audience the first two of these, but—as was his normal practice when nearing the end of a show—he took the opportunity to warn his audience that it would soon be time for them to leave.

"Before you go," he announced, "I'd like to show you two models of a rather different kind from a collection I'm building up. They are static ones which involve machinery that I've taught my fleas to operate."

The watchful Dean, who for years had so often experienced difficulty at social functions in getting people to go home at the proper time when they clearly wanted to stay longer, admired the easy manner in which Felix had started the process of moving out the present gathering.

From his store cupboard Felix lifted out his windmill which he had stuck on the bottom of a green-painted, inverted pudding basin to simulate a grassy hill, and stood it—as if on a large meadow—in the centre of the green-topped table.

It was a fine little model and in truth Felix was very proud to display it, irrespective of its flea connection, for he had spent many long, patient hours creating it. Not that this was a burden to him because during the long winter evenings he was never happier than when making new models for his show.

He had made a really attractive model of a wooden smock mill using very thin balsa wood planks laboriously cut using a razor blade, and individually stuck in place on an octagonal framework made with stiff wire, built up on a Meccano base. Most of the people present had been close enough to windmills of this type to recognise Felix's model as a very good, albeit very weenie, representation of the real thing. There were many of them about in the country and Felix had been particularly influenced by ones he knew well at Cranbrook and at Sandwich in Kent.

This form of regular-sided structure suited him because it was largely made of straight pieces of wood, thus avoiding the greater difficulty that would have faced him had he have chosen to make a tower-type mill, of fashioning curved surfaces. Since making it, however, he had acquired a large old metal pepper pot having a shape ideally suitable to use as the basis of a tower mill, so he had started work on it. By a happy chance its detachable top had a conical pointed shape that made it look almost purpose-built to form a realistic cap for the mill.

Though the interior of his smock mill was just an empty shell, at four levels corresponding to the mill's four floors, he had cut pairs of windows on opposite sides of the mill. There was a door at ground level, and part way up a balcony running all round the mill with access to it from a small door in the side. In this respect it was modelled on the mill at Cranbrook.

On the top of the mill was a typical cap which Felix had contrived to pivot so that it could be rotated to face the four sails into the wind in the usual way.

The four large sails, angled out slightly so that they were parallel to the sloping walls of the mill and far enough out to miss the balcony, were constructed from balsa wood, so as to be as light as possible. The tiny metal shaft they were mounted on ran right through the cap, passing through two pivots, one on each side, to connect directly to the shaft of one of Felix's flea-drum motors which he had conveniently mounted outside on the fantail structure.

Well above the fantail platform, at right angles to the main windmill sails, Felix had constructed the normal, wind-driven propeller device used to turn the cap into the wind. Also there, hanging down to the balcony, was the usual looped chain used to pull the cap round by hand when the wind was light—operated by a man walking round the balcony—the cap above turning in response to the chain as he pulled it. The tiny chain Felix had succeeded in making worked realistically.

Here, however, any comparison between his mill and a proper one ended, because prominently to be seen up there on the fantail platform was something without a counterpart in the real thing; a living creature was put there to turn the main sails, doing the job the wind normally did!

Felix's mill had only imaginary corn to grind; its purpose was to display the prowess of his versatile fleas. It was a dreamlike mill created for the fleas to amuse themselves on. In turn it served to entertain the monsters watching them, for whom they ground no life-sustaining flour, but on whose blood they would on the contrary gladly had fed if given half the chance to swap their location on the mill for a comfortable berth on the warm body of one of those so obviously very interested in them. Felix sometimes thought it a bit sad that the hardworking fleas were naively unaware that there was no warmth in the interest, and that they would be harshly unwelcome as guests.

When his audience had studied the tiny mill for a few moments, Felix took the brake off the flea-motor's drum, gave the sails a push to overcome their initial inertia and stood back to let it work by flea-power. To get it to go at all had been something of a trial to Felix. The reason was spotted very quickly by Joe, who summed it up in a comment that struck to the heart of the matter.

"That's one hell of a flea you've got up there," he said. "Those sails may be very light in weight but it still needs quite a bit of leverage to turn them. I see they go round once for every turn of the flea's treadle-drum, and that's no mean feat for that little fellow up there on the fantail. I should have thought you would have needed to gear it down for him."

"Blimey! It's clever of you to spot that straightaway," commented Felix. "I didn't think of it before I started. I'd thought that the sails being so light would make it easy for him. I began to regret ever making it, because I couldn't make it easy enough even for my strongest flea to turn for any length of time. And even then I had to give it a push to start it going at all. The flea's wind didn't blow hard enough—if you see what I mean!"

"What did you do, then?" asked Joe, looking puzzled. "You certainly haven't put any gearing in there to help him, but he seems to be coping all right."

"You're quite right—there are no gears. But I did fix him up with a bit of help, though!" Felix said rather archly. "Look—I'll show you."

With a grin, because the conversation had played right into his hands, allowing him a bit of extra opportunity for showmanship, he lifted off the conical-shaped roof of the cap, which he had arranged in the form of a simple, unfastened lid.

462

Working away, just down inside the cap was a second flea, treading another drum mounted in line with the drum outside, on the same simple shaft that drove the sails.

"It's a two flea-power job," explained Felix proudly. "I had to double up the engine room staff to make the mill turn at all. Of course I had to choose the two fleas carefully. These two are close friends. They get on together like a house on fire. Work very well together these two do, even though they can't see one another. They talk to each other all the time as they've only got the cap wall between them. They're side-by-side working two drums on the same shaft. They like that and it's peaceful up there when the mill is not working."

"How do you get them out to feed them?" asked Joe.

"Just unplug their tethering wires," replied Felix, putting the lid back on the cap. "I have to do the same on several of my models when I can't lift the whole motor out. It's easy to feed a flea on the end of a wire though. There's no problem with that at all. You just hold the wire and present the flea to your arm. When they've tanked up they are simply plugged into their model again and rest up there until there is work to do. It's a simply routine, nothing to it!"

For a few moments there was silence in the cabin as they watched the sails turning. Felix said nothing because he knew something was about to happen. After a short while it did. There as a faint 'clonk' from inside the mill and simultaneously the sails stopped turning.

"Hello! The wind's dropped!" somebody said, causing a laugh all round. "Or maybe they've knocked off for a cup of tea!"

"No, I know what's happened all right," said Felix, his face expressionless as usual. "Something's jammed the machinery driving the millstones. I heard a shout in there. The miller's a daft old blighter. It's time he retired and called it a day. He's always in trouble in there these days. He's probably gunged up his goolies in the grinding gear! That should give us some quick rising flour. He's a randy old devil, he is!"

The crowd laughed at the image this impromptu explanation evoked, of a doddering old elfin-sized miller sadly coming to grief inside the tiny mill that had stopped working so abruptly because of his failing abilities.

But Fanny inwardly winced and only the ghost of a smile creased her face. Then she frowned, glanced at Felix and gazed down thoughtfully at the little windmill. She was clearly not happy about her husband's bawdy remarks. She would have preferred him to remain more dignified as befits a professional man who is master of his own business, and an acknowledged expert in his specialist field!

Only the ultra observant Dean perceived this reaction on the part of the flea-man's wife, and stored it away in his mental catalogue of human behaviour patterns. He was interested in the way people related to one another. The couple were a strange pair, but in a way complementary to one another in the front they presented to the world. They intrigued him and were destined to feature, duly disguised, in a future story already germinating in his mind.

Felix did indeed know exactly what had happened inside the mill. He was having problems with it. Even the two fleas working together were not capable of turning the sails really satisfactorily for very long. There was development work still to do. Meanwhile, as a temporary expedient, he'd had to resort to winding a thread round the shaft and finding a weight to hang on it that was just heavy enough to keep the sails turning steadily while it dropped down the tower. Its arrival at the bottom was signalled by the tiny clonk they had heard.

One day he hoped to devise a simple gearing to allow the fleas to run faster while the sails turned very slowly, as windmill sails so often do in light winds. His direct drive, though simple for him to make, was too much for them. They needed a very low gear to cope easily so that they would be happy to keep running long enough to show off the windmill properly.

When the laughter following his comment about the unhappy fate of the miller had subsided, he picked up the model and put it away.

"I'm sorry about that," he said. "I'll have to put it right later. I haven't got time to mess about with it now. But I have one more model to show you before you go," he added, giving them all another gentle reminder that they were soon to depart.

For his last demonstration he placed upon the table a rectangular wooden platform about fifteen inches long and ten inches wide, standing six inches high. Its front and two ends were enclosed, but the long side facing Felix was open. He had things to do under there, out of sight of his audience.

In the top, a third of the way in from one end, he had cut a three-inch diameter hole to represent a well. Around it was built a half-inch high parapet. He had Boris to thank for the realistic brick-built appearance, yet very easy construction, of this well-head.

Undecided how to fabricate the circular structure so that it looked good, he had asked the advice of Boris who said he'd go away and think about it. He did better than that—he came back with the finished job! It was made of seven steel washers; four eighth-inch thick ones painted red, and three much thinner ones painted white.

There were vertical white lines at suitable intervals round the edge of the thick red washers, painted in to look like the mortar between a circle of bricks. All Felix had to do was stick one of the red washers around the hole as the first course of bricks; a thin white one on top of it as the mortar between courses; then simply interleave thick ones with thin ones to produce a neat looking circular wall of four courses of bricks. By making sure that the vertical white lines round the edge of one course fell between the corresponding lines on adjacent courses, Felix finished up with a very smart, professional-looking brick parapet around the top of his well. As a finishing touch Boris had painted the surface of the top washer grey, to represent a hard concrete rim on the well-head.

Felix used this well with both his windlass model and with one of his three cranes. With the windlass he treated it as an active well, but with the crane it served as a disused, abandoned well.

His windlass was constructed to look like a typical, simple, hand-cranked water-lifting machine, in essence just a pivoted roller on a wooden stand with an ornate, ridged wooden roof to protect the roller and its rope from the weather.

The windlass was neatly designed to fit snugly over the well. He could stand it in place and take it away again in a few moments. Its roller's axle had the usual handle at one end but the other end projected out a little way past the vertical post in order to carry the drum of a flea-motor.

Felix had made this particular drum with a diameter several times greater than that of the tiny, rope-winding roller. Its purpose was to give his flea the help it needed by providing it with plenty of leverage. The fact that this made the load come up the well very slowly, was in fact an advantage. It added to the suspense a bit and heightened the dramatic effect of the eventual appearance over the parapet of whatever was being lifted. The latter was not always as mundane as the expected bucket of water.

On the end of the white thread wound on the roller was a hook which carried a very lightweight silver bucket made for Felix by Gemstone George.

When demonstrating this model, Felix started the proceedings with the bucket pulled down through the well-head to rest on the bottom of his open-backed platform.

Sometimes he would put a little water in it, but more often than not he preferred to load it with some totally unexpected surprise. These always had to be of very light weight, and tucked under the platform in a box he had a variety of insects stored away; a little collection to which he added new specimens from time to time when chance provided them.

Flying insects were particularly suitable for this purpose because they often combined an impressive size and exotic experience, with very little weight. To see a daddy-long-legs appear over the edge of the parapet riding in a bucket could be relied upon to create much amusement.

Damsel flies were also always favourites of Felix. Their extremely delicate and pretty appearances made them very popular. So light were they that he could send up a 'married couple' if he were lucky enough to have them both in stock. The green-bodied female ones of the species he sought, with their four, almost transparent, pale green wings, were usually much more easily found than the posh blue males which had each of their flimsy wings marked with a distinctive mauve-coloured blob.

Felix always explained to his audience that the damsel fly women had more sense than their men folk because they chose to dress in pale green to merge with the landscape, whereas the men ponced around in blue with decorated wings and as a result got snapped up by birds, leaving a lot of widows in the community!

In a show as bizarre as his, nobody ever seemed to think it odd that the well should yield up in its bucket objects as curious and unlikely as these, instead of water. Usually there was silence as they watched the thin white thread steadily winding up on the roller of the windlass, and waited patiently for the bucket to appear out of the well. Its arrival carrying a passenger was always greeted with a great deal of interest and amusement.

With his present audience, however, Felix had chosen to show, not the windlass, but one of his cranes, and this he now placed upon the platform.

"Somebody has fallen down this disused well," he told them, "and the Police have called in the Fire Brigade to get him out!"

The model crane was a four-wheeled mobile one of the self-propelled type, with its engine mounted on the rectangular platform under a metal canopy. A slender jib of the open-framework kind, which Felix had made of stiff wire, carried a small pulley wheel at its tip. Hanging down from this was a black thread carrying a hook. The thread passed back from the pulley wheel down the back of the tapered jib, to a tiny metal bobbin around which it was wound.

Attached to the axle carrying the bobbin was a flea-motor, at present stationary because Felix had put its brake on. The crane was painted red, and on its metal back plate, in bold black letters, was printed **KENT FIRE BRIGADE**.

Felix pulled out a tiny locking-pin from the bobbin, leaving it free to turn on its spindle completely disengaged from the flea-motor. He allowed the hook to be lowered to the bottom of the well—out of sight of the audience—then turned his attention to attaching the hook to the load that had to be lifted out of the well.

This done, with a call of "Haul away—steady as she goes," he inserted the bobbin's locking-pin to engage with the shaft, took the break off his flea-motor and stood back to allow his well-trained crane driver to take over. As with the windlass, Felix had made the flea-motor's drum much larger in diameter than the take-up bobbin, to give the flea the leverage it needed to work the crane.

Slowly the thread tightened up and began to wind on to the bobbin. Felix had discovered a long time ago that fleas will work wonders and keep going a long time, provided they can 'walk' or 'run' fairly easily. Unlike work horses, their gigantic opposite numbers whose great size was beyond the capacity of a flea to comprehend, fleas will not strain away against a heavy load, striving to cope with it. This they refuse point blank to do. And there is no way of whipping them on to do so. That might well work with horses but certainly not with fleas. They will have none of it. All that sort of bullying treatment does to fleas is seemingly to make them even more determined to sit still—or rather squat still—and do nothing! Quite unlike their big brothers, they cannot be bullied into abject submission.

This steadfast refusal of the fleas to attempt to cope with any job that by instinct or calculation they judge too much for them, had repercussions when Felix designed new models. There were times when he had to carry out successive modifications to lighten the load, before the wheels began to turn. Every now and again he was forced to abandon a project altogether because his fleas let him know that he was asking too much of them. Though frustrating to him, Felix did not get annoyed at this. On the contrary, he respected the independent, determined spirit of his adopted small companions, and accepted their final judgement without demur.

In the present model, such development had led to him having to settle for very low gearing on the crane, so that the hauling up of a load was a long process.

Not knowing what to expect to see emerging from the danger of the disused well, the audience watched closely as the flea worked away on its drum.

When the stranded victim finally appeared above the parapet there was a gasp of surprise and delight from them all.

Swinging gently to and fro on the thread, its body supported in a tiny rescue sling, up popped a magnificent Emperor Dragonfly, the pride of Felix's collection. Turquoise and blue in colour, its head and body shone with an almost metallic sheen, while its four delicate wings—almost transparent and with a fine tracery of veins—were extended outwards to present a very wide wingspan.

Its huge eyes seemed to encompass the whole of the top and sides of its head. Curiously, as it slowly swung to and fro on the thread, it gave the impression that it was majestically scanning the faces of the people peering at it, deliberately turning to and fro, taking in the field of view presented to it on its deliverance from the depth of the well.

Once again the instinct Felix had for the dramatic enhanced the impact of his miniature model. The tiny flea providing the motive power to lift this burden was so utterly dwarfed by it that it seemed impossible for a flea to achieve such a remarkable feat. It would have been easy to imagine the flea, if it wished, being able to ride on the back of the powerful dragonfly as it tirelessly patrolled the stretch of water on the marshy land where it lived, swiftly darting here and there amongst the reeds, endlessly searching the area for its prey. In fact there was room on the back of the magnificent fly for a whole row of flea passengers to ride. But it would have seemed most unlikely that all of the tiny passengers, working together in unison, could ever rescue the monster if it were to land in trouble, never mind just one of them on its own.

When the strikingly attractive dragonfly was a few inches clear of the well-head, Felix applied the brake to the flea-motor's drum and picked up his forceps to lift the rescued creature off the crane's hook. Its sling was attached to a tiny ring which was simply slipped over the crane's hook, making it easy to put it on and take it off.

"Well done, Percy," he said, addressing the flea. "You've done a good job there, old son. A bloody good job. Your Dad would have been proud of you. Fanny and I are glad you are keeping up the family traditions."

As Felix gently replaced the handsome insect back inside his storage box beneath the platform, a lady standing nearby made an observation. "You speak as though his Dad is dead," she said, intrigued by his comment. "What happened to him?"

Felix's tone and manner had been such as to suggest a premature death, perhaps a tragedy of some sort.

"Heart attack!" responded Felix succinctly, contriving to look serious and sorrowful. "He went suddenly one day, sitting up there where his son is now. It was just one of those things. We'd had no warning he was unwell or we should have rested him. Saddened everybody, that did, especially his mates in the Fire Brigade crew. He was popular amongst the team. A likeable chap, one of the best. Still, it's nice to know his son has taken his place. Percy is a good lad. He's doing very well—as you've just seen."

The questioner was silent for a few moments, and strangely there was little or no sniggering at what Felix had said, preposterous though it may have been. His manner was convincing, an achievement again noted with some admiration by the closely observant Dean.

At length, to break the awkward silence, she made a further comment.

"I really can't think where a tiny thing like that flea gets all its strength from. For such a tiny weenie thing to be able to pull that huge dragonfly out of the well seems incredible. It's truly amazing! And to be able to jump so far, too!"

"It's all to do with marvellous special kinds of muscles in its legs and to those energy-storing pads under that hard-topped body that I told you about," said Felix, a trifle vaguely."I've tried to find out myself but nobody seems to know much about them. For their size they are some of the most powerful animals in the world. There are supposed to be over fifteen hundred different kinds of fleas in the world, forty in this country alone!"

Felix paused a moment to let this impressive piece of information sink in. He was clearly proud of the outstanding prowess of his fleas. Then he became a little philosophical.

"Beautifully designed creatures, aren't they?" he said thoughtfully. "Better than any engine any man could make, that's for sure! And they've got it all ways too. They're very powerful and they're highly intelligent. No wonder they have to feed on pure blood. Eating spuds and cabbages wouldn't keep extra-special animals like them alive! Wonderful creations, fleas are. Thinking back a bit, I expect at the time of the great Flood fleas were bright enough to make sure they got on Noah's Ark aboard old Noah! *And* riding on the animals as they went in two by two. Must have done, when you think it through! Yes, they are wonderful creations, no doubt about that. Wonderful. Beyond our understanding, fleas are! I don't suppose even the Archbishop of Canterbury understands them!"

This sudden unexpected reference to his Boss startled the attentively-listening Dean and jerked him out of his quiet reveries. Yet it was not inappropriate to his thoughts because he had detected an almost religious fervour in the flea-man's previous comments. Felix had appeared for a moment to be very close to delivering a little sermon on fleas. Had Felix been looking directly at him when he mentioned the Archbishop, the Dean would have thought his cover blown, and that, unlikely though it might seem, Felix had got him spotted. However, it was not so, and Felix did not pursue his philosophical observations any further. But his sudden unexpected mention of the Establishment sharpened the Dean's interest even more, and he watched the enigmatic flea-man wonderingly. Into his mind, by way of an instant minor inspiration, came a flitting name for him. Smiling to himself he silently dubbed him, Doctor of Flea-osophy, an appellation that was subsequently to appear against Felix's fictional representative in one of the Dean's future books.

This little discussion marked the end of Felix's show for the present session. Percy was the last performer he had time to present.

"Well, that's about it, folks," he said, picking up the model crane and stowing it away in his cupboard under the table. "That's about all I have time for," he added, stowing away his 'well' platform in the same place. "We hope you enjoyed our show."

Glancing at the clock as he bobbed up from behind the table he said, "We shall be starting our next show in about ten minutes' time. I can't spare long, but if you have any questions to ask, I'll be glad to answer them."

A lady standing near the back immediately took him up on this.

"Can you really tell the difference between the various breeds of fleas you use?" she asked. "They seem so small they all look the same to me—except for that huge mole-flea, of course."

"Yes, I certainly can," replied Felix emphatically. "I often get asked that. There are a lot of differences—not only in average size—but in several features. I've got drawings of all those I use myself, but there's no time to pass them around during a show, and they are too small to be seen by everybody if I just hold them up. But pretty soon now I shall be getting some large paintings to put on the wall in here, showing my main breeds. One of Sam Donatello's men who does a lot of his Fairground paintings for him, is making me big copies of my drawings. And he's doing them in colour so that I can show people details of them. You'd be surprised how different from one another they are."

"Are rabbit fleas much different from cat fleas?" asked the little man who had shown such an earnest interest in the proceedings. "I keep rabbits and my wife is always complaining that our cat is bringing rabbit fleas into the house."

"Well, that's wrong for a start!" commented Felix scornfully. "No self-respecting rabbit flea would ever think of jumping on a moggy. The other way round, maybe. But rabbit fleas are very particular what blood they suck. They wouldn't give you a thank you for a feed on a moggy!

It's strange you should have brought that point up, because rabbit fleas are unlike any others I know about. They can tell a rabbit from any other animal and just won't go on anything but a rabbit. Not unless they are starving hungry, they won't.

So you can tell you wife from me that wherever else her cat goes wandering around picking up fleas, they certainly don't come off your rabbits. Why should one get off where it wants to be and jump aboard a moggy when it hates the taste of a cat's blood? You're in the clear there, mate. No doubt about that. Your rabbits are not to blame."

"Thanks," said the little man gratefully, smiling with satisfaction. "That's a relief. I'm glad to learn that. I'll tell her what you said when I get home."

This display of authoritative knowledge, delivered with such utter confidence, was too much for the lurking smart-aleck to stomach. The flea-man was gaining far too much kudos for his liking. It irked him to witness that and his sour nature prompted him to react, abruptly and forcefully.

"Huh!" he grunted. "Huh! I don't believe that at all! What a load of balls! Fancy trying to pretend that a tiny little thing like a bloody flea can tell one hulking great animal from another. You must think we are all a lot of idiots making statements like that. That's an insult to our intelligence! What a load of bloody rubbish!"

This sudden broadside was too much for Felix. He looked—and undoubtedly was—absolutely furious.

"Fanny," he called out sharply, "how many people are waiting outside?"

His wife, visibly startled at this sudden reaction, popped her head out of the door.

"Twelve," she said. "No—wait a minute—two more have just wandered up—it's fourteen." She looked worried, for her husband was plainly very angry.

468

"Will you put up the ten-minute notice then, please," Felix said.

Fanny took up a blackboard on which was printed:

NEXT SHOW STARTS AT:

—then looked at the clock, added ten minutes to the time she read, chalked that calculated time on the board and took the board outside where it was placed in a prepared, prominent position.

This procedure was their normal practice. It served two purposes. It gave clear notice to those inside that their time was almost up, because the blackboard was always prepared ostentatiously in front of them, and—more importantly—it encouraged people waiting patiently outside not to wander off, as well perhaps as pulling in a few more folk passing by, who spotted the show was about to start and decided to join the queue.

Felix then turned his attention to the pain-in-the-neck who stood there smirking and wondering how the angry flea-man was going to get out of this one. He did not have long to wait . . . but he could not possibly have foreseen the consequences of his flagrant accusation.

Felix strode purposefully over to one of the two tables at the back of the cabin, took Fido off his lead and carried him to the table. For a moment the awkward cuss got worried, for he thought Felix was going to turn his dog on him so angry did he look. Instead of this drastic measure, however, he saw Felix put Fido on the table alongside the circus ring and instruct him to sit. His tone was very firm. Fido sat: promptly—no questions asked! The Boss meant what he said, and Fido sensed his determined mood only too well.

"Fetch Felicity over here, please, Fanny," he requested, rather curtly.

Meanwhile he went back to the rear table again and picked up Liz, the cat, which he sat on the demonstration table alongside Fido, but about a third of the way round the ring. For a moment he stroked the cat, which purred happily and settled down comfortably on the green cloth.

Taking the large, healthy-looking rabbit from Fanny, he put it on the table alongside the circus ring, midway between the cat and the dog.

"Give me the rabbit jar, please," he asked Fanny. She brought him over the glass jar in which was stored the remaining rabbit fleas of the day's reserve supply. There were four of them left in it.

"Keep your eye on Felicity, please Fanny," he requested. "Don't hold her unless she moves, but I'd like her to stay just exactly where she is."

Fanny of course now guessed what was going to happen and kept discreetly by Felicity without intruding on the action. A rabbit, unlike a dog or cat, does not always stay where it is put since it normally has less freedom of movement than they do and is glad to get out of its hutch for a while. Once let out, though, it is inclined to kick up its back legs with joy and bolt off anywhere-somewhere, for it is by nature a runner.

However, as it happened, Felicity was no trouble; she co-operated and stayed lying on the table. She seemed to know that it was not the time to play the fool.

"Now them, clever-Dick!" said Felix sharply."Watch this! In this jar I've got four rabbit fleas. I'm going to put them one at a time on the table in the middle of the circus ring and leave them free to go where they like. It will be entirely up to them. You needn't worry, though. Stink though you probably do, they won't jump on you. They'd rather starve first. Just watch where I put them and what they do."

Taking up the pipette he sucked up one of the four fleas into it and carefully blew it out plumb in the middle of the circus ring. There was silence in the cabin. Quite fortuitously the smart-aleck's rudeness had provided a situation of great interest. All eyes were on the tiny creature as it squatted momentarily in the otherwise empty ring, as solitary as a man alone at the centre of a very large meadow. Its dark brown, solid-looking body, tiny though it was, showed up clearly against the bright white background it stood upon.

For a few moments it hopped seemingly arbitrarily around the ring and then suddenly, with two impressive hops, it landed squarely on the back of the recumbent rabbit. There was a loud cheer from the audience.

Felix glanced at his tormentor, his eyebrows arched questioningly.

"Didn't hang about much, did he?" he asked. "I reckon he knew a rabbit from a dog or a cat when he saw one. Still, one flea doesn't prove anything. I know that. Let's have another go."

Felix was clearly enjoying himself and was evidently perfectly confident of the outcome of his demonstration. His adversary, on the contrary, glowered. A mind-reader would have detected a powerful wish emanating from his rather mean mind that the next flea would prove Felix wrong.

Once again Felix drew up a flea into his pipette and planted it squarely in the middle of the ring. It moved faster than the previous one, seeming more anxious to make a getaway. At first it hopped near Fido and the keenly watching sullen spoiler began to grin. But he was very quickly disappointed, for the flea, in a series of exploratory hops, moved about from place to place, then, with a long leap, disappeared into the rabbit's fur.

There was another excited cheer from the astounded audience. Plainly, nobody could possible fake this result. The flea had made its own decision. Felix was vindicated and his stock rose, to the satisfaction it must be said, of everybody except the one sullen man.

The little horse-flea man, a professed rabbit enthusiast, was clearly delighted. He made what many thought a fanciful comment.

"Do you know," he said to Felix with absolute conviction, "I saw that flea spin the air as it jumped towards the rabbit. It spun itself like Tich Freeman spins a cricket ball bowling for Kent!"

Several people chuckled at this assertion, but not Felix. "You're quite right," he said. "Absolutely right! Rabbit fleas do spin in the air as they land on a rabbit. It just goes to show how bright they are. They spin their bodies so they penetrate the rabbit's fur, and get through to safety as fast as possible. It's a well-known fact. Bloody clever they are. Bloody clever! Rabbit fleas have got their heads screwed on right, no doubt about that. They know that rabbits jump about a lot so they make sure they dive down deeply into the fur and don't break their necks by being chucked off the rabbit as soon as they land."

Full of confidence Felix sucked up the third flea and planted it, like the first two, smack in the middle of the ring. It sat still for a moment, hopped about a bit as though getting the lie of the land, then, with a sudden movement and two successive determined hops, landed fairly and squarely, not on the rabbit, but on the back of the cat!

"Oh dear!" exclaimed the clever-Dick with ill-concealed delight. "Dear-oh-dear! Something's gone wrong with the theory! A funny-looking rabbit that flea has chosen. A short-eared variety that purrs! How do you explain that, then, Mr. Flea-bloody-expert?" he asked, grinning maliciously at Felix.

Felix was not pleased. Not pleased at all. But he was not lost for an explanation.

"Ignorance, that's what!" he said. "Sheer bloody ignorance. That rabbit flea must be a plain idiot. There are ignorant people and there are fleas. You, of all people," he added, addressing the smirking spoiler directly, "ought to recognise ignorance when you see it. That flea is an exception. It's got your complaint. It was born ignorant!"

"Perhaps," intervened the little man hesitatingly, anxious to try to help Felix out of trouble, "perhaps that was a cat flea in the jar mixed up with the rabbit fleas. That would explain it."

"No, it was a rabbit flea all right. There's no mistake about that. I am quite certain of that. I could no more mistake a cat flea for a rabbit flea, than a cat for a rabbit," Felix replied.

"You've got the edge over that flea then, haven't you!" laughed the spoiler gleefully, snatching up this comment for the gift it was.

Felix bit his lip. He realised he'd handed the nasty man a dollop of ready-made ammunition on a plate. But he pressed on. He was not going to be defeated so easily if he could help it.

"Like I said," he persisted, "that flea is a Simple Simon sort of flea. Daft in the head. Off its rocker. There are ignorant men, ignorant women, ignorant boys, ignorant girls, ignorant horses, ignorant dogs, ignorant cats, ignorant cows and ignorant fleas. In all animals you find a few ignorant ones among a crowd. That's nature!"

"How do you find an ignorant cow in a field full of cows, then?" the spoiler asked Felix, grasping the opportunity to needle him with immense pleasure.

"Easy!" replied Felix without the slightest hesitation, his mind sharpened by the stimulus of being exposed to ridicule by the objectionable, sneering man. "A dog wouldn't be able to tell the difference between the smell of its shit and the smell of you!"

The crowd laughed loudly. Fanny winced with embarrassment feeling that Felix had lost ground by being so common, and the man himself looked furious for his snide remarks kept rebounding at him. Scowling at Felix he said, "The best thing you can do is put that last flea down in the ring. Let's have a look what that one can do. That should sort things out all right. My guess is that one will miss the rabbit as well. It will land on the dog, I reckon."

Felix silently took up his pipette, but before picking up the flea he decided to gamble his reputation on it, if only for the chance to put the obnoxious smart-aleck down once and for all.

"Think so, do you?" he said fiercely. "All right then, Mister bloody clever-Dick. Just watch this. I'll prove to you once and for all that if a rabbit flea that is normal is put near a cat, it will turn away and go look for a rabbit. You just watch!"

The little man saw danger immediately. He was plainly nervous on Felix's behalf.

"How do you know that last one is normal, Mr. Foden?" he asked anxiously. "That one might be ignorant too."

"True," said Felix, "it might! That's what that bloody clever-Dick hopes. But it won't be. It's the law of averages working. Its unlikely Fanny would have found two daft ones on Felicity this morning at one gathering. Hardly any chance at all. You'll see! My guess is this last flea will be normal. It's almost certain sure to be!"

The Dean, observing all this from his vantage point as an objective and detached observer, was astonished at the confidence of the flea-man, and even more impressed by the terrific atmosphere of expectation that had built up in the little cabin. Many a theatrical manager, he thought, would have given a very great deal to create such tension in a theatre. And they were all captivated by watching mere fleas! Hardly Shakespearean actors, he thought to himself, to his private, wry amusement.

There was utter silence in the room as Felix drew the last flea out of the jar and up into his pipette. The tension was palpable. Coolly and deliberately he blew the flea out again—not in the centre of the ring as he had been careful to do before—but near the side where the cat sat comfortably, impassively watching the proceedings.

For a moment or two the flea moved about a little and there seemed an extremely strong chance that it would escape from its vulnerable, exposed position by jumping up into the safe obscurity of the long hair on the adjacent cat. A haven was at hand. But it didn't! By some mysterious means it was attracted across the ring to the rabbit. It went direct to it in a series of hops, the last of which was a long, impressive, exuberant one, and quick as a flash it disappeared deep into the welcome sanctuary of the rabbit's fur, back where it had started early that morning! No doubt, as Felix and Fanny knew, migrating quickly and unerringly to join its mates behind Felicity's ears!

There was a spontaneous round of applause from the audience, most, if not all of whom were only too pleased that the unpleasant man had not won out over Felix.

"How about that, then!" exclaimed Felix, glaring triumphantly at his rival. "Does that satisfy you?"

The man visibly squirmed and was plainly annoyed that his outright challenge had rebounded upon him once again.

"That was just a sheer fluke," he said, aggressively. "Plain bloody chance that was. Just good luck. That's all!"

"Nonsense," intervened a well-dressed man standing nearby. "That was not a fluke or just good luck. The odds against the last flea finding its way across to the rabbit by chance, making it three out of four homing in on the rabbit, would be enormous. Not only that, the proprietor here actually put it alongside the cat to tempt it to choose that animal. He couldn't possible have been fairer. I think he's proved his point. Proved it beyond any doubt, I would say!"

"Hear hear!" called somebody else and there were general murmurs of agreement all round, mingled with further clapping of hands in support of what the speaker had said.

"Incidentally," the latter said, addressing his remarks to the little horse-flea man who stood near him, "I also saw that last flea spinning on its axis as it disappeared into the rabbit's fur. It's amazing that—it was actually spinning as if it flew through the air, just as you said you saw one of the others do. I'd never have believed it!"

All this praise, applause and outright support for the flea-man was too much for the disgruntled clever-Dick to stomach. He had to have another go.

"That's all very well," he grunted, with marked reluctance. "But I expect all fleas know their own hosts. He says only rabbit fleas can tell one animal from another," he added, addressing his remarks to the room in general. "My guess is if *they* can, then *all* fleas can. What he says about rabbit fleas being special is still all balls, I bet. A load of bloody boloney, like the rest of his crooked claptrap!"

Felix nearly exploded. "Stone the crows!" he burst out in obvious extreme exasperation. "You just never give up, do you? What a right bloody-minded miserable sod you are!"

Turning away, he called over to Fanny again.

"Fanny—pass me the cat jar, please," he requested, his manner stern and decisive. "This bloke is the most awkward bastard I've met in years."

Fanny glanced at him anxiously, but fetched the jar without comment and handed it to him. He took the top off and looked inside it.

"There are five cat fleas in here," he said. "Five, pure-bred cat fleas. They were collected off Liz here this morning," he added, pointing his finger to the contented cat sitting comfortably by the ringside. "Just watch again, you disbelieving bighead. Just watch. I'll do the same with these as I did with the rabbit fleas. Then perhaps you will believe me."

472

Without wasting time, for the pest was irritating him beyond measure and he had his next show to think about, Felix sucked up one of the cat fleas into his pipette and deposited it in the middle of the ring.

His audience was impressed. He certainly had the courage of his convictions, and didn't hesitate to put his reputation on the line!

And it paid off straightaway, because the tiny performer, on whom all eyes were focused, lost no time in departing the scene. Its purpose, were it to have expressed it, was to get the hell away while it had the chance. But it did *not* go to the cat! In two highly agile hops it disappeared straight into the rabbit's fur. Any triumph Felix felt was however very short lived. His quick-footed opponent instantly changed his tack.

"Ah! Now I see it all!" exclaimed the leech-like pest with undisguised joy. "Now I see what it's all about. You crafty bugger! The stink from that rabbit attracts all fleas, never mind rabbit fleas. That's blown your story for good and all, Mister Bloody Know-all Flea-man!"

Red in the face, clearly thoroughly annoyed and rattled by this sneering conclusion, Felix forbore to respond immediately to the taunting implication that he was a professional charlatan, just an out-and-out fraud.

Biting his lip, his expression set and unsmiling, he prepared to continue his demonstration, knowing that if the next cat flea opted for the rabbit his enemy would gloat with unbounded glee, but if it went to the cat he would claim it as proof of his original assertion.

Again the room was very quiet as he sucked up the flea and expertly planted it plumb in the middle of the ring. He was in luck. The flea didn't hesitate. With two rapid leaps it landed squarely on Fido's back and was lost to view immediately. Fido, who had been watching his master with close attention, spotted the flea fly towards him, gave a little bark as it landed, but failed in his quick attempt to nose it out and catch it.

"You spoke too soon," Felix said to the disappointed sceptic. "What are you going to suggest now? Because that one chose neither the rabbit nor the cat. Any minute now I expect you'll be telling me Fido pricked up his ears to look like a rabbit, or maybe made a mew like a moggy to muddle the flea! If so you can forget it. Fido won't be pleased to have somebody else's flea biting his guts!"

Fido, hearing his name mentioned, fixed his bright eyes on Felix and gave a sharp little bark.

"There you are," said Felix. "Fido confirms what I said."

"Balls!" said the clever-Dick sullenly. "You've still got more cat fleas in that jar of yours. Put another one down. You haven't proved anything yet. Put your flea where your mouth is!"

Felix was only too happy to do this. He reckoned he had now got the man well on the run. Well and truly boiled. In less than no time there was another flea in the ring. But unfortunately it confounded the issue and hopped about a bit until taking off in a mighty single leap to land on the sleepy cat sitting dozing by the ringside.

"That's one that's proved my point," said the man, triumphantly. "Straight to the cat, that one went. And it didn't hang about either. It made up its mind straightaway and jumped to the cat. Proves my point that does!"

"Proves your point, my arse!" exclaimed Felix indignantly, forgetting how neatly he had scored a minor victor over the loud-mouthed nuisance earlier on when he had used the same impolite expression. Only two people noticed it, however—Fanny who deplored it and the Dean who found himself sorry that Felix was slipping a bit in the control of his carefully cultivated, po-faced aplomb.

"Nuts! What absolute boloney!" continued Felix. "One out of three on the cat, with

473

only three animals to chose from. Now that really is chance working. Pure chance. It's exactly what you would expect from fleas that can't discriminate or who just don't care what they go on for a feed. There couldn't be better proof. Anyway, there are still two more fleas in the jar. You can see them jump as well."

The fourth flea when planted in the ring appeared less anxious to get out of sight than the previous ones and hung about a bit, apparently either taking the air, or making up its mind where to go. In a little while, though, it came to life and hopped across the ring in the direction of the cat, but changed its mind at the last minute and suddenly leapt sideways aboard the luckless Fido, who once again saw the enemy approaching, but could not move fast enough to catch it.

Felix's reputation was well and truly restored by these indeterminate, random results. But he had one more flea in the jar and offered it up for good measure. He was noticeably more relaxed now, having clearly won his battle. But there was no harm in rubbing it in. His opponent was on the ropes.

This last of the five provided an unexpected diversion and gave rise to much hilarity.

When Felix placed it in the centre of the circus ring, ignoring the animals altogether it moved towards the ringside between two animals and sat for a few moments not far from the edge, facing the audience.

Friar Tuck, standing at the front, his head bent over as near as possible to the ring because of his poor sight, was peering down intently through his thick pebble glasses, totally absorbed in the unfolding drama.

Suddenly, to the great delight of the audience, the flea jumped up to land on the barren terrain of the man's bald pate—skidded a bit in the perspiration standing out in beads up there—then hopped into the grey curly hair forming a dense fringe over his left ear.

There was a chorus of laughter all round. But the hapless man had lost sight of the flea and didn't know what the laughter was about. Felix moved quickly towards him and placed a hand on his shoulder.

"Stand quite still, Sir, please," he said respectfully. "I'm afraid the flea has jumped into your hair. Hold still—I'll soon have it out."

So saying he expertly moved Friar Tuck's hair about gently with his fingers, located the flea and sucked it up into his pipette.

"OK, I've got him," he said, carrying the pipette away. Abruptly though—staring intently at the pipette and studying its occupant with apparent disbelief—he stopped in his tracks and turned to face Friar Tuck.

Looking acutely embarrassed, he spoke very diffidently to the goggle-eyed man who was smiling good naturedly at him, evidently enjoying this unexpected outcome of Felix's final test.

"I'm sorry, Sir," said Felix, obviously feeling extremely awkward, "this is not the flea I put down on the table. It's a human flea—not a cat flea!"

There was another howl of laughter at this delightful twist in the turn of events. Friar Tuck took it in good part, for Felix—standing very close to him—had contrived to wink at him meaningfully without anyone noticing. The twinkle-eyed, chubby-faced man—bright and alert, whose sympathies were entirely with the flea-man—entered into the spirit of things. Felix had very unobtrusively inclined his head towards the smart-aleck as he winked, and Friar Tuck knew that the disruptive man was to be on the end of something. He was more than willing to co-operate.

"Good gracious me! Really! Well! How very embarrassing! Whatever next!" he spluttered, smiling broadly. "I haven't had a flea in my hair for years. Not since I was a boy. I catch the occasional flea from my dogs and cats, but they always get under my shirt—never on my head! Not that there's much up there to attract them unless they've got a passion for wide open spaces! And you say that is a human flea you have there? Are you sure?"

"Quite sure, no question about it," replied Felix, still contriving to look a bit shame-faced and apologetic. "But don't be embarrassed. I'm certain it didn't come in here riding on your head. I know too much about the ways of fleas to think that. I'm pretty sure I know quite well where it did come from. I'd lay a bet it came off our friend the clever-Dick standing just behind you. I thought he looked flea-bitten when he came in here, and I can see from here now that he's got flea bites all round his neck. Maybe that's why he's such a bloody-minded pain-in-the-neck all the time. He's a flea hater, that's for sure. We've all seen that. He won't give them credit for anything. No wonder he's been stirring things up in here from the moment he came in."

Felix paused a moment in his side-swiping apology, the crowd enjoying the fun, while the man under attack, now red in the face and clearly not at all happy, glared at him—for once speechless.

"I'm sorry about what's happened," Felix continued, to all appearances expressing genuine concern to the genial Friar Tuck. "But you stay behind and I'll soon find my cat flea. Don't worry, Sir. It's not your fault a flea-carrier like him should choose to stand near you. Mind you, I can well understand that flea wanting to get the hell off his lousy head. It won't have liked his attitude to my show, I'm quite sure of that."

There was much merriment as the people followed one another out of the door, many of them thanking Felix and Fanny on their way out for a thoroughly entertaining time. Except, that is, for the clever-Dick who, smarting with discomfiture and tasting the bitterness of defeat, slunk away feeling none too happy. As he reached the door, Felix called out to him.

"I say, friend clever-Dick," he said, grinning happily from ear to ear. "Do me a favour, will you? Don't come back, there's a good fellow! Go away and stay away, please. And try to be kind to your fleas!"

The man, not knowing how to respond to Felix's semi-jocular ribbing, conscious that to show anger would be yet another victory for the flea-man whom everybody else— except the departed flypaper lady—had seemed to find so likeable, scowled, but remained silent and went on his way. He was not a happy man!

Friar Tuck stayed behind as asked and spoke to Felix as soon as the people had moved away from him.

"I take it that *is* your cat flea you've got in there?" he grinned, pointing to Felix's pipette.

"Yes, of course," said Felix with a wide smile. "Thanks for being such a good sport. I couldn't resist the chance to wind up that nasty blighter a bit. He really did get under my skin. He's been doing his best to ruin my show so I thought I'd take the opportunity to raise a laugh at his expense and take the mickey out of him to square the account a bit. But perhaps it was a bit much of me to involve you like that."

"Glad to help," said Friar Tuck. "He deserved what he got. Mind you, in my opinion you handled him very well throughout. He came off worst, right from the first bell. He didn't succeed in scoring a single point. You didn't let him get away with anything. Anyway, I congratulate you on an ingenious and very entertaining show. I thoroughly enjoyed it."

"Thanks," said Felix. "It's kind of you to say that, and very encouraging to Fanny and me. We work hard to put on a good show, and apart from the odd ones now and again like that miserable old battleaxe of a woman who went off in a tizzy earlier on, and that bastard of a clever-Dick who has just left, most people seem to enjoy it in here."

"I'm quite sure they do! From what I've seen today I'm certain of that! There are always a few unpleasant people in any crowd. You mustn't let them bother you. Send them packing with 'a flea in their ear' as the saying goes! You of all people should be good at that," commented Friar Tuck laughingly.

With that the good natured old gentleman bid goodbye to Felix and Fanny, leaving that industrious, well-matched pair already busily engaged getting ready to start the next show.

The last to leave, having followed this final episode with close attention, was the Dean. While ostensibly watching with interest the antics of Fanny's healthy-looking white mouse which once again was happily treading away inside its rapidly spinning wheel, he had listened with quiet amusement to the exchange of words between Felix and the genial, rotund old boy who had been such a good sport in co-operating with Felix over the unexpected arrival, on his shining bald pate, of the wayward, highly energetic, escaping cat flea.

Unobtrusively the Dean made his way to the door and went on his way. As was his invariable practice he had played no personal part in the proceedings, but had remained throughout a silent, passive, highly discerning observer. It was a manner of behaviour that followed precisely an oft-quoted maxim from his North Country homeland, and one which had been much favoured by his taciturn father. Like him, the message—'hear all; see all; say nowt'—was blunt and uncompromising. The words were embossed on a bronze ornament below three monkeys, each having an appropriate posture that had stood on a mantelpiece in his childhood home and now functioned as a paperweight in his study.

He left, much impressed by the enigmatic Flea-man who, with his beguiling, so convincingly earnest and persuasive manner, managed to make even the most preposterous and outrageously unlikely assertion, seem curiously plausible. Perhaps it was that something about him evoked the support of his happy audiences so that they felt moved to go along with him, outrageous or not. Or maybe some were just disinclined to break the fascinating spell and preferred to live for a while in a world of fairytale make-believe.

The simple truth was that the fellow had succeeded in captivating upwards of twenty people for over half-an-hour with an intriguing entertainment, using as the basis of his unique show—of all the most bizarre creatures—a collection of assorted fleas methodically garnered from a variety of host animals, including human beings, then regularly fed with blood having an origin matching their generic personal parasitic preferences.

With a wry smile the Dean wondered how many priests in their pulpits and actors on their stages—with all their pomp, their panoply, their power, their props and their professional training—failed dismally day after day to achieve anything approaching this intense level of interest from those sitting at their feet seeking entertainment or inspiration.

It gave him food for thought, for he was well equipped by long experience to be able to make such comparisons objectively and fairly. He dwelt for a while upon the supreme irony of this demonstration of the fickle behaviour of a congregation of ordinary people.

With much inner amusement, he considered with delight what the reaction would be if somebody had the effrontery to suggest to the Archbishop of Canterbury, that a nondescript man mucking about with fleas in a small, shabby wooden hut, could excite a more enthusiastic response and a greater degree of genuine interest than a Bishop in a

Cathedral—perhaps—dare it be said—more even than could the Archbishop himself!

Oh dear! What sacrilege! What unworthy thoughts for a Dean on the Chief's staff! The Dean ought to have been ashamed of himself! But he wasn't! Not a bit! For he was profoundly atypical of his kind! An ecclesiastical oddball, if ever there was one.

From his own strictly private point of view the unlikely show had yielded a truly rich harvest, as unique as it was unexpected. Like Sam Donatello before him, it had been Larry Smith's well-chosen name for his unusual show, boldly painted on his intriguing headboard displayed above his cabin that had attracted him in to see the show, as he had been sauntering casually by. He made his way back to his holiday accommodation that day, determined to write the proprietor of Felix Foden's Flea Circus into a future story, dubbed, as he had already made up his mind, as a Professor of Flea-osophy—a fitting title for such a profound master of his subject!

So it was that from improbable beginnings Larry Smith achieved notable success riding on the backs of his tiny friends. Right from the start he was much encouraged because he knew they were instinctively fond of him! There was a quality of his blood that particularly attracted them, a blood-bond that gave him an unusual—perhaps for all he knew completely unique—ability to gain their confidence, to handle them without them being fearful of him, and to train them to go along with him in what, after all, were unflea-like activities that were indeed quite alien to their hereditary behavioural habits.

In his more meditative moments he thought that together, he and his fleas had singular inherited qualities that were by good fortune complementary: brought together by chance in a time of war, and maybe counting as one of the very, very few good things to come out of the greatest and most fearful war mankind had ever suffered.

In so far as they were capable of intellectual reasoning, he felt sure that his small comrades, being inveterate jumpers who appreciated a good jump when they saw one, were no doubt only too pleased that he had jumped on *their* bandwagon, for he gave welcome publicity to their little-known but truly phenomenal powers. This was a welcome change from the perpetual concentration of human beings on their manner of feeding, a blinkered and narrow-minded view of a very talented family—albeit of tiny stature—in the animal kingdom.

Perhaps, Larry felt, in the fullness of time, through his personal agency, they might achieve the universal respect they so richly deserved.

He hoped so, for he was sincerely fond of the little fellows and forever mindful of the way they had singled him out and befriended him, at the time of his darkest hours, in a German Prisoner-of-War Camp for British soldiers in the dark days of the 1914-1918 World War.

Chapter 31

A PEACEFUL SUNDAY AND PLEASANT DREAMS

for Boris the Driver and 'H.J.' the Dean

The fine weather spell continued the next day, and the sun rose over the now quiet and peaceful Fairground promising a pleasant day for the busy folk who ran it. Everything was closed down on a Sunday.

It was, however, not exactly a day of rest for everybody. There was much work to be done by many to clear up after the very busy Saturday that had followed what had so far proved to be a highly successful period at Hythe, and there were preparations to be made for next week. Business had been good and yesterday there had been a record crowd which, thanks to the warm and sunny day, had made the place a hive of activity until late in the evening, long after the SKWEC men had left for home.

Once he had tended his engine and settled it down to chuff away steadily, generating power for those doing maintenance work who were hooked to it and depended upon it for their supply of electricity, Boris was able to devote some time to his personal affairs and hobbies. He had to stay near at hand to watch over the Burrell, but it made little demands upon his time for it was only lightly loaded, so he was able to relax and enjoy whatever it was he was doing.

On such days as this he liked to set up his treadle fretsaw machine outside on the grass in the space between the engine and his caravan, alongside a trestle table on which he could spread his tools and materials, and get on with his model-making.

Because of his liaison with Felix and Fanny of Foden's Flea Circus, and his own particular interest in white mice and gerbils, he was these days often involved in work connected with their sideline business of selling white mice, together with cages and accessories for them. Today was one such day, for Fanny had expressly asked him to make up a small stock of mouse wheels for her since they were down to their last one.

Incongruous though it may have seemed to some people, the burly figure of Boris, associated as he was with the large, impressive steam engine thudding away by his side, could often be seen, not only busy manufacturing cages and other gadgets to do with white mice and gerbils, but also messing about tending his own small family of these tiny timid creatures that travelled with him.

The fact of the matter was, that the size of the creatures, and the scale of cages and equipment required for them, suited the scale of work he could do using his fretsaw machine and portable workshop. Because of the nature of his life, out and about all the year, with his threshing and steam-ploughing activities in the winter months, alternating with the Fairground commitment for the rather longer summer season, he really did need an absorbing hobby.

For some years now he had specialised in making three main products with his craftwork, using plywood as his basic material. These were dolls houses for girls, forts for boys to use with their lead soldiers, and cages for people who kept white mice and gerbils.

Of these three, it was his Tudor-style dolls houses which had been his main success. He did the work partly to earn extra money to enhance his income, and there was a continuing ready demand for them. Not only that, to go with these, when wanted, he was able to manufacture a whole range of furniture to a matching scale, which again was work ideally suited to his fret-working skills and small tools.

But this particular year, the arrival at Carlo's of Foden's Flea Circus had given a sudden impetus to his previously least-in-demand specialisation: his white mice work.

Felix and Fanny, who had joined Carlo's at the very start of the current season, had not been with the outfit long before their common interest was discovered. It happened that during his then just-ended steam-ploughing travels, Boris had nearly completed making a very posh, new white mouse cage for his own use, and it was this cage which was to provide his initial link with the Fodens.

Since boyhood he had liked to keep and breed these undemanding creatures. When at school, selling the young had brought him in a small extra income to supplement his pocket money. The cage he had made so recently was not only a very smart one but was also both convenient to use and easy to clean out. This latter facility was one not always remembered by people making and marketing fancy cages for animals and birds. His new cage was designed very much with this factor in view.

In essence it was of simple construction, just a long box with a hinged lid and a glass front. When the lid was raised, the glass front could be lifted out because the glass panel simply slid down grooves cut in each side-wall, its bottom edge locating neatly in a corresponding groove cut in the floor. The lid, hinged at the back, also had a groove cut in its front edge, so that the glass was firmly held all round. In effect, when the lid was closed, the glass panel was neatly fitted in a rectangular, slotted frame.

The box was eighteen inches long and twelve inches high. Seven inches up from the strong wooden bottom was another floor, this one made of more slender plywood, making the cage a two-storey luxury dwelling. Access to the upper-storey was via a sloping plywood ramp, fitted with matchsticks stuck across it at half-inch intervals. This 'staircase', angled up at 45°, passed through a hole in the 'bedroom' floor. The cage was ventilated by wire-gauze-covered rectangular slots cut in each of the three walls.

At one end of the upper floor, in a back corner, two extra pieces of plywood, fastened at right-angles to one another, slotted in to form a nesting box with access through a small hole in one side, much like a garden tits' nesting box.

Now and again Boris bred mice for sale, when he knew there was a specific demand for them.

As soon as a pair showed signs of building a nest, he helped them along by putting a supply of sundry pieces of torn-up paper, odd small pieces of cloth and cotton wool, feathers, dried grass and short lengths of soft string or wool, in a little heap on the bottom floor.

Almost as though obeying an instruction to do, the mice worked away, carrying this material bit by bit up the ramp and through the hole into their readymade hideaway upstairs, to construct a warm and comfortable nest, built in the form of a cosy, hollow ball.

Curiously, with his present breeding pair, the lady of the house usually stayed inside building the nest while her husband ran tirelessly up and down the stairway bringing up the material piece by piece and shoving it through the hole in the side of the nesting box. More often than not his wife was waiting at the hole and thrust her nose through to take the piece from him. It was not the first time Boris had witnessed this seemingly organised teamwork between a 'married couple' of mice, preparing for the arrival of a family.

Boris checked their progress in the business of nest building and raising a family by lifting the cage's lid now and again to look down into the privacy of the nesting box. The methodical, organised process of collecting the material and making the neatly-formed, cosy nest, always fascinated him, as did the development of the young.

Down below, in the quite spacious area there, he tried out a number of gadgets constructed for the entertainment and exercise of the inhabitants.

Chief amongst these, and by far the most popular device so far as they were concerned, was their treadmill-type wheel inside of which they appeared to enjoy spending endless time running hard, with great enthusiasm, to keep the wheel spinning away merrily.

Another device they seemed to appreciate was a seesaw arrangement. This he made from a length of plywood fitted with low side pieces to form a channel about ten inches long. It was pivoted at a point slightly off-centre so that one end rested down on the floor. A mouse would run up this, and as it passed the pivot the seesaw tipped up to form a chute down which the mouse ran, to pop out of the other end. Strangely enough, much like children, some of them would repeat the process over and over again, as though thoroughly enjoying the sensation.

But for popularity, the tread wheel won the day every time. Not only that, people seemed to like seeing mice working them, so they sold well.

By chance, soon after joining forces with Carlo's, Felix and Fanny had been wandering around the Fairground one Sunday morning, exploring the place with interest to get to know what exactly was there, when they came across Boris working at his table, putting the finishing touches to his new cage.

They had previously been introduced to Boris by Sam Donatello, but knew nothing about him beyond the fact that he was responsible for looking after Sam's newest and very impressive Burrell Showman's Engine, the pride of his small fleet, and also acted as the resident steam engine expert on the site.

They were immediately intrigued by his unusually palatial new home for white mice and their common interest was at once established. From then on they maintained a close liaison with Boris and quite soon joined forces with him in a common enterprise, for they saw in Boris a most useful source of practical back-up for their sideline.

Whereas Fanny was particularly interested in the livestock, Boris had little contact with the public, and his opportunities for selling mice were few, beyond occasional orders from people who knew him. On the other hand, though Felix did a lot of constructional work during the winter, he was far too busy with his show models to be able to spend much time during the summer season with cages and accessories, beyond the assembly now and again for his pre-fabricated sectional cages.

As the mice were more Fanny's interest than Felix's, it was mostly she who tended to do business with Boris. He was only too happy to have a regular outlet for his work, and during this first season with them it became obvious that they could co-operate very well, on a continuing basis, with mutual advantages to both.

That is how it was that on this pleasant Sunday, Boris had a definite purpose in his leisure pastime, and set about his task of manufacturing a small supply of four new mouse tread wheels, with a will.

As an efficient and capable craftsman, making things he had made many times before, he worked systematically, setting up something of a minor production line. He usually made a small quantity of each required part, prepared sufficient of each to cover the total number of finished units he was aiming at, and then spent a period assembling the completed end-products one after another, following an established sequence of operations that made the process seem easy, well-organised, and surprisingly fast.

Each mouse wheel required two, five-inch diameter plywood discs; thirty-eight 3½ inch-long metal rods to form the ring of treads; two brass washers for the centre pivot on the end discs; a twelve-inch metal rod for its supporting frame; and two brass end-spacers for which he used suitable washers.

Boris scribed a marking line around the discs, set a little way in from their rims, and used his callipers to step round the indented circles, pricking out marks at three-eighth-inch intervals. He then used a little hand-drill to make holes at these points to take the tread rods, and drilled a larger hole at the centres of the discs for their axles to pass through. When a brass washer had been stuck over each centre hole to form bearings, the discs were ready for assembly.

The plywood discs formed the main elements of the end product. It was his practice to keep a quantity of these in stock against future needs. They were very easily cut out using his fretsaw machine. One of each pair of discs had three entrance holes cut at equal intervals round its face, made large enough to admit a mouse with ease.

To assemble a complete wheel he placed the blank-faced disc of a pair flat on his table and with practised ease inserted a set of rods in the holes around the rim. The rods were cut from strong bicycle spokes and the size of the holes was such that the rods made a tight fit.

Using pointed-nosed pliers he then fitted the second, 'entrance-side' disc, carefully pushing each rod into its hole all the way round to locate it evenly before finally pushing them all firmly in. The ends of the rods finished up flush with the faces of the discs.

Having got this far the mouse wheel was nearly complete. It required only its support frame, the central part of which formed the wheel's axle. The twelve-inch rod, again made from a strong bicycle spoke, was first bent to make a flat-bottomed, U-shaped cradle. The mouse wheel, together with spacers each side of it, was slid on to the rod after the first of the two right-angled bends of the cradle had been made. When the second bend was made, the wheel was left snugly positioned in the centre of the frame.

Finally, the rod was bent outwards at each end, to give two convenient fixing spurs at right angles to the sides of the frame. In a cage these spurs were simply stapled to the underside of the top of the cage. Or in Boris's posh, two-storey apartment, were stapled under the bedroom floor.

For his present requirements Boris had close at hand, ready-prepared, sufficient materials to make four complete tread wheels.

He was busy assembling the second one when a young boy wandered over towards him and stood, a little diffidently, in front of his table and watched what he was doing. He had seen the lad some minutes earlier, standing gazing at the chuffing steam engine as it rocked gently to and fro with its regular relentless rhythm, seemingly fascinated by its huge, rotating flywheel and its shining, smoothly-working machinery. The fine Burrell Showman's Engine often attracted spectators, particularly children, and Boris always kept an eye on them though he'd never known anyone come to any harm, or take liberties by clambering aboard it.

Boris looked up at the rather nervous-seeming lad and greeted him with a broad, friendly smile.

"Hello, son," he said genially. "What's your name?"

The boy met his smile with a broad one of his own, and—evidently encouraged by this friendly reception—moved a little nearer to the table. But he did not reply to the question.

"Come to have a look at my engine, have you?" Boris asked, continuing to smile in a kindly way.

Again the boy said nothing, but still smiled at Boris, looking him directly in the eyes with an open, honest, innocent frankness which somehow tugged at Boris's heart-strings.

There was something unusual about the boy, a mute appeal which instantly alerted his attention. He had a curious impression that he was under appraisal. The boy appeared to be studying him intently as if trying to read his feelings, rather in the way that an animal, beckoned forwards—perhaps to take proffered food—will often stare long and hard before making tentative steps to move nearer in response to the invitation.

It was a fleeting feeling but a very positive one—initiated perhaps by the boy's absolute silence, stillness, and questioning watchfulness.

Boris was a sensitive man, very receptive to atmosphere and quick to assess the feelings of others. His mates called him a 'kind bloke', which summed up his nature in two words. Though short in words, it was a compliment only bestowed after long experience of a man's behaviour towards others. If used at all, it could be counted true.

Only a few moments had elapsed but Boris was very quickly acutely aware that the boy standing near him was on tenterhooks, as highly alert and nervous as a deer venturing from the shelter of its woodland safety, to stand, perfectly still, on the edge of a meadow.

Boris was quite incapable of being aware that the little lad was potentially scared of him without doing something about it immediately.

He reached down and picked up the first, already completed, tread wheel which he'd placed in a box by his side.

"I'm making wheels for white mice to play in," he said, holding it up by its frame for the boy to see and giving it a poke with a finger to set it spinning.

The boy's face lit up with instant recognition and delight. But he made no comment. His response, thought silent, was immediate. It was as meaningful as it was unexpected. He put his hands out, side by side, in front of his chest, facing downwards with fingers extended but curved to appear claw like and paddled his hands up and down rapidly.

"That's right," said Boris, nodding his head in agreement and beaming from ear to ear, "they get inside and tread it, making it whizz round and round."

Out of the corner of his eye he caught sight of movement and glanced sideways to spot a small girl who was walking up to look at his engine, towards the place where the boy had stood previously. It occurred to him that the two had probably come into the Fairground together, for he had seen no other people around.

The boy noticed his sideways glance and instinctively followed it—saw the girl, raced over to her, grabbed her by the hand and hurried her over to the table.

He pointed to Boris's mouse wheel with great excitement. As he did so he repeated his so vividly meaningful, paddling movement of his hands, then gesticulated with his hands, looking directly at the girl who was smiling happily and watching him intently. She nodded her head to him, apparently understanding what he meant, then turned to speak to Boris.

"He's my brother," she said. "He's not daft. But he can't speak. He's deaf and dumb. His name's Tom. My name's Emma. Tom's twelve and I'm ten. That's why he's bigger. But he doesn't go to school like I do. It's no good him going to school. Nobody could learn him anything."

Boris, taken aback but very moved by this brief, frank statement that had at once explained all with stark simplicity, responded immediately.

"Hello, Emma," he said, with a warm smile, so welcoming that it put the girl utterly at ease straight away. "Tom likes mice, does he?" he asked, with matching directness, but avoiding any reference to the boy's affliction.

"Yes," she said, nodding her head, smiling in agreement. "They're his favourite pets. He's got a white mouse of his own. He loves him. Sometimes he carries him around in his pocket!"

She turned to face her brother, whose eyes had moved from one to the other, aware he was being talked about. Bunching the fingers and thumb of her left hand to form a pointed mouse-like shape, she jabbed the forefinger of her right hand at him several times, smiling happily, her eyebrows raised high above her wide-open eyes, her whole expression being one of eager encouragement to him to respond.

She then made a series of expressive movements of her two hands, working them in unison, with her fingers and thumbs employed in slow, deliberate, rather bewildering ways, sometimes touching, sometimes making shapes in the air. Boris saw that the boy watched her with intense concentration.

483

Tom clearly understood what she meant, for his response was immediate. He nodded his head in vigorous confirmation of her message, smiling broadly, and making strange, toneless, very odd, unnatural-sounding noises, as he did so. The result of this rapid, mutual, private communication was that Tom knew, that Boris knew, that he'd got a mouse of his own and sometimes carried it in his pocket.

"He makes funny noises," Emma now informed Boris, by way of explanation of his odd behaviour. "It doesn't mean he's daft, though," she explained defensively, anxious so it seemed, to dispel any false impression about her brother at the outset.

"My Mum and Dad say he's never heard proper noises all his life so he can't copy them. He makes up noises of his own. But the doctor said he thinks Tom doesn't even hear those noises himself, in his head, either. They say it's wrong for people to make fun of his queer noises. It isn't fair. My Dad says he doesn't even know what a noise is. He says Tom's never heard a dog bark, or a bird sing, or anything else at all. Not even loud noises like the church bells. Not ever. Not since the day he was born. My Dad gets very angry when people say our Tom's daft."

"I'm sure he does," said Boris, with understanding, much moved both by what she'd said and by her earnest protection of her brother. "That's a very unkind thing for anybody to say."

"And he doesn't like people calling him Dumbo," she added, emphatically. "Most boys and girls call him Dumbo. So do some grown-ups. My Dad doesn't like it and tells them his name is Tom, not Dumbo. But it doesn't make much difference. He still gets called Dumbo."

Then, after a little pause, looking at her brother with what Boris saw to be true compassion and affection, she added touchingly, and sadly, "'Course, it doesn't make any difference to him really. He doesn't hear anything anyway. One day a big boy said to him, 'Dumbo, you're just stupid, you are. My rabbit's got more sense than you have. You'd better grow long ears like he's got. Then you might get to be as clever as he is.' Tom just grinned at him and everybody laughed. I didn't like that. That was nasty, wasn't it?"

"It was very nasty. Very nasty and very unkind," agreed Boris.

"It's sad," Emma said. "Tom's not unkind himself. He's very kind. He'd give anybody anything. He even gave that nasty boy a toffee after he'd said that to him. Most weeks he gives his sweets away. Gives away more than he eats, he does, most Saturdays. We get our pocket money on Saturdays."

She now turned her attention to the wheel Boris still held in his hand, which had so excited her brother that he had come racing across the grass to lug her over to see it.

"May I have a look at your mouse wheel please, Mister?" she asked.

"Of course you may," agreed Boris, passing the wheel to her.

She held it up by its two fixing lugs and Tom promptly gave it a poke with his finger to set it spinning. It clearly fascinated him.

"One day we saw one of these in a pet shop in Folkestone," she told Boris. "It was in a mouse cage in the window and a mouse was inside the wheel making it go. Mum couldn't get Tom away from the shop. She told our Dad about it when we got home and said Tom would have stood there all day if she'd let him!"

Tom tugged at his sister's arm and seemed to want to tell her something. She looked at him and he again made a serious of signs and gestures to her. It was clear to Boris that in his family they must have found ways over the years of communicating with Tom by a sign language of their own for she quickly turned to face Boris again and told him what it was all about.

"Tom wants to go home and fetch his mouse to show you, Mister," she said. "And

I know what he really wants, too. He would like to give his mouse a go in your wheel. Could his mouse have a ride in there, Mister? It's a very clean mouse and it wouldn't dirty your wheel at all. It's a very tame mouse. Would you let it have a go in the wheel?"

"Do you live near here, then?" asked Boris.

"Yes, just up the road," she replied. "We live in the first house down the lane that leads to the farm where my Dad works. That's our house over there," she added, pointing to a cottage over the far side of the adjacent field. "We can see your engine from our front garden. Shall I tell him he can go and fetch it?"

"Yes, of course you may," answered Boris, watching Tom's face and sensing the boy knew full well Emma was passing on his idea. "And his mouse is welcome to have a go in the wheel too, if he wants it to."

Emma turned to her brother and nodded vigorously, her beaming face communicating to him a happy permission to do what he wanted, and fetch his mouse.

Off he went, running across the grass as fast as he could go, past the chuffing engine, along the side of the Fairground and out on to the road.

"That's pleased him," Emma said, watching him go. "I expect my Mum will wonder what it's all about. But Tom will tell her I'm here with him so she won't mind him coming."

Boris noticed how naturally she had said this. Later on, when he thought about it, he reflected that in the 'telling' no words were involved since sounds didn't feature in Tom's world at all. It must, he figured, be a kind of talking with the eyes, with signs, shapes, touch, objects and actions forming a visual language, a language which had no words at all. The thought humbled him. It was not something to which he'd given much thought in the past.

He would have been surprised just how well Tom communicated within his small family circle, because of years of patience and loving care by his parents, and supported more and more by Emma.

But equally he would have been saddened had he have spent many days with the vulnerable young boy, to see how totally most people he met failed to realise he was a bright, intelligent lad and instead treated him like a nit-wit.

It was obvious to Boris that, though two years younger than her brother, Emma had learnt to take Tom under her wing and to some extent provide him with a link with his fellow beings. It was a link that was to last a lifetime, but was not all one-sided, for Tom was a good-hearted, kindly person, and a staunch, totally loyal companion to have around.

When Tom had gone off, Emma watched for a while as Boris continued to assemble his second wheel, comparing it with the completed one she still held in her hands.

"Why do you want these wheels?" she asked. "Are you making them for somebody's pet mice?"

"I'm making them for a lady who sells white mice and cages," he answered.

"Did you keep white mice when you were a boy?" she asked him.

"Yes, I did," replied Boris. "Still do, too!"

"Do you?" responded the girl, with surprise. "Have you got some here in the Fair with you?"

Boris, attracted by Emma's frank, open nature and her kindness towards her brother, thought he'd take a little time off from his work and show her his new cage.

"Come and look," he said, getting up from his table. "I'll show you two of mine that travel around with me to keep me company."

He led the way over to his small caravan. It was his habit on fine days to stand his

485

mouse cage out in the air. Well-provided for with its gauze-covered ventilation slots, it gave the box an airing and kept the mice in a healthy condition.

The cage stood on a folding table behind the caravan, between it and a wire fence that bordered the ground on that side, out of sight of people moving to and fro around the Fairground.

Emma gave an exclamation of surprise and delight when she saw the posh, comfortable home Boris had made for his privileged mice.

He tapped on the glass and one after the other the two mice, ever inquisitive and always ready to be fed tit-bits when their owner arrived at the cage, popped out of the nesting box upstairs where presumably they had been resting from their early morning exertions, and scuttled down the stairway. Boris always fed them first thing in the morning before he went about his duties, putting the food in their shallow metal feeding trays. They started their day with an early burst of activity, followed for the rest of the day with alternate periods of rest and movement.

Obligingly, one of them decided to show off in the wheel and—much to Emma's delight—scrambled into it and began to work it vigorously, with evident great satisfaction and enthusiasm.

Boris lifted the lid and showed her the inside of the nesting box in the corner, and also lifted out the glass to show her how he had arranged things so that the cage could be cleaned out easily. He always kept the floors covered with a layer of sawdust, and changed it once a week.

Emma was intrigued by the seesaw. Boris picked up one of the mice, popped it into the lower end and let it go so that it ran up the slope, tipped up the wooden channel, and nipped down the other side to run out of the far end.

Soon after they had returned to the worktable and Boris had resumed his construction of the next wheel, Tom came running back past the engine to join them.

Smiling from ear to ear he put his hand in his jacket pocket and took out a healthy-looking, well-fed white mouse, which he proudly held out for Boris to see. Boris took it from him, held it in the palm of his hand and gently stroked it, nodding his head with approval and smiling happily at Tom who was studying his reactions intently.

Handing it back to Tom, he picked up the completed mouse wheel and held it firmly with his two hands, with his elbows on the table to keep the wheel steady.

"Tell Tom to give him a go in the wheel, Emma," Boris said.

It took no time at all for Emma to convey this suggestion to Tom, who, grinning with pleasure, popped his mouse through one of the three entrance holes in the side of the wheel. Almost immediately it started to climb up the wires and set the wheel in motion. Soon it was running away like an old hand at the job, setting the wheel spinning merrily, much to Tom's visible delight.

Emma clapped her hands with joy when Tom looked at her gleefully, with obvious pride. Boris sensed that she was as much pleased by his happiness as by the athletic performance of his precious mouse.

"May I show Tom your mouse's house?" Emma asked Boris eagerly, as soon as they had retrieved the mouse from the wheel.

"Of course you may, Emma," agreed Boris. "You take him over to see it. You can show him inside, as long as you're careful not to let my mice out. Show him their nesting box and the seesaw. He'll like to see those things, I'm sure. And the stairway up to their bedroom too, I expect. Most people like to see them going upstairs to bed! But tell him not to put his own mouse in the cage, won't you? They might fight and we don't want them hurting one another, do we?"

"All right," said Emma. "I'll tell him to keep his mouse in his pocket."

Grabbing Tom's hand, Emma ran with him over to his caravan, having first got Tom to put his mouse safely away in his pocket again. Boris watched them go with a happy smile on his face, and sat at his table once again to resume his work. He rightly assumed they would be gone quite some time, examining his cage.

They had been there about five minutes when their father arrived on his bike to make sure they were not making a nuisance of themselves. He was a big, ruddy-faced, outdoor type of man who told Boris he'd been working in his garden when he'd seen Tom rush indoors to see his Mum, in a state of great excitement.

He had grabbed her by the hand, fetched his mouse out of its cage and pointed across the meadow to the Fairground where she could see Emma by the fence behind Boris's caravan. He had apparently made it plain that he wanted to take his mouse to show it to the engine driver man who was with Emma. She had let him go, but after a bit thought perhaps her husband ought to ride over to make sure they were not being a nuisance, especially as it was a Sunday and the Fair was closed.

Boris assured their Dad they were no trouble, and suggested he went over to the caravan to let them know he was there. He felt sure Tom would enjoy showing his Dad the cage. The rather diffident-seeming man, leaving his bike lying on the grass, went off to join his two children.

At length the three of them came walking back to the table to rejoin Boris who by that time had very nearly completed assembling the second wheel.

"Tom wants to show Dad his mouse working the wheel," Emma said."Would you mind?"

"Emma!" said her Dad sharply. "You've taken up enough of the gentleman's time already."

"No! Not a bit of it," Boris reassured him with a smile. "It's been a pleasure to have their company. He's welcome to give his mouse another spin. This is a Fairground after all! His mouse would expect to have a ride of some sort at a Fair, like everybody else!"

Emma laughed at that comment and passed on the good news to Tom.

Meanwhile Boris, sitting down at the table, picked up the completed wheel and held it ready again, as he had done before.

Tom, beaming with pleasure, popped his mouse inside and away it went as naturally as though it had been treading a mouse wheel all its life.

"He's good at that, isn't he, Dad?" exclaimed Emma. "He knew how to work it as soon as Tom put him in there!"

Boris noticed Tom watch his Dad and Emma closely as he looked up to make sure his Dad had seen his mouse perform. They were both gazing at the wheel and his Dad, catching his eye, nodded his head in marked approval and clapped his hands to show his appreciation of the mouse's clever efforts.

"It's a fine cage you've made over there for your mice," he said to Boris. "That's given me some ideas, that has. I think I'll quietly have a go at making one of those for Tom for Christmas. Reckon I'll have to make it at the farm, though, in our workshop there. Not much chance of keeping it a secret at home. Doesn't miss much, our Tom doesn't!"

"Will you really, Dad?" asked Emma, her face alight with expectation. "Tom would love that. So would I. It would be lovely to have a cage like that with a bedroom and a downstairs. Will you really make him one?"

"I'll have a try," said her Dad, laughing. "I've done it now!" he added, turning to Boris. "I sometimes forget with my two nippers here one pair of ears hears and one pair doesn't!"

"I promise I'll keep it a secret, Dad," assured Emma, smiling at him impishly.

Boris noted with some admiration how well the little family had learnt to live around Tom's sad affliction.

"Well, come on, you two," said their kind, good-tempered Dad. "Help him get the mouse out of the wheel, please, Emma. It's time we left this gentleman alone to get on with his work."

Boris waited until Emma had let Tom know it was time to go, and then lowered the wheel to the table so that they could retrieve the well-exercised mouse.

Tom's face showed that he'd rather stay longer and he looked longingly at the wheel when Boris put it down on the table.

The little group said goodbye to Boris and turned to start walking back past the engine, the man pushing his bike. But they didn't get far; Boris called them back. He had been teetering on the edge of a decision and now he had to obey his overwhelming compulsion to make it.

"Wait a minute," he called. "I'd like Tom to have this. He can take this one back with him. His mouse has taken a fancy to it!"

Boris walked towards them, holding out the mouse wheel and handed it to Tom who took it from him, looking decidedly puzzled. Anxiously he gazed up at his Dad, to see what it was he'd got to do.

"You can't do that!" said Tom's Dad to Boris, looking as worried as Tom was puzzled. "That's taken you a long time to make and cost you money. Let me buy it off you."

"No, you don't!" Boris said, grinning broadly. "Emma, you tell Tom that wheel is a gift for him from the Engine Driver. That's a fine mouse he's got there. He deserves a wheel to play in, especially as he's so good at working it! And make sure Tom understands that it's now his wheel for keeps. I don't want him to think he's got to bring it back again. I want him to know it's his for good. Then he will really enjoy having it."

Emma had no difficulty conveying the message and the sheer delight on Tom's face was something Boris remembered long afterwards.

"That's very, very kind of you," said Tom's Dad, hardly knowing what to say to their newly met, generous friend and uneasy lest in some way they were taking advantage of his kindness.

Boris reassured him, looking him squarely in the eyes, and smiling in a rather wistful way.

"Think nothing of it," he said. "That little lad deserves it. Life can't be easy for him, with his problem. I'm sure of that. But he's a fine, good-hearted little lad and I'd love him to take the wheel home with him today. And if you can't find room for it in his present cage, you'll have to hurry up and make the new one to put it in, for Christmas!"

"Oh! There's plenty of room in his present cage," laughed Tom's Dad. "You'll help me fit it in, won't you, Emma? We'll do it straightaway, as soon as we get home, shall we?"

"Yes please, Dad!" replied Emma, obviously overjoyed at the prospect of arriving home with the wheel and getting it into action as quickly as possible.

Boris stood and watched the little group walk off past his Burrell, and waved back as they turned to wave him goodbye. There were tears in his eyes as he listened to the deep voice of the man, and the happy, laughing voice of the thoughtful little girl, interspersed every now and again by the strange, toneless, meaningless, random sounds from Tom.

He knew that in the family Tom's total deafness would not stop him from leading a happy life, but he could not help being apprehensive about his future in the world at large. He had an uneasy suspicion that Tom had a rough ride ahead of him. All too often, Boris felt sure, Tom was destined to be brushed aside as a mindless idiot, and he could see a whole lot of hurt facing Tom unless, somehow, somebody could save him from it.

Boris was right in his assessment of Tom's predicament.

Tom was very much a spectator in the silent world which moved about him. Often he was a solitary figure, for except for his small immediate family, and to a lesser extent their close friends and relatives, people avoided him.

Since he could hear nothing at all, there was no reaction from him to sounds and voices, however loud. This lack of response meant that his facial expression appeared so vacant to strangers that they interpreted it as stupidity, evidence of a lack of ability to understand even the simplest thing.

This, coupled with the fact that quite at random he made unnatural noises—some people, perhaps for want of a better description rather than from malice, said he made animal noises—compounded the impression they gained of him and caused him to be treated as an idiot, incapable of reasoned thinking about anything at all.

Small wonder that Tom was often very hurt by the reaction of people to him, and wore an unhappy, puzzled look when, finding himself the centre of amusement and unkindness, there seemed to him to be nothing he could do except try to get away from them all and find someplace where he could be alone.

But his visual sense was made all the more acute because he relied entirely upon it. He studied facial expressions very intently. In the eyes he could detect kindness or meanness with the clarity of light or dark. And because he looked about him with an acuteness of interest that was much greater than that of a normal person, he saw much that others missed.

Strangely, animals and birds were much less afraid of him than of most human beings being around them. He had an affinity with them which, perhaps by instinct, they felt. They were naturally influenced by the fact that he had time for them and took pleasure in finding them food, for he perceived only too well that it was their perpetual hunt for food which preoccupied them most of their time.

Sometimes he would stand, as still as a stalking cat, but entirely without its menace, watching the behaviour of creatures in the garden and in the surrounding countryside. There was no doubt that he was recognised as posing no danger by some of those territorial animals and birds that lived permanently in and around their large garden at home. It seemed evident that he gained pleasure and companionship from their company when they moved about near him showing no fear. He knew about fear, and anybody watching him for long could not help noticing that he did everything he could to avoid scaring creatures in any way, however big or small they were. It was as though their nervous timidity was something he recognised and identified with only too well, so went out of his way to allay it, in whatever way he could.

As a practical man Boris could well understand that Tom had been stone deaf from birth for reasons which were no doubt permanent and beyond correction. But he thought it highly likely that Tom had the physical ability of talking normally if only he could be taught to do so. Unfortunately there didn't seem to be any way to teach him. He couldn't copy and presumably he couldn't possibly even imagine what a sound was.

Boris went to bed that night pondering the problem, certain that somebody, sometime, would find a way of teaching people like Tom to talk. Somehow sounds would have to be converted into some sort of sensation deaf people could feel or see, then copy and reproduce exactly, until by constant practice they could talk normally.

Maybe, he went on to think, they might even be taught to read and write, as well as talk, so being set free from their private prison into the world of words which would win them acceptance as normal people able to communicate with others—lacking then just the *one* ability, to hear sounds directly. They would be deaf, but not dumb. And not treated as nit-wits.

What really bugged Boris was little Emma's repeated insistence that her brother Tom was 'not daft'. Boris knew Emma was right. Even in so short a time he felt convinced that Tom was inherently bright. He simply had an un-started engine that needed a mechanic to set it running.

He eventually fell asleep with his mind fully occupied with these thoughts. And as so often happened with him, as with other problem-ponderers like him, his conscious thoughts crept into his sub-conscious mind and insidiously coloured, if not partially controlled, the curious part-rational, part-bizarrely irrational, unfathomable pictures being conjured up there in the kaleidoscopic mental melting pot of his unfettered, sleeping, yet free-running mind.

In the early hours of the morning he woke from a nightmarish dream in which Tom's head was wired up to an ingenious machine he'd invented for Tom in his garden shed workshop at home. Out of the rapidly dissolving confusion of impressions and details that filled his mind at the moment of waking, which try as he might—and he tried desperately—he could not recapture, one abiding picture remained sharply focused in his mind: Tom was sitting there in the shed, his face alight with pleasure, reading a copy of 'Just William'.

* * * * *

A few miles away from Hythe, comfortably installed in a well-furnished boarding house high on the cliff top overlooking the sea along the Leas area of Folkestone, another imaginative dreamer awoke at very much the same time as Boris. He also lay in bed trying hard to recapture details of the dream from which he had just awakened. It had been a delightful, amusing dream and sufficient of it remained in his mind for him to smile as he recalled the unlikely picture it presented.

In psychological make-up, his propensity to carry problems from late-night bedtime musings into dreams that became influenced by the subject of his end-of-the-day deep thinking, marked him as a man similar in many respects to Boris.

But his normal, everyday world was an entirely different one from that of Boris. It so happened that their respective dreams were both stimulated by experiences that weekend in Carlo's Fairground at Hythe; the one through the agency of white mice, the other through that of fleas!

For the awakened dreamer at Folkestone who lay smiling about the images left in his mind from his freshly-experienced dream, was the holidaying, story-writing Dean of the Church of England.

The aspiring future Dean of Canterbury was soon to travel back to the North of England to resume his clerical duties. He had spent his time on Sunday morning taking a pleasant walk in the sunshine along the famous marine promenade of the Leas, contemplating how he would weave into a future book some of the fascinating things he had witnessed the day before, in Foden's Flea Circus at the Fair in Hythe.

During the afternoon, knowing from long experience how important it is to record new encounters and ideas as soon as possible in order to capture the full impact of them before their pictures fade in the memory, he spent the afternoon in his room writing a series of notes which later would enable him to recapture the bizarre events vividly.

As he lay in bed that evening he had already started the enjoyable process of building a story around the image of Felix in his world of fleas, and in due course fell asleep with his mind full of these strange, almost unreal memories of the things he'd seen and the impressions he'd gained.

The Dean had a mischievous, impish streak to his nature. As a boy this had given rise to numerous pranks and escapades of usually a perfectly harmless kind, though sometimes to others a trifle irritating, if not positively annoying. As a Church dignitary it was a streak he had to suppress. But the innate impulse was still there, nonetheless.

Small wonder that in the conditions of total freedom from restraint enjoyed by his fertile mind during sleep, there were created in his dreams situations that were bizarre in the extreme.

It is probable that the slamming of a door along the corridor had awoken him in the midst of such a dream because he carried with him to his wakened state a vivid image that was typical of the unlikely happenings of his curiously mixed-up dreams.

The Archbishop of Canterbury, accompanied by his image-conscious wife—whose outwardly haughty manner, to be fair to her, belied an inner sense of fun known only to her close friends—had intruded during his slumbers into the Fairground world that was so occupying his mind. This was despite his habitual, deliberate total exclusion from his thoughts of all matters ecclesiastical during the period before he dropped off to sleep, for in sleep he sought escape from such serious subjects. His daytime dose from his combined cathedral and diocesan duties in Manchester was enough—quite enough—of this fare, for his appetite. When he slept he wanted none of it!

On this occasion, however, the unlikely intrusion of his professional C of E Boss into his happy dreams was most welcome, an unexpected bonus of added joy. For his mental picture, so vividly seen on wakening, absolutely delighted him and was to remain etched in his memory, to his lasting pleasure.

Seated upon a gaily-painted ostrich on Sam Donatello's most elaborate roundabout, dressed in all his splendid regalia—fit indeed to crown a King—sat the Archbishop, hurtling round and round, staring fixedly ahead, trying to look as dignified as possible and clearly not wishing to indicate that the procedure was in the least bit one which amused him!

By his side, in the next row of the three-abreast set of Gallopers, sat his haughty wife on a large white horse, similarly staring straight ahead as the horse rose and fell on its successive whirling journeys round and round. Again, by her expression and manner, she contrived to let it be known that such activities were really very much below her dignity.

In front of these two riders, behind them, and all around them, rode a sea of laughing, noisy, holidaymakers and local fairgoers. The two unsmiling visitors had, by some strange dream-world step, strayed into the Fairground at Hythe from the hallowed precincts of Canterbury Cathedral, and somehow got themselves mounted on Sam's Gallopers.

They were riding round and round, in a cocoon of supercilious isolation, to the accompaniment of the deafening blast of the Fairground Organ music, like two ghostly, unreal apparitions who had been transported there willy-nilly from another dimension of time and space.

The Dean clung on to this mental picture with much glee, smiling happily as he contemplated the embarrassing predicament of his Grace the Archbishop and his Lady!

He lay in bed savouring this delightful spectacle thrown up for his entertainment by the ingenuity of his subconscious mind. On reflection, wondering, as he so often did, by what process of random selection of memories, a particularly unlikely image such as this one arose, he concluded that the link between his Boss and the Fairground lay in Felix Foden's Flea Circus.

For the Dean remembered having thought about the Archbishops of York and Canterbury while watching the po-faced performance of Felix, and wondering at that time what their reaction would have been had they been able to see one of their Senior members of the Establishment watching the whimsical work of the enigmatic Flea Man. And not only that, watching him too with what was, most reprehensibly, very close interest and obvious amusement!

This reflection fired off his fertile imagination and pretty soon there was conjured up in his mind, another amusing picture to entertain him.

As he rested in a state of blissful comfort, half awake and half asleep, dozing away with his mind given full freedom and encouragement to play around and make what it would of the curiously contrasting combination of the Archbishop and the Flea Man, his imagination was stimulated by picturing the possibility of the Primate of All England poking his nose into Foden's cabin at the critical moment when Felix was launching his 'pièce de résistance': his Royal Navy Airship type SS Mk II!

It was the presence in his dream of his Grace and his Lady at the Fairground that made it reasonable to suppose that, driven by sudden curiosity, the Archbishop might well have had a quick peek inside to see what on earth could be happening in a place bearing the intriguing title of 'Felix Foden's Flea Circus'.

The Dean's imagination capriciously shifted the scene in his mind's eye to the privacy of the Archbishop's private apartments at Lambeth Palace in London, a place where he had been privileged to make occasional personal visits. He pictured a fireside domestic scene where his Grace and his Lady sat together in circumstances more fitting to their dignity than riding on Sam Donatello's Gallopers.

The Archbishop had been silent for some time. Something was clearly on his mind, for he looked worried and deep in thought. His wife discerned this and at length spoke to him, thinking perhaps that unburdening himself to her might help him to overcome whatever it was that was bothering him.

"What is troubling you, my dear?" she asked, her manner one of sympathetic consideration for his welfare.

"I'm concerned about something I saw in the Fairground down at Hythe yesterday," her husband replied. "I caught sight of 'H.J.' in rather unsavoury circumstances. As you know, he is well in line to become the next Dean of Canterbury—with my full backing of course. But what I saw yesterday troubles me. Troubles me most deeply, I'm afraid." His furrowed brow and worried expression reflected his deep concern.

"Good heavens!" she exclaimed, highly alert now with obvious interest. "Whatever's our Hughie been up to down there, then?" That there was the possibility of her learning something juicy and spicy was clearly evident in the tone of her voice, and the barely concealed expectant twinkle in her eyes.

"It's not exactly that he was personally doing anything reprehensible," replied his Grace, aware that he might have given the wrong impression and that his wife was eagerly awaiting a tit-bit of gratuitous scandal. "He was not actively doing anything himself. But he was present under circumstances which leave me to wonder, if, after all, his judgement, personal interests and sense of propriety may not be quite as impeccably suitable for this important office as I had thought."

"What were these unsavoury circumstances you speak of?" she asked, much intrigued. There was clearly something most unusual in the wind and she wanted to know about it.

"Well, when you were busy looking at the costume jewellery that so captivated your attention on that cheapjack Gift Stall place—let's see . . . what was it now . . . ah, yes . . . er 'Gemstone George's', the establishment was called, as I recall—while I was waiting for you when you were detained there," he explained, a slightly sardonic note in his voice registering his disdainful opinion of such a low-class-sounding Emporium, "I wandered off on my own for a short while."

He paused a moment, frowning thoughtfully, inwardly not too happy at divulging where he had gone, and the revelations he might be unable to avoid describing.

"Where did you go?" he wife asked, sensing his reluctance, and giving him a prod.

"The fact is," he continued, "I had a quick look in that Flea Show building we saw. You see, I really couldn't imagine what a Flea Circus could possibly be. I . . ."

"My God! That shouldn't present much difficulty," his wife interjected irreverently, her script under the deft control of the gleeful Dean, creating and observing the scene at one and the same time in his mischievous mind. "Just think of a Synod of the Church of England! A very appropriate image indeed, I'd have thought!"

The Archbishop's frown deepened, but he made no comment. He didn't like the allusion one little bit, but he let it pass having learnt by long experience that it was better to ride out such playful, disrespectful comments by his wife, for abysmal, humiliating defeat always followed any attempt to counter them. His dignity was best preserved by ignoring them.

"I was about to say," he continued, "I looked into the building and there was a small crowd of people in there watching what was happening. And standing on his own at the back, studying things with what I can only describe as a very keen interest, was 'H.J.', if you please! I could hardly believe my eyes! A Dean of my Church in a place like that! But it was 'H.J.' all right. There was no mistake about that! There he stood, as bold as brass!"

"Really, my dear!" his wife commented with some feeling. "What's wrong with that, for goodness sake? He's probably on holiday down there. Why should he not look in there if he wanted to? You were doing the same thing, after all! Be fair!"

This counter-attack threw his Grace a little. It was an angle that had not occurred to him. The sharp logic disturbed him.

"But you don't understand, Dorothy," he said. "I merely peeped in the door out of curiosity. 'H.J.' was actually inside there as one of the audience. He must have paid to go in. What's more, having seen the nature of the show, the disgusting crudity of the man running it and the depraved nature of his exhibits, one would have expected a man of his distinguished status to have walked out. But he must have stayed in there despite what he'd seen, from the very start. There was indeed a notice outside saying the next show would be starting shortly."

"What was it you saw that so upset you, then?" she pressed, getting more and more intrigued by the minute.

"I hardly like to describe it," her husband said. "The depravity of the scene appals me to recall. It's almost beyond belief that a Dean of my Church should find it entertaining to stand and watch such utter iniquity."

The apparent unwillingness of her husband to give specific details of what he had seen convinced her it must be something well worth hearing about.

"Good gracious, Godfrey," she said, "what an earth was going on in there? Some sort of public orgy or something?"

"No! No! No! —of course not!" he answered emphatically, startled now at his wife's unexpected and outrageous suggestion. "Nothing like that at all! How can you possibly imagine such a thing?"

"Because you're being so infuriatingly evasive, that's why!" she replied, impatiently. "For goodness sake tell me what you saw. I'm not a child!"

"Well, if you must know," he stated, so irritated by her insistence that he overcame his reluctance to talk about such a seamy sordid subject with his so-sophisticated and somewhat supercilious spouse, "if you really feel you have to know, they were all standing looking at an inflated male contraceptive, hovering over a table!"

His wife, though she tried very hard, could not suppress a stifled giggle of utter delight. She had the greatest difficulty in controlling herself sufficiently to pursue the incredible matter further. Clutching a handkerchief to her mouth she did her best—but with only limited success—to smother her spontaneous, delighted laughter.

"Do you mean to say they were all in there looking at a pumped-up French Letter?" she spluttered. "Oh! Oh! I say! How funny! How utterly priceless! What very strange entertainment! How absolutely wonderful! How unbelievably bizarre! But what on earth has a thing like that got to do with a Flea Circus, for heaven's sake?"

"That's just the point," he explained, not in the least pleased by her hilarity and startled by her use of so common an expression—most certainly not something she had ever said in his hearing before. "The man had blown the thing up with gas and fixed it up to look like an Airship. He'd got a cabin suspended underneath it, with dead insects sitting in it as passengers! And its two propellers, one in front and the other behind the cabin, were actually being driven round by live fleas on wires, which were treading on little drums to spin the propellers!"

She could hardly believe what she was hearing. The picture that arose in her mind's eye seemed too incredible to contemplate seriously. Her facial expression—one of highly amused incredulity—was noted by her husband, who was becoming increasingly displeased.

"Did you say he'd got insects riding in the cabin?" she managed to ask. "What was it supposed to be, then, a passenger-carrying Airship?"

"Well, no, not exactly," he replied. "It was supposed to be a model of a Royal Navy Submarine Spotting Airship, apparently. Painted on the side of it were the words Royal Navy, H.M. Airship S.S. Mark II. The insects sitting in the open-topped cabin represented the crew. In the front were two wasps, as the Pilot and the Co-Pilot/Navigator. Behind those, in pairs, were six honey bees dressed as sailors acting as submarine spotters."

His Grace, aware that far from being shocked, his wife was highly amused by what to him was a very sordid matter, felt irritated and aggrieved. She was indeed thoroughly enjoying his story, much more in fact, had he have known it, than she would have been by the orgy she had been beginning to think she was going to hear about. By comparison that would have been very mundane.

On an impulse, he thought she should have to suffer hearing the worst of it. Her reaction had not pleased him at all. She ought properly to have been shocked by the seamy story, not found it funny.

Very well! She should hear just how sordid the show was that 'H.J.' had found so absorbingly interesting.

"You might be equally as delighted," he said sarcastically, "to hear what names the sleazy fellow had chosen to give the craft's officers!"

"The two wasps, you mean, I presume?" she queried. She could not begin to imagine what names the man could possibly have given the ship's officers, which had obviously so adversely affected her affronted husband. But she was agog to find out! Alert and wide-eyed she hung on his words!

"That's right," he confirmed. "The Pilot was introduced to the august assembly as Captain Condom and the other wasp, if you please, the co-Pilot/Navigator that is, was introduced as Flying Officer . . . er . . . Flying Officer . . . er—let me see now, what was the name he gave him—ah yes!—I remember now—Flying Officer 'Spunkstopper'—that was the edifying name he chose for him!"

The Archbishop's attempt to give the impression he had some difficulty recalling the unsavoury name did not fool his observant wife. It was in fact emblazoned in banner headlines in his memory, and she knew it only too well. Over the years she had often seen him affect an innocent ignorance of some juicy expressions, or common man's earthy, non-academic terminology, implying to those around him that such matters were so far removed from his dignified eminence as to be completely beyond his ken.

Had he but known it, his affected hesitation merely added spice to the information he imparted to his wife. When the sound of the outrageous name finally impacted with her eardrums, the sheer incongruity of it nearly made her explode with delight and merriment. Totally unable to control her mirth any longer, the Archbishop's wife got up to leave the room.

His Grace was not amused. There was no sign of levity on his face, but instead he wore an expression of disgust and utter disapproval.

"I think you will agree," he concluded, adopting his most lofty and pompous manner which in private his wife was pleased to describe as 'going all-Archbishopy over her', "that a man capable of deriving pleasure from witnessing that kind of disgusting spectacle—indeed of actively supporting the staging of such depravity by paying to go in and see it—is a singularly unsuitable person to be appointed Dean of Canterbury. It really is unthinkable! Absolutely unthinkable! Quite out of the question!"

"Poor old Hughie," she spluttered, as she moved towards the door. "He should have kept away from pumped-up, flea-driven flying French Letters if he wanted to move to Canterbury Cathedral, shouldn't he! I must say, if he came now, whenever I saw his eyes raised to heaven I should wonder what it was that he was seeing floating in the firmament above him!"

Making a not very successful effort to control herself she opened the door and went out, but stopped short of fully closing it behind her. Overcome by a fit of devilment, she poked her head round the edge of the door to make a final comment before going off to find a private corner where she could giggle herself back to normality. She felt an irresistible urge to prick the outraged pomposity of her indignant husband, fully inflated as he now was by a chronic attack of priggish piety.

Driven by a desire to say something really dreadful, and inspired perhaps by an association of ideas deriving from the delightful mental image she had of the hilarious, surrealistic airship that had so offended his sense of propriety, she fired a devastating verbal missile at him.

Acting on an impulse she deliberately employed an awful, socially unacceptable, unforgiveable word, much used by vulgar people who knew no better, and occasionally by people of her close acquaintance who did. It was language which his Grace the Archbishop abhorred; and well she knew it!

"What a shame!" she said, in a tone of voice which she tried hard, despite her explosive condition, to make sound full of heartfelt sympathy. "What a very great shame! Fancy poor old 'H.J.' fouling up his preferment and fine, promising future, by standing in a sleazy little shabby shack, peering so professionally improperly at flying fucking fleas!"

This parting shot hit the Archbishop with the metaphorical impact of a high velocity bullet. He visibly winced. His eyes opened widely and his mouth dropped open. His expression was one of shocked, stunned disbelief.

Subsequently it cost him a lot of valuable prayer time trying to put right with the Almighty this awful, sinful transgression on the part of his wife.

For her part this aspect of the matter troubled his wife not at all. It was her belief, naive maybe by the standards of serious students of theology, that the Archbishop's Chief, having invented everything in the world, must surely have a holy sense of humour, and—while no doubt, in all fairness, applauding the sincerity of her husband—would witness the bizarre events with a tolerant, Fatherly smile—perhaps even with secret Heavenly glee!

* * * * *

The Dean, smiling with pleasure at his delightful reverie, sat up in bed and prepared to start another day.

But notwithstanding the fact that these unlikely events had been entirely generated by his highly imaginative and inventive mind, not to speak of his twisted sense of humour, joking apart he realised that if indeed his Boss did get to know that he had attended such an outrageous exhibition, and what's more actually enjoyed it, it could easily cost him his candidature for the post he coveted so much.

In this conclusion he was probably right, for his understanding of the true nature, not only of the Archbishop himself, but also of his wife, was penetrating and highly perspicacious—much more so than either of them could possibly have imagined.

So—very reluctantly because he had savoured the prospect—he decided that he would resist the temptation to relate the wonderful story of Felix Foden's Airship to his friends, or to anyone else for that matter, and simply reserve details of the bizarre show for inclusion in a story which would be published under the safe anonymity of his pseudonym.

As regards the proposed story itself, the germ of which was now firmly planted, as he went about his domestic preparations to start another day, his active and fertile mind played around with the delightful little scenes he had pictured in his mind during the day-dreaming reverie, and soon he concluded that this little cameo conjured up in his imagination was too good to lose. So, as was his habit, he took time out to jot down the essential skeletal details of it. And it was not long before he tentatively began to toy with the idea of writing it into his intended story built around the enigmatic Flea Man.

He liked the idea of the Archbishop of Canterbury—present at the Fair for whatever reason, maybe there in mufti with his wife just simply having a look round to see what was going on—taking a clandestine peek into the interior of the Flea Circus cabin at the critical moment he had pictured. And moreover, he also liked the idea of him seeing a senior member of the Ecclesiastical Establishment in there on his own enjoying the proceedings.

But of course it would be asking for trouble to allow himself to be the figure caught in there. In a story invented by an author ostensibly unknown personally to any of them, that would truly be dicing with potential disaster, and in the event carried no merit. It would simply draw attention to himself quite unnecessarily and maybe even blow his cover.

So, as a first possibility, he thought that he might—he just might—put the Archbishop of York inside there, to be seen in the seamy circumstances by his senior colleague and take it from there. Whether or not to convey this little cameo as part of the actual structure of the fictional story, or to carry it one step further from pretended reality by writing it in as a quirkish dream of one of the story's characters, he would have to decide. On balance, at a first judgement, it seemed to him that the 'dream' approach would stretch the limits of plausibility far enough.

However, all that being as it may, apart from the identity of the Church Establishment's covert member of the Flea Man's audience, much of these reveries was good stuff and could stand. So he recorded the salient details in his preliminary notes.

But being a prudent man, the Dean nonetheless determined that although he would write the story soon, while details were fresh in his mind, he would play for absolute safety and wait until he was well established in his hoped-for new appointment as the Dean of Canterbury before he had it published.

Once his feet were under the proverbial table, he would be difficult either to boot out, or to winkle out by devious means however crafty they might be. Like a lot of people he had leech-like powers of attachment once planted and the body of the Church of England was a difficult surface from which to prise off a determined hanger-on. It was his opinion that the higher one moved up the hierarchy, the better the surface became in this respect. A chap got to be bombproof: safe till Doomsday!

One hundred percent assurance of anonymity was also unattainable to those hiding under the protection of a pseudonym, so the wily fellow decided to get 'home and dry' before he exposed himself even to so remote a risk as a breach of publisher's security.

As a final prospective bonus arising from this delayed publication, he figured that when the story was in due course published, it would almost certainly find its way eventually to the inner sanctums of the Church. And, as then a member himself of the inner circle, he would be in a marvellous position to witness the reaction of the Principal Players to the revelation of their fictitious appearance as characters in a work of such dubious literary value!

He had a shrewd idea that the first of these characters to read the erudite work would be the Archbishop's wife, because he suspected, and with good reason, that her friends would delight in drawing her attention to it—not out of malice, but because they might well conclude that she would thoroughly enjoy it. And if by chance it didn't land in her hands by its own natural volition, he was quite crafty enough to engineer its arrival by devious means.

As to his Boss's reaction—that would be interesting indeed. Most interesting! A positive treat to look forward to with relish, and well worth the wait!

The abstract story would not of course be dated, and the period of the supposedly fictitious Archbishop would be unknown—although open to speculation by those interested.

But the Dean determined to endow his caricatured Archbishop of Canterbury with sufficient of the well-known habits, idiosyncrasies and behavioural mannerisms of the present incumbent to allow the man to see much of himself in the portrayed petulant and pompous Prelate—always assuming he knew himself well enough not to be so blissfully unaware of his outward appearance and of his personal reputation as perceived by others, that he missed the resemblance altogether.

Even so, others wouldn't fail to recognise him! Of that the Dean was sure, for he was confident enough in his own powers of invention and allusion to ensure that his story would be read by those close to the Archbishop, with gleeful appreciation on their part of the fictional character's role model.

Of one thing he was absolutely certain; the remarkable similarity between the two that he intended to establish, would not be lost on the Archbishop's wife. And knowing her as well as he did, he thought it highly likely that she might well innocently comment to her husband that he bore some similarity to his opposite number in the book—the comment being playful, of course! It would be delivered as a gentle little dig, too good-humoured to allow him to object without seeming stuffy and churlish. This was a skill she had developed to perfection. But the Dean knew that the point would register! The old boy would get the message! And what's more, if he hadn't read the story already, he would lose no time in doing so! All in all a gratifying little prospect: a potential situation full of pleasurable possibilities.

So an embryonic story was born that day in which the Principal Players were to be two Archbishops, one Archbishop's wife and a Professor of Fleaology.

A somewhat unlikely cast! But then the aspiring Dean of Canterbury was a most unlikely fellow! For by tortuous mental processes, known only to himself, he contrived to reconcile his devout Christianity with a widely-publicised, enthusiastic approval of the Godless Communism of the Soviet Union, which eventually earned him the unique description of 'The Red Dean'. The incorrigible priest was a pain to his perplexed peers, but in his perfidy the puzzlement produced by his open profanity gave much inner glee to the mischievous ecclesiastic as he impishly stirred his mess of pontifical pottage.

He was indeed a curious, enigmatic fellow whose anonymity in these books of the often decidedly blue kind, contrasted sharply with his high-profile writings of the red kind. So he was most amused by the title conferred upon him and was destined historically to be remembered as a man with a spiritual question mark over his head, illuminated by a pale, flickering halo which didn't seem to know if it should be there or not. Perhaps it reflected a flickering faith, a secret uncertainty no doubt shared by some other priests of even loftier status who would not care to admit it, even to themselves, but who would not let this stop them from blasting him with scornful, hypocritical comments, comments echoed by many piously outraged people.

Not that such reaction worried him. On the contrary, if anything he enjoyed them and digested them with pleasure. For he was as invulnerable as he was incorrigible—a most infuriating fellow whose sense of humour was like armour plating from which insults and criticisms bounced off as harmlessly as peas off a battleship, leaving no dent nor impression, their impact very frustratingly passing unnoticed, except perhaps for an appreciative smile.

Perversely, petulant people who got ratty with him simply provided the happy fellow with further material for his memory bank of acutely-observed patterns of human behaviour. All such gifts were gratefully received. They sometimes gave him inspiration and got written into stories!

From his cosy position of assured safety, he looked out on the world with a permanent beaming, benign and tolerant smile, as safe and snug as a bug in a rug. More secure indeed than a flea behind a rabbit's ear!

Chapter 32

CARLO'S FAIR MOVES TO DEAL

trouble on the road for Boris

Ten days later, on Wednesday morning, Carlo's Fair pulled out of Hythe heading for Deal in order to be there, installed and fully operational, before the start of the town's Carnival Week on the coming Saturday. It was their next-to-last move of the season. Their final destination was the Isle of Thanet where their stay was always fixed to cover the period when the Annual Thanet Ploughing Match took place.

It was customary for Sam Donatello to go off ahead of the main convoys of vehicles in his private car so that he arrived at their next site in advance of the remainder, to make final decisions about where the various rides and sideshows would be positioned. As his itinerary was largely a repeating one, he already had overall ground-plans for each regularly-visited site, but he always needed to finalise detailed plans on the day of each move, so that as people pulled in they could be directed where they had to go, without hold-ups and unnecessary troubles. In total there were so many vehicles, and so much equipment involved, that it was essential for the whole lot to be so organised that it flowed into a site in an uninterrupted, smoothly running stream.

Travelling with Sam were his wife Sandra, his fourteen-year-old son Charles Henry, and his eleven-year-old daughter Stella Mary. His son, whose names had been chosen after those of the first two generations of the Donatello family's fairground history—his Great-grandfather Carlo and his Grandfather Enrico—had just left school that summer and was now starting his working career with the family firm, destined, if all went well, eventually to become the next Boss of Carlo's Fairground Company.

It was only just after nine o'clock when, with a last word to Boris, Sam drove his very impressive-looking car out of the ground. Bought only a few weeks ago, and evidence itself of the prosperity of Carlo's Fairground Company, Sam's new car was the latest 1927 Alvis 12/50 Sports Tourer. Dark blue in colour, with four doors and a smart, superbly fitted, folding canvas hood, it was a fine, well-made car. There were many among those around the Fairground preparing to depart later that day, who paused in their activities to watch the car admiringly as it made its way out of the fairground.

Following their normal procedure, immediately afterwards Boris, with the help of two of Sam's trusted full-time staff, Stan Bowen and Stuart Robertson, completed his preparations for the journey. In less than half-an-hour after Sam had left, Boris drove his gleaming Burrell Showman's Engine out of the ground, towing behind him three vehicles; a fully-loaded, large trailer carrying the best part of Sam's largest set of Gallopers, followed by Sam's luxury caravan, and finally Boris's own small, personal caravan. Stuart rode on the engine footplate with Boris and Stan perched high up on the loaded trailer just behind them with a good view of the road ahead. From this high vantage point he was able to act as a look-out for Boris, to warn him of any potential difficulties or trouble ahead.

This routine enabled Boris and his two mates to arrive well ahead of the rest of the fraternity, allowing plenty of time for them to help Sam complete his reception arrangements, and also to get Sam's own domestic situation organised to the best advantage so that his family was safely settled into their well-equipped mobile home before the others flooded in.

The remainder were organised to leave at intervals in three separate convoys, split up like this to avoid clogging the roads with a single, very long convoy, which, in total, was too difficult to manage without trouble—especially on busy and often narrow roads.

Sam's most senior, full-time man always looked after the last convoy. He had the responsibility of seeing that Carlo's left behind them a site completely cleared of litter or rubbish of any sort. This ensured Sam's long-term relationships with Local Authorities remained good so that he was welcome again the next time round. Good venues, which he could visit regularly year after year, were an essential factor in his long-term prosperity.

Boris always looked forward to going to Deal, not least because of the presence there of the Royal Marines who had a large Depot in the area. Centred there was the Marine School of Music. He enjoyed listening to their military music and watching the parades and displays the Marines put on as part of the town's celebrations.

The weather was fine and they pulled out in high spirits. Moving from place to place suited Boris, and on a day like this he looked forward to the drive.

Unfortunately, on this occasion, the move did not go as smoothly as their well-organised journeys usually did. Through no fault of their own, about ten miles along the way they got tangled up in a road block due to an accident, and subsequently got involved in the business of clearing the way ahead.

Their involvement was voluntary—though not entirely altruistic—because they knew that coming up behind them would soon be a mass of vehicles from Hythe. The last thing Boris wanted was for that lot to bunch up in a very long line along the road, which would spell endless repercussions in an already difficult situation. And eventually it would cause near chaos when they all arrived at their new site in Deal.

The first indication Boris had that there was trouble ahead, though he didn't recognise it as such at the time, was the sudden absence of traffic coming towards him in the opposite direction. Normally a busy road, Boris had been congratulating himself on an unusually trouble-free run, towing the formidable, heavy and quite awkward train of vehicles at a good steady speed. But after a few miles of road empty of oncoming traffic he rounded a corner and saw—about three hundred yards up the road—why it was that he had run out of traffic coming the other way.

He could see in front of him a column of vehicles, including an East Kent bus and several lorries, parked nose to tail one behind the other, obviously facing a road blockage ahead.

Slowing down he brought his gleaming Burrell to a standstill some fifteen yards from the vehicle ahead. He was too old a hand to close up tightly, and habitually left himself space to manoeuvre especially when, as today, he had several vehicles hitched up in a train behind him. It was very difficult to back up without trailers jack-knifing, and all too easy to get hopelessly boxed in, when involved in a snarl-up of traffic on the road.

"Hang on, Stuart," Boris said to his mate, "I'll go and see what's up."

Jumping down from the driver's platform he spoke to Stan, who by this time had clambered right to the top of the trailer's highly-stacked load, to have a look ahead.

"Can you see what's happening, Stan?" he asked.

"Seems to be a big lorry right across the road, Boris," Stan said. "There's been an accident, I should think."

"Let's go and have a look," said Boris. "It's obviously been stuck there for some time for this lot to have collected. There must be a long tailback the other side too. We've met nothing coming the other way for quite a while."

"I noticed that," commented Stan, climbing down from his perch.

Together they walked up the road past the line of vehicles to join a small group of people standing watching the proceedings.

Boris spoke to the driver of the lorry at the front of the queue, who was sitting in his cab, drinking a flask of tea. He'd clearly been there quite a long time; frustration, if not indeed plain exasperation, showed on his face.

"What's up, mate?" Boris asked. "What's happened here?"

"The driver of that lorry stuck across the road told me he had to swerve to miss a silly bugger driving a motorbike too fast and passing a lorry coming towards him," said the frustrated driver. "He had to drive on the verge to avoid the motorbike and that trailer he was pulling swung sideways and its rear end slewed down the bank. It's got its nearside wheel down in the ditch and it's stuck fast there. The driver said it dragged his tail sideways and he's stuck across the road. The trouble is, the weight of that heavily-loaded trailer is hanging on the towing gear and it's all snarled up. The lorry can't budge either way until it's relieved of that load."

"Somebody needs to bring in a towing vehicle with a winch, then," commented Boris straightaway. "It shouldn't be too difficult to offload the trailer to free the lorry and let it drive off the road to let all the traffic through."

"That's right," agreed the driver. "That's exactly what they've just been trying to do. But the traction engine they brought along to tow it out with blew up!"

"Blew up!" exclaimed Boris, startled and immediately interested by the reference to a traction engine. "Do you really mean that?"

"It sounded like it," replied the driver. "It was parked where you see it now on the bank this side of the road and the blokes were over the other side getting the trailer hitched onto the towing cable when there was a kind of sharp bang from the engine and a terrific blast of steam that blew out all ways. There was a cloud of steam and ash all over the place. Nobody could get near it for a while. Something's definitely blown up!"

Boris meanwhile was staring across at the traction engine. He knew at once what had happened. The position of the engine, and the reference to clouds of steam and ash told him all too plain a story.

"That engine's blown its plug!" he stated categorically. "Not much doubt about that. That's negligence, that is. Sheer, bloody negligence!"

"What do you mean, Boris?" asked Stan, not himself a steam man.

"We'll go over and have a look to see if I'm right. Then I'll show you," replied Boris.

With that he strode off towards the stricken traction engine. The lorry driver, his interest awakened, jumped down from his cab and joined Stan following Boris to the engine.

One look was enough for Boris. It was parked nose down on the side of the grass bank which sloped downwards from their side of the road. Boris could see from the tracks its wheels had made that it had reached the scene by travelling along the meadow by the roadside and its driver had backed his rear end up the bank in order to present his towing gear to the road, pointing across to the front of the ditched trailer over the other side. He was over there at this moment with a small group of men, now engaged in taking off the cable they had so recently fastened, in order to retrieve it and wind it back by hand on to the winch of the now useless traction engine.

"What's happened then, Boris?" queried Stan. "Is it what you thought?"

"Low water level, that's what!" stated Boris emphatically, evidently disgusted by what he clearly regarded as a disastrous lack of competence on the part of the man who'd driven the engine. "There's no excuse for that, at all! Bloody disgraceful, that is! The bloke deserves the boot! Look, I'll show you."

Boris moved closer to the engine and explained what had gone wrong.

"With the engine parked nose down like this," he said, "the water in the boiler obviously runs to the front. If there's too little water in the boiler, the metal plate forming the top of the fire box at the back here loses its covering of water. In less than no time it's red hot—at least it would be without the safety plug. Without the plug the plate would buckle and the boiler really would blow up then. As it is, the safety plug has done its job. It's saved the life of the engine. And left a hell of a bloody mess for that stupid twit to clean up as well. Serves him right."

"What's the safety plug like?" asked the lorry driver, who had listened with interest to what Boris had said.

"It's a brass plug screwed into the top plate of the fire box," explained Boris. "The plug has a three-eighth inch hole bored up through its centre, which is filled with lead. If the water level is allowed to fall 'off the gauge', as we say, the plate heats up straight away, the lead melts and the high pressure steam from the boiler blows down through the hole, straight on to the fire. So the engine finishes up with the fire extinguished, the steam fully released, and one hell of a bloody mess left for the bloke who caused it, to clear up. But it lives to run another day, once a new plug has been screwed in."

"Clever that!" commented the lorry driver. "Simple but clever. Like so many answers to serious problems," he added admiringly.

Boris paused for a few moments, gazing at the mess with marked disapproval and distaste.

"There's the gauge," he then said, pointing to a glass tube mounted on the faceplate above the fire box. "No driver worth his job ever fails to keep a close watch on that. It should never be allowed to run low. There's a water injector on the engine, a tank of water mounted on the back and everything laid on to make the job easy. Sometimes people forget that going down a steep hill throws the water forwards in the boiler, so if the level is too low, the fire box top plate gets uncovered. But you wouldn't get a bloke who knows his stuff ever letting that happen."

Boris looked over the road at the group working there.

"Do you know what they've decided to do?" he asked the lorry driver.

"I heard one of them ask the driver of this traction engine if there is a phone nearby," he answered. "He himself happened to be working on the road up ahead a little way and drove back over the field to help out here. Somebody has gone off to telephone the nearest garage for help."

Boris began to feel sorry for the luckless engine driver whose attempt to help had landed him in such a mess. The man was clearly heading for a good dusting from his firm anyway. He decided to pitch in and help get them out of trouble himself.

"Come on, Stan," he said. "I'll go over and offer those blokes to pull that trailer away with my Burrell. That way we'll all get clear of the place quickly. Otherwise, we could be hanging about for a hell of a while."

"Could I help?" asked the lorry driver. "I want to get away as soon as I can. I'm on my way to Birmingham and I've got a long day ahead of me."

"Sure you can! Thanks!" said Boris. "The three of us together with Stuart will have them clear in no time at all."

The worried group of men over the road accepted the offer of help from Boris with much gratitude. And Boris forbore to comment to the engine driver, clearly identifiable by his sooty appearance and oily blue dungarees, about his unfortunate lapse in the care of his unhappy-looking machine over the road. He thought that the poor bloke had suffered enough and he looked worried sick.

It was a matter of only a few minutes for Boris and Stan to go back up the road, unhitch the Burrell, and bring it back along the field that bordered the road.

Stuart came along with them and Boris carefully backed his smart Showman's Engine up the bank so that his towing gear was conveniently placed with its rear end facing across the road.

On the back was a well-engineered winch system, much used in their fairground activities. Between them they soon pulled the steel cable across the road and fastened it on the towing gear of the heavily-laden trailer that was holding the lorry captive by trying to run downhill.

The group of men prepared themselves to knock off the trailer's towing hitch to free the lorry as soon as Boris had winched the trailer up far enough to take its weight off the lorry's towing bracket. Somebody also had the good sense to prepare blocks to place under the trailer's wheels, to prevent it running down to embed itself further in the ditch once Boris released his cable.

As is so often the case, the actual operation proved simple once the correct measures had been taken. In no time at all the lorry was free. Its driver had parked it well into the verge of the road and two-way traffic was able to flow again.

Boris, Stan and Stuart had to hurry back with the Burrell to hook it up and move off, much to the relief and pleasure of all those who had by now collected in a long line of vehicles behind their road train.

As, gathering speed, they chuffed past the scene of the accident, the now somewhat less anxious lorry driver, and the unhappy-looking traction engine driver who had simply set out to help him and landed himself in all sorts of trouble as a result, waved to them as they passed by.

"Thanks again, mate!" shouted the lorry driver.

Boris waved back to them and resumed his rather delayed journey to Deal, leaving behind the two men to sort out their problems. There was nothing that couldn't fairly easily be overcome in pulling the heavy trailer out of the ditch, but Boris knew both the two men would be messing about there for quite some time before they could pick up their respective jobs where they had left off when the mad-headed motorcyclist had caused the accident. He had been tempted to go the whole hog and pull the trailer out of the ditch himself. However, he knew from hard experience that snags could arise, and he could not risk the possibility that he might be delayed a long time if he got involved. Sam Donatello would not thank him if, by doing a good Samaritan act along the road, he finished up fouling up the smooth arrival of the mass of equipment on its way from Hythe to Deal. The task of shifting the whole lot from one site to another was difficult enough already, without adding unnecessary delays.

As it was, his intervention had cleared the road, to the benefit of all those held up, and Boris was on his way faster than he would have been if they had simply sat where they were and waited until the help that had been telephoned for, finally reached the scene. It could have been a long wait.

Despite these considerations, it bugged him a bit as he drove off, leaving the men waiting for help that he knew he could have given with his powerful Burrell, and he was silent for a while as he turned things over in his mind. The truth was that as a SKWEC man his natural inclination was to deal with the engineering problem, but his allegiance during the summer had to be to Carlo's. At length he broke his silence and spoke to Stuart who was standing by his side on the footplate, watching the road ahead.

"I don't suppose that bloody bloke on his motorbike even knows what a cock-up he caused," Boris commented to Stuart, who by now knew the whole story. "I expect he belted off up the road thinking how clever he'd been to get through the gap between the lorries. Half of them never know that other people have saved their lives when they tear around the roads like that."

As the driver of a slow, road-obstructing vehicle, Boris was all too accustomed to impatient drivers taking terrible risks to pass him, in the face of oncoming traffic. But it was something he could never come to terms with. Slow though the steam vehicles he drove were, stopping suddenly and safely—especially with trailers behind him, and considering the huge weight of the entire outfit—was not as easy as it might have seemed to faster traffic, whose drivers thought he should simply stop and give way. The trailer they had left behind them back up the road was not the first he had seen that had veered sideways and gone down into a ditch as a result of the vehicle towing it trying to slow down and swerve too quickly.

Fortunately, following the incident, the rest of the journey was covered in good time, and early in the afternoon Sam Donatello was pleased to see Boris pull onto the site at Deal. A little while later Sam's mobile home was in its chosen position, and his wife Sandra was able to get their domestic arrangements organised once again.

At intervals during the rest of the day the three convoys of vehicles arrived and were efficiently distributed over the large field to their assigned positions.

By Thursday evening the bulk of the work of building up the rides and settling in the various sideshows and booths was done. Final preparations were completed on Friday morning, and by early afternoon everything was ready for action.

The Fairground was scheduled to be open to the public early on Friday evening. By the advertised time the whole area was ablaze with coloured lights, and the familiar sound of fairground organs blasted out the well-known music to beckon in people from the neighbourhood.

As was usual, wherever they went, the first people to crowd into the ground were locals who enjoyed a preview of the Fair before the place really picked up its momentum. For most it was just the first of a number of visits to this large area of concentrated entertainment which landed annually on their doorsteps.

To those employed in the Fairground, one place was much like another. Once installed and up-and-going, they slipped automatically into their well-practised routines and just hoped that the weather would be kind to them, to make their stay a real success.

Business on that Friday evening was very good and augured well for their stay at Deal, especially if the fine weather continued. As was usual, there were some bugs in the system, and difficulties here and there to overcome as the organisation settled into its new location, but everything was running smoothly by the time the Fairground closed late that day.

Just before midnight, when all the rides were shut down, the place was quiet, and the last of the visitors had drifted away, Sam Donatello took his customary late-night walk around the extensive area. His walk had a dual purpose; a check that all was well, and an end-of-the-day bit of exercise for his fine Alsatian dog Max. It was really a security check, for it was not unusual, especially on Friday and Saturday evenings, for a few loiterers, often the worse for drink, to hang around noisily as potential sources of trouble—loath to bring their day's pleasure to an end by going home.

The sight of Sam, who was a big man with an authoritative manner, accompanied by his powerful dog which he habitually held on a short chain and leather leash, was quite sufficient to deter trouble-makers, and more often than not they left good-humouredly. It was no part of Sam's purpose to stir up trouble and—as the good business man he was—he steered a middle course between the need to look after the welfare of his extensive establishment and a desire to maintain a good relationship with the public on whose custom the Fairground fraternity depended.

On his way round he spotted Boris hurrying away from his caravan. He had the appearance of a man with a purpose, going somewhere specific rather than just strolling to take a breath of the brisk evening air before turning in for the night.

Sam smiled knowingly to himself.

"Off to get your fortune told, Boris?" he called, mischievously.

There was not much Sam didn't know about what went on around him, and Boris was well aware of this. Sam was right, as usual! He'd got it in one! Not that Boris minded much. He got on very well with Sam.

"Yes. Thought I'd just pop along and see that Crystal has settled in all right," he said, somewhat lamely.

"Don't make it last all night, then!" ribbed Sam. "Remember your age, Boris! Your engine is not quite as good as that brand new Burrell of yours, you know. We can't have you running out of steam! Goodnight, mate! Sleep well!"

"Goodnight, Sam," replied Boris, smiling ruefully. "Don't worry about me, though. I'm well protected from over-running. I've got two good balls on my governor, just like the Burrell has!"

Sam went on his way grinning to himself. He liked Boris's neat, bawdy retort. "Trust old Boris to pick up any reference to his beloved steam engine," he thought.

Boris was quite pleased with it too, considering it was off-the-cuff. So pleased in fact, that he resolved to tell Dame Crystal Star about it. This he subsequently did, much to her wry but rather qualified amusement at a well-chosen moment in the later proceedings when the reference had some natural relevance.

Though appreciating the wit, Dame Crystal was, however, not too happy about it because she was not too sure she wanted Sam to take too much for granted, nor that anybody else should either, come to that. She did not want it to be thought she was exclusively committed to one man. She was fond of Boris, but he was not the marrying kind in her view, nor come to that, was he her ideal man. And she still had her eye on the main chance. One day Mr. Just Right, just might, come along. Until then she took her pleasures where she could, though very selectively. But on this subject her thoughts were very private. It was not something she discussed with anyone.

Meanwhile her eyes were always open and every now and again a discerning man would vaguely sense that he was being regarded speculatively. She knew the feeling! But with the difference that there was nothing vague about her own perception of being regarded speculatively, for it was not as a potential permanent partner in marriage that she was aware of being so overtly personally assessed, almost every day of her life!

Shortly after nine o'clock the next morning, Boris—back to more mundane matters—busy working on his Burrell, settling it down ready for the Saturday just beginning—noticed a motorcyclist turn into the Fairground from the road.

The rider spotted him up on his engine and rode down the side of the field towards him. Boris watched him coming and immediately noticed both the characteristic blue and silver petrol tank of a Douglas machine, and also the unmistakable, smooth, satisfying sound of its twin-cylinder engine.

Like Joe, his close friend from SKWEC, Boris was a motorcycle enthusiast and something of a connoisseur of the wide range of models on the roads. As the bike drew near he recognised it as a model which had come on the market priced between forty and fifty pounds two years ago in 1925, and had subsequently earned wide acclaim.

It was a Douglas 'E.W.' model, fitted with their well-known 350cc horizontally opposed, 'fore-and-aft', flat-twin engine. Its two cylinders, lying along the axis of the machine, had the enviable reputation of providing a design concept that gave a perfectly balanced, smooth running, highly efficient engine, well proven since its first appearance, for reliability, ease of starting and high performance.

The bike had a three-speed gear box with a hand change mounted on the tank. Boris remembered that when it came on the market it introduced a departure from one feature that had previously been a hallmark of Douglas machines—their long, flat, parallel-sided, rectangular petrol tanks, decorated with the firm's attractive blue and silver colours. In this new model, the tank had evolved into a new, rounded, slightly sloping, nicely tapered design—while retaining the same well-known, widely recognised blue and silver paintwork.

Douglas machines were popular among private owners, for normal use. They had also achieved much success in TT races, where performance and reliability were essential qualities. A characteristic of Douglas bikes was their light weight compared to most other makes of similar engine power. It was a factor which affected road tax as well as performance. The tax, curiously, depended upon weight, not engine power, a fact regarded by some people as a vagary in the law, and by experts as an illogical anomaly.

The rider pulled up alongside the Burrell Showman's Engine and Boris stepped down from his perch to speak to him.

"Nice bike you've got there," Boris commented without preamble when the rider stopped his engine and turned, still seated on his saddle, to ask for assistance.

The visitor grinned in agreement, patting the tank of his bike affectionately.

"Motorbikes don't come any better, in my opinion, at least in the same price range," he said, with some pride. "But then, I'm biased I suppose. I've spent the last few years helping to make them!"

He then got down to the reason for his being there.

"Could you tell me where I can find the Wall-of-Death?" he asked. "I believe they're short of a rider and I've come to apply for the job! I read in the papers about the bloke getting killed and rode up from Bristol to Hythe yesterday to see if there was any chance of a job. I learnt that Carlo's had moved to Deal, so I stayed overnight in Hythe and have come on here now. Suit me wonderfully a job like that would. The more I thought about it, the more excited I got. So I dropped everything and decided to ride to Kent to try my luck. Perhaps I've been silly, but a chance like that may never come up for me again."

He paused a moment and then added, "I didn't discuss it with anybody. People have often said I'm too impulsive. Somebody would have tried to dissuade me from coming all this way on the off-chance of getting such a rare job—I'm quite sure of that. So I just jumped on my bike and here I am. And if I'm unlucky—well—I've enjoyed the ride."

Boris pointed out where the Wall-of-Death was situated, and confirmed that the outfit was indeed still one rider short, though he had heard that there had been a number of enquiries from would-be aspirants for the job, so far without success.

Apparently, with their show having been established only so very recently, the small team running the Wall-of-Death were hoping to find somebody with at least some knowledge of the business. They were none too keen to train a rider from scratch, although they realised that they might in the end have no choice unless they shipped an experienced rider over from the States where they had contacts with people in the business—an option that would have involved both much delay and expense.

Boris asked the visitor, who had introduced himself as Ivor Lukin, if he had ever ridden on the Wall-of-Death. It seemed that he did indeed have some experience, albeit as an amateur and of only very limited extent.

Ivor told Boris a little of his history. He was a man in his early thirties and while having only limited knowledge of the Wall-of-Death business, he certainly did know about motorbikes. He had started his working life with a firm in Bristol which specialised in them, and subsequently went to work for the actual Douglas firm itself.

This rang a bell with Boris, for he remembered having heard earlier that year that the Douglas factory, that was located near Bristol, had been virtually destroyed by a serious fire which had rocked the firm back on its uppers.

It was indeed this disaster which accounted for the presence of Ivor Lukin so many miles away from his home, looking for a new career in Kent. He told Boris that the Douglas firm had fortunately been able to save most of their stock of new machines and parts from the dreadful fire, but of course had to re-establish a virtually new factory before getting back into their stride again.

Meanwhile, like many others, Ivor was thrown on his own resources for a while. He had found temporary work in garages in and around Bristol, helping out here and there while waiting until his old job became available again.

Then, out of the blue came this possible opportunity in Kent. An outside chance though it obviously was, it was of immediate interest to Ivor. Strictly as a private venture, Ivor and some fellow members of a motorcycle club with which he had been associated for several years, had built a 'home-made' Wall-of-Death at Weston-super-Mare. It was their hope, eventually, to develop it into a part-time money-making activity by setting up a transportable outfit which they could possibly use at County Shows, Fêtes and Fairs, as well as in an Amusement Park near the seafront at Weston-super-Mare. Though still in the early stages of development, they were all enthusiastic about the project and hopeful they would in due course be able to get enough money together to fund the venture.

Boris thought that this experience, small though it was, might well give Ivor that essential edge over previous applicants to replace the man who had lost his life on the Wall, just two weeks ago at Hythe.

He wished Ivor good luck and watched him ride off slowly round the perimeter of the field, towards the Wall-of-Death. And he privately wished him still more luck too, should he get the job, for to Boris it seemed a very dangerous way of earning a living.

Ivor evidently made a good impression because later that morning he came back to tell Boris he had got the job subject to a one-month trial period, which he felt sure he could pass satisfactorily. Apparently, as Boris heard later that day, he had already demonstrated considerable skill on the Wall and showed no fear at all. This, with his extensive knowledge of the mechanics of motorbikes, made him a strong potential member of the depleted team.

Feeling very pleased with himself, Ivor went off to make his domestic arrangements. His first step was to drive all the way back to Bristol to organise his affairs and to pick up his essential belongings. It was a fine day and Boris rather envied him the ride, especially by the route he intended to take. He set off heading towards Dover and Folkestone, then along the coast road via Hythe, Dymchurch and Romney, passing on this road the fascinating Romney, Hythe & Dymchurch Miniature Railway, and on through Brighton—following, as far as he could, a coastal route to the West Country.

Boris waved him goodbye and listened appreciatively to the throaty, powerful sound of the twin-cylinder Douglas engine as Ivor accelerated happily up the road and away.

The following Tuesday afternoon, Ivor arrived back again in Deal and got himself fixed up at a Bed & Breakfast holiday boarding house, only a few minutes' walk from the Fairground.

During the evening, on his way to watch his new colleagues perform their current Wall-of-Death programme and to let them know he was safely back, ready to start work as soon as they wanted him to, he called to see Boris. Boris invited him to call at his caravan on his way out, for a drink and a chat, knowing that by the time the Wall-of-Death show ended, and Ivor had spent some time with those who ran it, the Fairground would be closed down for the day.

Ivor gladly accepted and in due course joined Boris in his small but cosy caravan. As Boris had suspected, Ivor's new colleagues were keen for him to join them as soon as possible, so he had arranged to make a start the very next morning, feeling very happy about the way things had turned out for him. Fortune had favoured him, for he had set off only the previous Friday morning on his long journey from Bristol, purely 'on spec', and it had come off; he was on the threshold of a new, exciting career in a world that was totally different from his previous industrial background. He was also pleased to have made a personal contact with somebody like Boris, who was able to answer his many questions about life with a travelling fair.

During the course of their conversation Boris asked Ivor if he had noticed the newly opened Romney, Hythe & Dymchurch Railway on his way along the coastal road. Ivor told him that he'd spotted the fascinating little trains on his way to Hythe on his first journey up from Bristol, and had in fact spent some time on that Friday evening looking at them. As he'd said before, he had spent the night at Hythe, having decided to leave the added journey to Deal, to locate Carlo's new site, until the first thing on Saturday morning.

Ivor had some interesting information about the railway, which, strangely enough, he'd discovered back home in Somerset. He was born in the village of Lympsham, between Burnham-on-Sea and Weston-super-Mare. His Dad still lived there and worked, as he had done all his life, on a farm in the area largely devoted to cattle and sheep. The countryside was very flat, much like that in the Dymchurch and Romney Marsh area.

When Ivor told his Dad about the wonderful little railway in Kent, his Dad had news for him. The miniature railway had nearly got built near his home in Somerset, and not in Kent at all!

Ivor, who had left home years ago, and lived in digs in Bristol, was unaware of any of this. It appeared that those planning the building of a miniature railway had selected two potential sites for it, one in Somerset and the other in Kent. They had to find a long run of flat land in an area where holidaymakers were around, in order to build a railway which could not only perform well using such small engines, but also be constructed at a reasonable cost and with a good chance of being a commercial success.

When surveying the possible route in Somerset, the railway people had visited his Dad's Boss because the projected line, if built, would have to pass across his farmland, assuming, of course, that a satisfactory financial agreement was subsequently arrived at. There were even rumours that Compulsory Purchase Orders might be sought to acquire the necessary land for the line, the justification being that the railway was intended to provide a scheduled public service. This possible legal development was viewed with marked disfavour by some people.

The proposed line would have started at Burnham-on-Sea near the terminus of the Somerset and Dorset Railway. From there it was to have run to the village of Brent Knoll, allowing a connection with the Great Western Railway whose Bristol to Exeter line passed through the station there.

Following its own new route, some distance from the GWR line, it was intended to run to a separate new station on the outskirts of Weston-super-Mare. A spur branch line to the Brean Down peninsular, where the Mendip Hills run down into the sea about a mile offshore, was also envisaged if it proved technically feasible.

The whole area of Burnham-on-Sea, Weston-super-Mare and the stretch of coast between them known as Brean Sands, was fast becoming increasingly popular as a holiday area. But building a suitable bridge over the Rive Axe presented a potentially costly problem and was one factor which influenced the final decision.

The project was an ambitious one, but in the event there proved to be too many technical, legal and financial difficulties involved in the total development, so it was dropped. The length of the miniature railway line would have been about eight miles.

The alternative site in Kent had a greater potential length of some fourteen miles. Added to this important advantage, the sighting of the new railway there, albeit a miniature one, would actually fulfil an existing need as no rail connection had hitherto existed between Hythe and Romney. Both from an engineering and from a commercial point of view, the Kent site had many advantages, so its choice was well justified.

Ivor's Dad was not the only one who was sorry when the Somerset project was dropped. Many people would have loved to have seen the fascinating miniature steam locomotives plying their way purposefully across the flat meadow lands. The sight of them, it was thought, would have added to the whimsical attraction of this misty edge of the Somerset wetlands.

Across the countryside, behind the barrier of sand dunes which stretched for miles along the coast, numerous scattered, stunted willow trees bent their pollarded heads over the drainage dykes they bordered. All of them, like the shrubs along the hedgerows, uniformly bent their bushy heads in the same direction, persuaded to do so by the strong prevailing westerly wind off the sea. This, by its persistent influence, imposed a permanent leaning aspect to the shapes of the bushes and trees exposed to it across the flat green landscape, and tilted the tall rushes, reeds and teasels that thrived thickly along the line of many of the ditches.

There were of course those who took the opposite view to Ivor's Dad, and were not at all sorry that the innovative railway project did not materialise but went elsewhere. They preferred to see the unusual, if not indeed unique countryside, left unchanged, as it had been for so many years. There was about it a tantalising quality, difficult to define, which to some people who felt its attraction strongly, seemed very vulnerable—almost as though it could slip away to be lost forever if its privacy and quietness were too much intruded upon.

The would-be developers of the Miniature Railway had soon become aware of strongly divided opinions about it and might well have stirred up a hornet's nest had they pursued it further. But the issue was quickly decided, and upon pragmatic rather than aesthetic grounds.

So the problem went away almost as soon as it had appeared—much like many a mist on the marshes—and was soon forgotten.

Boris was very glad the decision had gone in favour of the Kentish location for it was obvious from what he had seen while Carlo's was at Hythe, that it was already proving a great attraction and was clearly destined to become an increasingly important feature of this flat, marshy, coastal area.

Few local people, outside the group directly involved with the railway, were aware that it might well have gone to Somerset instead of Kent.

The next morning, full of enthusiasm, Ivor started his new and exciting job. He very quickly adapted to fairground life and settled in well with his new colleagues in the small team running the Wall-of-Death. He was well liked by them, and it was soon apparent that his one month's trial was a formality. He was there to stay!

His personal contacts with the Douglas firm in the West Country quickly proved invaluable to his new employers. They were in need of another machine. Instead of purchasing a second-hand one and spending a great deal of time modifying it for the special requirements of Wall-of-Death work, Ivor was able to negotiate a special deal with his old firm to provide them with a purpose-prepared bike.

There were always 'works' machines' around the factory. These were used continuously during development work, when modifications and experimental ideas were being tried out.

One of these was made available to Ivor and his new friends at a special price, with the main essential Wall-of-Death modifications already carried out in the factory. As part of the deal it carried with it much evidence of its origin, providing good advertising for the firm. It was attractively turned out bearing the blue and silver Douglas livery. This became Ivor's bike, and he was more than happy to have a Douglas engine beneath him during his dangerous displays on the Wall.

Confidence in the reliability of the machines they rode was a pre-requisite for the success of the riders. Any nagging doubts on this score would have seriously inhibited their performance since their lives depended upon their faultless running—especially when they were high up on the Wall. The sad death of Francis Fox at Hythe concentrated the attention of everybody on this important question of machine reliability. Ivor's complete confidence in his Douglas machine, based upon his own inside knowledge of how painstakingly careful the firm was in its manufacturing processes, rubbed off on the others, and over a period of time a strong link was developed between their particular Wall-of-Death and the Douglas firm. Although imponderable to quantify, there was no doubt in Ivor's mind that a good many Douglas bikes were sold as a result of this publicity. It was a feature of the Wall-of-Death that there was always a small group of motorcycle enthusiasts gathered around the bikes and their riders whenever an opportunity presented itself. And if Ivor were around, they could not help but be impressed by his partisan attitude towards his previous employer's products. He was very much a Douglas man!

On the last Saturday that Carlo's Fair was in Deal, Boris had an unexpected visit from his SKWEC Boss, Richard Livingstone, the firm's General Manager. Richard was accompanied by Frank Thrushton, his Workshops' Manager, recently seen by Boris at Hythe.

The two were at Deal and Walmer for the day for a specific purpose, not primarily to visit Carlo's. They had merely called in to see Sam Donatello on their way through, first thing in the morning, to settle some details with him about the work they were scheduled to do for Carlo's during their winter out-of-season rest period, the start of which was now only a few weeks away.

Frank was interested to learn from Boris that it looked as though a replacement had been found for the man so tragically killed on the Wall-of-Death at Hythe, during the evening of the day when Frank and his colleagues had seen an earlier performance while on their annual Works' Outing.

Ivor sounded a useful man to Frank, who was immediately alerted to the possibility that, with his engineering background at the Douglas Factory in the West Country, Ivor might perhaps be available during part of the winter period to work for a while at SKWEC where they were faced with a particularly heavy winter workload. Frank was short of skilled staff. Temporary extra staff of experienced men were not easily found in their rural area.

Subsequently, when they met Sam Donatello, they discovered that the Wall-of-Death people, who had joined Carlo's for the first time that year, were indeed going to park their equipment at Sam's winter quarters establishment where the rest of his own formidable array of Fairground paraphernalia was parked for annual maintenance work. It seemed highly probable that, like many of the Fairground fraternity not directly employed full-time by Sam, Ivor might well be looking for some temporary work to help him through the winter period.

Boris was asked to look into the matter, and in the event it all worked out well for Ivor. By one of those strokes of good fortune that play a crucial role in the way the careers of some people evolve, his chance meeting with Boris as his first contact on reaching Carlo's Fairground, proved a lucky break.

That year, and for several years following, Ivor's working career was assured. Apart from his highly specialised Wall-of-Death job, which, though thoroughly enjoyable and exciting, had no application elsewhere, he was to gain, during each winter off-season period, a wealth of engineering experience of a much wider variety than his previous work had been since this was exclusively on motorcycles.

Like Boris himself, Ivor settled into a comfortable routine of working for SKWEC each winter and spent the rest of the year travelling with Carlo's Fair.

These arrangements affecting Ivor were made, however, some weeks later on, after Carlo's had completed their last engagement of the year at the Isle of Thanet.

This was a regular arrangement, timed to coincide with the period during which the annual Ploughing Matches organised in the South East took place. There were two which Sam Donatello kept his eyes upon—the East Kent Ploughing Match and the Thanet Ploughing Match. Usually these were arranged to run consecutively.

The Isle of Thanet was a good place to site ploughing matches because of the very convenient, wide, flat areas of arable farmland, just inland from the sea.

Sam sited his Fairground at a point where it not only attracted people who were present in East Kent to attend the ploughing matches, but also pulled in many end-of-season holidaymakers from Ramsgate, Broadstairs, Margate, Westgate and Birchington-on-Sea. This concentration of holiday resorts in close proximity to one another made the Isle of Thanet a good location at which to site a Fair, and Carlo's sometimes made two trips per year there, one at the beginning of the season and the other towards the end.

It was a convenient place for Sam to start and to end his annual itinerary, because his own estate and winter quarters for all his Fairground equipment was only a few miles away.

Returning to the subject of Richard's and Frank's visit to Deal, the main reason for the trip had nothing to do with either the work of SKWEC or that of Carlo's Fairground.

Their day out was very much a pleasure jaunt, yet one with a serious purpose, pursuing things of historic interest which made a pleasant change from their normal professional engineering activities.

They were present in Deal primarily to do a good turn for a mutual friend and to give themselves a day off from their usual demanding duties.

Had they but have known it, their visit was to have far-reaching repercussions and in retrospect would appear to have been a Day of Destiny, a casual day that became a catalyst, causing results neither they nor even a clever clairvoyant like Dame Crystal Star could have foreseen.

Chapter 33

THE CALIFORNIAN CONNECTION
featuring the Duke of Wellington & the Cinque Ports

Richard's and Frank's visit to Deal had a Californian connection. Richard had received a letter from Walter Richtmeyer asking him a favour. At his Military Museum in San Francisco he had a section where famous figures from military history were featured.

He was currently researching the life of the Duke of Wellington. In some literature he had been studying he had seen a snippet of information linking Wellington with the fascinating corner of England that he had visited with so much pleasure when hunting down the story behind his fine, Spanish 17th century Flintlock Pistol.

When looking at his maps of the British Isles, his own affectionate name for this part of Kent was now 'Cannon Corner'. He had a permanent reminder of it proudly parked at the foot of the flagpole on the lawn outside his office!

Walter read that the Duke of Wellington ended his life at Deal, in residence at Walmer Castle where for twenty-three years, from 1829 to 1852, he had held the impressive-sounding title of Lord Warden of the Cinque Ports.

This brief reference intrigued him and he wondered if Richard could find time to discover a little more about it for him. He had plenty of information about Wellington's distinguished, active military career, but nothing more about the Deal connection, or about the Cinque Ports. It sounded interesting, the more so to Walter personally, who now felt that he had a special link with this corner of England which was an area steeped in military history.

Like a great many other people, Richard knew surprisingly little about the 'history on his own doorstep'. He had a vague idea he'd heard there was some special association between the 'Iron Duke' and Walmer Castle but couldn't remember what it was. He discussed it with Frank, who was none the wiser. But they both liked Walter and thought they ought to help him if they could.

Neither of them, as it happened, had ever visited the well-known castles at Deal and Walmer. The upshot was that they decided to treat themselves to a day out to put right this omission in their local historical knowledge. They chose a day when Carlo's was at Deal, so that they could combine some necessary SKWEC business with their personal outing.

Preparatory to this trip Richard spent some time looking up brief details of the history of the two Castles. It had always seemed odd to him that there should be two such formidable fortifications so close to one another at one point on the coastline. His first surprising discovery was that originally there had been three—not just two—all built at the same time, and all within a stretch of only about three miles along the coast.

The third one, known as Sandown Castle, had been on the opposite side of Deal Castle to that of Walmer Castle. Apparently, the sea broke through the outer wall of its moat in 1785, and the Castle subsequently suffered such severe encroachments by the sea that it no longer existed at all. It had finally been demolished by the War Office in 1863. He learnt that the site was now marked by an attractive rock garden which embodied the only remaining ruins.

Armed with this initial information, and having finished their business with Sam Donatello, Richard and Frank left Carlo's Fairground and set off to do some research on behalf of their friend living far away on the Pacific coast of America.

In the event they had a most interesting day, not only looking over Deal and Walmer Castles, but also exploring the area in general to get a sense of what the situation must have been like so many years ago when the Castles had been built. Though they had both been in the district many times before, it was surprising what a difference it made to have an object in view, instead of just wandering around idly glancing at all things in general and nothing in particular, as was usual when having a day out in a holiday resort.

Some days later, Richard sat down to write to Walter Richtmeyer, to convey the result of their researches. Realising that Walter's interest in the matter was professional, Richard did his best to assemble a real contribution to Walter's historical information for his Museum, and prepared his report in his usual methodical way.

When the package finally reached California some weeks later, Walter sat at his desk and studied the contents with much interest:

S.K.W.E.C. Ltd.,
Wingash,
Kent,
U.K.
22nd October 1927

Walter K. Richtmeyer Esq.,
Richtmeyer Military Museum,
San Francisco,
California,
U.S.A.

Dear Walter,

It has taken me some little while to reply to your letter. To be honest I was quite unable to answer your questions adequately, without first doing some research myself. Your letter had the salutary effect of making me realise how little I know about the history of this area in which I have spent my life. I must hasten to reassure you, however, that seeking the information you require has not imposed a burden upon me; on the contrary I have found the matters of absorbing interest.

I have not been alone in this. Frank has been alongside me in looking into this local history and has been equally interested in it. We decided to make your letter an excuse to give ourselves a day out, hunting down answers to your questions. The result was that we thoroughly enjoyed a very interesting day at Deal and the surrounding area, finding out things about the historical background to our home county, which we freely admit we both knew next to nothing about.

Having made this confession of prior ignorance, it occurs to me that it may not in the end prove to have been a disadvantage, for I have set about the matter in a systematic way in order to sift out the essence of what it is you want to know, from several centuries of English History. In other words I started from scratch!

It now falls to me to try to summarise this in as succinct a manner as I can.

On reflection I find that the information falls neatly into three packages. This I shall detail below under three headings, moving forwards in historical sequence from times long ago to the present day. It will be very much a layman's potted history, I'm afraid, but I hope you will find in it enough information for your purposes. Well, here goes:-

THE CINQUE PORTS

This name was given many centuries ago to a confederation of five English Channel Ports: Hastings, Romney, Hythe, Dover and Sandwich.

It was formed in the 11th Century, when each of these was an important port. Its purpose was to provide ships and seamen for the King, to patrol the English Channel and to transport the King's soldiers when and where necessary. In fact it provided the nucleus of the King's Fleet until the 14th Century.

In return for these maritime services the ports enjoyed corporate privileges, such as tax exemptions and authority to make their own bye-laws. The original rather vague arrangement seems to have become more formalised in the reign of Henry II (1154-1189).

The ports reached even greater importance in the 13th Century, after the loss of Normandy by King John. In 1268 the confederation became an independent administrative unit. A new Office was created, that of 'Lord Warden of the Cinque Ports', to head the organisation. It was in fact arranged as an extension of the powers of the authority of the Constable (i.e. Governor) of Dover Castle. This is a much older Castle than those we were concerned with at Deal, and well worthy of a separate study because its evolutionary history goes back a very long way.

Two other 'Ancient Towns' as they are called, Rye and Winchelsea, became 'linked' and associated with the confederation of five ports, as did thirty-two other places as 'minor members'.

Over the centuries, coastal erosion and the silting up of river mouths, together with the simultaneous growth of larger, deep water ports elsewhere along the South Coast of England, progressively reduced the importance of the five ports and their two linked 'Ancient Towns', as a confederation. Today only Dover remains of significance.

Sandwich, which was a very important port in ancient times, is now, in effect, an inland town, separated from the sea by a belt of flat marshy land and sand dunes, with access to the nearby sea via the narrow River Ouse only.

But the Historic Office and honorific title of Lord Warden of the Cinque Ports persists to this day, with however only occasional duties, which are largely ceremonial. The title confers an honour upon, rather than imposes a burden on, the distinguished person to whom it is granted.

DEAL, WALMER AND SANDOWN CASTLES

The first two of these still exist, but the third, Sandown, has long since disappeared due to encroachment of the sea. Its only remains now form part of a rock garden! I mention this at the outset, because neither Frank nor I even knew that there had ever been a third Castle at Deal. But now for some historic details of them.

These three Castles have a King Henry VIII connection. Like most people - certainly I must say at once by Frank and me - you probably think of Henry the Eighth firstly as the King who treated himself to many successive wives! His connection with the three Castles is in fact not un-associated with his wife-changing history. This briefly is the way it was, so far as I can understand, based upon information I have been able to gather from my brief local researches.

It seems that since 1535 the Pope had been getting more and more annoyed with King Henry VIII, and finally excommunicated him in 1538 because Henry had insisted upon divorcing his wife Catherine of Aragon, as well as amusing himself by dissolving the monasteries, confiscating their goods and calmly declaring himself to be the Supreme Head on Earth of the Church! Quite a claim!

Catherine happened to be an Aunt of the Holy Roman Emperor Charles V of Spain. All in all it was not a very happy state of affairs for his Holiness. The peeved Pope attempted to persuade Charles V of Spain to join forces with Francis I of France, invade England and cast out the intolerable upstart Henry VIII, who was bugging him so unmercifully.

This is where the Castles came into the picture. Henry VIII, and with him England itself, was faced with grave danger. His response, far from being intimidated, was to gather his forces and prepare a strong defence against invasion. The attack, if it came, was highly likely to fall in the region where the English Channel is at its narrowest. Only twenty-one miles, as no doubt you know, separates Dover and Calais.

In those days of sail a calm anchorage, preferably adjacent to a flat, low-lying landscape, was needed if a fleet were to stand a good chance of successfully landing large numbers of soldiers in fighting trim. Just such a place existed at Deal. Not far out from the coast are the Goodwin Sands. Between these natural, sea-breaking sand-banks and the coast lay a calm anchorage sheltered by the Goodwins and by the nature of the neighbouring coastline to the sides of the area.

Henry VIII was no doubt mindful of the fact that Julius Caesar himself landed on this foreshore in 55 and 54 BC, a success which Henry was obviously determined to deny his own potential enemies, nearly sixteen hundred years later!

So he built not one, but three Castles to protect the land from this tempting anchorage. They were started in 1538 and finished in 1540; quite an achievement, as I think you will agree!

The largest and most formidable one, Deal Castle, was in the centre. To the west of it, that is to say to its right looking out to sea, he built Walmer Castle; to the East came Sandown Castle. I should mention that these days, Walmer, Deal and Sandown are really all part of the same, continuous, small conurbation centred on Deal, not discrete, separated places.

The powerful Deal Castle, flanked by its smaller companions at Walmer and Sandown, would have presented any fleet trying to anchor and discharge troops, with the prospect of a devastating reception from the awesome battery of assembled cannons pointing directly out to sea from these three Castles. In the event, as you probably know, the enemy did not show up. No invasion materialised and the efficacy of Henry's defence was never tested.

Many people have speculated, in mock 'War Games', how the invasion, had it come, would have fared against this concentrated defence which fairly bristled with guns. You may care to study the history of the Castles since that time. Deal and Walmer Castles were, it seems, besieged in the Civil War, but surrendered after a short period to the Parliamentarians, the circumstances being far different from an invasion by a foreign army that first had to land, in very substantial force, from the sea. The Castles are said to have been put into a state of readiness on two subsequent occasions when invasion might have threatened; during the Dutch Wars of the 17th Century and again when invasion by Napoleon seemed imminent.

I have, however, simply endeavoured to find out how the Castles came to be there in the first place, rather than to study their history since then.

As for Sandown, in 1785 the sea broke through the outer wall of the Moat rendering the Castle 'barely habitable'. By 1863 the encroachments of the sea had become so serious that the War Office decided to pull down the remaining structure. As I said, a pleasant rock garden has now been created on its site, around the ruins, there having been no shortage of rocks! And I should add that Henry VIII did not confine his fortifications to this one place. It seemed to me, when I looked into the history of these three Castles for you, as though he had put all his eggs in one basket and gambled upon his enemies making their invasion at this point.

However, I discovered that this was not so. Though he considered the Deal area to be the most likely, he did make preparations at other places during the same period. Castles were built further round the coast beyond Dover, at Sandgate and at Camber. And on the other side of Deal, to guard against an attack up the Thames, block-houses armed with cannons were built at the neighbouring towns of Gravesend and Milton, with two more on the opposite side of the Thames at Tilbury.

Older Castles, such as Dover and at Queenborough on the Isle of Sheppey, were strengthened and more guns installed. But Queenborough Castle, I must hasten to tell you, like Sandown, is no longer there.

I must stress though, Walter, that my investigations have been only sketchy, but I must say, that superficial though they were, I found the subject very interesting.

It seems to me that this whole matter would make a very rewarding centre of study as a basis for an exhibition at your Military Museum. I have a picture in my mind of models of these Castles, with scale models of cannons and soldiers, etc., presenting a fascinating display. But then, maybe that's just the boy in me surfacing again! I always did like playing with toy soldiers and forts!

THE DUKE OF WELLINGTON'S ASSOCIATION WITH WALMER CASTLE

Walmer Castle became the official residence of Lord Wardens of the Cinque Ports in the 18ᵗʰ Century. Little of the original military character of the Castle now remains. Successive Lord Wardens have adapted the central part bit by bit, and built extensions out over the Bastions—in effect to make the Castle serve as a dwelling house. The walls of the original building are thirty feet thick at the base and fifteen feet above. Some foundation for a house!

The Duke of Wellington was Lord Warden from 1829 to 1852. He spent some time every year, often during the autumn, in residence at Walmer during the last twenty-three years of his life. There is an apartment at the Castle which is known as 'The Duke of Wellington's Room'. It is an irregularly-shaped room on the South side. Interestingly, it is preserved almost exactly as it was when the Duke lived there. Collected relics of his that are to be seen there include his bedstead; the chair in which he died, actually at the Castle on September 14ᵗʰ in 1952; his washing utensils; his desk; and the old camp chair that accompanied him on all his campaigns, including Waterloo.

The bedstead is very narrow indeed. In response to a remark about it he is said to have retorted, 'When it is time to turn round, it's time to turn out!' He was a very Spartan fellow it seems! His mattress in its old silk cover is still there. Over it is a velvet blanket that belonged to Blucher—a Prussian Field Marshall of Waterloo fame and a friend of Wellington's.

Also there are many small things of his—mirrors, teacups, boots, some of his letters, his old coffee pot and the case in which he carried his dispatches.

Strangely, the reading and writing desk is one at which he stood, not sat, to read and write. It is said that he usually preferred to stand for such activities rather than sit!

Frank, somewhat irreverently, said that he must have had either ants, or piles, in his pants!

I also noticed a copy of 'The Times' reporting the Battle of Waterloo; the actual dispatch case he used in the Peninsular Wars; his 'Wellington' boots (interestingly the first gumboots to be so described); and even a lock of his hair. The room developed into a collecting centre for 'Wellingtonaria', when it became known that it was being preserved as he had left it.

Also preserved as it was when he was there, is 'The Duke's Verandah' where the Lord Warden would stand and look out across the English Channel. It is said that every day the Duke took an early morning walk on the broad terrace. From the ramparts is a fine view through the trees, and over the sea, to the French coast.

We were told that Queen Victoria stayed at Walmer Castle twice during the period when Wellington was the Lord Warden, once in 1835, when she was only sixteen years of age, two years before she became Queen, and again later on with Prince Albert and their children as guests of the Duke, in rooms which may be seen by visitors.

Notes about enclosed documents and pictures

As we went around looking at things, Frank and I obtained any pamphlets and pictures we could for you, and also took a number of photographs ourselves, where the light was good enough. I enclose this material for you and hope it will be of interest. As you will see, there are several postcards included, which show views of the Castles. These are on sale in the shops for holidaymakers and tourists to buy, to post off to relatives and friends or keep as record of their visit.

You will find a copy I was lucky enough to obtain for you, of a rare photograph taken looking down on Deal Castle from a Royal Navy Airship in 1919, just after the World War. From this you will be able to see the form of the structure very easily.

The circular central building is the Keep, which has three floors. Built out from it are six semi-circular Bastions. You will see that, like the Keep, they are crenulated. These are surrounded by a yard beyond which are six more, much larger, semi-circular Bastions, whose outer walls go down into the large Moat.

Beyond this is the Castle's outer wall, which loops out like the petals of a flower to match the contour of the six large Bastions the other side of the dry and grassy Moat. The flat tops of the Bastions form Gun Platforms. You will notice a number of cannons disposed around these flat surfaces. The picture also shows up some of the fifty-three handgun ports near the foot of the six outer Bastions that look out over the Moat. One of the postcards shows a close-up view of some of these handgun ports.

Inside the Bastions is a continuous gallery, 440 yards long, running all the way round the Castle. Access to this gallery is from a passageway sloping down from the basement floor of the Keep. This passageway ends at the 'Sallyport', giving access to the Moat itself. Walking around this quarter-mile-long gallery connecting all the handgun ports, was aptly described as 'Walking the Rounds'. I found it very impressive in there—dark, silent and rather eerie!

The aerial photograph shows why it is that the three Castles are each often described as presenting an overall form rather like a 'Tudor Rose'. The inner Bastions around the central Keep, the curved-edged outer Bastions which interleave with the inner ones, then the looping perimeter wall itself, together make a symmetrical flower-like picture, when seen in plan-view from above. It is very much a 'curved' structure and considering its warlike purpose, a very attractive piece of architecture.

The Walmer and Sandown Castles, though smaller than Deal, with fewer Bastions and guns, followed this same Tudor Rose-like structure. These three Castles, all built in a space of about three miles of the coastline, really have to be regarded as an integrated defensive system.

One further thing would interest you. At Deal, in the basement of the three-storey Keep, there is an exhibition giving details of the purpose, design, construction, garrisoning and armaments of Henry VIII's Castles, and their subsequent history as part of the defence of England against invasion. I enclose a leaflet which gives some brief information about this exhibition.

We were told that the cannons standing around the Castles, some with little heaps of cannon balls beside them, are of mixed ages and origins. These days they are put there for decoration and interest. This is true of all historic military sites along the coast. Nobody seems to know much about cannons generally and it seems to me they are just plonked down irrespective of whether or not their age matches the location. Perhaps this is logical, though, because whilst the buildings, once erected, remained substantially the same, the cannons and weapons changed and improved over the years. This makes it difficult to see just what was available in Henry VIII's time. However, with your expert knowledge of the history of weapons, I expect you will be able to sort this out if you decide to create an exhibition about these Castles at your Museum.

Incidentally, whilst I remember it, Frank and I have often wondered if you have managed to find out the exact age and origin of the cannon our blokes dug up out of the soil of Kent with their steam plough.

We trust you will find this information helpful. Should your travels ever bring you to this corner of England again, we hope very much that you will call and see us here at SKWEC.

Yours sincerely, and with kind regards from Frank,

Richard Livingstone

P.S.

I mentioned War Games in my notes about Castles. Frank reminds me that a local retired Colonel we both know well, is an expert on the Napoleonic Wars and has set up a number of exhibitions from time to time to illustrate these. It is possible, should you have queries about the Duke of Wellington, that he might be able to help. He's a likeable man, not at all the crusty type! But the sort who would be glad to help. Now and again he brings visitors to look around our Depot. He's also interested in steam engines, you see, as well as in military matters. A bit like you yourself perhaps. His name and address is:-

> Colonel Gordon S. FitzWalter D.S.O.,
> Riverside House, Monkton Street,
> Littlebrook, Kent.

It might interest you to know that he spent many years in the East, especially in India, and also, I believe, in British Colonies in both East and West Africa. He served in

South Africa during the Boer War, retired in 1912 but returned to serve again during the 1914-1918 World War. His full name is Gordon Spencer FitzWalter and he was in the Royal Engineers.

His family roots are in Kent and he knows the County very well. He was in fact educated at King's School, Canterbury, a privilege indeed, for it is a fine school having a lifelong history of association with Canterbury Cathedral, and often said to be the oldest Public School in the Country. It was founded around AD598 when St. Augustine established the Cathedral itself. How's that for a school with a history! Can you wonder past pupils are proud to have been there? The Colonel certainly is - that's for sure! You may rest assured that he will not in the least mind should you write to him for information. In fact my guess is that he would welcome the contact with you in view of your mutual interests. As a matter of courtesy I shall of course tell him that I have passed his address to you.

* * * *

Walter Richtmeyer was delighted with the wealth of material he received from Richard in response to his enquiry. He had hesitated a little before seeking Richard's help, not wishing to presume too much upon the kindness of his new-found English friends. But long experience in his self-appointed task of hunting down historic material to enrich his already impressive collection of both artefacts and information in his Military Museum, had taught him that there was nothing quite the same as direct on-the-spot contact with people living where the history had been made. They could uncover information, or potential sources of it, much faster than could be done from far away. Often, it was difficult in the first place to discover to whom he could turn for assistance, and this itself sometimes necessitated a chain of letters to locate the right person.

Now he was very glad he had taken advantage of his fortuitous meeting with these 'Men of Kent'. His letter of thanks to Richard and Frank for their valuable assistance reflected the sincere gratitude he felt for their generous and willing efforts on his behalf. From the tone of Richard's letter he had been relieved to learn that their visit to Deal had in fact been enjoyable and rewarding to them both, and not a tedious duty gratuitously imposed upon them by him from afar.

But the matter did not end there. In the capricious way that chance contacts and off-the-cuff, often casual remarks by others sometimes have a profound effect upon subsequent events, a comment in Richard's letter sparked off a whole series of far-reaching repercussions.

Richard's almost light-hearted suggestion that Walter might perhaps consider creating a scale-model reproduction of the ancient fortifications along the coast of Kent, fell like a seed on warm and fertile ground.

Walter was immediately inspired by the concept which he at once saw would add a new dimension to his establishment. The idea of creating a whole new section to his Museum, where a mass of material could be concentrated in a series of model representations of historic buildings and events—each a theme dedicated to some topic likely to inspire interest in young and old alike—captured his imagination to such an extent that it became an absorbing new interest.

Castles and forts were always attractive subjects for models, and it was the thought of these more than anything else which had excited him. Like Richard, he had happy memories of being fascinated as a boy by wooden model forts, with soldiers, cowboys, Indians, horses, guns and carriages—all made of lead—to place carefully in and around them.

Looking at the pictures Richard had sent him brought these memories flooding back and fired his.imagination. Clearly there was a rich field here to be exploited.

Walter's success as a business man was in no small measure due to the energy and enthusiasm with which he entered into a new project.

Not a man to hang about dilly-dallying in a state of uncertainty about a possible new idea to enhance the attraction of his Museum, he made decisions rapidly, and having made them went about their exploitation with vigorous and infectious enthusiasm. He had a knack of seeking out and enlisting the support of people and organisations having particular knowledge and expertise, to assist him in developing new projects and ideas.

This new concept, conceived by a thoughtful, pipe-puffing, large and genial Englishman, sitting behind his desk in the quiet peaceful countryside of Kent, was no exception. No sooner did Walter start to mull the matter over in his mind, than his active, agile memory threw up an image that immediately inspired his imagination, and increased his initial impetus.

Perhaps it was another case of association of ideas, for the memory which had sprung to mind had in fact been registered there as a direct result of his contact with the man whose letter he now had in front of him.

The very thought of highly-professional, detailed scale-models of real world themes, reminded him straightaway of some of the wonderful things he had seen in his many recent visits to the Universal Film Studios in Los Angeles.

His liaison with the people there, who had latched on with such alacrity to the fascinating notion of creating a feature film telling the story of the discovery of the ancient cannon carrying its secret hidden Treasure Trove, dug out of the soil of Kent in the 'Garden of England', had opened up a new world to him.

And a vast world it proved to be. Established in 1915 by Universal Pictures, this mammoth complex had spread over four hundred and twenty acres on ground which, when he was a small boy, had been almost entirely occupied by chicken farms. Now it was the centre of a huge and fast growing new industry.

To Walter, the concentration of sheer human inventiveness and expertise he saw around him on his visits there, absolutely astounded him. And one facility he quickly discovered was the ingenious use of miniature models to be integrated into real life scenes by the talented photographic experts whose creativity so impressed him.

Now, by his good fortune in having friends within the vast organisation—and what was more, friends who were already so familiar with his connection with South East England—he had people with whom he could discuss his potential venture into the world of realistic modelling.

His first move was to write to his closest contact at the Studios—Max Selznick, the man who had taken up the story and directed the film about the ancient cannon with such enthusiasm and success.

Walter forbore to try to summarise what it was he wanted to discuss, but simply invited Max to call at the Museum, at his convenience, to have a look at another story from 'The Old Country' on which he was working, because it was proving of great interest.

He had a shrewd idea that Max might well see in it the possibility of another short feature film of the type much sought after as back-up short films to accompany the main film of a cinema programme. This was the particular responsibility of Max Selznick and his small innovative team, within the fast-expanding movie firm that employed him. It was he who had spotted and followed up, the newspaper story about Walter's Spanish Flintlock Pistol and its fascinating origin.

Meanwhile Walter was able to complete his work on the life of the Duke of Wellington, and embody the information provided by Richard about the matter of his appointment to the historic Office of Lord Warden of the Cinque Ports.

Having done this he immediately set to work to plan a first scheme for creating an exhibit, and centre of interest, around the building of fortifications by King Henry VIII of England, to oppose a possible invasion from the combined forces of Spain and France.

By the time Max Selznick fixed an appointment and came to see him at his Museum, Walter, with the aid of his skilled assistants, had already prepared what promised to be a very interesting display, though at this stage it was just an overall paper plan, lacking any attempt yet to solve the problem of the actual models that would form the three-dimensional heart of it.

Walter began by showing Max his work featuring the Duke of Wellington, and then told him about his letter of enquiry to Richard.

He had already decided that he could do no better than sit Max comfortably in his office, provide him with the correspondence, and leave him alone for a bit to read it through. Max, like Richard, had developed a soft spot for the beautiful, tranquil countryside of Kent. Moreover, Max knew the man whose letter he was to read, having accompanied Walter when they went to England to gather material for their 'Cannon' film.

On a pretext that he had a small matter to deal with, Walter went off and left Max to digest the material in peace and quiet. It was one thing to hand a man something to read and stand over him while he did so, but quite another to give the reader time to absorb the material on his own—time to have a really good look at it and, if necessary, back-track over parts of it again, to gain a clear grasp of what it was all about.

Walter's natural use of commonsense and practical psychology would have met with the approval of any serious student of business and industrial relations, and was another factor which lay behind his commercial success. He thought things through, and played his cards to maximum advantage. He timed his return nicely, for when he re-entered his office Max was shuffling the pages of Richard's letter back together, having just finished reading them.

"Interesting, that!" commented Max, looking up as Walter came in. "Richard Livingston's done a good job for you there. Fascinating corner of England that is, isn't it? The place sure oozes with history, doesn't it? Makes me want to go back there!"

"Me too!" agreed Walter with a smile. "Did you notice his suggestion about a modelled display of the Castles?"

"I did indeed," replied Max. "It struck me at once as a damn good idea!"

"Well, that's why I asked you to call," explained Walter. "Have a look at this."

Walter took Max over to a long table by the window where he had spread out his provisional plans for a possible layout of a model exhibition in the Museum of Henry VIII's preparations against the invasion of Kent. This, with the pictures and photographs Richard had sent him, provided a good idea of what might be created.

Not a man to dissemble, Walter came straight to the point.

"My difficulty here is the models," he stated. "I was wondering if it would be possible for me to commission the work to be done by some of your talented colleagues at the Studios. Even better, I got round to thinking that maybe your people might think the project interesting enough to make a feature film about. Much the same sort of approach as the 'Cannon' film. We could work together on it. I could undertake the historical research, and we could finish up with a new centre of interest at the Museum here, and a profitable film for you. What do you think?"

"As a matter of fact," smiled Max, amused by Walter's blatant opportunism, but not objecting to it for he shared the same trait, "as I read the material it already occurred to me that it could easily provide a very interesting basis for a documentary film. To be honest, I thought it was the possibility of that which persuaded you to call me in to see the material. Your problem of model-making did not of course occur to me. To us it is never a difficulty."

He paused a moment, looking down at the material thoughtfully, obviously weighing matters up in his mind. Then he continued.

"It's certainly an attractive proposition," he said. "It would be so easy to pack such a film with wonderful pictures of those historic towns mentioned in the bit about the Cinque Ports. Then, back-tracking in history, from local archives over in England, we ought to be able to come up with a fair picture of what the area around Deal looked like in the days of Henry VIII. Back at the Studios we could then create a pretty good modelled representation of the Castles, against a back cloth illustrating the general appearance of the place at the time."

Walter could hardly have hoped for a more encouraging first reaction to his suggestion. The two of them talked it over for a bit and Max determined to discuss it with his colleagues and decide whether they considered the project to be worth their while pursuing.

It wasn't long before Walter had a positive response from Max. His company at Universal Studios was certainly interested in the project.

The general impression was that the subject matter, properly handled, could hardly fail. There was widespread interest in America in historic Britain, and the nature of these ancient defensive buildings, nestling in their picturesque setting by the English Channel, couldn't be more photogenic.

Negotiations were conducted and a plan of action formulated. It was decided to start matters rolling the following spring. This had two advantages to the Film Company. Firstly it followed on nicely from their current work which at present was fully occupying them, and secondly it would give them the opportunity to do some filming in Kent when the countryside was at its best and the famous orchards were a mass of blossom.

Walter was more than happy to go along with this arrangement. It was agreed that a small party of them should travel to England together, to spend about six weeks in the Deal area gathering material for the film and exploring historical matters to get the background correct. From a financial point of view, Walter's potential interest was minimal compared with that of Universal Studios, but nonetheless his presence in the team was vital to them because it was to be his responsibility to get the history right. His interest was a long-term one concerning the development of the Museum; theirs by comparison was a short-term investment in a project that would give its greatest return in its initial launch period.

The intended film would be firstly a presentation of the modern appearance today of the historic towns constituting the five Cinque Ports, together with the two associated towns of Rye and Winchelsea, accompanied by a look at the surrounding countryside in springtime.

Secondly, it would include a reconstruction, to be made on their return to California, of the situation at the time when King Henry VIII had prepared his defences.

For the latter part of the assignment, detailed photographs of the Deal and Walmer Castles as they now appeared, with such records as Walter could unearth about their original appearance, and also that of the missing Sandown Castle, would constitute the essential data on which to prepare the models at the Studios. The eventual destination of the models made back at the Studios, would be Walter's Museum, once the film had been made.

The party was to include three photographic experts; two technicians; Max Zelznic and his personal assistant Martin Dewey; plus Walter himself.

Martin Dewey, an ex-journalist turned film researcher and scriptwriter, was an invaluable right-hand man to Max. When they went out and about together seeking material which involved personal relationships, Martin—who had a trained and penetrating mind—was much more perceptive and street-wise than Max. He was an astute observer, quick to grasp both the apparent outward essence of a matter—its surface appearance—and also to spot the often contrasting truth, or unstated nuances, below the surface. Max lacked this perspicacity. On occasions he was so blind to what to Martin was so obvious, that he was regarded by the latter as being incredibly naive for so talented a man, and was told by him that he ought to be more suspicious of people's motives for they were often not as nice as Max assumed them to be.

Equally as importantly, Martin had the talent to arrive back at base with all the necessary facts, either in cryptic shorthand, or stored in his excellent memory, with an accuracy which never ceased to amaze Max.

In these two respects, Martin's journalistic experience had given him strengths that complemented the professional skill of Max as a film maker, and the two made a powerful team in the development of documentary films.

On the trip to England Martin was to be worth his weight in gold because, in ways unforeseen when they all set out, there were to be a number of occasions where rich, potential material for future films fell fortuitously into their laps. Martin was there to record the essence of it, thoroughly and professionally in a way none of the others could have done. He also smelt a rat or two where those with him caught not the slightest whiff of anything unsavoury.

The plans were made, and in due course of time the day arrived when all of them were safely installed in a small, comfortable hotel in Deal, ready to begin their interesting assignment.

Everything went very well from the start. By prior arrangement they had decided to spend the first seven days visiting the five Cinque Ports, plus Rye and Winchelsea. This gave them plenty of material and ideas for their aim of taking home to the USA a photographic record of this section of the Kent and Sussex coastal towns, with the emphasis on selecting as many pictures as possible of buildings and features which dated far back in history. The weather was good and this initial period was more like a holiday than a working assignment.

Thereafter, for the next two weeks, Walter spent a good deal of time on his own, for his was a singular task—one of historical research—whereas, for part of the intended film material, the others necessarily had to work as a team under the direction of Max.

Once the initial programme was planned and settled, however, it was possible for Max, Martin and Walter to go off together, leaving the photographic team to complete the arranged work.

It was from these joint forays that unexpected results were to arise, not so much for the Military Museum—though there was some measure of benefit there as well—but much more so for the Film Company that, at a calculated risk to themselves, had financed the expedition for all of them. They were destined to achieve a much better return on their investment than they could reasonably have expected for the original single project. Very much better.

Soon after their arrival in Deal, Walter contacted Colonel FitzWalter and arranged to visit him at Littlebrook. Richard Livingstone of SKWEC, had, as a matter of courtesy, done what he'd said he would do, and told the Colonel several months ago that he had passed his name to Walter Richtmeyer in California in connection with Walter's enquiries about the Duke of Wellington.

The Colonel's reaction, as Richard knew it would be, was one of willingness to assist Walter in any way he could. It happened that Colonel FitzWalter was expecting Malcolm MacKenzie from Aberdeen to visit him shortly. He was coming to stay for a week or so, at the Colonel's invitation, to explore the area rather more thoroughly than he had been able to on his last visit, and also to see his ex-Royal Navy friends at Dover and Chatham.

In his usual organised way, Colonel FitzWalter decided to invite Walter and his fellow Americans Max and Martin, to come to see him when his Scottish visitor was there. He thought that Malcolm's presence would add interest to the meeting and assist him to entertain the Americans. It turned out to be an excellent idea and the day proved most interesting and enjoyable to them all.

Because of the reason for Richard Livingstone having put Walter in touch with the Colonel in the first place, it was natural for the Duke of Wellington to be the first topic of conversation, when—mutual introductions having been made—the group settled down over drinks in the comfortable lounge of Riverside House.

The Colonel told his visitors something of his interest in studying past military campaigns, and in an adjoining room—his 'Den' as he liked to call it—he showed them an example of the way in which he set about the task of trying to reconstruct battle scenes of earlier times. Walter was able to clear up some points concerning Wellington's life, and also gain many useful ideas about realistic and informative displays depicting the salient features of historic events and famous battles.

Malcolm MacKenzie's own interest in naval matters proved a point of contact, bringing him into the discussion. He told them that he was currently working on a model of Nelson's flagship, H.M.S. Victory, back in Aberdeen, which immediately alerted the interest of Walter, who was becoming involved with the world of models for the first time.

Colonel FitzWalter also had an interesting suggestion which later on Walter took up with enthusiasm. He thought that Nelson, a contemporary of the Duke of Wellington, would make an excellent centre of interest for Walter, who was not slow in spotting straightaway a potential source of assistance in this respect from Malcolm MacKenzie, a man he liked from the outset.

The Colonel, discussing the way in which Wellington's and Nelson's careers overlapped to some extent, mentioned the fact that surprisingly, so far as he could find out, the two never in fact seemed to have met. There was a story that they had passed one another in the lobby of the Admiralty on one occasion, but apparently without mutual recognition—or at least of showing any signs of it. He could not vouch for the accuracy of this story—it may have been apocryphal though he'd heard it from more than one source—but he had searched in vain for any records of the two having met, because it was a scene that he would like to have recreated. He observed, though, that Nelson was eleven years older than Wellington, who was in fact only thirty-six years old when Nelson, then forty-seven, was killed.

"Wellington," Colonel FitzWalter added, "went on to reach his eighty-fourth year!" This evidently reminded him of something for he went on to make some interesting observations.

"The two of them at least finished up close to one another," he smiled. "They are both buried in the Crypt of St. Paul's Cathedral!"

On an impulse he went to a long set of bookshelves along one wall of his cluttered Den, and took out a well-thumbed, chunky book of the Works of Tennyson. Flicking through the pages he soon found what he was looking for.

"Here it is," he said. "It's from Tennyson's 'Ode on the Death of the Duke of Wellington'. Some of you might be familiar with it. I'll read it to you—listen to this."

With that he read an extract, one that Walter was later to have attractively written out on an illuminated parchment, with a word of explanation, as a fitting last exhibit of his Duke of Wellington feature, at the Museum. Beside it, in a matching frame, he displayed photographs of the tombs of Nelson and Wellington, together with one of Wellington's huge funeral carriage which was kept on display in the Crypt. Some thought the carriage an incongruous object to place in the Crypt, but the Colonel disagreed and thought its presence was a tribute to the man who took his last ride upon it. These pictures were taken for Walter by Max's photographers at the Cathedral when on a visit to London during their stay.

The piece Colonel FitzWalter read was a poignant reminder to the Americans of the rich, historic, military heritage of which he was clearly very conscious and patriotically very proud, and it evoked a memory, not of storybook heroes, but of two very real famous men whose names were revered by the British.

The Colonel prefaced his reading by a simple philosophical comment.

"We all finish up just the same, simply as fellow men," he said. "We shed titles and ranks and uniforms and all marks of distinction, to meet our Maker as the simple men we are. Tennyson was conscious of this and speaks just of a sailor and a soldier meeting to rest together, the one arriving forty-eight years after the other."

Walter remembered this comment much later on when he decided upon a suitable title for his illuminated parchment.

The Colonel read the extract from Tennyson's poem with a depth of feeling far greater than those who judged him only by his somewhat stern and soldierly appearance would have thought him capable. But it would not have surprised a discerning man who long ago had been his wise, scholarly English Master at King's School, Canterbury. Perhaps—who knows—he heard Gordon Spencer FitzWalter now, and silently applauded his erstwhile pupil, now an aging man, who yet was still the boy he knew and understood so well.

Max, the film director, thought how well the pleasantly modulated voice would sound, over a movie picture of the Gun Carriage, covered by its proud Union Jack, as it made its slow, measured progress towards St. Paul's Cathedral in a military procession—splendid as only the British, with their long history and strongly-rooted traditions, could create so impressively. And Martin, the journalist—

—was alone to spy,
with his keen and ever watchful eye,
a tear on the cheek of the Colonel's face,
as he returned his book to its accustomed place.
But he did not marvel that it should be so,
or wonder how tears unbidden may flow,
for he had seen many a strong man silently weep,
when memories disturbed his waking sleep.

Who knows what moving scenes of past personal experiences had flitted across his mind, evoked by his own reading of these thought-provoking words which perhaps for him had strong emotional overtones. Observing him, Martin knew that the old soldier

527

must have been a better leader of his men in years gone by because he was at heart a simple, caring man—not a full-sized, unfeeling, living prototype of the lead soldiers he now had, set out on his War Games Table, across the room.

On occasions Martin had met men whose mould fitted this latter description. Their metallic, inhuman hardness frightened him, for they seemed to him to be as devoid of pity, as empty of compassion as the unblinking, fathomless eyes of a staring snake. They were the stuff of nightmares.

Colonel FitzWalter was clearly very far from being such a man, a fact that would have been wholeheartedly testified to by the many people he had met scattered around the world, and by men who had served under him, who remembered him with pleasure and with gratitude.

Walter's illuminated parchment finally appeared in the following form:

A Sailor welcomes a Soldier to St. Paul's Cathedral

"Who is he that cometh, like an
honour'd guest
With banner and with music, with solider
and with priest,
With a nation weeping, and breaking on
my rest?"

"Mighty Seaman, this is he,
Was great by land as thou by sea;
Thine island loves thee well, thou
famous man,
The greatest sailor since our world
began;
Now, to the roll of muffled drums,
To thee the greatest soldier comes;
For this is he,
Was great by land as thou by sea.

His foes were thine; he kept us free;
O give him welcome, this is he,
Worthy of our gorgeous rites,
And worthy to be laid by thee:
For this is England's greatest son,
He that gain'd a hundred fights,
Nor ever lost an English gun."

from

'Ode on the Death of the Duke of Wellington'
by
Alfred Tennyson (1809 – 1892)

(Poet Laureate from 1850)

Chapter 34

THE 'GARDEN OF ENGLAND' SERIES

movie-men from Los Angeles
strike gold in Kent

When comfortably seated back in the lounge, conversation turned to the way in which Malcolm MacKenzie, from the far north of Scotland, had first become associated with the village of Littlebrook in the heart of the Kentish countryside.

Starting at the beginning, Colonel FitzWalter told his visitors the story of the wandering tramp who ended his days dossing down at the foot of a local lime kiln, attracted there by the warm glow of its fire in the night sky.

This story, ending with the bizarre death of the Spindlecroft twins, captured the imagination of the Americans. It was a strange and fascinating series of events. With some awe they looked at Malcolm's gold pocket watch and passed it silently from one to the other, marvelling at its history and by what slender and improbable chance it had found its way back to the brother of the man whose twenty-first birthday present it had been.

Small wonder that Max Selznick, with growing excitement, realised that here in this quiet English village he had stumbled upon a true story that had all the potential of a wonderful, real-life, human-interest film. He made up his mind there and then to pursue it at a later date. However, he was determined not to get side-tracked at that moment but to let the day's visit take its natural course so that he could soak up the atmosphere and take away with him that evening an overall impression of the place and its people, making a mental note of anything of particular interest—such as the Spindlecroft story—to explore in detail afterwards.

Walter Richtmeyer, meanwhile, had immediately latched on to the description of the Spindlecrofts' collection of perfectly-scaled models, reflecting their craft as wheelwrights, that now formed a specialist section of Malcolm MacKenzie's fast developing Museum of Models, in Aberdeen. He perceived that he and Malcolm shared common interests and decided, subject to Malcolm's agreement, to arrange a brief visit to Aberdeen before returning to the States. There seemed to be a strong possibility of useful, mutual co-operation, more especially so since the Scotsman was currently working on a model of Nelson's flagship, Victory, and had a Royal Navy background himself.

Glancing at his watch the Colonel asked his visitors if they would like to take a stroll round the village before lunch, and this suggestion was accepted gladly because it was quite evident that the old-world atmosphere of the place held a great attraction for all of them.

Their route took them past a small group of quaint, very old, detached cottages, two of which had very recently been re-thatched. A third was in the process of being done and the fourth, as yet untouched, allowed of a 'before and after' comparison that illustrated what a striking difference new thatching made to the appearance of the dwellings. A new, neatly crafted straw peacock decorated the roof of one of them, contrasting sharply with three, well-weathered and bedraggled-looking birds waiting to end their days when the last roof was stripped.

There were two men working on the roof of the third cottage, well on their way to finishing it because they were busy crafting the ridge with split hazel wood which, being very flexible, could be bent over the capping on the apex. This wheat-straw ridge structure was very attractively constructed, built to do its job very well indeed, but looking more than just functional because it was held down by twisted hazel, the whole fashioned to appear much like a panelled quilt fastened right along the roof, making it snug and tight.

Both men were known to Colonel FitzWalter, who called out a greeting to them as the party paused for a few moments to watch the work in progress. He told his companions that the two were both local men who worked as a partnership, following in both cases the same trade as their fathers, who had taught them. The group watched the thatchers going about their ancient, traditional craft using methods and materials that had remained virtually unchanged in form for generation after generation.

It was a tranquil scene. The end-products looked very artistic indeed, and the cottages were provided not only with a new, well and truly watertight roof but one which included features and flourishes developed over the years to make buildings look extremely picturesque. Martin took a number of photographs of them before they moved off.

Beyond the cottages, not very far along the road, they reached the church, and the Colonel took his guests first of all to look at the grave of the solitary, wandering old soldier he had told them about.

As a result of the intervention of Malcolm MacKenzie, the man had ended his days in a named and well-cared for plot, and not, as might so easily have happened without the chain of events that had started by an act of kindness by the Spindlecroft twins, in an unnamed pauper's grave.

"Old Motty's doing a good job, as you can see, Malcolm," the Colonel commented to his Scottish guest.

"Yes, I was just thinking that," responded Malcolm. "I was quite sure that he would, of course—all the while that he's well enough to carry on, that is. Should he decide to give up his job here, though, you will remember to commission somebody else for me, won't you?"

"Our Motty won't give up if he can help it," smiled the Colonel. "But the Reverend Yelman and I have already discussed the matter. Don't worry, we'll see to it that the grave of your brother's old comrade from the Durham Light Infantry will not be forgotten and neglected in this quiet corner of his homeland where by chance he finished his days." Then, as an afterthought he added, "Sadly, as you know, he's got the Spindlecrofts here to keep him company. Like him they came much before their time. But there we are—that's life, I suppose. None of us knows what tomorrow holds."

They were about to wander off towards the church door when the Vicar entered the churchyard through the attractive old lych gate, spotted them and walked across to meet them.

Colonel FitzWalter introduced his American guests. The Vicar shook hands with each in turn, with a word of welcome to them, then turned to Malcolm MacKenzie and shook hands warmly with him.

"It's a pleasure to see you here again, Malcolm," he said. "I heard you were on your way down from Scotland to visit us again." Then, glancing down at the grave they were standing by he added archly, his eyes twinkling, "Checking up on our old and faithful servant Motty, are you? He's been doing his stuff, as you can see!"

"Malcolm's been reminding me to be sure to appoint somebody else if Motty gives in his notice," the Colonel interjected.

"Don't worry about that, Malcolm," interjected the Vicar. "Old Motty has no intention of retiring yet. He's got far too many friends in here to want to leave. I rather fancy he will keep on creeping here to have a chat with them and look after their graves right up until the day he finally joins them in the next world for good! But be assured we will look after matters for you when the time comes. We shall make sure that Simon Hepplethwaite's grave is never neglected. Edwin Jordan, our verger, knows all about the arrangements you have made and he keeps a watching brief on things like that."

This little exchange led to a brief explanation to the puzzled listeners about who 'Old Motty' was and why he was such a well-known local character.

The description of his activities and his alleged, remarkable psychic gifts, much amused the visitors and Max determined to explore the subject further when the opportunity arose. He sensed another unusual, weird story.

Before they left the graveside the Vicar added some comments about the quiet, unobtrusive Christian behaviour of the Spindlecroft brothers towards the totally unknown tramp for whom they had provided a last service. This he was proud and pleased to have an opportunity to do for he had been very moved by their gentle and genuine kindness. He even told them of the Spindlecrofts' own private contribution to the quality of the coffin and its fittings. Such deeds, he felt, should be made known to others, albeit quietly and discreetly.

The Vicar had his own logical reason for this personal opinion. It was his firmly-held view that the world would be better place if such acts of kindness did not go unnoticed, but received a little publicity—this not only for their good example but to counterbalance the unfailing, ready, and all too often positively eager widespread publicity given to all things unseemly.

Nor did he fail to tell the American visitors how Malcolm MacKenzie had stepped in to help his brother's comrade, so confirming what they had inferred from the conversation, that Malcolm had some proprietary interest in the ongoing care of the tramp's grave.

Reverend Yelman was rather sensitive on the subject of the exploitation of bad news and had some strong views about it. It was a point he had recently discussed with his brother-in-law who had been down on holiday for a few days from London where he was employed on the staff of one of the more sensational Sunday newspapers. The Vicar had been disturbed by his wife's brother's comment that so far as newspapers were concerned, bad news was always good news. It worked wonders for their circulation, he had said, a cynical view that the Vicar found hard to swallow.

"I find it difficult," he had responded at the time with lofty, disdainful aloofness, referring, rather to his wife's discomfiture, to the newspaper in question, "to come to terms with an organisation which avidly gathers news of crime, violence, cruelty, depravity, calamities, scandal and all manner of sleazy affairs and activities—not to mention its obsession with sexual excesses and perversions—in order to make the maximum amount of money exploiting the weaknesses of a naïve and gullible public!"

He had paused a moment after delivering himself of this decidedly devastating diatribe, weighing its content and searching for a suitable summing up, then concluding with a pomposity so priggish that his brother-in-law had felt like pricking him to see if he popped.

"It is nothing less—nothing less, I say— than deliberately profiting from iniquity. And this on Sundays, of all days!"

Despite his strongly-expressed aversion to such subject matter the Vicar nonetheless regularly read the paper himself—though very discreetly for it was purchased by his wife through a third party and was ostensibly nothing whatsoever to do with him! He salved his conscience, if now and again it were troubled, perhaps by the inclusion of a particularly reprehensible and outrageously juicy story which he had read with eager, close and lascivious interest, by the thought that he needed to know what was going on in the world so as to be aware of the unhealthy influences to which some of his parishioners were being exposed—those, that is, who were perverse enough to read it!

The Vicar's brother-in-law had listened politely to the damning diatribe, smiled to himself but diplomatically refrained from further comment. He was used to people pontificating about his scurrilous newspaper but was only too aware that the detailed accuracy of their vehemently expressed distaste revealed a pretty thorough reading of the paper by themselves.

Neither he nor his colleagues, and certainly not the paper's proprietors, were in the least put out by such attacks—not surprisingly as their circulation went up in direct proportion to them. Negative criticism of the outraged, self-righteous kind that they so regularly received, perversely provided positive progress for their increasingly popular publication, precisely the reverse of its intended effect! It was as good as lurid, titillating advertising and cost them nothing! So, week by week, with malice aforethought, they gleefully stirred their unwholesome pot and grew fat on it, much as the Red Dean did on his!

On leaving the neat, unpretentious but dignified last resting place of Simon Hepplethwaite with its nicely designed headstone bearing his name, the Vicar led his visitors to the shared grave of Herbie and Horace, the Spindlecroft twins.

Silently they grouped around to read its most unusual, perhaps unique, inscription, showing their identical birth and death dates, with the simple, accompanying epitaph. Nearby, in the family plot, they read the inscriptions on the graves of the twins' father, Samuel, and grandfather, Ebeneezer.

The Vicar explained how Ebeneezer Spindlecroft had founded the local firm in 1823. He told them a little of the family's history since that date and pointed out that the twins were the last of the family line; no more Spindlecrofts would be buried there.

He then, at their request, took them for a brief look over the church. It was an attractive old building and the Vicar was particularly proud of its fine, stained-glass windows. Having pointed these out and drawn attention to some of the main features of the building and its furnishings, he led them up the spiral stone steps in the corner of the tower to the belfry to see the array of six bells on which his enthusiastic team of bell-ringers practised their change-ringing repertoire regularly each week and sought to extend it by trying out other changes.

It happened that neither Malcolm MacKenzie nor the three Americans had ever been inside a bell tower and they stood for a while studying the bells and their mechanisms with interest. Each bell hung in its own frame from a strong wooden bar that was pivoted at both ends. The bar, called a bell's headstock, carried a large wooden wheel at one end. It was immediately evident that a bell was rung by pulling on a rope that passed round the grooved rim of its wheel. The large diameter of the wheels gave the leverage needed to pull the heavy bells up.

At the moment the bells were in their safe 'rest' position, hanging with their open ends downwards. When in action they were never at rest in this position; they were either perched with their mouths pointing upwards, balanced just off the vertical, or swinging in a circle downwards and up the other side to perch at the top once again—this time just off the vertical as before, but to the other side of the axis.

One pull of a bell's rope turned the wheel clockwise and swung the bell round in a complete circle one way. The next pull turned the wheel anti-clockwise and swung the bell back from where it had started. On each swing a freely suspended clapper hanging inside the bell hit its side to ring it, so that there were two strikes per one complete pulling cycle.

The Vicar went to the smallest of the six bells, the treble, and helped by Colonel FitzWalter who made sure the rope remained taut, heaved on its wheel until the bell was facing vertically upwards. On its headstock a wooden arm, mounted to point diametrically opposite in direction to the bell, swung down to locate itself on a slider arm at the bottom of the frame and stopped the bell from tipping over the top to swing down the other side.

"If you imagine all the bells set like this," he said, "then you can picture them as they all are when made ready by the ringers to go into action. As each rope is pulled, its bell swings down and rings once. On the next pull, because the rope has wound itself in the groove in the opposite direction, the bell swings back where it started from and gives another 'dong'. The first pull of the two is called the handstroke and the second the backstroke."

"That's neat," said Malcolm. "I must say, I've never stopped to consider what the mechanism in bell tower is like. I've seen the ringers standing in a circle on the ground floor pulling their ropes, but I've never seen what the ropes actually do."

"Bell-ringing is not as easy as it looks," commented the Vicar. "It takes new members a long time before they become truly proficient members of the team. Once they have mastered the actual art of pulling the bell, they then have to face a long period of training in order to learn how to function as one of the team. To begin with they get used to pulling 'rounds'. This is simply ringing the bells in sequence, starting with the highest note, the treble, and running down to the lowest one, the tenor. Twice through takes the bells back where they started. They call that one complete round. If you listen, you will hear a slight pause after each round of twelve, whereas you may not notice any interval between the two peals of six that make up the complete round."

"Then they start 'ringing the changes', don't they?" smiled Colonel FitzWalter. "From what I gather they can go on learning for the rest of their lives, can't they?"

"Yes, they can indeed," confirmed the Vicar. "They can ring the bells in a large number of different sequences, some much more pleasant to the ear than others. And of-course they change from one sequence to another as they go along—when they become expert, that is. It requires endless practice, but as you know, it becomes an absorbing hobby to those who really like it."

"With six bells that would give quite a sizeable number of possible changes, wouldn't it?" observed Colonel FitzWalter. "Seven hundred and twenty, I'm told," stated the Vicar. "It's an interesting subject. On their noticeboard down below, the Littlebrook team have a chart showing the number of changes possible for various numbers of bells. It's absolutely astounding. For eight bells it's over forty thousand, and for twelve it's just over four hundred and seventy-nine million, if you please! I can't vouch for the accuracy but that's what someone once worked out!"

"Do they get the chance to ring other sets of bells?" asked Max.

"Oh yes, they certainly do," replied the Vicar." The local team belongs to the Kent County Association of Bell Ringers and go off to other churches from time to time to get together with other teams."

"They even have access to a peal of twelve, don't they, Vicar?" interjected the Colonel. "Not may teams in the country can say that, so far as I know!"

"Surely there's no local church with twelve bells installed in it, is there?" queried Malcolm sounding somewhat surprised.

"No, you're right," confirmed the Vicar. "But curiously enough, not many million miles from here, at Birchington-on-Sea on the Isle of Thanet, there's a privately-owned bell tower built many years ago especially to contain a set of twelve bells. The local church could not accommodate them. It was built on an estate called Quex Park. Now and again the Littlebrook team go there and join up with local teams to practise ringing various changes on them. It's quite an experience, as you can imagine."

"It's an interesting bell tower, that one!" commented Colonel FitzWalter. "You can see it from miles around in that flat area. It's an elegant, white, metal tower with slender pinnacles that glint in the sunlight. It stands among the trees, well away from any other buildings. I'm told that in this area only Canterbury Cathedral has as many bells!"

"That's right," said the Vicar. "And of course, as you can imagine, it's a rare privilege to get to ring the Cathedral bells!"

Down below, the group looked at the place where the ringers stood and the Vicar showed them the nature of the ropes they pulled. He pointed out a rope's two main features—its doubled-over 'tail-end', and a section a few feet from the end where, over a length of some three feet, coloured wool is woven into it to form what is described as the 'sally', which provides a good grip for the ringer's hands.

Because of the way the rope is located in the rim of the wheel, at the end of the 'handstroke' the ringer is left with only the tail-end in his hands. More of the rope is taken up by the wheel on this stroke than on the other one. So, on the 'backstroke' the tail-end is gripped and pulled, but on the 'handstroke' the ringer has hold of the more comfortable 'sally' section of the rope.

Having described their technical details to his visitors, the Vicar then drew their attention to the change-ringing chart on the noticeboard, which he had mentioned to them earlier. The way in which the number of possible changes increased so staggeringly as the number of bells increased, astounded them. They expressed surprise at these figures and wondered about their accuracy. The Vicar said that he himself had been similarly sceptical when first he'd seen them, but the man who had produced the chart was pretty sure they were accurate. Apparently they had been passed to him by his uncle who worked in the famous Whitechapel Bell Foundry, London, founded by Robert Mot in 1570. Many historic bells had been cast there including the original American Liberty Bell. A picture of this famous bell, mounted in the Independence Hall at Philadelphia in Pennsylvania, was pinned on the noticeboard. The well-known crack in this historic bell could be clearly seen in the photograph. The presence of this picture provided the Americans with an unexpected link with home and they studied the board with interest.

Several pictures of other famous bells were also displayed, together with sundry snippets of information, including a note that in the year 1761 it was recorded that a relay of ringers rang 40,320 changes on eight bells in twenty-seven hours of continuous ringing in the large Norman tower of the village church at Leeds in Kent. The point was picked up by Walter Richtmeyer—always on the lookout for historical data—who there and then determined to try to see the church when he made a visit he had promised himself to the picturesque Leeds Castle near Maidstone.

The unlikely-looking numbers they saw on the chart are reproduced in the table below. Walter noticed an interesting correlation between the recorded marathon effort by the ringers at Leeds so many years ago and the figures set against a peal of eight bells in the intriguing chart. It seemed that the stalwart Men of Kent had clocked up a time that was just under the statistical par for the course.

Number of bells	Number of changes possible	Time needed to ring them at an average of 24 per minute			
		Years	Days	Hours	Minutes
4	24				1
5	120				5
6	720				30
7	5,040			3	50
8	40,320		1	4	
9	362,880		10	12	
10	3,628,800		105		
11	39,916,800	3	60		
12	479,001,600	37	355		

Leaving the bell tower the Vicar took them along the aisle to have a look at 'Old Faithful', the much-used, time-worn, very old church organ that had endured so long yet still sounded quite good, though often a trifle wheezy—and sometimes, through no fault of its own—decidedly so!

In a niche tucked away behind it they were amused to see where a volunteer had to sit, when the organ was in use, to work the lever of the hand-pumped bellows, an arrangement much like that in a blacksmith's forge.

The Vicar smilingly told them that one or other of the choir boys usually did the job on Sundays, finding it a rather pleasing alternative to sit in the cosy privacy behind there instead of performing their normal, high-profile duties. Frowning, he noticed as he was talking to them, that the random array of initials carved into the woodwork, some bearing dates of long ago, had grown some recent additions that were obviously freshly cut.

He made a mental note to give the boys in general yet another reminder that, glad though he was of their services, he did not want them to record their efforts for posterity in this way, wantonly damaging the fabric of the long-suffering old instrument in the process!

And to be more specific, he didn't need to be Sherlock Holmes to deduce that KWG and MM were almost certainly the recent artwork of two of his regular pumpers, the sons—bosom pals—of Bill Gunstone the saddler and Bill Martin the landlord of the Ship Inn, the two being somewhat reluctant vocalists in his current choir, who were often round the back of the organ together, working as a two-boy team!

The two boys were evidently having fun and games back there on Sunday mornings and would have to be trimmed—though gently because he was short of choir boys, a perennial problem of his.

Twice recently he'd had to speak to them for letting the air supply run low, a covert operation carried out much to the amusement of some of those listeners in the choir stalls who noticed the wheezy notes of the fading organ and knew very well why it teetered so perilously on the brink of total failure, then suddenly recovered strongly at full blast, only to fade away again moments later.

Skinny little Fanny Delaware, peering—head thrust forward—through her thick pebble lenses at her page of music, was distressed at this arbitrary variation in loudness which she felt the congregation might well attribute to the inadequacies of her performance. She had glanced anxiously over the top of her small, round, gold-framed glasses at her hero, the bearded parson high up in his commanding position in the pulpit, catching his eye with a look of mute appeal and letting him know by a shake of her head that the ropy rendition was not her fault.

These spasmodic failures of the pneumatic system did not please her at all. Not one little bit. Little of stature but big of heart, she put her all into her Sunday sessions at the organ. But she had found that any suggestion to the boys that something was amiss with their pumping activities was greeted by astonished, wide-eyed innocence, acted out with such conviction that an onlooker would perceive them as being hurt that their best efforts were not fully appreciated!

If she could have spared a foot from the organ's pedals she would gladly have attempted to pump the thing herself, as indeed she did with her old family harmonium that she practised on at home. But alas, the big church organ demanded lots of air and needed powerful lungs. In any case, both her feet had parts to play in the organ's music-making processes!

The vicar's guests, though noting his frowning, thoughtful countenance, were unaware of these domestic problems that engaged his mind as he showed them to the door and bade them a courteous goodbye.

When they left the church, Max, intrigued by the story of the wheelwright twins, asked the Colonel if it were possible for them to visit the premises where they had worked. Colonel FitzWalter was happy to agree and proceeded to explain to them how the business had in fact been bought out by a large firm from Ashford, Kent, where the twins' father, Samuel Spindlecroft, had been thoroughly trained as a wheelwright before joining forces with their grandfather in the family business at Littlebrook.

The premises had not changed very much at all since their death and nor had the wide-ranging nature of the work done there. It was a thriving business which the new owners had wisely left alone to maintain its connections, and was now staffed by four skilled men and an apprentice. Two of the men, Henry Foster and Bill Smythe, together with the boy Jack Thorpe, had been employees of the Spindlecrofts at the time of their deaths. The other two men had moved from the Ashford staff to work at Littlebrook. The man in charge was Henry Foster, now appointed as the foreman, working under the overall direction of a co-ordinating manager who visited them weekly from Ashford.

Colonel FitzWalter was very sure the men there would be willing to show them round, and this indeed proved to be the case. On arrival they were greeted warmly and shown various workshops and facilities by Henry Foster, following very much the same tour of inspection that Malcolm had done on his previous visit.

In view of what the Colonel had told them about the bizarre end to the lives of the two brothers, the Americans gazed about them in silence when at length they all stood in the small Chapel of Rest where the two men had been found on that fateful morning.

Parked side by side were the two biers on which they had lain. It was very quiet in the room for the Chapel had been sited in a position remote from the workshops and well away from the road that passed in front of the premises.

At length Malcolm spoke to Henry Foster, his voice hushed respectfully as seemed to befit the circumstances.

"Is that where they were when you found Herbie and Horace that morning?" he asked the foreman, nodding his head towards the two biers.

"Yes," replied Henry quietly, "the biers were just as you see them now. We leave them like that when not in use. Somehow we feel that's how they should be stood, close together, just as the brothers left them."

He hesitated a few moments and then added, "You may think it strange, but we kind of feel their presence here when it's very quiet. Especially first thing in the morning, and when we lock up at night. Bill and I sometimes feel we're still working for them. We half expect to go into the workshops one day and find them working at their benches again!"

"I can quite understand that," murmured Malcolm. "The whole place bears their stamp everywhere, doesn't it? And that of their dad, of course. I remember how they said their dad had trained them in the business, starting when they were just boys. And a strict taskmaster he was with them too, according to what they said. It's very much a Spindlecroft family business, isn't it? What a good thing it is that the Ashford firm has been able to keep it going. It would have been very sad to have closed it all down."

Max, listening to the quiet conversation, was very conscious of an unusual atmosphere in the place, and strongly aware that if he could recapture it in a movie, telling the story of the twins alongside that of a wandering hobo, he would have a very compelling film that would do very well in the States. And not only that, judging by past experience, it would probably be equally as successful exported back to be shown in the UK.

Martin, always the journalist, for his part was busy observing everything with great interest and automatically storing away images and impressions, though as yet he and Max had not even exchanged words on the possibility of a future feature film. The impact and obvious movie potential of the unusual sequence of events, set in the quaint surroundings, had hit them both quite independently of one another. But it was not until they got back to Deal that evening that they discussed it.

On leaving the wheelwrights' establishment the Colonel led them on a walk, pointing out places of interest as they went. Every now and again he passed a comment, which almost invariably excited their further interest and left them wishing they could linger awhile to see more.

As they stood looking at the Oast house he told them briefly how it fitted into the scheme of things in the business of producing beer. Later they were to see the hop gardens, already showing promise of a sea of healthy hop vines, but for the moment they looked with interest at the picturesque buildings.

"Fascinating place to visit during the hop-picking season," Colonel FitzWalter remarked. "Especially at night. I love the smell of the hops. It's a very eerie place, though. Very eerie indeed. The place is believed locally to be haunted and has been so for years, if what one hears is to be believed!"

"Do you believe the stories?" asked Walter whose strong interest in history had given him a feel for the strength of some age-old traditions and legends, and a disinclination to dismiss too lightly beliefs that had endured down the years. He was surprised at the Colonel's emphatic response.

"Difficult not to once you get in there in the middle of the night!" he said. "Some strange things go on in there, from all accounts. Not so long ago some visitors one evening got the fright of their lives in there!"

"What happened?" asked Walter, his interest now fully awakened.

"I don't know the whole story," replied the Colonel, "but from what I heard they were running some sort of amateur séance in there, holding hands at midnight and sitting in a closed circle in front of the Oast fire, trying to contact the spirit of a fellow who was killed in there exactly fifty years ago to that very day—so it was said. I understand that the man was the dryer-in-charge at the time. He was up in the cowl seeking to release a crow trapped somehow in the bearings, when a sudden gust of wind caught the cowl and swung it round sharply, wrenching the bar he was holding from his grip. He plunged right down that conical tower there and crashed to his death through the hop-drying surface, straight into the furnace below. His name, Timothy Twylock, is legendary around here."

"What a tragedy!" exclaimed Walter. "And what an awful way to die! But what happened at the séance to frighten them away so much?"

"All hell was let loose, apparently," answered the Colonel. "I don't know the details precisely but the experts reckon they must have released a poltergeist, or something like that. There was a series of sudden events—things flying about, noises, flashes of brilliant light, clouds of dust and ash—all that sort of thing—which left them all scared stiff. Even the rats bolted across the floor around their feet and out through a hole under the door so as to get the hell out of the Oast house, so I'm told. It caused quite a stir in the village at the time. Everybody was talking about it."

He paused a moment, looking up at the white-painted wind cowl high up on the peak of the Oast house tower, and then continued.

"I remember that at church the following Sunday the Vicar warned his congregation never to play around with the spirit world like that. 'There are powers we don't begin to comprehend,' he said, 'and people court disaster if they mess about with the occult and things they don't understand.' It's all very strange. Very strange indeed.

What I do know about the place, though, is that dogs just won't go in there unless you drag them in. Mine are certainly no exception. And they show evidence of being petrified with fear—the hairs on their neck stand up and they tuck their tails down between their legs! It's very curious—quite beyond my ken, that's for sure. Animals are often quick to sense an unnatural atmosphere. When something's abnormal they seem to sense it instinctively. It's a thing I met now and again in my travels out East. Best to keep one's nose out of that kind of psychic business, in my opinion."

The Americans looked at the old building wonderingly. In the sunshine it looked harmless enough; indeed it was extremely attractive in the well-known tradition of picturesque Kentish Oast houses. But they could well believe it might be another matter in the dead of night. Many old places are!

Max was once again keenly interested in the story. The more he saw and heard of life in the area the more sure he became that it held within it material for a whole series of highly entertaining stories that could be real money-spinners if expertly made into feature films.

By the time the party arrived back at Riverside House they had glimpsed, or heard about, many aspects of village life, and realised there was not much that could not be done within the district to sustain life in the largely farming community. The traditionally skilled crafts and trades associated with the countryside were all there on the spot, or within easy reach: blacksmiths, saddlers, wheelwrights, sawyers, thatchers, ladder and fencing makers, millers, cobblers, carpenters, plumbers, bricklayers, millwrights, carriers, licensed slaughterers, butchers, bakers, dairymen, poulterers, grocers, decorators, gunsmiths as well as motor mechanics, agricultural engineers and steam experts.

In his travels worldwide with the Army, Colonel FitzWalter—when in remote parts, off the beaten track— had many times reason to be thankful that among the men with him he could count upon there being a reservoir of skills, particularly from those brought up in rural areas, which enabled them to function entirely by relying upon their own resources wherever they happened to be.

After entertaining his visitors to lunch, Colonel FitzWalter packed them into his rugged, reliable workhorse of a car, a Clifton Tourer version of Austin's 20/40 model, and drove them around the surrounding countryside to see the nature of the farming carried out in the district. The robust car was typical of him—built like a battleship as he was wont to say—selected more as a general-purpose vehicle of the countryside than for any pretensions to elegance.

The Americans, accustomed to farming on the grand scale, were surprised to see the wide variety of activities that existed in the area within a small compass. There seemed to be something of everything: a wide variety of vegetables; soft fruit plantations; extensive orchards producing fruit of all kinds; corn fields; hop gardens; areas of woodland yielding both timber and game; pasture land for cattle and sheep; pigs; goats—indeed it would have been difficult to find anything needed that was not produced in the area. To the Californians, so far as they could see, only fruit needing a hotter climate such as oranges, lemons, grapefruits and bananas which they were so accustomed to seeing growing at home, were missing.

From a vantage point on a hill top on one side of the village, the Colonel stopped to point out buildings of particular interest in the valley below that they had not had time to visit.

Along the winding river running through the lush countryside they could see a water mill that had been grinding corn for generations past. Not too far away was an impressive Malt House with twin cowls like those on an Oast House, producing enough malt annually to keep Mackeson's, a large Kent brewery, supplied with its total requirement for manufacturing its well-known beer and associated products.

Across the far side of the valley, in the distance, perched on a prominent knoll, a tower windmill could be seen standing out against the skyline. Its sails were slowly turning in the moderate breeze as the mill, like its water-driven neighbour, did what it had done for so many years, grinding corn grown in the area to produce a range of high-quality flour for bakers, and meal for animal feedstuff.

The Americans expressed an interest in this attractive-seeming, distant windmill, so the Colonel obligingly drove them over to see it, taking a route past a hop garden and pausing on the way to show them the compound of 'hopper huts' where pickers from London spent several weeks each year on their annual holiday in the Kentish countryside.

Approaching the location of the windmill, he turned into the loop of the narrow road which skirted the knoll on top of which it was built and stopped the car at the end of the private lane which led up to the mill itself. They all got out and stood in a group looking up at the buildings.

For a while they stood in silence watching the large sails relentlessly sweeping round in the soft but steady breeze. It was a captivating sight. From this distance the swishing sails looked very large indeed, giving some indication of the formidable power they developed by their enormous leverage, working through the gearing within. The mill looked neat and well maintained and the deep rumble of its machinery could just be heard from where they were standing.

At length the Colonel said something which again alerted Max to the possibility of yet another topic for a future film feature.

"That old mill has seen its share of high drama," he said. "Not so long ago the Miller who owned it got himself gobbled up in its huge gear wheels up in the top there. It was a sickening business by all accounts!"

He paused a moment reflectively, frowning slightly, his face looking serious and thoughtful, and added, "It must have been a terrible way to die. He was not a man well-liked in the neighbourhood, and, I have to say, not much missed, but nobody could have wished him to die in such an awful way. My God, it must have been dreadful! Absolutely dreadful!"

"What happened?" asked Max, eager to prompt the Colonel to pursue the story further.

"I don't know exactly," answered Colonel FitzWalter. "It was a curious train of circumstances, though. One of those times when a peaceful routine that looks as if it will go on forever is suddenly shattered by the totally unexpected. Fate lashes out and reminds us not to become too complacent—not to take too much for granted.

The Miller didn't arrive home one night at his normal time and at length, when they went to see what was up, he was found pretty well cut in half by the huge gear wheels up in the top. He must have been there some time because there were signs that rats had been gorging themselves on the pools of his congealing blood and eating bits of his mangled flesh—so it was said at the time."

"What a horrible, gruesome thing to happen!" commented Max with a shudder. "It must have pretty awful for those who found him."

"It was indeed," exclaimed the Colonel emphatically. "It was said at the inquest that a safety bar gave way while he was up in the top trying to apply the brake to shut the windsails down for the night. Something was wrong with the mechanism, apparently. He pitched straight into the works, along with the bar, and the whole lot got crunched up and wedged in the main gearing mechanism. The wind was still trying to force the huge main gear wheel to turn and they had to go and fetch the Miller's number two from a local pub to turn the mill's cap out of the wind and manipulate the works to get him out."

"What a terrible shock it must have been for him!" said Max.

"As a matter of fact I think some people felt sorrier for him than for the Miller," stated the Colonel. "You can tell how little liked the Miller was by some who knew him well—I heard somebody in a local pub one night say he felt sorry for the rats that fed on him! 'Feeding on the Miller,' the chap said, 'must have given them a guts-ache worse than the rat poison he was forever putting down to get rid of them!' Hardly a charitable comment, I thought!"

"Not much of a compliment to the Miller, was it?" interjected Martin with a wry grin.

"Well, anyway, that was not the end of the story," went on Colonel FitzWalter. "There was a curious train of circumstance, like I said.

Not long afterwards, by a twist of Fate, the Miller's widow lost her life in a sad accident herself. She fell off her bike crossing a footbridge over the river by the local water mill you saw just now, and tumbled over the handrail into the deep and treacherous millpond. She was trapped and drowned. She, like her husband, died a lonely, accidental death. It was the sort of combination of circumstances that in parts of Africa I've been to would have been put down to the work of a witch doctor casting an evil spell on the family.

However, in the end, at least things turned out well for the Miller's number two. Nice chap, he is. A hard-working fellow who was much exploited by the Miller. But, as it transpired, he was fully recompensed for his years of servitude, as a result of these two tragedies. He and his wife inherited the windmill and the entire estate!

What happened was, when the Miller was killed, the wife relied entirely upon his number two to run the place for her, and very well he did it too. To secure his services she made him a partner in the business. But, unbeknown to him, the Miller's wife went further. Having no family of her own she had a will made out leaving all her property to him! Absolutely everything! So now the two of them are living happily in the Miller's luxury bungalow and the business is thriving. Life is sometimes more dramatic than fiction, isn't it? Fate works in mysterious way!"

"It certainly does," mused Max Selznick. "That's quite a story!"

Martin Dewey, the sceptic, said nothing. But his mind busied itself with the brief details he'd just heard, of this double tragedy. When something happened that was very bad for someone but turned out remarkably good for someone else, it always left him wondering. His years as an active journalist had left its mark on his thinking processes. He had been a very good journalist, a man with the proverbial 'nose', which had been used to the great advantage of his paper, so they had paid him accordingly. And his nose twitched now. His story sense was strongly alerted.

But he kept his own counsel. The ever-present danger of litigation against the paper for slander had taught him to steer a very delicate course between outright accusation and ostensibly innocent, vaguely expressed speculation hinting—with a light and delicate touch—at what he inwardly felt could well be the truth, yet which he dare not voice directly.

It was indeed Martin's command of the English language, and his faculty for subtlety of thought and expression, that had been spotted by the discerning Max Selznick at the Universal Studios. It led him to being attracted by a very good offer of substantially better financial rewards, to move over from journalism to become a film researcher and scriptwriter.

Max and Martin made a very good team. Much later that day, when they had said their goodbyes to their hospitable and helpful host, Colonel FitzWalter, at Littlebrook and returned to their temporary home at Deal, they compared notes—and with mutual excitement and enthusiasm they compared ideas about possible future plans while their minds were full of fresh memories and impressions, highly stimulated because of the compelling interest of what they had so recently seen and heard.

They determined to make time, once they had satisfied the demands of their current project at Deal, to return on their own to Littlebrook to do some further private research around the area.

At length, liaising with Walter, they were able to set aside a few days, during which Walter went to Aberdeen to spend some time with Malcolm MacKenzie, while they concentrated upon looking at potential future film projects at Littlebrook.

It worked out very well. Initially, hiring a car for a few days, Max and Martin immersed themselves in the local atmosphere in and around Littlebrook. By visiting several pubs in the area and getting into conversation with both publicans and their regular local clients as well as with tradesmen, they were able to collect a mass of interesting details about a variety of topics on which further investigations looked promising and worthwhile.

Their next move was to take along with them two of the photographic experts, not to prepare actual films yet but to provide them with all the salient pictures they would need back in the States, to plan what they eventually sifted out and crystallised to be potentially good film projects.

This they did, and finally left England for California, taking with them a wealth of extremely interesting material. Walter, for his part, had returned from Aberdeen leaving behind him a firm friend in Malcolm MacKenzie, with some agreed plans for future mutual co-operation.

Once back in America things went very well.

At the Universal Studios Max and a team went ahead to produce a film about the Cinque Ports of south eastern England in general and the fortifications built by King Henry VIII in particular. They had a wealth of material to work from and made a special feature of the castles at Deal and Walmer. Using photographs they had taken, and historic information gathered, excellent scale models were manufactured in co-operation with Walter Richtmeyer who, in due course, once the film was made, purchased the models and incorporated them in a special feature in his museum.

The film created a great deal of interest and a future, more wide-ranging one, was provisionally planned dealing with a general study of the castles and coastal fortifications of England.

Much more exciting to Max and Malcolm, however, for their next projects in the immediate future, was the material they had assembled about contemporary life in the Garden of England.

They had at their disposal several very promising human interest stories, following the successful one about the finding of the ancient cannon with its hidden Treasure Trove that had already achieved widespread interest and commendation. It made sense to capitalise on this success, following up the trail-blazing impact of the unusual film by producing others from the same part of the world.

The film company for whom Max Selznick worked decided to commission a series of films which for their own purposes they provisionally grouped under the title 'The Garden of England Series'. It was quite evident that there was enough material to provide the basis of several 'second-feature' films which could be produced over a period of time.

As a start it was decided to send a team to England to prepare the background material for three feature films dealing with the Tramp and the Wheelwrights, the

Haunted Oast House and the Drama in the Windmill. Max and Martin were key members of the team. In due course, full of enthusiasm, they set off once again for England.

Once they and their camera team reached Kent, however, and lived among the people of Littlebrook for an extended period, many other facets of the stories they were pursuing came to their notice with much else besides. This showed the existence of a very great deal more material than they had previously uncovered, opening up the prospect of other future projects.

One character whose name cropped up from time to time was 'Old Motty', as the locals called him, about whom they had first heard when in the churchyard on their previous visit. It was obvious, once they had met him briefly and seen him at his work, that he warranted special attention, so they determined to make enquiries about him as they went about their business. As a result of this the report about him written up in the County newspaper from Maidstone by the young reporter, Mike, came to their notice. They were much amused by this and Martin lost no time in contacting Mike to arrange a meeting with him. He was convinced by the style of the article that Mike was a fellow spirit and this proved to be the case when they met together in Maidstone. They got on very well and Martin was much entertained by what Mike had to tell him about his day's visit to the churchyard at Littlebrook. He came away with further copies of the article, plus copies of photographs Mike had taken at the time.

Investigating the Oast House story, they sought out the guests who had been present on the night in question and hunted down Percy Pringle the cobbler and then Taffy Thomas the woodcutter, to hear what they had to say about the psychic experiment in which the two had taken part, albeit somewhat reluctantly. Both told essentially the same story, each with the absolute conviction that they had witnessed manifestations of supernatural forces that had clearly frightened them in the extreme.

They were also much amused by the details they heard of Motty's part in the proceedings, and especially by his observations about his contact with the Spirit world, and in particular about the two soldiers who had overcome a technical difficulty by the simple expedient of swapping bones!

But they were the more intrigued because they perceived that neither Percy nor Taffy was inclined to dismiss Old Motty as a crank. Clearly they believed he had special powers and treated him as an eccentric loner with a shrewd and penetrating mind, who maybe knew a thing or two that was beyond their comprehension. It was obvious they stood in some awe of him and made no attempt to rubbish his utterances. Rather, they treated him with uneasy respect, preferring, it seemed, to keep him at arm's length and not to tangle with him.

In due course Max and Martin made it their business to winkle out Motty Marsh and talk at length to him themselves. They were richly rewarded, especially when they had lubricated Motty's tonsils with a few welcome pints of his favourite beer. His comments about some of the people whose names had come up in their investigations also gave them much food for thought. They concluded that the bent and grey-bearded old boy had very acute powers of observation and perception.

They decided it seemed sensible to photograph him in a variety of locations, including his beloved churchyard, so that they had him securely recorded in their archives to be embodied in any future film they might devise in which he could star—albeit by some well-chosen proxy back at the Studios. Tough though Motty Marsh undoubtedly was, there was no guarantee that the old fellow would still be around for long, so they made sure they had a permanent picture of him to work from when back in the States.

What they had to do when eventually they returned to California was to create movies which were a blend of snippets of film made in England, with mock-ups of scenes peopled by their own actors, so they needed to take home as comprehensive a record as possible of people, buildings and places so as to make their end-products realistic. More especially was this so because a not insignificant proportion of their final income would be expected to arise from the export of their work back to the UK. This challenge had been met in the past with films that had been acknowledged to achieve a high degree of realism. It was an accolade of which the film company was justifiably proud and sought to maintain.

So far as the haunted Oast House project was concerned, it was particularly important to have plenty of actual shots taken on location if they were to be able to re-create the authentic feel of the eerie atmosphere in the place at night-time. Having closely questioned two of the guests present during the much-talked about evening séance drama, they managed to talk in turn to Arthur Marchant, the dryer-in-charge, and to members of his team. These four men had been alerted in advance by Percy and Taffy that they might well be approached by the film men from America. The amorous pair were much excited about the possibility of a film being made about their frightening experience in the Oast House.

Arthur and his colleague had an earnest discussion on the matter and decided that they must at all costs stick to their story of the night's events. So far around the district everybody was convinced that what had happened was beyond doubt an authentic manifestation of psychic forces, even if there were some, perhaps, who suspected that the details had got exaggerated in the telling. In essence, the story was now accepted as historic fact, and the team of men involved was determined to preserve this belief.

The fact of the matter was that the business had now gone too far and they did not relish the consequences of revealing the truth at this late stage. To put it mildly, they would not have been popular! Too many people had been duped. But not only that, they were themselves convinced there really *was* something very eerie about the Oast House they worked in for so many hours during hop-picking time. Some people even admired them for being prepared to stay in there night and day for several weeks each year to do a scary job that just had to be done by somebody. There was a bit of kudos in it! So all in all they determined to stick to their guns, and this they subsequently did. No word of the truth ever escaped their lips!

The net result of this conspiracy was that Max and Martin received corroborative reports about what happened from everybody they spoke to. Not only that, the clear evidence of how genuinely scared Percy and Taffy had been, convinced them that something very unusual had indeed been experienced in the spooky old building at midnight as a result of the group getting together to invoke forces they did not understand.

The Vicar's comments had also been confirmation that something supernatural had taken place: a matter he considered serious enough to warrant his issuing a warning from the pulpit about the dangers of meddling with the Powers of Darkness.

Despite all of this, a nagging doubt remained in the mind of Martin at least. In the course of his journalistic career he had certainly come across instances when things had occurred that defied logical explanation. But more usually, he and his colleagues had uncovered bogus claims of spiritual powers amounting to nothing less than the fraudulent deception of the public for monetary gain.

He thought about it awhile and then came up with a possible way in which he could get another slant on the evening's strange events. There were two people whose evidence they had not been able to check—that of the two ladies from London, Clara and Glad, the guests of Taffy and Percy.

Since, if they made the film, these two would naturally have to be represented in their cast, Max agreed with him that it would be helpful to have photographs of them, and talk to them, to get some idea of what they were like. A trip to London by Martin would have the added advantage of affording a chance to get an independent check on the description of what was said to have happened in the Oast House, from two people not resident in Littlebrook and out of touch with the five men who had been present with them at the time, seated holding hands in a closed circle in front of the Oast's glowing furnace.

Arthur Marchant obtained their addresses for him from the farm bailiff, Ben Skinner, and Martin travelled to London by train to see if he could locate them. As luck would have it there was absolutely no problem and he was able to call upon them separately on the Saturday of his visit.

Both described the events in virtually identical terms. There was no question in Martin's mind but that they had indeed both experienced the phenomena he had heard about from the others. Not only that, but Clara actually stated that she felt a rat brush against her legs as it scuttled across the floor to disappear out of the door. Her description was so graphic that it clearly was something that had really happened; rats had for sure scuttled in terror out of the Oast House. It was not just imagination at work—of that Martin was absolutely certain.

Martin was convinced, and returned to Littlebrook not only with the photographs of the two ladies but also now quite sure in his own mind that there had been an unaccountable occult experience on that memorable night.

By the time they were ready to return to America the small team from Universal Studios had gathered a wealth of material for the films they had at present planned—four in number now, not three, because they had decided to devote one to the weird old character Motty Marsh, for whom they had developed a lasting affection.

They had never met anyone quite like Motty before, nor ever would again, they were sure. He was unique, and in their experience a one-off in the field of human eccentrics! In addition he was a natural actor who provided them with a wonderful character to portray. What was more, most of his generation had long since disappeared from the scene, although those of his personal acquaintance had clearly not severed their connection with his versatile mind and inner spiritual self. According to him he was in regular contact with them, which was indeed witnessed by others who had discreetly listened to him talking to them in the graveyard—including Mike, the reporter from Maidstone, whose entertaining article they had read with such amusement.

When the young reporter had journeyed down to Maidstone to investigate the activities of 'Old Motty', nobody—and certainly not Mike himself—could have had the slightest notion of the profound impact this assignment was to have on the future of the likeable, up-and-coming young man. For in discussing their plans for the series of 'Garden of England' films, it soon became only too apparent to Max and Martin that once back in California, very far away from the subject matter of their creative work, they were likely to find themselves, quite often, short of local knowledge. Moreover, this situation would be subject indeed to the probability that they might not only make mistakes, but also miss opportunities in the handling and presentation of their material.

It soon dawned upon them that what they really needed was to have a local expert from the area out there at the Studios with them. There was also the question of the local dialect, which for the sake of realism they hoped to reproduce—not least to enhance the acceptability of the films for export back to the UK.

The solution was immediately clear to Martin. If Max agreed, he suggested that they offer Mike a permanent job with them in California. Martin was a very experienced writer and journalist himself, and in Mike he could see precisely the right qualities to follow his own career path—from journalism to investigative research for films and also, later on, to actual script writing. Mike was already a quite accomplished investigative journalist; his handling of the Motty Marsh assignment had demonstrated that.

The outcome of this brainwave was a very happy one all round. Max agreed with enthusiasm; the offer was duly made to Mike; Mike accepted with equal enthusiasm, and the wheels began to turn with a minimum of delay.

Mike's editor at Maidstone, a man well advanced in his own life's working-span, saw a very bright and exciting future ahead for Mike in the States. He was not a man to stand in the young reporter's way: far from it. On the contrary, once he had satisfied himself that Mike was really serious in his enthusiasm to go, he did everything he could to facilitate Mike's early departure.

In this he was very successful; when the party from the Universal Studios returned to California, they took Mike with them!

Fortuitously for Mike, the assignment with which he was to be involved for his first few years was entirely concerned with matters connected with the UK. This necessitated occasional visits back to England, so his links with home were not abruptly severed. But in the long run he became a fully integrated member of the Film Company's team and loved his new life in Los Angeles.

One after another, the four films initially planned by Max and Martin were made. Each followed the success of the first two. The stories, in many ways so bizarre, proved extremely popular and intriguing to their audiences, as well as being readily accepted back in the UK.

In the course of time a more general, wider-ranging documentary film about historic English castles and Coastal Fortifications was also made. In this venture Walter Richtmeyer played an important part as the historical researcher and advisor, again to the mutual benefit both of the Film Company and of his own Military Museum enterprise.

Looking back years later, Walter Richtmeyer and Max Selznick—who became lifelong friends—were to reflect that when the steam ploughing team, busy in the peaceful, distant fields of Kent in England, had unearthed the ancient cannon, they had discovered not only a material Treasure Trove but also opened up a rich vein of potential treasure of a more abstract nature. The chain of events that followed the unearthing finally had repercussions which involved many millions of people and a great deal of money, for the number of people who actually got to see the films made in the Universal Studios of California was indeed measured in millions. The subject matter had an ongoing appeal, a whimsical, timeless quality that endured for many many years.

Neither did it do Walter Richtmeyer's enterprise any harm either. Not only did his Military Museum benefit substantially, but his idea of a parallel new venture, conceived when with the men of SKWEC in Kent, eventually became a reality.

The Theme Park he had envisaged, devoted to a large collection of Steam Engines and Fairground Equipment, was planned and developed adjacent to his Museum. At length it became by far the most profitable part of his total business enterprise. In fact it financed the purchase of many exhibits for the Military Museum, which otherwise could not have been afforded.

It must be said, however, that Walter's first love remained his Museum, despite the thriving success and greater public appeal of the new venture.

But he was lucky. He had an excellent, very talented and knowledgeable man to run his Theme Park for him: one Frank Thrushton, poached in the first place from HM Dockyards at Chatham in Kent by SKWEC, and finally poached from SKWEC of Kent by Mr Walter Richtmeyer of San Francisco, USA!

Frank's fortunes had been much enhanced by his move across the Atlantic to America. His future was very much more secure, as he had moved from an industry which was in decline because its technology was outdated, to one that existed purely to provide a permanent record of that very technology. The less familiar it became in everyday life and the quainter its huge and lumbering machinery appeared, the more fascinating it was to become to future generations. So for Frank the future was set fair.

But naturally, of course, there were times when he felt a little homesick, although he did have some permanent links with home to ameliorate these feelings when his mind turned to faraway Kent. At such times he went to have a look at the ancient cannon standing at the foot of Walter's impressive flagpole flying the Stars and Stripes so proudly, and indulged in a little nostalgia. And just inside the Museum was a picture of his group of happy SKWEC workmates loading the cannon onto a Sentinel Steam Wagon—and for good measure there was even one of those vehicles too, along with others of its kind from the UK, standing spruced-up and immaculate, on show in the Theme Park.

There was also another link with home. Every now and again Frank took himself off to Los Angeles to have a chat, and exchange reminiscences for a while, with his British friend Mike, one-time reporter from Maidstone, Kent, and now working away happily at the Universal Studios and settled there for life!

Little did the man, who so long ago jealously sought temporary safety for his worldly treasure by pushing it on a crude tray up the barrel of an ancient cannon lying half-buried in a ditch in the Kentish countryside, know what far-reaching repercussions there would be as a direct result of his private, furtive act.

Where he himself finished up, no one was ever to know. His precious treasure was left to sink out of sight into the cover of the rich wet soil, to remain hidden there until found so many years later by seven men of another, distant generation in a strange, new, unimagined, increasingly mechanised age.

For the Hand of Destiny plays in subtle and inscrutable ways with the blissfully unknowing people who form the pawns in its remorseless game of Fate, moving them seemingly at random to create, in an ever-unfolding story, life's infinitely variable pictures—each in its time so starkly and clearly seen—then so tantalisingly to fade and disappear for ever.

And there came a day when, with an impish smile, the Player—as if in answer to the unspoken wish of a sometimes lonely Englishman who looked out from his observation tower and gazed thoughtfully at a cosy, vacant, secluded corner in the Fairground adjacent to the Steam Engine Theme Park—reached out her hand to pluck Dame Crystal Star from her Kentish fairground to plant her, complete with her caravan, in the vacant spot that the lonely man looked at so wistfully.

But that is another story.

EPILOGUE

Life is just a Chequerboard
of Nights and Days,
Where Destiny with Man for
Pieces plays;
Hither and thither Moves and
Mates and Slays,
Then one by one, back in the
Closet lays.

From Edward FitzGerald's translation of the
Rubáiyát of Omar Khayyám